THE
MAMMOTH BOOK OF

BEST NEW HORROR

VOLUME TEN

Edited and with an Introduction by
STEPHEN JONES

CARROLL & GRAF PUBLISHERS, INC.
New York

Carroll & Graf Publishers, Inc.
19 West 21st Street
New York
NY 10010–6805

First published in the UK by Robinson Publishing Ltd 1999

First Carroll & Graf edition 1999

ISBN 0–7867–0690–2

Printed and bound in the EC

CONTENTS

ACKNOWLEDGMENTS

I would like to thank Sara Broecker, Bill Congreve, Andrew I. Porter, Jo Fletcher, Ellen Datlow, Mandy Slater, Aaron Sterns, Richard Dalby, Stefan Dziemianowicz, Gordon Van Gelder, David Pringle, Frederick S. Clarke, William K. Schafer, Barbara Roden and Christopher Roden, Peter Coleborn, Stuart Hughes and Andy Cox for their help and support. Special thanks are due to *Locus*, *Interzone*, *Science Fiction Chronicle*, *Variety* and all the other sources that were used for reference in the Introduction and the Necrology.

In memory of
JIM TURNER
(1945–99)
a good friend, and the man
who saved Arkham House.

INTRODUCTION

Horror in 1998

F OLLOWING A TWO-YEAR DECLINE IN NORTH AMERICA, a near-record number of genre books appeared in 1998. The total for horror titles was up slightly on the previous year, with around a quarter of those books published in the young adult market and more than 15 per cent of them featuring vampires.

However, the overall number of genre books published in Britain fell to its lowest for nearly a decade. Horror titles were down around 46 per cent on the previous year's figures, accounting for a mere 12 per cent of publishers' genre output (which was still 2 per cent above the share of the American market).

A new study revealed that romance books continued to lead all other genres in terms of book sales in America. The industry was worth more than $1 billion annually and accounted for nearly half of all mass-market paperbacks sold. Sales of romance titles nearly equalled the sales of all the other genres combined, including horror, science fiction, fantasy, mystery, thrillers and westerns.

German-owned international media company Bertelsmann AG, already owner of Bantam Doubleday Dell, purchased Random House in May for an estimated $1.3 billion. This resulted in a merger of the two publishers under the Random House name.

With a base of thirty-five million book and music club members worldwide, Bertelsmann announced an agreement with bookselling giant Barnes & Noble, Inc. to establish a joint venture with its Internet subsidiary, barnesandnoble.com. Under the agreement, Bertelsmann reportedly paid $200 million for a 50 per cent stake in the on-line service and each party also contributed $100 million capital. Launched in May 1997, barnes-andnoble.com became one of the twenty-five fastest-growing Web sites in the world, generating sales of $22 million for the six months ending 1 August 1998.

Meanwhile, in November Bertelsmann separately launched its own BooksOnline service in several European countries. The service used its new collaboration with barnesandnoble.com to offer customers worldwide the experience of shopping on-line for books in multiple languages.

In another major deal, Barnes & Noble acquired distribution giant Ingram Book Group for $200 million in cash and $400 million in stock, much to the consternation of many in the publishing and bookselling world. The purchase put Barnes & Noble in control of the primary distributor for its main on-line competitor, Amazon.com, and for most of the small chains and independent bookstores throughout the United States. The American Booksellers Association issued an official statement in which it considered the purchase to be "a devastating development that threatens the viability of competition in the book industry, and limits the diversity and availability of books to consumers."

In a separate case, the ABA and a number of independent booksellers filed an anti-trust lawsuit in March in the US District Court for Northern California, accusing Barnes & Noble and Borders bookstore chains of violating anti-trust laws by using their estimated combined annual buying power of $5 billion to receive secret preferential treatment from publishers. B&N chairman Len Riggio hit back with an open letter to the media denying the ABA's assertion that book superstores were responsible for the decline in independents and stated that there was no evidence of wrongdoing on the part of Barnes & Noble.

America's Crown Books filed for Chapter 11 bankruptcy in July after the new owner failed to find a buyer. This resulted in the closure of 79 of the chain's 174 stores. Having already returned many books to publishers earlier in the year, Crown was subsequently sued by its principal supplier, Ingram, who claimed payment for $10 million in books. Ingram eventually agreed to accept more returns and extend new credit to the chain in exchange for "super-priority" status as an unsecured creditor.

A £300 million agreement between Waterstones and Dillons bookshop chains became the biggest-ever deal in British book retailing, with the result that most of the Dillons branches were re-branded to Waterstones. The move put the combined 200-plus stores in a good position to gain further market share before potential rivals Borders could make substantial inroads into the UK market.

In 1997 the publishing industry was watching HarperCollins closely, amid the turmoil of restructuring, the cancellation of numerous titles, and rumours of bankruptcy. A year later the company reported that it had increased its operating profits by 200 per cent. While revenues stayed even at $737 million, profits increased from $12 million to $37 million. According to the annual report from parent company News Corp., the results were due to "a more focused publishing programme, decreased returns and some significant bestsellers." Fourth-quarter results for HarperCollins showed a $11 million operating profit, compared to only $1 million in 1997. Headed by publishing director John Silbersack, the HarperEntertainment imprint was launched in the autumn to cover all the media tie-ins being put out by Harper-Collins.

America's Leisure Books launched the Leisure Horror Book Club with two September titles, *Alone With the Dead* by Robert J. Randisi and *The Halloween Man* by Douglas Clegg.

French publisher Hachette Livre bought a 70 per cent equity stake in Britain's Orion Publishing Group and Macmillan (owned by German publisher Holtzbrinck) made a hostile £7.3 million takeover bid for Cassell (which included the Gollancz and Vista imprints). The Cassell Board of Directors had rejected the offer of £1 per share (a 122 per cent premium over the public valuation of 45 pence) when, in an unexpected move, Orion outbid Macmillan with £1.23 per share and bought the company.

Canadian publisher Commonwealth, who had entered into "joint contracts" (aka vanity publishing) with an estimated 2,000 authors and had an annual budget of $6 million, declared bankruptcy in March. With lawsuits threatened by disgruntled writers and employees, publisher Don Phelan went into hiding, only to resurface briefly to blame an "internal and external conspiracy" for his problems, saying he would represent himself in class action suits brought against the firm by its clients.

Despite an announcement in May that Stanislaus Tal's TAL Literary Agency had been sold to a company called Extreme Entertainment, it later emerged that Tal represented few if any authors and some royalties paid to the agency had never been reported.

The American Congress passed the Copyright Term Extension Act, adding a further twenty years to copyrights for individuals, bringing the length of copyright in the US up to life plus seventy years, and into line with the European copyright law which was amended in 1995. After vigorous lobbying by the Walt Disney Company (who was faced with losing its exclusive copyright to Mickey Mouse in 2003), another twenty years was added to the already existing seventy-five years of corporate copyrights. The Digital Millennium Copyright Act also gave full protection to work appearing on-line.

It was the summer of Stephen King. After his move in 1997 to Simon & Schuster for a $2 million advance and nearly 50 per cent of the profits, his big release for the year was the novel *Bag of Bones*. It was about bestselling author Mike Noonan, suffering from writer's block following the unexpected death of his wife and their unborn child, who found himself caught up in a supernatural mystery centred around Dark Score Lake and a town in the grip of a tyrannical millionaire. In America the book had a first printing of 1,360,000 copies from Scribner, backed by a $1 million promotional budget.

Despite his phenomenal popularity on both sides of the Atlantic, the author had not appeared at a public event in Britain for nearly fifteen years. To coincide with the publication of the new book, King visited London in mid-August for a rare promotional tour. Bottles of a special "King Lager" were available during the UK launch party, produced especially for the event by a London micro-brewery, and a commemorative signed edition of *Bag of Bones*, limited to just 2,000 copies, went on sale at London's Royal Festival Hall when King was interviewed by novelist and broadcaster Muriel Gray, read from his work, and answered questions in front of a capacity audience.

Books Etc. in association with Hodder & Stoughton gave away a free trade paperback omnibus to coincide with the publication of *Bag of Bones*. Only available from stores in the London area,

King etc. included a brief message from the author plus extracts from twelve of his novels.

Just in time for Christmas, Donald M. Grant, Publisher, re-released the first three books in King's *Dark Tower* series, packaged together at a suggested retail price of $110. This included a third printing of the first title in the series, *The Gunslinger* (1982), with a new dustjacket, and a second printing of *The Drawing of the Three* (1987), with a new dustjacket and ten new paintings by artist Phil Hale. The third book, *The Waste Lands* (1991), was a first edition. The set weighed a total of eight pounds and was available in a leatherette slipcase stamped on the spine in silver and maroon.

Dean Koontz's *Seize the Night* was the sequel to the author's *Fear Nothing*, and once again involved night-dweller Christopher Snow, who discovered more about the mutated gene virus infecting the inhabitants of Moonlight Bay and a secret government time-travel experiment. It was also released in a 750-copy signed, leatherbound, slipcased edition by Cemetery Dance Publications, illustrated by Phil Parks, along with a 52-copy lettered edition.

Anne Rice's *Pandora* was the first volume in the "New Tales of the Vampire" series, as Rice's undead characters David Talbot and Pandora returned from the author's previous books. It was followed by *The Vampire Armand*, which told the tale of the eponymous bloodsucker and leader of the Theatre des Vampires across the centuries.

The first volume in a new two-part series, Clive Barker's *Galilee: A Romance* was a Southern Gothic involving the eponymous male protagonist whose love affair with Rachel Pallenberg reawakened an old conflict between rival families. While the Gearys were rich and powerful, the Barbarossas were much darker and stranger.

Butterfly, *Crystal*, *Brooke*, *Raven* and *Runaways* comprised the "Orphans" series by V. C. Andrews® and marked a transition away from horror to young adult fiction for the late author. The story involved four teenage orphans who escaped from an evil foster home. Meanwhile, *Music in the Night* was the fourth in the Gothic horror "Logan Family" series under the Andrews byline, still probably written by Andrew Neiderman.

Thriller novelist Frederick Forsyth sold the American, Canadian and audio rights for *The Phantom in Manhattan* to New

Millennium Entertainment, a new publisher based in Beverly Hills, for an advance reported to be in the mid-seven-figure area. The novel was a sequel to Andrew Lloyd Webber's version of the Gaston Leroux classic, *The Phantom of the Opera*. New Millennium also planned to release the book in DVD format, while rumours of a stage version of *The Phantom in Manhattan* had already been circulating in theatrical circles for over a year. Forsyth had previously said he did not want to write another book, but apparently offered his services to Lloyd Webber at a dinner party in late 1997.

Published in America but not in his native Britain, Ramsey Campbell's psychological thriller *The Last Voice They Hear* involved an investigative journalist who was challenged by his long-missing brother to solve a series of murders, with his own family as the prize.

Although not usually known for their horror or dark fantasy work, Terry Brooks' *A Knight of the World* was the sequel to his bestseller *Running with the Demon*, while *Homebody* was a haunted house novel from Orson Scott Card.

Legacies was the second Repairman Jack novel from F. Paul Wilson ("writing as Colin Andrews" on the UK edition). The mysterious fixer became involved with a woman intent on destroying a house she had just inherited, and also the evil Arabs, Japanese agents, and American hit men who were out to discover the secrets concealed in the dilapidated mansion.

Charles Grant's "Millennium Quartet" continued with *Chariot*, the third novel in the series about the Four Horsemen of the Apocalypse. This time Plague used smallpox to wreak havoc in a world already at the mercy of Famine and Death, and only Las Vegas was spared. The author also launched a new series about a private occult investigation service with *Black Oak 1: Genesis* and *2: The Hush of Dark Wings*.

The Searchers: City of Iron by Chet Williamson marked the beginning of a new *X Files*-type trilogy about a team of three CIA agents investigating the supernatural. Phil Rickman's *The Wine of Angels* was the first in a series featuring new vicar Merrily Watkins and a mystery linked to a town's 17th century witch-hunts.

Set in the near-future, Peter James' *Denial* was about a psychiatrist who gave the wrong advice to a patient, an aging movie actress, who killed herself as a result. Her sociopath son held the doctor responsible and decided to avenge her death. *Soho Black* by Christopher Fowler concerned the high-pressure lifestyle of a failing film executive who dropped dead in a trendy bar one evening, and by doing so revitalised his career.

Michael Marshall Smith's *One of Us* was set in a world where dreams and memories could be accessed, a group of survivors confronted an ancient evil released from the *Chasm* by Stephen Laws, a horror writer discovered where he got his bizarre ideas from in *Straker's Island* by Steve Harris, and the myths behind the Arabian Nights and the secret history of Tut-ankh-amen's tomb were explored by Tom Holland in *The Sleeper in the Sands*.

Terror was the third in Graham Masterton's series about Jim Rook, a teacher with supernatural powers, while *House of Bones* was a young adult novel in the Point Horror series from the same author.

After his success in 1997 with the mainstream thriller *Bad Karma* (under the "Andrew Harper" pseudonym), Douglas Clegg's *The Halloween Man* marked a return to the horror field for the author. It was set in the quiet New England town of Stonehaven, which was filled with secrets of both natural and supernatural origin, including the terrifying figure of the title.

William Browning Spencer's *Irrational Fears* followed Jack Lowry, an alcoholic ex-professor trying to dry out. After witnessing the bizarre death of a fellow inmate in a hospital ward and being introduced to The Clear, a group of clean-cut young men who are the sworn enemy of Alcoholics Anonymous, Jack was transferred to a rural retreat where everyone gave thanks to H.P. Lovecraft's Elder Gods.

Greg Kihn's *Big Rock Beat* was a sequel to the author's *Horror Show*, also featuring director Landis Woodley, who this time became mixed-up in the production of a bizarre teen/monster beach movie.

Andrew Neiderman's *In Double Jeopardy* was about a female medical student who found herself involved with a man who behaved just like her brother-in-law, who had been executed for the brutal murder of her sister. *The Good Children* by Kate Wilhelm strayed into V.C. Andrews and Shirley Jackson territory with its tale of four young people trying to keep their family together in the face of lies, love, insanity and possible murder.

Joe R. Lansdale's *Rumble, Tumble* was the latest Hap and Leonard crime novel in which Hap Collins' girlfriend learned that her teenage daughter was part of a hellish prostitution ring and the two friends were forced to confront a biker army turned vice barons and stone-mad killers. Norman Partridge's *The Ten-Ounce Siesta* was the second volume in the enjoyable Jack Baddalach mysteries, in which the standard-issue good guy became involved with bikini girls with machine guns, cops with donuts, the heavyweight champion of the world, and a demon from Hell.

Voodoo Child by Michael Reaves was predictably set in New Orleans, while John Pritchard's *Dark Ages* took place in present-day Oxford but harkened back to earlier horrors. A massacre in the 12th century resulted in a modern-day haunting in Jenny Jones' *Where the Children Cry*. Mary Murrey's *The Inquisitor* concerned a depressed woman who became involved with pagan mythology, while a young widow joined a village coven of white witches in *The Witching Time* by Jean Stubbs.

John Evans' *Gordius* was a sequel to the author's *God's Gift*, Nick DiMartino's *A Seattle Ghost Story* was illustrated by Charles Nitti, and *Black as Blood* by Rob Chilson was a humorous novel about a body that would not stay dead.

Reporter-turned-sleuth Hollis Ball was helped by her husband's ghost in *Ghost of a Chance* by Helen Chappell, and David Beaty's *The Ghosts of the Eighth Attack* involved a RAF squadron in World War II haunted by phantom flyers from the First World War. A supernatural western set in Mexico, Loren D. Estleman's *Journey of the Dead* involved an ancient alchemist and the man who killed Billy the Kid.

A woman accused of murdering her husband claimed she was possessed by his first wife in *A Mind to Kill* by Andrea Hart, while in Richard La Plante's *Mind Kill*, a serial killer stalked his victims in their dreams. A psychic female criminal profiler tracked down a serial killer who took his victim's eyes in Joseph Glass' aptly-titled *Eyes*, and a psychic journalist investigated the death of a colleague in *Second Sight* by Beth Amos.

The spirit of a dead serial killer returned in Kimberly Rangel's *The Homecoming*, a woman's paintings were connected to a serial killer in *Retribution* by Elizabeth Forrest (Rhondi Salsitz), and the victim of a recently-released serial killer was apparently reincarnated in a musician in Roxanne Conrad's *Copper Moon*.

A serial killer menaced a near-future Glasgow in Paul Johnston's *The Bone Yard*, and *The Coffin Maker* by Jeffery Deaver featured quadriplegic detective Lincoln Rhymes matching wits with a killer who planned to eliminate three important witnesses in a grand jury trial. Will Kingdom's *The Cold Calling* was a police procedural involving yet another serial killer, as was Shaun Hutson's *Purity*.

In *The Last Days: The Apocryphon of Joe Panther* by Australian writer Andrew Masterton, a priest was suspected of being a brutal serial killer, while an isolated boarding house for children and a religious cult based on sex and the authority of a messianic figure featured in Carmel Bird's *Red Shoes*, another down-under novel, this one narrated by a guardian angel.

A woman about to commit suicide found an unconscious angel on the roof of her Manhattan apartment in Nancy A. Collins' romantic dark fantasy *Angels on Fire*. The eponymous prince of Hell inhabited a dead body in James Byron Huggins' *Cain*, and demon detectives set out to recover stolen crystal orbs in Camille Bacon-Smith's *Eyes of the Empress*.

Jeff Rovin's *Vespers* involved a police detective and a zoologist who discovered that millions of mutant killer bats had migrated to Manhattan. It was reportedly "soon to be a major motion picture". In *Dust* by scientist Charles Pellegrino, a maverick palaeobiologist discovered that Mother Nature was attempting to wipe-out mankind through a series of natural plagues and disasters. *Red Shadows* by Yvonne Navarro was a sequel to the author's *Final Impact* and set on a post-apocalyptic Earth that no longer rotated.

Frances Gordon's *Changeling* was based on the Rumpelstilt-skin fairy story, and *The Pit and the Pendulum* and *Frankenstein* were the latest erotic reworkings of horror classics in *The Darker Passions* series by Amarantha Knight (Nancy Kilpatrick).

Originally called *Dracula Cha Cha Cha* until the American publisher requested a change of title, *Judgment of Tears: Anno Dracula 1959* was the third in Kim Newman's acclaimed vampire series that mixed fact with fiction. Set in Rome on the eve of the wedding of Vlad, Count Dracula, to Moldavian princess Asa

Vajda, the vampire elders of the Eternal City were falling victim to a murderer known as the Crimson Executioner.

The undead Saint-Germaine was involved in a plague in 14th century France in *Blood Roses* by Chelsea Quinn Yarbro, and *Sisters of the Night: The Angry Angel* by the same author was the first in a packaged trilogy about Dracula's vampire "brides", illustrated by Christopher H. Bing. *Vampyrrhic* by Simon Clark concerned bloodsuckers nesting in a village in North Yorkshire, while a group of people inside a ring of standing stones were hurled back in time to a bloody past in the same author's *The Fall*.

Of Masques and Martyrs was the third volume in Christopher Golden's vampire "Shadow Saga", a computer programmer involved with role-playing games was apparently killed by one of the undead in Linda Grant's *Vampire Bytes*, and *The Undying* by Mudrooroo, a native Australian, was an unusual vampire novel and the second volume in the "Master of the Ghost Dreaming" series.

Blue Moon by Laurell K. Hamilton was the eighth instalment in the author's horror/crime series featuring vampire-hunter Anita Blake, who had to figure out a way to get her ex-boyfriend, high school teacher and werewolf Richard, out of jail after he was framed for attempted rape in Tennessee. The characters returned in *Burnt Offerings*, which involved an arsonist destroying businesses owned by the undead and a visit from the vampire's ruling council.

A Chill in the Blood was the seventh volume in P.N. Elrod's "The Vampire Files" series about undead private eye Jack Fleming in a post-prohibition Chicago, and *The Flesh, the Blood, and the Fire* by S.A. Swiniarski (S. Andrew Swann) involved police detective Stefan Ryzard investigating a vampire conspiracy and a series of "torso" murders in Depression-era Cleveland.

A vampire had been hiding for years inside the *Titanic* in Michael Romkey's *Vampire Hunter*, while in Miguel Conner's *The Queen of Darkness* vampires ruled a post-holocaust Earth.

One of Britain's most successful authors, Terry Pratchett was awarded the O.B.E. in the Queen's Birthday honours list for his services to literature. He also published his twenty-third "Discworld" novel, *Carpe Jugulum*, which involved the rulers of Uberwald, who just happened to be modern-thinking vampires.

Elvira: The Boy Who Cried Werewolf was the third in the

series by the camp TV horror host and John Paragon. Lycan-thropic detective Ty Merrick returned in *Manjinn Moon*, the third volume in Denise Vitola's mystery series set in the near-future. *The Passion* was a romantic tale about contemporary werewolves and a family secret by Donna Boyd, while a book of spells created a reluctant werewolf in Sandra Morris' dark fantasy *Green Moon and Wolfsbane*.

A female werewolf attempted to control her own destiny in ancient Rome in Alice Borchardt's historical dark fantasy *The Silver Wolf*. Borchardt is the sister of Anne Rice, who of course blurbed her sibling's book.

Shadow of the Beast was a first novel by Margaret L. Carter, about a werewolf roaming the dark streets of a town in Mary-land, while Julie Anne Parks' *Storytellers* involved a bestselling horror author menaced by a legendary Native American evil. Both books were published by DesignImage Group.

Michael Marano's ambitious début novel *Dawn Song* followed the lives of a gay man in 1990s Boston and a body-hopping succubus from Hell intent on stealing twenty male souls. The city was soon caught up in a supernatural struggle between two of Hell's demonic rulers against the backdrop of the Gulf War.

Respected short story author Caitlín R. Kiernan made her novel début with the paperback original *Silk*, about an emotion-ally disturbed woman named Spyder who invited the members of a struggling rock band into her world of blood rituals and vengeful spirits.

Published in the Do-Not Press' FrontLines series, *Head Injuries* by Conrad Williams was about a group of old friends reunited at a British seaside town during the off-season who were forced to confront the ghosts of their past.

A man suffering from a strange neurological disease repaired a sinister house and investigated the chain of deaths surrounding the property in Daniel Hecht's first novel *Skull Session*. Elizabeth Cody Kimmel's début novel *In the Stone Circle* was a young adult ghost story set in a haunted house in Wales, while *King Rat* by China Miéville was described as "urban Gothic" and set in London.

Valley of the Shadow by the brother-and-sister team of Earl Hardy and Naoma Hardy appeared from California's ReGeJe

Press, a modern woman searching for her lost son encountered ancient mythology in *Raven Stole the Moon* by Garth Stein, and a woman in a failing marriage was possessed by the soul of an exotic dancer in David L. Robbins' *Souls to Keep*.

Christa Faust's first book, *Control Freak*, was about a female writer researching a true-crime volume based on a grisly sex murder, who became involved in New York's sadomasochism club scene and developed into a natural dominant. Nalo Hopkinson's *Brown Girl in the Ring* won the Warner Aspect First Novel Contest and was set in a 21st century Toronto where Creole magic worked.

Ulysses G. Dietz made his début with the gay vampire novel *Desmond*, and Jay Kasker's *Out of the Light* involved more romantic vampires.

Movie tie-ins included *Blade* by Mel Odom, *Dark City* by Frank Lauria, *Fallen* by Dewey Gram, *Disturbing Behavior* by John Whitman, *Species II* by Yvonne Navarro, and *Godzilla* by Stephen Molstad.

Scott Ciencin continued his series of Godzilla novels aimed at both the adult and teenage markets with *Godzilla vs. the Space Monster, Godzilla at World's End*, and *Godzilla vs. the Robot Monster. Gargantua* was a novelization of the inferior TV monster movie by Robert K. Andreassi (Keith R.A. DeCandido).

A sequel to the 1941 movie starring Lon Chaney, Jr., *Return of the Wolf Man* by Jeff Rovin was the first and apparently only volume in a series based on Universal Studios' classic monster characters.

The X-Files: Fight the Future was the original title of the film by Chris Carter, "adapted" by Elizabeth Hand, and Ellen Steiber continued the series of young adult *X-Files* novelizations with *Hungry Ghosts*.

Replacing *The X-Files* as the hottest TV tie-in property was *Buffy the Vampire Slayer* with the novels *Night of the Living Rerun* by Arthur Byron Cover, *Return to Chaos* by Craig Shaw Gardner, and *Blooded* and *Child of the Hunt*, both by Christopher Golden and Nancy Holder. Holder was also responsible for the first book in the spin-off series, *The Angel Chronicles*, a young adult collection of three stories. Richie Tankersley wrote the second volume.

Once again proving that old vampires never die, *Forever Knight: These Our Revels* by Anne Hathaway-Nayne was based on the cancelled Canadian series, and actress Lara Parker revived her witch character Angelique from the old TV show *Dark Shadows* for the origin novel *Angelique's Descent*, described as "a tale of erotic love and dark obsessions".

Based on the graphic book and movie series created by James O'Barr, *The Crow: Quoth the Crow* by David Bischoff was about a dark fantasy writer forced to confront the evils he created to ultimately save his wife. Poppy Z. Brite's *The Lazarus Heart* had less to do with the series and was an original novel about a resurrected New Orleans photographer, framed for the murder of his lover, and the bizarre cast of characters he encountered. *Clash by Night* by Chet Williamson was another *Crow* novel and involved the destruction of a day-care centre by an extreme militia group and the ghost of a woman seeking revenge.

Ray Garton found himself reduced to writing the *Sabrina, the Teenage Witch* TV novelization *All That Glitters* under his own name, and the busy Nancy Holder also added to the series with *Spying Eyes*.

From California's Lucard Publishing, *Dracul: An Eternal Love Story* by Nancy Kilpatrick was a vampire novel based on a stage musical and came with an optional CD cast recording of the original San Diego performance.

Probably the two most unlikely crossovers of the year were *Star Trek the Next Generation/X-Men: Planet X* by Jan Michael Friedman, and the graphic novel *Tarzan versus Predator: At the Earth's Core* by Walter Simonson and Lee Weeks, in which Edgar Rice Burroughs' ape man and the alien hunter from the movies battled it out in Pellucidar.

White Wolf's *The World of Darkness* series, based on the role-playing games, continued with *To Speak in Lifeless Tongues* and *To Dream of Dreamers Lost* by David Niall Wilson, the second and third volumes respectively in "The Grails Covenant" trilogy, and *The War in Heaven* by Robert Weinberg, the third and final volume in the "Horizon War" trilogy. *The Winnowing* and *Dark Prophecy* by Gherbod Fleming were the final two volumes in the vampiric "Trilogy of the Blood Curse", *Dark Kingdoms* by Richard Lee Byers was an omnibus of three novels (two previously unpublished), and *The Quintessential World of Darkness* edited by Stewart Wieck and Anna Branscome contained three novels (one previously unpublished) by William Bridges, Rick Hautala and Edo van Belkom, along with two original stories by Kevin Andrew Murphy and Jody Lynn Nye.

Ravenloft: Shadowborn by William W. Connors and Carrie A. Bebris, and *Ravenloft: I, Strahd: The War Against Azalin* by P.N. Elrod were both based on the TSR role-playing vampire game.

Gabriel Knight: The Beast Within by Jane Jensen was the second novel based on the Gothic CD-ROM game, written by the game's creator.

Jonathan Carroll's *Kissing the Beehive* involved a bestselling paperback thriller writer who investigated a decades-old murder of a teenage beauty in his home town and encountered his most devoted fan, who called herself Veronica Lake.

Second Coming Attractions, the third novel from David Prill, was a funny and offbeat look at the Christian cinema industry which forced both the characters and reader to question their faith. With a nod to M.R. James and other authors of the supernatural, Andrew Klavan's *The Uncanny* involved a Hollywood producer who travelled to Britain to discover a real ghost story.

The Migration of Ghosts contained twelve original stories by Pauline Melville, while A.S. Byatt's *Elements: Stories of Fire and Ice* collected six reprints, all touched with magic, with at least two tales that could be considered horror.

The Collector of Hearts: New Tales of the Grotesque by Joyce Carol Oates contained twenty-seven stories, most of which were originally published over the past few years. Oates also edited *Telling Stories: An Anthology for Writers*, which included 111 stories, poems and non-fiction pieces designed as a learning tool for writers. Among the authors represented were Stephen King, H.P. Lovecraft, Harlan Ellison, Angela Carter and Oates herself.

The 1794 Gothic, *The Mysteries of Udolpho* by Ann Radcliffe, was reprinted by Oxford University Press in a new edition edited by Bonamy Dobree with an introduction and notes by Terry Castle.

Published as part of Penguin/Viking Children's Books "The Whole Story" series, Mary Shelley's *Frankenstein* reprinted the

1818 novel along with various pieces of art, including new illustrations by Philippe Munch.

Bram Stoker's Dracula Unearthed was yet another edition published by Desert Island Books, annotated and introduced by editor Clive Leatherdale, which included an introduction by Stoker to the 1901 Icelandic edition. From the same publisher, *Dracula: The Shade and the Shadow* edited by Elizabeth Miller contained twenty critical essays about Stoker's novel.

The Dream-Woman and Other Stories by Wilkie Collins collected eleven stories and an introduction by editor Peter Miles, *The Dedalus Book of French Horror: The 19th Century* included twenty-four stories translated by editor Terry Hale and Liz Heron, and Dover published *The Complete John Silence*, containing six supernatural stories about the psychic detective by Algernon Blackwood, edited by S.T. Joshi. Carroll & Graf's edition of *Thirty Strange Stories* was a welcome reissue of mostly horror and dark fantasy tales by H.G. Wells, with a new introduction by Stephen Jones.

John Evangelist Walsh's biography *Midnight Dreary: The Mysterious Death of Edgar Allan Poe* looked into the cause of the author's death, while Poe's *Selected Tales*, published by Oxford University Press, was a new selection, edited and introduced by David Van Leer. The Penguin/Signet Classic edition of Poe's *The Fall of the House of Usher* collected fifteen stories, a new introduction by Stephen Marlowe and an updated bibliography.

Books of Wonder's "Classic Frights" series of trade paperback reprints for young adults featured *The Fall of the House of Usher* by Edgar Allan Poe, illustrated by William Sayer; *Dracula's Guest* containing two stories by Bram Stoker, illustrated by Eric Shanower; *The Haunting of Holmescroft* by Rudyard Kipling, illustrated by Barb Armata; Mary E. Wilkins Freeman's *The Southwest Chamber*, illustrated by Margaret Organ-Kean; *Who Knows?* by Guy de Maupassant, illustrated by Jennifer Dickson, and *The Inexperienced Ghost* by H.G. Wells, *Casting the Runes* by M.R. James, *Man-Size in Marble* by E. Nesbit, *The Body Snatcher* by Robert Louis Stevenson and *The Monkey's Paw* by W.W. Jacobs, all illustrated by Jeff White.

Academy Chicago's edition of *The Monkey's Paw and Other Tales of Mystery and the Macabre* collected eighteen stories by

Jacobs, edited with an introduction by Gary Hoppenstand, while The Hazelwood Press published *The Monkey's Paw: A Facsimile of the Original Manuscript*, limited to just 300 copies.

The Witch's Tale was American network radio's first dramatic series devoted to tales of terror, conceived, written and directed by Alonzo Deen Cole. Subtitled *Stories of Gothic Horror from The Golden Age of Radio*, Dunwich Press collected thirteen of the radio show's original scripts as a limited edition trade paperback, edited by David S. Siegel. Two of the scripts were also re-created and broadcast live as a special Halloween programme on a west coast radio station on October 30th.

A trade paperback printing of *Tales of the Cthulhu Mythos* was significantly revised from the 1969 edition, with a new introduction by James Turner, and Arkham House finally reprinted Lovecraft's *Selected Letters III*.

After going out of print for a short while, and just in time to tie-in with Gus Van Sant's pointless shot-for-shot remake, Robert Bloch's classic *Psycho* was reissued with a new cover by Tor Books.

As usual, R.L. Stine ruled the young adult market with the first volume of "Goosebumps Series 2000", *Cry of the Cat*, plus *Fear Street: Camp Out* and *Fear Street: Scream, Jennifer*. Stine's *Fear Street: Seniors*, a new twelve-part series about a class of doomed students at Shadyside High School, began with *1: Let's Party*, *2: In Too Deep*, *3: The Thirst* and *4: No Answer*. *Fear Street Super Chiller 1: Stepbrother* was about a girl whose dreams revealed that her stepbrother murdered her in a previous life.

Although credited to R.L. Stine on the covers, the pseudonymously written *Fear Street Sagas* series continued with *11: Circle of Fire* (by Wendy Haley), *12: Chamber of Fear* (by Brandon Alexander), *13: Faces of Terror* (by Cameron Dokey), *14: One Last Kiss* (by Brandon Alexander), *15: Door of Death* (by Eric Weiner) and *16: The Hand of Power* (by Cameron Dokey).

It Came from Ohio! My Life as a Writer was a young adult biography of Stine written by the author "as told to Joe Arthur".

Christopher Pike's *The Hollow Skull* involved the inhabitants of yet another small town being taken over by an alien evil, while *Christopher Pike's Tales of Terror 2* collected five stories by the author.

Nightworld: Witchlight by L.J. Smith was the ninth in the series, and *Black Rot* and *Temper Temper* were the third and fourth volumes, respectively, in the *Weird World* series by Anthony Masters.

Four children battled with a city's supernatural forces in Celia Rees' *H.A.U.N.T.S.: H is for Haunting, A is for Apparition, U is for Undercover, N is for Nightmare* and *T is for Terror*, the first five volumes in a six-book series. M.C. Sumner's *Extreme Zone* series continued with *Dead End*, and *Monsters and My One True Love* by Dian Curtis Regan was the fourth and final volume in the "Monsters of the Month Club Quartet".

Kipton & the Voodoo Curse by Charles L. Fontenay was the tenth volume in "The Kipton Chronicles" series of SF mysteries, and involved Kipton investigating a voodoo curse on Mars.

The Flesh Eater by the excellent John Gordon was a variation on "Casting the Runes", about a mysterious club and its ghostly bogeyman. Theresa Radcliffe's *Garden of Shadows* was inspired by Nathaniel Hawthorne's story "Rappacini's Daughter", and Louise Cooper's *Creatures: Once I Caught a Fish, If You Go Down to the Woods* and *See How They Run* were the first three volumes in a series which reinterpreted old nursery rhymes.

Another small town was menaced by evil in *Darker* by Andrew Matthews, a girl defied her uncle and opened *The Boxes* by William Sleator, and a girl ended up at a Greek clinic run by gorgons in *Snake Dreamer* by Priscilla Galloway.

In *A Coming Evil* by Vivian Vande Velde, a young girl and a medieval ghost helped hide refugees from the Nazis. From the same author, *Ghost of a Hanged Man* was set in the Wild West. A boy encountered the ghost of an old actor in *The Face in the Mirror* by Stephanie S. Tolan, and a girl with agoraphobia could hear strange voices in *Angels Turn Their Backs* by Margaret Buffie.

Margaret Mahy's novella *The Horribly Haunted School* was about a boy who had an allergy to ghosts, and there were more spooks in *The Haunting* by Joan Lowery Nixon, *The Crow Haunting* by Julia Jarman, *The Ghost Twin* by Richard Brown, *The Ghost of Sadie Kimber* by Pat Moon, *The Ghost of Fossil Glen* by Cynthia DeFelice, *The Phantom Thief* by Pete Johnson, and *Blackthorn, Whitethorn* by Rachel Anderson.

A boy was pursued by an evil he could never escape in

Catchman by Chris Wooding, and there were more devilish happenings in *The Secret of the Pit* by Hugh Scott. *Vlad the Undead* by Hanna Lützen was a translation of the 1995 Danish novel about a young woman who read an account of a vampire in an old journal.

Andrew Bromfield translated *A Werewolf Problem in Central Russia and Other Stories*, a collection of eight tales by Victor Pelevin, first published in 1994. *Here There Be Ghosts* collected eleven stories (five reprints) and seven poems (one reprint) by Jane Yolen. *Shadows* was a collection of seven horror stories by James Schmidt, and *Somewhere Else* featured two ghost/time-travel stories by Leon Rosselson.

Classic Ghost Stories II edited by Glen Bledsoe and Karen Bledsoe contained eight stories by M.R. James, Henry James, Charles Dickens, Mary Wilkins Freeman and others, illustrated by Barbara Kiwak. *Great Ghost Stories* edited by Barry Moser collected thirteen tales by such authors as H.P. Lovecraft, H.G. Wells and Joyce Carol Oates. Edited by Alan Durant and illustrated by Nick Hardcastle, *Vampire & Werewolf Stories* contained eighteen stories and novel extracts by Bram Stoker, Richard Matheson and Jane Yolen, amongst others.

Neil Gaiman's *Smoke and Mirrors* collected thirty stories and poems. Subtitled "Short Fictions and Illusions", it was a reworking of his 1993 collection *Angels & Visitations*, with the addition of several new stories, including a couple original to the volume, plus a new introduction by the author.

The Cleft and Other Odd Tales was exactly what you would expect from acclaimed cartoonist Gahan Wilson. Twenty-four stories of weirdness, including the original title story, illustrated by the author/artist.

F. Paul Wilson's *The Barrens and Others* reprinted twelve stories from the late 1980s, plus a stage adaptation and a teleplay, with introductions by the author.

Published by Serpent's Tail, *Personal Demons* by Christopher Fowler collected seventeen stories (eleven original), including a new "Spanky" novelette. Kathe Koja's *Extremities* featured sixteen stories (two original) about human extremes.

Distributed as a promotional item through the UK's WHSmith bookstore chain, *When God Lived in Kentish Town & Others* was a small-format paperback containing four stories (three original) by Michael Marshall Smith.

Bradley Denton's *One Day Closer to Death* collected eight stories about the fate that awaits us all, including an original novella which was a coda to his novel *Blackburn*, featuring the sister of the eponymous serial killer. Published by The Book Guild, *The Venetian Chair and Other Stories* included twenty-two stories by Harry Turner.

Once Upon a Nightmare collected ten horror stories by Australian journalist John Michael Howson, while Bill Congreve's *Epiphanies of Blood: Tales of Desperation and Thirst* contained six mutant vampire stories (three original) and was published by Australia's MirrorDanse Books in an edition of 501 numbered copies.

Legends: Stories by the Masters of Modern Fantasy edited by Robert Silverberg was an anthology of new fiction which originally sold to Dutton/NAL for $650,000, before being resold to Tor Books. Although David Eddings and Terry Brooks eventually pulled out of the project, Terry Pratchett, Anne McCaffrey, Stephen King (a new "Dark Tower" story), Tad Williams, Robert Jordan, Robert Silverberg, Raymond E. Feist, Terry Goodkind, George R.R. Martin and Ursula K. LeGuin all contributed stories. The British edition came with two different covers, while in America Tor issued a boxed and leatherbound edition of 250 copies, signed by all the authors, for $250.00. These were apparently sold by lottery to book dealers only and, according to some reports, copies quickly surfaced for re-sale for as much as $1,000.

After a long delay, the latest Horror Writers Association anthology finally appeared in hardcover from CD Publications and paperback from Pocket Books. Unfortunately, *Robert Bloch's Psychos* was not really worth the wait. Despite a line-up that included Stephen King (a new novelette), Richard Christian Matheson, Charles Grant, Ed Gorman, Jane Yolen and others, it contained a selection of lacklustre serial killer stories that failed to live up to the expectation generated by the volume's title. Bloch died before the book was completed, but I suspect even he would have had difficulty saying anything positive about the tired tales included therein.

Dark Terrors 4: The Gollancz Book of Horror edited by Stephen Jones and David Sutton featured nineteen stories (one reprint) by such authors as Christopher Fowler, Neil Gaiman, Ramsey Campbell, David J. Schow, Roberta Lannes, Dennis Etchison, Poppy Z. Brite, Lisa Tuttle, Thomas Tessier, Michael Marshall Smith and Terry Lamsley.

Sirens and Other Daemon Lovers edited by Ellen Datlow and Terri Windling contained twenty-two erotic stories of magical, obsessional and irresistible love by Storm Constantine, Joyce Carol Oates, Tanith Lee, Edward Bryant, Neil Gaiman, Brian Stableford, Conrad Williams and others.

At 550-plus pages, *Dreaming Down Under* was a major new anthology of Australian speculative fiction edited by Jack Dann and Janeen Webb. It contained thirty-one stories by such Australian authors as Cherry Wilder, Lucy Sussex, Damien Broderick, Stephen Dedman, Terry Dowling, Aaron Sterns, George Turner, Robert Hood and Sean McMullen, plus a preface by Harlan Ellison.

Ellison was also one of the writers featured in *In the Shadow of the Gargoyle* edited by Nancy Kilpatrick and Thomas S. Roche, which included sixteen stories and a novel excerpt (three reprints) by Charles L. Grant, Neil Gaiman, Katherine Kurtz, Brian Lumley, Christa Faust and Caitlín R. Kiernan, Brian Hodge and others.

The Crow: Shattered Lives & Broken Dreams edited by J. O'Barr and Ed Kramer contained nineteen stories and ten poems based on O'Barr's graphic novel and movie series. Authors included Iggy Pop, Gene Wolfe, John Shirley and Nancy A. Collins, and it was illustrated by Bob Eggleton, Tom Canty, Don Maitz and others. A.A. Attanasio supplied the introduction.

Edited by Ric Alexander (Peter Haining), *The Unexplained: Stories of the Paranormal* contained twenty-one stories by Nigel Kneale, Ramsey Campbell, Richard Matheson, J.G. Ballard, Theodore Sturgeon, Arthur Machen, Basil Copper, Clive Barker, Harlan Ellison and others, including two originals by Graham Masterton and Richard Laymon and an introduction by Peter James. Under his own name, Haining also edited *The Mammoth Book of Twentieth-Century Ghost Stories*, which reprinted thirty tales from such unexpected authors as James Hadley Chase, Jack London, Stevie Smith, John Steinbeck, Muriel Spark, A. Merritt and P.G. Wodehouse, along with old hands Henry James, Agatha Christie, Arthur Machen, H.G. Wells, Arthur Conan Doyle and others.

Only available in a book club edition, editor Marvin Kaye's *Don't Open This Book!* was an anthology of thirty-nine dark fantasy stories (sixteen original) that included Tanith Lee, Ron Goulart and Patrick LoBrutto.

The Ex Files: New Stories About Old Flames edited by Nicholas Royle contained twenty-five original stories about the break-up of relationships, from such authors as M. John Harrison, D.F. Lewis, Pat Cadigan, Conrad Williams, Joel Lane, John Burke, James Miller and Michael Marshall Smith. Royle also edited *Neonlit: Time Out Book of New Writing Vol. 1*, the first in a series of annual anthologies which featured Christopher Fowler (with the very clever "Thirteen Places of Interest in Kentish Town"), Mike O'Driscoll, James Miller, Jason Gould, Christopher Kenworthy and Conrad Williams.

Editor and book packager Martin H. Greenberg celebrated the publication of his 1,000th book in a career so far spanning twenty-three years. With John Helfers he edited *Black Cats and Broken Mirrors*, which included seventeen original stories based around the premise that superstitions can come true from such authors as Bruce Holland Rogers, Nina Kiriki Hoffman, Peter Crowther and Charles de Lint.

Lawrence Schimel and Greenberg edited *Fields of Blood: Vampire Stories of the Heartland*, containing thirteen stories (four original) by Henry Kuttner, Nancy Holder, P.N. Elrod and others, and *Streets of Blood: Vampire Stories from New York City*, collecting another baker's dozen tales by such writers as Suzy McKee Charnas, Edward Bryant and Esther M. Friesner.

From the editorial team of Stefan Dziemianowicz, Robert Weinberg and Greenberg, *Horrors! 365 Scary Stories* was a massive, 700-plus page instant remainder anthology published by Barnes & Noble Books. It featured original short shorts by numerous horror authors, both new and established, including Peter Atkins, Steve Rasnic Tem, Don Webb, Brian McNaughton, Brian Hodge, Nancy Kilpatrick, Phyllis Eisenstein, Donald R. Burleson, Mandy Slater, Michael Marshall Smith, Wayne Allen Sallee, Edward Bryant, Lisa Morton, Brian Stableford, Yvonne Navarro and Hugh B. Cave.

A much better anthology from the same editorial team was *100 Twisted Little Tales of Terror*, also published by Barnes & Noble. It contained some excellent reprints by such well-known names as David J. Schow, Les Daniels, Karl Edward Wagner, Tanith Lee, H.P. Lovecraft, Frank Belknap Long, Fritz Leiber, Joe R. Lansdale, Thomas Ligotti, Kim Newman, R. Chetwynd-Hayes, Ramsey Campbell, Hugh B. Cave, August Derleth, John Shirley, Edward Bryant, Joel Lane, Michael Marshall Smith, Clark Ashton Smith and many more.

Stefan Dziemianowicz, Denise Little and Robert Weinberg edited the Barnes & Noble instant remainder *Mistresses of the Dark: 25 Macabre Tales by Master Storytellers*, which included reprints by Margaret Atwood, A.S. Byatt, Angela Carter, Daphne du Maurier, Patricia Highsmith, Shirley Jackson, Doris Lessing, Joyce Carol Oates, Ruth Rendell, Muriel Spark and Fay Weldon.

The Raven and the Monkey's Paw was an uncredited anthology of fifteen stories and eight poems. Eight of the tales and all the poems were by Edgar Allan Poe, and there were also classic reprints from W.W. Jacobs, Charles Dickins, Saki and Edith Wharton, amongst others. *Classic Ghost Stories* edited by John Grafton featured eleven tales of the supernatural by Charles Dickens, M.R. James, J. Sheridan Le Fanu and other familiar names, and Patricia Craig edited *12 Irish Ghost Stories* for Oxford University Press.

Hot Blood X was the tenth volume in the sexual horror series edited by Jeff Gelb and Michael Garrett. It included seventeen pieces of fiction (one reprint) from Ramsey Campbell, Graham Masterton, Lawrence Block, Nancy Holder, Melanie Tem, Brian Hodge, and Bentley Little, amongst others. *Demon Sex* edited by Amarantha Knight (Nancy Kilpatrick) contained eleven explicit horror stories (including one reprint by Neil Gaiman) from Thomas S. Roche, Edo van Belkom and Kilpatrick herself.

Lisa Tuttle edited *Crossing the Border: Tales of Erotic Ambiguity*, which included twenty-two stories (thirteen reprints). Although not really a horror book, it included stories by Poppy Z. Brite, Graham Joyce, Angela Carter, Joyce Carol Oates, Michael Blumlein, Nicholas Royle, Carol Emshwiller, Lucy Taylor, Neil Gaiman, Geoff Ryman and the editor.

The Ghost of Carmen Miranda and Other Spooky Gay and

Lesbian Tales edited by Julie K. Trevelyan and Scott Brassart, contained twenty-three stories (five reprints).

Most horror readers also probably passed on Otto Penzler's new crime anthology *Murder for Revenge*. If they did, they missed Peter Straub's remarkable novella "Mr Clubb and Mr Cuff", plus new stories by David Morrell, Joyce Carol Oates, Eric Lustbader, Lawrence Block and others.

The Year's Best Fantasy and Horror: Eleventh Annual Collection, ably edited as usual by Ellen Datlow and Terri Windling, weighed-in at more than 500 pages and contained thirty-seven stories, nine poems, and summaries by the editors, James Frenkel, Edward Bryant and Seth Johnson, along with the usual pointless list of "Honorable Mentions". *The Mammoth Book of Best New Horror Volume Nine* edited by Stephen Jones contained nineteen stories, only one of which (Stephen Laws' "The Crawl") overlapped with the Datlow/Windling volume.

Eternal Lovecraft: The Persistence of HPL In Popular Culture was edited by Jim Turner and published under his Golden Gryphon Press imprint. Described as ex-Arkham House editor Turner's farewell to H.P. Lovecraft, the retrospective anthology was split into three sections that contained eighteen reprints from Stephen King, Fritz Leiber, Nancy A. Collins, T.E.D. Klein and Harlan Ellison, amongst others.

Meanwhile, Arkham House itself returned to its dark fantasy roots with *Flowers from the Moon and Other Lunacies* by the late Robert Bloch, which contained twenty previously uncollected stories, mostly reprinted from *Weird Tales* and *Strange Tales*, edited and with an introduction by Robert M. Price. Also from Arkham, Peter Cannon edited *Lovecraft Remembered*, a collection of sixty-five reminiscences and other pieces about HPL by Robert Bloch, August Derleth, Robert E. Howard, Clark Ashton Smith and others, many reprinted from obscure sources.

Canada's Battered Silicon Dispatch Box revived Arkham's Mycroft & Moran imprint to publish *In Lovecraft's Shadow*, which collected all twenty-three of August Derleth's original Cthulhu Mythos stories, along with three poems (one original) and an essay, illustrated by Stephen E. Fabian. The same imprint also issued Derleth's *The Final Adventures of Solar Pons*, an original collection of early unpublished Sherlockian detective stories, comprising a novel, six stories (including two collaborations with Mack Reynolds) and a number of vignettes, edited by Peter Ruber.

Published by Fedogan & Bremer, *A Coven of Vampires: The Collected Vampire Stories of Brian Lumley* collected thirteen stories and a new foreword by the author. From the same imprint came Adam Niswander's *The Sand Dwellers*, a Lovecraftian Cthulhu Mythos novel set in the mountains of the American southwest. Both books were available in trade hardcovers plus 100-copy signed and limited editions.

From Britain's Pumpkin Books came *Ghosts and Grisly Things*, a collection of twenty of Ramsey Campbell's uncollected stories (one original) in simultaneous hardcover and trade paperback format. Pumpkin also published the first UK trade paperback and first world hardcover of Dennis Etchison's macabre murder mystery *Double Edge*, plus Nancy Kilpatrick's "Power of the Blood" vampire trilogy in uniform trade paperback editions, comprising the original novel *Reborn*, along with reprints of the first two volumes, *Child of the Night* and *Near Death*.

The début volume from Britain's Wandering Star imprint was a superbly designed and produced collection, *The Savage Tales of Solomon Kane* by Robert E. Howard. Profusely illustrated in colour and black and white by Gary Gianni, the slipcased hardcover was published in a signed edition of 1,050 copies, 100 publisher's copies, and 50 copies bound in goatskin. The book was accompanied by a CD recording of three Solomon Kane poems read by Paul Blake and a portfolio of Gianni's full-page plates. Bowen Designs Inc. also offered a cold-cast bronze sculpture based on Howard's sword-wielding puritan, designed by Gianni and sculpted by Randy Bowen.

Gauntlet Press issued a 40th anniversary edition of Ray Bradbury's classic collection *The October Country* with the original illustrations and unpublished sketches by Joe Mugnaini, an introduction by Dennis Etchison, an afterword by Robert R. McCammon, and a previously unpublished preface by Bradbury, originally written for the 1955 printing. It was limited to a 500-copy slipcased edition, signed by all the writers.

Also from Gauntlet, Richard Matheson's 1978 novel *What Dreams May Come* included a new introduction by the author, an introduction by Matthew R. Bradley, and an afterword by

Douglas E. Winter. It was published in a 500-copy signed and slipcased edition, while a deluxe edition contained an additional afterword by Richard Christian Matheson.

The younger Matheson also contributed an afterword to Gauntlet publisher Barry Hoffman's second novel, *Eyes of Prey*, a self-published sequel to his dark crime novel *Hungry Eyes*, in which that book's female protagonist tracked down a woman with her own murderous agenda.

The cleverly titled *Are You Loathsome Tonight?* was a new collection of twelve short stories by Poppy Z. Brite, published by Gauntlet. It included an odd introduction by Peter Straub, an afterword by Caitlín R. Kiernan, and several distinctive photo-illustrations by J.K. Potter (including some bizarre portraits of the author). The 2,000-copy limited edition was signed by all the writers.

Cemetery Dance Publications had another busy year with the launch of a new series of hardcover novellas featuring full-colour dustjackets, interior illustrations, full-cloth binding and acid-free paper. Each book was signed by the author in an edition of 450 numbered copies and twenty-six lettered copies (bound in leather and traycased). The first six titles were *The Wild* by Richard Laymon, *Spree* by Lucy Taylor, *411* by Ray Garton, *Untitled* by Jack Ketchum, *An Untitled Halloween Classic* by William F. Nolan and *Lynch* by Nancy A. Collins.

Also from CD came Laymon's *The Midnight Tour* and a reprint of his 1986 novel, *The Beast House*, both sequels to *The Cellar* and the third and second volumes respectively in the "Beast House Chronicles". Both volumes featured a new introduction and the author's preferred text, and were available in 400-copy signed and numbered editions and $175 deluxe lettered editions.

The Best of Cemetery Dance edited by Richard Chizmar was a massive retrospective volume, available in both trade and limited hardcover editions, containing sixty stories by such well-known names as Stephen King (with the terrible "Chattery Teeth"), Richard Laymon, Ramsey Campbell, Jack Ketchum, Poppy Z. Brite, Thomas Tessier, Hugh B. Cave, Richard Christian Matheson, Joe R. Lansdale, Nancy Collins, Peter Crowther, Norman Partridge and many others, along with interviews with Dean Koontz and the editor.

With an introduction by Tim Powers, writers such as Poppy Z. Brite, Ramsey Campbell, Douglas Clegg, Peter Crowther, Robert Devereaux, Nina Kiriki Hoffman, Nancy Holder, Jack Ketchum, Ed Lee, Elizabeth Massie, Thomas F. Monteleone, Yvonne Navarro, Norman Partridge, Lucy Taylor, Steve Rasnic Tem and Melanie Tem, and F. Paul Wilson were among those who contributed twenty-eight stories (two reprints) based around the tipped-in artwork of Alan M. Clark for *Imagination Fully Dilated*, co-edited by Clark and Elizabeth Engstrom. Cemetery Dance published a limited edition hardcover, signed by all the contributors, for $75. A deluxe leatherbound and slipcased edition with extra art was also available for $195.

Clark and Engstrom also teamed up for *The Alchemy of Love*, a collection of eight stories and pieces of art with an introduction by Jack Ketchum, which was released in a signed 500-copy hardcover edition by Oregon's Triple Tree Publishing.

Like Cemetery Dance Publications, Subterranean Press also launched its own series of short novels in hardcover format with Norman Partridge's *Wildest Dreams*. Plainly labelled "A Horror Novel" on the cover, it was a hard-boiled mystery in which psychic hit-man Clay Saunders was hired by tattooed villainess Circe Whistler to kill her father so she could gain control of his infamous Satanic cult in San Francisco. It was followed by Joe R. Lansdale's *The Boar*, which was written fifteen years ago (as *Git Back, Satan*) and had remained previously unpublished. The young adult adventure involved a fifteen-year-old boy's hunt for a monstrous boar, called Old Satan, in the Texas of the Great Depression. The books were available in, respectively, 500-copy and 750-copy signed and numbered editions and twenty-six lettered copies.

Originally announced as *Look Out, He's Got a Knife!* a few years ago, David J. Schow's collection *Crypt Orchids* finally appeared as a signed and numbered 500-copy hardcover from Subterranean. With an introduction by Robert Bloch (written in 1992), it was only fitting that several of the eleven stories (three original) and one stage play were inspired by the late author of *Psycho*. It was also available in a lettered edition.

From Dark Highway Press, Robert Devereaux's sexually explicit *Santa Steps Out: A Fairy Tale for Grown-ups* came with forewords by editors David Hartwell and Pat LoBrutto and illustrations by the ubiquitous Alan M. Clark.

Published by Mark V. Ziesing, *Black Butterflies: A Flock on the Dark Side* was a collection of seventeen horror stories (two original) by John Shirley, with a foreword by Paula Guran and illustrations by John Bergin.

Faces Under Water was the first volume in Tanith Lee's new dark fantasy series "The Secret Book of Venus", about a league of murderers in an alternate 18th century Venice, from the Overlook Connection Press. The same publisher issued a trade hardcover of Jack Ketchum's (Dallas Myr) 1986 novel *The Girl Next Door*, which retained the 1996 limited edition's introduction by Stephen King.

Obsidian Books published *The Exit at Toledo Blade Boulevard*, the first collection from Ketchum, containing twelve stories (six original), along with a memoir about the author's meeting in the 1980s with Henry Miller and an introduction by Richard Laymon. It was available in a signed and limited edition of 500 copies and 52-copy lettered and leatherbound edition in a matching traycase. Ketchum also contributed the introduction to the novel *Shifters* by Edward Lee and John Pelan, published by Obsidian in a signed and numbered edition of 375 copies.

Splatterspunk: The Micah Hayes Stories was a collection of five hardcore horror stories by Lee and Pelan, available in a limited trade paperback edition of 550 copies and a lettered hardcover from Sideshow Press.

From Florida's Necro Publications, *Portrait of the Psychopath as a Young Woman* by Edward Lee and Elizabeth Steffen concerned an emotionally disturbed advice columnist who attracted the attention of a crazed serial killer. It was available in a signed and limited trade paperback edition of 500 copies, a 150-copy signed hardcover and a deluxe lettered slipcased edition for $150. Also from Necro, Charlee Jacob's vampire novel *This Symbiotic Fascination* was available in a 100-copy hardcover edition and a 300-copy trade paperback, both of which were signed and numbered.

Terminal Fright Press published the aptly-titled *Terminal Frights* edited by Ken Abner, which featured twenty-two stories originally scheduled for the eponymous magazine or specially commissioned for the anthology from such writers as Peter

Crowther, Yvonne Navarro, J.N. Williamson, Tom Piccirilli and other regulars of the small press field. The same publisher also issued David Niall Wilson's novel *This is My Blood*, which combined vampires with the Bible's New Testament as an undead Mary Magdalene tempted Jesus Christ.

From Meisha Merlin Publishing, *BloodWalk* was an omnibus of Lee Killough's vampire detective novels, *Blood Hunt* (1987) and *Bloodlinks* (1988), with a new foreword by the author.

Limited to 500–600 copies each, the latest releases from Canada's busy Ash-Tree Press included *Binscombe Tales: Sinister Saxon Stories* by John Whitbourn, which collected fifteen linked stories (seven original) set in the southern England village where bizarre things always seemed to happen, and *The Night Comes On*, which included sixteen stories in the tradition of M.R. James by Steve Duffy. *The Fellow Travellers & Other Ghost Stories* by Sheila Hodgson contained twelve stories, several based on plot ideas by M.R. James and eight originally written as radio plays.

Edited and introduced by Hugh Lamb, *Out of the Dark: Volume One: Origins* by Robert W. Chambers was the first of two volumes and collected nine stories written prior to 1900, while *The Black Reaper* by Bernard Capes was a revised and expanded version of Lamb's 1989 Equation edition, collecting twenty-three stories with a revised introduction by the editor and a foreword by Ian Burns. *Nightmare Jack and Other Stories* by John Metcalfe collected seventeen stories and an afterword by Alexis Lykiard, and *Nights of the Round Table* by Margery Lawrence was a reprint collection of twelve stories from the 1920s. Both volumes were edited with an introduction by Richard Dalby.

The Clock Strikes Twelve and Other Stories by H.R. Wakefield contained all eighteen stories from earlier editions plus a further three uncollected tales, along with a new introduction by Barbara Roden. Jessica Amanda Salmonson edited both *Twilight and Other Supernatural Romances*, the first of two collections by Marjorie Bowen, containing seventeen stories, and *Lady Ferry and Other Uncanny People* which included eleven stories by Sarah Orne Jewett and a preface by Joanna Russ. The latter volume was the first in Ash-Tree's "Grim Maids" series, reprinting the supernatural fiction of unjustly neglected women writers.

Collected Spook Stories: The Terror by Night was the first in a series of five volumes collecting all E.F. Benson's strange and supernatural tales. Edited and introduced by Jack Adrian, it contained fifteen stories. Adrian was also the editor of *Aylmer Vance: Ghost-Seer* by Alice and Claude Askew, a collection of eight stories which was the first volume in Ash-Tree Press' Occult Detectives library, and *The Ash-Tree Press Annual Macabre 1998*, an anthology of six ghostly stories by authors not usually associated with the genre. These included W. Somerset Maugham, Arthur Ransome, Ford Madox Ford, E.C. Bentley, Hilaire Belloc and John Buchan.

Sarob Press in Wales launched a series of limited, numbered hardcovers with yet another edition of J. Sheridan Le Fanu's *Carmilla*, limited to 200 copies. It was followed by a 350-copy numbered edition of *Vengeful Ghosts* collecting eight stories (two original) by C.E. Ward, and *Skeletons in the Closet* by William I.I. Read collected nine stories (three reprints) involving Dennistoun, the World's Most Haunted Man.

Tartarus Press published a new edition of the 1907 novel *The Hill of Dreams* by Arthur Machen, with a new introduction by Mark Valentine, a 1954 introduction by Lord Dunsany and a previously unpublished introduction by the author. Featuring tipped-in illustrations by Sidney Sime, this was limited to 350 copies. Also from Tartarus, *The Collected Strange Papers of Christopher Blayre* reprinted author Blayre's three short story collections in a single volume.

The Child of the Soul and Other Tales contained four unpublished stories plus a letter by Count Stenbock, limited to 500 numbered copies from Durto Press. Atlas Press published Jean Ray's *Malpertius* in an English translation by Iain White.

Although he was better known as a writer of whimsical fantasy fiction, *The Boss in the Wall: A Treatise on the House Devil* was a genuinely creepy short novel based on a 600-page draft and a dream-inspired novella by the late Avram Davidson, completed by his ex-wife and editor Grania Davis. It came with brief but fascinating introductions by Peter S. Beagle and Michael Swanwick, and was published by San Francisco's Tachyon Publications in a softcover edition, a 100-copy signed and numbered hardcover, and a boxed and lettered edition of twenty-six copies.

Charlie's Bones by L.L. Thrasher was the first novel in a

proposed series featuring an amateur detective and her ghostly partner, from Colorado's Write Way Publishing.

After having his overdraft facility withdrawn by a new bank manager in October, British small press publisher Anthony Barker was forced to discontinue all his future publishing plans under the Tanjen imprint. Existing contracts with authors were cancelled and submissions were no longer invited as the remaining stock was sold off.

However, before the axe fell, Tanjen managed to publish *Scaremongers 2: Redbrick Eden* edited by Steve Saville. An anthology of twenty new and reprint (despite what it said on the copyright page) stories, it included such well-known names as Ramsey Campbell, Christopher Fowler, Stephen Laws, Kim Newman, Peter Crowther, Simon Clark, Nicholas Royle, Mark Morris and Joel Lane, amongst others. All royalties were donated to a charity for the homeless. The other final Tanjen title was *Mesmer*, a first novel by Tim Lebbon, in which a man who saw his murdered ex-girlfriend found himself in a world where the dead could live again.

From Britain's RazorBlade Press, Tim Lebbon's *Faith in the Flesh: The First Law/From Bad Flesh* collected two original novellas along with an introduction by Peter Crowther, while *The Dreaming Pool* by Gary Greenwood contained an introduction by Simon Clark.

The first three titles from new publisher The DesignImage Group were *The Darkest Thirst*, a trade paperback vampire anthology containing "Sixteen Provocative Tales of the Undead" by such authors as Robert Devereaux and Edo van Belkom; the vampire novel *Night Prayers* by P.D. Cacek, and *Carmilla The Return*, Kyle Marffin's contemporary retelling of J. Sheridan LeFanu's classic novella, set in Chicago. These were followed by another vampire anthology, *The Kiss of Death*, containing sixteen stories (three reprint) by Don D'Ammassa and others.

Silver Salamander Press published a collection of thirteen stories (five original) by Lucy Taylor entitled *Painted in Blood*. From the same imprint, *Falling Idols* by Brian Hodge was a trade paperback collection of seven stories (two original), available in a signed edition of 500 copies, along with a 300-copy hardcover edition and a 50-copy leatherbound version.

The first publication from Britain's The Alchemy Press was *The*

Paladin Mandates by Mike Chinn, which collected six stories (three original) about eponymous occult adventurer Damian Paladin, expertly illustrated by Bob Covington. Published as a slim hardcover by Airgedlámh Publications and The Alchemy Press, *Shadows of Light and Dark* collected thirty-two poems (twenty-one original) by Jo Fletcher in an edition of 250 numbered copies signed by the writer, artist Les Edwards, photographer Seamus A. Ryan, designer Michael Marshall Smith, and Neil Gaiman, who contributed the introduction.

From Boneyard Press, *Noise & Other Night Terrors* contained seven short stories (one original) and a novel extract by Newton E. Streeter, along with an introduction by Cindie Geddes. New Welsh imprint Oneiros Books published David Conway's début collection *Metal Sushi*, with an introduction by Grant Morrison.

The first in a new series of books published by Mythos Books and collectively titled "The Fan Mythos", *Correlated Contents* included six Cthulhu Mythos tales (two original) by James Ambuehl, introduced by Robert M. Price and illustrated by Jeffrey Thomas. Price also edited *The Innsmouth Cycle* for Chaosium, which contained thirteen stories and three poems.

Published by Armitage House, *Delta Green: Alien Intelligence* edited by Bob Kruger and John Tynes was an anthology of eight Lovecraftian stories based on the *Call of Cthulhu* role-playing game.

Leviathan 2: The Legacy of Boccaccio, published by The Ministry of Whimsy Press and edited by Jeff VanderMeer and Rose Secrest, contained four novellas by Richard Calder, Rhys Hughes, L. Timmel Duchamp and Stepan Chapman, interviews with the authors, and an essay about novella writing by David Pringle.

A follow-up to the 1997 anthology, *More Monsters from Memphis* was published in trade paperback by California's Zapizdat Publications, once again edited by Beecher Smith. It contained thirty-one stories set in the American south by Brent Monahan, Steve Rasnic Tem, Janet Berliner, Tim Waggoner, Tom Piccirilli, Tina Jens and others, including two by the editor.

Published by Space & Time, *Going Postal* edited by Gerard Daniel Houarner was an original paperback anthology of eighteen stories and one poem about people going crazy by such authors as Bentley Little, Gordon Linzner, Carlee Jacob, Tom

Piccarilli, Melanie Tem, Don Webb and James Dorr. *Harvest Tales & Midnight Revels* edited by Michael Mayhew contained nineteen horror stories to be read aloud on Halloween night and was published by California's Bald Mountain Books.

Subterranean Press continued its series of signed and numbered chapbooks with *Red Right Hand* by Norman Partridge, about a bank heist during the 1930s, and *Fugue on a G-String* by Peter Crowther (introduction by Ed Gorman), continuing the exploits of hardboiled private eye Kokorian Tate. Two more titles in the series released in time for Halloween were *The Night in Fog* by David B. Silva and *The Keys to D'Espérance* by Chaz Brenchley (introduced by Peter Crowther). These were each available in an edition of 250 copies and also twenty-six lettered hardcovers.

Also from Subterranean came *Testament: The Unpublished Prologues* by David Morrell, in which the author examined the writing of his 1975 thriller. It was available in numbered and lettered editions, both signed. *Monsters and Other Stories* by small press publisher/editor Richard Chizmar collected six recent tales, introduced by Edward Bryant. Subterranean's lettered edition also added an essay by Hugh B. Cave.

Candles for Elizabeth was an attractive chapbook from Meisha Merlin Publishing that collected three stories (one original) by Caitlín R. Kiernan, with an introduction by Poppy Z. Brite.

Steve Harris' *Challenging the Wolf* from The Squane's Press was limited to 500 copies and contained the original novelette of the title plus the first chapter from the unpublished novel *The Switch*.

Dark Raptor Press released chapbooks of *Expiry Date* by Scottish author Carol Anne Davis, the werewolf tale *The Case of the Police Officer's Cock Ring and the Piano Player Who Had No Fingers* by Ed Lee and John Pelan, *The Adventures of Threadwell the Tailor or Alterations Made While You Wait* by P.D. Cacek, and *Yours Truly, Jackie the Stripper* by Edo van Belkom. Each was limited to 333 signed copies.

Writhing in Darkness: Part I and *Part II* were a brace of chapbooks from California's Dark Regions Press which collected, respectively, nineteen and seventeen pieces of "horrific verse" by Michael Arnzen, with introductions by Wayne Edwards and John Grey. *Dark Tales & Light* by Bruce Boston was a collection of ten stories from Dark Regions, while *Poking the Gun: The Selected Poetry of John Grey* contained twenty-eight poems (seven original) along with an introduction by Michael Arnzen and illustrations by Dale L. Sproule. Each was limited to 125 signed copies.

Nice Guys Finish Last was the title of a story by Gary Jonas, which Barnes & Noble Books cut from the anthology *100 Wicked Little Witch Stories*. It was rescued by Oklahoma's Ozark Triangle Press, who published it in chapbook format. From the same imprint also came Jonas' *Curse of the Magazine Killers*, a collection of four stories which were sold to markets which subsequently folded before they could publish them.

Britain's Enigma Press kicked off its series of *Enigmatic Novellas* chapbooks with *Moths* by L.H. Maynard and M.P.N. Sims, followed by *The Dark Satanic*, a collection of two novellas by Paul Finch, and *Candlelight Ghost Stories*, two traditional ghost stories by Anthony Morris.

11th Hour Productions launched a series of *Twilight Tales* chapbooks featuring Chicago-area authors with *Tales of Forbidden Passion*, *Dangerous Dames*, *Strange Creatures* and *Winter Tales*, all edited by Tina L. Jens.

There was not much horror or dark fantasy in the eleven issues of *The Magazine of Fantasy & Science Fiction* published in 1998 under editor Gordon Van Gelder. Novelettes by Joyce Carol Oates and Tanith Lee were the standouts, and there was also fine fiction from Nina Kiriki Hoffman, Ian MacLeod, Ian Watson, Elizabeth Hand, Howard Waldrop and Phyllis Eisenstein. At least Douglas E. Winter's occasional book review column kept the flag flying for horror.

Edited by David Pringle, Britain's monthly *Interzone* continued to showcase some of the best imaginative fiction available, along with articles and reviews. Among the authors featured were Tanith Lee, Paul J. McAuley, Don Webb, Thomas M. Disch, Ian Watson, Gary Couzens, Michael Bishop, Cherry Wilder, John Whitbourn, Gwyneth Jones, Darrell Schweitzer, Ramsey Campbell and Kim Newman, plus interviews with Whitbourn, Jones, Stephen Gallagher, Sarah Ash, Dennis Etchison, John Shirley and Jack Williamson.

Under new publisher DNA Publications, *Worlds of Fantasy & Horror* changed its name back again to *Weird Tales*, but it remained a pale imitation of the legendary pulp magazine under the editorship of Darrell Schweitzer. Tanith Lee, Melanie Tem, Ian Watson, David J. Schow, Brian Stableford and S.P. Somtow were among the authors who contributed to the two over-sized issues published in 1998.

Cemetery Dance edited by Richard T. Chizmar included fiction by Thomas Tessier, Nancy A. Collins, Ed Gorman, Gary Raisor, Chaz Brenchley, Hugh B. Cave, Norman Partridge, Jack Ketchum, Poppy Z. Brite, Dennis Etchison, Douglas Clegg, Joe R. Lansdale and Norman Partridge, plus interviews with Tessier, Cave, Brian Hodge, Michael Marshall Smith, Edward Bryant, David Morrell, David B. Silva and Ramsey Campbell. With the tenth anniversary number, the magazine moved from a quarterly to a bi-monthly schedule and expanded its content per issue.

Andy Cox's glossy quarterly *The Third Alternative* included new fiction from Conrad Williams, Jason Gould, Rhys Hughes, Christopher Priest, James Lovegrove, Paul Finch, Joel Lane, Steve Rasnic Tem, Jeff VanderMeer and Tom Piccirilli, plus interviews with Priest, Graham Joyce, Jonathan Coe and Joyce Carol Oates. *Odyssey* edited by Liz Holliday published three issues with fiction by Darrell Schweitzer, Charles Stross, Richard Parks, Roz Kaveney and Ian Watson, interviews with Stephen Baxter and Tim Powers, and an appreciation of the late George Hay by David Langford.

After disappearing in 1994, *Amazing Stories*, the oldest of the science fiction magazines (created in 1926), was once again resurrected in July, this time by gaming company Wizards of the Coast. Unfortunately, despite an initial print-run of around 75,000 copies, the new contents were mostly limited to media tie-in fiction (including *Star Trek*), articles and reviews.

In June, Stephen King had a new short story, "That Feeling, You Can Only Say What it is in French" in the Summer Fiction Double Issue of *The New Yorker*.

The special S/M issue of Barry Hoffman's *Gauntlet: Exploring the Limits of Free Expression* included an interview with Clive Barker by Del Howison and fiction by Poppy Z. Brite. The following number featured Howison's interview with Richard Christian Matheson, a spoof interview with/by Brite, plus short fiction by Matheson and Richard T. Chizmar, and a novel excerpt from editor Hoffman.

Ténèbres: Toutes les couleurs du Fantastique was a new quarterly magazine launched in France that attempted to provide a professional market for fantastic literature. Edited by Daniel Conrad and Benoit Domis, the first three issues included fiction by Jay R. Bonansinga, Les Daniels, Stephen Dedman, Poppy Z. Brite, Christa Faust, Nancy Kilpatrick, John Brunner, Terry Dowling and Kim Newman, along with interviews with Dan Simmons, Brite, Faust, Kilpatrick and Newman.

Omni Online included a round-robin story written by Elizabeth Hand, John Clute, Kathleen Ann Goonan, Kim Newman and Jonathan Lethem, and another collaboration from Kelley Eskridge, Graham Joyce, Edward Bryant and Kathe Koja before the website was closed down in March, following the death of founder Kathy Keeton in 1997. Four former editors of the site, including Ellen Datlow, subsequently launched the new fiction webzine *Event Horizon* (http://www.eventhorizon.com/sfzine) five months later with fiction and columns by Terry Dowling, Pat Cadigan, Lucius Shepard, Jack Womack, Edward Bryant and others. Another round-robin story by Jay Russell, Elizabeth Massie, Roberta Lannes and Brian Hodge appeared over the November and December issues.

The March issue of the *Book and Magazine Collector* contained an overview of the career of "R. Chetwynd-Hayes: Master of the Macabre" by David Whitehead, along with a very useful bibliography and a guide to the current values of the author's first editions. The same issue also included articles on "Arthur Conan Doyle and the Paranormal", "Aubrey Beardsley and *The Savoy*" and the usual pages of bookseller ads. The annual SF, fantasy and horror issue of *AB Bookman's Weekly* in October featured a profile of Lord Dunsany by Henry Wessells, along with reviews and book dealer ads.

Dean Koontz was the featured writer in the December issue of *Publisher's Weekly's The Author Series* twenty-page supplement. During an informative interview with Jeff Zaleski, Koontz revealed that his presidency of the Horror Writers of America would haunt him forever, and that he resigned his office because of excessive political infighting in the organisation, particularly over awards. "I've written some horror," the author also admitted, "but I don't like horror."

Edited monthly by Frederick S. Clarke and Steve Biodrowski,

the always-excellent *Cinefantastique* included in-depth features on *Tomorrow Never Dies*, *Blade*, *Buffy the Vampire Slayer*, *Lost in Space*, *Species II*, *The X Files* movie, *Mulan*, *Virus*, *Mighty Joe Young*, and double-issues based around *The Outer Limits*, *The X Files* and *Star Trek: Deep Space Nine*.

Tim and Donna Lucas' indispensable *Video Watchdog* kept to its bi-monthly standard with features on David Lynch's *Lost Highway*, *The Lathe of Heaven*, the *Evil Dead* trilogy, the awful *Starship Troopers*, *Dracula* on video, and director Ulli Lommel, along with Douglas E. Winter's soundtrack column and all the news and reviews expected from one of the most intelligent and entertaining magazines in the field.

Edited by Dave Golder, the glossy monthly multi-media magazine *SFX* devoted cover features to *Starship Troopers*, *Buffy the Vampire Slayer*, *The X Files*, *Lost in Space*, *Godzilla*, *Star Wars*, *The Truman Show*, *Highlander: The Raven*, Uma Thurman, former Doctor Who Tom Baker and the top twenty sexiest people in SF!

Over at Visual Imagination, David Richardson's *Starburst* concentrated on science fiction with *Starship Troopers*, *Lost in Space*, *Babylon 5*, *Deep Impact*, *Godzilla*, *Star Trek: Insurrection*, *Armageddon*, *Star Trek: Voyager*, *Deep Space Nine* and the inevitable Las Vegas's *Star Trek: The Experience*. Meanwhile, David Miller's companion horror title *Shivers* celebrated its 50th issue and featured *The X Files*, *Buffy the Vampire Slayer*, *Scream 2*, *Wishmaster*, John Carpenter's *Vampires*, *Species II*, *Halloween H20* and *Blade*.

Sci-Fi Entertainment, the official magazine of the Sci-Fi Channel, was just one of a growing number of titles edited by Scott Edelman. It included features on *The X Files*, *Babylon 5*, *Sliders*, *Lost in Space*, *Xena Warrior Princess*, *Godzilla*, *Armageddon*, *Buffy the Vampire Slayer*, *Stargate SG-1*, *7 Days*, *Mercy Point* and various *Star Trek* movies and TV shows, along with British and American news and numerous ads.

The 16 October issue of the film magazine *Entertainment Weekly* contained a surprisingly knowledgeable list of "The Sci-Fi 100" (from *Star Wars* at No. 1 to *Independence Day* at No. 100), along with some interesting sidebar features.

Despite some administration problems, Necronomicon Press continued to churn out numerous small press booklets, mostly dedicated to H.P. Lovecraft and his fiction. Robert M. Price's *Crypt of Cthulhu* reached its 100th edition and along the way published a special Lin Carter issue commemorating the tenth anniversary of his death, which included an early story by the author and other tribute fiction.

Price also published HPL-inspired fiction and poetry in three issues each of *Cthulhu Codex* (featuring James Ambuehl, D.F. Lewis, Darrell Schweitzer and Richard L. Tierney), *Midnight Shambler* (with Adam Niswander, James Ambuehl, Stephen M. Rainey and Darrell Schweitzer), and *Tales of Lovecraftian Horror* (including W.H. Pugmire, Gary Myers, R.G. Capella and Peter Cannon).

S.T. Joshi edited three issues each of *Lovecraft Studies* and *The New Lovecraft Collector* (featuring Lovecraft news and releases around the world, including Joshi's ongoing series "The Works of H.P. Lovecraft: A Listing by Magazine"), plus an issue of *Studies in Weird Fiction* with articles on Clive Barker, H.P. Lovecraft and Frank B. Long, and Richard Matheson.

Knowledgeably edited by Stefan Dziemianowicz, S.T. Joshi and Michael A. Morrison, Necronomicon's quarterly *Necrofile: The Review of Horror Fiction* featured reviews by, amongst others, Brian Stableford, Chet Williamson, Peter Cannon and the editors, Ramsey Campbell's regular offbeat column, and an opinion piece by Stephen Jones.

Peter Enfantino and John Scoleri's *Bare●Bones* continued with articles about *The X Files* novels, interviews with cover artist Richard S. Prather and horror host Bob Wilkins, an index to *Tales of the Frightened* magazine, a look at the career of schlock director Jerry Warren, plus lots of other fascinating stuff.

Stuart Hughes and David Bell commemorated the eighth year of publishing their quarterly small press horror magazine *Peeping Tom* with stories by Stephen Gallagher, Steve Harris, D.F. Lewis, M.M. O'Driscoll, Derek Fox, Gavin Williams, Nicholas Royle, Chico Kidd and others.

Subtitled "A Magazine of Science Fiction & Dark Fantasy", Patrick and Honna Swenson's very professional-looking quarterly *Talebones* reached its thirteenth issue and included fiction and poetry by Stefano Donati, Trey R. Barker, Uncle River, Bruce Boston, Hugh Cook, Mary Soon Lee, Mark McLaughlin, Tom

Piccirilli and Don D'Ammassa, interviews with Spider Robinson, Bill Ransom, Jack Cady and K.W. Jeter, plus book reviews by Ed Bryant and Janna Silverstein.

Also sporting a full-colour cover, *Indigenous Fiction* edited by Sherry Decker made its début in August with fiction and poetry by Steve Lockley, James S. Dorr and others, plus an interview with Jeff VanderMeer.

Graeme Hurry's neatly designed *Kimota* published two special issues, dedicated to SF and horror, featuring fiction by Joel Lane, Paul Finch, Peter Crowther, David Sutton, D.F. Lewis, Stephen Bowkett and Derek M. Fox, along with an interview with Peter Hamilton and an article by Ramsey Campbell. The tenth issue of Mark McLaughlin's *The Urbanite* was published at Halloween and included fiction and poetry by W.H. Pugmire, John Pelan, Paul Pinn, Marni Scofidio Griffin and Caitlín R. Kiernan, based around the theme "On Whom the Pale Moon Gleams", while Gordon Linzner's twice-yearly *Space and Time* featured fiction by A.R. Morlan and Charlee Jacob.

Pendragon Publications' *Penny Dreadful: Tales and Poems of Fantastic Terrors* included work from John B. Ford, James S. Dorr and editor Michael Pendragon.

Writer and editor John B. Ford continued to build his small press publishing empire with *Ghouls & Gore & Twisted Tales*, a collection of fourteen stories illustrated by Steve Lines, and *The Derelict of Death*, a William Hope Hodgson pastiche co-written with Simon Clark. He also edited the final two issues of *Terror Tales*, featuring stories by Michael Pendragon, Paul Finch, Derek M. Fox and L.H. Maynard and M.P.N. Sims.

Mick Sims and Len Maynard also launched their own supernatural ghost and horror story magazine, *Enigmatic Tales*. The three perfect-bound issues featured fiction and poetry by John B. Ford, Bernard Capes, Paul Finch, Rhys Hughes, Steve Sneyd, A.F. Kidd, Peter Tennant and the editors, along with articles by Hugh Lamb and Richard Dalby.

The first volume of Steve Algieri's *Pulp Eternity* was a time-travel issue, with fiction by Cynthia Ward, Christopher Rowe and others. Published back-to-back, *Dark Regions/The Year's Best Fantastic Fiction* edited by Joe Morey and Morey and Mike Olson, respectively, featured fiction and poetry by Brian Lumley,

Brian Hodge and Bruce Boston. The ninth issue of Rod Heather's *Lore* included fiction from Stefan Grabinski, W.H. Pugmire and Elizabeth Massie, while the fourth issue of *Epitaph: Tales of Dark Fantasy & Horror* edited by Tom Piccirilli included an interview with Melanie Tem.

D.E. Davidson's *Night Terrors* celebrated its second anniversary with two issues that contained fiction by Hugh B. Cave and Don D'Ammassa. Canadian book dealer Raymond Alexander also included a new story by Cave in his first *My Back Pages* "magalog".

There were two issues of *Dreams of Decadence: Vampire Poetry and Fiction* edited by Angela Kessler, and *Vampire Dan's Story Emporium* edited by Daniel Paul Medici featured interviews with Janet Fox and Jim Baen.

The premiere issue of *Masque Noir* from editor Rod Marsden billed itself as "The New Wave of Australian Avant-Garde". Meanwhile, *Eidolon* 25–26 appeared a bit late, with stories by Terry Dowling and Rick Kennett, and *Aurealis* managed just one issue in 1998. *Altair* was the title of a new Australian speculative magazine edited and published by Rob Stevenson.

Issue 45 of Joe R. Christopher's *Niekas* was a special "Dark Fantasy" number with essays about Stephen King, H.P. Lovecraft and others by such contributors as Mike Ashley, S.T. Joshi, Sam Moskowitz and Darrell Schweitzer (who was also interviewed). Issue 72 of *Foundation: The Review of Science Fiction* edited by Edward James included an article about Suzy McKee Charnas plus an interview with the author.

The 9th issue of *Horror Magazine* from Dark Regions Press featured interviews with Joe R. Lansdale, Yvonne Navarro, Darrell Schweitzer and Suzy McKee Charnas, plus a report on the 1997 World Horror Convention.

Still the leading news and reviews magazine of the F&SF field, *Locus* celebrated its 30th year of publication with interviews with Tim Powers, Tanith Lee, Joan Aiken, S.P. Somtow, Stephen Baxter, Paul J. McAuley, Nelson Bond, Lucy Taylor, P.D. Cacek, Peter Straub and many others. Andrew I. Porter's news and reviews magazine *Science Fiction Chronicle* managed only five issues in 1998 (one up on the previous year), and included interviews with Charles L. Grant and Tanya Huff.

The Ghost Story Society's excellent journal *All Hallows* published three perfect-bound editions edited by Barbara Roden and Christopher Roden that contained stories by Rhys Hughes, Paul Finch, Tina Rath and Simon MacCulloch. They also included reviews, news columns and non-fiction by Roger Dobson, Richard Dalby, David G. Rowlands and others about *The Twilight Zone*, Charles L. Grant, Robert Aickman, Arthur Conan Doyle, and *The Innocents*.

Given a welcome re-design by editor Debbie Bennett, The British Fantasy Society's bi-monthly newsletter, *Prism UK*, featured articles by Mark Chadbourn, Mike Chinn, Meg Turville-Heitz, Simon Clark and Stephen Gallagher, interviews with Whitley Streiber, Peter Atkins, Graham Joyce and Stephen King, and regular columns from Nicholas Royle, Tom Holt and Chaz Brenchley, along with all the usual news and book and media reviews. *Dark Horizons* No. 37 was edited and produced for the Society by Peter Coleborn, Mike Chinn and Phil Williams and included fiction from Simon MacCulloch, Rick Cadger, Paul Finch, Mark McLaughlin and D.F. Lewis, plus an article by Storm Constantine. The BFS also published its first major paperback and hardback release, *Manitou Man: The Worlds of Graham Masterton* by Graham Masterton, Ray Clark and Matt Williams. Containing ten tales of sex, death and terror (three original), a critical analysis of the author and a complete Masterton bibliography, the book was limited to a 300-copy paperback edition and a 100-copy deluxe cased edition signed by the three authors plus cover artist Les Edwards, illustrator Bob Covington, editor David J. Howe, and Peter James, who supplied the introduction.

The Horror Writers Association Newsletter finally found its direction under editor Meg Turville-Heitz, appearing on schedule and with each issue packed with news, controversy and a lively letters column.

Issue 16 was the final edition of Aaron Sterns' *Severed Head: The Journal of the Australian Horror Writers*, as AHW president Bryce Stevens decided to close down the organisation in February because of lack of finances.

The Governing Body of Britain's The Vampyre Society agreed unanimously to wind down the Society in 1998. The action was taken following the resignation of six committee members in April. Meanwhile, The Vampire Guild continued to publish

Crimson, which included an interview with Stephen Laws and an article on Mexico's mythical Chupacabra.

Issue 8 of *That's Clive!*, the magazine of the official German Clive Barker fanclub, included interviews with Barker (who also contributed several pieces of artwork) and Peter Atkins, articles about Stephen Jones and the H.R. Giger museum, plus related news and reviews. An irregularly-published news magazine about Stephen King and his work, editor George Beahm's *Phantasmagoria* changed its format with the eighth issue to a larger, more-easily readable layout, with extra photos and content.

George Beahm also published the non-fiction study *Stephen King from A to Z: An Encyclopedia of His Life and Work*, with an introduction by Michael R. Collings and illustrated with photos, movie stills and artwork. *Stephen King: America's Best-Loved Bogeyman* was yet another biography of the author by Beahm, with an introduction by Stephen J. Spignesi plus sixteen pages of photos.

Spignesi's own *The Lost Work of Stephen King: A Guide to Unpublished Manuscripts, Story Fragments, Alternative Versions, and Oddities* included more scrapings from the bottom of the barrel, published by Carol Publishing/Birch Lane Press. Part of the Chelsea House *Modern Critical Views* series, *Stephen King* edited by Harold Bloom collected fifteen essays about the author and his work by Clive Barker, Chelsea Quinn Yarbro and others, along with a bibliography.

Published by Borgo Press, *Scaring Us to Death: The Impact of Stephen King on Popular Culture* was a significantly expanded and updated second edition of a 1987 book by Michael R. Collings. Also from Borgo, Tony Magistrale substantially revised and updated his 1991 Starmount book *The Shining Reader* as *Discovering Stephen King's The Shining*.

Discovering Dean Koontz edited by Bill Munster was Borgo's revised edition of the 1988 volume *Sudden Fear*, collecting ten critical essays by Richard Laymon, Elizabeth Massie and others, with an introduction by Tim Powers and an afterword by Joe R. Lansdale.

Joy Dickinson's travel guide *Haunted City: An Unauthorized Guide to the Magical, Magnificent New Orleans of Anne Rice* was published in a revised and updated edition. *Manly Wade Wellman: The Gentleman from Chapel Hill: A Working Bibliography* was the third updated edition of the booklet from Galactic Central Publications edited by Phil Stephensen-Payne and Gordon Benson, Jr.

Joan Kane Nichols' *Mary Shelley: Frankenstein's Creator: First Science Fiction Writer* was a young adult biography, while Betty T. Bennett's *Mary Wollstonecraft Shelley: An Introduction* was aimed at older readers who wanted to discover more about the woman who wrote *Frankenstein*.

A series of critical essays about the author of "The Yellow Wallpaper" were collected in *A Very Different Story: Studies on the Fiction of Charlotte Perkins Gilman*, edited by Val Gough and Jill Rudd for Liverpool University Press.

California's Night Shade Books published *The Necronomicon Files: The Truth Behind The Legend* edited by Daniel M. Harms and John Wisdom Gonce III, which collected essays about the history and rumours surrounding H.P. Lovecraft's fictional book of magic. Along the same lines, Armitage House offered Fred L. Pelton's *A Guide to the Cthulhu Cult*, supposedly written in 1946 by a delusional paranoid. A revised and expanded second edition of *Encyclopedia Cthulhiana* by Daniel Harms was a reference guide to H.P. Lovecraft's Mythos from Chaosium.

Published by Deadline Press, *A Writer's Tale* was an autobiographical volume in which Richard Laymon talked about his experiences writing and publishing within the horror genre.

In *Northern Dreamers: Interviews with Famous Science Fiction, Fantasy, and Horror Writers*, editor Edo van Belkon interviewed twenty-two fellow Canadian authors, including Nancy Baker, Charles de Lint, Candas Jane Dorsey, Phyllis Gotlieb, Tanya Huff, Nancy Kilpatrick and Robert Charles Wilson.

Reflections on Dracula: Ten Essays by Elizabeth Miller appeared from Transylvania Press, *Piercing the Darkness: Undercover with Vampires in America Today* was a revealing look at contemporary underground vampire culture by Katherine Ramsland, and *The Vampire: A Casebook* was an academic study of the legends, edited by Alan Dundes.

From Scarecrow Press, *Vampire Readings: An Annotated Bibliography* by Patricia Altner covered almost 800 items and was indexed by author and title, while *The Vampire Gallery: A*

Who's Who of the Undead was a guide to bloodsuckers from the past two centuries by the often unreliable Gordon J. Melton.

St. James Guide to Horror, Ghost, and Gothic Writers edited by David Pringle looked at more than 440 fiction authors, arranged alphabetically with an emphasis on the 20th century. Mike Ashley and Brian Stableford were contributing editors, and there was an introduction by Dennis Etchison.

In *Screams of Reason: Mad Science and Modern Culture*, David J. Skal explored the concept of the mad scientist in literature and the media, while Marina Warner's *No Go the Bogeyman: Scaring, Lulling and Making Mock* was a critical look at figures of terror from fairy tales to horror fiction.

Edited by Clive Bloom, *Gothic Horror: A Reader's Guide from Poe to King and Beyond* contained more than thirty excerpts and essays on horror by Poe, Freud, Barker and others, including a chronology of "Significant Horror and Ghost Tales" and a selected bibliography. Susan Jennifer Navarette looked at 19th century literature and society in *The Shape of Fear: Horror and the Fin de Siècle Culture of Decadence*.

Waterstone's Guide to Science Fiction, Fantasy & Horror turned out to be an idiosyncratic reference work edited by staff members Paul Wake, Steve Andrews and Ariel for the British bookstore chain. Despite such contributors as Stephen Baxter, Ramsey Campbell, John Clute, Neil Gaiman and Anne McCaffrey, and the inclusion of an interview with Michael Marshall Smith, the book contained some curious omissions.

A decade after the original volume appeared, Carroll & Graf reprinted a revised and updated edition of the Bram Stoker Award-winning *Horror: 100 Best Books* edited by Stephen Jones and Kim Newman.

Part of Visible Ink Press' seemingly never-ending series of movie reference guides, *Videohound's Horror Show: 999 Hair-Raising, Hellish and Humorous Movies* by Mike Mayo included an alphabetical listing of reviews and special "Hound Salutes". *The Sci-Fi Channel Encyclopedia of TV Science Fiction* was a guide to various series from the past five decades by Roger Fulton and John Betancourt.

The Avengers: The Making of the Movie by Dave Rogers was certainly more interesting than the film it was promoting, as was

The Official Godzilla Compendium: A 40-Year Retrospective by J.D. Lees and Marc Cerasini, which appeared in time to tie-in with the big-budget remake.

"They're Here . . ." Invasion of the Body Snatchers: A Tribute contained essays about the classic 1956 SF movie by Stephen King, Tom Piccirilli and others with an introduction by Dean Koontz. It was edited by the film's star, Kevin McCarthy, and Ed Gorman.

The Making of The X-Files was an illustrated look at the creation of the feature film by Jody Duncan, while *I Want to Believe: The Official Guide to The X-Files* was the third in a series of illustrated episode guides by Andy Meisler.

Christopher Golden and Nancy Holder's *Buffy the Vampire Slayer: The Watcher's Guide*, the official companion to the hit show, was a confusingly-designed look at the first two seasons, complete with background information and an exclusive interview with creator Joss Whedon. However, *Buffy X-Posed* by Ted Edwards was an unauthorised biography of actress Sarah Michelle Gellar that also included an episode guide plus black-and-white-photos.

All I Need to Know About Filmmaking I Learned from The Toxic Avenger by Lloyd Kaufman and James Gunn was the former's autobiography and charted the history of his Troma distributing company. At the other end of the spectrum, *James Whale: A New World of Gods and Monsters* by James Curtis was a biography of the famed Hollywood director.

McFarland's expensive reference works included *Of Gods and Monsters: A Critical Guide to Universal Studio's Science Fiction, Horror and Mystery Films 1929–1939* by John T. Soister, *Italian Horror Films of the 1960s: A Critical Catalogue of 62 Chillers*, an A-Z guide by Lawrence McCallum, and Tom Weaver's *Science Fiction and Fantasy Film Flashbacks: Conversations with 24 Actors, Writers, Producers and Directors from the Golden Age*, which included interviews with John Badham, Edward Dmytryk and Debra Paget.

From the same publisher came John Kenneth Muir's *Wes Craven: The Art of Horror*, while Brian J. Robb's *Screams & Nightmares: The Films of Wes Craven* appeared from Titan Books.

Batman: Animated by Paul Dini and Chip Kidd was a beautifully produced, full-colour look at the stylised TV cartoon series based on the classic DC Comics character.

Also superbly designed by Chip Kidd, *Superman: The Complete History: The Life and Times of the Man of Steel* was impeccably researched by Les Daniels.

From Collectors Press, *Pulp Culture: The Art of Fiction Magazines* was a marvellously illustrated history of pulp magazines edited by the knowledgeable Frank M. Robinson and Lawrence Davidson and featuring full-colour reproductions of more than 400 mint-condition covers. It was also available as a limited edition hardcover.

William Gibson contributed the introduction to *The Art of the X-Files* edited by Marvin Heiferman and Carole Kismaric. *The Haunted Tea Cozy* was Edward Gorey's very strange reworking of Charles Dickens' *A Christmas Carol*.

Published by Morpheus International, *Barlowe's Inferno* contained various personal views of Hell by artist Wayne Barlowe, with an introduction by Tanith Lee, and *The Fantastic Art of Beksinski* collected the paintings of Polish artist Zdzislaw Beksinski. Also from Morpheus, *H.R. Giger's Retrospective: 1964–1984* was a translation of a 1984 German edition, covering two decades of the artist's work.

For Underwood Books, Arnie Fenner and Cathy Fenner edited *Icon: A Retrospective Collection by the Grand Master of Fantastic Art*, the single largest collection of Frank Frazetta's work ever published. It also included text by Rick Berry, James Bama and William Stout, along with an illustrated biography. Besides the trade edition, it was published in a deluxe slipcased edition of 1,200 copies containing an extra sixteen pages of art, and as a $300 leatherbound traycased edition of 100 copies which included an unpublished Frazetta drawing. Also from Underwood and edited by the Fenners, *Spectrum 5: The Best in Contemporary Fantastic Art* included more than 300 pieces of art from over 180 artists, selected by a jury system. The only hardcover edition appeared from the Science Fiction Book Club.

From Mythos Books came *The Lovecraft Tarot*, a handsome-looking set of seventy-eight illustrated cards by David Wynn and illustrator D.L. Hutchinson, accompanied by a ten-page booklet.

A \$200 CD-ROM compilation of the complete archives of *Heavy Metal* magazine was withdrawn from sale when a number of contributors complained that they had not been notified about the project nor offered any compensation for the re-use of their work.

Night of the Living Dead co-author John A. Russo and composer/computer artist Vlad Licina launched Midnight Comics in November. The imprint kicked off with *Children of the Dead*, a three-issue mini-series by Steven Hughes, Phil Nutman and John Russo, based on a proposed film written by Russo, that examined the lives of a "special" group of youngsters born during the zombie plague. A special CD soundtrack was composed and recorded for the series by Vlad and The Dark Theater.

Winter's Edge II, a special from DC Comics/Vertigo, featured a new story about Death written by Neil Gaiman and illustrated by Jeffrey Jones, plus stories by other hands featuring the Golden Age Sandman Wesley Dodds, John Constantine, Tim Hunter and several more characters. Meanwhile, artist Yoshitaka Amano produced a new *Sandman* poster as part of the tenth anniversary of Gaiman's character.

Dark Horse comics launched a new series based on the popular TV show *Buffy the Vampire Slayer*, written by Andi Watson and illustrated by Joe Bennett. As a special promotion, a five-page colour *Buffy* strip scripted by Christopher Golden appeared exclusively in the 21–27 November issue of *TV Guide*. Along with its ongoing regular series, Dark Horse also published a three-issue *Buffy the Vampire Slayer: The Origin* mini-series, based on Joss Whedon's 1992 movie, from the creative team of Dan Brereton, Golden and Bennett.

Also from Dark Horse came *The Curse of Dracula*, a three-part series in which veterans Marv Wolfman and Gene Colan (reunited from Marvel's *Tomb of Dracula* two decades earlier) teamed up for a contemporary version of Stoker's story. The same publisher also revived its licence for *The Terminator*, written by Alan Grant and illustrated by Steve Pugh.

Image's new Cliffhanger imprint added *Crimson* to the lineup, which was artist Humberto Ramos' unique look at vampires, and Britain's Games Workshop launched a series of black and white *Warhammer* comics set in the popular fantasy gaming world.

*   *   *

At the 70th Academy Awards presentation in Los Angeles, James Cameron's overblown *Titanic* (which features a supernatural coda) tied with the Oscar record set by *Ben-Hur* (1959), picking up mostly technical awards for Visual Effects, Sound Effects Editing, Sound, Original Score, Film Editing, Costume Design, Cinematography, Art Direction, Director and Best Picture. Rick Baker and David LeRoy collected the Make-up award for their work on *Men in Black*.

To celebrate a century of American films, in 1998 the American Film Institute created a highly controversial list of the 100 Best American Movies, based on the recommendations of a 1,500 member panel, including President Bill Clinton. *Citizen Kane* was voted the top film, but the list was so skewed towards contemporary titles that Steven Spielberg was the most chosen director and nothing by Buster Keaton, Greta Garbo or Fred Astaire was even listed. Only nineteen of the final 100 were genre titles: 6: *The Wizard of Oz*; 11: *It's a Wonderful Life*; 12: *Sunset Boulevard*; 15: *Star Wars*; 18: *Psycho*; 22: *2001: A Space Odyssey*; 25: *E.T. The Extra-Terrestrial*; 26: *Dr. Strangelove*; 43: *King Kong* (1933); 46: *A Clockwork Orange*; 48: *Jaws*; 49: *Snow White and the Seven Dwarfs*; 58: *Fantasia*; 60: *Raiders of the Lost Ark*; 61: *Vertigo*; 64: *Close Encounters of the Third Kind*, 65: *The Silence of the Lambs*; 67: *The Manchurian Candidate*, and 87: *Frankenstein* (1931).

Starring Vince Vaughn as the nutty Norman Bates and Anne Heche as his shower victim, director Gus Van Sant's superfluous colour remake of Alfred Hitchcock's *Psycho* was quickly forgotten. However, ten years after the murder by strangulation of actress Myra Davis (the voice of Norman Bates's mother and Janet Leigh's body double in the Hitchcock original), Los Angeles detectives used DNA evidence to charge a 31-year-old man with her death and with another, similar killing.

Jamie Lee Curtis returned as Laurie Strode, once again menaced by Michael Myers' homicidal Shape in *Halloween H20*, based on a treatment by Kevin Williamson. The title actually celebrated the series' twentieth anniversary and had nothing to do with water. Meanwhile, police in Riverside, California, reported that a 15-year-old boy claimed that the character of Myers from the latest sequel directed him to stab and strangle a 62-year-old woman who was babysitting other children in his home. The boy, who was found with the knife believed to have been used in the attack, was arrested and placed in a facility for psychiatric observation.

Survivor Jennifer Love Hewitt and her friends found themselves on a vacation from Hell as they were stalked by the hook-handed killer of the derivative sequel *I Still Know What You Did Last Summer*. *Disturbing Behaviour* should have been called *The Stepford Kids* as bad teenagers were turned into "A" students by an experimental psychiatric facility, and more stupid teens were bumped off by an unseen serial killer in *Urban Legend*. Scott Reynolds' *The Ugly* was a gruesome serial-killer story set in New Zealand, while Neil Jordan's *The Butcher Boy* was based on the novel by Patrick McCabe.

Scriptwriter Kevin Williamson once again plundered the past and rehashed some old movie plots for Robert Rodriguez's *The Faculty*, in which a group of teen students discovered that their teachers were really body-stealing aliens.

The most successful film of the year was *Armageddon*, starring Bruce Willis, Ben Affleck and Steve Buscemi. Despite being overlong and filled with clichés, Michael Bay's big-budget disaster movie worked, thanks to memorable characters, strong performances and superb special effects as a team of oilworkers were sent into space to destroy a huge asteroid that was on a collision course with Earth. Mimi Leder's *Deep Impact* covered similar ground, as a comet hit the Earth, causing a giant tidal wave which decimated the American east coast and thankfully drowned star Téa Leoni.

Despite a massive publicity campaign in America, the huge boxoffice take for Roland Emmerich and Dean Devlin's misguided $120 million reworking of *Godzilla* was still considered a disappointment. *Daily Variety* reported that the film had trouble in Japan as well. Even though it broke records there when 500,000 people turned out to see it on the opening day, ticket sales dropped considerably during the second week.

In Stephen Sommers's underrated *Deep Rising*, the likeable Treat Williams found himself unwittingly involved in a raid on a cruise ship and discovered that most of the crew and passengers had been killed by giant flesh-eating worms from the ocean depths. Ron Underwood's remake of the 1949 RKO movie *Mighty Joe Young* also used some impressive special effects to bring the eponymous fifteen-foot ape to life.

The X Files movie followed on directly from the fifth season of the TV series, as FBI agents Mulder and Scully (David Duchovny and Gillian Anderson) finally uncovered what was really behind all the conspiracies and cover-ups. It also included a flying saucer climax that was straight out of *The Thing from Another World* (1951).

Alex Proyas' wonderfully *noir*-ish *Dark City* involved Rufus Sewell as a man framed as a serial killer who discovered that he and everyone else were living in outer space, where a dying race of alien "Strangers" (who looked like Clive Barker creations) possessed the bodies of the dead and could stop time.

A big opening weekend for the fast, flashy and violent vampire action movie *Blade*, based on the Marvel Comics character, quickly led to rumours of a sequel to again star Wesley Snipes as the moody half-undead, half-human killing machine. The arty *Wisdom of Crocodiles* starred Jude Law as a psychic vampire who fed off the positive emotions that existed in his victims' blood streams, while John Carpenter's *Vampires*, based on John Steakley's 1990 novel, was one of the director's worst movies, thanks to a dumb script (Don Jakoby), laughable performances (especially James Woods), unconvincing special effects and the obvious low budget. Even so, it was still way ahead of *Razor Blade Smile*, a woefully cheap-looking vampire thriller that simply didn't have the talent or budget to match the high concepts of 26-year-old writer/director Jake West. It also marked a sad end to the career of actor David Warbeck.

As Death, Brad Pitt took a holiday in the interminable *Meet Joe Black*. Based on the novel by Richard Matheson, Robin Williams had a colourful look at the after-life in *What Dreams May Come*, and Michael Keaton came back from the dead to revisit his children as a silly-looking snowman in *Frost*.

Al Pacino's Satanic John Milton hired hotshot lawyer Keanu Reeves for his Manhattan law firm in *The Devil's Advocate*, based on the novel by Andrew Neiderman. Denzel Washington played a detective attempting to catch a body-hopping demonic killer in *Fallen*, and Universal successfully revived its killer-doll franchise with *Bride of Chucky*, in which the possessed plaything was reanimated by voodoo and teamed up with his sexy psychopath girlfriend played by Jennifer Tilly.

An adaptation of Christopher Bram's superior gay novel *Father* of *Frankenstein*, Bill Condon's *Gods and Monsters* was an overlong and occasionally plodding look at the final months of retired film director James Whale, expertly played by Ian McKellan. McKellan also appeared as a former Nazi being blackmailed by a 16-year-old student in Bryan Singer's *Apt Pupil*, based on the story by Stephen King.

Based on the novel by executive producer Dean Koontz, *Phantoms* starred Peter O'Toole and Ben Affleck investigating a small town where a blob monster had caused everyone to disappear.

Produced by star Oprah Winfrey, *Beloved* was a Civil War ghost story that flopped at the boxoffice. Sandra Bullock and Nicole Kidman played witchy sisters looking for love in *Practical Magic*, and the long-delayed Spanish film *Killer Tongue* involved a woman infected by an alien rock.

Natasha Henstridge returned as a sexy alien shape-changer still looking to get laid in the laughable *Species II*. *Star Trek: Insurrection*, the third film to feature *The Next Generation* crew, suffered from a weak storyline but did include an evil race of facelifting aliens, and Kurt Russell battled a cyborg warrior on another planet in the futuristic flop *Soldier*.

Joe Dante's subversive dark comedy *Small Soldiers* was set in a small town which became a battleground for voice-activated toys fitted with munitions chips.

Vincenzo Natali's student film *Cube* resembled an overlong *Twilight Zone* episode, as a group of strangers found themselves trapped in a endless maze of interlocking cubes, some of which contained lethal traps. In *Sphere*, based on the novel by Michael Crichton, Sharon Stone, Dustin Hoffman and Samuel L. Jackson discovered an alien artifact underwater which gave them the power to unconsciously manifest their dark sides.

Lost in Space starring William Hurt, Gary Oldman, Matt LeBlanc and Mimi Rogers was loosely based on the 1960s TV show about the space family Robinson. Supposedly inspired by the same period, Jeremiah Chechik's *The Avengers* was an incompetent travesty of the cult sci-spy show, with Ralph Fiennes and Uma Thurman lacking any screen chemistry as John Steed and Mrs. Peel, and Sean Connery hamming it up as the villain. It reportedly lost $40 million and became the third biggest boxoffice disaster of all time after *Inchon* and *Heaven's Gate*.

It was hard to believe that yet another version of *The Phantom of the Opera*, starring a maskless Julian Sands, was the movie Italian cinemagoers said they wanted to see from co-writer/ director Dario Argento.

The anniversary re-release of William Friedkin's 1973 classic *The Exorcist* in Britain meant extra business for the clergy, who were inundated with requests for spiritual guidance from moviegoers overwhelmed by the experience. BBC Radio 4 also broadcast a half-hour programme entitled *Lucifer Rising – 25 Years of "The Exorcist"*, in which journalist Mark Kermode interviewed writer William Peter Blatty and director William Friedkin.

Although it didn't have much to do with the author, *Bram Stoker's Shadowbuilder* was quite an impressive direct-to-video horror thriller involving a black magic demon that used the dark to kill off its victims. Don Coscarelli reworked his 1979 film again as *Phantasm IV*, once more featuring Angus Scrimm as the Tall Man, and Christopher Walken returned as the psychopathic angel Gabriel in *Prophecy 2*. Ahmet Zappa, David Carradine and Fred Williamson all turned up in Ethan Wiley's *Children of the Corn V: Fields of Terror*.

Curse of the Puppetmaster and *Subspecies 4* were the latest entries in executive producer Charles Band's direct-to-video series, while *Frankenstein Reborn!* and *Werewolf Reborn!* were the first two titles in Band's *Filmonsters!* series aimed at teenagers.

Scooby-Doo on Zombie Island was an enjoyable direct-to-video cartoon feature in which the cowardly dog and his pals met up with some scary E.C. Comics-style zombies, however *Addams Family Reunion* was a disappointing video entry in the live-action series, with Tim Curry and Daryl Hannah taking over the roles of Gomez and Morticia.

With his daughter Sara Jane and co-stars Adrienne Corri and Christopher Lee among those present on November 23rd, an English Heritage Blue Plaque was unveiled at the birthplace of horror film star Boris Karloff, who was born William Henry Pratt in Peckham, south London, in 1887.

Steve Barron's *Merlin* was a magical TV mini-series that looked at the myths and legends of Arthurian Britain from the perspective of the eponymous sorcerer (Sam Neill) and other supernatural characters. *Peter Benchley's Creature* was another fun mini-series, in which scientist Craig T. Nelson and his family encountered a mutated monster land shark, created during the Vietnam war and accidently released by treasure hunters.

A series of underwater earthquakes released a family of mutated salamanders that had grown to gigantic proportions in *Gargantua*, a cable TV monster movie made without any sophistication by Bradford May. Wes Craven "presented" *Don't Look Down*, a Halloween TV movie in which Megan Ward played a reporter afraid of heights.

Stephen Tompkinson was the wimpy hero who uncovered a plot by a mysterious pharmaceutical company to develop a drug that caused those who took it to share their thoughts in the three-part series *Oktober*, based on the novel by writer/director Stephen Gallagher.

When a million year-old giant artifact was discovered in hyperspace, writer/executive producer J. Michael Straczynski reworked familiar themes from both H.P. Lovecraft and Nigel Kneale into *Babylon 5: Thirdspace*, the second in a series of TV movies based on the SF show, and David Hasselhoff certainly looked the part as special agent *Nick Fury* in the TV movie based on the Marvel Comics character. When dubbed scientist Udo Kier predicted that sun spots would result in the Earth experiencing a new ice age, various west coast characters whined and panicked as it got cold in the count-the-clichés disaster movie *Ice*.

Veteran Debbie Reynolds played a witchy grandmother who had to stop an evil warlock from returning the powers of darkness to the colourful world of ghosts and monsters in the Disney TV movie *Halloweentown*.

The best genre show to début during the 1998 TV season was the Fox Network's grim *Brimstone*, in which Peter Horton played dead police officer Ezekiel Stone who made a deal with the Devil (John Glover) to return to Earth and recover 113 escaped souls from Hell. Unfortunately, it was soon cancelled.

Meanwhile, the Wes Craven/Shaun Cassidy series *Hollyweird*, which was also being prepared for a fall début on Fox, was never aired after the network decided to make some major changes in the show, including bringing in an all-new cast. It was supposed to be about three midwest teenagers who brought their local-access cable TV show about unsolved murders and bizarre night-life to Hollywood.

At least *Buffy the Vampire Slayer* continued to build upon its solid fan base with strong characterizations and surprisingly dark stories, as the high school vampire-hunter (Sarah Michelle Gellar) and her friends discovered that Willow's new boyfriend Oz was the werewolf terrorizing Sunnydale; a jealous science student used a potion to turn himself into the kind of man he thought his girlfriend wanted him to be; a Nigerian demon mask belonging to Buffy's mother brought the recently dead back as homicidal zombies; an experimental DNA process had the side-effect of turning school swim-team members into monstrous gill-men, and Buffy's undead boyfriend Angel (David Boreanaz) escaped after spending centuries in Hell, only to be confronted by his many victims.

Buffy cast members also selected their all-time favourite music videos on the 1998 MTV Halloween special, *Videos That Don't Suck*, which also included a behind-the-scenes look at the series, and Fox Consumer Products announced its own *Buffy* clothing line aimed at teenage girls.

Chris Carter's phenomenally popular *The X Files* came up with a couple of scary episodes amongst the usual aliens and con-spiracy plots. In "Folie à Deux" a man holding his colleagues as hostages tried to convince Mulder (David Duchovny) that his boss was really a mind-clouding insectoid monster that had been turning its victims into blank-eyed zombies, while in "Bad Blood" Mulder was accused of staking a pizza delivery boy because he believed he was a vampire. As the surprise ending revealed, the whole trailer park community was made up of the glowing-eyed undead. Unfortunately, the killer doll episode "Chinga", co-scripted by Stephen King and creator Carter, turned out to be a big disappointment.

Lance Henriksen's Frank Black had little more than a cameo in the best *Millennium* episode, "Somehow, Satan Got Behind Me", in which four demons in human guise got together in a donut shop to discuss how things were going with their soul collecting. The rest of the second season plodded on, despite some major plot changes.

Poltergeist The Legacy, the series about the members of a San

Francisco-based secret society who protect others from the super-natural, returned with a two-part story in which anthropologist Alex Moreau (Robbi Chong) was bitten by an old friend while visiting New Orleans and soon found herself transforming into a vampire.

Psi Factor: Chronicles of the Paranormal was hosted by an unconvincing Dan Aykroyd and supposedly inspired by the actual case files of The Office of Scientific Investigation and Research. Adding Matt Frewer and Michael Moriarty to the second season, O.S.I.R. investigators looked into the case of a family who had survived for more than a century without aging by drinking fresh blood, and travelled to swamp country to investigate the case of two murdered brothers who were brought back from the dead by their family as putrefying zombies.

Ultraviolet was a moody six-part British serial in which a police detective (Jack Davenport) found himself recruited by a covert organisation dedicated to eradicating modern-day vampires in a secret war being fought on the streets of contemporary London.

Malcolm McDowell brought a nice dark edge to his role as Mr. Rourke in the ill-fated revival of *Fantasy Island*, and Jeremy Piven was either the eponymous Roman god or a madman in the light-hearted *Cupid*.

In *Charmed*, Shannen Doherty, Holly Marie Combs and Alyssa Milano starred as the three Halliwell sisters, who dis-covered they were witches. Using a magic recipe book found in the attic of their San Francisco home, the trio solved crimes of a supernatural nature. Mark Dacascos played a musician brought back from the dead seeking revenge in *The Crow: Stairway to Heaven*, which was based on the books and movies created by James O'Barr.

The usually tedious *Star Trek: Deep Space Nine* managed at least one memorable episode ("Far Beyond the Stars") that looked at racism in the 1950s against the background of the SF pulp magazines.

Debra Messing portrayed bioanthropologist Dr Sloan Parker, who uncovered the existence of a new species dedicated to the annihilation of mankind in the underrated *Prey*. Robert Lee-shock was the new lead in *Earth Final Conflict*, playing body-guard Liam Kincaid, a man more than human who was caught in the struggle between the alien Taelons and the human Resistance.

Sliders also revised its cast as Jerry O'Connell, Cleavant Derricks, Kari Wuhrer and the talentless Charlie O'Connell continued to travel ("slide") between parallel Earths on the Sci-Fi Channel and discovered an apparently haunted hotel and a digitised world where their real bodies wandered around as zombie-like "Empties". *7 Days* was a time-travel series about an ex-CIA agent (Jonathan LaPaglia) who had to save the Earth on a weekly schedule.

Following a 1996 pilot movie, *The Vanishing Man* finally made it to British TV screens for an inane six-part series starring the irritating Neil Morrissey as undercover agent Nick Cameron, who turned invisible whenever he came into contact with water. Even worse was the BBC Scotland and Sci-Fi Channel-produced *Invasion: Earth*, which was shown in six fifty-minute episodes (each costing a reported $1.2 million). Written by Jed Mercurio, this tale of aliens from another dimension invading a remote Scottish village was one of the most ludicrously inept science fiction shows ever broadcast in the UK.

Having apparently lost the title they wanted (see above), Steven Spielberg's DreamWorks SKG produced the *anime*-style cartoon *Invasion America* in three hour-long segments. Despite a cast of well-known voices (including Leonard Nimoy), old ideas and poor animation didn't help. DreamWorks and Spielberg had more success with *Toonsylvania*, featuring the gruesome comedy cartoon adventures of Igor (Wayne Knight), Dr Frankenstein (David Warner) and his dumb Monster Phil, along with the zombie family of *Night of the Living Fred*.

The Simpsons Halloween Special IX was also fun as Homer's new hairpiece was possessed by the revenge-seeking spirit of an executed criminal, Bart and Lisa were sucked into an Itchy and Scratchy cartoon on TV, and Maggie turned out to be the offspring of alien commander Kang. Even better was *The Angry Beavers* episode "The Day the World Got Really Screwed Up!", an hilarious Halloween special narrated by Peter Graves in which beavers Daggett and Norbert ended up at the home of "B" movie actor Oxnard Montalvo where they battled monsters controlled by an evil vampiric alien intelligence from another dimension.

Guest voices included Adrienne Barbeau, William Schallert and Jonathan Haze.

Van-pires was a syndicated live action and computer-animated series in which a group of teens attempted to stop parasites from sapping the Earth of all its natural gases. The Fox Saturday morning cartoon *Godzilla: The Series* was a vast improvement over the flashy movie it was based on, and Saban's cartoon *Monster Farm* was set on a rural farm full of monsters, including vampiric rooster Cluckula, Jekyll and Hyde sheep Dr. Woolly, monster pig Frankenswine, living-dead bull Zombeef and Egyptian mummy Cowapatra.

A quartet of transforming mummies with superhuman powers ("With the strength of Ra!") and their sacred cat protected a twelve year-old San Francisco skateboarder, who was the reincarnation of an Egyptian prince in the cartoon *Mummies Alive!* The inevitable action toys followed.

Goggle Watch: The Horror of the House of Goggle Part13 was a daily half-hour children's series featuring the Goggle Family who decided to turn their guest house into a themed hotel, "Goggle House of Horror". Even more infantile was the BBC's *Julia Jekyll and Harriet Hyde*, in which a schoolgirl (Olivia Hallinan) periodically transformed into a hairy giant monster.

A juvenile spin-off from the Kevin Sorbo show *Hercules the Legendary Journeys*, *Young Hercules* involved the teenage son (Ryan Gosling) of Zeus and his friends battling the fanged followers of the evil god Bacchus over several half-hour episodes.

Based on the short-lived 1991–92 series, *Eerie Indiana "The Other Dimension"* involved Mitchell Taylor (Bill Switzer) and his friend Stanley (Daniel Clark), who discovered that weirdness was spilling into their world via an inter-dimensional television signal.

The New Addams Family was an unfunny half-hour comedy series based upon the creepy characters created by Charles Addams. At least it included a welcome guest appearance by John Astin (the original Gomez from the 1964–66 series) and the excellent Nicole Fugère as Wednesday.

Inspired by the 1989 hit film and characters created by Stuart Gordon, Brian Yuzna and co-executive producer Ed Naha, *Honey, I Shrunk the Kids* followed the usually-bizarre exploits of scientist Wayne Szalinski (Peter Scolari) and his family.

The title of Kevin Brownlow's slightly disappointing cable TV documentary, *Universal Horror*, was something of a misnomer as it also included material from several other studios. The History Channel's *In Search of History* series featured two well-researched documentaries based around genre themes: *Legends of the Werewolves* looked at lycanthropes both real and fictional, while *The Real Dracula* investigated the life of *Dracula* author Bram Stoker and the historical facts behind the character. However, E! Entertainment's *Mysteries & Scandals: Bela Lugosi* was a sleazy, tabloid-style exposé of "the tormented life" of the actor that simply rehashed rumour, innuendo and myths as it concentrated on the end of Lugosi's career as an alcoholic and drug addict.

For computer-users, The Learning Company/Red Orb, a division of Mindscape, released *Blackstone Chronicles: An Adventure in Terror*, a game for the PC that was based on John Saul's series of books set in and around a haunted asylum.

The 8th World Horror Convention was held in Phoenix, Arizona, over the weekend of 7–10 May. Guests of honour were Brian Lumley, Bernie Wrightson and publisher Tom Doherty, with John Steakley as Toastmaster. The Media Guest, Tom Savini, failed to show up.

The Bram Stoker Awards were presented by the Horror Writers Association at a banquet on 6 June in New York City, with Douglas E. Winter as the Keynote Speaker and Edward Bryant as Toastmaster. The winners were *Children of the Dusk* by HWA President Janet Berliner and George Guthridge in the Novel category; *Lives of the Monster Dogs* by Kirsten Bakis for First Novel; "The Big Blow" by Joe R. Lansdale (from *Revelations/ Millennium*) for Long Fiction/Novelette; "Rat Food" by Edo van Belkom and David Nickle (from *On. Spec* magazine) for Short Story; Karl Edward Wagner's *Exorcisms and Ecstasies* edited by Stephen Jones for Collection, and Stanley Wiater's *Dark Thoughts: On Writing* for Non-Fiction. Both William Peter Blatty and Jack Williamson were presented with Life Achievement Awards, a Specialty Press Award was given to Richard Chizmar for *Cemetery Dance* magazine and CD Books, while Sheldon Jaffery received the Board of Trustees's 1998 Hammer Award for his service to the HWA.

Winners of the International Horror Guild Award were announced at the Dragon*Con Awards Banquet on Friday 5 September in Atlanta, Georgia. The Lifetime Achievement award went to Hugh B. Cave; Ramsey Campbell's *Nazareth Hill* was voted Best Novel; *The Throne of Bones* by Brian McNaughton won in the Collection category; the Best Anthology award went to *Revelations/Millennium* edited by Douglas E. Winter; *Drawn to the Grave* by Mary Ann Mitchell won First Novel; "Coppola's Dracula" by Kim Newman (from *The Mammoth Book of Dracula*) won in Short Form; "Cram" by John Shirley (from *Wetbones* 2) was Best Short Story; Stephen R. Bissette was Best Artist; Best Graphic Story went to *Preacher: Proud Americans* by Garth Ennis and Steve Dillon, and Best Publication was *Necrofile* edited by Dziemianowicz, Joshi and Morrison. Although nominations were made in the film category, judges Edward Bryant, Hank Wagner and Fiona Webster abstained from presenting an award.

The 1998 British Fantasy Awards were presented at FantasyCon XXII in Birmingham, England, on Sunday 13 September. Voted for by members of the British Fantasy Society and FantasyCon, the winners were announced at the Awards Banquet by Master of Ceremonies Ramsey Campbell and Guests of Honour Freda Warrington and Jane Yolen. *Light Errant* by Chaz Brenchley won the Best Novel award (The August Derleth Fantasy Award); Best Short Story was Christopher Fowler's "Wageslaves" (from *Destination Unknown/Secret City: Strange Tales of London*); *Dark Terrors 3: The Gollancz Book of Horror* edited by Stephen Jones and David Sutton was voted Best Anthology; Jim Burns was Best Artist; the Best Small Press Award went to *Interzone* edited by David Pringle; D.F. Lewis was presented with the Special Karl Edward Wagner Award, and a Special Convention Award was announced for past BFS President Kenneth Bulmer.

Only the location saved one of the worst-ever organised World Fantasy Conventions, held in Monterey, California, over 29 October to 1 November. Guest of Honour was Gahan Wilson, Special Guests were Frank M. Robinson, Cecelia Holland and Richard Laymon, and Richard A. Lupoff was Toastmaster. The winners of the World Fantasy Awards, selected by a panel of judges, were announced at an anti-climactic buffet lunch. The Special Award – Non-Professional went to Fedogan & Bremer for book publishing; the Special Award – Professional was won by *The Encyclopedia of Fantasy* edited by John Clute and John Grant; Best Artist was Alan Lee; Best Collection went to *The Throne of Bones* by Brian McNaughton; the Best Anthology was *Bending the Landscape: Fantasy* edited by Nicola Griffith and Stephen Pagel; "Dust Motes" by P.D. Cacek (from *Gothic Ghosts*) won for Best Short Fiction; Richard Bowes' "Streetcar Dreams" (from *The Magazine of Fantasy & Science Fiction*, April 1997) was voted Best Novella, and the Best Novel was *The Physiognomy* by Jeffrey Ford. Life Achievement Awards were announced for editor Edward L. Ferman and writer Andre Norton.

California-based dealer Barry R. Levin announced that Peter F. Hamilton had won his Collectors Award for 1998 for Most Collectible Author of the Year. The limited Tor edition of Robert Silverberg's anthology *Legends* was Most Collectible Book of the Year, and Britain's George Locke received the special Lifetime Collectors Award for His Unique Contribution to the Bibliography of Fantastic Literature.

Ten years is a long time. It's even longer in publishing. The past decade has not been kind to horror fiction, with the erosion of the mid-list and the cancellation of genre imprints resulting in the all-but-collapse of the commercial field.

Which makes it all the more remarkable that the *Best New Horror* series has reached this landmark number of volumes. This is mostly due to the tenacity of Nick Robinson of Britain's Robinson Publishing and Kent Carroll and Herman Graf of America's Carroll & Graf Publishers. Despite various changes of title and format, they have continued to publish and support this series of anthologies in the face of industry apathy to the genre.

If not for them, I could not have reprinted more than 1.5 million words of the best horror fiction to have appeared over the past ten years.

I have always said that the aim of this series is to present a representative sampling of stories which are being nominally published under the description of "horror", or "dark fantasy" or whatever the publishers' current nomenclature for the genre is.

That is why I have been proud to select work by such new and up-and-coming authors as Thomas Ligotti, Kim Newman, Michael Marshall Smith, Poppy Z. Brite, Neil Gaiman, Kathe Koja, Douglas E. Winter, Terry Lamsley, Brian Hodge, Grant Morrison, Roberta Lannes, Norman Partridge, Storm Constantine, Ian R. MacLeod, Elizabeth Massie, Nicholas Royle, Elizabeth Hand, Graham Joyce, Caitlín R. Kiernan, Chaz Brenchley, Joel Lane, Conrad Williams, Donald R. Burleson, D.F. Lewis and many others alongside more established names such as Peter Straub, Ramsey Campbell, Brian Lumley, Clive Barker, Harlan Ellison, F. Paul Wilson, Robert R. McCammon, Dennis Etchison, Charles Grant, Jonathan Carroll, Gene Wolfe, M. John Harrison, Iain Sinclair, Tanith Lee, T.E.D. Klein, Graham Masterton, Kate Wilhelm, Richard Laymon, Gahan Wilson and Thomas Tessier, to name only a few. Sadly, others like Karl Edward Wagner, Robert Bloch, Manly Wade Wellman, John Brunner and Robert Westall are no longer with us, but their work lives on, preserved in the pages of this series and elsewhere.

In fact, *Best New Horror* has published a total of 239 stories and novellas and one poem in its ten-year history. During that period only two authors have ever refused a request to reprint their work – it just so happens that they are the two biggest-selling names in horror on either side of the Atlantic. Go figure.

Best New Horror has also been fortunate enough to win the World Fantasy Award, the British Fantasy Award and The International Horror Critics Guild Award, as well as being nominated on several other occasions. To everyone who voted for the book and has supported it over the years, my sincere thanks.

I would also especially like to thank Ramsey Campbell, who co-edited the first five volumes with me and who remains this series' spiritual inspiration. I continue to strive to match his taste, skill and intelligence with every new edition.

But what of the future? As the new Millennium arrives and the horror field claws its way back from the brink of the abyss and begins to find its commercial voice again, *Best New Horror* will hopefully be there to chart its resurgence and supply a few pointers along the way. This series will continue to discover the most exciting new names in dark fiction (in all its myriad forms) and present them alongside some of the best-known authors currently working in the field.

At its best, horror fiction is amongst the most imaginative and challenging work being published today, and *Best New Horror* will continue to reflect that literary excellence into the 21st century.

I hope you'll be along for the ride . . .

The Editor
May, 1999

CHRISTOPHER FOWLER

Learning to Let Go

CHRISTOPHER FOWLER'S LATEST NOVEL IS TITLED *Calabash*. His other recent books include two new collections of short stories, *Uncut* and *Personal Demons*, and the novel *Soho Black*. Among his earlier work is *Roofworld* (currently being developed as a big-budget action horror movie), *Rune*, *Red Bride*, *Disturbia*, *Spanky* and *Psychoville* (also in development). *Menz Insanza* is a large graphic novel from DC Comics/Vertigo, illustrated by John Bolton.

" 'Learning to Let Go' came from my desire to get away from traditional 'horror' stories," explains the author. "I had read many tales that were similarly constructed, and few seemed to contain any of the author's actual experiences. So I began with a very traditional take on such tales – the journey into mystery – and gradually pulled it apart until I found something I related to myself – at which point I discovered that I no longer wished to write traditional horror stories.

"So this is a closure, if you like, the last of my 'old style'. For a while after I stopped writing altogether, trying to work out what to do; but once the bug is in you it's hard to let go – hence the title – and I finally struck out in an entirely new direction, which is my latest novel. As they say, if you don't burn your bridges now and then, you never grow!"

E VERYONE HAS A STORY TO TELL, he reminded himself. Whether it really happened, to them or to someone else, is irrelevant. What's important is that they believe some part of it, no matter how small. The most ludicrous and unlikely narrative might yield a telling detail that could lodge in a person's mind forever.

Harold Masters smiled at the thought and was nearly killed as he stepped off the kerb on the corner of Museum Street. The passing van bounced across a crevice in the tarmac and soaked his trousers, but the doctor barely noticed. He raised his umbrella enough to see a few feet ahead and launched himself perilously into the homegoing traffic, his head clouded with doubts and dreams. Why were his pupils so inattentive? Was he a poor storyteller? How could he be bad at the one thing he loved? Perhaps he lacked the showmanship to keep their interest alive. Why could they create no histories for themselves, even false ones?

Fact and fiction, fiction and fact.

What was the old Hollywood maxim? *Nobody knows anything.* Not strictly true, he thought. Everyone has some practical knowledge, how to replace a lightbulb, how to fill a tank with petrol. But it was true that most information came second-hand, even with the much-vaunted advent of electronic global communication. You couldn't believe what you saw on the news or read in the papers, not entirely, because it was written with a subtle political, commercial or demographic slant, so why, he wondered, should you believe what you read in a washing machine manual or see on a computer screen? A taxi hooted as he hailed it, the vehicle's wing mirror catching at his coat as he jumped up on to the opposite kerb.

Dr Harold Masters, at the end of the twentieth century:

Insect-spindled, grey, dry, disillusioned, unsatisfied, argumentative (especially with his wife, whom he was due to meet on the 18:40 p.m. train from Paddington this evening), hopeful, childish, academic, isolated, impatient, forty-four years old and losing touch with the world outside, especially students (he and Jane had two of their own – Lara, currently at Exeter University, and Tyler, currently no more than a series of puzzling postcards from Nepal).

Dr Harold Masters, collector of tales, fables, legends, limericks,

jokes and ghost stories, Professor of Oral History, off to the coast
with his wife and best friend to deliver a lecture on fact and
fiction, was firmly convinced that he could persuade anyone to
tell a story. Not just something prosaic and blunted with repeti-
tion, how granny lost the cat or the time the car broke down, but
a fantastic tale spun from the air, plotted in the mouth and shaped
by hand gestures. All it took, he told himself and his pupils, was a
little imagination and a willingness to suspend belief. Peregrine
Summerfield disagreed with him, of course, but then the art
historian was a disagreeable man at the best of times, and had
grown worse since his girlfriend had left him. He made an
interesting conversational adversary, though, and Masters looked
forward to seeing him tonight.

Thank God we persuaded him to come out and spend the
weekend with us, he thought as he left his taxi and walked on to
the concourse at Paddington Station. Peregrine had suggested
cooking dinner for the doctor and his wife this weekend, but his
house doubled as his studio and was cluttered with half-filled
tubes of paint, brushes glued into cups of turpentine, bits of old
newspaper, pots of cloudy water and stacks of unfinished can-
vasses. Besides, they were bound to argue about something in the
course of the evening, and at least this way they would be on
neutral ground. Or rather, running over it, for they had arranged
to meet in the dining car of the train.

Masters spent too long in the station bookshop quizzing one of
the shelf stackers on her reading habits, and nearly forgot to keep
an eye on the time. Luckily the dining carriage was situated right
at the platform entrance, and he was able to climb aboard
without having to gallop down the platform.

"Darling, how nice of you to be on time for once." Jane, his
wife, kissed him carefully. "I felt sure you'd miss it again. Perry's
not made it yet, either. I bribed the waiter to open up the bar and
got you a sherry. God, you're soaked. I thought you were going to
get a taxi. Do you want me to put that down for you?" She
pointed to his dripping briefcase.

"Um, no, actually, I've something to show you." Masters
seated himself and dug inside, removing a handful of yellowed
pages sealed in a clear plastic envelope. "Thought you'd be
interested in seeing this. I might include it in the lecture."

Jane had hoped for a little social interaction with her husband before he plunged back into his ink-and-paper world. Concealing her disappointment, she accepted the package and slipped the pages from their cover. She was good at masking her emotions. She'd had plenty of practice. "What's it supposed to be?"

"It was found in a desk drawer in a Dublin newspaper office when they were clearing out the building. Miles passed it to me for verification."

With practised ease, Jane slipped the yellow pills into her cupped hand and washed them down with her sherry. "You really want me to look at this now?"

"Go on, before Perry gets here," pleaded Masters. He was like an irritating schoolboy sometimes; he would hover over her, driving her mad if she didn't read it straightaway. Reluctantly, she perused the battered pages.

"Obviously it's meant to be a missing chapter from Bram Stoker's *Dracula*, revealing the fate of Jonathan Harker. But if it was real, it would have to be part of an earlier draft." Jane tapped the pages level. "The quality of the writing is different, too coarse. It wouldn't fit with the finished version of the book at all." She studied the pages again. "It's a fake. I think it's pretty unlikely that Bram Stoker would write about oral sex, don't you? The ink and the paper look convincingly old, though."

"Damn." Masters accepted the pages back. "You saw through it without even reading it properly. Miles went to the trouble of using genuine hundred-year-old ink, too. It's his entry for a new course we're starting called 'Hidden Histories'."

"Did you really expect me to believe it was the genuine article?"

"Well, I suppose so," he admitted sheepishly.

"Honestly, you and Miles are as bad as each other."

"Well, I believed it," he moped. "But then, I always believe the stories I'm told."

Jane smiled across the top of her glass. "Of course you do. Remember how convinced you were that the Hitler diaries were real?"

"I *wanted* them to be real. To learn about the inside of that man's brain, didn't you?"

"No, Harold, I didn't." She looked out of the window. "We're moving. I hope Perry got on board."

"Jesus, that was close thing. I wasn't expecting it to leave on time." Peregrine Summerfield was standing beside them, attempting to tug his wet tweed jacket away from his body while a waiter pulled ineffectually at a sleeve.

"Perry, you're getting water over everything."

"I was trying to choose a paperback. Nearly missed it. On Hallowe'en, too, that would have been an omen, eh? It's pissing down outside. Hallo, darling." He kissed Jane. "The tube smelled like an animal sanctuary, all wet hair and coats. Anyone ordered me a drink? What have you got there?" He pointed at the plastic-coated pages on the table as he sat down beside Masters' wife.

"Something for my lecture on fact and fiction."

"Oh?" Summerfield thudded down into his chair and eagerly accepted a drink from Jane, carefully guiding the sherry glass over his beard.

"Yes, it purports to be – well, it's actually –"

"Jane, you're looking bloody gorgeous, as ever," Summerfield interrupted, "beats me how you do it on a shitty night like this. What's on the menu apart from their god-awful watery vegetables, I wonder? Let's see if we can get one of these pimply louts to open some wine, shall we?"

He made a beckoning gesture at Masters. "Come on, then, I know you're dying to tell someone about your talk tomorrow. What have you got planned for these poor students?"

"I thought I'd talk about how fact and fiction have switched places since the war."

"What do you mean?"

"Well, you have to look at the history of storytelling. For me, one of the most important dates in the last century was the 28th of December, eighteen hundred and eighty-one."

Summerfield gave a shrug. "Why?"

"On that day the first public building was illuminated with electricity for the first time ever, at the Savoy Theatre." Masters leaned forward conspiratorially. "Just think of it. With the click of a switch, twelve hundred electric lamps cast darkness from the room. The myths and mysteries of the past were thrown aside by the bright, cold light of scientific reason. No more shadows. No more hidden fears. No more cautionary tales of bogeymen and ghouls. And in the week of the winter solstice! As if man was determined to prove the dominance of light over darkness!

"Fiction once involved the telling of tales by candlelight. With electricity to help us separate fact from fiction, everything was clearly designated. Before the advent of television life was simpler. You went to work, you came home, you listened to the radio, you read a book; it was hard to mix your home life with your fantasy life. Now, through, the lines are blurred. People have phoney job titles and meaningless career descriptions. They spend their days lying to each other about what they do for a living, trying to make their work sound more interesting than it is, then they go home and watch gritty, realistic soap operas on TV. No wonder their kids are confused about what's real and what isn't. People write to soap stars as if they were real characters. And with so many companies spoon-feeding us entertainment, no wonder we're losing the power to create our own fantasies. No wonder that we're not believed even when we've achieved the fantastic. Inexplicable mysteries occur every day, in every life. It's how we choose to read them that defines us as individuals."

"Oh please," Summerfield exploded, "you might as well ask me to believe in Roswell, Area 51, crop circles, Nessie and all that Fortean stuff. You want to believe in the paranormal because you secretly think there has to be something more to the world than just this." He pointed out of the window. It had grown dark outside. They had already left the suburbs. A glimmer of buttery light showed above the brow of a passing hill.

"Perhaps I do, but that's not the point. It's important to keep an open mind."

"Then you'll never make any decisions in your life. You'll be like a child forever."

"Wait a minute, let's simmer down a little." Jane Masters held up her hand for peace. The table was becoming rowdy earlier than usual. A pair of diners in black plastic witch-hats were staring at them. "Where are we?"

"I'm not sure. It's too dark to see."

"Besides," Summerfield ploughed on, "getting someone to believe in something is simply a matter of theatricality and good presentation. If I wanted you to believe a strange story, I could easily make you do it. Especially on a night like tonight, of all nights." He emptied the wine bottle. At this rate, thought Masters, we'll be crocked before we reach the coast. The air pressure in the carriage altered as they entered a tunnel, sucking out the flame from the little orange pumpkin-candle the waiter had placed on their table.

Summerfield turned to the others, his command of the table absolute, and raised his hands. For the next few minutes he told a tale, the odd affair of a businessman who became imprisoned within an ancient London building. At the conclusion he sat back and drained his glass. He looked from Jane to Harold Masters and permitted himself a satisfied smile.

"Well?" he asked. "You do believe me, don't you? I hope you do, because Jonathan Laine is an old friend of mine, and the story came from his own lips. He couldn't live with the guilt of his secret, and subsequently killed himself. They found him at the bottom of the Thames, somewhere down at the Dartford estuary. So stick that in your pipe and smoke it."

They broke the conversation as their starters arrived. The train seemed to be travelling at an unusually laborious pace, and was lumbering through the flat open countryside toward the lights of a distant town. Heavy rain began to thrash the sides of the carriage. It was as if they had entered a car wash. Toward the end of the meal, Masters raised his glass. "I'd like to propose a toast, seeing as it's Hallowe'en and the perfect time for creepy stories. Jane, perhaps you'd like to tell one."

"Oh no, Harold, I'd rather not," begged Jane, throwing a desperate glance at Summerfield.

"Don't tell me all these years of hearing my stories hasn't rubbed off on you just a little bit." Masters gave a pantomime wink.

"I can't help you, Jane," said Summerfield. "Go on, join in the spirit of the thing. Show us what being with Harold has taught you."

Jane shot him a look of betrayal that had the force to knock over a large piece of furniture.

"All right, then," she conceded, "I'll tell you a story I first heard many years ago. I was a young girl, impatient to become an adult. It taught me something about the nature of time."

As the train crept on through the rain she began her story, about a powerful sultan and the winding of a thousand clocks. By the time she had finished, she looked close to tears. "I always liked exotic stories," she explained, blowing her nose. "They let you forget mundane things for a while." Harold had already lost interest, and was looking over at the next table. She followed his eyeline and saw three students, a pale-faced girl and two boys, staring at them as if they were mad. "Godby, is that you? And Saunders?" asked Masters.

"Yes, sir."

"Good God, lad, am I to have no privacy? As if I don't see enough of you during term. How many more of you are there?"

The first of the group spoke up. His accent was American. "Just me and Kallie, sir. And this is Claire." A bony, whey-faced girl seated between them gave an awkward smile.

That's all we needed, thought Jane with a sinking heart, *to be stuck with Harold's students for the rest of the journey*. They were doomed never to have time to themselves. These days it seemed that there were always other people in the room all talking at once, colleagues from the museum, hyperactive pupils, aged academics, never any of her friends, never any special private moments together, no wonder she –

"Are you going to tell any more stories?"

"I can't believe it," Masters announced to the rest of the group, "surely we're not in the presence of students displaying an interest? They don't noticeably do so in any of my lectures. Yes, we may well tell more stories," he replied, "but you can only join in if you bring a tale of your own to the table."

"Preferably a true one," added Summerfield, just being awkward. He did not enjoy the company of the young; they tired him with their fatuous observations, and made him feel fat and old and unattractive. "And you must present it in the form of a proper story, with voices and acting and everything. And most important of all, you have to bring your own wine."

Outside, sheet lightning illuminated the fields, like someone momentarily flicking on a light. "We're drinking cider," the first student replied, holding out his hand. "I'm Ben. From Colorado originally, but I'm studying here now." The introductions continued around the table. "I've got a story from my creative writing course. It's based on something I read in an old newspaper." Ben dug into his backpack and pulled out a folder filled with scissored articles. "Here's the original clipping." He held it up for everyone to see. " '*Human civilisation, it seems, has flourished during a 10,000 year climactic ceasefire. Hostilities may be about to resume. – Independent On Sunday, 18th February 1996.*' We had to develop a story from a factual starting point, and this is what I came up with."

"All right, but you have to convince us that it might really be true," warned Masters. "Let's hear what today's youth have to offer in the way of narrative ability. The floor of the carriage is yours."

Ben cleared his throat.

"You could have warned me it was set in the future," complained Harold Masters after he had finished. "That counts as science fiction and I don't like science fiction." The student sheepishly returned the clippings to his bag.

"So you didn't like the story, Harold?" asked Summerfield, surprising himself with his decision to defend the boy.

"I didn't say that. It's just that it can't be true because it hasn't happened yet."

"But it's a possible future, one of many. Who knows what will happen to us? And who's to say it isn't happening right now in a parallel universe?"

"Well, I liked it," said Jane, refilling her glass. "Although I think the wine has gone to my head a little. Maybe that's making me more susceptible."

"Perhaps." Summerfield checked his watch. "It's getting late. We should all be growing susceptible. The floodgates to the supernatural world are open tonight, remember. What time do we get to the coast?"

"A little after eleven," Jane replied. "I informed the hotel of our arrival time. They weren't terribly happy about it." She turned to the students. "Where are you three off to?"

"Hallowe'en party. We have friends who rent a house on the edge of Dartmoor."

"I bet your pals have some interesting tales to tell about mysterious goings-on on the moors, eh?" said Summerfield.

"No." Claire grimaced as though the idea was the stupidest she had ever heard. "They just smoke dope all day and play video games."

"Couldn't you revive the tradition of oral history and get them to make up some stories?" asked Masters.

"Oh for God's sake, Harold," Jane exploded, "that's not what young people want to do with their time."

"As the father of two children, Jane, I think I can safely say that I know how the juvenile mind operates."

"Do you? I find that hard to believe. Our offspring are certainly not children, they're not even teenagers any more, and not only do I not know who Lara has been seeing lately or where Tyler is, I'm not entirely sure I would recognise either of them if they sent me recent photographs." She was referring to the snapshot their son had mailed from Nepal earlier in the year. The emaciated young man with the shaved head and the wispy beard seemed to bear no resemblance to the thoughtful child who used to sit beside her at night writing endless fantastic stories in his school exercise book.

"I'm working on a story at the moment," said Kallie.

"It's not set in the future, is it?" asked Masters cautiously.

"No, London Docklands, in the present day. I read about electromagnetic pollution somewhere. Microwaves can create hot spots, areas rippling with forcefields stronger than the most powerful ocean cross-currents. The story's about a corporation that accidentally creates them in its offices."

"Sounds a bit far-fetched." Summerfield wrestled another wine bottle away from the concerned waiter and overfilled everyone's glasses as the train hammered over a set of points.

"Big business as the evil bogeyman, it's an ever-popular target for student paranoia," complained Masters, unimpressed. "There's no human dimension in the stories of the young. Too many issue-led morality tales, the sort they have on American television shows, nothing from direct experience."

"Oh for God's sake," snapped Jane, "people can only reflect the times in which they live. There are no traditional heroes left, no explorers, no captains, no warriors. I don't know why you expect so much from others. One thing that years of listening to you has taught me is that you're incapable of telling a decent story. It's a talent you singularly lack, because you have no perception. You're best off leaving it to other people."

Shocked by her own honesty, she stopped herself from saying any more. An uncomfortable atmosphere settled on the table. Stung, Masters stared out into the rainswept darkness, avoiding his wife's angry gaze.

"Come on, chaps, let's not get personal." Summerfield clapped his hands together and startled Jane, who was gazing glumly into her wine, hypnotised by the steady movement of the train. Most of the carriage was deserted now. Even the guard was dozing in an end seat, his head lolling on his shoulder. It was as though they had been freed from the shackles of time and place, the co-ordinates that underpinned their lives slipping quietly away into the night.

Claire shifted across the aisle to the opposite seat and faced them. "I've got a story," she said mischievously. "About some friends of mine who got locked in a pub." And she told it, although it didn't sound true.

"Well." Jane cleared her throat at the end, slightly flummoxed. "That was certainly *frank*. Although I'm not sure it's really a fit subject to turn into a dramatic piece."

"Some people are uncomfortable around the subject of sexuality," mumbled Claire, meaning older people, meaning her. The senior members of the group were a little embarrassed by the girl's intensity, although it obviously did not bother Kallie or Ben. Jane drained her glass and pushed back into her seat, unsettled by what she had heard. Masters cleared a spot on the window and peered out. "My watch has stopped. I thought we'd be able to see the sea by now. Doesn't the train run along the coast for the last hour?"

"There's not much of a moon."

"Even so, you should be able to see something."

The carriage shifted across a set of uneven points, and the overhead lights flickered. Electricity crackled somewhere beneath their feet.

"Maybe we're on the Hallowe'en train to hell." Summerfield looked around. Jane was half asleep. Suddenly the train lurched hard and shuddered to a hard halt, its brakes squealing. Wine bottles and glasses toppled on tables, and several pieces of luggage bounced down from the overhead racks.

"What on earth . . ."

Jane blearily pulled herself upright. "Are we there?"

"God knows where we are." The doctor pressed his forehead against the window. "It's pitch black out there. I can't see a thing."

Ben retrieved his backpack from beneath his seat. "I'm going to ask someone."

"You needn't bother asking the guard," said Masters, pointing. "He seems to have wandered off."

"Maybe he's dead," Summerfield stage-whispered, "drugged,

shot with a poison dart, a minor character in an Agatha Christie play, someone whose Rosencrantz-like role exists simply to fulfil a duty to the plot."

"Now who's muddling fact and fiction?" Masters asked uncomfortably. He turned to his wife. "Are you warm enough?"

"You've noticed it too, then." The heating had gone off. They could hear the steady tick of the radiators cooling all along the carriage. Jane sensed that there was something wrong, as if the world had slipped a notch deeper into darkness. Panic was descending on her like a cold veil of rain. She dug into her purse for the tablets Dr Colson had prescribed, but could not find them. She had taken two earlier. What had she done with the rest of the packet? When she turned to her husband, she found that he was making his way along the aisle toward the exit.

There *was* something wrong. She needed the tablets to stop her from worrying. She dumped the purse out on to the table and began scrabbling through the contents. The foil sheet glittered between her fingers as she popped out two of the yellow capsules. Claire pulled a mobile phone from her bag and checked it. "No reception," she said casually. "Anyone else?"

"Wait." Jane retrieved a small black square from her coat and flipped it open. "None here either. The service isn't reliable in heavily wooded areas."

At the front of the carriage, Masters pushed down the train window and peered out into the darkness, his breath condensing in the invading night air. He looked back along the curving track, but could see nothing until the moon cleared the clouds.

When the lunar light finally unveiled the landscape, he saw that there were no other carriages behind them. Theirs had been uncoupled from the main body of the train, and released into what he could only assume was a siding. It sat by itself on a gravelled incline, with low hills rolling away on either side. The sea was not in sight, not where it should have been.

He tried to see ahead in the other direction, and could make out a vague dark shape beside the track, a large, squat building of some sort. Clearly there had been a mistake, some kind of accident. He decided to head back and give a cautious report to the others.

"Well, we have no power to move by ourselves," said Summerfield, when the situation had been explained. "As I see it, we have two choices. We can stay here and freeze our nuts off, hoping that somebody finds us, or we can head for the building you saw and try to find a telephone that works."

"I don't understand how this could have happened." Jane looked over at the students, annoyed that they could be so calm and still, and by the way they sat apart, implying some kind of private pact of solidarity that did not exist among their elders. "Isn't anyone worried at all?"

"There's not really much to worry about," said Summerfield. "This sort of thing happens all the time. You always read about trains overshooting their stations and passengers having to walk down the track in the dark."

"I'm not walking along the track – we could be electrocuted!"

"I'm not saying we all do, but someone should. This looks like an old branch line. Suppose a connection came loose and we got separated when we went over the points back there? It could happen, even with advanced information systems. Perhaps nobody will be aware that there's a carriage missing until the train reaches its destination. Maybe not even then."

"Harold, I think your imagination is bypassing your common sense," Summerfield admonished. "Let's face it, you've never been much good in a crisis. Let's try and be logical about this. The carriage coupling must have made a noise when it disconnected. Doesn't anyone remember hearing it?"

Masters looked around. "And what happened to the guard? When I last saw him he was asleep in the end seat there."

They searched the carriage, not that there were any places where someone could be concealed. The toilet was empty. The six of them were the only passengers left on board. Kallie pulled his coat down from the overhead rack. The others began donning their top coats. As they were doing so, the lights began to dim to a misty yellow. Jane released a miserable moan.

"I was going to stay in tonight," said Claire, checking her hair in the window. "There was a weepie on TV. But I decided to join these two. Right now I could be snuggled up indoors with a tub of ice cream watching Bette Davis going blind."

"Was *Dark Victory* on tonight?" asked Kallie. "I love that film."

"Yeah, but I think it was sandwiched between *Curse of the Demon* and *Tarantula*."

"How can you people just chatter on as if nothing is wrong?" Jane snapped.

"Yeah, you're right," Claire agreed, "let's all panic instead. What exactly is in those little pills you're taking, by the way?"

"I also suggest we make for the building further along the line," said Masters. "Unless anybody wants to stay here."

"I've got a torch in my bag," Kallie offered.

"Well, I'm not stepping foot outside of this carriage." Jane dropped back into her seat just as the overhead lights faded completely. "Oh, *great*."

"Jane, you cannot stay here."

"Can't I? Watch me."

"I just don't think we should split up, that's all."

"Yeah," Claire cut in, "look what happens when they do that in movies. Somebody gets a spear through them."

"Please, Jane, you're making things awkward."

"Do whatever you want," snapped Jane. "I'm staying here. You can make your own decision for once in your damned life."

"Then I say we go," said Masters, hurt.

"You can't leave your wife here by herself," Summerfield protested.

"You're right, Peregrine. Would you mind staying with her? We shouldn't be gone too long."

"But I was going to come with you." He looked hopelessly at Jane, who was clearly anxious for him to stay. "Oh, all right. We'll wait for you to return."

"Okay, who else is coming?" asked Masters. The students already had their bags on their backs. "Are you sure you'll be all right, darling?"

"I'll be fine, I'll settle once you go –"

"This is Southern England in autumn, Harold, not Greenland in January," said Summerfield. "Go on, piss off the lot of you, and come back with a decent explanation for all of this."

The four of them made their way to the end of the carriage, leaving behind Jane Masters and Peregrine Summerfield, who layered themselves in sweaters and nestled beneath an orange car blanket that made them look like a pair of urbanised Buddhist monks.

It was lighter outside. The moon gave the surrounding wooded hills a pallid phosphorescence. A loamy, wooded scent of fungus and decayed leaves hung in the air. The track appeared as a luminous man-made trail in the chaotic natural landscape. They saw that the carriage must have rolled by itself for at least half a mile before coming to a stop at the bottom of the incline. The grass around them was heavily waterlogged, so they stayed in the centre of the track. Kallie kept his torch trained a few feet ahead.

"How far do you think it is?" he asked, pointing to the distant black oblong beside the track.

"I don't know. Half a mile, not much more."

"We could have a sing-song," said Masters. "Claire, what kind of music do you like?"

"Trance techno and hard house," Claire replied. "You don't 'sing' it."

"Anyone else know any songs?"

"*Please*," she begged, "the first person to start singing gets a rock thrown at them. Ben, tell another story, just a short one."

"Okay," said Ben. "The woman it happened to is a friend of my mother's, and she's not nuts or anything. At least," he added darkly, "she wasn't until this happened." And he told the tale of the lottery demon.

"Sounds to me like her boyfriend left her and she couldn't handle it," said Masters.

Claire gave a scornful hoot. "Typical middle-aged male viewpoint."

"So what are we saying here, that for every positive action there is a reaction?" asked Kallie, "like you can't win without making someone else suffer? Thanks for the morality play."

"No," said Ben defensively, "just that luck works in both directions. Look at tonight. If we hadn't booked the dining car and then stayed late over our meals, if we hadn't joined your table, we wouldn't be in this fucking mess now."

Something hooted in the rustling hillside at their backs. The black bulk loomed a few hundred yards ahead. Masters was freezing. His left shoe was taking in water. He hated leaving Jane, but knew she was not strong enough to walk through unknown terrain in the dark. "Don't worry, there will be a logical explanation for this," he assured the others. "There always is."

They reached a concrete ramp and began to climb. "It's a station," said Ben, shining his torch ahead. "*Milford*. Ever heard of it?"

They climbed on to the platform and approached the low brick box that functioned as the main building. Masters tried the door of the waiting room, but it was locked.

"Do you think it still operates?" asked Claire. "It's unmodernised. They've got wooden slat benches instead of those curved red steel ones with the little holes. And look at the lights. They've got tin shades."

"It can't still be used," said Ben, shining his torch through the window of the ticket hall. "Take a look at this." The others crowded around in the halo of light. The ticket machines inside had been vandalised. The timetables were heavy with mildew and drooped down like rolls of badly-hung wallpaper. Several of the floorboards were rotten and had fallen through.

"Can you see a phone?" asked Claire.

"You're joking. If there is one, it's going to be out of service. Try your mobile again."

A silence. Only the sound of their breath and the wind in the trees while Claire tried to get a service signal. She tipped the device to the light. "Still nothing."

"We should at least try to work out where we are. Did anyone see if we passed Exeter?"

"I don't know, Ben," Kallie suddenly shouted, surprising everyone. "This was your idea, remember? I'm from the city, I don't visit places with trees unless they're the indoor kind in big pots, like the ones you get in malls. If you told me to expect rabid fruit-bats and rats the size of Shetland ponies I'd believe you because I don't *know* about outdoor stuff, this is not *me*, all right?"

"You might have told us before you decided to tag along," said Claire. "I'm freezing. What are we going to do?"

"I guess we either walk back to the carriage or pass the night here," Masters replied.

"I'm not walking all the way back. Anyway, there's no more heat or light in the carriage than there is here. Oh shit, listen to that." From above came the sound of rain on slates.

"That does it, we all spend the rest of the night in the waiting room," said Ben firmly. "It makes the most sense."

"Oh, you get to decide what's good for everyone, do you?" Claire snapped. "Of course, you're *American*."

"Just what is that supposed to mean?"

"Just that you always boss people about."

"Only if we know what's best for them."

"You're trying to make up for being beaten in Vietnam and the Gulf by telling everyone else what to do."

"At least we're capable of making life-decisions, which is more than you guys. I suggest you try it sometime."

"Great advice coming from a country where people eat with their fingers and send money to TV evangelists."

"Now you're being offensive."

"Come on, you two, give it a rest." Kallie pushed between them and led the way back to the waiting room. They had to break the lock to get the door open, but found a dry fireplace with dusty bundles of wood stacked beside it.

"I read that bird-watchers use places like these as hides," said Masters, digging out his lighter. Outside, the rain began pounding the roof. It took a few minutes for the wood to catch, but soon they had a moderate amount of light and heat. Paint hung in strips from the ceiling, but the floor appeared to have been recently swept.

"I'm going to use the john," said Ben, rising from the corner where he had been seated glaring balefully at Claire. "If you hear a crash it's me kicking the lock off, okay? Give me your flashlight." He pulled the waiting room door open. "Hey, listen to that rain."

"This is like the station in *Brief Encounter*." Claire hunched down inside her overcoat. Kallie had already fallen asleep. "I've seen it dozens of times on TV and I always want the ending to be different."

"I'm surprised you like it at all," said Masters. "Surely your generation prefers more recent stuff. You'd rewrite the ending, then?"

"Only in my head. Don't you ever do that, change the endings of things?"

"All the time, Claire."

Kallie fell asleep in front of the fire. The rain was still pounding the platform roof. "Ben's been a long time. Do you think we should go and look for him?"

"No, it's okay, I'll go," said Masters, forcing his aching limbs into action. He checked his watch but condensation clouded the face. As he picked his way along the dark platform, he tried to imagine what had been responsible for stranding them here. The carriage had been coupled at both ends. There had been a guard in the carriage with them. None of them had been paying much attention – they'd been too busy grandstanding each other with crazy stories. Perhaps they'd missed some kind of emergency announcement. But didn't the staff always come around and check the carriages if there was a problem? In this day and age surely people were protected from accidents of fate? Wet leaves plastered the backs of his legs as he walked. He reached the door of the ladies' toilet, but found that it was still locked. There was no sign that Ben had ever reached this far.

He turned slowly around and studied the dim forms about him. No sound but for wind and rain. But there was a faint glimmer of light, no more than a pencil beam, from somewhere near the far end of the platform. As he reached it, he realised that it had to be from Ben's torch, and it was coming from the underpass to the other platform. Wary of slipping on the wet steps, he descended.

"They've probably found a telephone by now and called someone," said Summerfield vaguely. "There's really nothing to worry about." He and Jane sat side by side in the pitch-black carriage, protected from moonlight by the hill behind them, as the art historian emptied the last of the wine into his glass. At least she had stopped crying now.

"I want to know why this is happening," she said finally.

"That's like trying to explain the moon, or the course of people's lives."

"It's all so random, and it shouldn't be. We've been telling each other stories all night, but they're not like life because they have plots. Nothing is left to chance. All this – there's no plot here, just a stupid accident, someone not doing their job properly." She wiped her nose with a tissue. "I don't want to be worried all my life. I'm tired of always thinking of others. When the children were ill, when my mother died, when Harold had his breakdown I was always the strong one. I had the answers and the energy to go on. It seems like there was never a moment in my life when I wasn't prepared to face disappointment. I feel like a fictional cliché, the academic's neurotic wife, and only *I* know that I'm not in someone else's story, that I'm real. Well, I don't want to be like that any more. I want someone else to take care of the worrying for a while. I want to go away somewhere warm and quiet. Where could I go, Peregrine?"

"I know a story about a special place," he whispered.

"Is it real, though?"

"No, of course not. I don't know anything about real places."

"But you must do. You're so much more practical than Harold."

"Darling, I'm not real, any more than you are. In your heart you must know that." And she knew he was right, for she remembered nothing before boarding the train.

Masters reached the bottom of the dripping tunnel and peered ahead. He could see nothing but the glare of the flashlight. "Ben?" he called, and the reverberation of his voice was lost in the falling rain.

The torch lay in a shallow puddle. He picked it up and allowed the beam to cross the walls. There was no sign that anyone had been here. He continued through the underpass to the other side, but a rusted iron trellis barred the way to the opposite platform, so he made his way back.

When he reached the waiting room once more, he found it deserted. The fire burned low in the grate. Kallie's jacket was still lying across one of the benches, but the three students had disappeared as completely as if they had never existed. Masters was a rational man. He tried to remember their faces, but found he could no longer conjure their features in his mind. Shocked, he dropped down into the nearest seat and tried to understand what was happening.

They had been on a train, and the carriage had become separated, and they had walked to the station . . . Jane and Peregrine were still waiting for him, that much he remembered. He had just decided to walk back to them when he heard a distant pinging of the lines. Impossible, of course, but it sounded as though a train was coming. He ran out on to the platform and peered into the murky night as the sound grew louder.

Now he saw the bright, empty carriages swaying around the bend ahead, heard the squeal of brakes as the locomotive pulled into the station and came to a sudden stop before him. The green-painted carriage threw yellow rectangles of light on the platform. It bore the initials GWR on its doors. The compartments were separate and lined with colourful prints of British holiday resorts. The seats had antimacassars on their backs. The train was a flawless reproduction of one from his childhood, but why? And how? And surely it occupied the same line as their poor stalled carriage?

He had barely managed to climb inside and shut the door before it lurched off once more, running to its timetable as surely as Alice's white rabbit, and as Masters fell back into the seat he thought; this is a memory, an idealised moment from the past, correct in the details down to the curious acrid smell of such carriages and the itchy bristles of the seat, but not something that's really happening now – merely a culmination of fragments seen and experienced, not fact but fiction, someone else's fiction.

He pushed down the window and leaned from it, searching the track ahead. Where the stalled carriage should have been was nothing at all, no carriage, no track, no hills or sea, no night or day, just nothing.

And he thought; I've fallen asleep like one of my students, that's all it is. There's nothing to be afraid of. It's simply that I've lost the ability to tell reality and fantasy apart. Right now it seems I'm fictional but I know I'm real, for I have real memories. He thought hard and tried to recall something, a moment so exact and specific to his life that it would prove he was real, so that the fiction would break up around him like an unfinished short story. He tried to think of Jane and Peregrine, whom he knew had been having an affair for nearly two years, but could not conjure a single past memory from either of them. He thought about this evening, and the way it conformed to the most absurd conventions of a typical Hallowe'en short story; the stormy night, the train ride, the mystery destination, the tale-telling guests. Stay calm, he told himself, and remember, remember, he repeated as the train hurtled toward a stomach-dropping oblivion, remember something real and true, remember the last time you were truly happy.

And then a real moment came to him.

A dead, hot day in mid-July. The air is countrified, dandelion spores rising gently on warm thermals, the lazy drone of a beetle alighting on dust-dulled hedge leaves. A suburban summertime, where the South London solstice settles in a sleepy yellow blanket over still front gardens.

Westerdale Road has its characters; the bad-tempered widow who appears in her doorway at the sound of a football being kicked against a wall, the deaf old couple whose pond freezes over every winter, so that they have to thaw their goldfish from a block of ice in a tin bath beside the fire. Some of the houses have Anderson shelters in their gardens, converted to tool-sheds in time of peace. Others still keep chickens, a distinctive sound and smell that excites the neighbourhood cats. Further along the street is a "simple" man who sits on his front step smiling inanely in the bright sunlight.

Masters forced himself to remember, to stop himself from ceasing to exist. These weren't his memories, he realised with a shock, they belonged to someone else entirely. What were they doing in his head?

Many street names conjure pastoral imagery; "Combedale Road", "Mycenae Road", "Westcombe Hill". At noon the silent sunlight scorches the streets. Housewives stay deep within the little terraced houses, polishing sideboards, making jellies, listening to wirelesses in cool shadowed rooms. Their men are at work, mopping their brows in council offices, patrolling machine-room floors, filling out paperwork in dusty bank chambers. Their children are all at school, reciting their tables, catching beanbags, and in the break following lunch there is a special treat; the teacher unlocks a paddock behind the playground of Invicta Infants, and here is a haven from the hot concrete, a small square meadow of close-cropped emerald grass hemmed in with chicken-wire. Here we are allowed to lie on our stomachs reading comics, passing them between each other. It is peaceful, warm and quiet (the teachers do not tolerate the vulgarity of noise) and although we are in a suburban street, it feels like the heart of the country-side. And here is the heart of all remembered happiness.

Confused, Masters began crying as the carriages dissolved around him and tumbled away through the night sky, the foundations of his life evaporating as he fought to recall anything at all that made him human.

What was it about this area, what did it possess to make it so special, so irreplaceable and precious? A few roads, a pond behind a wall where sticklebacks were trapped in jars and dragonflies skimmed the oily water, a railway line with a narrow pedestrian tunnel beneath it, a station of nicotine-coloured wood and rows of green tin lamps along the platform. Some odd shops;

a perpetually deserted furniture showroom, damp and dark, its proprietor standing ever-hopefully at the door, a model railway centre, a tobacconist selling sweets from large jars, a rack of Ellisdons Jokes on a stand, none of them living up to their packet descriptions, a chemist with apothecary bottles filled with coloured water and a scale machine, green and chrome with a wicker weighing basket, a bakery window filled with pink and white sugar mice, iced rounds, meringues and Battenburg cake. An advertisement painted on a wall, for varnish remover of some kind, depicting a housewife happily pouring boiling water from a kettle on to a shiny dining room table. Cinema posters under wire. A hardware shop with tin baths hanging either side of the door.

This confluence of roads and railway lines is bordered by an iron bridge and an embankment filled with white trumpet-flowered vines, and populated by families with forgotten children's names; Laurence, Percy, Pauline, Albert, Wendy, Sidney. No ambitions and aspirations here, just the stillness of summer, the faint drone of insects, bees landing on flowerbeds in the police station garden, tortoises and chickens sheltering from the heat beneath bushes, cats asleep in shop windows with yellow acetate sunscreens, and life being lived, a dull, sensible kind of life, unfolding like a flower, the day loosening as slowly as a clock spring – an implacable state which children thought would never change, but which is now lost so totally, so far beyond reach that it might have occurred before Isis ruled the Nile.

The lecturer had no memories of his own because he did not truly exist. Just like any flesh and blood human being, the creation that was Harold Masters reached his time unexpectedly and without resolution, and so dissolved into a tumble of threadbare tissues. With no plot momentum to drive him and no memories of his own, just borrowings from the mind of his creator, he turned over and over into nothing and was gone. And in that moment, he was the most real.

The storyteller in the mind's eye of Harold Masters sits at his chipped writing desk staring up at shelves of books, his eye alighting on an old 78 rpm record, and it dawns on him that he took Masters' name from the label, which features a dog and a gramophone. He wonders how many other characters' names came from spines of books and recollections of friends. A video of

Brief Encounter, a copy of *Dracula*, a photograph of New York, a lottery ticket, a drawing of a phoenix, a brandy bottle, a hotel brochure, a dog's collar, an Arsenal scarf, childhood notes. He looks for the patterns that shape his own life and finds only tarmac, concrete and steel, the dead carapace of something lost to all but his mind's eye.

His own past is as dead as his – and Masters' – recollection of it.

Dr Beeching closed the branch lines, road planners cut the streets in half, smashed down the houses, constructed swathes of concrete through the hills, the roads, the railways, the gardens, and like a bush cut through at the root, everything familiar died. The shops of his childhood were boarded up, homes falling to the wrecking ball, friends divided, families relocated. Now oil-drenched vibrations pulse the once-still air. A bright patch of pavement remains where once he stood with his face to the sun, free as the sky.

That was his reality.

Everything now is fiction.

They feel different, he notes, fact and fantasy. The former rooted in observation and experience, the latter bound by publishers' conventions. Sitting in the small cold study, the storyteller determines to leave behind his outmoded world of locked-room mysteries and vampire soaps in search of something real. But how hard will it be to leave such a cosy niche for a place with endless horizons and no parameters? Even letting go has a learning process.

He pushes back his chair and goes to the open window, inventing as hard and as fast as he can. It is a beautiful spring morning, and the breeze causes his eyelids to flutter. There is brine in the air. He looks down from the window-ledge at the thin white clouds racing far beneath, then loosens his belt and steps out of his trousers. It only takes a moment to remove his T-shirt, pants and socks. Drawing a deep breath, he walks confidently out on to the rope-covered surface of the springboard, determined not to show that he is scared.

How the releasing of shackles makes his body feel lighter than air.

Poor old Harold Masters, not being allowed to finish his story. It was so obvious to see where his tale was going that there was simply no reason for the author to finish it himself, not when his readers could put together the clues and do the job for him. The burden is always on the author to rediscover ways of surprising his audience, and that task has been fulfilled, albeit in a rather unorthodox manner.

It's good to be standing at the edge, he tells himself, bouncing lightly on the balls of his feet. There's a new world ahead. As the old century closes, he can leave behind his plots and characters. There are some excellent practitioners of the art who seem more than happy to close up the store behind him. There will always be the attraction of lies.

His body is pale and unused to such exposure. The clouds below appear as if seen from an airplane window. He moves further to the end of the board and gives a few experimental bounces. Then he bends his knees, jumps into the air, comes down on to the board and straightens his legs. The tension released in the board springs him high into the air, so high he feels he could punch a hole in the sky. For a brief moment it seems as if he could stay like this forever.

And for those who are left back on the ground, blinking in the sharp sunlight, those who are all too familiar with where they have been, the question for them now is how not to look back, how not to look down, but where to begin.

Where to begin.

And the answer, of course, is right – here.

NEIL GAIMAN

The Wedding Present

NEIL GAIMAN HAS HAD A BUSY YEAR promoting his bestselling fairy tale for adults, *Stardust*, and working on the movie version for Miramax. For the same company he scripted the English language version of Hayao Miyazaki's *anime*, *Princess Mononoke*, and he is currently developing the film version of his BBC-TV series *Neverwhere*.

On the publishing front, he is writing a scary children's book entitled *Coraline*, a novel with the working title *American Gods*, a picture book called *The Wolves in the Walls*, and a Japanese *Sandman* tale titled *The Dream Hunters*.

"I had the idea for the story about ten years ago – at a friend's wedding reception," Gaiman reveals. "I was sitting at the next table to Ray Harryhausen. I thought "I'll write a story and give it to the happy couple as a wedding present," and then I realised what the story was about and decided that they might not appreciate being given it as a present. So I didn't write it. I decided to wait until some friends got married who'd like it.

"The weeks went by and the months and the years. And when people got married, I always wound up getting them towels or toasters or things, because I thought they might not appreciate the story.

"And then, last year, I was writing the introduction to my short story collection *Smoke and Mirrors*. I was trying to talk about where stories came from, and I mentioned that there were stories I had never written – and it occurred to me that the right wedding would probably never come along, so I might as well write the story anyway.

"So I did. I put it in the Introduction to *Smoke and Mirrors*. People who don't read introductions will never know there was a story in the collection that they never read."

A FTER ALL THE JOYS and the headaches of the wedding, after the madness and the magic of it all (not to mention the embarrassment of Belinda's father's after-dinner speech, complete with family slide-show), after the honeymoon was literally (although not yet metaphorically) over and before their new suntans had a chance to fade in the English autumn, Belinda and Gordon got down to the business of unwrapping the wedding presents and writing their thank-you letters – thank you's enough for every towel and every toaster, for the juicer and the bread-maker, for the cutlery and the crockery and the teasmade and the curtains.

"Right," said Gordon. "That's the large objects thank-you'd. What've we got left?"

"Things in envelopes," said Belinda. "Cheques, I hope."

There were several cheques, a number of gift tokens, and even a £10 book token from Gordon's Aunt Marie, who was poor as a church mouse, Gordon told Belinda, but a dear, and who had sent him a book token every birthday as long as he could remember. And then, at the very bottom of the pile, there was a large brown, business-like envelope.

"What is it?" asked Belinda.

Gordon opened the flap, and pulled out a sheet of paper the colour of two-day-old cream, ragged at top and bottom, with typing on one side. The words had been typed with a manual typewriter, something Gordon had not seen in some years. He read the page slowly.

"What is it?" asked Belinda. "Who's it from?"

"I don't know," said Gordon. "Someone who still owns a typewriter. It's not signed."

"Is it a letter?"

"Not exactly," he said, and he scratched the side of his nose and read it again.

"Well," she said, in an exasperated voice (but she was not really exasperated; she was happy. She would wake in the morning and check to see if she were still as happy as she had been when she went to sleep the night before, or when Gordon had woken her in the night by brushing up against her, or when she had woken him. And she was). "Well, what is it?"

"It appears to be a description of our wedding," he said. "It's very nicely written. Here," and he passed it to her.

She looked it over.

```
It was a crisp day in early October when Gordon Robert
Johnson and Belinda Karen Abingdon swore that they
would love each other, would support and honour each
other as long as they both should live. The bride was
radiant and lovely, the groom was nervous, but ob-
viously proud and just as obviously pleased.
```

That was how it began. It went on to describe the service and the reception clearly, simply, and amusingly.

"How sweet," she said. "What does it say on the envelope?"

"*Gordon and Belinda's Wedding*," he read.

"No name? Nothing to indicate who sent it?"

"Uh-uh."

"Well, it's very sweet, and it's very thoughtful," she said. "Whoever it's from."

She looked inside the envelope to see if there was something else in there that they had overlooked, a note from whichever one of her friends (or his, or theirs) had written it, but there wasn't. So, vaguely relieved that there was one less thank you note to write, she placed the cream sheet of paper back in its envelope, which she placed in a box-file along with a copy of the Wedding Banquet menu, and the Invitations, and the contact sheets for the wedding photographs, and one white rose from the bridal bouquet.

Gordon was an architect, and Belinda was a vet. For each of them what they did was a vocation, not a job. They were in their early twenties. Neither of them had been married before, nor even seriously involved with anyone. They met when Gordon brought his thirteen-year-old Golden Retriever, Goldie, grey-muzzled and half-paralysed, to Belinda's surgery to be put down. He had had the dog since he was a boy, and insisted on being with her at the end. Belinda held his hand as he cried, and then, suddenly and unprofessionally, she hugged him, tightly, as if she could squeeze away the pain and the loss and the grief. One of them asked the other if they could meet that evening in the local pub for a drink, and afterward neither of them was sure which of them had proposed it.

The most important thing to know about the first two years of their marriage was this: they were pretty happy. From time to time they would squabble, and every once in a while they would have a blazing row about nothing very much that would end in tearful reconciliations, and they would make love and kiss away the other's tears, and whisper heartfelt apologies into each other's ears. At the end of the second year, six months after she came off the pill, Belinda found herself pregnant.

Gordon bought her a bracelet studded with tiny rubies, and he turned the spare bedroom into a nursery, hanging the wallpaper himself. The design was covered with nursery rhyme characters, with Little Bo Peep, and Humpty Dumpty, and the Dish Running Away With the Spoon, over and over and over again.

Belinda came home from the hospital, with little Melanie in her carrycot, and Belinda's mother came to stay with them for a week, sleeping on the sofa in the lounge.

It was on the third day that Belinda pulled out the box-folder, to show her wedding souvenirs to her mother, and to reminisce. Already their wedding seemed like such a long time ago. They smiled at the dried, brown thing that had once been a white rose, and clucked over the menu and the invitation. At the bottom of the box was a large brown envelope.

"*Gordon and Belinda's Marriage*," read Belinda's mother.

"It's a description of our wedding," said Belinda. "It's very sweet. It even has a bit in it about Daddy's slide-show."

Belinda opened the envelope and pulled out the sheet of cream paper. She read what was typed upon the paper, and made a face. Then she put it away, without saying anything.

"Can't I see it, dear?" asked her mother.

"I think it's Gordon playing a joke," said Belinda. "Not in good taste, either."

*   *   *

Belinda was sitting up in bed that night, breast-feeding Melanie, when she said to Gordon, who was staring at his wife and new daughter with a foolish smile upon his face, "Darling, why did you write those things?"

"What things?"

"In the letter. That wedding thing. You know."

"I don't know."

"It wasn't funny."

He sighed. "What are you talking about?"

Belinda pointed to the box-file, which she had brought upstairs and placed upon her dressing-table. Gordon opened it, and took out the envelope. "Did it always say that on the envelope?" he asked. "I thought it said something about our wedding." Then he took out and read the single sheet of ragged-edged paper, and his forehead creased. "I didn't write this." He turned the paper over, staring at the blank side as if expecting to see something else written there.

"You didn't write it?" she asked. "Really you didn't?" Gordon shook his head. Belinda wiped a dribble of milk from the baby's chin. "I believe you," she said. "I thought you wrote it, but you didn't."

"No."

"Let me see that again," she said. He passed the paper to her. "This is so weird. I mean, it's not funny, and it's not even true."

Typed upon the paper was a brief description of the previous two years for Gordon and Belinda. It had not been a good two years, according the typed sheet. Six months after they were married Belinda had been bitten in the cheek by a Pekingese, so badly that the cheek needed to be stitched back together. It had left a nasty scar. Worse than that, nerves had been damaged, and she had begun to drink, perhaps to numb the pain. She suspected that Gordon was revolted by her face, while the new baby, it said, was a desperate attempt to glue the couple together.

"Why would they say this?" she asked.

"They?"

"Whoever wrote this horrid thing." She ran a finger across her cheek: it was unblemished and unmarked. She was a very beautiful young woman, although she looked tired and fragile now.

"How do you know it's a *they*?"

"I don't know," she said, transferring the baby to her left

breast. "It seems a sort of *they*-ish thing to do. To write that and to swap it for the old one and to wait until one of us read it . . . Come on, little Melanie, there you go, that's such a fine girl . . ."

"Shall I throw it away?"

"Yes. No. I don't know. I think . . ." She stroked the baby's forehead. "Hold onto it," she said. "We might need it for evidence. I wonder if it was something Al organised." Al was Gordon's youngest brother.

Gordon put the paper back into the envelope, and he put the envelope back into the box file, which was pushed under the bed and, more or less, forgotten.

Neither of them got much sleep for the next few months, what with the nightly feeds and the continual crying, for Melanie was a colicky baby. The box-file stayed under the bed. And then Gordon was offered a job in Preston, several hundred miles north, and since Belinda was on leave from her job, and had no immediate plans to go back to work, she found the idea rather attractive. So they moved.

They found a terraced house in a cobbled street, high and old and deep. Belinda filled in from time to time at a local vets, seeing small animals and house pets. When Melanie was eighteen months old Belinda gave birth to a son, whom they called Kevin, after Gordon's late grandfather.

Gordon was made a full partner in the firm of architects. When Kevin began to go to kindergarten, Belinda went back to work.

The box-file was never lost. It was in one of the spare rooms at the top of the house, beneath a teetering pile of copies of *The Architect's Journal* and *Architectural Review*. Belinda thought about the box-file, and what it contained, from time to time, and, one night when Gordon was in Scotland overnight consulting on the remodelling of an ancestral home, she did more than think.

Both of the children were asleep. Belinda went up the stairs into the undecorated part of the house. She moved the magazines and opened the box, which (where it had not been covered by magazines) was thick with two years of undisturbed dust. The envelope still said *Gordon and Belinda's Marriage* on it, and Belinda honestly did not know if it had ever said anything else.

She took out the paper from the envelope, and she read it. And then she put it away, and sat there, at the top of the house, feeling shaken and sick.

According to the neatly-typed message, Kevin, her second child, had not been born; the baby had been miscarried at five months. Since then Belinda had been suffering from frequent attacks of bleak, black depression. Gordon was home rarely, it said, because he was conducting a rather miserable affair with the senior partner in his company, a striking but nervous woman ten years his senior. Belinda was drinking more, and affecting high collars and scarves, to hide the spider-web scar upon her cheek. She and Gordon spoke little, except to argue the small and petty arguments of those who fear the big arguments, knowing that the only things that were left to be said were too huge to be said without destroying both their lives.

Belinda said nothing about the latest version of *Gordon and Belinda's Marriage* to Gordon. However, he read it himself, or something quite like it, several months later, when Belinda's mother fell ill, and Belinda went south for a week to help look after her.

On the sheet of paper that Gordon took out of the envelope was a portrait of a marriage similar to the one that Belinda had read, although, at present, his affair with his boss had ended badly, and his job was now in peril.

Gordon rather liked his boss, but could not imagine himself ever becoming romantically involved with her. He was enjoying his job, although he wanted something that would challenge him more than it did.

Belinda's mother improved, and Belinda returned within the week. Her husband and children were relieved and delighted to see her come home.

It was Christmas Eve before Gordon spoke to Belinda about the envelope.

"You've looked at it too, haven't you?" They had crept into the children's bedrooms earlier that evening and filled the hanging Christmas stockings. Gordon had felt euphoric as he had walked through the house, as he stood beside his children's beds, but it was a euphoria tinged with a profound sorrow: the knowledge that such moments of complete happiness could not last; that one could not stop Time.

Belinda knew what he was talking about. "Yes," she said. "I've read it."

"What do you think?"

"Well," she said. "I don't think it's a joke any more. Not even a sick joke."

"Mm," he said. "Then what is it?"

They sat in the living room at the front of the house with the lights dimmed, and the log burning on the bed of coals cast flickering orange and yellow light about the room.

"I think it really is a wedding present," she told him. "It's the marriage that we aren't having. The bad things are happening there on the page, not here, in our lives. Instead of living it, we are reading it, knowing it could have gone that way and also that it never did."

"You're saying it's magic, then?" He would not have said it aloud, but it was Christmas Eve, and the lights were down.

"I don't believe in magic," she said, flatly. "It's a wedding present. And I think we should make sure it's kept safe."

On Boxing Day she moved the envelope from the box-file to her jewellery drawer, which she kept locked, where it lay flat beneath her necklaces and rings, her bracelets and her brooches.

Spring became summer. Winter became spring.

Gordon was exhausted: by day he worked for clients, designing, and liaising with builders and contractors, by night he would sit up late, working for his own self, designing museums and galleries and public buildings for competitions. Sometimes his designs received honourable mentions, and were reproduced in architectural journals.

Belinda was doing more large animal work, which she enjoyed, visiting farmers and inspecting and treating horses, sheep and cows. Sometimes she would bring the children with her on her rounds.

Her mobile phone rang when she was in a paddock trying to examine a pregnant goat who had, it turned out, no desire to be caught, let alone examined. She retired from the battle, leaving the goat glaring at her from across the field, and thumbed the phone open. "Yes?"

"Guess what?"

"Hello darling. Um. You've won the lottery?"

"Nope. Close, though. My design for the British Heritage Museum has made the shortlist. I'm up against some pretty stiff contenders, though. But I'm on the shortlist."

"That's wonderful!"

"I've spoken to Mrs Fulbright and she's going to have Sonja babysit for us tonight. We're celebrating."

"Terrific. Love you," she said. "Now got to get back to the goat."

They drank too much champagne over a fine celebratory meal. That night in their bedroom as Belinda removed her earrings, she said, "Shall we see what the Wedding Present says?"

He looked at her gravely from the bed. He was only wearing his socks. "No, I don't think so. It's a special night. Why spoil it?"

She placed her earrings in her jewellery drawer, and locked it. Then she removed her stockings. "I suppose you're right. I can imagine what it says, anyway. I'm drunk and depressed and you're a miserable loser. And meanwhile we're . . . well, actually I *am* a bit tiddly, but that's not what I mean. It just sits there at the bottom of the drawer, like the portrait in the attic in *The Picture of Dorian Gray*."

" 'And it was only by his rings that they knew him.' Yes. I remember. We read it in school."

"That's really what I'm scared of," she said, pulling on a cotton nightdress. "That the thing on that paper is the real portrait of our marriage at present, and what we've got now is just a pretty picture. That it's real, and we're not. I mean," she was speaking intently now, with the gravity of the slightly drunk, "Don't you ever think that it's too good to be true?"

He nodded. "Sometimes. Tonight, certainly."

She shivered. "Maybe really I *am* a drunk with a dog-bite on my cheek, and you fuck anything that moves and Kevin was never born and – and all that other horrible stuff."

He stood up, walked over to her, put his arms around her. "But it isn't true," he pointed out. "This is real. You're real. I'm real. That wedding thing is just a story. It's just words." And he kissed her, and held her tightly, and little more was said that night.

It was a long six months before Gordon's design for the British Heritage Museum was announced as the winner, although it was derided in *The Times* as being too "aggressively modern", in various architectural journals as being too old-fashioned, and it was described by one of the judges, in an interview in the *Sunday Telegraph*, as "a bit of a compromise candidate – everybody's second choice."

They moved to London, letting their house in Preston to an

artist and his family, for Belinda would not let Gordon sell it. Gordon worked intensively, happily, on the museum project. Kevin was six and Melanie was eight. Melanie found London intimidating, but Kevin loved it. Both of the children were initially distressed to have lost their friends and their school. Belinda found a part-time job at a small animal clinic in Camden, working three afternoons a week. She missed her cows.

Days in London became months and then years, and, despite occasional budgetary setbacks, Gordon was increasingly excited. The day approached when the first ground would be broken for the museum.

One night Belinda woke in the small hours, and she stared at her sleeping husband in the sodium yellow illumination of the streetlamp outside their bedroom window. His hairline was receding, and the hair at back was thinning. Belinda wondered what it would be like, when she was actually married to a bald man. She decided it would be much the same as it always had been. Mostly happy. Mostly good.

She wondered what was happening to the *them* in the envelope. She could feel its presence, dry and brooding, in the corner of their bedroom, safely locked away from all harm. She felt, suddenly, sorry for the Belinda and Gordon trapped in the envelope on their piece of paper, hating each other and everything else.

Gordon began to snore. She kissed him, gently, on the cheek, and said, "Shhh." He stirred, and was quiet, but did not wake. She snuggled against him and soon fell back into sleep herself.

After lunch the following day, while in conversation with an importer of Tuscan marble, Gordon looked very surprised, and reached a hand up to his chest. He said, "I'm frightfully sorry about this," and then his knees gave way, and he fell to the floor. They called an ambulance, but Gordon was dead when it arrived. He was thirty-six years old.

At the inquest the Coroner announced that the autopsy showed Gordon's heart to have been congenitally weak. It could have gone at any time.

For the first three days after his death, Belinda felt nothing, a profound and awful nothing. She comforted the children, she spoke to her friends and to Gordon's friends, to her family and to Gordon's family, accepting their condolences gracefully and gently, as one accepts unasked-for gifts. She would listen to other people cry for Gordon, which she still had not done. She would say all the right things, and she would feel nothing at all.

Melanie, who was eleven, seemed to be taking it well. Kevin abandoned his books and computer games, and sat in his bedroom, staring out of the window, not wanting to talk.

The day after the funeral her parents went back to the countryside and they took both the children with them. Belinda refused to leave London. There was, she said, too much to do.

On the fourth day after the funeral she was making the double bed that they had shared when she began to cry, and the sobs ripped through her in huge, ugly spasms of grief, and tears fell from her face onto the bedspread and clear snot streamed from her nose, and she sat down on the floor suddenly, like a marionette whose strings have been cut, and she cried for the best part of an hour, for she knew that she would never see him again.

She wiped her face. Then she unlocked her jewellery drawer and pulled out the envelope. She opened it, and pulled out the cream-coloured sheet of paper, and ran her eyes over the neatly-typed words. The Belinda on the paper had crashed their car while drunk, and was about to lose her driving license. She and Gordon had not spoken for days. He had lost his job, almost eighteen months earlier, and now spent most of his days sitting around their house in Salford. Belinda's job brought in what money they had. Melanie was out of control: Belinda, cleaning Melanie's bedroom, had found a cache of five and ten pound notes. Melanie had offered no explanation for how an eleven-year-old girl had come by the money, had just retreated into her room and glared at them, tight-lipped, when quizzed. Neither Gordon nor Belinda had investigated further, scared of what they might have discovered. The house in Salford was dingy, and damp, such that the plaster was coming away from the ceiling in huge, crumbling chunks, and all three of them had developed nasty, bronchial coughs.

Belinda felt sorry for them.

She put the paper back in the envelope. She wondered what it would be like to hate Gordon, to have him hate her. She wondered what it would be like not to have Kevin in her life, not to see his drawings of aeroplanes or hear his magnificently tuneless renditions of popular songs. She wondered where Melanie – the other Melanie, not *her* Melanie but the there-but-for-the-Grace-of-God Melanie – could have got that money from, and was relieved that her own Melanie seemed to have few interests beyond ballet and Enid Blyton books.

She missed Gordon so much it felt like something sharp being hammered into her chest, a spike, perhaps, or an icicle, made of cold and loneliness and the knowledge that she would never see him again in this world.

Then she took the envelope downstairs to the lounge, where the coal-fire was burning in the grate, because Gordon had loved open fires. He said that a fire gave a room life. She disliked coal fires, but she had lit it this evening out of routine and out of habit, and because not lighting it would have meant admitting to herself, on some absolute level, that he was never coming home.

Belinda stared into the fire for some time, thinking about what she had in her life, and what she had given up; and whether it would be worse to love someone who was no longer there, or not to love someone who was.

And then, at the end, almost casually, she tossed the envelope onto the coals, and she watched it curl and blacken and catch, watched the yellow flames dancing amidst the blue.

Soon, the wedding present was nothing but black flakes of ash which danced on the updraughts and were carried away, like a child's letter to Santa Claus, up the chimney and off into the night.

Belinda sat back in her chair, and closed her eyes, and waited for the scar to blossom on her cheek.

PETER ATKINS

Adventures in Further Education

PETER ATKINS WAS BORN IN LIVERPOOL and now lives in Los Angeles. The scriptwriter of such movies as *Hellbound: Hellraiser II*, *Hellraiser III: Hell on Earth*, *Hellraiser: Bloodline* and *Fist of the Northstar*, his first two novels were *Morningstar* and *Big Thunder*.

The author is currently working simultaneously on his third novel and a screenplay version of the same story, tentatively scheduled for filming in early 2000. The screenplay has been retitled *Prisoners of the Sun* by its producers, but Atkins is keeping his original title *The Source of the Nile* for the novel. He also has a collection of his short fiction out from Pumpkin Books which has as its centrepiece his screenplay for the movie *Wishmaster* which, according to *Variety's* year-end charts, was the most successful independent feature of 1997.

As he explains, " 'Adventures in Further Education' was written for *Horrors! 365 Scary Stories*, an anthology where the upper limit for length was 750 words. I sold the editors five stories – of which this one, at 630 words, was the longest! Like the protagonist, I once had a teacher who tapped his pen on his desk but, unlike Kenny, I didn't continue the experiment . . ."

K ENNY TAPPED THE PEN on the surface of his desk for the seventeen thousand, four hundred and thirty-sixth time.

There was nothing the matter with him. It wasn't like it was an obsession or anything. It wasn't like he didn't do anything else. Since his sixth-grade teacher had first introduced the idea to him twenty years ago, he'd done all the normal things – he'd graduated from high school, he'd graduated from college, he'd met Tiffany, fallen in love, married, fathered two children, and found himself a perfectly respectable job with a perfectly respectable firm. There was nothing unusual about Kenny except his little hobby. And that's all it was – a hobby. he didn't bother anybody with it. In fact, nobody knew he did it, not even Tiffany. It was just a hobby, an interest, an experiment that nobody else had ever had the patience to see through.

Mr Neill had only tapped *his* pen five times, for example.

"So it's theoretically possible," Mr Neill had said, sounding almost as bored as the fifty twelve-year-olds who were doing their best to pretend to listen to him, "that, if you kept tapping this pen on this desk long enough, one time it would just slip through the surface."

He'd been giving the class a glimpse of the New Physics, a taste of the theories that were revolutionising the way scientists looked at the world, a hint that the matter that made up the forms of this world which everyone accepted as solid and separate was in fact all one and that only probability kept everything as it was and kept our reality apart from a multiverse of others.

Kenny hadn't been particularly interested in the theoretical and metaphysical implications of what Mr Neill was saying. He was twelve years old, for Christ's sake. He'd just thought it would be really fucking cool to see a pen slip through a desk and had been disappointed when, after his fifth tap, Mr Neill had put his pen down and moved on to something else.

Quietly, and without drawing anybody's attention, Kenny had started tapping his pen. And counting.

Seventeen thousand, four hundred and thirty-seven. Seventeen thousand, four hundred and thirty-eight.

It wasn't the same desk, of course. it was the sixth desk since he'd started. But it was the same pen (dry now of ink, chewed up and useless for anything but its secret purpose), and that had to count for something.

The phone rang. Kenny picked it up, dealt with the call, hung up. He laid the pen down throughout the call and it didn't bother him at all. After all, he wasn't crazy. Life had to be lived. Work had to be done. His experiment required patience and tenacity, and Kenny prided himself on possessing plenty of both.

Seventeen thousand, four hundred and thirty-nine. Seventeen thousand, four hundred and forty. Seventeen thousand, four hundred and . . .

The pen slid effortlessly and smoothly into the desk.

Kenny, letting go instinctively, threw himself back in his chair, an adrenal shock of surprised fulfillment shooting through his entire body. He looked up, ready to shout his triumph to the rest of the large open-plan office.

But the office wasn't there.

Kenny was staring at a kaleidoscope world of shifting, flickering lights, a surfaceless void with an unimaginably distant vanishing point near which huge amorphous shapes twisted and writhed in a constant fury of becoming. Lightning in colours he couldn't name seared across the infinite and multi-hued sky in jagged shards the size of which he couldn't conceive. Alien winds screamed their impossible being in warring cacophonies of notes he couldn't believe at volumes he couldn't bear.

Had he still had hands, Kenny would have grabbed at his chair (had there still been a chair). Had he still had a mouth, Kenny would have screamed. Had he still had eyes, Kenny would have closed them.

Had he still had his pen, Kenny would have started tapping.

KATHE KOJA

Bondage

KATHE KOJA LIVES IN THE Detroit area with her husband, artist Rick Lieder, and her son. Her Bram Stoker Award-winning début novel, *The Cipher*, appeared in 1991, since when she has published *Bad Brains*, *Skin*, *Strange Angels* and *Famished*, plus the short story collection *Extremities*.

Her short fiction (including several collaborations with Barry N. Malzberg) has appeared in such magazines and anthologies as *Omni*, *The Magazine of Fantasy & Science Fiction*, *Dark Voices 3, 5* and *6*, *Still Dead: Book of the Dead 2*, *A Whisper of Blood*, *Little Deaths*, *The Year's Best Horror Stories* and *Best New Horror 3* and *5*.

According to the author, "My own sense is that 'Bondage' is as close to a pure morality play as anything I've done."

S HE WAS SHAPED LIKE SCULPTURE: high bones, high forehead, long fingers silver-cool against his skin as they lay side by side in the deep four-poster, princess-bed draped in lace and gauze and "Don't ever buy me a ring," she said; those fingers on his belly, up and down, up and down, tickling in his navel, playing with his balls. "I don't like them."

Even her voice, as calm and sure as metal. "Why not?" he said.

"They're just –" Fingertips, nipping at his thighs. "They're bondage gear."

"Bondage, sure. Like a wedding band, right?"

And her shrug, half a smile, one-elbow rise to reach for her drink: that long white back, faint skeleton trail of bones and "What do you know about bondage?" her smile wider now, canine flash. "B & D, S & M. You ever do that, any of that?"

Have you? "No," he said. "I'm not into pain."

"It's not about pain," she said, "or anyway it doesn't have to be. Bondage and *discipline*," tapping his chest for emphasis. "Who's on top." She drank what was left in the glass, set it back on the floor, climbed atop him so her breasts were inches from his mouth. "Like now," she said.

Her taste of perfume, of faintest salt: long legs hooked high above his hips, strong and growing stronger, wilder as she rode him, head straining back, back, as if she would twist that long white body into a circle, bend it like sculpture, like metal and stone and when he came it was too soon, fast and over and she was looking at him and almost smiling, lips spread to show those little pointed teeth.

"Not so bad, was it?" she said. "Woman superior?"

"But that's not the same thing," he said, still breathless. "Not the same thing at all."

Next day's dinner, some Tex-Mex place she loved: plastic cacti, the waiters in ten-gallon hats and reaching for her bag beneath the table, reaching and: a box, gift box embossed black-on-black, SECRET PLEASURES and "Here," she said with half a smile. "For you."

"What's this for?" he said.

"No reason. – Go on, open it," and he did, something soft and limp inside and, curious, he unfolded that softness, spread it flat on the table between them: supple white leather oval, no true eyes, gill-slit where the mouth should be and "Pretty cool, isn't it?" she said. Tangle of black strings, one black grommet on each side, simple as desire itself. "Do you like it?"

"Where'd you get this?" The box in hand again, examination and "From a sex store," she said, "downtown. Thumb cuffs and cock rings, nipple clamps. Piercing jewelry." Touching the mask. "And these."

And a server there to refill their water glasses, frank stare at the mask on the table: "What's that?" Eighteen, nineteen years old, faint drift of acne across his forehead beneath the ludicrous hat. "For Halloween?"

"No," she said before he could speak, "no, it's for sex. A sex toy," and the boy laughed a little, hasty to fill the glasses and be gone and "Why'd you have to say that?" he said, annoyed. At the work station see the boy with another server, their tandem turn to stare and she laughed, reached to take the mask and place it back inside the box.

"No reason," she said. "Just part of the game."

And later in bed, kisses and nipping fingers, playful hands on his thighs but he was waiting, he knew it would come and: reaching for her glass she retrieved as well the box, SECRET PLEASURES and the featureless face within, white face waiting for flesh to fill it, carry it, make it move and "Go on," she said, "I bought it for you, put it on."

"I will if you will."

"You first," and she helped him adjust it, tie the dangle of strings so the mask lay comfortably close, leather so soft it might have been a second skin: *Who am I?* wiped clean of all expression, no mouth to sulk or smile and "Mmmmm," her hands now on his face, petting, stroking the mask. "You should see how you look."

"I look like nothing," he said. Strange to feel the movement of muscles when he spoke, feel his lips against the mask like some alien skin. "Everyman."

"The bogey-man," and she laughed, leaning back, back against the pillows, cheekbone flush and reaching, reaching to bring his face to her breasts: "Your turn," she said. "Your turn to be on top."

It grew hot, inside the mask; he didn't mind.

"Your turn." Raining outside, monotony of thunder and she crabby in quilts, ugly nightgown and "Your turn," he said again, dangling the mask by its strings: caul from some secret birth, some unborn self and "Go on," he said, feeling his hardon press his trousers as facial bones might press the mask: a slight straining, the pressure of rising heat and the mask did not fit her quite as well, hung slightly beneath her chin but he tightened the strings again – "Ow," more annoyance than real pain, her voice softer somehow because dampered, muffled by the slit which did not completely meet her lips. "It's too tight," faint her voice but he left it that way, no portion of her features visible, nothing but faceless white.

"Lie down," he said.

"Oh, not here," yet without true complaint, she was not attending, she was feeling the mask with her fingers, curious to press against cheekbones and chin and "You know I tried this on before," more than half to herself. "But not so –"

"Lie down," he said; he was already naked. Thunder like the echo of a beating heart, giant's heart in rhythm with his own; pulse of blood and rain on the roof, a clutch of claws, her body bent obedient on the landscape of the quilts: and afterwards, half-turned from him: "You hurt me," she said, touching herself, pale hands between her legs. "Don't be so rough."

The mask on the floor like a self discarded; no one; anyone. Everyman. "I'm sorry," he said. "I didn't mean to."

The next time he lay below her, masked and silent: *don't move*, that was the game, *no matter what don't move*: clamped thighs, her juddering breasts and she bit him, bright teeth in the shoulder hard enough to leave a bruise: nipping and pinching with her nails, scratches on his chest, his back and he had to fight not to shift or move, not to push her away, to lay absolutely still even as he came, sweep of red pleasure and she above in reckless motion, hair sweat-wild and tumbled, panting as if she had no air and "Oh, *yes*," collapsing down to lie beside him, one leg stretched companionably across his two, thigh high on his hip and without moving anything but his fingers he pinched her, quick and brutal on her inner thigh and in perfect reflex she slapped him, very hard, across the face, both sound and impact deadened by the presence of the mask.

Neither spoke.

Some time after that he fell asleep, woke much later to find her curled far across the bed and himself still in the mask: sweat dried to an itch across his cheekbones, the differing itch of his overnight beard, fingers clumsy with fatigue against the strings.

Waking to true morning he found it crumpled on the floor, spoor and element of dream made to follow the sleeper all the way to the waking world.

* * *

"I'm sorry," she said. She might have been crying, earlier, in the shower; she had kept the bathroom door closed; her eyes were clear but swollen, pink and sore around the lids. "I never meant to hit you."

I'm sorry too. "Let's forget it," he said. "Okay?"

The next time they made love they did not use the mask: plain faces, closed eyes and although it was good – with her it was almost always good – still he missed it, the heat within that stasis, visible and not, here and not-here: but said nothing, did not mention it at all.

He wondered if she missed it, too.

Dinner: carryout Thai in little lumps, he had waited too long to leave the office, stuck twice in traffic in a heavy storm; so much rain, lately. The food on his plate gone slick and cold, eating alone, clicking through channels and outside another sound, her car in the driveway: half-rising to open the door, let her in and "Hi," wet and breathless, hair stuck to her face, raincoat spatter and "Oh good," she said, "you got dinner." Side by side on the sofa and now that she was home he opened a bottle of wine, two bottles, still on the sofa and he started to undress her, blouse and bra, hooks and eyes and "Wait," she said, voice lightly slurred and warm from the wine. "Just wait a minute," and gone then as he stripped, lay back on the sofa, rain on the roof and all at once the white face, peering at him, mouth expressionless but beneath, he knew, a smile.

"Peekaboo," she said and inside him the sudden surge, heat pure and rising like mercury, like the tempo of the storm and "Let me wear it," he said, up on one elbow, rising to reach for the strings, "and then you can –"

"No," from above him, pale and remote. "It's not your turn."

That stare: he could not see her eyes and inside him then a differing surge, something grey and chilly, like metal, like falling rain.

SECRET PLEASURES: between a video store and a deli, glass door opaque and inside the rachet and thump of industrial music, steel-toned racks to display the shiny harnesses, leather hoods and thigh-high boots and below the counter a glass case of jewelry, piercing jewelry like little iron bars, dumbbells, hooks and circles and "Can I help you?" from a tall thin boy in leather, boots and jacket, head to toe and "Masks," he said. "I want to see the masks," and after all it was very easy to say, no doubt the clerks had already seen it all, this boy with his thin cheeks and ragged hair leading him to the display carousel, to show him what there was to see: buckles and loops and ribbon ties, leather and rubber all faces he might wear, desires he might claim if only for a night and "That one," he said, pointing with the tip of one finger. "Let me see that one."

Red leather harsh as meat exposed, no plain oval but the true mask, face-shaped and stitchery like scars, strangely peaked at the eyebrows and "What're these supposed to be?" he asked, touching the peaks. "Horns?"

"Those are darts," the clerk said. "To make it fit tighter. See?" and positioned to his face, buckled on and the clerk stepped back so he might use the mirror: eyes kept closed for a moment, wanting tactile information, wanting the feel of the mask before any decision sight might make: this one much tighter than the other, stiffer, more formal; this mask would not fit *her* at all – and he opened his eyes to the mirror, to see himself a stranger: sex become power, desires become demands, demands made as orders and when the clerk told him the price he shrugged a little, more than he meant to spend but what difference did that make?

His credit card on the counter, bright and toy-like, the clerk brushing hair from his eyes: "Do you want a box or anything? A gift box?"

"No," he said. "Just put it in a bag."

Raining, still, and nearly dark as he pulled into the driveway, heart in peculiar race and he called her name when he entered, made his voice normal, called her name again as he walked through the darkened house with the bag tight in his hand, room to room: nothing: she was nowhere so circle back to the living room, silent and dark, rain like voices to make a chorus, secret chorus in a language all its own as

"Here I am," her voice, very quiet and then again, as if he had not heard: "Here I am."

Past the sofa, in the corner where wall met wall and she was naked: and hooded, draped in a hood so shapeless and so black as to give no breath of the female, no hint of the human inside. If there were eye-slits, he did not see them; there must be holes for breathing, but in this light he could not be sure. Gaze without words but an alien shudder, as if some other creature, bullet-shaped, past fathoming, were rising from the fragile flesh of her body, the sloping shelf of shoulders made from bone.

The bag made a sound as it touched the floor; his fingers trembled on the straps, the heavy red buckles of the mask.

"I brought you something," he said.

Silence: arms crossed, her breath in hitching motion, both of them waiting for him to strip and cross the room.

CHAZ BRENCHLEY

The Keys to D'Espérance

CHAZ BRENCHLEY HAS MADE A LIVING as a writer since he was eighteen, and 1999 marks his twenty-third anniversary in the job. He is the author of nine thrillers, most recently *Shelter*, and is also the creator of a major new fantasy series, *The Books of Outremer*, based on the world of the Crusades. He is a prize-winning former poet and has also published three fantasy books for children and close to 500 short stories in various genres.

He was Crimewriter-in-Residence at the St. Peter's Riverside Sculpture Project in Sunderland, which he describes as "a bizarre experience" and which led to the collection *Blood Waters*. His novel *Dead of Light* is currently in development as a movie, and he won the British Fantasy Society's 1998 August Derleth Fantasy Award for the sequel, *Light Errant*.

" 'The Keys to D'Espérance' is one of those very rare stories that I wrote because I had to, without any market in mind," explains the author. "I was – as ever – broke, and supposed to be working on a book that was already late; and for a month there was nothing I could do but put that aside and work on 'D'Espérance'. Which then sat around for years, waiting for the right publisher to turn up.

"I was so pleased when Bill Schafer of Subterranean Press offered to do it as a chapbook, that was perfect. It is very much the first of a series of stories about the house, in which I hope to write obliquely about the history of Britain through this century. I have the next couple of stories in my head, only waiting for me to find the time to write them."

A CTUALLY, BY THE TIME THE KEYS CAME, he no longer believed in the house.

It was like God, he thought; they oversold it. Say too often that a thing is so, and how can people help but doubt? Most facts prove not to be the case after all, under any serious examination. Even the Earth isn't round.

One day, they said, *D'Espérance will be yours. You will receive it in sorrow*, they said, *and pass it on in joy. That is as it is* they said, *as it always is, as it should be.*

But they said it when he was five and he thought they meant for Christmas, they'd never make him wait to be six.

When he was six they said it, and when he was seven and eight and nine.

At ten, he asked if he could visit.

Visit D'Espérance? they said, laughing at him. *Of course you can't, you haven't been invited. You can't just visit. You can't call at D'Espérance. In passing*, looking at each other, laughing. *You can't pass D'Espérance.*

But if it was going to be his, he said at twelve, wasn't he entitled? Didn't he have a right to know? He'd never seen a painting, even, never seen a photograph . . .

There are none, they said, and, *Be patient*. And, *No, don't be foolish, of course you're not entitled. Title to D'Espérance does not vest in you*, they said. *Yet*, they said.

And somewhere round about fifteen he stopped believing. The guns still thundered across the Channel, and he believed in those; he believed in his own death to come, glorious and dreadful; he believed in Rupert Brooke and Euclidean geometry and the sweet breath of a girl, her name whispered into his bolster but never to be uttered aloud, never in hearing; and no, he did not believe in D'Espérance.

Two years later the girl was dead and his parents also, and none of them in glory. His school would have no more of him, and the war was over; and that last was the cruellest touch in a long and savage peal, because it took from him the chance of an unremarked death, a way to follow quietly.

Now it must needs be the river, rocks in his pockets and thank God he had never learnt to swim. There would be notice taken, that was inevitable; but this would be the last of it. No more family, no one more to accuse or cut or scorn. The name quite gone, it would simply cease to matter. He hoped that he might never be recovered, that he might lie on the bottom till his bones rotted, being washed and washed by fast unheeding waters.

Quite coldly determined, he refused to lurk withindoors on his last long day. At sunset he would go to the bridge, *rocks in my pockets, yes, and no matter who sees, they shan't stop me*; but first he would let himself be seen and hissed at and whispered about, today as every day, no craven he. It was honour and honour only that would take him to the river; he wanted that clearly understood.

So he walked abroad, returning some books to the public library and setting his accounts with the last few merchants to allow him credit. He took coffee in town and almost smiled as the room emptied around him, did permit himself the indulgence of a murmured word with the cashier on his way out, "Please don't trouble yourself, I shan't come back again."

And so he went home, and met the postman at the door; and was handed a package, and stood on his doorstep watching as the postman walked away, wiping his hand on his trousers.

The package was well wrapped in brown paper, tied with string and the knots sealed. It was unexpectedly heavy for its size, and made softly metallic noises as he felt its hard angles shift between his fingers.

Preferring the kitchen in his solitude to the oppressions of velvet and oak, of photographs and memories and names, he went straight through and opened the package on the long deal table under the window.

Keys, three separate rings of keys: brass keys and bronze and steel, keys shorter than his thumb and longer than his hand, keys still glittering new and keys older than he had ever seen, older than he could believe, almost.

For long minutes he only held them, played with them, laid them out and looked at them; finally he turned away, to read the letter that had accompanied them.

An envelope addressed to him in neat copperplate, nothing extravagant; heavy laid paper of good quality, little creased or marked despite its journeying in with the keys. A long journey, he noted, unfolding the single sheet and reading the address at the top. His correspondent, this remitter of keys was apparently a country solicitor; but the town and the company's name were entirely unfamiliar to him, although he had spent two months now immersed in his parents' affairs, reading everything.

My dear lad, the letter said – and this from a stranger, strange in itself – *I believe that this will reach you at the proper time; I hope you may learn to view it as good news.*

In plain, you are now the master of D'Espérance, at least in so far as such a house may ever be mastered by one man. The deeds, I regret, you may not view; they are kept otherwhere, and I have never had sight of them. The keys, however, are enclosed. You may be sure that none will challenge your title, for so long as you choose to exercise it.

I look forward to making your acquaintance, as and when you see fit to call upon me.

Yours, etc.

His first impulse was to laugh, to toss the letter down, his resolution quite unchallenged, quite unchanged. Just another house, and what did he want with that? He had one already, and meant to leave it tonight and forever.

But he was a boy, he was curious; and while he would welcome death, while he meant to welcome it, *come, sweet Death, embrace me*, he was very afraid of water.

His hands came back to the keys and played upon them, a silent music, a song of summoning. Death could surely wait a day, two days. So could the river. It was going nowhere; he'd be back.

And so the train, trains, taking him slow and dirty into the north country. Soon he could be anonymous, no name to him, just a lad too young to have been in the war, though he was old enough now. That was odd, to have people look at him and not know him. To have them sit just across the compartment and not shift their feet away from his, not lour or sniff or turn a cold, contemptuous, ostentatious shoulder.

One woman even tried to mother him, poor fool: not knowing what a mother meant to him, bare feet knocking at his eyeballs, knocking and knocking, *knock knock*. He was cold himself then, he was savage, gave her more reason than most had to disdain him, though still she wouldn't do it.

And at last there were sullen moors turned purple with the season, there was a quiet station with a single taxi waiting and the locals hanging back, *no, lad, you take it, it's only a ten-minute walk into the town for us and we know it well, it's no hardship*.

He wouldn't do that, though. Their kindness was inappropriate, born of ignorance that he refused to exploit; and he had no need of it in any case. It was after six o'clock, too late to call on the solicitor, and he didn't plan to seek lodgings in town. His name was uncommon, and might be recognised. Too proud to hide behind a false one, he preferred to sleep in his blanket roll under whatever shelter he could find and so preserve this unaccustomed anonymity at least for the short time he was here.

Leaving the station and turning away from the town, he walked past a farm where vociferous dogs discouraged him from stopping; and was passed in his turn by a motor car, the driver pausing briefly to call down to him, to offer him a ride to the next village. He refused as courteously as he knew how, and left the road at the next stile.

Rising, the path degenerated quickly into a sheep-track between boulders, and seemed to be taking him further and further from any hope of shelter. He persevered, however, content to sleep with the stars if it meant he could avoid company and questions. Whenever the path disappeared into bog, he forced his way through heather or bracken until he found another; and at last he came over the top of that valley's wall, and looked down into an unexpected wood.

He'd not seen a tree since the train, and here there were spruce and larch below him, oak and ash and others, secret and undisturbed. And a path too, a clear and unequivocal path, discovered just in time as the light faded.

He followed the path into the wood, but not to its heart. He was tired and thirsty, and he came soon to a brook where he could lie on his stomach and draw water with his hands, fearing nothing and wanting nothing but to stay, to move no more tonight.

He unrolled his blankets and made his simple bed there, heaping needles and old leaves into a mattress between path and brook; and only at the last, only a little before he slept did he think he saw the girl flit between trees, there on the very edge of vision, pale and nameless as the light slipped.

Pale and nameless and never to be named; nor seen again except like this, a flicker of memory and a wicked trick of the light. He closed his eyes, not to allow it passage. And breathed deeply, smelling sharp resins and the mustiness of rot, and so cleared his mind, and so slept.

Slept well and woke well, sunlight through trees and a clean cool breeze and no fear, no anger, nothing but hunger in him. With the river's resolution to come, all else was resolved; there was, there could be nothing to be afraid of except that last great terror. And why be angry against a town he'd left already, a world he would so shortly be leaving?

Breakfast was an apple from his backpack, eaten on the march: not enough for his belly, but that too was no longer the driving force it had been. He had higher considerations now; with time so short, a grumbling gut seemed less than urgent.

Oddly, with time so short, he felt himself totally unhurried. He would walk back the way he had come, he would find his way into the town and so to the solicitor – but not yet. Just now he would walk here, solitary among trees and seeking nothing, driven by nothing . . .

Which is how he came to D'Espérance, called perhaps but quite undriven: strolling where others before him had run, finding by chance what was his already, though he meant to take only the briefest possession.

The path he took grew wider, though no better cared for. Tree-roots had broken it, in places the fall of leaves on leaves had buried it; but logic and light discovered its route to him, not possible to lose it now. It turned down the slope of the valley and found the brook again, and soon the brook met something broader, too shallow for a river, too wide for a stream. The path tracked the water until the water was suddenly gone, plunging through an iron grid into a culvert, an arch of brick mounded by earth. Steps climbed the mound, and so did he; and standing there above the sound of water, he was granted his first sight of D'Espérance.

* * *

Never any doubt of what he saw. He knew it in that instant, and his soul sang.

The house was dark in its valley, built of stone washed dark by rains and rains. Even where the sun touched, it kept its shadow.

A long front, with the implication of wings turned back behind, though he couldn't see for certain even from this elevation, with the house full-face and staring him down. A long front and small windows, three storeys and then a mansard roof with dormers; in the centre a small portico sheltering a high door, and he wasn't sure even the largest of his keys would open such a door. Wasn't sure that it deserved to.

No lights, no movement: only dark windows in a dark wall, and the sun striking brightly around it.

Between himself and the house there were formal gardens wrecked by growth, rampant hedges and choked beds; but the hedges and beds stood only as a frame to water. Long stone-lined pools were cut strict and square at the corners, though they were green and stagnant now and the jutting fountainheads were still; and below the gardens, lapping almost at his feet lay the deeper, darker waters of a lake. No need for the return journey after all. No need for anything more, perhaps, now that he'd seen the house. He could run down the slope before him, twenty yards at a good flying sprint and he'd be too fast to stop. And so the plunge into cold cold water and the weight of his pack, the saturated blankets, even the keys helping to drag him down . . .

But this side of all that water, on the verge of unkept grass between trees and lake stood a building, a small lodge perhaps, though its weight of stone and its leaded dome spoke of higher ambition. Ivy-clad and strange, seemingly unwindowed and half-way at least to a folly, it must look splendid from the house, one last positive touch of man against the dark rise of the wood. And it would be a shame not to have set foot in any part of D'Espérance, all this way for no more than a glimpse; shame too to go on an impulse, on a sudden whim, seizing an unexpected opportunity. No, let it at least be a decision well thought through, weighed carefully and found correct. Nothing hasty, no abrupt leap into glory or oblivion. He needed to be sure of his own motives, to feel the balance of his mind undisturbed; there must be no question but that it was a rational deed, in response to an untenable situation.

So no, he didn't take the chance to run. He walked carefully down the steep slope and turned to parallel the lake's edge as soon as the ground was level, skirting the last of the trees, keeping as far from the water as he could. Looking across to the further shore, where the gardens' gravel walks ended in a stone balustrade and a set of steps leading down into the lake, he saw a man he thought might have been his father. Blindfold and blundering in the bright dry light, the man teetered on the steps' edge, on the rim of falling; and then there was dazzle burning on the water as a soft breeze rippled the sun, and when his eyes had cleared he could no longer see the man.

It is a truism that anything seems larger as you get closer, that you lose perspective; but here he thought it was the other way, that his eyes had made him think the lodge small because they couldn't credit the house with being so very large. It must be so, although he wasn't looking at the house now to make comparisons. This near, the lodge took everything. Squat and massive it sat below its dome and drew him, dragged him forward; he thought that it was so dense it made its own gravity, and that he was trapped now, no way out.

The lodge had double doors that faced the water, too close for his liking, only three low steps and half a dozen flagstones between them. In echo of the house, there was a small pediment above the high doors, with columns to support it in a classic portico. Still no proper windows. He could see a thin run of glass at the cupola's foot, between lead and stone; but even with that, even at this season with the sun low enough to strike through the doorway at the height of the day, it was going to be dark in there.

No lock on the doors, though, no need to struggle with the keys. He climbed the steps, laid his backpack down, set his shoulder to one of the doors and pushed.

There was rust in the hinges, and it spoke to him: its voice was cold and harsh, it said "Guilty," and then it squealed with laughter.

He jumped back, sweating, clutched at a column for support and looked out across the lake again. Saw nothing, no movement, no man.

Stood still, listened; heard the blood hiss and suck in his ears, heard his heart labour behind his ribs, eventually heard birdsong and the soft lapping of the lakewater, a more distant rushing which must be the underground flow to feed and freshen it.

The door stood ajar, silent now, its greeting spoken and its accusation or its judgment made. He stepped forward and pushed again, and it swung wide with no sound beyond the grating of rust in its hinges.

Not a lodge, then. Surely a folly after all.

He stood in the doorway, and the sun threw his long and slender shadow across an enamelled iron bath. One of eight, all set in a circle, radiating; and at the centre a square-tiled pit, a plunge-bath large enough for a dozen men to share.

There was nothing else in the great circular chamber except for wooden slat benches around the sides, dark with mould and damp. The walls were adorned with intricate murals, figures from history painted in the Pre-Raphaelite style, though the light was too dim for him to identify the scenes portrayed.

A bathhouse, he thought, *a bathing-house*. This vast construction, and it was only a place to bathe, *ensemble* or *en famille*; and that with the lake outside, just there, wide and deep and surely more attractive . . .

Perhaps there'd been a club, a bathing-club, the local gentlemen anxious to preserve their modesty or their ladies' blushes. That or something like it: nothing else could explain so much labour, so much expense to such frivolous effect.

But frivolous or not it was here, and so was he. If D'Espérance could spawn a structure so large and strange at such a distance, then he thought his keys could stay where they were, safely in his pack. Something he lacked, to take him up to the house. He'd settle for this, at least for today. The child is father to the man; there were lessons here to be learned, aspects of the parent surely reflected in its idiot son.

He thrust the door as wide as it would go and then opened the other also, to let in as much light as he could, and to allow the breeze to freshen the musty air. Some few cracks in the domed roof added a little further light to what the door gave, and that high circle of glass below the dome, but this must be the most it ever saw by nature. He thought they would have needed lamps, those who used it. Whatever they used it for.

Still, there was enough to see by. Stepping inside, he could see a gallery now, circling just at the wall's height, below that ring of glass and the dome's first curving: all wrought iron, the gallery, and likewise the spiral stair that led up to it from behind the door. *That must have been for strangers*, he thought, *for observers, non-participants*.

Now he was concerned about the murals, he thought at the very least they must be lewd. Some provincial Medmenham set he imagined building this bathhouse, ambitious to reproduce the Hell-Fire Club in their own gardens. But lowering his eyes tentatively to look, expecting grave disappointment, expecting a grand fancy rendered simply sordid, he found nothing like it.

King Arthur and Excalibur he found, Oberon and Puck he found, Wayland in his smithy and other men or fairies that he couldn't identify, but all surely harmless even to his nervous sensibilities.

And all flaking too, some cracking as the plaster bulged behind them or staining darkly from beneath. Seeing one crack too long, too straight for nature, he went closer and found the outline of a door within the picture, found a painted leather strap to tug it open.

And tugged, and first saw the mirror that backed the door, that showed him his own shape marvellously moving in this still place. Then saw the closet behind the door, with its hooks and bars for hanging clothes, its slatted shelves for towels and other necessaries.

Closed that door and looked for others, found them regularly spaced around the chamber; and none hid anything more than an empty closet, until the last.

On the other side of the double doors was the iron spiral leading up; here, as though in secret reflection behind its concealing door, was a stone spiral leading down, leading into darkness.

Bold he could be, curious he certainly was; but he needed a light in his hand before he ventured those narrow steps. And hot food in his belly, that too.

One thing at least he'd learned in his time at school, though not from his teachers. Like many a boy before him, he'd befriended the local poachers for the sake of an occasional salmon or grouse

to scorch over his study fire and eat with his fingers, with his
friends. At the start of term he'd brought them bottles of brandy
filched from his father's cabinet; in return they'd taken him out
more than once, shown him how to make a snare and where to set
a night-line.

Those skills would feed him now. There must be fish in the
lake; there were certainly rabbits in the wood's fringe, he'd seen
signs of them already. He hadn't thought to bring fishing line or
wire, why should he? He wasn't here for sport. But he could
improvise. He had bootlaces, there were springy willow-shoots
growing by the water. No need to visit the town, even to shop for
what would ensure he need not visit again.

Sitting on the steps in the sunshine while water rippled before
him, that water reflecting clouds and light and nothing of the
great dark house, he reflected on the house; and almost felt he had
a duty there at least, if none to family and reputation gone or a
name that was meaningless now, himself the last shamed bearer
of it. He should go to the solicitor, and ask how arrangements
might be made. If he had to be honest, *I shall be dead soon, and
the house needs an heir*, then so be it. He could do that, once.
More than once, he thought not; but once would be sufficient.

Something screamed in the wood behind him, with the voice of
a young girl. He started, shifted on the warming stone, and went
to check his snares.

Already there was a rabbit kicking, held tight around the neck
and its feet barely in contact with earth. He gathered wood for a
fire, laid it in the portico and lit it with flint and tinder from his
pack; then he fetched the rabbit. Carried it still living to his fire,
though it lay still as a dead thing in his hands, only its eyes alive.
Those he killed first, with a pencil. Contrary to all his tutors'
lessons he let it die slow and suffering, tutor himself now and pain
all his lesson, the real world his theme.

"See it?" he whispered, poking with his pencil, digging gently.
"See the light, little brother, see the *light*?"

What the rabbit saw, of course, was darkness: which was what
he saw also, whichever way he looked, into the bathhouse or out
across the lake. Shapes woven from shadow moved in the
shadows inside, avoiding the last of the sun's fall across the
floor; or they moved darkly in the water, under the glitter of light.

Ragged gunfire sounded through the wood and birds rose like

smoke, screaming on the wind. *A posse shooting crows*, he thought; but he still thought himself alone in this valley, and he didn't believe that anyone would shoot at crows with a .303.

Later, as his fire hissed under the rabbit's dripping quarters, he heard sounds of soft knocking, dull and rhythmic.

Sat and listened; and no, not knocking after all. Sounds of kicking. Slow, steady, unremitting, a foot thudding into flesh and breaking bone.

He tended his fire, but his hands were trembling now.

Sitting in the twilight, licking greasy fingers – not wanting to go to the lake to wash, not while it was light enough to see what moved within the waters – he thought he saw words scratched black across the red disc of the sun.

Guilty he thought was said again, and other words he couldn't read for the fire in his eyes, but they might have been names. His father's or his mother's, the girl's or his own. It didn't matter which. Any name was a betrayal.

He thought he should leave this valley before the games turned worse than cruel, before they remembered the real world and turned to blood. Not at night, though, he wouldn't leave at night. The wood had been friendly to him once; but there was coming in and there was going out, and they were different. He felt a little like an eel in a basket, trapped without trying. Come the morning, he'd test that. Not now.

So he made his bed in the portico, on hard stone because there were too many shadows in the long grass moving, too many murmurs coming up. Between the wood and the water, even the bathhouse seemed to offer something of protection.

Something, perhaps; but not enough. Waking in the cold night, he felt a moist warmth on his face and smelt sour breath, smelt blood.

Heard his own breathing change, heard his blood rush. Stiffened every muscle not to move, not to roll away; and thought there was no greater giveaway, no louder announcement, *I'm awake!*

An unshaven cheek brushed his, dry lips kissed him, and he held himself rock-still. A voice moaned in whispers, and he wouldn't moan back. Then touch again and harder this time, hard to hold against such pressure as the man's face stropped itself against his. Skin and stubble and the bone beneath: and something else he felt, wouldn't open his eyes to see it but he felt coarse cloth, a blindfold.

And then there was nothing but the hard sounds of breathing, and the sounds of footsteps gone too quickly. He couldn't hear water, but he thought the man had walked straight into the lake.

In the morning he found a thread of linen caught in his own soft stubble. He tied it in a coil and put it in his wallet for safe-keeping, where he might have put a lock of someone's hair; and no, he couldn't think of leaving now. Too much of betrayal already, too much of guilt.

Besides, the wood would never pass him through. He tested that. He went back to the culvert, and tried to walk the path upstream; and tree-roots tripped him, leaves hid hollows under-foot where he fell and hurt his ankle, might have broken it. Where the path slid beneath his feet and he could barely scramble back to solid ground, watching earth crumble into water, there he gave it up, there he turned and came back; but it had been nothing more than a token in any case, he'd only meant to scout.

No escape from the valley, then. Not by the wood, at least. There must be a road, however ill-kept; but between himself and any road the house lay, massive and dissuasive. *My house*, he thought; but that was a legal fiction at best, and more of a brutal joke. Even at this distance, he was learning a little. The lesson was that D'Espérance didn't belong, it wasn't owned. It might, on suffer-ance, permit; but he was not yet ready to confront what that would mean, being accepted by D'Espérance.

So no, not that way. He wouldn't even skirt the borders of the house; this was closer than he liked already, in its ambit even this further side of the lake.

Locked out of the wood, not ready for the house and no water-baby, never that, there was only the bathhouse left him. This much he could encompass, heavy as it was, as it might prove to be. This much he could carry, for a while. *For a brief while*, his thoughts reminded him, and were still.

In the best of the light, with the doors wide, he went in with a pale torch burning and opened the door to the spiral stair.

Walking down in sinking circles, he smelt must and mould and dead air. The flame flickered, making shadows dance around him; but that was only mechanical, the action of light unfiltered by strangeness, he could understand that and not fear it.

Distant sounds of rushing, like a hard wind contained: he thought of the culvert, and the hurry of hidden water.

The stair turned one final time, and brought him into a high cold chamber lined with brick, dark with moisture. This too was dedicated to the mechanical, though, and nothing to fear. His weak torch showed him pumps and boilers, copper pipes and iron, gauges and valves. His eye traced the run of pipes, what would be the flow of the water; he followed it, he learned it, he loved it. This was how he wanted the world to be, all in order and all explaining itself.

Until his torch went out; and this was not how he wanted the world to be, utterly dark and cold and empty, nothing in reach of his groping hands.

Groping, his hands found nothing but his eyes did. *Knock knock*, cool and stiff like fingers but not that, not fingers: lightly knocking against his eyes and knocking again like crooked fingers while he only stood there, too much knocked upon.

Moaning, he heard his voice say "Mama"; but all moans sound more or less like Mama, and he hadn't called her that since he was a child, not since he was very small indeed.

He stepped backwards, away from the knocking; and kept his hands rigidly at his sides not to grope again, not to feel.

Not to find.

His feet found a wall for him, and he kept his shoulder against it until they came to the rise of the stairs. And so up, still in darkness and that rushing sound in his ears changing now, turning rhythmic, turning to kicks; and the door closed at the top but his barging shoulder crashing it open and his stumbling feet carrying him out into the cool and shadowed bathhouse which was so much warmer, so very much brighter than what lay below.

And still he couldn't leave, and wouldn't. Not if she were here too, and the girl somewhere in the wood, perhaps: that early glimpse no trick of light or memory, those sounds of kicking no folly of his mind.

He saw his father again across the lake, bound and blindfold, a khaki figure in an early light although the sun was setting.

Beset by his own senses, he struggled for that numb normality he'd worn like a cloak before. Horror was unexceptional, pockets were a proper place for rocks, one deep plunge and never rising after was a fit deed in a nothing, nothing world.

But poking at a rabbit's eyes wouldn't do it now, wouldn't keep him. Not where his father's eyes were too much on his mind, where his mother dangled always in his thoughts, where the girl might be watching from the wood.

What could keep him, the only thing that might keep him from the slip, from sliding through terror and into its undermath, would be to walk that slip's edge, to hang on terror's lips against its speaking. To go back into the bathhouse and take possession of the dark below, where his mother currently possessed it.

Gathering cobnuts and filberts at the wood's edge, his back turned to whatever threatened in the water, he heard a snuffling that might have been tears and saliva backed up in a sobbing girl's throat. He heard a scratching that might have been a girl's desperate nails digging furrows in the path, and then a steady heavy thud-and-scrape that sounded like nothing so much as a boot falling and falling, and its metal studs scraping on the path between falls as the foot drew back and lifted to fall again. He could hear breathing too, hard grunts tied to the same rhythm.

He lifted his head expecting to see her, expecting to see her kicked; and saw instead a bloated pink-brown rump swing and rub against a tree, hard enough to shake the trunk. And it swung away and swung back, thud and scrape, and it was only a pig after all: a great sow twice or thrice his weight, let forage in the wood or else – more likely, he thought, out here where no one was – escaped its sty and living feral. Unless D'Espérance did this too, throwing up animals unexpectedly and when they were most desired.

He needed this sow badly, and lacked the means to take her.

Means could be made, though. Made or found.

He slipped away quietly, not to disturb her at her scratching, not to startle her off into the depths of the wood where he might not be allowed to follow. If this was her current rooting-ground, then above all he wanted her to keep to it.

He blunted his knife cutting at ash-saplings, hacking them away from their roots. With the blade given an edge again on the granite steps of the portico, he spent the evening trimming and whittling until he had an armoury of sorts, three straight poles each sharpened at one end. He hardened the points in his fire, remembering an engraving in a book that showed cavemen doing the same; and the work absorbed him so that he forgot to look over the water before the light failed, to see if his father were there.

He still listened for the creak of rope in the bathhouse or sounds of kicking in the wood, as he turned his spears in the glowing ashes; but he heard neither tonight, only the sow's noise among the trees. He might have chased her then, but that he was learning to fear the dark, or those things that were couched within it. Instead he trusted her still to be there in the morning, and lay all night fretting in his blankets, doubting her.

Up at first light, he found the sow moved on; but didn't need his acquired skills to track her. A blindfold man could have followed this trail, the broken undergrowth and the furrowed earth.

He caught up with her quickly, and with no hindrance from the wood: no tripping roots, no hanging branches tangling in his hair. There was hunting, apparently, and there was trying to leave, and they too were different.

Slowing as soon as he heard the sow's heedless progress, he crept close enough to sight her rump again; and ah, he wanted to do this hero-style, one mighty cast to fell her swift and sure.

But this wasn't sport, there was no one to applaud, and his spears weren't made for throwing. Silent as he knew how, as he had been taught, he slid forward into the wind and the sow never heard him, her great flap ears trailing on the ground as she snouted under leaves and bushes, eating nuts and acorns, eating insects, eating frogs.

At three yards' distance he set two spears to stand against a tree, and hefted the other in both hands above his head. The sow moved one, two casual paces forward, blithe in her size and strength, and oh, she was big, she was just what he needed; and he took a breath and ran and thrust, all his strength in his arms as he stabbed down, driving the spear's haft deep as he could into the sow's flank.

She screamed, as he was screaming as he stabbed: high and shrill both of them, vicious and unrestrained. But he thought she'd run, or try to; and she didn't run. She turned, although her hind leg failed her where the spear jutted from it, and her eyes were red in the shadowed wood, and her festering yellow teeth were snapping at him; and he tried to jump backwards, and he fell.

Sprawled on his back, he looked up into a canopy of branches baring themselves before winter, and he saw his mother twist above his head, lolling at the rope's end. Her bare feet swayed and turned, one way and the other, feeling in the absence for his eyes.

He screamed again, and rolled; and though he only sought to roll away from his mother, he was sprayed with slaver from the sow's jaws as her bite just barely missed him. Gasping and shaken he scrambled away, and the sow strained to follow, hauling her weight unsteadily on three legs, slipping and rising again, squealing in pain and fury.

Up at last, he wanted only to run; but his eyes snagged on his two spare spears, and this was what they were for, after all, he'd never expected to finish her with one. So he snatched up one of them, holding it two-handed again against her sheer mass; and as she came at him open-mouthed, he rammed its dark point into what was soft at the back of her throat.

And barely released his grip in time as her jaws threshed about its haft, where it jutted out between them; but she was a spent force now, crippled and gagged, blood colouring her leg and frothing between her teeth. He could take time to recover his last spear, time to consider his aim before thrusting.

Trying for her heart, he didn't find it. She fell away, though, all her efforts on breathing now, no fight left in her; and he could work the spear deeper, turning and thrusting and leaning on it like pushing a stick into the earth. At last something vital gave, be it her heart or her spirit. One last shudder, and then the slow moan of leaking air with no breath behind it, and she was dead.

And he lifted his head, ready to howl if he needed to; and his mother was gone, there was no body dangling, wanting to knock, *knock knock* against his eyes in this dappled daylight.

He butchered the sow where she lay, bloody on a bed of dead leaves. There was no other choice; he couldn't possibly have dragged her back to the portico for a cleaner dismemberment.

He hewed at her with his short-bladed knife, and this was butchery indeed, up to the elbows in blood and ankle-deep in the run of her spilt guts with the stink of her rising all about him. The knife slipped often in his slimy hands, so that he added his own blood to hers; but he worked all day, and at last had all the pieces of her laid out on cool clean stone under the shelter of the pediment. Then he could wash, he could strip off his fouled clothes and wash those also, naked under the cold sun; and briefly he had no fear of the lake, he watched only with exhaustion and no hint of terror as dark shapes rose to question his shadow only a little further out, where the lake-bed suddenly fell steep away.

Because he had no other way to do it, he built a slow fire beneath one of the iron tubs in the bathhouse, and laid pieces of pork inside it on a bed of well-scrubbed stones. As the bath and the stones heated, so fat melted and ran down to spit and hiss on hot enamel; and this was what he needed, not the meat.

While the lard rendered, he made crude pots from clay he'd dug with his fingers from the lake's edge. Baking in the fire's ashes, several of them cracked or flindered; but some survived well enough to use, he thought.

Pork for dinner, roasted dry but he wouldn't heed that. The skin had gone to crackling; as he crunched it something roiled and stirred the water, far out in the centre of the lake. He heard his father cry out in the darkness, and he heard a staccato rattle of gunfire; and he heard his mother's slow choking; and louder than any, louder than all of those he heard the sounds of kicking.

His father came to him again when he should have been sleeping. Wet serge warned him, smelling strongly in the damp air; cracking his eyelids barely open showed him an outline against the sky, the glint of moonlight on buckles.

He heard boots shift on stone, he heard each separate breath like a groan. But no kiss this time, no touch at all; and after his father was gone, what he heard until he slept was his mother's rope creaking in the wind, as she dangled somewhere close at hand. He wouldn't open his eyes again to look, but he thought perhaps she was up between the pillars of the portico, that close.

*　　*　　*

In the morning, he scooped a potful of lard from the bath and set it to melt by his cooking-fire outside. Threads drawn from a blanket and plaited together made a wick; he laid that across the pot and let it sink, with ends trailing out on either side.

When he lit them in the shadows behind the bathhouse door, they made more soot and smell than light; but they made light enough to work by. Light enough to reclaim the cellars from his mother, perhaps, though she could dangle as well in light as darkness.

She couldn't knock, *knock knock* at his eyes in the light, and that was what counted.

He made as much light as he could, three lamps each with two wicks burning at both ends, twelve guttering flames to save him. He carried them down one at a time, and even the first time there was no body swinging at the head of the stairs, nor any at the foot, nor in the chamber below: only the boilers and the pumps and the constant rushing sound of water.

By his third trip down, coming from light into light with light right there in his hands, he felt secure until he looked more closely at the machinery. All the surfaces were coated in a sticky black mixture of dust and grease, generations old; but two words gleamed out at him in the light he'd brought, shining where someone had written them with a finger in that clagging muck. One of course was *Guilty*, and *Coward* was the other.

One quick sobbing breath, staring, seeing the finger in his mind – fine and delicate for sure, trembling a little perhaps with the enormity of it all – and then he turned abruptly, and saw the box of tools in the corner, half-hidden under dark and heavy piping.

A galvanised iron bucket, and a wooden box of tools: hammers and screwdrivers and wrenches, everything he could possibly need. No can of grease, but he didn't need grease now, he had his bathful of rendered fat. He could sieve that through his shirt to get the grit out. Not first, though. Cleaning came first; and first for cleaning were the boilers that bore those two accusations, those truths.

Days he worked down there, days and into the nights sometimes, cleaning and greasing and taking apart, sketching plans and patterns of flow with charred sticks on the tiled floor. His parents left him largely undisturbed, his father no longer crossing the lake, his mother only distantly dangling. If they were making room for the girl, if it was her turn now, she was being slow to show; and he wasn't waiting.

Not consciously, at least. Consciously, he was learning how to plumb.

At last, the turn of a great brass stopcock brought water gushing through the pipes. The furnace burned hot and fast on gathered wood; and as soon as pressure started to build, the first leaks showed where rubber had perished and his rabbitskin-and-pork-fat improvisations wouldn't hold. He patched as best he could, and set the bucket to catch the worst of the drips. It didn't matter, he was only testing the system, and there was a drain in the floor in any case. If it wasn't blocked.

Sweating, he refilled the furnace and threw a lever, and the pump started to knock, *knock knock*. Knocked and failed, and knocked again. More leaks, jets of steam now, clouding out the light; briefly he thought the show was over for the day, *knock knock* and nothing more.

But again a knock, and a faster knocking; the rhythm changed abruptly, hard and steady and unfaltering now, and he thought of course of kicking; and the girl came walking to him out of the steam and oh, she was so afraid.

She wore white, as she had when last he saw her. Her fingers plucked at the fabric of her dress, her eyes were wide and panic-lost and all her body was trembling. Her mouth shook so much, at first she could say nothing.

There was nothing he could say, and nothing he wanted said between them; but she tried, and tried again, and at last:

"They shot your father," she said. "They took him out and shot him. For cowardice," she said; and she had said all this before though not like this, not so dreadfully afraid. "There was a court martial and they found him guilty, and they shot him."

Her voice had been hard before, hard and accusatory. *You lied to me*, it had been saying, *you're a coward too*. There had been no tears then, and none of the pleading, none of the terror he saw in her pallid face.

Then as now, he had been unable to speak at all; then as now, she had gone driving heedlessly on, far past what was honourable or decent. And yes, he was an expert on honour by then, he'd seen it from both sides and knew it better than any.

"Your mother," she said, though she clearly, she so much didn't want to. "That's why she, why she hanged herself," she said. "For shame," she said, "she hanged herself for shame."

Let herself dangle in the dark for him to find when he walked clean into her, her bare toes *knock knock* against his blinded, desperate eyes.

"You should do that too," she said, "why not? Why don't you? A coward and the son of a coward, and your mother the only honourable one among you all, why don't you just jump in the river? Too scared, I suppose," she said, answering herself. "I should have known then, when I realised you were a water-funk. Once a coward, always a coward. Like father, like son . . ."

And that was all she said, because it was all she had said the first time. After that it was only crying out, and grunting.

And now as then, and this was what she'd been so afraid of: that it would happen again as it had, that it would have to.

And of course it did. He swung wildly, and felt the solidity of her against the back of his hand as she sprawled at his feet; and *feet, yes*, already he was kicking.

Kicking and kicking, but not to silence her this time, not for shame. Only because she was there, as his parents were intermittently there, in their intermittent deaths; and the thing was there to be done, and so he did it.

Felt better, second time. Not good, never that; but better. She cried, but not him. No choking, no fire in his throat or eyes, neither anger nor grief could find him. Fear might have found him, perhaps, but he wasn't afraid of this.

Neutral at last, he kicked until his feet lost her in the steam, until she was entirely gone from there.

And then he felt his way up the stairs and out into the bath-house where a couple of taps were hissing and spitting, scalding to his hand as he turned them on.

He scrubbed one of the baths as best he could, and washed every piece of clothing that he'd brought. He laid them out on the portico steps, and came back naked to fill the bath again.

Lying back with his eyes closed, with burning water lapping at his ears and the corners of his mouth, he thought that nothing was finished, even now; but it didn't seem to matter. Let his father stumble blindfold against death, let his mother dangle, let the girl come for kicking when she chose. Or when he called her. The world was wider, much wider than this; and here he was only on the fringes of it yet, he hadn't even been up to the house . . .

Later, in the darkness, when his clothes were dry, he thought he might walk down to the lake and into the water. He would be borne up, he thought, and carried over, because in his pockets he carried the keys to D'Espérance.

But actually, he slept; and in the morning he walked the other way, he walked into town looking for the solicitor.

STEPHEN LAWS

The Song My Sister Sang

STEPHEN LAWS LIVES AND WORKS in Newcastle upon Tyne. To date he has published ten horror-thrillers – *Ghost Train*, *Spectre*, *The Wyrm*, *The Frighteners*, *Darkfall*, *Gideon* (winner of the Children of the Night Award), *Macabre*, *Daemonic*, *Somewhere South of Midnight* and *Chasm* – which have been widely translated around the world.

His award-winning short stories have appeared in various magazines, newspapers and anthologies (most recently in *Best New Horror 9*), and he is the regular host of the Manchester Festival of Fantastic Films. His first solo collection of short stories, *The Midnight Man*, was recently published by Darkside Press.

"The abandoned open-air swimming pool which is the centrepiece of 'The Song My Sister Sang' really did exist," Laws reveals. "The central character's description of the place is completely factual. His memories of playing there, the sights and sounds – they're all mine. The history of the place is also true. It remained derelict for many years, just as described in the story. The place always haunted me, and I knew that one day – when I had the right story – it would feature in my work in some form or other.

"When I was writing my novel *Somewhere South of Midnight*, a friend of mine, who works for the local authority responsible for the place, managed to get permission for me to get through the padlocked gate with a video camera. I spent a half-day exploring the pool, the sluices, the derelict changing rooms with their rusted curtain rails and disintegrated tile floors. It was perfect for what I had in mind – the setting for a confrontation between the novel's main character and a professional hit man.

"I'd just finished writing the sequence when my friend rang me to say: 'You're never going to believe this – but the council has just approved plans to demolish the place and build an outdoor sea-life feature on the site.' Three months later, the swimming pool was bulldozed out of existence. I suppose I could have just left the sequence as it was, but somehow it didn't feel right. Perhaps I thought that using a real-life setting, when that setting no longer existed, was dating the book somehow. So I rewrote the sequence for the novel, creating a fictional derelict health club up on the promenade overlooking the site where the swimming pool used to be.

"But this strangely haunting place just wouldn't leave me alone. I knew that there was a story there somewhere, waiting to happen. Eventually, it did. When Steve Saville asked me for a contribution to his anthology *Red Brick Edens* and its theme of urban decay, I knew then that the location had found not only its story but also its home. The swimming pool has gone forever – all that remains is twenty minutes of incredibly eerie video footage on a shelf in my study. And, of course, 'The Song My Sister Sang'."

F OR MOST PEOPLE living along the North-East coast, the Big Event that summer was what happened to the coast-line and its wild-life.

Just say the words *Edda Dell'Orso* and see what kind of reaction you get from the local fishermen who ply their trade out of North Shields Quay. The captain and crew of that ill-fated tanker never made it out of the wreck alive, so the Inquiry could only reach an open verdict; even though they'd had the specialists and the engineers and the aquamarine people from Blyth out there to try and find out why the tanker had drifted so close to shore. Close enough to become grounded; close enough to gash one of its main tanks on seabed rocks, close enough to cover the entire length of beach for ten miles on either side with a smothering sea-blanket of crude oil.

That, they'll tell you, was the horror that marred last summer.

They're wrong. The real horror wasn't to do with the fouled-up beaches and the near-death of the local fishing industry. It might have all begun with the *Edda Dell'Orso*, but the real horror was . . . how do I put it? . . . much more personal than that.

It happened in the abandoned swimming pool on Tynemouth beach. Derelict and boarded up. Rotting under the salt-spray and the sun and the cruel sea winters. That's where the real horror began.

And where I might have lost my sanity.

Very soon now, I'll know for sure.

The open-air swimming pool had been a real crowd-puller, from its opening at the turn of the century right up until its closure in the 1960s. Built in an oval-shape, below the cliffs on Tyne-mouth beach, its sluices were open to the sea. One side faced the cliffs, the other out to the sea; the rounded end of that oval looking down on clustering rocks where children climbed and hunted for crabs and winkles. Back then, the pool itself had been tiled in blue and white; the surface of the water glittering under the summer sun like molten silver. I played there as a kid, with my sister; just before the place was closed. And every time I try to get a picture of it as it was then, I always seem to get *sounds* instead. The sound of the sea, beyond the walls and in the sluices. The cries of children splashing and diving matched by the wheeling cries of seagulls overhead. The cliff side of the pool was bordered by the pumping station and its chlorine tanks. There was a side gate there, with a steep and tightly winding set of stairs that took you straight up to the promenade above. The main building housed the changing area. Inside was a maze of mini-corridors with individual tiled cubicles. Plastic curtains hung from the overhead rails. Again, the sounds come back to me. It seemed that the place was always filled with laughter; echoing screeches as kids ran and played; the slap of bare feet on tiled floors as they dashed in and out of those cubicles, consumed by holiday excitement. Lots of Scottish accents, I remember.

Bloody funny, that. The accents, I mean.

Every "factory-fortnight", all the shipyard workers from the River Tyne would pack the family up to Scotland for the tradi-tional family holiday in cheap digs on the sea front. At the same time, all the shipyard workers from the Clyde would do the same thing, and head down here to Tynemouth and Whitley Bay.

Staying in the same cheap bed and breakfasts, and doing pretty much everything their Geordie compatriots would be doing north of the border. I often wondered why everyone didn't just stay where they were. Anyway, I seemed to make a lot of Scottish holiday friends back then. Close as blood-brothers for two weeks, then gone forever after. Even though Amy and I were local kids, that swimming pool was an exotic visit for us; maybe two or three times a year, in a good summer.

And then that terrible, terrible thing happened.

No one ever told me this, but I reckon it was Amy's death that led to the closure of the pool. Two weeks after the funeral, the gates were chained. Thirty-odd years later, and the place still haunted me.

First, let me tell you what happened on that Thursday morning when the *Edda Dell'Orso* ran aground.

I guess you must have seen the television news reports about the oil slick that washed ashore and what it was doing to the seagulls and the guillemots. I've heard it said that more people were enraged about what was happening to the seabirds than what had happened to the crew. Right or wrong, I guess people felt that it was the men's fault at root, and that the "dumb" animals were suffering the consequences. I'm an animal lover, that's why I spend so much of my spare time working with the RSPCA and the RSPB; but I would never put animals before people, the way that some animal lovers do. Anyway, there was one hell of an outcry.

And I was down there on Tynemouth beach with the other volunteers, doing my bit. Trying my best not to scare to death the oiled-up gulls and the other seabirds which were bobbing on that tide of black filth; carefully trudging waist-deep through all that foamed-up crude oil in my waders and trying to get the poor buggers passed back to shore without getting my eyes pecked out. A difficult job in more ways than one; mess around too much trying to get your hands on a seabird and the chances are that it'll die of fright before you're able to get it back to where it can be cleaned. Same thing with the cleaning operation. The washing and cleaning is a gruelling, painstaking operation. No matter how careful you are, it's an arduous and distressing experience for them, and it wouldn't be the first time I've had a bird suddenly just die in my hands while I was trying to get the oil and the shit out of its plumage, no matter how gentle I was trying to be.

It was a particularly distressing experience on that Thursday morning. The oil was so thick close to shore that the waves just weren't "breaking" anymore. Undulating black ripples flowed around me as I worked. A lot of the birds had been early morning feeders, and we hadn't got there until just after ten. Consequently, there were a lot of dead gulls as we made our slow way south down the beach. A lot had drowned in that oily morass, others had struggled to be free, their wings hopelessly gummed until they'd died of exhaustion.

And all the time we worked our way down the beach, I was aware that we were getting nearer and nearer to the abandoned swimming pool. I tried to keep its presence out of my mind, tried not to let those memories overwhelm me. To a great extent, it worked. The needs of those birds were so immediate that they outweighed the bitter memories. But even though the waves weren't breaking because of the heavy overlay of oil, I could still hear the sussurant rush of the sea further out, and every once in a while, it brought it all back to me with a vividity that made me want to turn around and wade back to the beach. Luckily, there were twelve of us out there that morning, all relying on each other; so the thought of letting them all down, in what was a painstaking team effort, kept me going.

Then someone cried: "Over there!"

I turned to look back. It was Lorna Jackson. At first I thought she'd hurt herself, when I saw that there was a dark smudge right across her brow. Then I realised that it was oil, wiped there accidentally by her own hand. She was pointing urgently down the beach and when I turned to look I could see what had so alarmed her. A seabird had become trapped in one of the swimming pool's sluices; a three-foot-round aperture set into the base of the pool's sea wall. The rocks and the wall were stained by years of green and yellow sea-encrustment, but now the area around that sluice and the rim of the aperture were smeared with the *Edda Dell'Orso*'s jettisoned filth. Right in the middle of that opening, wings flapping in distress as it bobbed up and down on a black mass, was a gull. Unlike most of the birds we'd come across, it still had a glimmer of white in its wings. Perhaps it had just come down on the rocks beside the sea wall, too hungry for pickings to take any notice of its fellows' fate; but it didn't seem to be as badly oiled-up and that in itself made it a prime candidate for rescue.

"I'll get it!" I yelled, before anyone else could respond, and surged back to the beach. It was maybe fifty yards to the sea wall.

I've thought about why I responded so quickly.

Sometimes I think it's to do with everything I've just told you. The bird not being so badly oiled-up and everything. Now I know it had to do with something altogether different. There were a million and one reasons why I should have kept away from that swimming pool after what happened to Amy. I've said it was a place that haunted me. More than that. On the grim grey days of my depressions, when nothing in the world seemed to make sense anymore, or when I was tottering on the edge of that pit of melancholy, almost ready to let myself fall . . . my thoughts always returned to that swimming pool, no matter how much I tried to prevent it.

Maybe that day I had a chance to grasp the nettle.

Perhaps I saw the opportunity to do something I'd thought about doing for a long time.

Not so much bearding the lion in its den, because there was no fucking lion in there. Just the echoes of those bygone days, keeping me awake at night. Now, I had a chance to go where I'd dreaded. Does that make sense? I didn't want to go in there, *couldn't* have gone in there just with the idea of laying my personal demons to rest. But hell, now there was a *reason*. That bird would die. And maybe . . . just maybe . . . setting foot in there might go some way to easing my pain. Even as I watched, the bird was being sucked in through the sluice, out of sight and into that hateful place. There was a collective moan behind me as it vanished, but I turned as I ran, oil splattering the sand from my waders, and I waved:

"Okay. It'll be okay. I've got it."

There was a concrete ramp on the beach, maybe a hundred feet long, leading right up to the rusted and padlocked front gate of the swimming pool. The fence was wire mesh, so I knew that I could climb it if I had to. Not knowing whether my sense of urgency had to do with the plight of the bird, or my need to just get in and out of there as quickly as possible, I hopped the last few feet on either foot as I pulled off my oil-stained waders and dropped them on the ramp. I yanked at the padlock and a fine cloud of brown rust furled and blew away on the sea-breeze. The fence seemed to vibrate away on all sides; a strange noise, like the "singing" that sometimes comes from telegraph wires. That sound affected me badly and I didn't know why. Back on the beach, the others were continuing with their job, but were still watching me. Gritting my teeth, I hooked my fingers through the mesh and climbed.

The fence was about twenty feet high, and I had no problem with heights. But my heart was hammering as I swung my legs over the top and began the climb down to the other side. When I hit bottom, I still clung to that fence, sweat making my shirt stick to my back and running in itchy rivulets down my face. I screwed my eyes shut. Then, with an angry curse I pushed myself around, ran past the empty lifebelt stand and came face to face with the cracked and rusted fountain that I had played in as a kid.

Back then, it had been a wonderful conical pyramid of bright blue and white paint, standing by the shallow end of the open air pool. There had been steps there, so that the kids could climb up and stand beneath a glittering curtain of breath-catching, cold sea water. Now, it was just a cracked and stained mass. I barely had a chance to take it in. Or the graffiti-ridden walls and the yawning, empty doors and windows of the changing area block off to my right.

All I could see was the swimming pool itself.

No more glittering water. No more sparkling blue and white tiles.

The surface of the pool was a black mass, undulating and shifting as if there was something alive beneath it. Rubble, shattered spars of wood and tangled ironwork had been dumped into that pool, but it was impossible to make anything out clearly. Hundreds of gallons of the *Edda Dell'Orso*'s crude oil had been sucked in through the sea-sluices and had coated the entire surface. But it was not this that made the sight so obscene. It was what the tanker's spilled load had brought with it. The tide and the clinging oil had sucked more than one seabird in through that sluice. There were birds all over that undulating mass. Maybe a hundred, maybe more. It was impossible to tell. Most of them were dead, and the only flash of white feathers I could see was down by the sluice itself, where the bird had been sucked in. It flapped and struggled as it was carried further into that seabird's graveyard on the rippling ebony surface.

I ran forward, knowing that there was no way I could wade

into that pool. I'd have to find something to pull the gull into the side. I glanced at the abandoned changing rooms as I ran alongside the pool to where the bird was struggling. The echoing sounds of kids laughing and of bare feet slapping on cold tile floors somehow seemed very real to me. Now, I didn't know whether I was doing the right thing by coming in here, or whether I was just going to make the dreams and the memories even worse than they already were. It was replaying in my head now, the day when Amy died. I didn't want it to, but just being in this place brought it back with a horrifying intensity.

It had been my birthday party the day before, and Amy had stolen all the attention as usual. It was supposed to be my day. A special day when Mam and Dad could show me that they loved me just as much as her. But sure enough, just when it seemed that everything was going well; when the kids were all playing and I was feeling really good – the party was brought to a halt when Amy told everyone that she wanted to sing her song and do her dance. And I remember looking at Mam and thinking: "They won't let her do it. They won't let her spoil the party. Any other time, any other day. But not now. Not at my birthday party . . ."

And Mam had told everyone to be quiet and had picked Amy up and put her on the table, and even though the other kids had seen it all before, they were made to be quiet, and Amy was asked . . . was asked . . . to do her song and her dance. I could have cried and begged and ranted, in the way that a nine-year-old will, but I was just so hurt. So hurt, that I couldn't say a thing. My throat was constricted as I stood there and watched Amy be made the centre of attention as she sang . . .

I tried to push those memories out of my mind, but it was impossible. The seagull's movements had become weaker. It raised one oil-covered wing as if it was trying to wave at me. In another moment, it must succumb.

And Amy began to sing:

"Ain't she sweet? I ask you, ain't she neat? Now I ask you very con-fi-dentially: Ain't! She! Sweet!"

Her little feet began to pound out that tap-dance rhythm on the table and the kids shuffled and watched and God how I wanted that table to collapse beneath her, or for her to miss a step and fall and begin crying and . . .

There was a broken spar of wood lying by the side of the pool. I picked it up. The wood was so rotten that it was crumbling in my hands even as I hoisted it out over the surface of the oil.

The next day we had gone to the beach. The sun was shining and there were lots of families all encamped on the same stretch of sand that I'd just come from. But inside, I was feeling over-shadowed in a way that I'd often felt. I wanted to be alone, that's why I asked Mam and Dad if I could go on up to the swimming pool. Dad had insisted that I take Amy with me. After all, I was the older brother and it was my job to look after my little sister. That constricted feeling was in my throat again. Couldn't I do anything without having her along in tow? Didn't they realise that I wanted some time for myself? I sulked, but they made me take her. We were already in swimming costumes, so there was no need to use the changing facilities.

"Keep in the shallow end," Mam had said.

I was able to reach the seagull with the spar, but the bird began to panic, even though I was being as gentle as I possibly could. Its one free wing began to flap and splatter the oil, and I began to make shushing noises as if I was dealing with a small child.

"Easy . . . easy . . ."

I didn't want to take her. They shouldn't have made me take her. What the hell were they thinking about, Mam and Dad? I was only nine years old, Amy was seven. What did they think I was? Amy's nursemaid?

Slowly and gradually, I drew the seagull in to the side. Its wing ceased to flap. It looked at me with one blank eye, giving in to its fate.

There were other kids there. Kids my own age. Amy wanted to play, began to cry when I said she had to stay there in the shallow end while I went to play with those others. I knew why she wanted to come. She just wanted to be the centre of attention, as usual; would probably sing that bloody song again and just embarrass me. So I left her there while I made new friends. And the first I knew that something had gone wrong was when that woman screamed . . .

Still making that shushing sound, I reached out and gently took the bird by its wing. It didn't resist. It just kept looking at me as if it knew that I was going to rend it apart and devour it. I let go of the spar and it slid soundlessly beneath the surface of the oil. I had the bird now and lifted it to the side; long tacky threads of oil spattered and flurried in the sea breeze.

. . . and when I looked back down to the shallow end, I could see three men ploughing through the water; could see one of them lunging down and dragging something from the bottom and the woman was just screaming and screaming, making the other kids down there begin crying too, as . . .

The seagull was dead. Its head lolled on its neck. Its one eye was still blank and staring. I could feel that constriction in my throat again; just as if I was nine years old once more. What had I done by coming into this place again? How could I have been so stupid as to believe that I could exorcise those memories? I lay the bird at the poolside and crouched down on my haunches, looking back to the shallow end.

And then, about six feet out from where I sat, something moved beneath the oil.

I saw it from the corner of my eye. At first, I thought it might be sunlight reflecting on that ebony surface. I stared at the place where I thought I'd seen movement. It came again. Something that flapped out of the oil, smaller than a seagull's wing, but with the same kind of movement. Another sea bird, trapped beneath the surface and trying to rise. I looked for the spar, then remembered that I'd let it drop into the pool. Frantically, I searched around for something else. Now, it seemed as if there was a chance to make good on my failure. If I could save even one bird from this morass, then somehow it seemed that my desperation need not be so intense. There was nothing at hand. Perhaps back there in the changing rooms . . .?

But then there was new movement, something so strange and graceful and eerie that I could only sit there and watch.

A swan was rising from the oil.

What I had at first assumed to be a wing was a swan's head breaking the surface. Because now that swan's head was rising and I could see its long and graceful black-coated neck as it emerged slow and dripping from the pool. But there was something wrong with that neck now. It had been broken in the middle. It was bending at an impossible angle as the neck emerged from the oil and . . .

This was no swan's head, no swan's neck.

It was a hand, and an arm; now bending at the elbow as something came up out of the pool.

A head crested from the oil. Long hair, black and dripping.

And all I could do was sit, frozen and terrified, as the woman finally stood up in the pool, so completely covered in black filth that she might have been a statue carved out of basalt. She was motionless now, facing me, as if waiting for me to do something. But all I could do was sit there and stare. The woman's eyes opened, two white orbs in that hideous black visage.

I opened my mouth, but I couldn't say a word.

And then the woman began to sing.

The voice was ragged and halting, as if she had been under that oil for a long, long time, and had perhaps forgotten how to use her voice properly. Her face remained blank, but her eyes never left me as she sang.

"*Ain't . . . she . . . sweet? I ask you . . . ain't she neat . . .?*"

That's when I must have fainted, because it seemed that the black oil was everywhere then, filling my eyes. The horror of what I was seeing and hearing was too unbearable. I remember hearing:

"*. . . ask you very con-fi-dentially . . .*"

And then there was nothing.

There were no dreams, no nightmares. Just this terrible buzzing in my ears and a dreadful taste in my mouth. I knew then, even in that dark place behind my eyes, that I was asleep at home and in bed. I had been drinking again. And when I finally surfaced from that sleep, I would have a king-sized hangover. I would wake up and realise that everything about the swimming pool and the thing that had emerged from it was an alcohol-induced nightmare. Something was wrong with the mattress on my bed. It felt too hard, too uncomfortable. I struggled to wake . . . and felt concrete. Dislocated and afraid, I jerked out of that sleep and struggled to rise.

I was still lying by the side of the swimming pool.

It was still daytime.

The oil lay thick and dark and heavy on the surface of the pool.

And not ten feet from where I lay, the young woman was still there.

She had pulled herself to the edge of the pool, had tried to crawl out of that black mass, but her strength had given out at the last. She had hauled her upper body out of the pool, her arms stretched before her and her fingers clawing at the concrete. Oil lay spattered around her; thick streamers of the damned stuff. But her lower body and legs were still in the pool, hidden beneath the oil.

Instinctively, I recoiled, backing away until I sat heavily and groggily on the concrete steps which led up to the derelict changing rooms. The ringing was still in my ears and I struggled to contain my nausea. I looked at my watch and realised that I couldn't have been unconscious for more than a few minutes. Remembering the others back on the beach, I decided to run and get help.

But then the woman groaned and one hand groped feebly as she tried to haul herself the rest of the way out of the pool.

I hesitated, thinking: *This can't be happening.*

The woman groaned again, unable to pull herself any further.

But she's alive. The least you can do is get her out of that pool and then you can run for help.

Unsteadily, I moved back to the poolside.

"It's alright . . . you're all right . . ."

I didn't want to touch her, was still struggling to contain the feeling that I hadn't woken up yet and that this was an ongoing nightmare. I'd had a terrible shock when I'd seen her emerging like that, but I must have imagined that she was singing that song. I *must* have. The woman tried to lift her head to look at me, but was too exhausted. Fumbling at her face, she tried to brush the straggling long hair away.

"*Please* . . ." Her voice was so faint that I could hardly hear it. "*Help me.*"

And without being aware that I'd made the decision to help, I was suddenly kneeling beside her. I took one arm. It felt terribly cold. I pulled, but the woman hadn't the strength to assist, and she remained half-in, half-out of the pool. Standing, I took her under the armpits and hauled her from the oil, leaving a great black trail on the concrete lip. For the first time, I realised that she was naked; her frame slender and slight. Perhaps it was the oil coating her from head to foot. When she was clear of the pool, I turned her over and helped her to sit.

"You wait here," I began. "I'm going to get help."

"*No,*" she replied, gagging as oil flowed from her lips. My God, was she going to die?

"You're going to be all right, I promise. But I need to get a doctor and . . ."

And the woman opened her eyes to look at me.

"*Dean,*" she said, calling me by my first name.

Everything is fractured, after that. I've tried to put the pieces together in my mind, but a lot of it just doesn't make sense. I seem to remember crying and laughing at the same time, calling my sister's name. That might be wrong; that might just be all in my mind. But I do remember those eyes, because suddenly that was all I could see. The whites of those eyes were somehow shocking, set into that black-oil sculpted face. The irises were so green that they sparked, and looking at them somehow hurt my own eyes. They were growing larger as I looked. And then I seem to remember something to do with the side gate to the swimming pool; the gate behind the changing block beyond which lay a steep flight of stone stairs, leading up the cliffs to the seafront parade and its rows of hotels.

Something to do with a length of corroded steel pipe that was lying around.

Something to do with enormous effort on my part.

I think, although I can't be sure, that I smashed the lock and chain on that side gate. And we must have climbed those stairs. We must have, because that's where I'd parked my car. I must have wrapped my own jacket around her, helped her into that car. Perhaps there were people up there; staring in astonishment at us. I seem to recall faces. Perhaps not.

I must have driven home to my flat.

Because the next thing I remember clearly is standing in my living room, just outside the bathroom. I was staring at that door, and when everything around me registered properly again, I realised that the shower was on. I could hear the water hissing. I raised my hand to shove the door open, but something made me stop. I looked around, trying to convince myself that I wasn't still dreaming. Yes, this was my living room; just as I'd left it earlier that day. When I tried to move, my legs were weak. I staggered, clutching at the sofa, and ended up at the window looking down to the street, six floors below. It was evening, and my car was in its usual place.

And there was a dark stain on the pavement, from the car to the communal entrance. As if someone had spilled something there. From this distance, it looked horribly like blood.

I squinted at my watch. I'd lost about nine hours.

I braced my hand on the window sill and shook my head. When I turned and looked around again, I expected somehow that everything would have changed; that this strange dream would take a different turn. But the living room was just as I'd left it that morning before heading off to the beach. I suddenly felt nauseous and took a step back towards the bathroom. Fear cramped my stomach with the sudden knowledge that Amy . . . she . . . whatever . . . was in there. It acted like an inner safety valve, preventing me from throwing up then and there.

What *was* in there?

"Amy . . .?"

When the telephone rang, it was like some kind of electric shock. My teeth clamped shut so hard that I nicked my tongue, and my mouth filled with blood. With the second ring, I realised that I wasn't going to have a heart attack. By the third, the fear had returned with a sickening intensity. It suddenly became important that whoever or whatever was in the bathroom not be disturbed by the sound. Staggering across the room, I snatched up the receiver.

"*Dean?*"

It was Lorna.

"Yes . . ."

"*What the hell are you playing at?*"

"Sorry?"

"*We've been worried sick about you. What happened to you? Where did you go?*"

"Go? I'm not sure what . . . I mean . . ."

"*You ran off to the pool to get that poor bird, and then you just vanished from the face of the earth. Have you any idea what trouble you've caused? When you didn't come back we went to look for you and you were nowhere . . . nowhere . . . to be seen. Christ, we've had the coastguard and the police out. We thought you'd gone into that fucking pool, or something. They've sent people down to drag the bloody thing. So what happened . . .?*"

"I'm sorry, Lorna. Something . . . something happened . . . and I had to leave and . . ."

"*You had to leave? I mean, without saying anything to any-one? Without telling any of us? You . . . you shit! We've been worried sick. Well . . .*" Unmistakeably, anger building out of control. "*look . . . look . . . you can telephone the fucking police and the coastguard and tell them to call off the search, and while you're at it you can tell them why you . . .*"

"Goodbye, Lorna."

I put down the receiver. My hand was shaking badly.

Beyond the bathroom door, the sound of the shower had suddenly ceased.

It had been turned off.

I stood there, looking at the door. A part of me knew that I should just turn and get out of that apartment as fast as I could. But I couldn't move. I tried, but I was rooted to the spot.

Something was going to happen.

And there was nothing I could do.

I tried to speak, but my voice choked in my throat.

My heart was hammering. I could feel the blood pulsing in my temples.

And that's when I heard the singing again. So low as to be almost inaudible. Sly, and hideously mischievous.

"*Ain't . . . she . . . sweet?*"

"Oh Christ, Amy. I didn't mean to leave you in the pool."

Somehow, my voice sounded like the voice of the nine-year old I'd once been.

"*I . . . ask . . . you. Ain't . . . she . . . neat?*"

"It can't be you. Is it you? Amy, I'm so *sorry* . . ."

The sorrow erupted from me. Thirty years of contained grief. The tears flowed down my cheeks to mingle with the blood in my mouth. It was the salt taste of the sea.

"*Dean,*" said that voice, with a sibilant echo that must surely be impossible in there.

"Yes?"

"*Come and open the door, Dean.*"

"Oh God, Amy. I can't . . ."

"*Come and open the door!*"

"I'm afraid . . ."

There was laughter then. Girlish laughter; low but still somehow echoing, and with a terrifying sense of intent.

"*Come let me taste your tears.*"

Suddenly, I was moving. There was no conscious effort on my part. The voice was drawing me to it, and there was nothing I could do.

Through the blurred vision of my grief and my terror, I saw my own hand reach forward for the bathroom door as I stumbled forward.

The telephone began to ring again. It sounded thin and distant, nothing to do with me at all.

I watched my hand turn the handle, saw the door swing open.

Beyond, I could see only steam from the shower. Some inner and distant part of me knew that there shouldn't be steam in here at all. There was never steam when I showered. But it was there, and all the details of the bathroom were shrouded in that swirling, undulating mass. Ragged wisps and rapidly dissolving tentacles swirled over the threshold into the living room, dissolving before they reached me.

"*Come here, Dean*," said something hidden from sight.

In terror and grief, I stepped into the bathroom and felt the warm embrace of the steam.

And that's when everything becomes fractured again.

Something happened in there, but it's as if my mind is either incapable of comprehending it, or that the horror was so great that it shuts off every time I try to understand what was being done to me. I'm trying to think of it now; trying to get impressions, but nothing will register. I know it's in there, locked in my head, but nothing will come.

When it ended, the nightmare had changed location again.

The first thing I became aware of was the wind. It smelled of salt and seaweed, and when my vision cleared I could see the sea. I was standing on a beach, and moonlight was shining on the water. When I looked down, I could see that I was standing on shale, not sand. I'd spent enough time on the north-east coast to know that I was a great deal further south than Tynemouth or Whitley Bay. There was no oil on the water.

I turned to look away from the sea and to the ragged cliffs behind me. The movement was too much for me, as if I'd been standing in the same position for hours and my limbs had frozen. I fell to my knees, retching. When I'd finished, something made me look back to the sea.

She was standing in the water, silently watching me.

I knew that she hadn't been there before, that there was no way she could have suddenly appeared like that. But there she was, the water troughing around her naked legs. The moonlight silhouetted her from behind. I could see no details of her face or, thank God, those eyes.

"Please . . ." I began.

I knew that if she began to sing that song again, I must surely go mad.

But she didn't say a word. She just stood motionless, watching me.

I lowered my head once more, feeling the nausea swelling within me.

When I looked up again, she had moved closer. But it was as if she hadn't moved at all. As if she had somehow *floated* closer to shore. The water foamed around her shins, but she was still in the same motionless position.

"*Dean.*"

The voice echoed impossibly once more. I moaned and waited for the end.

"*Stand up.*"

I staggered to my feet. I had no will to resist.

"*Come closer.*"

I took three shambling steps to the water's edge. We were perhaps six feet apart, but I still could not see her face. I don't know how long we just stood like that, facing each other. A part of me wondered if we'd stay like that forever, frozen in that tableau; with the hushing of the sea, the smell of salt and weed, and the flickering of moonlight on the water.

"*Stay away from Deep Water,*" she said at last.

". . . why? . . ." I barely recognised my own small voice.

"*My sisters and I feed there.*"

This time, she did move. Three languid steps towards me. For the first time, I realised that there was no trace of oil on her naked body. Her long hair moved around her shoulders in the wind, as if it had a life of its own. And now I could see that her eyes were closed. I knew then that she could still see; knew with utter certainty that she could see into my mind and read everything that was there.

She raised a graceful arm and placed her hand on my shoulder.

It's difficult to tell you what happened next.

I can't really tell you how, but I *felt* something then.

Something hideous.

She remained in that position, and there was no physical change in her. But that touch of her hand brought images in my mind; images that still haunt my nightmares. I seemed to see something that looked like a sea anemone; something with tentacle-like clusters surrounding barbed and voracious mouth-parts, moving greedily like the mandibles of a crab or a sea spider. I felt the cold touch of scales, the fetid breath of something that fed on the corpses of the drowned. I don't know if I screamed or not, but I felt that I must have.

My senses still swimming, I watched her turn from me and walk back into the sea. She moved with that same languid grace, the hair swirling around her head. She didn't dive into the water, didn't swim away. She just kept on walking until the water had reached her shoulders. When it reached her neck, she half-turned her head to look back at me as if she was going to say something else.

But she said nothing.

And in the next moment, the water covered her head and she was gone.

I wasn't aware that I'd fallen to my knees.

For a long, long time I just knelt there, staring out across the moonlit water, listening to the wind.

When dawn began to creep up behind me, I staggered to my feet and headed for the rough path that wound up the cliffs. My car was parked up there, crude oil smeared on the back seat.

I didn't look back at the sea when I climbed into the car and headed home.

So there you have it.

End of story.

And all I have are the bad dreams and the unanswered questions. Was it Amy? Or was it something that only looked human when it wanted to, and could pretend to be anyone it wanted to be by reading minds? Was it my sister, a grown woman thirty years later? Or one of those whom Ulysses had heard, when he was lashed to the mast of his ship while his companions' ears were filled with wax? In the darkest moments, I wonder if those who drown become what I saw and experienced that day.

Come let me taste your tears, she had said.

What did she find there that prevented her from doing what she was created to do?

Stay away from Deep Water. My sisters and I feed there.

Why did she spare me and warn me?

The beaches are clean again. I spend a lot of time down at Tynemouth, on the beach and looking out to sea. Usually at night. The water has a strange attraction for me. I know that one day soon, I'll have to go out there, no matter what she said.

Tonight, I heard sounds across the dark water. That's why I've written all of this down.

It sounded like whales, calling to each other.

But perhaps it was just another siren-song as the sisters moved through the deep.

They've demolished the swimming pool now. It was sealed and drained before the work could commence. No one expected what they found in there. It was the Captain of the *Edda Dell'Orso* and one of the crew. Sucked in through the sluices with the oil slick. They say their faces were eaten away by fish. Except that there were no living fish in that black morass.

So many unanswered questions.

And as much as I used to hate the song my sister sang, there are times when I stand on that beach in the moonlight and with the sea-wind coming in cold and harsh from the east, I pray with all my heart that I might hear it again. Sung in that strange, echoing voice.

Some day soon, I'll find out whether it really did happen, or whether I've just lost my mind. I'll hire a skip, and head for Deep Water. Maybe then, if she's watching and she can still taste my tears, she'll have to do what she refrained from doing that day.

I won't be afraid, I won't resist.

Because perhaps . . . just perhaps . . . I'll have the answers to all those questions before the waters close over my head and I submit to her caress.

KIM NEWMAN

A Victorian Ghost Story

KIM NEWMAN'S NOVELS INCLUDE *The Night Mayor*, *Bad Dreams*, *Jago*, *The Quorum*, *Back in the USSA* (with Eugene Byrne), *Life's Lottery*, *An English Ghost Story* and his multiple award-winning epic historical vampire novel, *Anno Dracula*, plus its sequels *The Bloody Red Baron* and *Judgment of Tears* (aka *Dracula Cha Cha Cha*). A fourth book in the sequence is planned, titled *Johnny Alucard*.

His short fiction is collected in *The Original Dr Shade and Other Stories*, *Famous Monsters* and the forthcoming *Seven Stars* and *Unforgivable Stories*, while two recent chapbooks are *Andy Warhol's Dracula* and *Where the Bodies Are Buried*. Recent non-fiction volumes from the author include *Millennium Movies: End of the World Cinema* and *BFI Classics: Cat People*.

"AMONG THE BLESSINGS OF CIVILISATION," began Ernest Virtue, his shrewd glance passing over us, one by one, "can any be more profound and yet simple than oak paneling? Its humble stoutness, derived from the most English of trees, serves us as our forefathers were served by the blockstones of their castles. Observe the play of firelight upon the grain. Does it not seem like armour? In a room lined with oak panels, one is safe, shielded from all harm, insusceptible to all fear. If not for oak paneling, I would not have the fortitude to tell you this story.

"Wondrous indeed is it to plump oneself in a comfortably-stuffed leather armchair in the heart of a metropolis and find oneself at peace, the raucous sounds of the outside world muffled, the pestilential fogs of the capital banished. Add to the picture a roaring fire providing both light and warmth, the after-effects of a hearty meal, generous measures of fine old brandy and healthy infusions of pungent cigar smoke, and one might think oneself transported from the cares of the quotidian world to a higher realm even than that ruled over by our own dear Queen, God rest the soul of her beloved Prince Consort Albert. Without such an Elysian refuge, a man might be maddened by London. For this city is the most haunted place on Earth."

In the club-room, the topic of the evening had turned to the beyond, and we were telling ghost stories. Colonel Beauregard had conjured the hill-spirits of far-off India, detailing the unhappy fate of a degenerate officer who meddled with the native women and incurred the wrath of a little brown priest. The Reverend Mr Weeks had countered with a story of phantoms in a ruined abbey on an abandoned isle in the Hebrides, and of an unwary delver after treasure driven out of his wits by an intelligence that seemed composed of creeping, writhing kelp.

We were pleasantly stirred from the torpor that follows a substantial meal, awakened by brandy and terror, thirsty perhaps for more of both.

I had not expected Virtue – Mr Ernest Meiklejohn Virtue, of the brokerage firm of Banning, Clinch and Virtue – to enter into the field and contribute a story. I had written him up for the illustrated press some months earlier and had formed the opinion that he was a man entirely of this world. Somewhat past middle age, with a barrel of a body and a generosity of grey whiskers about his chops to compensate for a growing expanse of baldness upon his dome, he was a man of substance. If not for the quality of his clothes, he might pass as an ageing prize-fighter or the chucker-out in a rowdy hostelry. It was said that many who confronted him on the floor of the Exchange yielded for fear that he would extend his financial attacks into the arena of physical assault. Needless to say, away from the bearpit of the stock market, he had a reputation as the most charitable and mild-mannered of souls.

"I have in these last months become victim to a particularly pernicious species of apparition," Virtue continued. "Gentlemen, you see before you a man persecuted beyond endurance, persecuted by spectres."

I drew in breath. From his solemn countenance, I could tell Virtue was not joshing us. The Colonel and the Reverend had passed on tales given them by colleagues who were themselves not the primary parties in the events recounted. Both had endeavoured, in the spirit of the thing as it were, to embroider, to add their own details, increasing the horripilating effects of their anecdotes. In comparison, Virtue seemed to offer the uncut, unpolished stone of experience.

Even in the warmth of the club-room, I felt a chill. The brandy I sipped stung my mouth.

"London is full of fog," Virtue continued. "Sulphurous, clinging, lingering, choking fog. As you know, it makes the streets seem like river-beds and turns us all into bottom-crawlers, probing blindly, advancing step by step. A moment's lapse of concentration and one is lost. All this is familiar to you. But I tell you there are creatures in the fog, unperceived by all but a few. These entities harbour a singular hostility, a resentment almost, for those of us who enjoy the comforts of the living."

The Reverend Weeks nodded sagely. Colonel Beauregard's hand went to his thigh, where, were he in uniform, his pistol would have been.

"I first became aware of these infernal spirits some months ago. I was, I confess, particularly pleased with myself that day. I'd concluded a nice piece of business, manipulating the market in an especially cunning manner so that my own cause was victorious and my rivals routed. I need not trouble you with details, but Weeks – who profited not a little from being let in on my machinations – can testify to the neatness of the trick. It would not be overstating the situation to say that fortunes changed hands that afternoon. The *Times* noted, somewhat predictably, "Virtue is Triumphant".

"While I indulged in a celebratory tot with my allies, accepting in all good grace the muttered tributes of fallen foes, the first real fog of autumn gathered in the streets. It rose like a tide of soup around scurrying pedestrians, washing against the thighs of the cabmen perched on their seats, closing over the backs of their horses. It is my custom to walk from the Exchange to my house in Red Lion Square, abjuring the comfort of a hansom for the sake of exercise. It is important to maintain the body, for flesh is the cloak of the soul and clothes should always make a statement, testifying to the man who wears them. I set out, flushed with my success . . ."

". . . and with good spirits, I'll be bound," said Beauregard.

Virtue inclined his head. "A dram of whisky, no more. I have, of course, considered that my experience might have been shaped by an intoxication unperceived by myself. Indeed, this is what I later tried desperately to tell myself. However, that came afterwards.

"I am familiar with my route home. I was often given to expressing the sentiment that I daresay I could find my way to my front door blindfold. This sudden fog, which you might remember being of remarkable consistency, put my rash boast to the test.

"I must have made a misturn, for I walked for some considerable time, far longer than it should have taken me to return myself safely to my own doorstep. The outlines of the buildings that I perceived through the yellow wafting curtain of the fog did not resolve themselves into the familiar contours of Red Lion Square. I was going over and over in my mind the triumph of the day, allowing myself something of the sin of pride in appreciating my own cleverness. Strategic minor purchases like the opening feints of a fencing match diverted those who opposed my interests until I was ready to deliver the elegant killing thrusts that secured my victory. I saw columns of figures piled up like heavenly bricks, and neglected to pay attention to the earthly stones beneath my feet.

"At length, I brought myself up short and looked around.

"It is a very queer sensation indeed to find oneself utterly alone in the middle of London. The fog hung so thickly as to be impenetrable, seeming almost to have coalesced about my person. If I reached out, my hand grew indistinct and then disappeared entirely from my sight. The effects of the fog were by no means restricted to the obscuring of my sense of sight. It was of that singular texture, that dampness and stickiness, that clings to one's clothes and can sometimes never be washed away, that gums up your eyes and makes your nostrils flow, that tickles the throat, that seems to invade your anatomy and clog your chest and heart. That taste we Londoners can never entirely be free of was strong in my mouth, to the point of vileness. It was as if the fog had targeted me of all the millions of the city, and wrapped me in its woolly, stinking shroud, isolating me from my fellows, holding me fast in one spot.

"I would have continued to walk, but in my unlovely gloating I had lost all sense of direction. The sun was setting, and the yellow of the fog turning to a darker hue, tendrils of brown and black winding through it. But this change of light was general, not from a specific direction that would have enabled me at least to fix a compass point. Dread fingertips touched my heart, coldly caressing. Terror sparked in my brain. It was my impulse to move, to run from the spot, to career blindly into the opaque cloud that clung to the streets, to keep running until I was free of this gathering gloom. Yet I was still Ernest Meiklejohn Virtue, Lion of the City, Master of the Exchange. I have iron in my soul. I resisted the impulse to panic, recognising it from many a hairy moment on the market floor, knowing that if I held fast I would prevail.

"I *felt* them, first.

"Something brushed past me, about the size of a big dog but clad in damp ragged cloth not sleek smooth fur. Something that went on two shod feet, yet was not what I would consider a child. Something that was all bones and hurry. I was molested slightly, poked and prodded, and had good cause to clamp a protective fist about my gold watch. Then the creature was gone. All I saw of it was a mop-head of twiggy hair, like a flying bird's nest, at about waist-height, zooming away into the fog. I heard footfalls clatter, and then it was gone.

"What had it been?

"There were others. It was at an intersection, it seems, and these creatures passed every which way at will, jostling me one way and another. I glimpsed sparkling eyes, and felt hard little shoulders. I heard their mewlings, which were not the cries of animals and yet bore little resemblance to the patterns of civilised speech. I was possessed, I admit, with a loathing that went deeper than my intellect. An instinctive revulsion that made me shrink inside my clothes with each rude touch. I was sure their touch left deposits upon my person, and that these substances would prove even less susceptible to cleaning away than the miasmal filth of fog. They chattered and stank and jeered and passed by.

"It could only have taken a minute or so. The creatures were soon gone. I found myself breathing hard, sucking into my lungs yet more of the ghastly fog, which made me cough and splutter all the more. I bent double. I was drowning in the city's visible stench."

Virtue took a swig of brandy and sloshed it around his mouth, trying to wash away the remembered taste. He had become quite agitated in the recounting of his experience, offering none of the eye-rolls and leers with which the Colonel and the Reverend had punctuated their tales. His ghost story was of a different quality. I found myself feeling a little of the horror Virtue claimed to have felt, but tempered by a distance, a quarrelsome need to question. I bit my tongue, and let him continue.

"When I straightened up, a miraculous transformation was taking place, as if in answer to a prayer I had not dared to voice. The fog was thinning, as it sometimes does. Good clean transparent air rushed in from somewhere and diluted the muddy clouds, reducing it to streamers of ropy substance and a ground-covering of thin white mist. A draught hurried the worst of the stuff away, and I could again make out something of the situation in which I found myself.

"Naturally, I felt a surge of joy at my deliverance. But it froze in my breast. The scene disclosed was not that which I had expected.

"Simply put, I was transported. From the London we know to another realm entirely, a Stygian parody of the city, entirely loathesome in its crepusculence.

"I stood on a street washed with filth. More mud than stone, more ordure than mud. Buildings stood all around, walls stooped over to make a tunnel of this thoroughfare. The ill-fit bricks bulged in places, allowing foul water to dribble. There were smashed street lamps, none lit. Fires burned in the night, within the buildings or in barrels set on the street, but heat and light were swallowed by the darkness and cold of this unnatural place. A nearby sign was splashed with dirt, unreadable. I knew that I was, in a more profound sense than I could imagine, lost.

"This place was inhabited. That is the worst of it.

"The first ghost I got a good look at inspired me not to horror but to pity. It was a waif-like thing, with huge liquid eyes and a tiny knot of a mouth, clad only in a vest-like singlet that disclosed wasted arms and grubby bare feet. I was unsure of its sex, for it wore a shapeless cap of some rough material over its hair, but I knew that it was not alive as we are. This was some poor lost soul, wandering.

"It saw me and stretched out a hand, palm up, beseeching.

"I had much this creature wanted, I was sure, but nothing I could give. Its eyes grew wetter and its head angled to one side. I heard its painful moan, a wordless begging. I stifled the pity that sprang up unwanted in my breast, and was on my guard against this ghostly thing. I fancied malice in its eye. That this creature loved me not, would do me harm if it could, was not to be trusted.

"There were others, roughly in the shapes of men and women, but clad as even the lowest savage of India would never clothe himself, in the meanest of rags. I was assaulted by details. Rotten teeth, marbled eyes, grimy clawnails, fungus swatches of hair, great scabs, mismatched buttons.

"Had these once been people?

"They came out of their dwellings and gathered around me, like a pack of dangerous dogs.

"You are spirits," I declared, "and you cannot harm a Christian soul. Begone!"

"My words gave them pause. My mental strength returned. I was better than these creatures. I was alive. They could only touch me if I let them. My moment of weakness was past.

"I still had to escape from this place. And to do so, I would have to turn my back. I believe this is the most courageous thing I have ever done.

"I turned and walked away, loudly reciting the Lord's Prayer. As I knew they would not, the ghosts did not rush at me from behind. I was too strong for that, and they knew me for their better.

"But I heard barks of laughter, horribly close to human sounds of mirth. As I plunged into a bank of thickening fog, returning I hoped to the world of the living, my cheeks burned with an inexplicable embarrassment. The ghosts mocked me, jeering at my back, possessed by a cruel hilarity that cast me out of their region as surely as my feet carried me away, into the fog again.

"Now, I was running almost, at least walking briskly. I began on the psalms. After some interval, I collided with a police constable in Farringdon Road and was able from there to make my way home."

The Reverend Mr Weeks nodded sagely, and Colonel Beauregard scowled in sympathy. I felt as if I had myself been transported beyond the rational world, into Ernest Virtue's hellish half-city.

"I thought, that night as I prepared for my bed, my horrible experience was at an end. I imagined this moment, when I would retell it to good friends within a room of stout oak and know I was beyond the reach of those ghosts. I slept soundly, untroubled by what had occurred. The world was back as it should be, and my place in it was fixed and secure.

"But that laughter had followed me.

"Three days later, in the street outside the Exchange, I heard that laughter again. I looked about, startled, rudely breaking off a conversation. It was broad daylight, if overcast. A great many brokers stood about in groups, discussing the day's business. Amid so many frock coats and top hats, it was hard to catch a glimpse of the tattered cloak. But it was there, I was sure. The quality of the laugh was not human. It came from the beyond.

"That was not the only incident. I have been certain, always when outside, when on the street, that I have seen a shadow or heard a cry which could only betoken the presence of one or more of that ghostly crew, escapees from that dreadful place abroad in the city of the living. Have they followed me back? Or have they always been among us, unseen by the many, maddening the few cursed souls who have awoken to their presence?

"I have been touched again. Their hands sometimes grip the skirts of my coat as I pass. Their fingers poke and prod. My watch is lost to them. I don't know when it was stealthed away, but when I found it was gone, I also found a blue bruise on my belly, where the watch must have pressed.

"They love us not, these ghosts. They envy the life we have. They are needy, with a hunger we cannot understand. They would take everything from us if they could. And if they can not have what we have, they will tear us down and destroy all we hold dear, out of spite. I must be strong, must remain strong. Else the world will spin out of its orbit and be lost in the darkness."

"Now, now, old man," said the Colonel. "Chin up."

"Yes, Colonel. I keep my chin up. I keep my back straight. I keep my heart closed. I can resist."

I expected our clergyman to have something to say, but the

Reverend Mr Weeks had nodded sagely off to sleep. In itself, that gave me a chill none of the stories had raised.

"For a while, it was dreadful," Virtue continued. "Even in broadest daylight and in the most respectable thoroughfares, I was aware of them. They slouch among us, clinging to their gutters and alleys, boldly meeting our glances, trying with their guttural noises to harry our minds. London is thick with these monsters. I was woken up to their presence, and wondered what spell had been cast over me so that I should be cursed with the power of seeing those things that should decently remain invisible. They are parodies of life, loathsome and pitiable, despicable and damned. Their corruption is complete, and yet they yearn even as we do, for the light, for the warmth. I know you must find this hard to credit, for had another tried to persuade me of this before my experience in the fog I would have deemed him mad. But these ghosts are among us. All the time."

An excitement, almost a rage, had built up in me as Virtue spoke. I had expected one of the others to cut him off, to rend apart his strange misconception. And yet it fell to me.

"Surely," I began, "your ghosts are nothing supernatural. The place you have described is simply a slum. Sadly, many such are to be found in London. Your ghosts are just the poor, no more."

Virtue's eyes fixed me like the lights of a hostile gunboat.

"The poor!" he exclaimed. "The Poor!?!"

There was a terrifying force inside him.

"The unfortunate," I continued. "Beggars and wastrels, no doubt. The human detritus of our city, those who through birth or inclination have found themselves settling on the bottom."

"This is London," Virtue said, with a ferocious certainty. "The most prosperous city in the world. No such creatures exist, not naturally. My dear friend, of this I am sure as eggs is eggs. For me, the curtain has lifted and I have seen a hellish world beyond."

I was horrorstruck by something new in Virtue's tone. A spark of pity, for me that I could be so deluded as to believe his phantoms to be people like ourselves.

"Colonel Beauregard, Mr Weeks," I appealed.

Neither worthy – for Mr Weeks was now awake again – joined my position.

"This is a case of spectral persecution," Virtue insisted. "It will be resisted. If you ignore them, I have found, they go away. For I am winning my private war. This last week, they have been fainter presences. I can still see them, but I have to weaken and direct my gaze at a fixed shadow to be sure. I have been successful in willing myself free of persecution. By ignoring the ghosts, I deny them substance. Within days, I shall have banished these apparitions entirely. Oak panels are my armour. My mind is my sword."

Somehow, his conviction swayed me. I came to see his experience as he did himself. I still held in my mind my original assumption, but in my heart I knew I relied too much on my mind.

There were ghosts. This city was spectre-plagued. Mr Ernest Meiklejohn Virtue was haunted.

I added my own story to the collection, to conclude the evening. It was hurried, I confess, a confection of hooded monks and a hook-clawed madman, with lovers united beyond the grave and a villain harried over a cliff by the bloodied floating faces of his victims.

The company broke up, and departed the club to the quarters of the compass.

It was not a foggy night, but it was moonless. I watched Virtue stride off vigorously, down a street ill-lit by faint gaslight. He marched almost, swinging his cane like a lance, looking straight ahead and not into any of the alleys that fed into the street, whistling a hymn that spoke of the rich man in his castle and the poor man at the gate, He made them high and lowly and ordered their estate. In some of the alleys were huddles that breathed and stretched out empty hands. He walked past, unseeing.

For Virtue, the haunting was almost over.

But a horror worse than all the crawling severed hands, floating green shrouds, chattering skulls and ambulant scarecrows pitched in together clung to the stones of this prosperous city, impinging when it had to on the main thoroughfares but festering always in the shadows beyond the gaslight, wrapping the hearts of men and women like you and I in a misery more profound than the sufferings of any wailing spectre bride or seaweed-dripping wrecker's revenant. I remembered Virtue's convictions, of his own rectitude and of the strength of oak panels.

I resolved to model myself on him, and walked home, holding my breath in the darks between the pools of lamplight, arriving safely at my own oak-lined fortress.

That night, I saw no ghosts.

BRUCE
HOLLAND ROGERS

The Dead Boy
at Your Window

It's been a good year for Bruce Holland Rogers. His ghost story "Thirteen Ways to Water" (from the anthology *Black Cats and Broken Mirrors*) won the 1999 Nebula Award from the Science Fiction and Fantasy Writers of America, and the following story was the winner of the Horror Writers Association's Bram Stoker Award.

The author contributes a regular column to the writing magazine, *Speculations*, about meeting the spiritual and psychological challenges of full-time fiction writing, and he is currently working on a collection of short-short short stories with the support of an Individual Artist Fellowship from the state of Oregon.

About "The Dead Boy at Your Window", he recalls, "This story began with a writing exercise I assigned myself: Write a story about a lie. I was quite surprised to discover the consequences of this particular lie."

I N A DISTANT COUNTRY where the towns had improbable names, a woman looked upon the unmoving form of her newborn baby and refused to see what the midwife saw. This was her son. She had brought him forth in agony, and now he must suck. She pressed his lips to her breast.

"But he is dead!" said the midwife.

"No," his mother lied. "I felt him suck just now." Her lie was as milk to the baby, who really was dead but who now opened his dead eyes and began to kick his dead legs. "There, do you see?" And she made the midwife call the father in to know his son.

The dead boy never did suck at his mother's breast. He sipped no water, never took food of any kind, so of course he never grew. But his father, who was handy with all things mechanical, built a rack for stretching him so that, year by year, he could be as tall as the other children.

When he had seen six winters, his parents sent him to school. Though he was as tall as the other students, the dead boy was strange to look upon. His bald head was almost the right size, but the rest of him was thin as a piece of leather and dry as a stick. He tried to make up for his ugliness with diligence, and every night he was up late practicing his letters and numbers.

His voice was like the rasping of dry leaves. Because it was so hard to hear him, the teacher made all the other students hold their breaths when he gave an answer. She called on him often, and he was always right.

Naturally, the other children despised him. The bullies sometimes waited for him after school, but beating him, even with sticks, did him no harm. He wouldn't even cry out.

One windy day, the bullies stole a ball of twine from their teacher's desk, and after school, they held the dead boy on the ground with his arms out so that he took the shape of a cross. They ran a stick in through his left shirt sleeve and out through the right. They stretched his shirt tails down to his ankles, tied everything in place, fastened the ball of twine to a buttonhole, and launched him. To their delight, the dead boy made an excellent kite. It only added to their pleasure to see that owing to the weight of his head, he flew upside down.

When they were bored with watching the dead boy fly, they let go of the string. The dead boy did not drift back to earth, as any ordinary kite would do. He glided. He could steer a little, though he was mostly at the mercy of the winds. And he could not come down. Indeed, the wind blew him higher and higher.

The sun set, and still the dead boy rode the wind. The moon

rose and by its glow he saw the fields and forests drifting by. He saw mountain ranges pass beneath him, and oceans and continents. At last the winds gentled, then ceased, and he glided down to the ground in a strange country. The ground was bare. The moon and stars had vanished from the sky. The air seemed gray and shrouded. The dead boy leaned to one side and shook himself until the stick fell from his shirt. He wound up the twine that had trailed behind him and waited for the sun to rise. Hour after long hour, there was only the same grayness. So he began to wander.

He encountered a man who looked much like himself, a bald head atop leathery limbs. "Where am I?" the dead boy asked.

The man looked at the grayness all around. "Where?" the man said. His voice, like the dead boy's, sounded like the whisper of dead leaves stirring.

A woman emerged from the grayness. Her head was bald, too, and her body dried out. "This!" she rasped, touching the dead boy's shirt. "I remember this!" She tugged on the dead boy's sleeve. "I had a thing like this!"

"Clothes?" said the dead boy.

"Clothes!" the woman cried. "That's what it is called!"

More shriveled people came out of the grayness. They crowded close to see the strange dead boy who wore clothes. Now the dead boy knew where he was. "This is the land of the dead."

"Why do you have clothes?" asked the dead woman. "We came here with nothing! Why do you have clothes?"

"I have always been dead," said the dead boy, "but I spent six years among the living."

"Six years!" said one of the dead. "And you have only just now come to us?"

"Did you know my wife?" asked a dead man. "Is she still among the living?"

"Give me news of my son!"

"What about my sister?"

The dead people crowded closer.

The dead boy said, "What is your sister's name?" But the dead could not remember the names of their loved ones. They did not even remember their own names. Likewise, the names of the places where they had lived, the numbers given to their years, the manners or fashions of their times, all of these they had forgotten.

"Well," said the dead boy, "in the town where I was born,

there was a widow. Maybe she was your wife. I knew a boy whose mother had died, and an old woman who might have been your sister."

"Are you going back?"

"Of course not," said another dead person. "No one ever goes back."

"I think I might," the dead boy said. He explained about his flying. "When next the wind blows . . ."

"The wind never blows here," said a man so newly dead that he remembered wind.

"Then you could run with my string."

"Would that work?"

"Take a message to my husband!" said a dead woman.

"Tell my wife that I miss her!" said a dead man.

"Let my sister know I haven't forgotten her!"

"Say to my lover that I love him still!"

They gave him their messages, not knowing whether or not their loved ones were themselves long dead. Indeed, dead lovers might well be standing next to one another in the land of the dead, giving messages for each other to the dead boy. Still, he memorized them all. Then the dead put the stick back inside his shirt sleeves, tied everything in place, and unwound his string. Running as fast as their leathery legs could manage, they pulled the dead boy back into the sky, let go of the string, and watched with their dead eyes as he glided away.

He glided a long time over the gray stillness of death until at last a puff of wind blew him higher, until a breath of wind took him higher still, until a gust of wind carried him up above the grayness to where he could see the moon and the stars. Below he saw moonlight reflected in the ocean. In the distance rose mountain peaks. The dead boy came to earth in a little village. He knew no one here, but he went to the first house he came to and rapped on the bedroom shutters. To the woman who answered, he said, "A message from the land of the dead," and gave her one of the messages. The woman wept, and gave him a message in return.

House by house, he delivered the messages. House by house, he collected messages for the dead. In the morning, he found some boys to fly him, to give him back to the wind's mercy so he could carry these new messages back to the land of the dead.

So it has been ever since. On any night, head full of messages, he may rap upon any window to remind someone – to remind you, perhaps – of love that outlives memory, of love that needs no names.

RAMSEY CAMPBELL

Ra*e

RAMSEY CAMPBELL IS SOMEONE ELSE who enjoyed a good year in 1999. No sooner had he travelled to Atlanta, Georgia, to collect the Grand Master Award at the ninth World Horror Convention, than he was back in Los Angeles receiving the Horror Writer Association's Bram Stoker Award for Life Achievement.

Recent books by the author include the novels *The Last Voice They Hear*, *The House on Nazareth Hill*, *The One Safe Place*, *The Long Lost* and the forthcoming *Silent Children*, plus such collections as *Waking Nightmares*, *Strange Things Stranger Places* and *Alone With the Horrors*.

" 'Ra*e' was another tale written to an order that proved less firm than it had promised to be," reveals the author. "Jeff Gelb and Lonn Friend, editors of the *Hot Blood* series of anthologies, asked various people to write a long story about one of the seven deadly sins. You will have guessed which attracted me. Alas, for whatever reason, the project failed to find a publisher, and so although I completed the first draft of the tale in early 1996, I saw little point in revising such a lengthy piece to be touted elsewhere. For a while a second volume of *Dark Love* seemed imminent, and apparently both editor Nancy Collins and her publishers wanted me in it, but it too faded and vanished. The story finally appeared in my latest collection, *Ghosts and Grisly Things*, published by Pumpkin Books."

"YOU'RE JOKING, LAURA. You're just doing your best to madden your mother and me. You're not going out like that either."

"Dad, I've already changed once."

"And not for the better, but it was better than this. Toddle off to your room again and don't come back down until you've finished trying to provoke us."

"I'll be late. I am already. There isn't another bus for an hour unless I go across the golf course."

"You know that's not an option, so don't give your mother more to worry about than she already has. You shouldn't have wasted all that time arguing."

"Wilf –"

"See how your mother is now. Perhaps she can be permitted a chance to speak before you have your next say. What is it, Claire?"

"I think she can probably go like that rather than be waiting in the dark. I know you'd give her a lift if you weren't on patrol. I only wish I could."

"Well, Laura, you've succeeded in getting round your mother and made her feel guilty for not being able to drive into the bargain. I'm sorry, Claire, that's how it seems to me, but then I'm just the man round here. Since my feelings aren't to be allowed for, I'll have to try and keep them to myself."

"Thanks, mum," Laura said swiftly, and presented her with a quick hug and kiss. Claire had a momentary closeup of her small pale face garnished with freckles above the pert snub nose, of large dark eyes with extravagant lashes which always reminded her how Laura used to gaze up at her from the pram. Then the fourteen-year-old darted out of the room, her sleek straight hair as red as Claire's five years ago swaying across the nape of her slim neck as her abbreviated skirt whirled around the inches of bare thigh above her black stockings. "Thanks, dad," she called, and was out of the front door, admitting a snatch of the whir of a lawnmower and a whiff of the scented May evening.

Wilf had turned his back as she'd swung away from her mother. He sat down heavily in the armchair beside the Welsh dresser on which ranks of photographs of Laura as a baby and a toddler and a little girl were drawn up. He tugged at the knees of his jogging pants as he subsided, and dragged a hand across his bristling eyebrows before using it to smooth his graying hair. "Better now?" said Claire in the hope of dislodging his mood.

He raised his lined wide face until his Adam's apple was almost as prominent as the two knuckles of his chin. "I was serious."

"Oh, now, Wilf, I really don't think you can say your feelings are swept under the carpet all that much. But do remember you aren't the only –"

"About how she dresses, and don't bother telling me you used to dress that way."

"I could again if you like."

"I'm still serious. You were older, old enough your parents couldn't stop us marrying. Besides which, girls weren't in the kind of danger they are these days."

"That's why we have folk like you patrolling. Most people are as decent as they used to be, and three of them live in this house."

He lowered his head as if his thoughts had weighed it down, and peered at her beneath his eyebrows. "Never mind hiding in there," she said with the laugh she had increasingly to use on him. "Instead of thinking whatever you're thinking, why don't you start your patrol early if you're so worried and see her onto the bus."

"By God, you two are alike," he said, slapping his thighs so hard she winced, and pushed himself to his feet.

"That's us women for you."

The front door thumped shut, and Claire expelled a long breath through her nose. If only he wouldn't disapprove quite so openly and automatically of all that Laura was becoming – "What's wrong?" she blurted, because he had tramped back in.

"Nothing you've spotted." He played the xylophone of the stripped pine banisters as he climbed the stairs to the parental bedroom. She'd begun to wonder what was taking him so long when he reappeared, drumming his fingernails on his neighbourhood patrol badge, which he'd pinned to his black top over his heart. "Found it in with your baubles," he said. "Now maybe I've some chance of being taken notice of."

In the photograph he seemed determined to look younger, hence threatening. It still made her want to smile, and to prevent herself she asked "Who's out there at the moment, do you know?"

"Your friend Mr Gummer for one."

"No friend of mine. He'd better not come hanging round here if he sees you're away."

"You'd hope putting on one of these badges would make him into a pillar," Wilf said as he let himself out of the house.

Claire followed to close the filigreed gate at the end of their cobbled path after him, and watched him trot along the street of large twinned houses and garages nestling against them. Perhaps she was being unfair, but Duncan Gummer was the kind of person – no, the *only* person – who made her wish that those who offered to patrol had to be vetted rather than merely to live in the small suburb. Abruptly she wanted him to show himself and loiter outside her house as he often found an excuse to do while he was on patrol: she could tell him she'd sent Wilf away and see how he reacted. She had a vision of his moist lower lip exposing itself, his clasped hands dangling over his stomach, their inverted prayer indicating his crotch. She wriggled her shoulders to shrug off the image and sent herself into the house to finish icing Laura's cake.

She was halfway through piping the pink letters onto the snow-white disc when she faltered, unable to think how to cross the t of "Happy Birthday" without breaking her script. How had she done it twelve months ago and all the times before? She particularly wanted this cake to be special, because she knew she wouldn't be decorating many more. Perhaps it was the shrilling of an alarm somewhere beyond the long back garden with its borders illuminated by flowers that was putting her off, a rapid bleeping like an Engaged tone speeded up. She imagined trying to place a call only to meet such a response – a sound that panic seemed to be rendering frantic. Nervousness was gaining control of her hands now that Wilf had aggravated the anxiety she experienced just about whenever Laura left the house.

She'd spent some time in flexing her fingers and laying down the plastic tool again for fear of spoiling the inscription – long enough for the back garden to fill up with the shadow of the house – before she decided to go out and look for him. Laura would be fine at the school disco, and on the bus home with her friends, so long as she'd caught the bus there. Having set the alarm – she needn't programme the lights to switch themselves on, she would only be out for a few minutes – Claire draped a linen jacket over her shoulders and walked to the end of the road.

The Chung boys were sluicing the family Lancia with buckets of soapy water and a great deal of Cantonese chatter. Several mowers were rehearsing a drowsy chorus against the improvised percussion of at least two pairs of shears. The most intrusive sound, though not the loudest, was the unanswered plea of the alarm. When Claire reached the junction she saw that the convulsive light that accompanied the noise was several hundred yards away along the cross street, close to the pole of the deserted bus stop at the far end, against the baize humps of the golf course. As she saw all this, the alarm gave up. She turned from it and caught sight of Wilf.

He mustn't have seen her, she thought, because he was striding away. Shrunken by distance, and obviously unaware that his trousers were a little lower than they might be – more like a building worker's than any outfit of the architect he was – he looked unexpectedly vulnerable. She couldn't imagine his tackling anyone with more than words, but then members of the patrol weren't supposed to use force, only to alert the police. She felt a surge of the old affection, however determined he seemed these days to give it no purchase on his stiff exterior, as she cupped her hands about her mouth. "Wilf."

At first she thought he hadn't heard her. Two mowers had travelled the length of their lawns before he swung round and marched towards her, his face drawn into a mask of concern. "What is it? What's wrong?"

"Nothing, I hope. I just wanted to know if you saw her onto the bus."

"She wasn't there."

"Are you sure?" Claire couldn't help asking. "She'd have been in time for it, wouldn't she?"

"If it came."

"Don't say that. How else could she have gone?"

"Maybe she got herself picked up."

"She'd never have gone in anybody's car she didn't know, not Laura."

"You'd hope not. That's what I meant, a lift from a friend who was going, their parents, rather."

The trouble was that none of Laura's friends would have needed to be driven past the bus stop. Perhaps this had occurred to Wilf, who was staring down the street past Claire. A glance showed her that the streetlamp by the bus stop had acknowledged the growing darkness. The isolated metal flag gleamed like a knife against the secretive mounds of the golf course. "She should be there by now," Claire said.

"You'd imagine so."

It was only a turn of phrase, but it made her suspect herself of being less anxious than he felt there was reason to be. "She won't like it, but she'll have to put up with it," she declared.

"I don't know what you mean."

"I'm going to phone to make sure she's arrived."

"That's – yes, I should."

"Are you coming to hear? You aren't due on the street for a few minutes yet."

"I thought I'd send your favourite man Mr Gummer home early. You're right, though, I ought to be with you for the peace of mind."

If he had just the average share, she reflected, she might have more herself. It took her several minutes to reach the phone, as a preamble to doing which she had to walk home not unduly fast and unbutton the alarm, by which time there was surely no point in calling except to assure herself there wasn't. The phone at the disco went unanswered long enough for Wilf to turn away and rub his face twice; then a girl's voice younger than Claire was expecting, and backed by music loud enough to distort it, said "Sin Tans."

"Hello, St Anne's. This is Laura Maynard's mother. Could I have a quick word with her?"

"Who? Oh, Lor." As Claire deduced this wasn't a mild oath but a version of Laura's name, the girl said "I'll just see."

She was gone at once, presumably laying the receiver down with the mouth toward the music, so that it amplified itself like a dramatic soundtrack in a film. Claire had thought of a question to justify the call and no doubt to annoy Laura – they'd established when she must be home, but not with whom or how – when the girl returned. "Mrs Maynard," she shouted over an upsurge of the music, "she's not here yet, her friend Hannah says."

"You obviously wouldn't know if her bus happened to run."

"Yes, Hannah was on it, but it was early at Lor's stop."

"I understand," said Claire, compelled to sound more like a

grown-up than she felt. "Could you ask her to ring home the moment she gets there? The moment you see her, I mean."

"I will, Mrs Maynard."

"Thanks. You're very –" The line went dead, and Claire hung up the receiver beside the stairs, next to the oval mirror in which Wilf was raising his hunched head. Two steps like the heaviness of his expression rendered palpable brought him round to face her. "She's not there, then," he said.

"Not yet."

"Not much we can do, is there? Not till she gets home, and then I'll be having a good few words."

"Don't work yourself up till we know what happened. You always assume it's her fault. I may just nip out to see . . ."

"I can look if you like while you're waiting for her to call. See what?"

"She'll speak to the machine if we aren't here. I know she wouldn't go across the golf course by herself, but maybe someone she knew went with her if they missed the bus too. If anyone's still playing I can ask if they saw her. It's better than sitting at home thinking things there's no need to think."

"I'll come with you, shall I? If there are any golfers they may be miles apart."

He so visibly welcomed being motivated that she couldn't have refused him. "You set the lights and everything while I go on ahead," she told him.

The twilight was quieter, and almost dark. The mowers had gone to bed. Though she could hear no sound of play from the golf course she made for it, having glanced back to see that Wilf was following, far enough behind that she had a moment of hoping a call from Laura had delayed him. By the time he emerged from their street Claire was nearly at the bus stop.

Smaller flags led away from it, starting at the first hole. The clubhouse was nearby, though screened by one of the thick lines of trees that had been grown to complicate the golf. Claire heard the whop of a club across the miles of grass and sandy hollows, and the approach of a bus, reminding her that it was at least an hour since Laura had left the house. "Come on, Wilf," she urged, and stepped off the concrete onto the turf.

Tines of light from the clubhouse protruded through the trees; one thin beam pricked the corner of her eye. A stroke that sounded muffled by a divot echoed out of the gloom. "I'll find them," she called, pointing towards the invisible game, "while you see if anyone at the clubhouse can help. Show them your badge."

Her last words jerked as she began to jog up a slope towards a copse. Having panted as far as the clump, she glanced at Wilf. "Get a move on," she exhorted, but her words only made him turn to her. She waved him onward and lurched down the far side of the slope.

Her cry brought Wilf stumbling towards her, halting when she regained her balance. "What now?" he demanded, his nervousness crowding into his voice. "What have you –"

"Nearly fell in a bunker, that's all," she said, grateful to have an excuse for even a forced laugh. She took a step which placed the bulk of the copse between her and Wilf and cut off the light from the clubhouse, and looked down.

This time she didn't cry out. "Wilf," she said with the suddenly unfamiliar object she used for speech; then she raised her voice until it became part of the agony she was experiencing. "Wilf," she repeated, and slid down into the bunker.

The slope gave way beneath her feet, and she felt as if the world had done so. The darkness that rose to meet her was the end of the lights of the world. It couldn't blind her to the sight below her, though her mind was doing its best to think that the figure in the depths of the sandpit wasn't Laura – was the child of some poor mother who would scream or faint or go mad when she saw. None of this happened, and in a moment Laura was close enough to touch.

She was lying face down in the hollow. Her skirt had been pulled above her waist, and her legs forced so wide that her panties cut into her stockinged legs just above the knees. The patch of sand between her thighs was stained dark red, and the top of her right leg glistened as if a large snail had crawled down it. Her fists were pressed together above her head in a flurry of sand.

Claire fell to her knees, sand grinding against them, and took hold of Laura's shoulders. She had never known them feel so thin and delicate; she seemed unable to be gentle enough. As Laura's face reluctantly ceased nestling in the slope, Claire heard the whisper of a breath. It was only sand rustling out of Laura's hair –

more of the sand which filled her nostrils and her gaping mouth and even her open eyes.

Claire was brushing sand out of Laura's eyelashes, to give herself a moment before the glare of her emotions set about shrivelling her brain – she was remembering Laura at four years old on a day at the seaside, her small sunlit face releasing a tear as Claire dabbed a grain of sand out of her eye – when she heard Wilf above the bunker. "Where are –" he said, then "Oh, you're – What –"

She shrank into herself while she awaited his reaction. When it came, his wordless roar expressed outrage and grief enough for her as well. She looked up to see him clutching at his heart, and heard cloth tear. He was twisting the badge, digging the pin into his chest. "Don't," she pleaded. "That won't help."

He wavered at the top of the bunker as if he might fall, then he trudged down the outside of the hollow to slither in and kneel beside her. She felt his arms tremble about her and Laura before gripping them in a hug whose fierceness summed up his help-lessness. "Be careful of her," she hardly knew she said.

"I did it."

She almost wrenched herself free of him, his words were so ill-chosen. "What are you saying?"

"If I hadn't made her miss her bus by going on at her . . ."

"Oh, Wilf." She could think of nothing more to say, because she agreed with him. His arms slackened as though he felt unworthy to hold her and Laura; she couldn't tell if he was even touching her. One of them would have to get up and fetch someone – he would, because she found she couldn't bear the thought of leaving Laura to grow cold as the night was growing. But there was no need for him to go. Someone was observing them from above the bunker.

The emotion this set off started her eyes burning, and she might have scrambled up the slope to launch herself at the intruder if he hadn't spoken. "What are you people up to in there? This is private property. Please take your—" His voice faltered as he peered down. "Dear Christ, what's happened here?" he said, and was irrelevant to her fury – had been as soon as she'd grasped he wasn't the culprit. Nothing but finding them might bring to an end the blaze of rage which had begun to consume every feeling she would otherwise have had.

*   *   *

"Mrs Maynard."

She could pretend she hadn't heard, Claire thought, and carry on plodding. But a supermarket assistant who was loading the shelves with bottles of Scotch and gin nodded his head at her. "There's a lady wants to speak to you."

"Mrs Maynard, it is you, isn't it? It's Daisy Gummer."

Claire knew that. She was considering speeding her trolley out of the aisle when her exit was blocked by a trolley with a little girl hanging onto one side – a six- or seven-year-old in the school uniform Laura had worn at that age. Claire's hands clenched, and she swung her trolley round to point at her summoner.

Mrs Gummer was in her wheelchair, a wire basket on her lap. The jacket and trousers of her orange suit seemed designed to betray as little of her shape as possible. Her silver curls were beginning to unwind and grow dull. Her large pale puffed-up face made to crumple as her eyes met Claire's, then rendered itself into an emblem of strength. "Has to be done, eh?" she declared with a surplus of heartiness. "It's not the men who go out hunting any longer."

The little this meant to Claire included the possibility that the old woman's son wasn't with her, not that his absence was any reason to linger. Before Claire could devise a reply that would double as a farewell, Mrs Gummer said "Still fixing up people's affairs for them, are you? Still tidying up after them?"

"If that's what you want to say accountants do."

"Nothing wrong with using any tricks you know," Mrs Gummer said, performing a wink that involved pinching her right eye with most of that side of her face. "Duncan's done a few with my money at his bank." As though preparing to reveal some of them, she leaned over her lapful of tins. "What I was going to say was you keep working. Keep your mind occupied. I wished I'd had a job when we lost his father."

"That would have helped you forget, would it?"

"I don't know about forget. Come to terms would be about the size of it."

"And what sort of terms would you suggest I come to?" Claire heard herself being unpleasant, perhaps unreasonable, but these were merely hints of the feelings that constantly lay in wait for her. "Please. Do tell me whatever you think I should know."

The old woman's gaze wavered and focused beyond her, and

Claire had an excuse to move out of the way of whoever was there. Then she heard him say "Here's the soap you like, mother, that's gentle on your skin. Who's your friend you've been talking to?"

"You know Mrs Maynard. We were just talking about . . ." Apparently emboldened by the presence of her son, Mrs Gummer brought her gaze to bear on the other woman. "How long has it been now, you poor thing?"

"Three months and a week and two days."

"Have they found the swine yet?"

"They say not."

"I know what I'd do to him if I got hold of him, chair or no chair." Mrs Gummer dealt its arms a blow each with her fists, perhaps reflecting on the difficulties involved in her proposal, before refraining from some of another wink as she said "They'll be testing the men round here soon though, won't they? It isn't just fingerprints and blood these days, is it?"

The possibility that the old woman was taking a secret delight in this sickened Claire, who was gripping her trolley to steer it away when Duncan Gummer said "I shouldn't imagine they think he's from our neighbourhood, mother."

He'd taken his position behind the wheelchair and was regarding Claire, his eyes even moister than his display of lower lip. "They've told you that, have they?" she demanded. "That's the latest bulletin for the patrol."

"Not officially, no, Mrs Maynard. I'm sure Mr Maynard would have told you if they had. I was just thinking myself that this evil maniac would surely have had enough sense, not that I'm suggesting he has sense like ordinary folk unless he does and that's part of how he's evil, he'd have kept his, his activities well away from home, would you not think?" He looked away from her silence as a load of bottles jangled onto a shelf, and let his lip sag further. "What I've been meaning to say to you," he muttered, "I can't blame myself enough for not being out that night when I was meant to be on patrol."

"Don't listen to him. It's not true."

"Mother, you mustn't —"

"It was my fault for being such a worn-out old crock."

"That's what I meant. You weren't to know. You mustn't take it on yourself."

"He thought I was turning my toes up when all I was was passed out from finishing the bottle."

"Can't be helped," Claire said for the Gummers to take how they liked, and turned away, to be confronted by the liquor shelves and her inability to recall how much gin was left at home. She was letting her hand stray along the relevant shelf when Mrs Gummer said "You grab it if that's what you need. I know I did when his father left us."

Claire snatched her hand back and drove her trolley to the checkout as fast as the shoppers she encountered would allow. She couldn't risk growing like Mrs Gummer while Laura went unavenged. Time enough when the law had taken its course for her to collapse into herself. She arranged her face to signify that she was too preoccupied to talk to the checkout girl, and imitated smiling at her before wheeling out the trolley onto the sunlit concrete field of the car park.

Tasks helped advance the process of continuing to be alive, but tasks came to an end. At least riding on the free bus from the supermarket to the stop by the golf course was followed by having to drag her wheeled basket home. She might have waited for Wilf to drive her if waiting in the empty house hadn't proved too much for her. His need to go back to work had forced her to do so herself, and on the whole she was glad of it, as long as she could do the computations and the paperwork while leaving her colleagues to deal face to face with clients. She didn't want people sympathising with her, softening the feelings she was determined to hoard.

As she let herself into the house the alarm cried to be silenced before it could raise its voice. Once that would have meant Laura wasn't home from school, and Claire would have been anxious unless she knew why. She wouldn't have believed the removal of that anxiety would have left such a wound in her, too deep to touch. She quelled the alarm and hugged the lumpy basket to her while she laboured to transport it over the expensive carpet of the suddenly muggy hall to the kitchen, where she set about loading the refrigerator. She left the freezer until last, because as soon as she opened it, all she could see was Laura's birthday cake.

She'd thought of serving it after the funeral, but she would have felt bound to scrape off the inscription. That still ended at the unfinished letter – the cross she had never made. She'd considered burying the cake in the back garden, but that would have been too final too soon; keeping it seemed to promise that in time she would be able to celebrate the fate of Laura's destroyer. She reached into its icy nest and moved it gently to the back of the freezer so as to wall it in with packages. While Wilf rarely opened the freezer, she could do without having to explain to him.

He ought to be home soon. She might have made a start on the work she'd brought home from the office, except that she knew she would become aware of trying to distract herself from the emptiness of the house. She wandered through the front room, past the black chunks of silence that were the hi-fi and video-recorder and television, and the shelves of bound classics she'd hoped might encourage Laura to read more, and stood at the window. The street was deserted, but she felt compelled to watch – to remember. Remember what, for pity's sake? She'd lost patience with herself, and was stepping back to prove she had some control, when she saw what she should have realised in the supermarket, and grew still as a cat which had seen a mouse.

"Wilf?"

"Love?"

"What would you do . . ."

"Carry on. We've never had secrets from each other, have we? Whatever it is, you can say."

"What would you do if you knew who'd, who it was who did that to Laura?"

"Tell the police."

"Suppose you hadn't any proof they'd think was proof?"

"Still tell them. They'll sort out if there's proof or not. If you tell them they'll have to follow it up, won't they? That's what we pay them for, those that do, that you haven't fixed up not to pay tax."

"I'd be best phoning and not saying who I am, wouldn't I? That way they can't find out how much I really know."

"Whatever you say, love."

He had to agree with her, since he wasn't there: he'd left home an hour ago to be early at a building site. She couldn't really have had such a conversation with him when he would have insisted on learning why she was suspicious, and then at the very least would have thought she was taking umbrage which in fact she was too old and used up to take. She knew better, however. If Duncan Gummer had been as obsessed with her as she'd assumed him to be, how could be have needed his mother to identify her at the supermarket? Now Claire knew he'd used his patrolling as an excuse to loiter near the house because he'd been obsessed with Laura, a thought which turned her hands into claws. She had to force them to relax before she was able to programme the alarm.

The suburb was well awake. All the surviving children were on their way to school; a few were even walking. The neighbourhood's postman for the last four months had stopped for a chat with a group of mothers being tugged at by small children. Less than a week ago Claire would have been instantly suspicious of him – of any man in the suburb and probably beyond it too – but now there was only room in her mind for one. She even managed a smile at the postman as she headed for the golf course.

The old footpath, bare as a strip of skin amid the turf, led past the first bunker, and she made herself glance in. It was unmarked, unstained. "We're going to get him," she whispered to the virgin sand, and strode along the path to the main road.

A phone box stood next to the golf course, presenting its single opaque side to a bus stop. Claire pulled the reluctant door shut after her and took out her handkerchief, which she wadded over the mouthpiece of the receiver. Having typed the digits that would prevent her call from being traced, she rang the police. As soon as a female voice, more efficient than welcoming, announced itself she said "I want to talk about the Laura Maynard case."

"Hold on, madam, I'll put you through to –"

"No, you listen." Now that she was past the most difficult utterance – describing Laura as a case – Claire was in control. "I know who did it. I saw him."

"Madam, if I can ask you just to –"

"Write this down, or if you can't do that, remember it. It's his name and address." Claire gave the information twice and immediately cut off the call, which brought her plan of action to so definite an end that she almost forgot to pocket her handkerchief before hanging the phone up. She stepped out beneath a sky which seemed enlarged and brightened, and had only to walk to the stop to be in time for an approaching bus. As she grasped the metal pole and swung herself onto the platform of the bus she was reminded how it felt to step onto a fairground ride. "All the way," she said, and rode to the office.

* * *

"Claire? I'm back."

"I was wondering where on earth you'd got to. Come and sit and have a drink. I've something I've been wanting to –"

"I'm with someone, so –"

"Who?"

"No need to sound like that. Someone you know. Detective Inspector Bairns."

"Come in too, Inspector, if you don't mind me leaving off your first bit. I don't suppose you'll have a drink."

"I won't, thanks, Mrs Maynard, not in the course of the job. Thank you for asking."

She wasn't sure she had – she was too aware of the policeman he'd made of himself. His tread was light for such a stocky fellow; the features huddled between his high forehead and potato chin were slow to betray any expression, never including a smile in her limited experience, but his eyes were constantly searching. "Do have one yourselves," he said.

"I'll get them, Claire. I can see you're ready for a refill."

"You'll have the Inspector thinking I've turned to the bottle."

"Nobody would blame you, Mrs Maynard, or at any rate I wouldn't." Bairns lowered himself into the twin of her massive leather armchair and glanced at Wilf. "Nothing soft either, thanks," he responded before settling his attention on Claire.

She smiled and raised her eyebrows and leaned forward, none of which brought her an answer. "So you'll have some news for me," she risked saying.

"Unfortunately, Mrs Maynard, I have to –"

Wilf came between them to hand Claire her drink on his way to the couch, and in that moment she wished she could see the policeman's eyes. "Sorry," she said for Wilf as he moved on, and had a sudden piercing sense that she might be expected to apologise for herself. "You were saying, please, go on."

"Only that regrettably we still have nothing definite."

"You haven't. Nothing at all."

"I do understand how these things seem, believe me. If we can't make an immediate arrest then as far as the victim's family is concerned the investigation may as well be taking forever."

"When you say not immediate you mean . . ."

"I appreciate it's been the best part of four months."

"No, what I'm getting at, you mean you've an idea of who it is and you're working on having a reason to show for arresting him."

"I wish I could tell you that."

"Tell me the reason. Us, not just me, obviously, but that's what you mean about telling."

"Sadly not, Mrs Maynard. I meant that so far, and I do stress it's only so far, we've had no useful leads. But you have my word we don't give up on a case like this."

"No leads at all." Claire fed herself a gulp of gin, and shivered as the ice-cubes knocked a chill into her teeth. "I can't believe you've had none."

"We and our colleagues elsewhere questioned everyone with a recorded history of even remotely similar behaviour, I do assure you." The policeman looked at his hands piled on his stomach, then met her eyes again, his face having absorbed any hint of expression. "I may as well mention we received an anonymous tip last week."

"You did." Claire almost raised her glass again, but wasn't sure what the action might seem to imply. "I suppose you need time to get ready to follow something like that up."

"It's been dealt with, Mrs Maynard."

"Oh." There was no question that she needed a drink before saying "Good. And . . ."

"We're sure it was a vindictive call. The informant was a woman who must bear some kind of grudge against the chap. Felt rebuffed by him in some way, most likely. She didn't offer anything in the way of evidence, just his name and address."

"So that's enough of an excuse not to bother with anything she said."

"I understand your anger, but please don't let it make you feel we would be less than thorough. Of course we interviewed him, and the person who provided his alibi, and we've no reason to doubt either."

Claire had – Mrs Gummer had admitted to having been asleep – but how could she introduce that point or discover the story the old woman was telling now? "So if there's no news," she said to release some of her anger before her words got out of control, "why are you here?"

"I was wondering if either of you might have remembered anything further to tell me. Anything at all, no matter how minor it may seem. Sometimes that's all that's needed to start us filling in the picture."

"I've told you all I can. Don't you think I'd have told you more if I could?"

"Mr Maynard?"

"I'd have to say the same as my wife."

"I'll leave you then if you'll excuse me. Perhaps it might be worth your discussing what I asked when I'm gone. I hope, Mrs Maynard . . ." Bairns was out of his chair and had one foot in the hall before he said "I hope at least you can accept we're doing everything the law allows."

She did, and her rage focused itself again, letting her accompany him to the gate and send him on his way. The closing of his car door sounded like a single decisive blow of a weapon, and was followed by the reddening of the rear lights. The car was shrinking along the road when she saw Duncan Gummer at the junction – saw him wave to Bairns as if he was giving him a comradely sign. The next moment his patrolling took him out of view, but she could still see him, as close and clear in her mind as her rage.

"Who is this? Hello?"

"It's Claire Maynard."

"It wasn't you that kept ringing off when my mother answered, was it?"

"Why would I have done that, Mr Gummer?"

"No reason at all, of course. My apologies. It's got us both a little, well, not her any longer, she's sound asleep. What can I do for you?"

"I wanted to discuss an idea I had which I think might be profitable."

"I don't normally talk business outside business hours, but with you I'm happy to make an exception. Would you like to meet now?"

"Why don't you come here and keep me company. We can talk over a couple of drinks."

"That sounds ideal. Give me ten minutes."

"No more than that, I hope. And I shouldn't bother troubling your mother if she needs her sleep."

"Don't worry, I'm with you. Softly does it. I'm all in favour of not disturbing anyone who doesn't have to be."

"I'll be waiting," Claire said with a sweetness she imagined she could taste. It made her sick. She heard him terminate the call, and listened to the contented purring of the receiver, the sound of a cat which had trapped its prey. When she became aware of holding the receiver for something to do while she risked growing unhelpfully tense she hooked it and went to pour herself a necessary drink.

She loaded ice into the tumbler, the silver teeth of the tongs grating on the cubes, then filled the remaining two-thirds of the glass almost to the top. More room needed to be made for tonic, and she saw the best way to do that. The tumbler was nearly at her lips when she opened the gin bottle and returned the contents to it. She mustn't lose control now. To prove she had it, she crunched the ice cubes one by one, each of them sending an intensified chill through her jaw into her skull until her brain felt composed of impregnable metal. She had just popped the last cube into her mouth when she saw Gummer's glossy black Rover draw up outside the house. She bit the cube into three chunks which she was just able to swallow, bringing tears to her eyes. They were going to be the last tears Gummer would cause her to shed, and her knuckles dealt with them as she went to let him in before he could ring the bell.

Whether his grin was meant to express surprise or pleasure at her apparent scramble to greet him, it bared even more of his lower lip than usual until he produced a sympathetic look. "I'm glad you felt able to call," he said.

"Why wouldn't I?"

"Well, indeed," he said as though to compliment her on being reasonable, and she had to turn away in order to clench her teeth. "Close the door," she said once she could.

The finality of the slam gave her strength, and by the time he followed her into the front room she was able to gaze steadily at him. "What's your taste?" she said, indicating the bottles on the sideboard.

"The same as you'll be having."

"I'm sure you'll have a large one," she told him, and managed to hitch up one corner of her mouth.

"You've found me out."

Whatever answer that might have provoked she trapped behind her teeth as she busied herself at the sideboard. Perhaps after

all she would have a real drink instead of pretending a tonic was
gin; his presence was even harder to bear than she'd anticipated.
Already the room smelled as though it was steeped in the after-
shave he must have slapped on for her benefit. When she moved
away from the sideboard with a glass of gin and tonic in each
hand she found him at the window through which she didn't
know how many times he might have spied on Laura. "Please do
sit down," she said, masking her face with a gulp of her drink.

"Where will you have me?"

"Wherever you're comfortable," said Claire, retreating to the
armchair closest to the door. As she'd handed him his glass she'd
touched his fingertips, which were hot and hardly less moist than
his underlip. The thought of them on Laura almost flung her at
him. She forced herself to sit back and watch him perch on the
edge of the nearer end of the couch.

"Strong stuff," he said, having sipped his drink, and put it on
the floor between his wide legs. "So it's a financial discussion
you're after, was that what I understood you to say?"

"I said profitable. Maybe beneficial would have covered it
better."

"Happy to be of benefit wherever I can," Gummer said and
showed her the underside of his lip, which put her in mind of a
brimming gutter. "Do I recall the word company came up?"

"Nothing wrong with your memory."

"I wouldn't like to think so. Not like my mother's," he said,
and glanced down between his legs while he retrieved his glass.
Once he'd taken another sip he seemed uncertain how to
continue. She wanted him in a state to betray himself by the
time Wilf came back. "So what kind of company do you
prefer?" she said.

"Various. Depends."

"Whatever takes your fancy, eh?"

"You could say that if the feeling's mutual."

"Suppose it isn't reciprocated? What happens then?"

"Sometimes it is when you dig a bit deeper. You think there's
nothing, but if you don't let yourself be put off too soon you find
what the other person's feelings really are."

Claire brought her glass to her mouth so fast that ice clashed
against her teeth. "Suppose you find you're wrong?" she said, and
drank.

"To tell you the truth, and I hope you won't think I've got too big a head, so far I don't believe I ever have."

"Would you know?"

"I'm sorry?"

Claire lowered her glass with as much care as she was exerting over her face. "I said, would you know?"

"I hope so this far."

His gaze was holding hers. He still thought they were discussing a possible relationship. While she swallowed an enraged mirthless laugh she won the struggle to form her expression into an ambiguous smile. "So what are your limits?"

"There's always one way to find out," he said, and revealed his wet lip.

"You don't think you should have any."

"As long as one takes care, and we know to do that these days. It isn't as though one's committed."

"Wouldn't it come down to not being found out even if you had a partner? I know you're good at not being."

"As good as I need to be, right enough."

That was almost too much for Claire, especially when, having planted her glass on the carpet to distract herself, she looked up to be met by the sight of his dormant crotch. Wilf ought to be home in a few minutes, she reminded herself. "And what age do you like best?" she managed to ask.

"Nothing wrong with a mature woman. A good deal right with her, as a matter of fact, and if I may say so –"

"Nothing wrong about younger ones either if you're honest, is that fair?"

"I won't deny it. Teaching them a thing or two, that's pretty special. There again, and you'll tell me if I'm flattering myself, sometimes even when it's a lady of our generation –"

"You bastard."

"Forgive me if I expressed myself badly. It wasn't meant as any kind of insult, I do assure you. Mature was what I meant, not so much in years as –"

"You swine."

"I think that's a little much, Claire, may I call you Claire? I'm sorry if you're touchy on the subject, but if you'll allow me to say this, to my eyes you –"

"I remind you of a younger woman."

"My feelings exactly."

"A young girl, in fact."

"Ah." He faltered, and she saw him realise what he could no longer fail to acknowledge. "In some ways that's absolutely true, the best ways, may I say, only I suppose I thought that under the circumstances –"

"You loathsome filthy stinking slimy pervert."

She saw his lip draw itself up haughtily, and was reminded of a snail retreating into its shell. "I fear there's been some misunderstanding, Mrs Maynard," he said, and rose stiffly to his feet. "I understand your being so upset still, but my mother will be wondering where I am, so if you'll excuse me –"

Claire was faster. She swung herself around her chair with the arm she'd used to shove herself out of it, and trundled the heavy piece of furniture into the doorway. Having wedged it there, she sat in it and folded her arms. "I won't," she said.

"I really must insist." He held out his hands as if to demonstrate how, once he crossed the yards of carpet, he would grasp her or the chair. "I'm truly sorry for any error."

"You think that should make up for it, do you?"

"To be truthful, I don't know what more you could expect."

He didn't believe he had been found out, she saw – perhaps the idea hadn't even occurred to him. "Maybe you will when you see your mistake," she said and made her arms relax, because her breasts were aching as they hadn't since they were last full of milk.

"It'll be easiest if you tell me."

"You think I should make it easy for you, do you?" Her mouth had begun to taste as foul as her thoughts of him, and she would have swallowed more than the taste if her glass had been within reach. "Try this for a hint. Maybe you should have kept your mother out of my way."

"You've drifted away from me altogether. Let me suggest in your interest as much as mine –"

"Or found a way to stop her talking. You're good at that, aren't you?"

"Some understanding can usually be reached if it has to be. I assume that when you decide to let me go you won't be telling –"

"Like Laura never did."

"Well, really, Mrs Maynard, I must say that seems rather an unfortunate –"

"Unfortunate!" Claire ground her shoulders against the chair rather than fly at him – ground them so hard that either the chair or the doorway creaked. "That's your word for it, is it? How unfortunate would you say she looked the last time you saw her?"

He took a breath to give Claire yet another swift response; then his mouth sagged before clamping shut. He rubbed the side of one hand across his lips, and she imagined how he might have wiped his mouth as he sneaked away from the golf bunker. She stared at his face to see what would come out of it next, until he spoke. "It *was* you."

This was far less than the response she wanted, in fact nothing like it, and she continued to stare at him. "It was you who kept ringing off, wasn't it, till I was there to answer. What didn't you want my mother to hear?"

"Maybe I shouldn't have rung off. For all I know she's good at keeping secrets, especially if she thinks she's protecting her son."

"Why should she think –" His eyes wobbled and then steadied as though Claire's gaze had impaled them. "My God, that was you as well. You didn't just call us."

"Seems as though I might as well have."

"You tried to put the police onto me."

"If only they'd done their job properly. You wouldn't be here now. You'd be somewhere, but I'd have to put up with that being less than you deserved, I suppose. Only you are here, just the two of us for the moment, so –"

Gummer turned to the window as if he'd observed someone – Wilf? The street was quiet, however, and it occurred to her that he was considering a means of escape. She lurched out of the chair and grabbed the bottle of gin by its neck. "Don't bother looking there. You're going nowhere till I've finished with you," she said.

"Mrs Maynard, I want you to listen to me. I know you must –" He was almost facing her when he stopped and rubbed his lip and gave her a sidelong look. "Finished what exactly?"

"Guess."

"I don't believe I have to. Profitable was what you said this was going to be when you rang, wasn't it? If I may say so, God forgive you."

"You mayn't. You'd better –"

"Whatever you think about me, you were her mother, for heaven's sake. You're expecting me to pay you to keep quiet, aren't you? You're trying to make money out of the death of your own child," he said, and let his mouth droop open.

It was expressing disgust. *He* was daring to feel contemptuous of *her*. His wet mouth was all she could see, and she meant to damage it beyond repair. She seemed less to be raising the weapon in her hand than to be borne forward by it as it sailed into the air. His eyes flinched as he saw it coming, but his mouth stayed stupidly open. She had both hands on the weapon now, and swung it with all the force of all the rage that had been gathering for months. "Claire," he cried, and tried to dodge, lowering his head.

For a moment she thought the bottle had smashed – that she would see it explode into smithereens, as bottles in films always did when they hit someone on the head. Certainly she'd heard an object splintering. When his mouth slackened further and his eyes rolled up like boiled eggs turning in a pan she thought he was acting. Then he fell to a knee which failed to support him, and collapsed on his side with a second heavy thud. As if the position had been necessary for pouring, a great deal of dark red welled out of his left temple.

When it began to stain the carpet she thought of moving him or placing towels under his head, but she didn't want to touch him. He was taken care of. She peered at the bottle, and having found no trace of him on it, replaced it on the sideboard before returning to her chair. She supposed she ought to move the chair out of the doorway, not least to bring her within reach of her drink, but the slowness that had overtaken her since the night she'd found Laura's body was becoming absolute, and so she watched the steady accumulation of the twilight.

In time she had a few thoughts. If Mrs Gummer was awake she must be wondering where her son was. She'd had decades more of him than Laura had lived, and soon enough she would learn he was only a lump on the floor. Claire considered drawing the curtains, but nobody would be able to see him from the pavement, and in any case there was no point in delaying the discovery of him. The discoverer was most likely to be Wilf, who would still have to live here once she was taken away, and she oughtn't to leave him the job of cleaning up after her, though perhaps the carpet was past cleaning. When she narrowed her eyes at the blind mound of rubbish dumped in her front room, she couldn't determine how far the stain had spread. It annoyed her on Wilf's behalf, and she was attempting to organise and speed up her thinking sufficiently to deal with it when she saw him appear at the gate.

It wasn't guilt which pierced her then, it was his unsuspecting look – the look of someone expecting to enjoy the refuge of home at the end of a long day. He couldn't see her for the dimness. He wasn't as keen-eyed as a patrolman should be, Claire found herself thinking as she stumbled to face the chair and drag it out of the doorway. That was as much as she achieved before he admitted himself to the house. "Claire?" he called. "Sorry I was longer than I said. Some old dear thought a chap was acting suspicious, but when I tracked him down would you believe he was one of our patrol. Where are you?"

"In here."

"I'll put the light on, shall I? No need for you to sit in the dark, love." He came into the room and reached for the switch, but faltered. "Good Lord, what's . . . who . . ."

Claire found his hand with one of hers and used them to press the switch down. "My God, that's Duncan Gummer, isn't it?" he gasped, and his hand squirmed free. "Claire, what have you done?"

"I hope I've killed him."

Wilf stared at her as if he no longer knew what he was seeing, then ventured to stand over the body. He'd hardly begun to stoop to it when he recoiled and hurried to draw the curtains. He held onto them for some seconds, releasing them only when their rail started to groan. "Why, Claire? What could –"

"It wasn't half of what he did to Laura."

"He –" Wilf's face convulsed so violently it appeared to jerk his head down as he took a step towards Gummer. Claire thought he meant to kick the corpse, but he controlled himself enough to raise his head. "How do you know?"

"His mother lied about his alibi. Either she said she was awake when she was asleep or she knew he wasn't at home when he said he was, when – when he . . ."

"All right, love. It's all right." Wilf veered around the body and offered her his hands, though not quite close enough for her to touch. "How did you find that out?"

"She let it slip one day and he tried to shut her up."

"Why couldn't you have told the police?"

"I did."

"You – oh, I get you." He was silent while he dealt with this, and Claire took the opportunity to retrieve her glass, not to finish her drink but to place it out of danger on the sideboard. Gummer's body seemed such a fixture of the room that she was practically unaware of blotting out her sense of it as she picked up the glass. The clunk of the tumbler on wood recalled Wilf from his thoughts, and he said almost pleadingly "Why didn't you tell *me*?"

"What would you have done?"

He stepped forward and took her hands at last. "What do you think? When the police didn't listen, probably the same as you. Only I wouldn't have done it here where it can't be hidden."

"It's done now. It can't be helped, and I don't want it to be."

"I wish to God you'd left it to me." He stared around the room, so that she thought he was desperate for a change of subject until he said "What did you use?"

"The gin. The bottle, I mean. It did some good for a change."

"I won't argue with that."

Nevertheless he relinquished one of her hands. Before she knew what he intended, he was hefting the bottle as though to convince himself it had been the weapon. "Don't," she protested, then saw her concern was misplaced. "It doesn't matter," she said. "Your fingerprints would be on it anyway."

"So would yours."

"What are you getting –"

"Just listen while I think. We haven't much time. The longer we wait before we call the police, the worse this is going to look."

"Wilf, it can't look any worse than it is."

"Listen, will you. We can't have you going to prison. You'd never survive."

"I'll have to do my best. When everyone knows the truth –"

"Maybe they won't. You used to think he was sniffing round you. Suppose that got out somehow? I know how lawyers think. They'll twist anything they can."

"He wasn't interested in me. It was Laura."

"You say that, but how can you prove it in court? Your instincts are enough for you, I know that, for me too if I even need to tell you. But they won't be enough if his mother sticks to

her story, and if your lawyer tried to break her down too much
think how that would look, them harassing an old woman with
nobody left in the world."

"All right, you've shown me how wrong I am," Claire said,
feeling not far short of betrayed. "Any suggestions?"

"More than a suggestion."

He reached out and drew his hand down her cheek in a slow
caress as he used to when they hadn't long been married, then
patted her face before sidling around her into the hall. She had no
idea of his intentions until he unhooked the phone. "Wilf –"

"It's all right. I'm going to make it all right. Hello." Though he
was gazing so hard at her it stopped her in the doorway, the last
word wasn't addressed to her. "Detective Inspector Bairns,
please."

"Wilf, wait a minute. Ring off before he can tell who you are.
Don't stay anything till we've –"

"Inspector? It's Wilfred Maynard. I've killed the man who took
our daughter from us."

Claire grabbed the doorframe as her knees began to shake. She
would have snatched the phone from him if it hadn't been too
late. Instead she sent herself into the room as soon as she felt safe
to walk. She could hardly believe it, but she was hoping she
hadn't killed Gummer after all. She fastened her fingertips on the
wrist of the sprawled empty flesh. She held it longer than made
sense, she even said a prayer, but it was no use. The lump of flesh
and muscle was already growing cold, and there wasn't the
faintest stirring of life within.

"I'll be staying here, Inspector. I give you my word. I wouldn't
have called you otherwise," she heard Wilf say. She walked on
her unwieldy brittle legs into the hall in time to see him hang the
receiver. "Wilf," she pleaded, "what have you done?"

"Saved as much that we've got as I could. I know I can take
prison better than you can. Quick now, before they come. Help
me get my tale straight. How did you bring him here? Was he just
passing or what?"

She thought of refusing to answer so that Wilf couldn't prepare
a story, but the possibility that their last few minutes together
might be wasted in arguing was unbearable. "I called him at
home."

"Will Mrs Gummer know?"

"He said she'd be wondering where he'd got to."

"You hadn't long come in from gardening, had you? Did anyone see him arrive?"

"Not that I noticed."

"Just say he stopped when he saw you gardening and you invited him in. And when you'd both had a drink you accused him over Laura, and I came home just in time to hear him say what?"

"I don't know. Wilf –"

" 'You can't prove anything.' That's as good as a confession, isn't it, or it was for me at any rate. He was shouting, so he didn't hear me, because I let myself in quietly to find out what the row was. How many times did you hit him?"

"Do you have to be so calculating about it? I feel as if I'm already in court."

"I have to know, don't I? How many times?"

"It just took the once."

"That's fine, Claire. Really it is." He offered her his hands again, and finding no response, let them sink. "It'll be manslaughter. I heard Laura's name and him saying you couldn't prove it, and that was enough. There was a moment when I lost control, and then it was done and there was no turning back. That's how it must have been for you, am I right? They'll believe me because that's how these things happen."

He must be trying to live through her experience, but she felt no less alone. "Do they, Wilf?"

"Wait, I've got it. They'll believe me because I couldn't have had any other reason to kill him. It's not as though I could have imagined anything was going on between you two, even if you did imagine he fancied you."

Even in the midst of their situation, that felt cruel to her. "Thank you, Wilf."

"I have to say it, haven't I? Otherwise they might get the wrong idea. Look, there's a good chance the court will be lenient, and if it isn't I wouldn't be surprised if there's a public outcry. And I can't imagine I'll have too bad a time of it in jail. It's his kind that suffer the worst in there, not the ones who've dealt with them."

"You sound as though you're looking forward to being locked up."

"What a thing to say, Claire. How could anyone feel like that?"

As she'd spoken she'd known the remark was absurd, yet his need to persuade her it was made it seem less so. "Why would I want anything that's going to take me away from you?" he said.

Claire had a sense of hearing words that didn't quite go with the movements of his mouth. No, not with those – with his thoughts. Before she could ponder this, she heard several cars braking sharply outside the house, and a rapid slamming of at least six doors. "Here they are," Wilf said.

The latch of the gate clicked, and then it sounded as though not much less than an army marched up the path. The doorbell rang once, twice. The Maynards looked at each other with a deference that felt to Claire like prolonging the last moment of their marriage as it had been. Then Wilf moved to open the door.

Bairns was on the step, and came in at once. Five of his colleagues followed, trying to equal his expressionlessness, and Claire didn't know when the house had felt so crowded. "He's in the front room, Inspector," Wilf said.

"If you and Mrs Maynard would stay here." Bairns' gaze had already turned to his colleagues, and a nod sent two of them to stand close to the Maynards. He paced into the front room and lingered just inside, hands behind his back, as a prelude to squatting by Gummer's body. He hardly touched it before standing up, and Claire felt as if he'd confirmed her loathing of it. "I must ask you to accompany us to the police station, Mr Maynard," he said.

"I'm ready."

"You too, Mrs Maynard, if you will. You'll understand if I ask you not to travel in the same car."

"In that case do you mind if I give my wife a cuddle, Inspector? I expect it may be her last for a while."

The policeman's impassiveness almost wavered as he gave a weighty nod. Wilf took hold of Claire's shoulders and drew her to him. For a moment she was afraid to hug him with all the fierceness in her, and couldn't quite think why. Of course, he'd scratched himself with his patrolman's badge that night on the golf course. The scratches would have healed by now, not that she had seen his bare chest for years. When he put his arms around her she responded, and felt him trying to lend her strength, and telling her silently to support his version of events. They remained embraced for a few seconds after Bairns cleared his throat, then

Wilf patted her back and pushed her away gently. "We'd best get this over and done with then, Inspector."

Bairns had been delegating men to drive the Maynards. He directed an unambiguously sympathetic glance at Claire before turning a more purposeful look on Wilf. Wilf was going to convince him, she thought – had already convinced him. She had never realised her husband could be so persuasive when he had to be. She saw him start towards the front door, matching his pace to that of his escort as though he was taking his first steps to his cell. Her sense of his persuasiveness spread through her mind, and in that instant she knew everything.

"I'll drive you whenever you're ready, Mrs Maynard," a youngish policeman murmured, but Claire was unable to move. She knew why Wilf had seemed relieved at the prospect of the sentence he was courting – because he'd been afraid he might be jailed for worse. Everything made its real sense now. Nobody had been more obsessed with the way Laura dressed and was developing than Wilf. Claire remembered accusing Gummer of being attracted to a girl as a preferred version of an older woman she resembled. The accusation had been right, but not the man.

"Mrs Maynard?"

She saw Wilf's back jerking rhythmically away from her, and imagined its performing such a movement in the bunker. For a moment she was certain she could emerge from her paralysis only by flying at him – but she was surrounded by police who would stop her before she could finish him off, and she had no proof. She'd nursed her rage until tonight, she had hidden it from the world, and she could do so again. She felt pregnant with its twin, which would have years to develop. "I'm ready now," she said, and took her first step as her new self.

Wilf was being handed into the nearest police car as she emerged from the house. Shut him away, she thought, keep him safe for me. His door slammed, then the driver's, but apart from a stirring of net curtains the activity went unacknowledged by the suburb. As Claire lowered herself stiffly into the next car, Wilf was driven off. One thing he needn't worry about was her confirming his tale. She would be waiting when he came out of prison, and she could take all that time to imagine what she would do then. Perhaps she would have a chance to practise. While she was waiting she might find other men like him.

LAWRENCE WATT-EVANS

Upstairs

LAWRENCE WATT-EVANS WAS BORN AND RAISED in Massachusetts, but after sojourns in Pennsylvania and Kentucky he is now firmly settled in the Maryland suburbs of Washington, D.C. He is a full-time writer of horror, fantasy, and science fiction, with more than two dozen novels and a hundred short stories to his credit, as well as articles, comic books, poetry, etc.

In 1988 he was nominated for a Nebula and won the Hugo Award and the *Asimov's* Readers' Poll Award for his story "Why I left Harry's All-Night Hamburgers". He served two years as president of the Horror Writers Association (1994–1996), and his most recent novels are *Touched by the Gods* and *Dragon Weather*.

T HEY'RE SO DAMN LOUD UP THERE. Yelling and fighting, and then that thumping – I guess it must be folk dances or something.

They could show a little consideration, couldn't they?

And then there was the time they left the water running and it leaked through the bathroom ceiling and damn near flooded the place, and of course it was the weekend and we couldn't get hold of the landlord until Monday – no, Tuesday, it was a long weekend! And there was wet plaster falling all over the sink and the floor. And stains everywhere.

I tell you, if we could find a decent apartment we'd have been out of this rathole years ago.

And they won't talk to us when we see them in the halls, when I shout at them they just walk right on by like they didn't even hear me. I went up there once to complain, but they wouldn't answer the door.

Maybe they were busy; I think their refrigerator must have broken down or something, because even with the door closed I could smell something rotten.

They can't be very clean.

Anyway, tonight was the last straw, more yelling, and singing this awful high-pitched song, like something the Arabs sing in one of those old movies, and then thumping about and I swear I heard the furniture breaking.

"I've had enough," Jack said, and I agreed and said he should call the cops, and he said no, he'd settle it himself, and he went up there.

There was more yelling then, and banging, but then it stopped. I guess he talked some sense into them.

I wish he'd get back, though. There's something dripping through the ceiling again.

It's not water, though, it must be paint.

It's bright red.

CAITLÍN R. KIERNAN

Postcards from the King of Tides

CAITLÍN R. KIERNAN'S SHORT FICTION has appeared in such anthologies as *Love in Vein II*, *Dark Terrors 2* and *3*, *Dark of the Night*, *White of the Moon*, *Silver Birch*, *Blood Moon*, *Darkside*, *The Year's Best Fantasy and Horror* and *Best New Horror*.

Her first novel, *Silk*, was published in 1998 and has so far received both the International Horror Guild and Barnes & Noble Maiden Voyage awards for best first novel. She also writes the graphic novel series *The Dreaming* for DC Comics/Vertigo. A collection of her short fiction, *Tales of Pain and Wonder*, is forthcoming from Gauntlet Publications, and her second novel, *Trilobite*, will appear from Penguin/Roc. The author also publishes her own irregular newsletter, *Salmagundi*, and her official website is http://www.negia.net/~pandora, which she shares with Poppy Z. Brite and Christa Faust.

As Kiernan reveals, "I think that the ocean has always affected me the way that outer space affects a lot of people – that same dizzying sense of awe at the vastness of it, at the unknown. A lot of my childhood was spent by the sea, and it was always fascinating and terrifying at the same time. It still is.

"In 'Postcards from the King of Tides', the main thing I wanted to do was communicate these feelings about the sea, in particular, the way that my first visit to the Pacific coast of Oregon and northern California affected me. There aren't many things I love as much as the sea, but there aren't many things that frighten me as much, either. The title was suggested by George Darley's poem, 'The Rebellion of the Waters' (1822)."

H ERE'S THE SCENE: The three dark children, three souls past twenty but still adrift in the jaggedsmooth limbo of childhoods extended by chance and choice and circumstance, their clothes impeccable rags of night sewn with thread the color of ravens and anthracite; two of them fair, a boy and a girl and the stain of protracted innocence strongest on them; the third a mean scrap of girlflesh with a blacklipped smile and a heart to make holes in the resolve of the most jaded nihilist but still as much a child as her companions. And she sits behind the wheel of the old car, her sagegrey eyes straight ahead of her, matching their laughter with seething determination and annoyance, and there's brightdark music, and the forest flowing around them, older times ten hundred than anything else alive.

The winding, long drive back from Seattle, almost two days now, and Highway 101 has become this narrow asphalt snake curving and recurving through the redwood wilderness and they're still not even as far as San Francisco. Probably won't see the city before dark, Tam thinks, headachy behind the wheel and her black sunglasses because she doesn't trust either of the twins to drive. Neither Lark nor Crispin have their licenses, and it's not even her car; Magwitch's piece- of-shit Chevrolet Impala, antique '70s junk heap that might have been the murky green of cold pea soup a long, long time ago. Now it's mostly rust and bondo and one off-white door on the driver's side. A thousand bumper stickers to hold it all together.

"Oooh," Lark whispers, awevoiced, as she cranes her neck to see through the trees rushing past, the craggy coast visible in brief glimpses between their trunks and branches. Her head stuck out the window, the wind whipping at her fine, silkwhite hair and Tam thinks how she looks like a dog, a stupid, slobbering dog, just before Crispin says, "You look like a *dog*." He tries hard to sound disgusted with that last word, but Tam suspects he's just as giddy, just as enchanted by the Pacific rain forest, as his sister (if they truly *are* brother and sister; Tam doesn't know, not for sure, doesn't know that anyone else does either, for that matter).

"You'll get bugs in your teeth," he says. "Bugs are gonna fly right straight down your throat and lay their eggs in your stomach."

Lark's response is nothing more or less than another chorus of "ooohs" and "ahhhs" as they round a tight bend, rush through a break in the tree line and the world ends there, drops suddenly away to the mercy of a silveryellowgrey sea that seems to go on forever, blending at some far-off and indefinite point with the almost colorless sky. There's a sunbright smudge up there, but sinking slowly westward, and Tam looks at the clock on the dash again. It's always twenty minutes fast, but still, it'll be dark a long time before they reach San Francisco.

Tam punches the cigarette lighter with one carefully-manicured index finger, nail the color of an oil slick, and turns up the music already blaring from the Impala's tape deck. Lark takes that as her cue to start singing, howling along to "Black Planet", and the mostly bald tires squeal just a little as Tam takes the curve ten miles an hour above the speed limit. A moment in the cloudfiltered sun, blinding after the gloom, before the tree shadows swallow the car whole again. The cigarette lighter pops out, and Tam steals a glance at herself in the rearview mirror as she lights a Marlboro: yesterday's eyeliner and she's chewed off most of her lipstick, a black smudge on her right cheek. Her eyes a little bleary, a little red with swollen capillaries, but the ephedrine tablets she took two hours ago, two crimson tablets from a bottle she bought at a truck stop back in Oregon, are still doing their job and she's wider than awake.

"Will you sit the fuck down, Lark, before you make me have a goddamn wreck and kill us all? Please?" she says, smoky words from her faded lips and Lark stops singing, pulls her head back inside and Crispin sticks his tongue out at her, fleshpink flick of I-told-you-so reproach. Lark puts her pointy, black boots on the dash, presses herself into the duct-taped upholstery, and doesn't say a word.

They spent the night before in Eugene and then headed west, followed the meandering river valleys all the way down to the sea before turning south toward home. Almost a week now since the three of them left Los Angeles, just Tam and the twins because Maggie couldn't get off work, but he'd told them to go anyway;

she didn't really want to go without him, knew that Lark and Crispin would drive her nuts without Magwitch around, but the tour wasn't coming through L.A. or even San Francisco. So she went without too much persuading, *they* went, and it worked out better than she'd expected, really, at least until today.

At least until Golden Beach, only thirty or forty miles north of the California state line and Crispin spotted the swan neck of a *Brachiosaurus* towering above shaggy hemlock branches and he immediately started begging her to stop, even promised that he wouldn't ask her to play the P.J. Harvey tape anymore if she'd Please Just Stop and let him see. So they lost an hour at The Prehistoric Gardens, actually paid money to get in and then spent a whole fucking hour wandering around seventy acres of drippywet trees, listening to Crispin prattle on about the life-sized sculptures of dinosaurs and things like dinosaurs, tourist-trap monstrosities built sometime in the 1950s, skeletons of steel and wood hidden somewhere beneath sleek skins of wire mesh and cement.

"They don't even look real," Tam said, as Crispin vamped in front of a scowling stegosaur while Lark rummaged around in her purse for her tiny Instamatic camera.

"Well, they look real enough to *me*," he replied and Lark just shrugged, a suspiciously complicit and not-at-all-helpful sort of shrug. Tam frowned a little harder, no bottom to a frown like hers, and "You are really such a fucking geek, Crispy," she said under her breath but plenty loud enough the twins could hear.

"Don't call him that," Lark snapped, defensive sister voice, and then she found her camera somewhere in the vast, blackbeaded bag and aimed it at the pretty boy and the unhappy-looking stegosaur. But, "A geeky name for a geeky boy," Tam sneered, as Lark took his picture; Crispin winked at her, then, and he was off again, running fast to see the *Pteranodon* or the *Ankylosaurus*. Tam looked down at her wristwatch and up at the sky and, finding no solace in either, she followed zombie Hansel and zombie Gretel away through the trees.

After The Prehistoric Gardens, it was Lark's turn, of course, her infallible logic that it wasn't fair to stop for Crispin and then not stop for her and, anyway, all she wanted was to have her picture taken beside one of the giant redwoods. Hardly even inside the national park and she already had that shitty little camera out again, sneaky rectangle of woodgrain plastic and Hello Kitty stickers.

And because it was easier to just pull the fuck over than listen to her snivel and pout all the way to San Francisco, the car bounced off the highway into a small turnaround, rolled over a shallow ditch and across crunchsnapping twigs; Lark's door was open before Tam even shifted the Impala into park and Crispin piled out of the back seat after her. And then, insult to inconvenience, they made Tam take the photograph: the pair of them, arm in arm and wickedsmug grins on their matching faces, a mat of dry, cinnamon needles beneath their boots and the boles of the great sequoias rising up behind them, primeval frame of ferns and underbrush snarl all around.

Tam sighed loud and breathed in a mouthful of air so clean it hurt her Angeleno lungs and she wished she had a cigarette, then *Just get it the fuck over with*, she thought, sternpatient thought for herself. But she made sure to aim the camera just low enough to cut the tops off both their heads in the photo.

Halfway back to the car, a small squeal of surprise and delight from Lark and "*What?*" Crispin said, "What is it?" Lark stooped and picked up something from the rough bed of redwood needles.

"Just get in the goddamned car, okay?" Tam begged, but Lark wasn't listening, held her discovery out for Crispin to see, presented for his approval. He made a face that was equal parts disgust and alarm and took a step away from Lark and the pale yellow thing in her hands.

"*Yuck,*" he said, "Put it back down, Lark, before it bites you or stings you or something."

"Oh, it's only a banana slug, you big sissy," she said and frowned like she was trying to impersonate Tam. "See? It can't *hurt* you," and she stuck it right under Crispin's nose.

"*Gagh,*" he moaned, "It's *huge,*" and he headed for the car, climbed into the back seat and hid in the shadows.

"It's only a banana slug," Lark said again. "I'm gonna keep him for a pet and name him Chiquita."

"You're going to put down the worm and get back in the fucking car," Tam said, standing at the back fender and rattling Magwitch's key ring in one hand like a particularly noisy pair of dice. "Either that, Lark, or I'm going to leave your skinny ass standing out here with the bears."

"And the sasquatches!" Crispin shouted from inside the car and Tam silenced him with a glare through the rear windshield.

"Jesus, Tam, it's not gonna *hurt* anything. Really. I'll put it in my purse, okay? It's not gonna hurt anything if it's inside my purse, right?" But Tam narrowed her mascara smudgy eyes and jabbed a finger at the ground, at the needle-littered space between herself and Lark.

"You're going to put the motherfucking worm *down*, on the ground," she growled, "and then you're going to get back in the motherfucking car."

Lark didn't move, stared stubbornly down at the fat slug as it crawled cautiously over her right palm, leaving a wide trail of sparkling slime on her skin. "No," she said.

"*Now*, Lark."

"No," she repeated, glanced up at Tam through the cascade of her white bangs. "It won't hurt anything."

Just two short, quick steps and Tam was on top of her, almost a head taller anyway and her teeth bared like all the grizzly bears and sasquatches in the world. "Stop!" Lark screeched. "Crispin, make her stop!" She tried too late to turn and run away, but Tam already had what she wanted, had already snatched it squirming from Lark's sticky hands and Chiquita the banana slug went sailing off into the trees. It landed somewhere among the ferns and mossrotting logs with a very small but audible *thump*.

"Now," Tam said, smiling and wiping slug slime off her hand onto the front of Lark's black Switchblade Symphony t-shirt. "Get in the car. *Pretty* please."

And for a moment, time it took Tam to get behind the wheel and rev the engine a couple of times, Lark stood, staring silent toward the spot in the woods where the slug had come down. She might have cried, if she hadn't known that Tam really would leave her stranded there. The third rev brought a big puff of charcoalsoot exhaust from the Impala's noisy muffler and Lark was already opening the passenger-side door, already slipping in beside Tam.

She was quiet for a while, staring out at the forest and the stingy glimpses of rocky coastline, still close enough to tears that Tam could see the wet shimmer in the windowtrapped reflection of her blue eyes.

*   *   *

So the highway carries them south, between the ocean and the weathered western slopes of the Klamath Mountains, over rocks from the time of Crispin's dinosaurs, rocks laid down in warm and serpent-haunted seas; out of the protected cathedral stands of virgin redwood into hills and gorges where the sequoias are forced to rub branches with less privileged trees, mere Douglas fir and hemlock and oak. And gradually their view of the narrowdark beaches becomes more frequent, the toweringsharp headlands setting them one from another like sedimentary parentheses.

Tam driving fast, fast as she dares, not so much worried about cops and speeding tickets as losing control in one of the hairpin curves and plunging ass-over-tits into the fucking scenery, taking a dive off one of the narrow bridges and it's two hundred feet straight down. She chain smokes and has started playing harder music, digging through the shoe box full of pirated cassettes for Nine Inch Nails and Front 242, The Sisters and Nitzer Ebb, all the stuff that Lark and Crispin would probably be whining like drowning kittens about if they didn't know how pissed off she was already. And then the car starts making a sound like someone's tossed a bucket of nails beneath the hood and the temp light flashes on, screw you Tam, here's some more shit to fuck up your wonderful, fucking afternoon by the fucking sea.

"It's not supposed to do that, is it?" Crispin asks, back seat coy, and she really wants to turn around, stick a finger through one of his eyes until she hits brain.

"*No*, Einstein," she says instead, "It's not supposed to do that. Now shut up," settling for such a weak little jab instead of fresh frontal lobe beneath her nails. The motor spits up a final, grinding cough and dies, leaves her coasting, drifting into the breakdown lane. Pavement traded for rough and pinging gravel and Tam lets the right fender scrape along the guardrail almost twenty feet before she stomps the brakes, the smallest possible fraction of her rage expressed in the squeal of metal against metal; when the Impala has finally stopped moving, she puts on the emergency brake and shifts into park, turns on the hazard lights.

"We can't just stop *here*," Lark says, and she sounds scared, almost, staring out at the sun beginning to set above the endless Pacific horizon. "I mean, there isn't even a *here* to stop at. And before long it'll be getting dark . . ."

"Yeah, well, you tell that to Magwitch's fine hunk of Detroit dogshit here, babycakes," and Tam opens her door, slams it closed behind her and leaves the twins staring at each other in silent, astonished panic.

Lark tries to open her door, then, but it's pressed smack up against the guardrail and there's not enough room to squeeze out, just three or four scant inches and that's not even space for her waif's boneangle shoulders. So she slides her butt across the faded, green naugahyde, accidentally knocks the box of tapes over and they spill in a plasticloud clatter across the seat and into the floorboard. She sits behind the wheel while Crispin climbs over from the back seat. Tam's standing in front of the car now, staring furiously down at the hood, and Crispin whispers, "If you let off the brake now, maybe we could run over her," and Lark reaches beneath the dash like maybe it's not such a bad idea, but she only pulls the hood release.

"She'd live, probably," Lark says, and "Yeah," Crispin says, and begins to gather up the scattered cassettes and return them to the dingy shoe box.

The twins sit together on the guardrail while Tam curses the traitorous, steamhissing car, curses her ignorance of wires and rubber belts and radiators, and curses absent Magwitch for owning the crappy old Impala in the first place.

"He said it runs hot sometimes, and to just let it cool off," Crispin says hopefully and she shuts him up with a razorshard glance. So he holds Lark's hand and stares at a bright patch of California poppies growing on the other side of the rail, a tangerineorange puddle of blossoms waving heavy, calyx heads in the salt and evergreen breeze. A few minutes more and Lark and Crispin both grow bored with Tam's too-familiar indignation, tiresome rerun of a hundred other tantrums, and they slip away together into the flowers.

"It's probably not as bad as she's making it out to be," Crispin says, picking a poppy and slipping the sapbleeding stem behind Lark's right ear. "It just needs to cool off."

"Yeah," she says, "Probably," but not sounding reassured at all, and stares down the precarious steep slope toward the beach, sand the cinder color of cold apocalypse below the grey shale and sandstone bluff. She also picks a poppy and puts it in Crispin's hair, tucks it behind his left ear, so they match again. "I want to look for sea shells," she says "and driftwood," and she points at a narrow trail just past the poppies. Crispin looks back at Tam once, her black hair wild in the wind, her face in her hands like maybe she's even crying, and then he follows Lark.

Mostly just mussels, long shells darker than the beach, curved and flaking like diseased toenails, but Lark puts a few in her purse, anyway. Crispin finds a single crab claw, almost as orange as the poppies in their hair with an airbrush hint of blue, and she keeps that too. The driftwood is more plentiful, but all the really good pieces are gigantic, the warped and polished bones of great trees washed down from the mountains and scattered about here, shattered skeletons beyond repair. They walk on warm sand and a thick mat of sequoia bark and spindletwigs, fleshy scraps of kelp, follow the flotsam to a stream running down to meet the gently crashing sea, shallowwide interface of saltwater and fresh. Overhead, seagulls wheel and protest the intrusion; the craggy rocks just offshore are covered with their watchful numbers, powdergrey feathers, white feathers, beaks for snatching fish. *And pecking eyes*, Lark thinks. They squawk and stare and she gives them the finger, one nail chewed down to the quick and most of the black polish flaked away.

Crispin bends and lets the stream gurgle about his pale hands. It's filled with polished stones, muted olive and bottle green pebbles rounded by their centuries in the cold water. He puts one finger to his lips and licks it cautiously and "Sweet," he says. "It's very sweet."

"What's that?" Lark says and he looks up, across the stream at a windstunted stand of firs on the other side and there's a sign there, almost as big as a roadside billboard sign and just as gaudy, but no way anyone could see this from the highway. A great sign of planks painted white and lettered crimson, artful, scrolling letters that spell out, "ALIVE AND UNTAMED! MONSTERS AND MYSTERIES OF NEPTUNE'S BOSOM!" and below, in slightly smaller script, "MERMAIDS AND MIRACLES! THE GREAT SEA SERPENT! MANEATERS AND DEVILFISH!"

"Someone likes exclamation points," Lark says, but Crispin's already halfway across the stream, walking on the knobby stones protruding from the water and she follows him, both arms out for balance like a trapeze acrobat. "Wait," she calls to him, and he pauses, reluctant, until she catches up.

The old house trailer sits a little way up the slope from the beach, just far enough that it's safe from the high tides. Lark and Crispin stand side by side, holding hands tight, and stare up at it, lips parted and eyes wide enough to divulge a hint of their mutual surprise. Lark's left boot is wet where she missed a stone and her foot went into the stream, and the water's beginning to seep past leather straps and buckles, through her hose, but she doesn't notice, or it doesn't matter, because this is that unexpected. This old husk of sunbleached aluminum walls, corrugated metal skin draped in mopgrey folds of fishing net, so much netting it's hard to see that the trailer underneath might once have been blue. Like something a giant fisherman dragged up from the sea, and finally, realizing what he had, this inedible hunk of rubbish, he left it here for the gulls and the weather to take care of.

"Wow," Lark whispers, and Crispin turns, looks over his shoulder to see if maybe Tam has given up on the car and come looking for them. But there's only the beach, and the waves, and the birds. The air that smells like dead fish and salt wind, and Crispin asks, "You wanna go see?"

"There might be a phone," Larks says, still whispering. "If there's a phone we could call someone to fix the car."

"Yeah," Crispin replies, like they really need an excuse beyond their curiosity. And there are more signs leading up to the trailer, splinternail bread crumbs teasing them to take the next step, and the next, and the next after that: "THE MOUTH THAT SWALLOWED JONAH!" and "ETERNAL LEVIATHAN AND CHARYBDIS REVEALED!" As they get close they can see other things in the sandy rind of yard surrounding the trailer, the rusting hulks of outboard motors and a ship's wheel nailed to a post, broken lobster cages and the ivorywhite jaws of sharks strung up to dry like toothy laundry. There are huge plywood and canvas façades leaned or hammered against the trailer, one on either side of the narrow door and both taller than the roof: garish seascapes with whitefanged sea monsters breaking the surface, acrylic foam and spray, flailing fins like Japanese fans of flesh and wire, eyes like angry, boiling hemorrhages.

A sudden gust off the beach, then, and they both have to stop and cover their eyes against the blowing sand. The wind clatters and whistles around all the things in the yard, tugs at the side-show canvases. "Maybe we should go back now," Lark says when the wind has gone, and she brushes sand from her clothes and hair. "She'll wonder where we've gone . . ."

"Yeah," Crispin says, his voice grown thin and distant, distracted, and "Maybe," he says, but they're both still climbing, past the hand-lettered signs and into the ring of junk. Crispin pauses before the shark jaws, yawning cartilage jaws on nylon fishing line and he runs the tip of one finger lightly across rows of gleaming, serrate triangles, only a little more pressure and he could draw blood.

And then the door of the trailer creaks open and the man is standing in the dark space, not what either expected if only because they hadn't known what to expect. A tall man, gangly knees and elbows through threadbare clothes, pants and shirt the same faded khaki; bony wrists from buttoned sleeves too short for his long arms, arthritis swollen knuckles on his wide hands. Lark makes a uneasy sound when she sees him and Crispin jerks his hand away from the shark's jaw, sneakchild caught in the cookie jar startled, and snags a pinkie, soft skin torn by dentine and he leaves a crimson gleaming drop of himself behind.

"You be careful there, boy," the man says with a voice like water sloshing in a rocky place. "That's *Carcharodon carcharias* herself hanging there and her ghost is just as hungry as her belly ever was. You've given her a taste of blood and she'll remember now . . ."

"Our car broke down," Lark says to the man, looking up at his face for the first time since the door opened. "And we saw the signs . . ." She points back down the hill without looking away from the man, his cloudy eyes that seem too big for his skull, odd, forwardsloping skull with more of an underbite than she ever thought possible and a wormpink wrinkle where his lower lip should be, nothing at all for the upper. Eyes set too far apart, wide nostrils too far apart and a scraggly bit of grey beard perched on the end of his sharp chin. Lank hair to his shoulders and almost as grey as the scrap of beard.

"Do you want to see inside, then?" he asks, that watery voice, and Lark and Crispin both look back toward the signs, the little stream cutting the beach in half. There's no evidence of Tam anywhere.

"Does it cost money?" Crispin asks, glances tentatively out at the man from underneath the white shock of hair hiding half his face.

"Not if you ain't got any," the man replies and blinks once, vellum lids fast across those bulging eyes.

"It's getting late and our car's broken down," Lark says and the man makes a noise that might be a sigh or might be a cough. "It don't take long," he says and smiles, shows crooked teeth the color of nicotine stains.

"And you've got all the things that those signs say in there?" Crispin asks, one eyebrow cocked, eager, excited doubt, and the man shrugs.

"If it's free, I don't expect you'll be asking for your money back," as if that's an answer, but enough for Crispin and he nods his head and steps toward the door, away from the shark jaws. But Lark grabs his hand, anxious grab that says "Wait," without using any words, and when he looks at her, eyes that say, "This isn't like the dinosaurs, whatever it is, this isn't plaster and plywood," and so he smiles for her, flashes comfort and confidence.

"It'll be something cool," he says. "Better than listening to Tam bitch at us about the car, at least."

So she smiles back at him, small and nervous smile and she squeezes his hand a little harder.

"Come on, if you're coming," the man says. "I'm letting in the flies, standing here with the door wide open."

"Yeah," Crispin says. "We're coming," and the man holds the door for them, steps to one side, and the trailer swallows them like a hungry, metal whale.

Inside, and the air is chilly and smells like fish and stagnant saltwater, mildew, and there's the faintest rotten odor somewhere underneath, dead thing washed up and swelling on the sand. Crispin and Lark pause while the man pulls the door shut behind them, shuts them in, shuts the world out. "Do you live in here?" Lark asks, still squeezing Crispin's hand, and the old man turns around, the tall old man with his billygoat beard and looking down on the twins now as he scratches at the scaly, dry skin on his neck.

"I have myself a cot in the back, and a hot plate," he replies and Lark nods; her eyes are adjusting to the dim light leaking in through the dirty windowpanes and she can see the flakes of dead skin, dislodged and floating slowly down to settle on the dirty linoleum floor of the trailer.

The length of the trailer has been lined with wooden shelves and huge glass tanks and there are sounds to match the smells, wet sounds, the constant bubble of aquarium pumps, water filters, occasional, furtive splashes.

"Wonders from the blackest depths," the old man sighs, wheezes, sicklytired imitation of a carnie barker's spiel, and "Jewels and nightmares plucked from Davy Jones' Locker, washed up on the shores of the Seven Seas . . ."

The old man is interrupted by a violent fit of coughing and Crispin steps up to the nearest shelf, a collection of jars, dozens and dozens of jars filled with murky ethanol or formalin, formaldehyde weakteabrown and the things that float lifelessly inside: scales and spines, oystergrey flesh and lidless, unseeing eyes like pickled grapes. Labels on the jars, identities in a spideryfine handwriting, and the paper so old and yellow he knows that it would crumble at his most careful touch.

The old man clears his throat, loud, phlegmy rattle and he spits into a shadowmoist corner.

"Secrets from the world's museums, from Mr. Charles Darwin's own cabinets, scooped from the sea off Montevideo in eighteen hundred and thirty-two . . ."

"Is that an octopus?" Lark asks and the twins both stare into one of the larger jars, three or four gallons and a warty lump inside, a bloom of tentacles squashed against the glass like something wanting out. Crispin presses the tip of one finger to the glass, traces the outline of a single, dimewide suction cup.

The old man coughs again, throaty raw hack, produces a wadded and wrinkled, snotstained handkerchief from his shirt pocket and wipes at his wide mouth with it.

"*That*, boy, is the larva of the Kraken, the greatest of the cephalopods, Viking-bane, ten strangling arms to hale dragon ships beneath the waves." And then the old man clears his throat, and, in a different voice, barker turned poet, recites, " 'Below the thunders of the upper deep, / Far, far beneath in the abysmal sea, / His ancient, dreamless, uninvaded sleep / The Kraken sleepeth . . .' "

"Tennyson," Lark says and the old man nods, pleased.

Crispin leans closer, squints through the gloom and dusty glass, the clouded preserving fluids, and now he can see something dark and sharp like a parrot's beak nested at the center of the rubbery molluskflower. But then they're being hurried along, past all the unexamined jars, and here's the next stop on the old man's tour.

Beneath a bell jar, the taxidermied head and arms and torso of a monkey sewn onto the dried tail of a fish, the stitches plain to see, but he tells them it's a baby mermaid, netted near the coast of Java a hundred years ago.

"It's just half an old, dead monkey with a fish tail stuck on," Crispin says, impertinent, already tiring of these moldy, fabricated wonders. "See?" and he points at the stitches in case Lark hasn't noticed them for herself.

The old man makes an annoyed sound, not quite anger, but impatience, certainly, and he moves them quickly along, this time to a huge fish tank, plateglass sides so overgrown with algae there's no seeing *what's* inside, just mossygreen like siren hair that sways in whatever dull currents the aquarium's pump is making.

"I can't see anything at all in there," Crispin says, as Lark looks nervously back past the mermaid toward the trailer door. But Crispin stands on his toes, peers over the edge of the tank, and "You need to put some snails in there," he says. "To eat some of that shit so people can see . . ."

"*This* one has no name, no proper name," the old man croaks through his snotclogged throat. "No legend. This one was scraped off the hull of a Russian whaler with the shipworms and barnacles and on Midsummer's Eve, put an ear to the glass and you'll hear it *singing* in the language of riptides and typhoons."

And something seems to move, then, maybe, beyond the emerald scum, feathery red gillflutter or a thousand jointed legs the color of a burn and Crispin jumps, steps away from the glass and lets go of Lark's hand. Smug grin on the old man's long face to show his yellowed teeth, and he makes a barking noise like seals or laughing.

"You go back, if you're getting scared," the old man says and

Lark looks like that's all she wants in the world right now, to be out of the trailer, back on the beach and headed up the cliff to the Impala. But Crispin takes her hand again, this very same boy that's afraid of banana slugs but something here he has to see, something he has to prove to himself or to the self-satisfied old man and "What's next, sea monkeys?" he asks, defiant, mock brave.

"Right here," the old man says, pointing to something more like a cage than a tank. "The spawn of the great sea serpent and a Chinese water dragon," planks and chicken wire on the floor, almost as tall as the twins and Crispin drags Lark along toward it. "Tam will be looking for us, won't she?" she asks, but he ignores her, stares instead into the enclosure. There's muddy straw on the bottom and motionless coils of gold and chocolatebrown muscle.

"Jesus, it's just a stupid python, Lark. See? It's not even as big as the one that Alexandra used to have. What a rip-off . . ." and then he stops, because the snake moves, shifts its chainlink bulk and now he can see its head, the tiny horns above its pearlbead eyes, and further back, a single, stubby flap of meat along one side of its body that beats nervously at the air a moment and then lies still against the filthy straw.

"There's something wrong with it, Crispin, that's all," Lark says, argument to convince herself, and the old man says, "She can crush a full-grown pig in those coils, or a man," and he pauses for the drama, then adds, resuming his confident barker cadence, sly voice to draw midway crowds – "Kept inside a secret Buddhist monastery on the Yangtze and worshipped for a century, and all the sacrificial children she could eat," he says.

The flipper thing on its side moves again, vestigial limb rustle against the straw, and the snake flicks a tongue the color of gangrene and draws its head slowly back into its coils, retreating, hiding from their sight or the dim trailer light or both; "Wonders from the blackest depths," the old man whispers, "Mysteries of the deep, spoils of the abyss," and Lark is all but begging, now. "*Please*, Crispin. We should go," but her voice almost lost in the burbling murmur of aquarium filters.

Crispin's hand about her wrist like a steel police cuff, and she thinks, *How much more can there be, how much can this awful little trailer hold*? When she looks back the way they've come, past the snake-thing's cage and the green tank and the phony mermaid, past all the jars, it seems a long, long way; the dizzying impression that the trailer's somehow bigger inside than out and she shivers, realizes that she's sweating, clammy coldsweat in tiny salt beads on her upper lip, across her forehead and leaking into her eyes. *How much more?* but there's at least *one* more, and they step past a plastic shower curtain, slick blue plastic printed with cartoon sea horses and starfish and turtles, to stand before the final exhibit in the old man's shabby menagerie.

"Dredged from the bottom of Eel Canyon off Humboldt Bay, hauled up five hundred fathoms through water so inky black and cold it might be the very moment before Creation itself," and Crispin is staring at something Lark can't see, squinting into the last tank; cold pools about Lark's ankles, one dry and one still wet from the stream, sudden, tangible chill that gathers itself like the old man's words of cold, or heavy air spilling from an open freezer door.

"And this was just a *scrap*, boy, a shred ripped from the haunches or seaweed-crusted skull of a behemoth . . ."

"I can't see anything," Crispin says, and then, "*Oh*. Oh shit. Oh, Jesus . . ."

Lark realizes where the cold is coming from, that it's pouring out from under the shower curtain and she slips her sweatgreased hand free of Crispin's grasp. He doesn't even seem to notice, can't seem to stop staring into the murky, ill-lit tank that towers over them, fills the rear of the trailer from wall to wall.

"And *maybe*," the old man says, bending very close and he's almost whispering to Crispin now, secrets and suspicions for the boy twin and no one else. "Maybe it's growing itself a whole new body in there, a whole new organism from that stolen bit of flesh, like the arm of a starfish that gets torn off . . ."

Lark touches the folds of the curtain and the cold presses back from the other side. Cold that would burn her hand if she left it there, lingered long enough. She glances back at the old man and Crispin to be sure they're not watching, because she knows this must be forbidden, something she's not meant to see. And then she pulls one corner of the shower curtain aside, and that terrible cold flows out, washes over her like a living wave of arctic breath and a neglected cat box smell and another, sharper odor like cabbage left too long at the bottom of a refrigerator.

"Fuck," Crispin says behind her. "No fucking way," and the old man is reciting Tennyson again.

"There hath he lain for ages, and *will* lie/Battening upon huge sea worms in his sleep,/Until the latter fire shall heat the deep . . ."

There is dark behind the shower curtain, dark like a wall, solid as the cold, and again, that vertigo sense of a vast space held somehow inside the little trailer, that this blackness might go on for miles. That she could step behind the curtain and spend her life wandering lost in the alwaysnight collected here.

". . . Then once by man and angels to be seen," the old man says, somewhere back there in the World, where there is simple light and warmth, "In roaring he shall rise and on the surface die."

Far off, in the dark, there are wet sounds, something breaking the surface of water that has lain so still so long and she can feel its eyes on her then, eyes made to see where light is a fairy tale and the sun a murmured heresy. The sound of something vast and sinuous coming slowly through the water toward her and Crispin says, "It moved, didn't it? Jesus, it fucking *moved* in there."

It's so close now, Lark thinks. *It's so close and this is the worst place in the world and I* should *be scared, I should be scared shitless*.

"Sometimes it moves," the old man says. "In its sleep, sometimes it moves."

Lark steps over the threshold, the thin, tightrope line between the trailer and this place, ducks her head beneath the shower curtain and the smell is stronger than ever now. It gags her and she covers her mouth with one hand, another step and the curtain will close behind her and there will be nothing but this perfect, absolute cold and darkness and her and the thing swimming through the black. Not really water in there, she knows, just *black* to hide it from the prying, jealous light – and then Crispin has her hand again, is pulling her back into the blinding glare of the trailer and the shower curtain falls closed with an unforgiving, disappointed *shoosh*. The old man and his fishlong face is staring at her, his rheumy, accusing eyes, and "That was not for you, girl," he says. "I did not show you that . . ."

She almost resists, wrenches her hand free of Crispin's and slips back behind the curtain before anyone can stop her, the only possible release from the sudden emptyhollow feeling eating her up inside, like waking from a dream of Heaven or someone dead alive again, the glimpse of anything so pure and then it's yanked away. But Crispin is stronger and the old man is blocking the way, anyhow, grizzled Cerberus standing guard before the aquamarine plastic, a faint string of drool at one corner of his mouth.

"Come on, Lark," Crispin says to her. "We shouldn't be here. We shouldn't ever have come in here."

The look in the old man's eyes says he's right and already the dream is fading, whatever she might have seen or heard already bleeding away in the last, watercolor dregs of daylight getting into the trailer.

"I'm sorry," Crispin says as they pass the shriveled mermaid and he pushes the door open, not so far back after all, "I didn't want you to think I was afraid."

And "No," she says, "No," doesn't know what to say next, but it doesn't really matter, because they're stumbling together down the trailer's concrete block steps, their feet in the sand again, and the air is filled with gentle twilight and the screaming of gulls.

Tam has been standing by the stream for half an hour, at least that long since she wandered down to the beach looking for the twins, after the black man in the pick-up truck stopped and fixed the broken fan belt, used an old pair of pantyhose from the back seat of the Impala and then refilled the radiator. "You take it easy, now, and that oughta hold far as San Francisco," he said, but then she couldn't find Lark or Crispin. Her throat hurts from calling them, near dark now and she's been standing here where their footprints end at the edge of the water, shouting their names. Getting angrier, getting fucking scared, the relief that the car's running again melting away, deserting her for visions of the twins drowned or the twins lost or the twins raped and murdered.

Twice she started across the stream, one foot out and plenty enough stones between her and the other side to cross without getting her feet wet, and twice she stopped. Thought that she glimpsed dark shapes moving just below the surface, undulating forms like the wings of stingrays or the tentacles of an octopus or squid, black and eellong things darting between the rocks. And never mind that the water is crystal clear and couldn't possibly be more than a few inches deep. Never mind she *knows* it's really nothing more than shadow tricks and the last glimmers of the setting sun caught in the rippling water. These apprehensions too instinctual, the thought of what might be waiting for her if she slipped, sharp teeth eager for stray ankles, anxiety all but too deep to question, and so she's stood here, feeling stupid, calling them like she was their goddamn mother.

She looks up again and there they are, almost stumbling down the hill, the steep dirt path leading down from the creepy old trailer, Crispin in the lead and dragging Lark along, a cloud of dust trailing out behind them. When they reach the stream they don't even bother with the stepping stones, just splash their way straight across, splashing her in the bargain.

"Mother*fucker*," Tam says and steps backwards onto drier sand. "Will you please watch what the fuck you're doing? Shit . . ." But neither of them says a word, stand breathless at the edge of the stream, the low bank carved into the sand by the water; Crispin stares down at his soggy Docs and Lark glances nervously back toward the trailer on the hill.

"Where the hell have you two bozos been? Didn't you hear me calling you? I'm fucking hoarse from calling you."

"An old man," Lark gasps, wheezes the words out, and before she can say anything else Crispin says, "A sideshow, Tam, that's all," speaking quickly like he's afraid of what Lark will say if he doesn't, what she might have been about to say. "Just some crazy old guy with a sort of a sideshow."

"Jesus," Tam sighs, pissytired sigh that she hopes sounds the way she feels and she reaches out and plucks a wilted poppy from Crispin's hair, tosses it to the sand at their feet. "That figures, you know? That just fucking figures. Next time, Magwitch comes or your asses stay home," and she turns her back on them, then, heading up the beach toward the car. She only stops once, turns around to be sure they're following and they are, close behind and their arms tight around one another's shoulders as if they couldn't make it alone. The twins' faces are hidden in shadow, night-shrouded, and behind them, the sea has turned a cold, silvery indigo and stretches away to meet the rising stars.

MICHAEL
MARSHALL SMITH

Everybody Goes

MICHAEL MARSHALL SMITH'S DÉBUT NOVEL, *Only Forward*, won the British Fantasy Society's August Derleth Fantasy Award in 1995. His second novel, *Spares*, has been optioned by Steven Spielberg's DreamWorks SKG, while his latest, *One of Us*, is being developed as a movie by Di Novi Pictures and Warner Bros.

He has had his short fiction published in anthologies and magazines on both sides of the Atlantic, including several volumes of the *Darklands*, *Dark Voices*, *Dark Terrors*, *The Year's Best Fantasy and Horror* and *The Best New Horror* series. He is a three-time winner of the British Fantasy Award for Best Short Story, and has been nominated three times for the World Fantasy Award. His short fiction is collected in *When God Lived in Kentish Town & Others* and *What You Make it*.

As the author recalls, "This story is loosely based on a time when my family lived in Armidale, in New South Wales, Australia. One Sunday we went out to visit the family of a school friend of mine, who lived in the outback. While the parents chatted about grown-up stuff, my friend took me into the bush.

"It was a hot day, and the land was flat and featureless. We found this little canyon in the middle of the open plain, much as described in the story, with steep walls and a door floating in the pond at the bottom. In retrospect, I suppose that if someone had taken the trouble to drag a piece of rubbish that heavy to it then we can't have been that far from civilisation – but in my memory we were on the surface of Mars. We messed around, as boys will, and we had fun, and then we walked home through the stillness. It was a good day."

I SAW A MAN YESTERDAY. I was coming back from the waste ground with Matt and Joey and we were calling Joey dumb because he'd seen this huge spider and he thought it was a Black Widow or something when it was just, like, a *spider*, and I saw the man.

We were walking down the road towards the block and laughing and I just happened to look up and there was this man down the end of the street, tall, walking up towards us. We turned off the road before he got to us, and I forgot about him.

Anyway, Matt had to go home then because his family eats early and his Mom raises hell if he isn't back in time to wash up and so I just hung out for a while with Joey and then he went home too. Nothing much happened in the evening.

This morning I got up early because we were going down to the creek for the day and it's a long walk. I made some sandwiches and put them in a bag, and I grabbed an apple and put that in too. Then I went down to knock on Matt's door.

His Mom answered and let me in. She's okay really, and quite nice-looking for a Mom, but she's kind of strict. She's the only person in the world who calls me Peter instead of Pete. Matt's room always looks like it's just been tidied, which is quite cool actually though it must be a real pain to keep up. At least you know where everything is.

We went down and got Joey. Matt seemed kind of quiet on the way down as if there was something he wanted to tell me, but he didn't. I figured that if he wanted to, sooner or later he would. That's how it is with best friends. You don't have to be always talking. The point will come round soon enough.

Joey wasn't ready so we had to hang round while he finished his breakfast. His Dad's kind of weird. He sits and reads the paper at the table and just grunts at it every now and then. I don't think I could eat breakfast with someone who did that. I think I would find it disturbing. Must be something you get into when you grow up, I guess.

Anyway, *finally* Joey was ready and we left the block. The sun was pretty hot already though it was only nine in the morning and I was glad I was only wearing a T-Shirt. Matt's Mom made him wear a sweatshirt in case there was a sudden blizzard or something and I knew he was going to be pretty baked by the end of the day but you can't tell moms anything.

As we were walking away from the block towards the waste ground I looked back and I saw the man again, standing on the opposite side of the street, looking at the block. He was staring up at the top floor and then I thought he turned and looked at us, but it was difficult to tell because the sun was shining right in my eyes.

We walked and ran through the waste ground, not hanging around much because we'd been there yesterday. We checked on the fort but it was still there. Sometimes other kids come and mess it up but it was okay today.

Matt got Joey a good one with a scrunched-up leaf. He put it on the back of his hand when Joey was looking the other way and then he started staring at it and saying "Pete . . ." in this really scared voice; and I saw what he was doing and pretended to be scared too and Joey bought it.

"I told you," he says – and he's backing away – "I *told* you there was Black Widows . . ." and we could have kept it going but I started laughing. Joey looked confused for a second and then he just grunted as if he was reading his Dad's paper and so we jumped on him and called him Dad all afternoon.

We didn't get to the creek till nearly lunch time, and Matt took his sweatshirt off and tied it round his waist. It's a couple miles from the block, way past the waste ground and out into the bush. It's a good creek though. It's so good we don't go there too often, like we don't want to wear it out.

You just walk along the bush, not seeing anything, and then suddenly there you are, and there's this baby canyon cut into the earth. It gets a little deeper every year, I think, except when there's no rain. Maybe it gets deeper then too, I don't know. The sides are about ten feet deep and this year there was rain so there's plenty of water at the bottom and you have to be careful climbing down because otherwise you can slip and end up in the mud.

Matt went down first. He's best at climbing, and really quick. He went down first so that if Joey slipped he might not fall all the way in. For me, if Joey slips, he slips, but Matt's good like that. Probably comes from having such a tidy room.

Joey made it down okay this time, hold the front page, and I went last. The best way to get down is to put your back to the creek, slide your feet down, and then let them go until you're hanging onto the edge of the canyon with your hands. Then you just have to scuttle. As I was lowering myself down I noticed how far you could see across the plain, looking right along about a foot up from the ground. There's nothing to see for miles, nothing but bushes and dust. I think the man was there too, off in the distance, but it was difficult to be sure and then I slipped and nearly ended up in the creek myself, which would have been a real pain and Joey would have gone on about it forever.

We walked along the creek for a while and then came to the ocean. It's not really the ocean, it's just a bit where the canyon widens out into almost a circle that's about fifteen feet across. It's deeper than the rest of the creek, and the water isn't so clear, but it's really cool. When you're down there you can't see anything but this circle of sky, and you know there's nothing else for miles around. There's this old door there which we call our ship and we pull it to one side of the ocean and we all try to get on and float it to the middle. Usually it's kind of messy and I know Matt and Joey are thinking there's going to be trouble when their Moms see their clothes, but today we somehow got it right and we floated right to the middle with only a little bit of water coming up.

We played our game for a while and then we just sat there for a long time and talked and stuff. I was thinking how good it was to be there and there was a pause and then Joey tried to say something of his own like that. It didn't come out very well, but we knew what he meant so we told him to shut up and made as if we were going to push him in. Matt pretended he had a spider on his leg just by suddenly looking scared and staring and Joey laughed, and I realised that that's where jokes come from. It was our own joke, that no one else would ever understand and that they would never forget however old they got.

Matt looked at me one time, as if he was about to say what was on his mind, but then Joey said something dumb and he didn't. We just sat there and kept talking about things and moving around so we didn't get burnt too bad. Once when I looked up at the rim of the canyon I thought maybe there was a head peeking over the side but there probably wasn't.

Joey has a watch and so we knew when it was four o'clock. Four o'clock is the latest we can leave so that Matt gets back for dinner in time. We walked back towards the waste ground, not running. The sun had tired us out and we weren't in any hurry to get back because it had been a good afternoon, and they always finish when you split up. You can't get back to them the next day, especially if you try to do the same thing again.

When we got back to the street we were late and so Matt and Joey ran on ahead. I would have run with them but I saw that the man was standing down the other side of the block, and I wanted to watch him to see what he was going to do. Matt waited back a second after Joey had run and said he'd see me after dinner. Then he ran, and I just hung around for a while.

The man was looking back up at the block again, like he was looking for something. He knew I was hanging around, but he didn't come over right away, as if he was nervous. I went and sat on the wall and messed about with some stones. I wasn't in any hurry.

"Excuse me," says this voice, and I looked up to see the man standing over me. The slanting sun was in his eyes and he was shading them with his hand. He had a nice suit on and he was younger than people's parents are, but not much. "You live here, don't you?"

I nodded, and looked up at his face. He looked familiar.

"I used to live here too," he said, "When I was a kid. On the top floor." Then he laughed, and I recognised him from the sound. "A long time ago now. Came back after all these years to see if it had changed."

I didn't say anything.

"Hasn't much, still looks the same." He turned and looked again at the block, then back past me towards the waste ground. "Guys still playing out there on the 'ground?"

"Yeah," I said, "It's cool. We have a fort there."

"And the creek?"

He knew we still played there: he'd been watching. I knew what he really wanted to ask, so I just nodded. The man nodded too, as if he didn't know what to say next. Or more like he knew what he wanted to say, but didn't know how to go about it.

"My name's Tom Spivey," he said, and then stopped. I nodded again. The man laughed, embarrassed. "This is going to sound very weird, but . . . I've seen you around today, and yesterday." He laughed again, running his hand through his hair, and then finally asked what was on his mind. "Your name isn't Pete, by any chance?"

I looked up into his eyes, then away.

"No," I said. "It's Jim."

The man looked confused for a moment, then relieved. He said a couple more things about the block, and then he went away. Back to the city, or wherever.

After dinner I saw Matt out in the back car park, behind the block. We talked about the afternoon some, so he could get warmed up, and then he told me what was on his mind.

His family was moving on. His dad had got a better job somewhere else. They'd be going in a week.

We talked a little more, and then he went back inside, looking different somehow, as if he'd already gone.

I stayed out, sitting on the wall, thinking about missing people. I wasn't feeling sad, just tired. Sure I was going to miss Matt. He was my best friend. I'd missed Tom for a while, but then someone else came along. And then someone else, and someone else. There's always new people. They come, and then they go. Maybe Matt would return some day. Sometimes they do come back. But everybody goes.

TANITH LEE

Yellow and Red

TANITH LEE BEGAN WRITING AT the age of nine. After school she worked variously as a library assistant, shop assistant, filing clerk and waitress before spending a year at art college.

She published three children's books in the early 1970s, but it was only when DAW Books published her novel *The Birthgrave* in 1975, and thereafter twenty-six other titles, was she able to become a full-time writer. To date she has published nearly sixty novels, including such recent titles as *White as Snow*, *A Bed of Earth* and *Venus Preserved*, plus nine collections of novellas and short stories. Her radio plays have been broadcast by the BBC and she scripted two episodes of the cult TV series *Blake's 7*.

Tanith Lee has twice won the World Fantasy Award for short fiction, and in 1980 she was awarded the British Fantasy Society's August Derleth Award for her novel *Death's Master*.

"I am a great admirer of, amongst others, M.R. James . . .," reveals the author. "His influence on me, in this story, is perhaps evident only to myself."

From the Diary of Gordon Martyce:

9th September 195–: 7:00 p.m.
Coming down to the old house was at first interesting, and then depressing. The train journey was tedious and slow, and after the second hour, over and again, I began to wish I had not under-

taken this. But that would be foolish. The house, by the quirkiness of my Uncle's will, is now mine. One day I may even live in it, although for now my job, which I value, and my flat, which I like, keep me in London. Of course, Lucy is terribly interested in the idea of an old place in the country. I could see her eyes, lit by her second gin, gleam with visions of chintz curtains, china on the mantlepiece, an old, dark, loudly-ticking cloak. But it is not that sort of house – I knew that even then, never having seen inside it in my life. As for Lucy, I am never sure. She has stuck to me for five years, and so I have not quite given up on the notion of one day having a wife, perhaps a family. Quite a pretty woman, quite vivacious in her way, which sometimes, I confess, tires me a little. Well, if it comes to that, she can do what she wants with the house. It is gloomy enough as it stands.

Beyond the train, the trees were putting on their September garments, brown and red and yellow, but soon a drizzle began which blotted up detail. It was raining more earnestly when I reached the station and got out. I had only one small bag, the essentials for a stay of a couple of nights. That was good, for there was no transport of any kind.

I walked to the village, and there was given a cup of tea, the keys, and a lift the last mile and a half.

Johnson, the agent, let me off on the drive. He had offered to take me round, but I said this was not necessary. There is a woman, Mrs Gold, who comes in every day, and I was told, she would have put things ready for me – I trusted this was true.

The rain eased as I walked along the last curve of the drive. Presently I saw the house, and recognized it from a photograph I had observed often enough in my Father's study. A two-storey building, with green shutters. Big oaks stood around it that had done the walls some damage, and introduced damp. I supposed they could be cut down. Above, was my Grandfather's weather-vane, which I had never been able, properly, to make out in the photograph, but which my Father told me was in the shape of some Oriental animal deity. Even now, it remained a mystery to me, between the leaves of the oaks and the moving, leaden sky.

I got up the steps, and opened the front door, and stepped into the big dark hall. The trees oppress this house, that is certain, and the old stained glass of the hall windows change the light to mulberry and spinach. However, I saw through into the sitting room, and a fire had been laid, and wood put ready. A touch on a switch reassured me that the electricity still worked. On the table near the door I found Mrs Gold's rather poorly spelled note. But she had done everything one could expect, even to leaving me a cold supper of ham and salad, apple pie and cheese. She would be in tomorrow at eleven. I need have no fears.

I looked round. I am not fearful by nature. I always do my best, and am seldom in a position to dread very much. A childhood visit to the dentist, perhaps, for an especially painful filling – something of that apprehension seized me. But it was the nasty dark light in the hall. My Uncle died in this house not three months ago. Before him, he had lost his family, his wife and sister, and two sons. Before them another generation had perished. As Shakespeare points out, it is common for people to die.

Going through into the sitting room, I have put a match to the fire. This has improved things. On a sideboard stands a tray with brandy, whisky and soda. Though it is early for me, I shall pour myself a small measure. I gather the boiler is at work, and I can count on a hot bath. I do not want a chill.

10th September: 2:00 *p.m.*
The house is a mausoleum. Lucy be blowed, I think I shall sell it. Last night was dreadful. Creaks and groans of woodwork, an eldritch wind at the windows and down the chimneys. I read until nearly two a.m. Then at three I was woken by a persistent owl hooting in the garden trees. I am not a country person. I longed for my warm city flat and the vague roar of traffic.

However, this morning early I went over the place thoroughly, from attic to cellar. There are a great many rooms, more than I should ever want, and the heating would be prohibitive. It is very old fashioned, those thick, bottle-green and oxblood curtains favoured by our grandfathers – evidently by mine, and my Uncle William, too – enormous cliffs of furniture, and endless curios, some of them I expect very valuable, from the East – Egypt, India and China. I am not particularly partial to any of this sort of thing. I find the house uncomfortable, both physically – it is cold and damp – and aesthetically.

At about eleven thirty, the not very punctual Mrs Gold arrived. I was not surprised. Women are generally unreliable. I have learnt this from Lucy. Nevertheless, I commended Mrs Gold on keeping

YELLOW AND RED223

the house clean, which she has more or less done, and on the supper left for me yesterday. She is a large woman, constructed like a figurehead, with severe grey hair. She began, of course, at once to tell me all about my Uncle, and what she knows of my Grandfather before him. She is, naturally, as her class nearly always are, fascinated by details of all the deaths. It was with some difficulty that I got her to resume her work. Going into the library, I then took down some boxes of photographs, and began to go through them, more to pass the time than anything else. The agent is coming tomorrow, to discuss things, or I would have tried to get home today.

The photographs, most of which have dates and names written on the back, are generally displeasing, many the dull, antique kind where everyone stands like a waxwork, as the primitive camera performs its task. My grandfather was a formidable old boy, with bushy whiskers, in several scenes out in some foreign landscape, clutching his gun, or his spade, for he had been involved in one or two famous excavations, in the East. Here he had taken his own photographs, some of which had appeared in prominent journals of the day. These, obviously, were not among the general portraits, nor was I especially interested to look them out. My father had been wont to tell me, at length, how Grandfather Martyce had taken the very first photograph inside some remarkable ancient tomb. I had found this, I am afraid, extremely boring, then, and scarcely less so now. I have, too, forgotten the location. Lucy has often commented that I am not a romantic. I am glad to say I am not.

Eventually Mrs Gold finished her ministrations, and I went down to learn her wages, which were modest enough. She had put into the oven for me, besides, a substantial hot-pot.

"Your Uncle was very fond of those, I must say," she announced. "He relied on me, once the old cook had retired. Mrs Martyce was often ill, you understand, Miss Martyce too. I had a free hand."

I said something gallant about her cooking. She ignored this.

"It was a great worry," she said, "to see them waste away. First the boys, and then the sister and the wife. Your Uncle was the last to go. He was very strong, fought it off, so to speak. The doctors couldn't find anything wrong with him. But it was the same as with the ladies, and the children."

I privately thought that no doubt a reliance on elderly country doctors was to blame here, but I nodded lugubriously, and was apparently anticipated.

"Your Grandfather now," persisted this tragic choric Mrs Gold, glowering on me in the stone kitchen, the pans partly gleaming at her back from her somewhat hard work upon them, "he was the same, but they put it down to some foreign affliction, bad water, those dirty heathen foods. You understand, Mr Martyce – your Uncle, Mr William Martyce, was only in the house a year before he first fell ill. And before that, never a day's indisposion." I noted that, not only did she employ words she could not, probably, spell, but that she was also able to invent them.

"It seems an unfortunate house," I said. She appeared to wish me to.

"That's as may be. The cook was never out of sorts, nor any of the maids, while they had them. And I've never had a day in bed, excepting my parturiton." I assumed she meant childbirth, and kept a stern face. Mrs Gold was certainly most serious. She said, "If I was you, sir, I'd put this house up for sale."

"That might be an idea," I said.

"Not that I want to cause you misgivings."

"Not at all. But it will be too big for me, I'm sure."

When she had gone, I ate the beef sandwiches she had left me, and was grateful her meals were more cheerful than her talk, although I have jotted down here her two interesting words, to make Lucy laugh.

10th September: 6:00 p.m.
I do not like this house. No, I am not being superstitious. I believe there is not a fanciful bone in my body. But it depresses me utterly. The furnishings, the darkness, the chilliness, which lighting all the fires I reasonably can – in the sitting room, dining room, my bedroom, the library – cannot dispel. And the things which so many would find intriguing – old letters in bundles, in horrible brown, ornate, indecipherable writing – caskets of incenses and peculiar amulets – such items fill me with aversion. I want my orderly room with its small fire that warms every inch, my sensible plain chairs, the newspaper, and a good, down-to-earth detective novel.

I have already taken to drink – a whisky at lunch, and now another before dinner – and even this went awry. I am not a man who spills things. I have a sound eye and a steady hand. However, sitting over the fire in the library, crouching, should I say, with pure ice at my back, I was looking again at some of the more recent photographs. These comprised a picture of my Uncle and his sons on the lawn before the house, and some oddments of him, pruning a small tree, standing with a group I took to be the local vicar and various worthies of the nearby village. In these scenes, my Uncle is about forty, and again about fifty. He looks hale enough, but I had already gathered from the delightful Gold that he was, even then, frequently laid low.

Finally I put the pictures down on the side table, and rested my whisky, half full, beside them. I then stood up to reach for my tobacco. I have often seen Lucy have little accidents like this. Women are inclined to be clumsy, I find, something to do with their physique, probably. In brief, I knocked the table, the whisky glass skidded over it, and upset its contents in four sploshes, one on each of the photographs.

I gave a curse, I regret to say, and set to mopping up with my handkerchief. The pictures seemed no worse for the libation, and so I went downstairs to refill my glass. Having looked in on the hot-pot, I decided to give it another half hour, and came back reluctantly upstairs, meaning to try to find some book I could read – my own volume was finished during the early hours this morning. There was not much doing in this line, but at last I found some essays on prominent men, and this would have to serve. Returning to the fire in haste, I there found that each of the photographs on which the alcohol had spilled was blotched with an erratic burn. I must say, I had no notion malt whisky could inflict such a wound, but there, I am not a photographer.

This annoyed me. Although I have no interest in the photographs particularly, I know my Father would have had one, and for his sake, I would not have desecrated them. I am not a Vandal. I feel foolishly ashamed of myself.

I began to think then about my Father and my Uncle William, of how they had lost touch with each other, and how, oddly, we had never been on a visit to this house. One assumes there had come to be a rift between the two men. There was a marked difference in age. Even so, I recall my Father speaking of my Uncle as the former neared his end. "Poor William," he said. "What could I do?" I had not wanted to press him, his heart was giving out.

Irritated, uneasy and out of sorts, I have pushed the damaged photographs together, and come down again, to eat of Mrs Gold's bounty.

10th September: *10:30 p.m.*
Something very odd. How to put this down . . . Well, I had better be as scientific as I can. I had forgotten my book, and, deciding on an early bed, since I am feeling rather fatigued – the country air, no doubt – I came up to the library to collect the volume. It lay on the table, and going to pick it up, I saw again the spoiled photographs.

While I had been downstairs dining, something had gone on. The stains had changed, rather they had taken on a colour, deep swirls of raw red and sickly yellow. This was particularly unpleasant on the black and white surface of the original scenes. I examined each photograph in turn, and all four were now disfigured in this way. I had already resolved that it was no use crying over spilt milk, or whisky, to be more precise, and was about to put them down again, when something else arrested my attention.

Of course, I am aware that random arrangements or marks can take on apparently coherent forms – the "faces" that one occasionally makes out in the trunks of old trees, for example, or the famous Rorschach inkblot test. Yes, the random may form the seemingly concrete, and mean very little, save in the realms of imagination and psychiatry.

However. However – where the whisky had burned the photographs, a shape had been formed, now very definite, and filled in by rich, bilious colour. Not in fact a shape that I could recognize – yet, yet it was consistent, for in each of the four pictures, it was almost exactly the same. And it was – it is – a horrible shape. Most decidedly that. I do not like it. There is something repulsive, odious, about it. I suppose that is because it is like some sort of *creature* – and yet a creature that can hardly, I would think, exist.

Then, I am being rather silly. I had better describe what I see. What is the matter with me?

There, I have had another whisky – I shall certainly have a thick head in the morning! – and I will write this down with a steady hand.

The thing that the whisky has burnt out in the photographs is, in each one, identical, allowing for certain differences of – what I shall have to call – posture, and size. It has the head of a sort of frog, but this is horned, with two flat horns – or possibly ears – that slant out from its head sideways. The body is bulbous at the front, and it has two arms or forelegs, which end in paws, resembling those of a large cat. The body ends not in legs, but in a tail like that of a slug. This is all bad enough, but in the visage or head are always two red dots, that give the impression of eyes.

It is a beastly thing. I fear I cannot convey how vile, nor what a turn it has given me.

The varying size of the – what shall I call it? – apparition? – is another matter. I can only conclude the whisky fell in a smaller drop here, a larger there. Although that is not what I recollect quite. It seemed to me my drink had spread in roughly equal splashes on each photograph. But there.

In these two, where my Uncle William prunes the tree, the thing is quite small. But here, where he is in conversation with the vicar and the worthies, it is larger. And here, where William is standing with his sons, the thing is at its largest.

It is so curiously placed in this view, that it seems to recline at William's very feet, spacing its paws for balance. In relation to the man and boys, it is the equivalent of a medium-sized dog. I cannot escape the illusion that it has not grown bigger, but – got nearer. That way madness lies.

If there were a telephone here, I would put a call through to Saunders, or Eric Smith, even to Lucy. But there is no telephone. Perhaps, a good thing. What would I say?

I know I am behaving in an irrational and idiotic manner. I must pull myself together.

I have put the photographs back on the table and turned them face down. I shall go up and take a couple of aspirins. Obviously, in months to come, I will reread these entries and laugh at them.

11th September: *11:00 a.m.*
Johnson, the agent, arrived efficiently at ten, and we perfunctorily discussed my plans. I had no hesitation in telling him that I would probably wish to put the house up for sale. I passed a restless

night, mostly lying listening to the grim silence of this place. I would have been glad for the creaking of the boards I had heard on my first night, even for the boisterous owl. But both failed me. Everything seemed locked in the cupboard of the darkness, and now and then, like a child, I sighed or moved about, to make some sound.

I got a little sleep for an hour or so after dawn, and came down bleary-eyed but resolved. I had put myself into a foolish state over those confounded burns on the photographs. Perhaps this is the price for allowing myself to become a middle-aged bachelor. No matter. I am going back to London this evening. Back to traffic and fog and lights, and human company if I wish it. I must take myself in hand. I do not want to become one of those querulous neurasthenic fools one reads of. Good God, I have gone through a World War, and although luck put me out of the way of most of the action, I was ready enough to do my part. Is some childish horror going to undo me now?

As he was leaving, Johnson recommended that I seek out the vicar. "If you want to know anything about your Uncle's tenancy here, that is."

"Oh, yes. A Reverend Dale, I believe."

"That's right. He's getting on, but pretty spry. A wise old bird."

I said that I might not have the time, but thanked Johnson all the same. What, after all, did I want to know? My Grandfather's forays in the East did not interest me, and all the rest seemed decline, disease, and death. Charming points of conversation – besides, the bubbling Mrs Gold had already rejoiced me with enough of all that.

"Incidentally, Johnson," I said, as I saw him to the door, "I suppose there is some use of photography in your business."

"There is," he agreed.

"I wonder if you've ever heard of – alcohol making a burn on a photograph?"

"Well, I never have," he said. He thought deeply. "It might, perhaps. But not anything pure, I wouldn't have thought."

"Whisky," I said.

"From a still, maybe. Not the stuff in a bottle. Why do you ask?"

"Oh, something a friend told me of."

Johnson shrugged and laughed. "A waste of a good beverage," he said.

When he was gone, I made a decision. It was because I had begun to feel angry.

Mrs Gold was not to come today until three, but she had left me another cold plate. This I tried to eat, but did not really fancy it, although I had had no breakfast.

Eventually I took the largest soup tureen I could find from the kitchen, and the whisky decanter, and went up to the library. The quickest way to be rid of my "monster" was to carry out an experiment. It was quite simple. I would place a selection of photographs in the tureen and pour over them enough whisky to cover them entirely. Either nothing would happen to them, or they would burn – burn all over into yellow and red. And that would be that. No random marks, no possible coincidences of shape. No doubt the pictures that I spoiled underwent some flaw in their reproduction, or there was some weakness in the material on which they were printed. I was confident, to the point of belligerence, that by this means I should be free of the horror I had unwittingly unleashed. As for ruining more photographs, if I did so, there comes a point where one must put oneself first.

I set the tureen down on the big table in the library. Outside, the birds were singing. There was a view of the lawn, and the big oaks, golden and crimson in the dying of the leaves. It is a sunny day.

I took three photographs from the box more or less at random, a scene of my Uncle and his son by the little summer house, the two boys playing some game under the trees when they were small. To this selection I added one of the former casualties, the photograph of my Uncle pruning the tree. One thing I had made sure of, the three new scenes were of different dates, and had therefore been processed on other paper.

Dropping the four into the bowl, I poured in a geneerous measure of the whisky. A waste, as Johnson had said.

I have come away to write this, leaving a proper space of time, and now I am going back to look. There will be nothing, I believe, or complete obliteration. I am already beginning to feel I have made an idiot of myself. Perhaps I will tear out these pages.

11th September: *6:00p.m.*
The walk down to the village, just under a mile and a half, took me longer than it should have. I arrived feeling quite done up, and

went into the little pub, which had some quaint name I forget, and had a brandy and soda.

Across the green was the vicarage, a picturesque building of grey stone, and behind it the Norman church, probably of interest to those with an historical concern. When I got to the vicarage door, and knocked, a homely fat woman came and let me in, all smiles, to the vicar's den. It was a nice, masculine place, redolent of pipe smoke, with a big dog lying on the hearth, who wagged his tail at me politely.

The Reverend Dale greeted me, and called for tea, which the fat nymph presently brought with a plate of her own shortbread. This tasted very good, although I am afraid I could eat no more than a bite.

The vicar let me settle myself, and we talked about ordinary things, the autumn, elements of the country round about, and of London. At last, leaning forward, the old man peered at me through his glasses.

"Are you quite well, Mr Martyce?"

"Perfectly. Just a trifle tired. I haven't slept well at the house."

He looked long at me and said, "I'm afraid people often don't."

I took a deep breath. "In what way?" I asked.

"Your family, Mr Martyce, has been inclined to insomnia there. The domestics have never complained. Indeed, I never heard a servant from there that had anything but praise for the house and the family. Mrs Allen, the former cook, retired only when she was seventy-six and could no longer manage. She was loath to go."

"But my family – there has been a deal of illness."

"Yes, I'm afraid that is so. Your Grandfather – he was before my time, of course. And his wife. Your father was long from home, and his brother, Mr William, was sent out into the world at twenty . . . before there was any – problem at the house. The two brothers did not at first choose to come back. And your father, I think, not at all. He lived to a good age?"

"He was nearly eighty. There was quite a gap between him and William – my Grandfather's travels."

"Eighty – yes, that's splendid. But poor William did not do so well. He was, as you know, only sixty-two when he succumbed. His wife was a mere fifty, and your Aunt in her forties. But, in later life, she had never been well."

I tried a laugh. It sounded hollow. "That house doesn't seem very healthy for the Martyces."

Reverend Dale looked grave. "It does not."

"And what explanation do you have for that, sir?"

"I fear that, although I am a man of God, and might be expected to incline to esoteric conclusions, I have none."

I said, flatly, "Do you think there is a malevolent ghost?"

"I am not supposed to believe in ghosts," said the Reverend Dale. "However, I can't quite rid myself of a belief in – *influences*."

A cold tremor passed up my back. I deduce I may have gone pale, for the vicar got up and went over to his cabinet, from which he produced some brandy. A glass of this he gave me – I really must put a stop to all this profligate drinking! I confess I downed it.

"You must understand," he said, "I'm speaking not as a man of the cloth, but simply – as a witness. I've seen very clearly that, in the Martyce family, those who spend much or all of their time at the house, sicken. Some are more susceptible, they fail more swiftly. Some are stronger, and hold at bay or temporarily throw off the malaise, at first. Your Grandfather lived into his nineties, yet from his sixties he had hardly a day without severe illness. Perhaps, in a man of advancing years, that is not uncommon. And yet, before this time, he was one of the fittest men on record, apparently he put the local youth, who are hardy, to shame. Again, some who aren't strong, also linger in a pathetic, sickly state – your Aunt was one of these. She succumbed only in her adult years, but then her life was a burden for her. One wondered how she bore with it. Even she, at length . . . " he sighed. "Her end was a release, I am inclined to think. A satisfactory cause of death meanwhile has never been established. In your Grandfather's case, necessarily it was put down to old age. As with his wife, since she died in her sixties. In the cases of others, death must be questionable. Or unreasonable. As with your Uncle's two sons. They were fourteen and nineteen years."

"I assumed some childish malady –"

"Not at all. Clemens was their doctor, then. I will reveal, he confided in me somewhat. He was baffled. The same symptoms – inertia, low pulse, some vertigo, headache, an inclination not to eat. But no fever, no malignancy, no defect. You will perhaps know, William's health was poor enough to keep him out of the War. He was utterly refused."

I said, briskly, "Well, I'm leaving tonight."

"I am glad to hear that you are."

"But, I had intended to put the house up for sale —"

"I think you need have no qualms, Mr Martyce. Remember, no one who has lived there, who is not a member of your family, has ever been ill. If anything, the reverse."

"A family curse," I said. I meant to sound humorous and ironic. I did not succeed.

The Reverend Dale looked down upon his serviceable desk.

"I shall tell you something, Mr Martyce. You are, evidently, a sensible man. I can't guarantee my words, I'm afraid. The previous incumbent of the parish passed them on to me. But he was vicar in your Grandfather's time. It seems your Grandfather, always a regular churchgoer when at home, asked for an interview. This was about three years after his final return from the East. He was getting on in years, and had recently had a debilitating bout of illness, but recovered, and no one was in any apprehension for him, at that time." The vicar paused.

"Go on," I said.

"Your Grandfather it seems posed a question. He had heard, he said, of a belief among primitive peoples, that when a camera is used to take a photograph, the soul is caught inside the machine."

"I've heard of this," I said. "There is a lack of education among savages."

"Quite. But it appears your Grandfather asked my predecessor — if he thought that such a thing were truly possible."

I sat in silence. I felt cold, and wanted another brandy, but instead I sipped my tepid tea.

"What did he say, your predecessor?"

"Naturally, that he did not credit such an idea."

"To which my Grandfather said what?"

"It seems he wondered if, rather than catch a human soul, a camera might sometimes snare . . . something else. Something not human or corporeal. Some sort of spirit."

Before the eye of my mind, there passed the memory of how my Grandfather had photographed so many exotic things. And of the pictures taken inside the ancient and remarkable tomb. I am not given to fancies. I do not think it *was* a fancy. Like a detective, I strove to solve this puzzle.

I stood up before I had meant to, I did not mean to be rude.

The old man also rose, and the dog. Both looked at me kindly, yes, I would swear, even the dumb animal had an expression of compassion.

"Excuse me," I said, "I have to hurry to be sure of my train."

"You're not returning to the house?" said the Reverend Dale.

"No. It's all locked up. The cleaning lady has been and gone. I promised her she'd be kept on until any new tenants take over. They must make their own arrangements."

"I think you have been very wise," said the vicar.

He himself showed me to the door of the stone house. "It's a lovely afternoon," he said. "You look rather exhausted. That cottage there, with the green door. Peter will drive you to the station. Just give him something towards the petrol."

I shook his hand, and like some callow youth, felt near to tears.

In future I must take more exercise. It is not like me to be so flabby. Thank God, Peter was amenable.

I have written all this down in the train. It has not been easy, with the jolting, and once I leaned back and fell fast asleep. I am better for that. I want to make an end of it here, and so return into London and my life, clear of it.

No, I cannot say I know what has gone on. When I put the four photographs into the tureen and poured in the whisky, I thought myself, frankly, an imbecile.

I had left them for perhaps twenty minutes, possibly a fraction longer. I approached the table with no sense of apprehension. Rather, I felt stupid.

Looking in, I saw at once, but the brain needs sometimes an interim to catch up with the quirkiness of the eye. So I experienced a numbing, ghastly dread, but even so I took out the photographs one by one, and laid them on the newspaper I had left ready.

The original had not altered. That is, the photograph, already damaged, of my Uncle by the tree. It had not changed, nor the mark, the yellow and red mark, that had the shape of a horned creature with forelegs and the hind body of a giant slug. There it still was, quite near to him but yet not close. There it was with its blind red dots of eyes, brilliant on the black and white surface of that simple scene.

The other three images are quickly described, and I should like to be quick. The whisky had affected them all only in one place. And in that place, always a different one, exactly similarly. The demon was there. The same. Absolute.

Where the two boys are playing as children, it is some way off, among the trees. It is coiled there, as if resting, watching them, like a pet cat.

In the photograph of William and his wife and sister – my Aunt – the thing is much nearer, lying in the grass at their feet – again, again, like some awful pet.

But it is the last picture, the most recent picture of my Uncle William's younger son, it is *that* one – They are standing by the summer house. The boy is about thirteen, and the date on the back, that the whisky has blurred, gives evidence that this is so.

They do not look so very unhappy. Only formal, straight and stone still. That is probably the very worst thing. They should be in turmoil – and the boy – the boy should be writhing, flailing, screaming –

The demon is close as can be. It has hold of the boy's leg. *It is climbing up him.* Its tail is coiled about his knee – Oh God, its head is lying on his thigh. The head has tilted. It gazes up at him. It has wrapped him in its grip. He does not – *he does not know.*

I shall write no more now. I do not want to open this diary again. The lights of London will be coming soon, out of the autumn dusk. Smells of smoke, cooking, and unhygenic humanity. Thank God. Thank God I have got away. Thank God. Thank God.

From a letter by Lucy Wright to her friend J.B.:

1st November 195-:
Your letter did cheer me up a bit, though I cried a bit after. Yes, I'd love to come for a visit, and it would help to get my mind off – this. Then, I feel guilty. But what can I do? I was totally in the dark. I didn't know. He never confided in me. I don't understand.

I'd always known Gordon was a bit of an old stick-in-the-mud. But he was kind and hardworking, and I did hope he'd get round to popping the question one day. No one else has made any offers. And of course, he was well-off. Not that that was my main reason. But, well, I've never been rich, and it would be nice, not to worry all the time, where the rent's coming from, or if you can afford a new pair of nylons.

The funny thing was, when he came back from that house of his uncle's in the country (and strangely he wouldn't discuss that at all), he couldn't see enough of me. We were out every night, like a couple of twenty-year-olds. The pictures, concerts, even dinners in a lovely little restaurant up West. And he made a real fuss of me. He even bought me roses. I thought, this is it. He's going to ask me now. And I thought, I can change him, get him to brighten up a bit. But then – well it was a funny thing that happened. It was really silly and – nasty. Peculiar.

It was my birthday – that was the time he gave me the roses – and one of my cousins, Bunty, well she sent me a really lovely present. It was a little camera. What do you expect – I wanted to use it. And one night when Gordon and I were in that nice restaurant, I was showing him the camera, and the manager, who knows Gordon, came up and said, "Let me take a picture of you, Mr Martyce, and your young lady." Well I was a bit giggly – we'd had some lovely wine – and I was all for it, but Gordon got really funny. No, I mean he got he really angry, sort of well – frightened, red in the face – but the manager just laughed, and he took the photograph anyway, with me very nervous and Gordon all hard and angry and scared. The manager said Gordon would have to be less camera-shy, for the wedding.

I thought, Gordon's angry because he feels he's being forced to think about that, about getting married. And he doesn't want to. And that depressed me, because things had seemed to be going so well. So it ended up a miserable evening. And he took me home. And – well. That was the last time I saw him. I mean, the last time I *saw* him. Because I don't count the funeral. How can I? They had to close the coffin. Anyway. He was dead then. I'm sorry. Look, a tear's fallen in the ink. What a silly girl. Crying over a man that didn't even want me.

Of course, I did speak to him just once more, on the telephone. He rang me up about a week after the dinner, and he said he was going to collect the films – the photographs, you see. And I was glad he'd rung me, so I said yes. I was a bit embarrassed, because the rest of the film was all of my family, dad and mum, and Alice and the babies, and it was the first time I'd taken any photographs, and I was sure they'd be bad.

But then I didn't hear again, and the next thing was, the policeman coming round in the afternoon, just as I was trying to get money in that rotten meter that's so stiff. My washing was everywhere – it was Saturday – but he didn't look. He helped me with the meter and then he put me in a chair, and he told me. Gordon had gone out on the Northern Line and – well, you know. He'd fallen under a train. Well they said, he'd thrown himself under. People had seen him do it. But how can I believe that? I mean, Gordon. It must be a mistake. But then, where was he going? He doesn't have any relatives, and no friends out that way. Didn't have. Well.

But I was so glad to get your kind letter. You see, I went round to Gordon's flat this afternoon, they let me, because there were a few things of mine there, a couple of books I tried to get Gordon to read – I don't think he did – and some gloves I'd left, little things – oh, and a casserole dish I'd bought him. It was a nice one. I thought I'd better have it, now.

And on the table in his room, there were the photographs. The police had obviously been there, because things were a bit disturbed, not the way Gordon would have left them. But the odd thing was, these photographs were lying on a newspaper, and they'd stuck to it, so they must have got wet. And – there was a strong smell of whisky, as if he'd spilled some. Maybe he had. He'd been drinking more lately, more than I'd known him do. I remember he said something strange – something about using a spirit to show a spirit. But he was always too clever for me.

Any way, I did look at the photographs, and I wondered if I could take them home, but I wasn't sure, so I didn't, though I can't see that they'll be any help to the police or anyone. Actually, I hadn't done too badly for a beginner. The ones of the babies are really nice, though I'd made Alice look a bit fat, and she wouldn't like that. The last one was the one the manager at the restaurant took of Gordon and me, and it was really a pity. I admit, it made me cry a bit. Because, it would have been nice to have a picture of him and me together, something to remember him by. It wasn't just that we looked really daft – me all grinning and silly, and Gordon so puffed up and upset. No, there was this horrible big red and yellowish mark on the picture – I suppose something went wrong when it was taken, perhaps some light got in, or something, that can happen, can't it?

The funny thing is, I can't explain this, but there was something – something really awful about this mark. It sounds crazy and you'll think I'm a proper dope. You know what an imagination I've got. You see, it looked to me like a funny sort of animal – a sort of snake thing, with hands – and a face. And the oddest part of all, it was in just this place that it looked as if it was sitting square on Gordon's shoulders, with its tail coming down his collar, and its arm-things round his throat, and its face pressed close to his, as if it loved him and would never let go.

STEVE RASNIC TEM

What Slips Away

STEVE RASNIC TEM HAS PUBLISHED HUNDREDS of short stories in such magazines and anthologies as *Fantasy Tales*, *Weirdbook*, *Whispers*, *Twilight Zone*, *Crimewave*, *The Magazine of Fantasy & Science Fiction*, *The Third Alternative*, *New Terrors 1*, *Shadows*, *Cutting Edge*, *Dark at Heart*, *Forbidden Acts*, *MetaHorror*, *Dark Terrors 3*, *Horrors! 365 Scary Stories*, *Bedtime Stories to Darken Your Dreams*, *White of the Moon*, *The Year's Best Fantasy and Horror* and previous volumes of the *Best New Horror*.

His first (and to date, only) novel, *Excavation*, was published in 1987, and he won the 1988 British Fantasy Award for his story "Leaks". A collection entitled *Ombres sur la Route* appeared in France several years ago, and a new collection is forthcoming from Ash-Tree Press.

About the following story, Tem recalls: "I visited Memphis numerous summers as a child, and I found it to be a rather exotic place compared to my native southwest Virginia. The other element generating the story is the years we've spent remodelling and restoring our Victorian home (all sixteen rooms of it). I finished the final area last summer (the attic).

"With each trip to the hardware store/lumber yard I found myself muttering: 'This is the last 2 × 4 I will buy in my lifetime, this is the final section of sheet rock, this is the last bucket of joint compound, etc. etc'."

T WO OF HIS NEIGHBORS have died in as many weeks. Another has lost his mind, or his past, Taylor's not sure which. The fellow at the end of the street electrocuted himself while rebuilding his roof: a raised hammer, a cable shedding black insulation and hung too low. The man's wife says he had no business up there in the first place – he was always doing too much, remodeling the house every few years whether it needed it or not, and besides he had no depth perception.

Walter across the street had been another weekend remodeler. He was putting in a new tub on the second floor, the good-for-nothing son-in-law helping him carry the thing. Walter had a heart attack, but if that hadn't killed him the torturous fall through water-rotted flooring would have. Now the son-in-law lies out on a towel each day beside a blue cooler full of cold ones.

Taylor has never met the fat man who wanders up and down their street in overalls, but he's been told the poor fellow owned the big green Queen Anne – worked at fixing it up most every day of his adult life, and after forty years the bank took it away. A fall down the stairs on moving day and something important must have slipped away, because the fat man no longer knows his own name.

Some days their street smells like a kid's birthday party. Other days it's a dead mule washed up along the Mississippi.

Many nights Taylor wakes up from some bad dream of the past and the fear is so strong in him he can smell it coming out of his pores, a smell like the solvents he uses to strip decades off the woodwork and clean his tools: a rotten soup of ancient tint and discoloration. "It's two a.m. in the Bluff City," the radio tells him, and sometimes it tells him the day and sometimes the year and he decides to take it at its word because right at this moment he has no clue. The bedroom's been torn up for over a year, walls demolished down to studs and the original knob-and-tube wiring, exposing the rusted narrow pipes used to supply the gas lights of the last century, and then it's three a.m. in the Bluff City, then four, and staring out his window – the casement gone, paint flakes working their way under his fingernails – all he can see moving on this street in midtown Memphis is someone else's memories, shadows walking with the power of regret, and "it's a killer out there," the radio reminds him. "The hottest summer in years. Mr J.T. Reynolds of our fair city died of heatstroke this afternoon, trying to put in a new attic exhaust fan, they tell me. Those old houses, well, you just gotta watch your step. Best take it easy, friends."

Taylor looks out over the dark trees to another row of street lamps. J.T. Reynolds had a pretty little house a block away. And that makes four. *What's that smell*? he thinks, his face flushed with damp heat and something else. *What's that smell*?

It's just another one of those things that slips away, he decides, stumbling down steps with no railing, grabbing a beer out of the greasy brown ice box, and so *many* things just slip away. You don't think about them for a time and before you know it they're gone, and will no longer hold in the mind however much you try. You cannot will some things to stay.

Like some smells, he thinks, going out to the porch, stepping around what is missing from the porch, the things he's torn away. Taylor cannot remember the smell of his mother's perfume, although he recalls it as a dramatic fragrance he'd been exposed to, surely, every day of his life from birth until his twenties. He would have been twenty-three, maybe twenty-four, when he'd finally left, only to return here years later to discover that his mother's smell had slipped away from this house, gone into the dark with her lace doilies, flowery dresses, and white bowls full of jelly beans.

Angela's smell, now that was something else. Like lemons, something to do with the lotion she likes so much. And the kids, hair and faces scented like sunlight in sheets, Beth's with a touch of strawberry, Andy's lemony like his mother's. Angela promised to bring them by for a visit – "Not that you'll notice" – but he hasn't laid eyes on them in months, and can count on their remembered smells only to suggest a child's revenant in their darkened rooms.

His kids had hated all the remodeling as much as his ex – no, he wouldn't call her that – Angela had. Beth said she had "visitors" in her room, splinter people with doorknob eyes. Andy just said the shadows were all funny and he hated the holes in his walls. Angela said this was no way for kids to live.

Taylor talked to them about how important a sense of *history* was, how their house had stood when Memphis was an important slave market, and about the underground railroad, and the thousands who had died in the yellow fever epidemics, some in this very neighborhood, how 70,000 lay buried under the shady trees of Elmwood Cemetery.

"*I hate his tree,*" Beth suddenly cried, pointing out the window at the distorted bark of a century-old oak. "He's always making faces at me!"

"You're always telling them the worst things about the past," Angela accused him, the day she took their kids away.

It occurs to him now he might turn the power back on to that part of the house. He completed the new wiring only a few weeks after Angela made her escape – his kids straining to see him through the back window as the taxi sped off. But filling those empty rooms with bright, new light would only make him feel worse.

An aroma of licorice stains the air behind him, coming from that section of the porch he'd took out last week. He found his dad's old cigarette lighter on the exposed ground, nested in a paste of black leaves and rotting rags – the old man must have lost the thing, what?, a good thirty years ago. Taylor should know – his father was so sure he'd stolen it he'd whipped him 'til he bled, the memory of that time stinking of leather, warm piss.

As the memory strides around him, grey porch wood creaking under its prodigious weight, Taylor takes another swig from his Blue Moon Ale, refusing to turn around, to grant that grim-faced recollection the satisfaction of his fear.

"Daddy?" Stupid thing to ask, but he's almost finished the bottle, so what better time to ask a dead man questions?

His father doesn't answer, but that smell of licorice – the old man gnawed it constantly – permeates the muggy air. Suddenly Taylor feels nauseated by it, tosses the rest of the bottle into the weedy lawn.

"I'm going to finish this place," he speaks through the stench. "You didn't get it done, Grandpa didn't get it done. I'm getting it done." His head swims in the heat. A shadow floats across his vision, brown and slightly distorted, as if seen from inside an amber beer bottle. *It's a killer out there.* "Once Angela sees how it turns out, she'll understand better. People are going to read about it in the paper." The house settles around him, groaning in its disordered sleep. *I'll wake you yet,* he thinks. But a house this old should be done with all its settlings, and Taylor sniffs the air with unease. A few remaining wheaty fumes of beer. The irises from next door smelling a little like orange blossoms, sausage and red beans cooking a few doors down the street. The straggly surviving azaleas in his own yard have no smell, although a lot was promised by the showy pink flowers of months back. He has a vague memory that azaleas smelled when he was a kid, smelled like flannel comfort and a lukewarm bath after supper, but now he can't be sure.

"Taylor? That you on those rickety old steps?"

He watches Jack Rayburn stumble out of the weeds crowding the front gate. "They ain't rickety. Rebuilt 'em last month."

"Well, I sure wish you'd trim this monkey jungle back a tad. 'Bout to scratch hell out of me."

"Too much hell to scratch out, Jack. Least in my lifetime."

Jack chuckles and sits down beside him. Taylor didn't want company tonight, but he finds he's glad to see his old friend.

"Here, brought you a Moon Pie." Jack slaps the disk of chocolate-covered cardboard into Taylor's hand. "Got it at the Circle K at Madison and McLean. I think that lady clerk is a man, what you think?"

"I think I wish my daddy'd lived long enough to buy cigarettes there. He might've asked that lady out."

"Well, here's to the sonovabitch!" Jack takes a big bite out of a Moon Pie of his own.

"Jesus, Jack. Ain't it a little hot for that crap? Here, let me get you a beer."

"It's four in the morning, Taylor boy. Having spent a goodly part of this fine evening at Betty Boop's Karaoke Club, I'm disinclined to imbibe further. Sorry you declined to join me, you inimical bastard." Jack wiggles the remaining bit of Moon Pie. "Breakfast time." He chews sloppily, frothing his lips white and brown. "Don't . . . tell . . . me," he says around another bite. "You're working this late?"

"Sometimes when I can't sleep, I think of a way to figure out doing a thing, and I like to start it, right then." He tries to move his head away from Jack's sickly sweet, Moon Pie smell. "Used to drive Angela crazy."

"Unreasonable woman. She and the kids back, yet?"

"No. I haven't heard from her."

"Course not. If she was here, you wouldn't be out on the porch drinking, and thinking up additional ways to torment this ancient southern structure."

"Leave it, Jack. You'll see, it's going be a showplace."

"I used to hear your daddy say that all the time, when we were kids, every time I came over. He'd sit in a broke-down davenport over, there where once-upon-a-time you had a porch, with a beer in one hand and a cigarette in the other, and tell both us kids his big plans for his 'showplace.' Never saw him lift a hammer."

"Tell me you never saw *me* with a tool."

"Oh, you're *way* different from your daddy. Beer in one hand, hammer in the other." Jack finishes his snack. "You know you keep on like this, you'll end up like Bobbie Thompson."

"Wait . . . what's happened to Bobbie?"

"I'm sorry – I thought you knew. Chimney fell on him out in that old shack of his. I kept telling him to hire a mason, but I guess he wanted to save some money and fix the brickwork himself. It was that old and crumbly stuff, should've been torn down a long time ago. This remodeling business – I don't know – I think it's for the birds."

And that's five. It's a killer, friends.

Despite his declared misgivings Jack eventually accepts a beer, and then a couple more. Taylor stops himself after six – the more he drinks the sharper the fragrance of licorice, seasoned by a bitter cigarette smoke slipping out from under the steps.

"Before Daddy died he said this place was starting to look like an Orange Mound crackhouse. Said the whole neighborhood was going that way. He acted like it was my fault."

"Your daddy's idea of beautiful was that velvet portrait of Elvis as bullfighter hanging in The Lamplighter. You should've gotten Angela and the kids out here a long time ago."

"This place has been in the family almost a century and a half – you don't just leave a home like this."

"History's a bitch, Taylor. After all those folks died in the yellow fever epidemics, what did the good citizens of Memphis do? Twenty-five thousand of them left. You're always talking about the importance of history – can't you learn from what they did? You're the one drug me up to Elmwood to see the long mass grave where they buried some of 'em. All those bodies with no names."

"But that's what I mean. I want to make a name for myself. If I restore this house good enough, maybe somebody will remember me."

"History feeds on names, my friend. That's pretty much all that making a name is worth. The past is a damned monster, or at least it can be. Better to have your children remember you, and their children if you're lucky enough to live that long. Jesus Christ, Taylor, you gave up your kids for this goddamn house! You let your future slip away for a past that wasn't all that great to begin with."

The stench of cigarettes burns Taylor's eyes. What other reason does he have to be crying? "I don't know how to explain it any better. The past is just so much bigger a place to live in, you know? It's so big it's hard to think of much else sometimes. Like the Mississippi – you live by it long enough you don't believe you're thinking about it much at all when in fact it waters just about every sensation you have. It's down in your bowels and in your walk – the pull and the flow and just the sheer size of it locks you into its rhythm."

They talk into the new perfumes of morning, another night slipping away almost without Taylor noticing its passage.

Some time around dawn Taylor wakes up to light and air like the inside of a yellow bottle, and although he can sense the heat he cannot feel its presence. Jack lies only a few feet away, stretched out on his back in the weeds. The recollection of week-long summer sleepovers, a smaller but no less ornery Jack refusing the offer of ratty old blankets, hangs a smile on Taylor's stiffened face. "Hey, Jack, come on. We're too old for this shit."

He nudges Jack with his boot. Brownish air drifts through the yard, and now his mouth tastes of stale cigarettes. He wipes his face with a hand sore with morning, attempts to loosen his tongue.

"Come on, Jack. I got beds inside. Things look pretty messed up, but I still got beds."

Licorice and beer, cigarettes and azaleas. Taylor lifts his head and stares around the yard. Fragrance has come back to the azaleas, but was that the way they used to smell? Like garbage and exhaust and lettuce gone to black soup at the back of the refrigerator? Shadows shift across the yard and shift again, and he supposes the sun must be rising awfully fast to create such a dramatic change. Light suddenly knifes his eyes, a crack in his yellow bottle. "Jack? I can't stay out here, Jack."

He rises and goes to his friend, who stares up at him with wide eyes and a nosebleed, his face more yellow than Taylor's morning. "Jack!" His mouth is open but he doesn't say anything. Taylor can see that his friend's gums have been bleeding, and there's a web of bloody vomit on the chin. "Jack," he whispers softly, but his friend is gone into a yellow fever dream. *The past is a monster, Taylor boy.* "Damn, Jack. You're number six," he says, and staggers back. *Something's here*, he thinks, *something vast and old as the river*.

The house reels behind him, and when he turns around he throws his hands up over his face, sure it's going to topple onto him. Windows swim in amber heat. Shingles flutter away like paper. Out of the door a boundless shade like a nicotine stain oozes across the missing boards and down the steps, through the weeds and out the gate, a faint hint of dead fish and stagnant water in its wake.

"It's slipping away, Jack, it's slipping away!" he cries and stumbles after, hands held out like a needy child.

But sometimes it just gets away from you. Sometimes it all just slips away. And chasing the past is like trying to recapture the breath that's just left you, stinking of loss and regret, now floating out beyond the gate, now out on the river, making its own way to the sea.

DENNIS ETCHISON

Inside the Cackle Factory

DENNIS ETCHISON IS A WINNER of both the World Fantasy Award and the British Fantasy Award. His first two short story collections, *The Dark Country* and *Red Dreams*, are currently back in print from EMR Books, and a new (fourth) collection is due from DreamHaven, illustrated by J.K. Potter. He has also recently compiled the art book *Horror of the 20th Century* for Collectors Press, and his Hollywood *noir* novel *Blue Screen* is forthcoming.

About the following story, Etchison explains: "One evening in 1997, my wife Kris and I ran into Peter and Dana Atkins at Dark Delicacies bookstore, a favourite haunt of horror writers in Southern California. The occasion was a street fair sponsored by the local merchants along Burbank's Magnolia Boulevard. At some point Dana and I decided to search out a shop called It's a Wrap, featuring clothes worn only once or twice in movies and TV shows filmed at the studios nearby, much of it with expensive designer labels and offered for re-sale at ridiculously low prices. There were rumours of Armani suits for $150.

"Before we got there, a woman with a clipboard sidled up to us and asked if we would like to attend the screening of a new television pilot. Dana had already spotted It's a Wrap. I needed her advice about the women's clothing inside so that I'd know whether to go back for Kris. 'No, thanks,' I said. 'It pays fifty dollars,' said the woman. That sounded like a painless way to cover the cost of some Oscar-winning threads. We both signed on, and a month later I found myself in a theatre owned by a market research company. The dreary sitcom I saw that day was soon forgotten, and the cash I received was quickly squandered, but certain details remained with me. The two-way mirrors, for example. The hi-tech monitoring equipment I glimpsed on the way out. And the unreadable expressions of the young women who worked at the testing facility. What sort of person, I wondered, takes such a job – and why? Was it only for the salary? Or were there were other, more secret reasons?

"Dana never followed up, and her husband, who is a horror writer, wasn't offered the gig. A pity. I can't guess what story he might have written, but I'm sure it would have been a good one, very different from mine and worth a lot more than fifty bucks. The reasons to be afraid are all around, if you make it your business to look for such things."

U NCLE MILTIE DID NOT LOOK VERY HAPPY. Someone had left a half-smoked cigar on his head, and now the wrapper began to come unglued in the rain. A few seconds more and dark stains dripped over his slick hair, ran down his cheeks and collected in his open mouth, the bits of chewed tobacco clinging like wet sawdust to a beaver's front teeth.

"Time," announced Marty, clicking his stopwatch.

Lisa Anne tried to get his attention from across the room, but it was too late. She saw him note the hour and minute on his clipboard.

"Please pass your papers to the right," he said, "and one of our monitors will pick them up . . ."

On the other side of the glass doors, Sid Caesar was even less amused by the logjam of cigarette butts on his crushed top hat. As the water rose they began to float, one disintegrating filter sloshing over the brim and catching in the knot of his limp string tie.

She forced herself to look away and crossed in front of the chairs to get to Marty, scanning the rows again. There, in the first section: an empty seat with a pair of Ray-Bans balanced on the armrest.

"Sixteen," she whispered into his ear.

"Morning, Lisa." He was about to make his introductory spiel before opening the viewing theater, while the monitors retrieved and sorted the questionnaires. "Thought you took the day off."

"Number Sixteen is missing."

He nodded at the hallway. "Check the men's room."

"I think he's outside," she said, "smoking."

"Then he's late. Send him home."

As she hurried toward the doors, the woman on the end of row four added her own questionnaire to the pile and held them out to Lisa Anne.

"Excuse me," the woman said, "but can I get a drink of water?"

Lisa Anne accepted the stack of stapled pages from her.

"If you'll wait just a moment –"

"But I have to take a pill."

"Down the hall, next to the restrooms."

"Where?"

She handed the forms to one of the other monitors.

"Angie, would you show this lady to the drinking fountain?"

Then she went on to the doors. The hinges squeaked and a stream of water poured down the glass and over the open toes of her new shoes.

Oh great, she thought.

She took the shoes off and stood under the awning while she peered through the blowing rain. The walkway along the front of the AmiDex building was empty.

"Hello?"

Bob Hope ignored her, gazing wryly across the courtyard in the direction of the adjacent apartment complex, while Dick Van Dyke and Mary Tyler Moore leaned so close to each other that their heads almost touched, about to topple off the bronze pedestals. They had not been used for ashtrays yet today, though their nameplates were etched with the faint white tracks of bird droppings. She hoped the rain would wash them clean.

"Are you out here? Mister . . .?"

She had let Angie check them in this morning, so she did not even know Number Sixteen's name. She glanced around the courtyard, saw no movement and was about to go back inside, when she noticed someone in the parking lot.

It was a man wearing a wet trenchcoat.

So Number Sixteen had lost patience and decided to split. He did not seem to be looking for his car, however, but walked rapidly between the rows on his way to – what? The apartments beyond, apparently. Yet there was no gate in this side of the wrought-iron fence.

As she watched, another man appeared as if from nowhere. He had on a yellow raincoat and a plastic-covered hat, the kind worn by policeman or security guards. As far as she knew the parking lot was unattended. She could not imagine where had he come from, unless there was an opening in the fence, after all, and the guard had come through from the other side. He stepped out to block the way. She tried to hear what they were saying but it was impossible from this distance. There was a brief confrontation, with both men gesturing broadly, until the one in the trenchcoat gave up and walked away.

Lisa Anne shook the water out of her shoes, put them on and turned back to the glass doors.

Marty was already into his speech. She had not worked here long enough to have it memorized, but she knew he was about to mention the cash they would receive after the screening and discussion. Some of them may have been lured here by the glamor, the chance to attend a sneak preview of next season's programs, but without the promise of money there was no way to be sure anyone would show up.

The door opened a few inches and Angie stuck her head out.

"Will you get *in* here, girl?"

"Coming," said Lisa Anne.

She looked around one more time.

Now she saw a puff of smoke a few yards down, at the entrance to Public Relations.

"Is anybody there?" she called.

An eyeball showed itself at the side of the building.

Maybe this is the real Number Sixteen, she thought. Trying to get in that last nicotine fix.

"I'm sorry, but you'll have to come in now . . ."

She waited to see where his cigarette butt would fall. The statues were waiting, too. As he came toward her his hands were empty. What did he do, she wondered, eat it?

She recognized him. He had been inside, drinking coffee with the others. He was a few years older than Lisa Anne, late twenties or early thirties, good-looking in a rugged, unkempt way, with his hair tied back in a ponytail and a drooping moustache, flannel shirt, tight jeans and steel-toed boots. A construction worker, she thought, a carpenter, some sort of manual labor. Why bother to test him? He probably watched football games and not much else, if he watched TV at all.

As he got closer she smelled something sweet and pungent. The unmistakable odor of marijuana lingered in his clothes. So that's what he was up to, she thought. A little attitude adjustment. I could use some of that myself right about now.

She held out her hand to invite him in from the rain, and felt her hair collapse into wet strings over her ears. She pushed it back self-consciously.

"You don't want to miss the screening," she said, forcing a smile, "do you?"

"What's it about?" he asked.

"I don't know. Honest. They don't tell me anything."

The door swung open again and Angie rolled her eyes.

"Okay, okay," said Lisa Anne.

"He can sign up for the two o'clock, if he wants."

Number Sixteen shook his head. "No way. I gotta be at work."

"It's all right, Angie."

"But he missed the audience prep . . ."

Lisa Anne looked past her. Marty was about finished. The test subjects were already shifting impatiently, bored housewives and tourists and retirees with nothing better to do, recruited from sidewalks and shopping malls and the lines in front of movie theaters, all of them here to view the pilot for a new series that would either make it to the network schedule or be sent back for retooling, based on their responses. There was a full house for this session.

Number Sixteen had not heard the instructions, so she had no choice. She was supposed to send him home.

But if the research was to mean anything, wasn't it important that every demographic be represented? The fate of the producers and writers who had labored for months or even years to get their shows this far hung in the balance, to be decided by a theoretical cross-section of the viewing public. Not everyone liked sitcoms about young urban professionals and their wacky misadventures at the office. They can't, she thought. I don't. But who ever asked me?

"Look," said Number Sixteen, "I drove a long ways to get here. You gotta at least pay me."

"He's late," said Angie. She ignored him, speaking as though he were not there. "He hasn't even filled out his questionnaire."

"Yes, he has," said Lisa Anne and ushered him inside.

The subjects were on their feet now, shuffling into the screening room. Lisa Anne went to the check-in table.

"Did you get Number Sixteen's?" she asked.

The monitors had the forms laid out according to rows and were about to insert the piles into manila envelopes before taking them down the hall.

Marty came up behind her. "Which row, Miss Rayme?" he said officiously.

"Four, I think."

"You think?" Marty looked at the man in the plaid shirt and wrinkled his nose, as if someone in the room had just broken wind. "If his form's not here –"

"I know where it is," Lisa Anne told him and slipped behind the table.

She flipped through the pile for row four, allowing several of the questionnaires to slide onto the floor. When she knelt to pick them up, she pulled a blank one from the carton.

"Here." She stood, took a pencil and jotted 16 in the upper right-hand corner. "He forgot to put his number on it."

"We're running late, Lees . . ." Marty whispered.

She slid the forms into an envelope. "Then I'd better get these to the War Room."

On the way down the hall, she opened the envelope and withdrew the blank form, checking off random answers to the multiple-choice quiz on the first page. It was pointless, anyway, most of it a meaningless query into personal habits and lifestyle, only a smokescreen for the important questions about income and product preferences that came later. She dropped off her envelope along with the other monitors, and a humorless assistant in a short-sleeved white shirt and rimless glasses carried the envelopes from the counter to an inner room, where each form would be tallied and matched to the numbered seats in the viewing theater. On her way back, Marty intercepted her.

"Break time," he said.

"No, thanks." She drew him to one side, next to the drinking fountain. "I got one for you. S.H.A.M."

"M.A.S.H," he said immediately

"Okay, try this. *Finders*."

He pondered for a second. "*Friends?*"

"You're good," she said.

"No, I'm not. You're easy. Well, time to do my thing."

At the other end of the hall, the reception room was empty and the doors to the viewing theater were already closed.

"Which thing is that?" she said playfully.

"That thing I do, before they fall asleep."

"Ooh, can I watch?"

She propped her back against the wall and waited for him to move in, to pin her there until she could not get away unless she dropped to her knees and crawled between his legs.

"Not today, Lisa."

"How come?"

"This one sucks. Big time."

"What's the title?"

"I don't know."

"Then how do you know it sucks?"

"Hey, it's not my fault, okay?"

For some reason he had become evasive, defensive. His face was now a smooth mask, the skin pulled back tautly, the only prominent features his teeth and nervous, shining eyes. Like a shark's face, she thought. A residue of deodorant soap rose to the surface of his skin and vaporized, expanding outward on waves of body heat. She drew a breath and knew that she needed to be somewhere else, away from him.

"Sorry," she said.

He avoided her eyes and ducked into the men's room.

What did I say? she wondered, and went on to the reception area.

A list of subjects for the next session was already laid out on the table, ninety minutes early. The other monitors were killing time in the chairs, chatting over coffee and snacks from the machines.

Lisa Anne barely knew them. This was only her second week and she was not yet a part of their circle. One had been an editorial assistant at the *L.A. Weekly*, two were junior college students, and the others had answered the same classified ad she had seen in the trades. She considered crashing the conversation. It would be a chance to rest her feet and dry out. The soggy new shoes still pinched her toes and the suit she'd had to buy for the job was damp and steamy and scratched her skin like a hair shirt. She felt ridiculous in this uniform, but it was necessary to show people like Marty that she could play by their rules, at least until she got what she needed. At home she would probably be working on yet another sculpture this morning, trying to get the face right, with a gob of clay in one hand and a joint in the other and the stereo cranked up to the max. But living that way hadn't gotten her any closer to the truth. She couldn't put it off any longer. There were some things she had to find out or she would go mad.

She smiled at the monitors.

Except for Angie they barely acknowledged her, continuing their conversation as though she were not there.

They know, she thought. They must.

How much longer till Marty saw through her game? She had him on her side, but the tease would play out soon enough unless she let it go further, and she couldn't bear the thought of that. She only needed him long enough to find the answer, and then she would walk away.

She went to the glass doors.

The rain had stopped and soon the next group would begin gathering outside. The busts of the television stars in the court-yard were ready, Red Buttons and George Gobel and Steve Allen and Lucille Ball with her eyebrows arched in perpetual wonderment, waiting to meet their fans. It was all that was left for them now.

Angie came up next to her.

"Hey, girl."

"Hey yourself."

"The lumberjack. He a friend of yours?"

"Number Sixteen?"

"The one with the buns."

"I never saw him before."

"Oh." Angie took a bite of an oatmeal cookie and brushed the crumbs daintily from her mouth. "Nice."

"I suppose. If you like that sort of thing."

"Here." She offered Lisa Anne the napkin. "You look like you're melting."

She took it and wiped the back of her neck, then squeezed out the ends of her hair, as a burst of laughter came from the theater.

That meant Marty had already gone in through the side entrance to warm them up.

"Excuse me," she said. "It's showtime."

Angie followed her to the hall. "You never miss one, do you?"

"Not yet."

"Aren't they boring? I mean, it's not like they're hits or anything."

"Most of them are pretty lame," Lisa Anne admitted.

"So why watch?"

"I have to find out."

"Don't tell me. What Marty's really like?"

"Please."

"Then why?"

"I've got to know why some shows make it," she said, "and some don't."

"Oh, you want to get into the biz?"

"No. But I used to know someone who was. See you."

I shouldn't have said that, she thought as she opened the unmarked door in the hall.

The observation booth was dark and narrow with a half-dozen padded chairs facing a two-way mirror. On the other side of the mirror, the test subjects sat in rows of theater seats under several 36-inch television sets suspended from the ceiling.

She took the second chair from the end.

In the viewing theater, Marty was explaining how to use the dials wired into the armrests. They were calibrated from zero to ten with a plastic knob in the center. During the screening the subjects were to rotate the knobs, indicating how much they liked what they saw. Their responses would be recorded and the results then analyzed to help the networks decide whether the show was ready for broadcast.

Lisa Anne watched Marty as he paced, doing his schtick. He had told her that he once worked at a comedy traffic school, and she could see why. He had them in the palm of his hand. Their eyes followed his every move, like hypnotized chickens waiting to be fed. His routine was corny but with just the right touch of hipness to make them feel like insiders. He concluded by reminding them of the fifty dollars cash they would receive after the screening and the discussion. Then, when the lights went down and the tape began to roll, Marty stepped to the back and slipped into the hall. As he entered the observation booth, the audience was applauding.

"Good group this time," he said, dropping into the chair next to hers.

"You always know just what to say."

"I do, don't I?" he said, leaning forward to turn on a tiny 12-inch set below the mirror.

She saw their faces flicker in the blue glow of the cathode ray tubes while the opening titles came up.

The show was something called *Dario, You So Crazy*! She sighed and sat back, studying their expressions while keeping one eye on the TV screen. It wouldn't be long before she felt his hand on her forearm as he moved in, telling her what he really thought of the audience, how stupid they were, every last one, down to the little old ladies and the kindly grandfathers and the working men and women who were no more or less ordinary than he was under his Perry Ellis suit and silk tie. Then his breath in her hair and his fingers scraping her pantyhose as if tapping out a message on her knee and perhaps today, this time, he would attempt to deliver that message, while she offered breathless quips to let him know how clever he was and how lucky she felt to be here. She shuddered and turned her cheek to him in the dark.

"Who's that actor?" she said.

"Some Italian guy. I saw him in a movie. He's not so bad, if he could learn to talk English."

She recognized the co-star. It was Rowan Atkinson, the slight, bumbling everyman from that British TV series on PBS.

"Mr Bean!" she said.

"Roberto Benigni," Marty corrected, reading from the credits.

"I mean the other one. This is going to be good . . ."

"I thought you were on your break," said Marty.

"This is more important."

He stared at her transparent reflection in the two-way mirror.

"You were going to take the day off."

"No, I wasn't."

The pilot was a comedy about an eccentric Italian film director who had come to America in search of fame and fortune. Mr Bean played his shy, inept manager. They shared an expensive rented villa in the Hollywood Hills. Just now they were desperate to locate an actress to pose as Dario's wife, so that he could obtain a green card and find work before they both ran out of money.

She immediately grasped the premise and its potential.

It was inspired. Benigno's abuse of the language would generate countless hilarious misunderstandings; coupled with his manager's charming incompetence, the result might be a television classic, thanks in no small measure to the brilliant casting. How could it miss? All they needed was a good script. She realized that her mind had drifted long enough to miss the screenwriter's name. The only credit left was the show's creator/producer, one Barry E. Tormé. Probably the son of that old singer, she thought. What was his name? Mel. Apparently he had fathered a show-business dynasty. The other son, Tracy, was a successful TV writer; he had even created a science-fiction series at Fox that lasted for a couple of seasons. Why had she never heard of brother Barry? He was obviously a pro.

She sat forward, fascinated to see the first episode.

"*Me, Dario!*" Benigni crowed into a gold-trimmed telephone, the third time it had rung in less than a minute. It was going to be his signature bit.

"*O, I Dream!*" she said.

"Huh?"

"The line, Marty. Got you."

The letters rearranged themselves automatically in her mind. It was child's play. She had almost expected him to come up with it first. They had kept the game going since her first day at AmiDex, when she pointed out that his full name was an anagram for *Marty licks on me*. It got his attention.

"You can stop with the word shit," he said.

He sounded irritated, which surprised her. "I thought you liked it."

"What's up with that, anyway?"

"It's a reflex," she said. "I can't help it. My father taught me when I was little."

"Well, it's getting old."

She turned to his profile in the semidarkness, his pale, clean-shaven face and short, neat hair as two-dimensional as a cartoon cutout from the back of a cereal box.

"You know, Marty, I was thinking. Could you show me the War Room sometime?" She moved her leg closer to his. "Just you and me, when everybody's gone. So I could see how it works."

"How what works?"

She let her hand brush his knee. "Everything. The really big secrets."

"Such as?"

"I don't know." Had she said too much? "But if I'm going to work here, I should know more about the company. What makes a hit, for example. Maybe you could tell me. You explain things so well."

"Why *did* you come here?"

The question caught her offguard. "I needed a job."

"Plenty of jobs out there," he snapped. "What is it, you got a script to sell?"

The room was cold and her feet were numb. Now she wanted to be out of here. The other chairs were dim, bulky shapes, like half-reclining corpses, as if she and Marty were not alone in the room.

"Sorry," she said.

"I told you to stay home today."

No, he hadn't. "You *want* me to take the day off?"

He did not answer.

"Do you think I need it? Or is there something special about today?"

The door in the back of the room opened. It connected to the hall that led to the other sections of the building and the War Room itself, where even now the audience response was being recorded and analyzed by a team of market researchers. A hulking figure stood there in silhouette. She could not see his features. He hesitated for a moment, then came all the way in, plunging the room into darkness again, and then there were only the test subjects and their flickering faces opposite her through the smoked glass. The man took a seat at the other end of the row.

"That you, Mickleson?"

At the sound of his voice Marty sat up straight.

"Yes, sir."

"I thought so. Who's she?"

"One of the girls – Annalise. She was just leaving."

Then Marty leaned close to her and whispered:

"*Will you get out?*"

She was not supposed to be here. The shape at the end of the row must have been the big boss. Marty had known he was coming; that was why he wanted her gone. This was the first time anyone had joined them in the booth. It meant the show was important. The executives listened up when a hit came along.

"Excuse me," she said, and left the observation booth.

She wanted very much to see the rest of the show. Now she would have to wait till it hit the airwaves. Was there a way for her to eavesdrop on the discussion later, after the screening?

In the hall, she listened for the audience reaction. Just now there must have been a lull in the action, with blank tape inserted to represent a commercial break, because there was dead silence from the theater.

She was all the way to the reception area before she realized what he had called her.

Annalise.

It was an anagram for Lisa Anne, the name she had put on her application – and, incredibly, it was the right one. Somehow he had hit it. Had he done so naturally, without thinking, as in their word games? Or did he know?

Busted, she thought.

She crossed to the glass doors, ready to make her break.

Then she thought, So he knows my first name. So what? It's not like it would mean anything to him, even if he were to figure out the rest of it.

She decided that she had been paranoid to use a pseudonym in the first place. If she had told the truth, would anybody care? Technically AmiDex could disqualify her, but the family connection was so many years ago that the name had probably been forgotten by now. In fact she was sure it had. That was the point. That was why she was here.

Outside, the rain had let up. A few of the next hour's subjects were already wandering this way across the courtyard. Only one, a woman with a shopping bag and a multi-colored scarf over her hair, bothered to raise her head to look at the statues.

It was disturbing to see the greats treated with such disrespect.

All day long volunteers gathered outside at the appointed hour, smoking and drinking sodas and eating food they had brought with them, and when they went in they left the remains scattered among the statues, as if the history of the medium and its stars meant nothing to them. Dinah Shore and Carol Burnett and Red Skelton with his clown nose, all nothing more than a part of the landscape now, like the lampposts, like the trash cans that no one used. The sun fell on them, and the winds and the rains and the graffiti and the discarded wads of chewing gum and the pissing of dogs on the place where their feet should have been, and there was nothing for any of them to do but suffer these things with quiet dignity, like the fallen dead in a veterans' cemetery. One day the burdens of their immortality, the birdshit and the cigarette butts and the McDonald's wrappers, might become too much for them to bear and the ground would shake as giants walked the earth again, but for now they could only wait, because that day was not yet here.

"How was it?" said Angie.

"The show? Oh, it was great. Really."

"Then why aren't you in there?"

"It's too cold." She hugged her sides. "When does the grounds crew get here?"

"Uh, you lost me."

"Maintenance. The gardeners. How often do they come?"

"You're putting me on, right?"

She felt her face flush. "Then I'll do it."

"Do –?"

"Clean up. It's a disgrace. Don't you think so?"

"Sure, Lisa. Anything you say . . ."

She started outside, and got only a few paces when the sirens began. She counted four squad cars with the name of a private security company stenciled on the doors. They screeched to a halt in the parking lot and several officers jumped out. Did one of them really have his gun drawn?

"Oh, God," said Angie.

"What's going on?"

"It's the complex. They don't like people taking pictures."

Now she saw that the man in the dark trenchcoat had returned. This time he had brought a van with a remote broadcasting dish on top. The guards held him against the side, under the call letters for a local TV station and the words EYEBALL NEWS. When a cameraman climbed down from the back to object they handcuffed him.

"Who doesn't like it?"

"AmiDex," Angie said solemnly. "They own it all." She waved her hand to include the building, the courtyard, the parking lot and the fenced-in apartments. "Somebody from *Hard Copy* tried to shoot here last month. They confiscated the film. It's off-limits."

"But why?"

"All I know is, there must be some very important people in those condos."

"In *this* neighborhood?"

She couldn't imagine why any VIP's would want to live here. The complex was a lower-middle-class housing development, walled in and protected from the deteriorating streets nearby. It had probably been on this corner since the fifties. She could understand AmiDex buying real estate in the San Fernando Valley instead of the overpriced Westside, but why the aging apartments? The only reason might be so that they could expand their testing facility one day. Meanwhile, why not tear them down? With its spiked iron fences the complex looked like a fortress sealed off against the outside world. There was even barbed wire on top of the walls.

Before she could ask any more questions, the doors to the theater opened. She glanced back and saw Marty leading the audience down the hall for the post-screening discussion.

She followed, eager to hear the verdict.

The boys in the white shirts were no longer at the counter. They were in the War Room, marking up long rolls of paper like doctors charting the vital signs in an intensive care ward. Lights blinked across a bank of electronic equipment, as many rack-mounted modules as there were seats in the theater, with dials and connecting cables that fed into the central computer. She heard circuits humming and the ratcheting whir of a wide-mouthed machine as it disgorged graphs that resembled polygraph tests printed in blood-red ink.

She came to the next section of the hall, as the last head vanished through a doorway around the first turn.

The discussion room was small and bright with rows of desks and acoustic tiles in the ceiling. It reminded her of the classrooms at UCLA, where she had taken a course in Media Studies, before discovering that they didn't have any answers, either. She merged with the group and slumped down in the back row, behind the tallest person she could find.

Marty remained on his feet, pacing.

"Now," he said, "it's your turn. Hollywood is listening! How many of you would rate –" He consulted his clipboard. "– *Dario, You So Crazy!* as one of the best programs you've ever seen?"

She waited for the hands to go up. She could not see any from here. The tall man blocked her view and if she moved her head Marty might spot her.

"Okay. How many would say 'very good'?"

There must not have been many because he went right on to the next question.

" 'Fair'?"

She closed her eyes and listened to the rustle of coat sleeves and wondered if she had heard the question correctly.

"And how many 'poor'?"

That had to be everyone else. Even the tall man in front of her raised his arm. She recognized his plaid shirt. It was Number Sixteen.

Marty made a notation.

"Okay, great. What was your favorite scene?"

The silence was deafening.

"You won't be graded on this! There's no right or wrong answer. I remember once, when my junior-high English teacher . . ."

He launched into a story to loosen them up. It was about a divorced woman, an escaped sex maniac and a telephone call to the police. She recognized it as a very old dirty joke. Astonishingly he left off the punchline. The audience responded anyway. He had his timing down pat. Or was it that they laughed *because* they knew what was coming? Did that make it even funnier?

The less original the material, she thought, the more they like it. It makes them feel comfortable.

And if that's true, so is the reverse.

She noticed that there was a two-way mirror in this room, too, along the far wall. Was anyone following the discussion from the other side? If so, there wasn't much to hear. Nobody except Marty had anything to say. They were bored stiff, waiting for their money. It would take something more than the show they had just seen to hold them, maybe *Wrestling's Biggest Bleeps, Bloopers and Bodyslams* or *America's Zaniest Surveillance*

Tapes. Now she heard a door slam in the hall. The executives had probably given up and left the observation room.

"What is the matter with you people?"

The woman with the multi-colored scarf hunched around to look at her, as Marty tried to see who had spoken.

"In the back row. Number . . ."

"You're right," she said too loudly. "It's not poor, or fair, or excellent. It's a *great* show! Better than anything I've seen in years. Since –"

"Yes?" Marty changed his position, zeroing in on her voice. "Would you mind speaking up? This is your chance to be heard . . ."

"Since *The Fuzzy Family*. Or *The Funnyboner*." She couldn't help mentioning the titles. Her mouth was open now and the truth was coming out and there was no way to stop it.

Marty said, "What network were they on?"

"CBS. They were canceled in the first season."

"But you remember them?"

"They were brilliant."

"Can you tell us why?"

"Because of my father. He created them both."

Marty came to the end of the aisle and finally saw her. His face fell. In the silence she heard other voices, arguing in the hall. She hoped it was not the people who had made *Dario, You So Crazy!* If so, they had to be hurting right now. She felt for them, bitterness and despair and rage welling up in her own throat.

"May I see you outside?" he said.

"No, you may not."

The hell with Marty, AmiDex and her job here. There was no secret as to why some shows made it and other, better ones did not. Darwin was wrong. He hadn't figured on the networks. They had continued to lower their sights until the audience devolved right along with them, so that any ray of hope was snuffed out, overshadowed by the crap around it. And market research and the ratings system held onto their positions by telling them what they wanted to hear, that the low-rent talent they had under contract was good enough, by testing the wrong people for the wrong reasons, people who were too numb to care about a pearl among the pebbles. It was a perfect, closed loop.

"*Now*, Miss Rayme."

"That isn't my name." Didn't he get it yet? "My father was Robert Mayer. The man who wrote and produced *Wagons, Ho!*"

It was TV's first western comedy and it made television history. After that he struggled to come up with another hit, but every new show was either canceled or rejected outright. His name meant nothing to the bean-counters. All they could see was the bottom line. As far as they were concerned he owed them a fortune for the failures they had bankrolled. If he had been an entertainer who ran up a debt in Vegas, he would have had to stay there, working it off at the rate of two shows a night, forever. The only thing that gave her satisfaction was the knowledge that they would never collect. One day when she was ten he had a massive heart attack on the set and was whisked away in a blue ambulance and he never came home again.

"Folks, thanks for your time," Marty said. "If you'll return to the lobby . . ."

She had studied his notes and scripts, trying to understand why he failed. She loved them all. They were genuinely funny, the very essence of her father, with his quirky sense of humor and extravagant sight gags – as original and inventive as *Dario, You So Crazy!* Which was a failure, too. Of course. She lowered her head onto the desktop and began to weep.

"Hold up," said Number Sixteen.

"Your pay's ready. Fifty dollars cash." Marty held the door wide. "There's another group coming in . . ."

The lumberjack refused to stand. "Let her talk. I remember *Wagons, Ho!* It was all right."

He turned around in his seat and gave her a wink as she raised her head.

"Thank you," she said softly. "It doesn't matter, now."

She got to her feet with the others and pushed her way out.

Farther down the hall, another door clicked shut. It was marked Green Room. She guessed that the executives from the other side of the mirror had decided to finish their argument in private.

Marty grabbed her elbow.

"I told you to stay home."

"You're hurting me," she said.

"But you just wouldn't take the hint, would you?"

"About what?"

"You can pick up your check in Payroll."

"Get your hands off me."

Number Sixteen came up next to her. "You got a problem here?"

"Not anymore," she said.

"Your pay's up front, cowboy," Marty told him.

"You sure you're okay?" asked Number Sixteen.

"I am now."

Marty shook his head sadly.

"I'll tell them to make it for the full two weeks. I liked you, you know? I really did."

Then he turned and walked the audience back to the lobby.

Farther down the hall, she saw Human Resources, where she had gone the first day for her interview, and beyond that Public Relations and Payroll. She didn't care about her check but there was a security door at the end. It would let her out directly into the courtyard.

Number Sixteen followed her.

"I was thinking. If you want some lunch, I've got my car."

"So do I," she said, walking faster.

Then she thought, Why not? Me, with a lumberjack. I'll be watching Martha Stewart while he hammers his wood and lays his pipe or whatever he does all day, and he'll come home and watch hockey games and I'll stay loaded and sit up every night to see *Wagons, Ho!* on the Nostalgia Channel and we'll go on that way, like a sitcom. He'll take care of me. And in time I'll forget everything. All I have to do is say yes.

He was about to turn back.

"Okay," she said.

"What?"

"This way. There's an exit to the parking lot, down here."

Before they could get to it the steel door at the end swung open.

The rain had stopped and a burst of clear light from outside reflected off the polished floor, distorting the silhouette of the figure standing there. A tall woman in a designer suit entered from the grounds. Behind her, the last of the private security cars drove off. The Eyeball News truck was gone.

"All set," the woman said into a flip-phone, and went briskly to the door marked Green Room.

Voices came from within, rising to an emotional pitch. Then the voices receded as the door clicked shut.

There was something in the tone of the argument that got to her. She couldn't make out the words but one of the voices was close to pleading. It was painful to hear. She thought of her father and the desperate meetings he must have had, years ago. When the door whispered open again, two men in grey suits stepped out into the hall, holding a third man between them.

It had to be the producer of the pilot.

She wanted to go to him and take his hands and look into his eyes and tell him that they were wrong. He was too talented to listen to them. What did they know? There were other networks, cable, foreign markets, features, if only he could break free of them and move on. He had to. She would be waiting and so would millions of others, an invisible audience whose opinions were never counted, as if they did not exist, but who were out there, she was sure. The ones who remembered *Wagons, Ho*! and *The Funnyboner* and *The Fuzzy Family* and would faithfully tune in other programs with the same quirky sensibility, if they had the choice.

He looked exhausted. The suits had him in their grip, supporting his weight between them, as if carrying a drunk to a waiting cab. What was his name? Terry Something. Or Barry. That was it. She saw him go limp. He had the body of a middle-aged man.

"Please," he said in a cracking voice, "this is the one, you'll see. *Please* . . ."

"Mr Tormé?" she called out, remembering his name.

The letters shuffled like a deck of cards in her mind and settled into a new pattern. It was a reflex she could not control, ever since she had learned the game from her father so many years ago, before the day they took him away and told his family that he was dead.

Barry E. Tormé, she thought.

You could spell a lot of words with those letters.

Even . . .

Robert Mayer.

He turned slightly, and she saw the familiar nose and chin she had tried so many times to reproduce, working from fading photographs and the shadow pictures in her mind. The two men continued to drag him forward. His shoes left long black skidmarks on the polished floor. Then they lifted him off his feet and he was lost in the light.

Outside the door, a blue van was waiting.

They dumped him in and locked the tailgate. Beyond the parking lot lay the walled compound, where the razor wire gleamed like hungry teeth atop the barricades and forgotten people lived out lives as bleak as unsold pilots and there was no way out for any of them until the cameras rolled again on another hit.

Milton Berle and Johnny Carson and Jackie Gleason watched mutely, stars who had become famous by speaking the words put into their mouths by others, by men who had no monuments to honor them, not here or anywhere else.

Now she knew now the real reason she had come to this place. There was something missing. When she finished her sculpture there would be a new face for the courtyard, one who deserved a statue of his own. And this time she would get it right.

The steel door began to close.

Sorry, Daddy! she thought as the rain started again outside. I'm sorry, sorry . . .

"Wait." Number Sixteen put on his Ray-Bans. "I gotta get my pay first. You want to come with me?"

Yes, we could do that. Simple. All we do is turn and run the other way, like Lucy and Desi, like Dario and Mr Bean, bumbling along to a private hell of our own. What's the difference?

"No," she said.

"I thought –"

"I'm sorry. I can't."

"Why not?"

"I just . . . can't."

She ran instead toward the light at the end, hoping to see the face in the van clearly one last time as it drove away, before the men in the suits could stop her.

KELLY LINK

The Specialist's Hat

KELLY LINK LIVES IN Somerville, Massachusetts. She has worked in bookstores, libraries and as a babysitter. She once won a trip around the world by answering "because you can't go through it" to the question, "Why do you want to go around the world".

Her short fiction has appeared in *Asimov's Century* and, more recently, in *Fence* and online on *Event Horizon*. She won the James Tiptree Award in 1997 for her story "Travels with the Snow Queen", which also happens to be the title of her collection from Edgewood Press.

"This story comes from three places," explains the author. "A friend of my father's was describing a house that he had lived in as a child, where he rode his bicycle upstairs, in the enormous attic. In Raleigh, North Carolina, at an outdoor folklore exhibit, I read a piece of oral history about snake whisky. Finally, in the Peabody Museum in Boston, I found the chant for the Specialist's Hat, although the hat, of course, was missing."

"WHEN YOU'RE DEAD," Samantha says, "you don't have to brush your teeth."

"When you're Dead," Claire says, "you live in a box, and it's always dark, but you're not ever afraid."

Claire and Samantha are identical twins. Their combined age is twenty years, four months, and six days. Claire is better at being Dead than Samantha.

The baby-sitter yawns, covering up her mouth with a long white hand. "I said to brush your teeth and that it's time for *bed*," she says. She sits crosslegged on the flowered bedspread between them. She has been teaching them a card game called Pounce, which involves three decks of cards, one for each of them. Samantha's deck is missing the Jack of Spades and the Two of Hearts, and Claire keeps on cheating. The babysitter wins anyway. There are still flecks of dried shaving cream and toilet paper on her arms. It is hard to tell how old she is – at first they thought she must be a grownup, but now she hardly looks older than them. Samantha has forgotten the baby-sitter's name.

Claire's face is stubborn. "When you're Dead," she says, "you stay up all night long."

"When you're dead," the babysitter snaps, "it's always very cold and damp, and you have to be very, very quiet or else the Specialist will get you."

"This house is haunted," Claire says.

"I know it is," the babysitter says. "I used to live here."

> Something is creeping up the stairs,
> Something is standing outside the door,
> Something is sobbing, sobbing in the dark;
> Something is sighing across the floor.

Claire and Samantha are spending the summer with their father, in the house called Eight Chimneys. Their mother is dead. She has been dead for exactly 282 days.

Their father is writing a history of Eight Chimneys, and of the poet, Charles Cheatham Rash, who lived here at the turn of the century, and who ran away to sea when he was thirteen, and returned when he was thirty-eight. He married, fathered a child, wrote three volumes of bad, obscure poetry, and an even worse and more obscure novel, *The One Who is Watching Me Through the Window*, before disappearing again in 1907, this time for good. Samantha and Claire's father says that some of the poetry is actually quite readable, and at least the novel isn't very long.

When Samantha asked him why he was writing about Rash, he replied that no one else had, and why didn't she and Samantha go play outside. When she pointed out that she was Samantha, he just scowled and said how could he be expected to tell them apart when they both wore blue jeans and flannel shirts, and why couldn't one of them dress all in green and the other pink?

Claire and Samantha prefer to play inside. Eight Chimneys is as big as a castle, but dustier and darker than Samantha imagines a castle would be. The house is open to the public, and during the day, people – families – driving along the Blue Ridge Parkway will stop to tour the grounds and the first story; the third story belongs to Claire and Samantha. Sometimes they play explorers, and sometimes they follow the caretaker as he gives tours to visitors. After a few weeks, they have memorized his lecture, and they mouth it along with him. They help him sell postcards and copies of Rash's poetry to the tourist families who come into the little gift shop.

When the mothers smile at them, and say how sweet they are, they stare back and don't say anything at all. The dim light in the house makes the mothers look pale and flickery and tired. They leave Eight Chimneys, mothers and families, looking not quite as real as they did before they paid their admissions, and of course Claire and Samantha will never see them again, so maybe they aren't real. Better to stay inside the house, they want to tell the families, and if you must leave, then go straight to your cars.

The caretaker says the woods aren't safe.

Their father stays in the library on the second story all morning, typing, and in the afternoon he takes long walks. He takes his pocket recorder along with him, and a hip flask of Gentleman Jack, but not Samantha and Claire.

The caretaker of Eight Chimneys is Mr Coeslak. His left leg is noticeably shorter than his right. Short black hairs grow out of his ears and his nostrils, and there is no hair at all on top of his head, but he's given Samantha and Claire permission to explore the whole of the house. It was Mr Coeslak who told them that there are copperheads in the woods, and that the house is haunted. He says they are all, ghosts and snakes, a pretty bad-tempered lot, and Samantha and Claire should stick to the marked trails, and stay out of the attic.

Mr Coeslak can tell the twins apart, even if their father can't; Claire's eyes are grey, like a cat's fur, he says, but Samantha's are *gray*, like the ocean when it has been raining.

Samantha and Claire went walking in the woods on the second day that they were at Eight Chimneys. They saw something.

Samantha thought it was a woman, but Claire said it was a snake.
The staircase that goes up to the attic has been locked. They
peeked through the keyhole, but it was too dark to see anything.

> And so he had a wife, and they say she was real pretty. There
> was another man who wanted to go with her, and first she
> wouldn't, because she was afraid of her husband, and then she
> did. Her husband found out, and they say he killed a snake and
> got some of this snake's blood and put it in some whiskey and
> gave it to her. He had learned this from an island man who had
> been on a ship with him. And in about six months snakes
> created in her and they got between her meat and the skin. And
> they say you could just see them running up and down her legs.
> They say she was just hollow to the top of her body, and it kept
> on like that till she died. Now my daddy said he saw it.
> — An Oral History of Eight Chimneys

Eight Chimneys is over two hundred years old. It is named for the
eight chimneys which are each big enough that Samantha and
Claire can both fit in one fireplace. The chimneys are red brick,
and on each floor there are eight fireplaces, making a total of
twenty-four. Samantha imagines the chimney stacks stretching
like stout red tree trunks, all the way up through the slate roof of
the house. Beside each fireplace is a heavy black firedog, and a set
of wrought iron pokers shaped like snakes. Claire and Samantha
pretend to duel with the snake-pokers before the fireplace in their
bedroom on the third floor. Wind rises up the back of the
chimney. When they stick their faces in, they can feel the air
rushing damply upward, like a river. The flue smells old and
sooty and wet, like stones from a river.

Their bedroom was once the nursery. They sleep together in a
poster bed which resembles a ship with four masts. It smells of
mothballs, and Claire kicks in her sleep. Charles Cheatham Rash
slept here when he was a little boy, and also his daughter. She
disappeared when her father did. It might have been gambling
debts. They may have moved to New Orleans. She was fourteen
years old, Mr Coeslak said. What was her name, Claire asked.
What happened to her mother, Samantha wanted to know. Mr
Coeslak closed his eyes in an almost wink. Mrs. Rash had died the
year before her husband and daughter disappeared, he said, of a

mysterious wasting disease. He can't remember the name of the poor little girl, he said.

Eight Chimneys has exactly 100 windows, all still with the original wavery panes of handblown glass. With so many windows, Samantha thinks, Eight Chimneys should always be full of light, but instead the trees press close against the house, so that the rooms on the first and second story – even the third-story rooms – are green and dim, as if Samantha and Claire are living deep under the sea. This is the light that makes the tourists into ghosts. In the morning, and again towards evening, a fog settles in around the house. Sometimes it is grey like Claire's eyes, and sometimes it is gray, like Samantha's.

> *I met a woman in the wood,*
> *Her lips were two red snakes.*
> *She smiled at me, her eyes lewd*
> *And burning like a fire.*

A few nights ago, the wind was sighing in the nursery chimney. Their father had already tucked them in, and turned off the light. Claire dared Samantha to stick her head into the fireplace, in the dark, and so she did. The cold, wet air licked at her face, and it almost sounded like voices talking low, muttering. She couldn't quite make out what they were saying.

Their father has been drinking steadily since they arrived at Eight Chimneys. He never mentions their mother. One evening they heard him shouting in the library, and when they came downstairs, there was a large sticky stain on the desk, where a glass of whiskey had been knocked over. It was looking at me, he said, through the window. It had orange eyes.

Samantha and Claire refrained from pointing out that the library is on the second story.

At night, their father's breath has been sweet from drinking, and he is spending more and more time in the woods, and less in the library. At dinner, usually hot dogs and baked beans from a can, which they eat off of paper plates in the first-floor dining room, beneath the Austrian chandelier (which has exactly 632 leaded crystals shaped like teardrops) their father recites the poetry of Charles Cheatham Rash, which neither Samantha nor Claire cares for.

He has been reading the ship diaries which Rash kept, and he says that he has discovered proof in them that Rash's most famous poem, *The Specialist's Hat*, is not a poem at all, and in any case, Rash didn't write it. It is something that the one of the men on the whaler used to say, to conjure up a whale. Rash simply copied it down and stuck an end on it and said it was his.

The man was from Mulatuppu, which is a place neither Samantha nor Claire has ever heard of. Their father says that the man was supposed to be some sort of magician, but he drowned shortly before Rash came back to Eight Chimneys. Their father says that the other sailors wanted to throw the magician's chest overboard, but Rash persuaded them to let him keep it until he could be put ashore, with the chest, off the coast of North Carolina.

The specialist's hat makes a noise like an agouti;
The specialist's hat makes a noise like a collared peccary;
The specialist's hat makes a noise like a white-lipped peccary;
The specialist's hat makes a noise like a tapir;
The specialist's hat makes a noise like a rabbit;
The specialist's hat makes a noise like a squirrel;
The specialist's hat makes a noise like a curassow;
The specialist's hat moans like a whale in the water;
The specialist's hat moans like the wind in my wife's hair;
The specialist's hat makes a noise like a snake;
I have hung the hat of the specialist upon my wall.

The reason that Claire and Samantha have a baby-sitter is that their father met a woman in the woods. He is going to see her tonight, and they are going to have a picnic supper and look at the stars. This is the time of year when the Perseids can be seen, a shower of white sparks falling across the sky on clear nights. Their father said that he has been walking with the woman every afternoon. She is a distant relation of Rash, and besides, he said, he needs a night off and some grown-up conversation.

Mr Coeslak won't stay in the house after dark, but he agreed to find someone to look after Samantha and Claire. Then their father couldn't find Mr Coeslak, but the babysitter showed up precisely at seven o'clock. The baby-sitter, whose name neither twin quite caught, wears a blue cotton dress with short floaty sleeves. Both Samantha and Claire think she is pretty in an old-fashioned sort of way.

They were in the library with their father, looking up Mulatuppu in the red leather atlas, when she arrived. She didn't knock on the front door, she simply walked in and then up the stairs, as if she knew where to find them.

Their father kissed them goodbye, a hasty smack, told them to be good and he would take them into town on the weekend to see the Disney film. They went to the window to watch as he walked into the woods. Already, it was getting dark, and there were fireflies, tiny yellow-hot sparks in the air. When their father had entirely disappeared into the trees, they turned around and stared at the baby-sitter instead. She raised one eyebrow. "Well," she said. "What sort of games do you like to play?"

> *Widdershins around the chimneys,*
> *once, twice, again.*
> *the spokes click like a clock on the bicycle;*
> *they tick down the days of the life of a man.*

First they played Go Fish, and then they played Crazy Eights, and then they made the baby-sitter into a mummy by putting shaving cream from their father's bathroom on her arms and legs, and wrapping her in toilet paper. She is the best baby-sitter they have ever had.

At nine-thirty, she tried to put them to bed. Neither Claire nor Samantha wanted to go to bed, so they began to play the Dead game. The Dead game is a let's pretend that they have been playing every day for 274 days now, but never in front of their father or any other adult. When they are Dead, they are allowed to do anything they want to. They can even fly by jumping off the nursery beds, and just waving their arms. Someday this will work, if they practise hard enough.

The Dead game has three rules.

One. Numbers are significant. The twins keep a list of important numbers in a green address book that belonged to their mother. Mr Coeslak's tour has been a good source of significant amounts and tallies: they are writing a tragical history of numbers.

Two. The twins don't play the Dead game in front of grown-ups. They have been summing up the baby-sitter, and have decided that she doesn't count. They tell her the rules.

Three is the best and most important rule. When you are Dead, you don't have to be afraid of anything. Samantha and Claire aren't sure who the Specialist is, but they aren't afraid of him.

To become Dead, they hold their breath while counting to thirty-five, which is as high as their mother got, not counting a few days.

"You never lived here," Claire says. "Mr Coeslak lives here."

"Not at night," says the baby-sitter. "This was my bedroom when I was little."

"Really?" Samantha says. Claire says, "Prove it."

The baby-sitter gives Samantha and Claire a look, as if she is measuring them: how old; how smart; how brave; how tall. Then she nods. The wind is in the flue, and in the dim nursery light they can see the milky strands of fog seeping out of the fireplace. "Go stand in the chimney," she instructs them. "Stick your hand as far up as you can, and there is a little hole on the left side, with a key in it."

Samantha looks at Claire, who says, "Go ahead." Claire is fifteen minutes and some few uncounted seconds older than Samantha, and therefore gets to tell Samantha what to do. Samantha remembers the muttering voices and then reminds herself that she is Dead. She goes over to the fireplace and ducks inside.

When Samantha stands up in the chimney, she can only see the very edge of the room. She can see the fringe of the mothy blue rug, and one bed leg, and beside it, Claire's foot, swinging back and forth like a metronome. Claire's shoelace has come undone, and there is a bandaid on her ankle. It all looks very pleasant and peaceful from inside the chimney, like a dream, and for a moment, she almost wishes she didn't have to be Dead. But it's safer, really. She sticks her left hand up as far as she can reach, trailing it along the crumbly wall, until she feels an indentation. She thinks about spiders and severed fingers, and rusty razorblades, and then she reaches inside. She keeps her eyes lowered, focused on the corner of the room, and Claire's twitchy foot.

Inside the hole, there is a tiny cold key, its teeth facing outward. She pulls it out, and ducks back into the room. "She wasn't lying," she tells Claire.

"Of course I wasn't lying," the baby-sitter says. "When you're Dead, you're not allowed to tell lies."

"Unless you want to," Claire says.

> Dreary and dreadful beats the sea at the shore.
> Ghastly and dripping is the mist at the door.
> The clock in the hall is chiming one, two, three, four.
> The morning comes not, no, never, no more.

Samantha and Claire have gone to camp for three weeks every summer since they were seven. This year their father didn't ask them if they wanted to go back and after discussing it, they decided that it was just as well. They didn't want to have to explain to all their friends how they were half-orphans now. They are used to being envied, because they are identical twins. They don't want to be pitiful.

It has not even been a year, but Samantha realizes that she is forgetting what her mother looked like. Not her mother's face so much as the way she smelled, which was something like dry hay and something like Chanel No. 5, and like something else too. She can't remember whether her mother had gray eyes, like her, or grey eyes, like Claire. She doesn't dream about her mother anymore, but she does dream about Prince Charming, a bay whom she once rode in the horse show at her camp. In the dream, Prince Charming did not smell like a horse at all. He smelled like Chanel No. 5. When she is Dead, she can have all the horses she wants, and they all smell like Chanel No. 5.

"Where does the key go to?" Samantha says.

The baby-sitter holds out her hand. "To the attic. You don't really need it, but taking the stairs is easier than the chimney. At least the first time."

"Aren't you going to make us go to bed?" Claire says.

The baby-sitter ignores Claire. "My father used to lock me in the attic when I was little, but I didn't mind. There was a bicycle up there and I used to ride it around and around the chimneys until my mother let me out again. Do you know how to ride a bicycle?"

"Of course," Claire says.

"If you ride fast enough, the Specialist can't catch you."

"What's the Specialist?" Samantha says. Bicycles are okay, but horses can go faster. "The Specialist wears a hat," say the baby-sitter. "The hat makes noises." She doesn't say anything else.

> When you're dead, the grass is greener
> Over your grave. The wind is keener.
> Your eyes sink in, your flesh decays. You
> Grow accustomed to slowness; expect delays.

The attic is somehow bigger and lonelier than Samantha and Claire thought it would be. The baby-sitter's key opens the locked door at the end of the hallway, revealing a narrow set of stairs. She waves them ahead and upwards.

It isn't as dark in the attic as they had imagined. The oaks that block the light and make the first three stories so dim and green and mysterious during the day, don't reach all the way up. Extravagant moonlight, dusty and pale, streams in the angled dormer windows. It lights the length of the attic, which is wide enough to hold a softball game in, and lined with trunks where Samantha imagines people could sit, could be hiding and watching. The ceiling slopes down, impaled upon the eight thickwaisted chimney stacks. The chimneys seem too alive, somehow, to be contained in this empty, neglected place; they thrust almost angrily through the roof and attic floor. In the moonlight, they look like they are breathing. "They're so beautiful," she says.

"Which chimney is the nursery chimney?" Claire says.

The baby-sitter points to the nearest right-hand stack. "That one," she says. "It runs up through the ballroom on the first floor, the library, the nursery."

Hanging from a nail on the nursery chimney is a long, black object. It looks lumpy and heavy, as if it were full of *things*. The baby-sitter takes it down, twirls it on her finger. There are holes in the black thing, and it whistles mournfully as she spins it. "The Specialist's hat," she says.

"That doesn't look like a hat," says Claire. "It doesn't look like anything at all." She goes to look through the boxes and trunks that are stacked against the far wall.

"It's a *special* hat," the baby-sitter says. "It's not supposed to look like anything. But it can sound like anything you can imagine. My father made it."

"Our father writes books," Samantha says.

"My father did too." The baby-sitter hangs the hat back on the nail. It curls blackly against the chimney. Samantha stares at it. It nickers at her. "He was a bad poet, but he was worse at magic."

Last summer, Samantha wished more than anything that she could have a horse. She thought she would have given up anything for one – even being a twin was not as good as having a horse. She still doesn't have a horse, but she doesn't have a mother either, and she can't help wondering if it's her fault. The hat nickers again, or maybe it is the wind in the chimney.

"What happened to him?" Claire asks.

"After he made the hat, the Specialist came and took him away. I hid in the nursery chimney while it was looking for him, and it didn't find me."

"Weren't you scared?"

There is a clattering, shivering clicking noise. Claire has found the baby-sitter's bike and is dragging it towards them by the handlebars. The babysitter shrugs. "Rule number three," she says.

Claire snatches the hat off the nail. "I'm the Specialist!" she says, putting the hat on her head. It falls over her eyes, the floppy shapeless brim sewn with little asymmetrical buttons that flash and catch at the moonlight like teeth. Samantha looks again, and sees that they *are* teeth. Without counting, she suddenly knows that there are exactly fifty-two teeth on the hat, and that they are the teeth of agoutis, of curassows, of white-lipped peccaries, and of the wife of Charles Cheatham Rash. The chimneys are moaning, and Claire's voice booms hollowly beneath the hat. "Run away, or I'll catch you and eat you!"

Samantha and the baby-sitter run away, laughing, as Claire mounts the rusty, noisy bicycle and pedals madly after them. She rings the bicycle bell as she rides, and the Specialist's hat bobs up and down on her head. It spits like a cat. The bell is shrill and thin, and the bike wails and shrieks. It leans first towards the right and then to the left. Claire's knobby knees stick out on either side like makeshift counterweights.

Claire weaves in and out between the chimneys, chasing Samantha and the baby-sitter. Samantha is slow, turning to look behind. As Claire approaches, she keeps one hand on the handlebars and stretches the other hand out towards Samantha. Just as she is about to grab Samantha, the baby-sitter turns back and plucks the hat off Claire's head.

"Shit!" the baby-sitter says, and drops it. There is a drop of blood forming on the fleshy part of the baby-sitter's hand, black in the moonlight, where the Specialist's hat has bitten her.

Claire dismounts, giggling. Samantha watches as the Specialist's hat rolls away. It gathers speed, veering across the attic floor, and disappears, thumping down the stairs. "Go get it," Claire says. "You can be the Specialist this time."

"No," the baby-sitter says, sucking at her palm. "It's time for bed."

When they go down the stairs, there is no sign of the Specialist's hat. They brush their teeth, climb into the ship-bed, and pull the covers up to their necks. The baby-sitter sits between their feet. "When you're Dead," Samantha says, "do you still get tired and have to go to sleep? Do you have dreams?"

"When you're Dead," the baby-sitter says, "everything's a lot easier. You don't have to do anything that you don't want to. You don't have to have a name, you don't have to remember. You don't even have to breathe."

She shows them exactly what she means.

When she has time to think about it, (and now she has all the time in the world to think) Samantha realizes with a small pang that she is now stuck indefinitely between ten and eleven years old, stuck with Claire and the baby-sitter. She considers this. The number 10 is pleasing and round, like a beach ball, but all in all, it hasn't been an easy year. She wonders what 11 would have been like. Sharper, like needles maybe. She has chosen to be Dead, instead. She hopes that she's made the right decision. She wonders if her mother would have decided to be Dead, instead of dead, if she could have.

Last year, they were learning fractions in school when her mother died. Fractions remind Samantha of herds of wild horses, piebalds and pintos and palominos. There are so many of them, and they are, well, fractious and unruly. Just when you think you have one under control, it throws up its head and tosses you off. Claire's favorite number is 4, which she says is a tall, skinny boy. Samantha doesn't care for boys that much. She likes numbers. Take the number 8 for instance, which can be more than one thing at once. Looked at one way, 8 looks like a bent woman with curvy hair. But if you lay it down on its side, it looks like a snake curled with its tail in its mouth. This is sort of like the difference between being Dead, and being dead. Maybe when Samantha is tired of one, she will try the other.

On the lawn, under the oak trees, she hears someone calling her name. Samantha climbs out of bed and goes to the nursery window. She looks out through the wavy glass. It's Mr Coeslak. "Samantha, Claire!" he calls up to her. "Are you all right? Is your father there?" Samantha can almost see the moonlight shining through him. "They're always locking me in the tool room. Goddamn spooky things," he says. "Are you there, Samantha? Claire? Girls?"

The baby-sitter comes and stands beside Samantha. The baby-sitter puts her finger to her lip. Claire's eyes glitter at them from the dark bed. Samantha doesn't say anything, but she waves at Mr Coeslak. The baby-sitter waves too. Maybe he can see them waving, because after a little while he stops shouting and goes away. "Be careful," the baby-sitter says. "*He*'ll be coming soon. It will be coming soon."

She takes Samantha's hand, and leads her back to the bed, where Claire is waiting. They sit and wait. Time passes, but they don't get tired, they don't get any older.

Who's there?
Just air.

The front door opens on the first floor, and Samantha, Claire, and the baby-sitter can hear someone creeping, creeping up the stairs. "Be quiet," the baby-sitter says. "It's the Specialist."

Samantha and Claire are quiet. The nursery is dark and the wind crackles like a fire in the fireplace.

"Claire, Samantha, Samantha, Claire?" The Specialist's voice is blurry and wet. It sounds like their father's voice, but that's because the hat can imitate any noise, any voice. "Are you still awake?"

"Quick," the baby-sitter says. "It's time to go up to the attic and hide."

Claire and Samantha slip out from under the covers and dress quickly and silently. They follow her. Without speech, without breathing, she pulls them into the safety of the chimney. It is too dark to see, but they understand the baby-sitter perfectly when she mouths the word, Up. She goes first, so they can see where the fingerholds are, the bricks that jut out for their feet. Then Claire. Samantha watches her sister's foot ascend like smoke, the shoelace still untied.

"Claire? Samantha? Goddammit, you're scaring me. Where are you?" The Specialist is standing just outside the half-open door. "Samantha? I think I've been bitten by something. I think I've been bitten by a goddamn snake." Samantha hesitates for only a second. Then she is climbing up, up, up the nursery chimney.

AVRAM DAVIDSON & GRANIA DAVIS

The Boss in the Wall: A Treatise on the House Devil

AVRAM DAVIDSON (1923–1993) NEEDS VERY LITTLE introduction. He was one of the great voices of imaginative fiction. The author of more than 200 short stories and many longer works, he won the Hugo, Ellery Queen, Edgar and World Fantasy awards, including the latter for Life Achievement. He was also nominated for the Nebula in every category.

Grania Davis was Avram Davidson's former wife, life-long friend, and sometime collaborator. Her fantasy novels based on oriental legends include *The Rainbow Annals*, *Moonbird* and *Marco Polo and the Sleeping Beauty* (with Davidson), while her short fiction also reflects her travels abroad.

Although Avram Davidson's work was largely out of print at the time of his death, Grania Davis has undertaken to get his fiction back into publication, helped by friends in the SF and fantasy community. With Robert Silverberg she co-edited the 1998 collection *The Avram Davidson Treasury*, which included thirty-eight stories, each introduced by a noted author, while *The Investigations of Avram Davidson*, co-edited with Richard A. Lupoff, is a recent collection of mystery stories.

"What a long, strange trip 'The Boss in the Wall' has been," reveals Davis. "Avram had a weird dream in the early 1980s. I don't remember exactly when. The dream became a rough, sprawling 600-plus page novel manuscript, about a strange creature in American folklore. When I first read it, it blew me away. After Avram's health declined, I set to work to complete the novel, as I had already done with *Marco Polo and the Sleeping Beauty* (1988).

"(Aside: In classical music, 'Completed By' is a recognized byline. Different versions of Mozart's 'Requiem' were post-humously Completed By different living composers. Perhaps we should consider this usage.)

"There was interest in the *Boss* novel, but editors changed positions, and somehow the book never got published. Avram began to work on a novella-length version of the story, but that also slipped through the cracks of the publishing process. After his death, I really wanted to see 'Boss' in print. I began the job of completing the novella, incorporating important segments from the novel, including material of my own. This version was supposed to be published in a fine magazine – which promptly ceased publication. Was 'Boss' jinxed, or what?

"Finally, Jacob Weisman, at Tachyon Publications in San Francisco, rose to the challenge. He published the completed novella, *The Boss in the Wall: A Treatise on the House Devil*, with thoughtful introductions by Peter S. Beagle and Michael Swanwick, and a truly creepy cover by Michael Dashow. 'Boss' was placed on the ballot by the Nebula Jury, which reaches out to smaller publishers like Tachyon. What a great surprise!

" 'The Boss in the Wall' is a powerful, strange, funny tale. This was Avram's last major work (along with *Virgil III: The Scarlet Fig*). 'Boss' has been well-received, as I always hoped it would be. To quote from the story: '. . . The dreadful secret, so long concealed, has begun to escape from its dreadfully long conceal-ment.' "

– And he dwelleth in desolate cities, and in houses which no man inhabiteth –

– Job XV, 28

To say that the office looked dirty and shabby was to say that water looked liquid and wet. Newspapers, documents, magazines, clippings, files and folders lay stacked and slipped and scattered. Someone was thrusting his hand into a large manila envelope. Someone was turning the pages of an old illustrated publication. Someone was going through a scrapbook, moistening loose corners with a small glue-brush. On one webby wall was a sign: THE CONTRACT NEVER EXPIRES. *None of the men was working hard or working fast, none of them seemed interested in what he was doing, and whatever they were all doing, they gave the impression of having been doing it for a long, long time.*

I.   What Larraby's Got

The not-crisp card read:

Edward E. Bagnell
Professor of Ethnology
Sumner Public College

Curator Larraby of the Carolina Coast Museum looked up from the card. "Still sticking to 'Ethnology,' are they?" His tone was civil, even amiable, but there was a something in his eyes beyond the usual mere shrewdness.

"Yes sir, they are. Still sticking to 'Public', also." Bagnell was sure there was something sticking to the Curator's manner, inside the ruddy, well-worn face, lurking around the corners of the well-trimmed gray mustache and the picturesquely tufty silvery eyebrows. The Curator asked a few questions about Sumner Public College: Was Macrae getting on with his study of so-called "Moorish" mountain people? Was SPC having the usual small-college trouble with trustees who wanted more money spent on football than on music, say, or scholarship – *real* scholarship? Then there was a pause, and then the odd expression ceased to be odd at all, and was now plain to see.

Slyness.

And with that came the very slow, very quiet, "Well, what can I do for you, Professor Bagnell?"

Out with it.

"I understand that you have a Paper-Man here under lock and key, Curator Larraby."

At once: "Yes I *thought* that was what you – don't know how I knew, but I – *what did you say?*" The slyness was gone, it was quite gone. The ruddy face was now quite red, the slightly jowely mouth hung agape. "*What* did you say?"

"A Paper-Man or Paper-Doll or Paper-Doll Man. A Hyett or Hetter or Header. A Greasy-Man or String-Fellow. A Rustler or Clicker or Clatterer. And/or other names. Though I assume . . . I'm sure you know."

For a moment, silence. Then an audible swallow, a shake, as though the heavy, aging body had been set slightly askew and needed to be set right. A shudder, and then the slumped old man said, "This assumption cannot be allowed to get into the newspapers or the newsreels. This . . ."

The newsreels! Bagnell had never seen a newsreel, anymore than he had ever seen a passenger pigeon or a Civil War veteran. "Oh God no! That's the last thing we would want!"

The effect was galvanic. The curator was on his feet. "I require another name, and then we'll see how sure you are that I know."

Bagnell said, "*The Boss in the Wall.*" Larraby was out the door before Bagnell was finished, but he was waiting in the hall.

"I was, as I said, sure that was what you wanted, young man. Pardon me, Professor. But I figured you'd go about it *slyly.*" The older man put his arm through Bagnell's, and the gesture at once dissipated all mistrust. "I'm taking you to the top of the tower, it's up these stairs, and I may lean on you quite a bit: no elevator. Slowly. Good."

The stairs were swept clean and smelled of old wood and polish, but as they went up higher a strong odor of disinfectant became predominant. "– And if you *had*, why, I'd have hustled you right out of here. And here's the key, Dr Bagnell. The *first* key."

Inside the tower was a locked room which required a second key, and inside this was a modern steel cabinet with two keyholes; alongside it stood an open jug of creosol. "Tower door locked behind us? Make sure. Lock this one and swing the night-bolt too. Now, got a strong stomach?"

Bagnell said that he had helped to find and bury hurricane and flood victims. He now noticed another odor in the rather small room, a strong one, entirely different from the tarry reek of the disinfectant.

"Had such experience? Well, useful. Don't say it's better, don't say it's worse; different. Clean different." He was gently inserting a key. "But not clean. *God*, no." He looked up, withdrew the key. "Oh, forgot. Got a handkerchief? Put some of that bay rum on it; you may feel that you want it in a hurry." On a small table in the corner was, of all things, a bottle of that once-widely-used gentlemen's lotion and hair-tonic. Bagnell had thought it had gone out with newsreels. Was that the source of the other odor? *God*, no! Bagnell obediently scattered some spicy bay rum on his handkerchief. Larraby had the second key in and out.

Inside were two perfectly ordinary large cardboard cartons with laundry soap logos on them. "*Two*? I thought there was *one*."

"Think twice. There is." And so there was.

It was in two pieces.

The trousers and jacket were antique, and dull with dirt and some sort of grease; the words *corpse fat* came swift into Bagnell's mind. On one bony foot, and it was as though the skin had been scraped thin before being replaced over the bones – and the skin was filthy beyond anything he had ever seen before, was a part of something doubtless once a shoe. The jacket was torn; it was worn-torn and it was ripped-torn, and beneath it was part of a shirt. And the shirt-part was worst of all, for it must have once been white. No other color could ever have become so ghastly grey, and here and there were stains of other colors, though none was bright.

"Breathe through your handkerchief, and don't get too close as you lean over it."

Bagnell obeyed. Though not before an accidental breath gave him knowledge of the actual smell. A breath was enough. It was not what he had imagined it might be. The smell was organic, he was sure of that, but it was nothing like any organic – or for that matter inorganic – odor he had ever been exposed to before. It was worse than mere decay or decomposition, worse than any disease, worse – He had covered his nose but he could, even despite the scented distillation of the bay and the thick rank creosol, taste it; he covered his mouth as well.

Pieces of shredding yellowed-filthied paper poked out here and there: from under the ragged ankle-edge of the trouser cuff. From out of the gap where the fly had been, the tattered paper protruded like a codpiece. Worn and stained paper formed a sort of ghastly lace jabot high in front. And all of it that he could see showed awful and ugly stains, and even some of the stains had stains.

Larraby took up an exceedingly long pair of rather odd tongs and turned the upper torso half-over; it must have been very light for him to do it with one hand. "Look there." There was an immense hole beneath the left shoulder-blade. And it had been stuffed, there was no other word for it, stuffed with paper.

Larraby said, through his own handkerchief mask, "Of course we never attempted to examine all the paper, but I can inform you that it seems to consist mostly of the special election supplement of the New York *Herald* of November whatever-it-was, 1864, which proves nothing; old Greeley shipped his weekly edition all over the country."

Bagnell's eyes were darting here and there, noting the claw-like hand encrusted with far more than a century's (perhaps) filth, noticing the rubbed-out part of the sleeve from which protruded a something grimy and grim which was likely an elbow. Noticing . . . *not* noticing –

"The head's not there."

"Oh." Bagnell's eyes were again darting.

"The head's not *here*, is what I mean. Don't bother looking for it. Seen enough?"

Bagnell thought he'd probably seen enough.

"But I've got a photograph of it downstairs." And Larraby went to locking up the cabinet. Then Bagnell let them out. Then Larraby locked up behind them.

"A photograph of –?"

"– Of the head. Want to know what the fellow said? Fellow who brought the body to us? Do, eh? A'*right*! – Steady; going down is not so easy for me as some might think. – Said he saw *it*, that thing upstairs, saw it lying on the floor of . . . a certain old building. Said he saw a rat scuttle over and start to gnaw at one of its feet. Said – you ready for this? A'*right*, said he saw the thing catch the rat with its *foot* – the *thing's* foot. Said he saw it jerk the rat up and heard the rat squeal. Ever hear a rat give a death-squeal when some gant old tiger-she-cat with a dirty kitten catched hold of it? And he said that thing, old Boss-Devil, began to eat the rat. That dried-up old horror, supposedly dead a hundred years, with flesh as sere as a mummy's, *began to eat the rat.* Could it happen? *God*, no! *Did* it happen? *God*, yes!"

As for the head; it was a good photo.

The mouth was still mostly full of teeth, visible beneath the writhed-up lip, and seemed to Bagnell very capable of clicking and clattering – and perhaps – of killing a rat . . . a very large rat, too. The nose was sunken but was by no means gone. Something had happened to one ear – how many times might it have offered itself as bait for rats, if rats were what it wanted; lying on rotting floors in rotting buildings by moonlight or in moondark, in forgotten tumuli behind now-vanished pest-houses? – Something had happened to one ear and one eye was closed – but one eye wasn't. It was likely no more than a trick of the light, but the eye seemed to be looking watchfully out of one squinted corner. The eye seemed to have a very definite expression and seemed (as such things often will) to be looking directly at Bagnell, who did not in any way like the look. It was not what Bagnell would think of as fearful. The look was . . . what?

Sly.

He shuddered. Curator Larraby, once again just another on-the-way-to-being-old-man said, somewhat smugly, "Ah. Now it catches up with you. Here. Something I keep on hand, case of snakebite. Have one with you." After the first sip, the second sigh, the curator said, "Save you the trouble of asking. No, you may not have a copy. Want a photograph of the head, direct you to Dr. Selby Abott Silas, scholar, rogue and thief, and most unworthy damned Yankee rat and rascal, holder of the magniloquent title of Principal Steward of the General Museum of the Province of Rhode Island and Providence Plantations. Details on request. Some other time. Further questions? Brief ones . . ."

As Bagnell made a last and fruitless look towards the flat and locked steel box with the photo of the Paper-Man's head, and made to go, one further question came to him.

Larraby made no objection to answering. The man who had brought in the thing upstairs, in two pieces plus the head, brought them in a gunny sack; the man was a well-known manslayer. "Had killed two Negroes, well, was *tried* for two. Half-black, half-Catawba Indian; a Mustee, we used to call them. And after he'd done a year or so in the penitentiary, where by the way he behaved himself, and I'm sure no one stole *his* cigarettes or tried to commit a crime against nature upon *him*, ho no! Well, while he was away there'd been some breakage here, theft and vandalism, so we pulled some strings, got Mustee a parole by offering him the job of second night-watchman; midnight to eight a.m.. He looks like *Australopithecus maledictus*, and you may be sure that *no* one comes around here now who's got no lawful business. Mustee has no morals, no religion, feared of *nothing*, keeps his contracts. Gave him one hundred silver dollars for his find, and a big bottle of over-proof rum. – Hm, maybe I'll give Mustee a ticket to Providence, Rhode Island. Hm, think about it." Larraby thought about it as he reached for a lamp.

"Let me put some more lights on. Old newspapers, yes, indeed. Keep out the cold, they do. Wonder what *you*'ll do, next time you hear a rustle in the dark. *Your* life has been changed forever. Well, nobody twisted your arm; you can always sell insurance. Mind your step on your way out."

"How did Mustee kill those two, ah, Negroes?"

Larraby, winding a light scarf, looked at him eye to eye. "Broke their necks," he said. "Quote me for one single word in print about this, I'll ruin your career without compunction."

And that was the first time Bagnell actually saw one.

So he informed his friend, Dr Claire Zimmerman, when he called her later that day. In the past that call would have been heralded by the almost-necromantic words: *This is Long Distance Calling*. But neither of them remembered that, and neither had seen a newsreel. The past was sending them different messages . . . far more distant and dangerous.

Excerpt From the Interim Committee Report:

"How many appearance, or maybe we should say sightings, have been reported, would you say?" asked Branch.

"Don't know," said Bagnell.

"Define your terms," said Claire Zimmerman. "How reported, to whom reported?"

"Well, it should be possible to find out. That would help combat it, wouldn't you think?" asked Branch. "Do we even know, for instance, how many authenticated cases there are of one of them doing actual bodily harm to a human being?"

"How authenticated, by whom authenticated? Oh, there are accounts, sure. Bite wounds and scratches, mostly, and talk of festering and amputations," said Bagnell. "We just don't *know*. We think the Boss in the Wall is scaring us. Maybe *he* thinks we're scaring him. How many of them are there? We don't know. Do they know we're on to them and that we're after them? Can they communicate with each other? *Do* they? We don't know. Are they suffering from some kind of unknown virus, and if so, is the disease still spreading? Has it infected and infested some of the filthy derelicts we see lying in the doorways of old buildings? Are the drifters sliding and sickening and deteriorating into Paper Men? We don't know. What's it all about – and what can we really *do* except burn down every old house in the country?"

II.   The Old House

The new house was very old, and Elsa Beth Smith and Professor Vlad Smith loved it at once.

Partly they had come to see it because of the cottage cheese fight of the people next door, and partly it was because of Uncle Mose, that fine old rogue.

College Residence Building Number Three had been, like all Bewdley College's new Residence Buildings, military housing during the war. *The* War; World War Two. "A duplex!" was Elsa Beth's first exclamation on entering her and Vlad's new home – a brave cry which ignored the stained walls, leak-marked ceilings, pokey kitchen, and warping walls and doors and window-frames. The buildings had not been built to last. They were, in fact, *not* lasting, they were decaying fast, but people still lived in them all the same. And among the people were the people next door, Professors Albert and Anna Murray, husband and wife. The Murray marriage was not going too well, and a hearty sneeze penetrated the thin partition between the two families.

"Smell this," – Anna Murray coming out on the porch.

"Throw it out," – Albert Murray, nose in paper.

"Throw out a whole carton of cottage cheese?"

"Don't throw it out then, *dammit*!" Albert bellowed.

Inside their house, Vlad and Elsa Beth's four-year-old daughter, Bella says softly, "Abbert and Amma are fighting again." A slight and sallow child, resembling her father. Not precocious. She has her ways, what child has not? And the mere way she has of standing in a doorway with a wry, dry look on her small face makes her parents wonder how the doorway ever existed before Bella came to stand in it.

Her parents do not directly reply. They consider their options. "The rents in quaint old Bewdley City are out of sight," sighs Elsa. She was once a strawberry blonde, but since Bella was *in utero*, Elsa's hair has darkened to a light brown. Her face, with its slight suggestion of a double chin, looks very thoughtful. She is a talented painter and she is very nice.

Not long thereafter came Uncle Mose's letter.

Uncle Mose wrote: "Moses Stuart Allenby is looking around for a sponge to throw in. I am tired of robbing widows and orphans, and I'm going to make you kids an offer. Elsie Bessey knows I'm quiet and clean in my habits. Mostly I sit in my room studying subversive publications like *The Wall Street Journal*, play a little jazz on my gramophone, take walks and watch birds. Want to relax at home, but must have a home, and have no desire to sleep on your sofa. So here's the offer: All around small towns are perfectly suitable houses which never appear on any real estate lists because they are too old and unfashionable. Beware of Grecian pillars, cost another fifty thou and who needs them? Here are the magic words: *A quick sale for $25,000 cash.* Your local land agent will blench and swallow nervously. Then he will run around like a roach in rut season. You'll be surprised how fast he comes up with something usually thought unsaleable. Old, old houses are solidly built or they wouldn't have survived to be old, old. Uncle Mose was a farm boy, built and repaired many a barn and old house before leaving on the milk train to the city. Uncle Mose will leave lovebirds alone to bill and coo, and will often baby-sit little Bella, teach her to play poker and dance the hootchie-cootchie."

"There's the house, Professor, to the right," said realtor Bob Barker with a toothy smile.

The words formed in Vlad's mind: *That house wasn't even built in the 19th century*. He saw a small replica of Andrew Jackson's Hermitage, with squared wooden pillars, lacking even a lick of plaster, holding up the verandah's second story. Not

Grecian at all – just an old, old house that George Washington never slept in.

"Let's go in, if you folks are ready," Bob Barker said. They were ready. "Got to tell you honestly that this house is almost devoid of your modern conveniences. No electricity, no telephone, but no problem there, the lines run right past the place. It's well-water, but the pump is inside the house. There is just merely one bathroom, and it empties into a ciss-pool. Watch out for the far end of the porch, got a rotten place there." The key kept in a niche in the sill was modern. That was perhaps the only thing which was.

"I love it, I love it," said Elsa Beth. "I love it, I love it," said she.

Uncle Mose came two days later.

"My *God*, Uncle Mose," said Vlad, "what is that you've got with you?" It was grey with reddish lights in its pelt, and it was huge, and it panted at them and lolled its tongue. "It's big as a cow!"

Bella said, "*That's* no cow, that's a *big dog*."

"You're right little Belly. A St Hubert Hound named Nestor. Fine with kids, but burglars watch out! Where's some iced tea? Where's our new house? Settle down Mose," he advised himself. Moses Stuart Appleby had been rather tall and his shoulders still hinted at broadness. He was, as always, immaculate. "I'm all packed and weighed and ready for freighting, soon as I'm sure. Ready to go? *I'm* ready to go. Let's fill a big thermos with iced tea, Elsie Bessy."

They stopped in town for him to mail a letter, and an aged black man rose to confront them in clothes washed threadbare-clean. "You the folks buyin' ol' Rustler house nigh the river?"

"Was that its name, Russel? I didn't know that," said Vlad. "It's on old River Road, though. Yes."

The old man nodded. His skin was gray and his eyes were glazed with age. "That's it. I born here, call me Pappa John. Can I pleased to give you folks some kindly advice? They is three warnings. Firstly, get you a cat. They *hates* cats. Nextly, keep you a fire. They *feared* o' fire. And lastly, please folks, *never* get between one o' *them* and the *wall*." He nodded his ancient head. Vlad, understanding not one word, thanked him and went on into the post office. And then the town sped by . . . and a country lane, with old oak trees dripping Spanish moss.

"There it is."

Uncle Mose looked and said nothing, until they went up on the wide verandah which ran all around the house. "Hey, look there. A tree. A lilac tree. Some old-time housewife planted a lilac bush, and now it's grown taller than the house. Well, let's open her up."

Faint broom tracks showed that some attempt at house-cleaning had been made more recently than the planting of the lilac bush. Faint tremors and echoes in the old, old house. How old? Maybe in the title-deed. Maybe not. Were the Russels that old Pappa John mentioned the original owners? What was Uncle Mose doing? Uncle Mose was leaning over with his ear against the wall. Catching Vlad's questioning eye, he gestured for Vlad to do the same. At first Vlad heard something like the sound of the sea in a seashell. After that came fainter and odder sounds. A rustling . . . a far-off clicking.

A breath lightly brushed his neck and Vlad jumped. It was Uncle Mose; "Hear anything?"

"Rats, maybe."

"Rats don't rustle. Rats don't click. We'll put out some rat-traps, then we'll see."

Attempts, rough and rude enough, had been made to keep the old house in order. In one room the ancient roses of the wall-paper bloomed faintly, almost evoking a ghostly perfume. Elsewhere the walls were papered only with yellowing, tattered newspaper. In one large closet, "Whew, kind of musty in here," said Vlad.

"Whew is right. Worse than that."

"Dead rat under the floorboards, or inside the wall?"

Uncle Mose shrugged. "Old houses, Lord, how they retain. Maybe the moldy diapers of a baby who died a hundred years ago. Well, no problem. Open all the doors and windows, have the place scrubbed down from attic to cellar."

Back home, and effusively greeted by the great hound Nestor, and by Bella fresh and pink-cheeked from her nap. They had drinks. They discussed the house. They all agreed they loved the house. Discussion had reached a pleasantly high level when there was a piercing scream.

Tonight at the Murrays' it was Anna's turn to scream.

Vlad hastened to speak. "Say, why don't we have a cook-out somewhere? A picnic?"

"Oh, good!" said Elsa. "Hey! why don't we have it at the new house?" Then Elsa had her great and wonderful idea: "Why don't we *sleep* out there tonight in sleeping bags? To celebrate, I mean."

"All in favor, say Aye," directed Uncle Mose, and he insisted that everything was to be his treat. And they got lots of everything.

At the old house: "The steaks are doing just fine," said Uncle Mose. "I want to check something out. Bring some flashlights and come along." He walked into the house with long strides, and what he wanted to check out was soon revealed. "Nothing in this trap, nothing in that one. Let's take a look in the cellar . . . nothing. Traps are clean as a whistle. As near as I can see, there isn't a rat in the whole place."

Elsa said, of course, that she was delighted to hear it. "And I'm pleased to see how thick the walls are. It'll stay cooler in the summer and warmer in the winter. My mother always said that high ceilings and thick walls are healthy."

Nestor moved his huge head delicately. Nestor had been doing his own checking-out, and was still alert.

Bella said, "This is our new house." The grown-ups were pleased. Yes, they said, this was their new house. Without changing her slow and level tone, Bella said, "I don't like it." Then she repeated, "I don't like it." Nor did she say anymore.

When the steaks were ready, they took their seats on the front steps. The steaks were tender and very, very good.

Later, upstairs in the rose-papered room, sleeping bags side by side, Elsa said, "You know, for an old bachelor, my uncle knows a thing or two. The gentle way he convinced Bella to share the downstairs room tonight, without a single protest. He must know this is a sort of special honeymoon thing. You and me."

Vlad did not immediately answer. He rolled over so his sleeping-bag slightly overlapped hers. "Your place or mine," he whispered.

Afterwards, Vlad went down to use the antique toilet behind the stairs. The door of one room opened a crack; lamplight and shadow. "Vlad?" said Uncle Mose.

The door opened wider. The great St Hubert hound appeared, his master close behind. "Would you be kind enough to let Nestor out the front door for a minute? Same errand as you. Let him back in when you're ready. Didn't want to leave Bella alone in case she woke up, first time in a strange house."

"Sure. Let's go, Nestor." The dog came forward, gave Vlad a sociable sniff, waited until the front door was opened, and ambled off into the night. Vlad turned back, flashlight in hand, toward the water closet under the stairs.

"Oh, by the way, Uncle Mose; that funny sound we heard that time, when we were listening at the wall? The rustling and, uh, clicking? I heard it again a few minutes ago, when I happened to have my ear against the floor."

"Look into it in the morning. On about your business now, your wife might be nervous alone upstairs. G'night." The older man nodded, retreated into his chamber. Those two words were the last ones Vlad would ever hear him clearly say.

The plumbing rushed and gurgled loudly. Vlad stood by to make sure the ancient equipment suffered no overflowing; then went to the front door. Nestor appeared at once. "Good boy." Light still showed beneath the closed door of Mose's room.

Then the things began to happen.

In what order did the things happen? Some things happened simultaneously, and there was no time to pause and think. The first thing was absolutely astonishing in itself. Nestor flung himself into the air, absolutely vertically; his feet even left the floor. Then he hurled himself, still upright, against the closed door with the crack of light beneath it. Before his immense body slammed against the door, Bella began to scream in a thin and terribly high tone which Vlad had never heard from her before. At once there was an answering scream from Elsa upstairs and, more or less at the same time, Nestor's body slammed against the door. Uncle Mose roared and his feet ran, tramping, inside the room which had gone dark. Nestor howled and tried to break down the door. Vlad flung himself upon the door, and fell against Nestor instead. He tried to hold his light steady to see and grasp the door-knob.

Still Nestor howled, still the old man stumbled inside the closed room, and still Bella screamed. – And the door opened and Vlad staggered into the room and tried desperately not to lose his balance. The noises Uncle Mose made were not roars any longer; Uncle Mose it was who staggered, lurched, fell upon his back and rolled to his side. Bella had stopped screaming, and was utterly silent. Nestor flung himself across the room and the house shook.

Elsa came screaming in, and then she did absolutely the worst thing she could possibly have done – and somehow Vlad knew absolutely that she was going to do it. She seized the arm of the hand in which he held the flashlight, and she tugged down on it as she called her daughter's name, and the flashlight swung wildly up and down until he managed to get it into the other hand.

Nestor was throwing himself against the wall and clawing at the wall, howling and slathering, and something fell from his mouth. Vlad reeled as he tried to dislodge his wife and to focus the flashlight. Then Elsa let go of Vlad's arm and ran to pick up her child, who was arching and thrashing and kicking and making sharp howling sounds. Elsa picked her up, but Bella's arms and legs still moved and jerked convulsively.

What else was in the room? Something else had been in the room. Someone else had been in the room. Something . . . someone filthy and frightful and foul had been in the room.

There to one side was the Coleman lamp, and Vlad forced himself to calm his hands and to relight the lamp, and the room filled with hissing light. No one else and nothing else was in the room now.

Still the huge dog flung himself against the wall. Then it stopped.

Bella stopped her frightful convulsions. She hung limp in her mother's arms, even when Elsa had fallen on her knees onto the sleeping bag, pressed her ear against the tiny chest, lifted her horrified face to him and nodded slightly.

Nestor stepped delicately on huge feet to his master, nuzzled him and licked him, and began to utter a deep and moaning lament. Was the old man dead? Vlad slowly got down beside the body and said, "Uncle Mose? Nestor? Uncle Mose?" Slowly he placed his ear against the fallen man's chest. There was no rustling sound he heard, no clicking. He heard no sound at all. Nestor sniffed again and began to howl.

The long, slow, cold nightmare continued. Call the police, deputy sheriffs, sheriff's deputies. The hospital: "Well, it's shock, basically. Your little girl is of course the most affected, but your wife too is in shock. I'm afraid you aren't in too good shape yourself."

– Take these . . . sign these . . . tell us again, Professor, exactly what happened: questions asked by the doctors and by the police.

Shock, Professor. Your only child has ceased to be a little girl who stood in a doorway and turned your heart with a single look. She became a wind-up doll which screamed and thrashed, except when the doll wound down and looked dully out of unfocused eyes. *Shock, to use simple language, short-circuits the nervous system.*

"What did she see that caused this shock? What sort of creature, sir? It is difficult for us to believe, you see, because your wife doesn't report anything like that. Don't be offended, sir, but you too have suffered a severe shock of some sort . . ."

"What the hell, Branch, what the hell?"

Vlad's old friend, and fellow Professor of Folklore David Branch looked at him and said, "Nobody knows what the hell, Vlad. We have to take this one step at a time."

"Why was Uncle Mose's funeral and cremation over so quickly . . . why was his collar so high?" Then another thought sprang into Vlad's mind. "Where's Nestor?"

"He's at Dean Jorgenson's farm; it's in the next county, so the sheriff can't get him to shoot."

"*What*? Why would they shoot Nestor?"

"Well, mainly because they were afraid of him. This great brute was leaping around, terribly upset, and next thing a deputy got the idea that, well, maybe Nestor had killed the old man – Impossible? Why, impossible?"

"I told them the dog wasn't *in* the room . . . when it began to happen."

"Well, they didn't know that and, um, I heard that Mose had some sort of *marks* on his throat that might have killed him so – Anyway, Nestor ran off and Dean Jorg heard about it, and called the trembling beast into his van and drove him across the county line, so Nestor's all okay. What next?"

"I want to go back to that damned old house . . . and I need some plastic bags."

At the supermarket, leaning on the back of a superannuated cart containing aluminum cans, empty bottles, and odds and ends of light junk was someone whom Vlad recalled meeting. Remembrance was mutual. Stopping his wagon, the old black man said,

"I sorry, sir, about you daddy." Why bother with a correction? Vlad nodded, sighed. "Must be you daddy fo'get, done git between it and the wall . . . fine ol' gentleman."

Vlad stared. Remnants of thought came whirling by, as if caught in a gale. "What do you mean, Pappa John? Get between *what* and the wall . . . what wall?"

The age-glazed eyes in the furrowed face looked at him. "Them bad things as we finds sometimes in old houses. Them Rustlers or Clickers . . . them Paper Men. The *Boss*, sir, the Boss in the Wall. How the lady and the lee girl? *The Boss done stole the lee girl's soul and you gots get it back.*"

He pushed off, leaving Professor Branch looking after him, leaving Vlad with his mouth twitching. "Did you understand what old John meant, Branch?"

"I believe I do, which is not to say that I believe it as facts."

"I should tear that damned house apart . . . find evidence."

They drove beyond the small town and along the country road. The old house looked far different in late afternoon sunshine than it had at night. In the room where Uncle Mose and Bella had cheerfully agreed to spend the night lay a well-worn red rubber toy.

Vlad pointed out to Branch a portion of the wall deeply and recently scored by talons. "Those are Nestor's claws, I guess." He put his ear against the wall; heard nothing. "It's hollow," he said.

"It would be. Proves nothing by itself."

Vlad abruptly said, "Ah, that's what I came for." He pointed to something in the corner. "It was in her hand, and she dropped it when I picked her up." He took the plastic bags out of his pocket.

Branch knelt and looked, then he sniffed. This time it was *his* face that writhed. "Paper. It looks like old newspaper . . . well, this is an old house. What a godawful stench. You say it was in your wife's hand?"

"No, it wasn't my wife," said Vlad, as he carefully used one plastic bag to scoop the object into another. "It was my daughter who had it clutched in her hand. It was Bella."

No further search could legally be made of the house, and no walls would be torn apart. According to the sheriff's department, the deceased died from a stroke or a heart attack, possibly following an attack by a dog or some other animal. Case closed.

*   *   *

At the hospital, Elsa woke up and took a light supper, then she slept again. Bella's condition was unchanged. Elsa's aunt, Uncle Mose's sister, invited them to stay at her big house in the country after they were released. Elsa softly told Vlad that she thought the change would do her and Bella good. Vlad reluctantly agreed.

"Jesus, Branch, what should I do?" said Vlad when they returned to College Housing. "It is my belief that Uncle Mose died of a severe bite in the throat by some sort of degenerate or derelict creature, for lack of better words, and that's what terrified my wife and daughter, and messed up our lives. That's what I told the doctors and the sheriffs, and nobody believed me. No autopsy was done before his body was cremated, and . . ."

"Do? Well the first thing to do is take Doctor Branch's prescription of a big drink of whatever booze you have on hand, and then you are going to lie down and pretend to sleep. I will put on some sleepy-type music and . . . ah, I'd like to look through your files. I promise not to read any love notes or old paternity warrants; I want to look for learned matter. Folkloric shop stuff, okay?"

Pretending to sleep was, as expected, succeeded by genuine slumber. Then by awakening and finding Branch reading by lamplight. "What's that you're reading, Branch?"

"I thought you'd never ask." He tilted up an old red folder mended with tape. "Look familiar?"

Vlad felt that it did look familiar, that he knew what was in it, and somehow he did not *like* what was in it. He recalled a small voice saying, "Is this our new house? I don't *like* it." He leaned his head on his hand and choked back tears.

Branch shoved the folder over to Vlad, who slowly opened and leafed through it. What was this on yellowed paper, laboriously typed in old-fashioned typescript? *Transcript of Alleged Rare Pamphlet Allegedly Entitled "The Treatise on the House Devil."* And this: a sheaf of sundry papers, typed and penned and machine copied on various sorts of copy-machines, attached by a large rusting paper clip, and labeled *Bagnell's Notes.* An item caught his eye; *Preliminary Survey of the Folklore of Two Ohio River Tributaries*: "I had the usual difficulties: first you must find your source. Then you must make him talk. Then you must make him stop talking. Or her. In fact it was from a her that I learned a folk remedy for pubic lice which is too gross for learned journals. Also I heard the following account which might interest you: Near a place called Wide Waters, where two large boats could pass each other, was a tower. It was originally as tall as a three-story building, but then kind of crumbled. Some say it was used as a shot-tower or a lighthouse. Others say it was built by a wicked Frenchman to remind himself of France. He was cruel to his slaves and nearly starved them to death. Well, as soon as Lincoln freed the slaves, they mixed up a big batch of cement and carried over a big pile of stones, and walled their evil old master – their *Boss* – inside the tower. Then all the former slaves ran off. There were no windows in the tower, just little slits. And before anybody came around and found him, long after he must have died, they say he got so thin he was able to poke his hands through the slits and wave them around. And they say you can still sometimes see the skeletal hands of the cruel 'Boss in the Wall' waving through the slits on stormy nights.

"You can recognize elements of countless Old World legends of cruel leaders walled in towers, such as the Sultan of Baghdad and the Mouse Tower on the Rhine. Though the skeletal hands waving through the slits may be strictly a local touch."

"Okay, Branch, okay. I got it now; I remember," Vlad wept. "Why didn't I remember it before?"

Branch had poured moderate drinks for both of them from a bottle, sipped his own and gestured to his old friend to do the same. "Here's a possible explanation. Why did you originally forget it? Because you *forgot*, that's why. Who the hell remembers everything? Every wife in the world feels compelled to shove some of her husband's old crap out of sight, and you had other things to do, so you forgot. Then you went to the old house, and just the sight of the place, or some little sound or smell started to bring back memories. But you didn't *want* the memories. You and your wife and uncle wanted the old house, and the memories weren't very nice. So your mind suppressed them. Until that moment. Let's say that your uncle had some kind of stroke, or fit of convulsions. He couldn't breathe, so he clawed and tore at his own throat. Suppose your daughter woke up and saw him, and she started to scream and scream." Branch took another sip and continued, "Suppose that what you saw was so terrible, your mind couldn't admit that you saw it. You *had* to be seeing something else. Your mind, so to speak, *slipped* down, down into the sub-basement. And down there in the mud and jumble, your mind found something. It found those old tales that old Pappa John had babbled about, and it *substituted* those old terror-tales for the terrible thing you were really seeing. All of this in an instant, of course, but the memory lingers on. Maybe your little girl's defense was to retreat into convulsions and unconsciousness."

Vlad groped for words. He felt as if he were on the edges of a deep, dark wood. "Is that what you really think happened? That my buried memories of all those damned old legends made me think I saw . . ."

From outside the dark woods came a deep sigh. "That's certainly one explanation, and I advise you to consider it," said Branch, tossing down the rest of the whiskey.

Later, much later Vlad's breath came softly and regularly from the couch. Branch slipped silently out of the room, took up the telephone, and walked as far into the kitchen as its long cord would allow. He turned on the light and a water tap, then dialed a number. Waited.

"Doctor Edward Bagnell, please. Hello, Ed? This is Branch. Yes, I know what time it is. Have a pen and paper? Okay, listen carefully. The House-Devil, Paper-Man, Boss in the Wall; well, I want to report another sighting."

III.   Vlad's Quest

How sweetly the small old town smelled in the early summer rains. It seemed to smell of cedar and citronella and water and mint.

Annie Jenkins, Dean Jorgenson's housekeeper said, "Was it one of those *tramps*, one of those *awful* ones? The Lord knows where they come from or why – luckily not often – oh they don't *do* anything violent, not lately, they don't even *steal*, the ones I'm thinking of. We used to call them Paper Men when I was a girl, because they put newspapers under their old clothes to keep warm in winter, though why in *summer*? – Don't even steal, which is very odd if you think of it, they being so poor they can't even afford soap or second-hand clothes. Oh those filthy rags. Just the sight of them, oh and the *awful* smell of them. I asked my husband what *causes* them, every so often you know. Harry said it was 'slum clearance'. Harry says some awful old abandoned building is torn down somewhere, and then those dreadful derelicts have no place to hide, and so they just wander off, they shamble around, and sometimes they turn up *here*. Thank the Lord they don't seem to stay. I have no idea where they *go*, but they don't stay here. Was it one of those –? And to think of the sheriff accusing that sweet big dog. Why, when you gave him a shirt his old master had worn, Nestor took it to his bed in the barn, laid the shirt on the straw, and rested his head on it all that day."

Dean Jorgenson said, tapping his huge hairy fingers on his desk-top, "Well, good, Stewart. I told Vlad he could take the summer off if he took someone with him. I'm glad it's you. He likes you; says you have a good mind and a good sense of humor. Fortunately this is still a private college and I can finagle you some graduate credits, and something out of the special funds without having to justify it to six state legislative committees. Consider that done. And you, in turn, won't let him get morbid and obsessive about . . ." He searched for a word, gazed at Jack Stewart with troubled eyes and concluded, " . . . *it.*"

Vlad looked as if he was fairly well recovered from a bad drunk, but Jack knew that if you *looked* it, you weren't recovered at all. It wasn't until they were bedding down for the first night, in a worn-down motel, that Vlad began to loosen up and talk.

"I understand Jorg's going to do some creative bookkeeping, and get you some grad credits. Good. Officially we're going on just another fun folklore ramble," he ran his fingers over his tired face. "Good clean bright stuff; children's jump-rope jingles, Paul Bunyan tales of the lower Appalachians, Old Darky stories about Mr Buzzard. But unofficially you are going to be my keeper, eh? We, that's *you*, kid, are going to keep me, that's *me*, kid, from getting into anything gamy or gritty. No folkloric spelunking. But no such luck, kid. God bless poor dear old Jorg, but I'm going after such little-known legends as the Clickers, the Rattlers, and I don't mean snakes, I mean the Greasy Man, Paper-Man, the Boss in the Wall, see?"

Jack Stewart ran his own fingers through his molasses-colored curly hair, murmured about a shower, looked up and asked, "Why?"

"Why? Because I saw a specter haunting an old house, and it killed my uncle and sent my little girl into convulsions and my wife into a deep depression and, my god, it was *awful*! *Why* was it there? What *was* it, what *is* it? Nobody believes that I really saw it. Hardly anybody in academe even *knows* the legend, let alone believes it. Allbright does. We're going to see Allbright. I've got to find out more about the legend, more about what I saw. I've got to find something that will help my wife and my daughter, help us put our lives back together. Bagnell knows about the legend. We're going to see Bagnell. And . . . after that, well, we'll *see*. See?"

Stewart, in turn, liked Vlad's mind and sense of humor. But now he saw a man slumped in unhappiness, confusion, pain. There was much that he wanted to know about what happened. Much he dared not ask, which he knew would be revealed later. So he merely said, "I see."

Vlad kicked off his shoes, rapidly undressed, said he was too tired for a shower. "Have one in the morning. Too tired even to put on the jammies. Maybe I'll put them on in the morning, too. Going to stay up reading? Try the Gideon Bible, Job xv, 28, as a starting text. Leave the light on in the bathroom, if you like. *Night*."

Jack turned on his reading light. Gideon Bible? Well, there weren't many things you *could* do in a motel room. Job, huh, xv . . . 26, 27, ah . . . His finger traced its way to the verse.

28. *And he dwelleth in desolate cities, and in houses which no man inhabiteth* . . .

Jack Stewart decided to leave the light on in the bathroom.

Robert E.L. Allbright lived amidst the dense green kudzu vines, way away from anywhere, and very far away from the highways. The hand he held out was large and reddened and splotched . . . a description of his face, as well. His eyes were red-rimmed and he blinked a lot. "I hope, Professor, that you may have had my letter?" asked Vlad Smith politely. Blink. Blink. "In which I said that I'd like to talk with you about the possible origins of the legends of the Paper-Man, or the Boss in the Wall?" Blink. Blink.

It was not clear if Allbright had led them into his office or his dining room. At one end of a table strewn with books and papers, a late teenaged boy was sitting beside a sort of barricade erected out of old law-books, eating breakfast cereal and milk. "My grandson, Albert S.J. Allbright. In theory he is reading law with me. When he is finished he will be a foremost authority on the foreclosure of mules." His voice had fallen into the flattening tones of the increasingly deaf.

The boy slightly turned his head and raised his hand to it, as though to wipe away Rice Crispies and, looking straight at Stewart said, low-voiced, "You got a joint?"

Stewart opened his mouth to reply, looked at his elders and turned his own head slightly.

The boy got up and shuffled dishes. "Go git you some coffee," he said.

"Give you a hand," said Stewart.

"Well," said Allbright, "I got your letter, where did I put that shoe box?" He rummaged among the many shoe boxes and other things on the table. "Put it – Florsheim Shoes – here." He took up the shoe box, turned it over. A sheaf of typescript settled down on the table. Inasmuch as the width of the average shoe box is somewhat less than that of the average sheet of typing paper, someone had neatly trimmed the papers. The idea had something of the simplicity of genius.

"Here 'tis," Allbright said, "Here 'tis. *A True Account Prepared From The Original Testimony, of the Capture and Death of a Paper-Man on the Lands and Domains of Jim Oglethorpre Allbright, Esquire, as edited by his Grandson, Professor Robert E.L. Allbright. With Notes and Commentaries.* – Sorry I don't have a clear copy to give you. Like to look at it?"

"Well," said Vlad, slightly bowled over. "I'd like to . . . yes . . . I'd like to talk with you about it. I'd like you to tell me about it, if you don't mind."

Allbright said there was mighty little to tell. "He was located, as my diagram shows, my map here, he was found in one of the old tobacco barns we used to have. And it was set fire to, and he was seen as he ran off, and he was tracked down. My Great Grandmother was at hand, and she rallied the Negras, and they behaved very bravely, yes sir. My Grandfather was at war at the time, and his old mother guarded the fort, so to speak, and gave them courage. Because generally speaking they would have fled like deer from such an apparition; who could blame them?"

Who indeed, thought Vlad bleakly.

"As it was, they stoned him with stones until he died."

"*What?*"

Old Allbright slowly nodded his massive, mottled head. "It is what happened, Professor Smith. To be sure." He looked at Vlad directly. "There were skeptics, aren't there always? Some of them said he was a Union prisoner, escaped from Andersonville Prison. Prison *camp*, we would call it nowadays. Some said *that* was why he was so gant. Well, no one denies that Andersonville was very bad. What comes of putting a Dutchman in charge of things. A Switzerdutchman. Starved his prisoners, the scoundrel. Went back to Switzerland during the war, went and returned by running the blockade. How much you want to bet he put a lot of money in one of those banks over there?"

Jack Stewart and the younger Allbright returned, carrying a tray with coffee and mugs, which they set on the table.

"As for the other skeptical account, why, some said that the creature killed was a Confederate deserter who had stripped off his uniform so as not to be identified, and had taken up some rags of old clothes from who knows where, maybe from a farmhouse in the middle of a battlefield. You know there was an old farmhouse right in the midst of the Battle of Bull Run, and an old lady died in that house during the battle, and who knows what went on in there. And as for the creature's gant condition, maybe he hadn't eaten well while he was hiding and skulking. He was discovered in the tobacco barn and tobacco is a filthy weed. I like it, but it's not *nourishing*, which might explain his extreme thinness, and if hunger left him too weak to bathe in a creek, his extreme filthiness – *if* the explanations of the skeptics be true. I have offered this fully-documented account to no less than four-teen publications, and would you believe that ten of them decisively declined, and that four did not even reply?"

Jack said, rather abruptly, "If you tell it, sir, I would believe it. Otherwise I would not."

Vlad also looked surprised. "I should think that such an account of the myth in action would be very acceptable, con-sidering the historical period, and from someone of your stature in the field."

"My stature in the field. Well, well." Blink. Blink. His reddened face grew redder yet, but his voice remained flat. "If you had spent as much time in the Groves of Ac*adee*mee as I have, it would perhaps surprise you less." He poured coffee.

Later in the car Vlad said, "I don't mind telling you that I was feeling just a bit spooked."

The kudzu vines sped by, sped by. There seemed to be hardly anybody around, and the few people they saw didn't seem to be doing anything. Surely they did not, could not, eat the damned stuff.

"Know what you mean," Jack Stewart said. "What'd you think of that boy, buried alive out here, no wonder he couldn't think of anything except grass."

"Well, you can't smoke kudzu."

"He said a funny thing, we were sort of rapping about that and this. Well *I* did most of the talking about old Paper-Man, and he said, 'You know Larraby's got one locked up, don't you?' And I said, 'No, who's Larraby, and what's he got?' And then he took a looooong toke, and he said, 'Well, if you don't know who Larraby is, then I don't know what he's got.'"

Vlad said, "We can ask Ed Bagnell at Sumner Public College."

And then conversation faded away in the face of endless green tangles of kudzu . . . kudzu.

Dr Edward Bagnell was on the telephone: "Dr Claire Zimmerman, please. Claire? Ed. Do you have your little slate and pencil there? Okay, Listen. On whatsoever excuse, I want you to go to Rhode Island and see Dr Silas Abbott Selby of the Providence Plantations Museum; this refers to the Paper-Man Project. It's of gross importance and intense confidence; you will go and question Selby about a rumor that he has a Paper-Man's head. *Don't* scream into the phone, for God's sake. Heard it from Curator Luke Larraby of the Carolina Coast Museum, who has Selby in the sights of his Parrott guns – that's confidential. I doubt if one visit will get you a peep, but be prepared to keep at it. It may require a slightly less severe costume and manner; that's up to you. That's all. Kiss, kiss."

Silas Selby had another view of the matter. He sipped Fundador, and looked at Claire over the rim of the glass. Her cropped dark hair framed her round face. They were in the W. Waldo Brown Room, endowed by the philanthropist of that name, some said in order to have a quiet place to drink brandy without his wife.

"Larraby has no training as a museum specialist whatsoever," he said flatly. "He was an architect, and sort of a house doctor for old houses, patching them up, I mean. By and by he began to do work for the old museums down there in Carolina. Well, they were short all kinds of trained people, and he was a quick study, enthusiastic and willing to turn his hand to anything, willing to read up and become the local authority on anything; just the sort of man they needed when the curatorship fell vacant." Selby sipped his brandy, gazed at Claire, and let his eyebrows rise and fall.

"Well, somehow or other Luke had acquired a local mummy. Ante-bellum, post-bellum, or just plain bellum. There are places throughout the world where the soil tends to preserve bodies laid to rest, and such bodies sometimes turned up down Luke's way in places unexpected. I think they became sort of cult objects, who can say why? People went mum when one asked, and people looked at each other out of the corners of their eyes. Local name for them was 'Paper-Men' or 'Paper Doll,' because the local lovers of grue and ghoulishness had been in the habit of padding their wasted bodies with old newspapers under the clothes, which made them look less gant and skeletal, chests less fallen in, stomachs less shrunken and so on. The ancient Egyptians used small sacks of cedar sawdust for the same purpose, after all. It is reminiscent of old Jeremy Bentham, stuffed and mounted and in his best clothes, attending the annual meetings of the . . . whichever society. – Now perhaps I should not be *tell*ing you all this, Doctor Zimmerman, may I call you Claire? But I feel I can count upon your –?"

He peered at her again over his wine-glass. She assured him (again) that he might count on her.

"More brandy, Miss Zimmerman, or a biscuit? Very well, though I hate to be a solitary drinker." Selby sipped his own. "I was visiting the provincial museums, and had to go about checking it ever so circumspectly. Couldn't come right out and demand to see it. Well, Larraby kept that Paper Doll thing hidden in a Rinso box in a *broom* closet! It was in three pieces, in totally deplorable condition. A great troll of a janitor was lurking around. Details shall be spared you. 'Luke, confound it, this should be kept in a moisture- and temperature-controlled, sealed case.' "

"Couldn't agree with you more," said Larraby.

"Then why isn't it?"

"Haven't got one, is why. Besides, our fragrant friend might spook the city senseless."

" 'And there should be a series of tests made, examinations, measurements, tissue samples. Let me give this some thought.' To make the matter short, a complex plan was worked out. Some recently acquired shekel medallions would be sent to Larraby as sort of hostages, and the head of his precious mummy would be sent north to Rhode Island to be tested, *teeth* for example. Meanwhile I looked into getting a proper sealed case for it. But after a very short time, old Luke Larraby began demanding his, um, object back, and making ridiculous charges that the shekels weren't authentic. Said the shekel medallions, of 18th century European manufacture, had been represented as actual 2nd century shekels of the last Jewish Commonwealth, which was certainly *not* stipulated in the agreement. Said his miserable mini-museum had now provided a more secure repository than the broom closet. Well, the tests take a long time, so Silas Abbott Selby stood firm." The empty glass came down firmly on the table and his eyes firmly held Claire's.

"And I am not likely to yield, my dear Miss, ah, my dear Doctor Zimmerman, for in strictest confidence, there is a great deal of mystery about this whole thing. The tests are inconclusive, but I can disclose that the tests show no traces of such chemical embalming agents as arsenic or formaldehyde or anything more modern. Though what they did disclose was both interesting and puzzling. Certain tissues are inconsistent with . . . the state of certain sinew fragments, soft tissue, brain matter and spinal matter, epidermal cells . . . but I have no wish to be prolix. Oh, the press would like nothing more, nothing better than to compare us, by 'us' I mean the Carolina Coast Museum and the General Museum of the Province of Rhode Island and Providence Plantations, compare us to Burke and Hare. Ha ha."

"Oh, surely you need not rush away now. A glass of Fundador? Do let me pour you, our Fundador is famous – well, I have very much enjoyed. And should you hear, should you just hear any of, ha ha ha, *Curator* Larraby's, he has *no* degree in museum science, you know, of his complaints against this ancient and august institution, older than our Republic, well, ha ha, just consider the source. Allow me to help you with your wraps – well, Goodnight, Miss, Doctor Zimmerman. Claire."

In a semi-senile tortoise shuffle came Dr H. Brown Roberts. "Who was that young woman, Selby? Surely you were not entertaining a personal female guest in these semi-Senatorial chambers, endowed by Uncle Waldo Brown, eh? Looked like a flapper to me. Eh?"

Framed in the arch of the ancient gallery, Dr Roberts wagged his snowy head. His white-thatched nostrils gleamed. "Well, I suppose it doesn't signify. I'm only old Harry Roberts, and I don't signify, though I *am* still on the Budget Committee. I guess I know a flapper when I see one, and I know a good bottle of Fundador when I see one, so pour me a glass, Silas Selby. Call me a Brandy Baptist if you like, what care I; I'm only old Harry Roberts and my years of labor don't signify. Pour me *two* glasses of good Spanish brandy, or I'll tell the Budget Committee about your stinking old head, and what will they say about *that*? – Ah. Hah ha. Mmmm. Tell you I know a flapper when I see one."

Edward Bagnell, Doctor of Philosophy, friend of Dave Branch, and holder of other distinctions greeted Vlad Smith and Jack Stewart in the Elephant Room of Sumner Public College's Museum of Ethnology. The Elephant Room contained a rather large and awful oil painting of the progress of some Hindu maharaja, the gift of a long-ago benefactor. The painting's cleaning was fiercely resisted on the grounds that it was best left obscured.

Bagnell waved them to a large leather sofa. "I daresay you'd like to know *why* it's Sumner *Public* College? *Every*body wants to. I am able to dispel the mystery. The founding fathers and the one founding mother put the word in to show that the college was a serf to neither church nor state. As some still *are*. How do you like the Elephant Room? It looks like the antechamber of a rather seedy club, but here the Department of Ethnology holds out by being part anthropology, part folklore, and part whatever. We claim to have pioneered the inter-disciplinary study; haw. And *here* is where the ethnologists gather to drink embalming fluid, as wine is only allowed on campus for certain ceremonial occasions. How is Allbright doing?"

Stewart took the reply upon himself. "Old man gives the

impression that he's mostly letting the kudzu grow over him, but he isn't really. And the boy makes cryptic statements such as 'Larraby's got one locked up.' " He repeated what he had told Vlad and concluded, "You have any idea what that means, Dr Bagnell?"

Ed Bagnell shrugged. "Probably that Larraby, whoever he may be, has a report on the legend, and is keeping it locked up until he's ready to publish. Typical academic paranoia, eh Vlad?"

After answering no more than a grunt, Vlad slowly began to speak of his own and immediate problem. Of encountering by moonlight in the old uninhabited house, something so hideous, noisome, foul that he might have thought it was madness to think it was real. Only to find the sight so real as to drive his small daughter past terror and hysteria. "Do you understand why I'm trying to find out . . ." he waved his hands helplessly, ". . . *what* the damned thing was? That, that *van*ished in an instant? One minute it was there, another minute *nothing* was there, as though, just as though it *had* come out of the wall. The police say 'Tramp' – it was no tramp! The only thing it resembled was that old legend, and that's why I'm here, Ed. In my file on the legend is a collection of items labeled *Bagnell's Notes*. I won't go so far as to say they are yellowed, but they are far from crisp. May I ask how *you* got interested in the legend of the Paper-Man, or whatever name you call it by?"

"I got interested when I read an unpublished paper on it, and remembered I'd long ago met a possible informant, and hadn't realized it. One day when I was a kid, I was walking in a strange part of town and I came to an old house, abandoned and all overgrown. I thought I'd go in and look around, when a creepy old man hobbled from out of nowhere, with torn old clothes, and just a few teeth grinding in stubbly jaws, and he smelled very funny. Later an old lumberjack said to me, as if reading my mind, 'Don't go in that old house, boy, a Boss in the Wall lives there. They're crazy people who think they're dead, and they wrap themselves in paper, and they rattle like snakes and bite like snakes, so don't go in there, boy.' "

Stewart paid the ultimate compliment. He sat straight up and said, "No shit?"

"But I decided that poor old man was just a bum or tramp, who staked out a place for himself and didn't want me inside. Years later I read the unpublished item, and all the elements fit, so naturally I became interested. I wrote a paper on the subject, and mine remains unpublished too. So there you are, gentlemen."

"What conclusions did you come to, for example, about the origins of the legend?" asked Vlad.

Bagnell shrugged. "It's like trying to trace down the origins of a fog. The fog exists and you can see it, but it always seems to begin somewhere else. Compare it to other American legends, that is, you can trace groundhog stories to badger stories, but then you trace them right back to groundhogs. Sometimes we folklorists take every possibility into consideration except the human longing for a good yarn, which sometimes means a good *scary* yarn." A twig snapped in the fireplace and Bagnell said, "If fireplaces were concealed inside walls, they might be called *snappers*. All the legends are attached to old houses, and old houses often creak. They attract drifters and outcasts of broken minds and unclean habits, who remind us of childhood terror-tales of ghosts and skeletons and god knows what. And so a legend evolves."

Vlad asked if Bagnell had anything new to show him. Bagnell suggested he might call Dave Branch, but Vlad remainded him that it was Branch who had sent him to Bagnell.

"Well," Bagnell said, "I don't know what to tell you, Vlad, I just don't know what to tell you."

Vlad did not move for a while, then he let himself sink back in the chair. Behind him hung a beautiful photograph, an enlargement in sepia of a group of Ainu at a long-ago American world's fair. They gazed through the camera as from some lost continent, too dignified to show their infinite bewilderment and their vast sense of doom.

After Vlad and Jack departed, Bagnell picked up the phone: "Dr Bagnell returning Dr Branch's call. Hello, Dave? Yes, I know you hadn't called; that's just a ploy, never fails – *sly*. Listen, one Vladimir Smith Ph.D.. He's tracking the Paper-Man legend. I just have one question: you *didn't* mention the Committee to him, did you? No, good, that's fine. Back to your learned discourses. Bye."

"Rawheaded Bloody Bones" may be an undifferentiated spook, but it is certainly vividly different from the rather enigmatic "The Boss in the Wall" which, to some informants,

*suggests an image of the human mind trapped inside the skull,
and which has been reported from Mobile, Alabama to Jack-
sonville, Florida, and on up the Atlantic Coast for a few states
more. "Rawheaded Bloody Bones" would not remind you
right away of the "Greasy-Man" of Corpus Christi, Brownsville and Porta Isabella (all Texas). In all these places, however, "Greasy-Man" is also known as "String-Fellow" or "The
String-Fellow." It's been conjectured that the latter name may
come from the jerky, puppet-like walk attributed to the phenomenon. In New Orleans, of course, where every superstition
flourishes, most of these names may be found, plus, as might
be expected, the* zomby–zumbi–jumbie–duppy *group of names
(see* Limekiller): *with the important difference that no "Paper-
Man" etc. has ever been alleged "held to service or labor." In
other words, Zomby may have been at one time a slave, but
Paper-Man was not.*

– Bagnell's *Notes*

Bagnell had arranged for Vlad and Jack to stay in a college
guesthouse where Bagnell, himself, had recently stayed while his
house was being painted. In the drawer of a nightstand Vlad
found a sheaf of forgotten papers, labeled *Duplicate of Dr
Bagnell's Committee Report*. Vlad felt a twinge of scruple. Should
he read it? But what has been duplicated can hardly be personal.
So . . .

"Mr Ernest Anderson is a trapper in a nearby state. He and his
family moved into a structure known locally as 'the Old Linsey
Mill.' The exterior is brick, but the inside is built of more eclectic
materials. The main mill building has been closed for years, and
the family lives in part of it. From the start of their residence there,
it seems there were odd noises and odd smells, and one of the
children claimed to have seen something. Mr Anderson, being a
trapper, set a number of traps. On the night of the given date, a
loud noise was heard from the second floor, described as the
rattling and thrashing of a creature caught in a trap. Mr Anderson
and other male relatives left the living quarters to rush upstairs,
but then they heard loud screams and ran back to the living
quarters, because one of the children was having some sort of fit."

Here Vlad's blood ran cold as he continued reading . . .

"Mr Anderson drove the child to the West County Medical

Center, and it wasn't until much later that he was able to check the upstairs trap. It had been sprung, and inside the trap was a badly crushed, but easily identifiable human foot that seemed to be in a mummified condition. There was no sign of blood, and there was an immensely strong and fetid odor. I asked Mr Anderson if the force of the trap being sprung could have severed the foot from the ankle. He answered, and remember that he has long been a trapper; he said that the foot had been gnawed off."

Attached to the pages was an envelope, and inside the envelope was a horrible close-up photograph. Of the foot. Vlad let the pages flutter away. He tried to swallow, but found that he could not. After a while he got up and went for a glass of water.

"You all right, Vlad?" asked Jack from the adjoining room.

"No, I am not."

"Want to tell me about it?"

"No, I don't." Vlad gave him the papers. Jack read them and looked up with an expression part-puzzled, part-unhappy. Vlad handed him the envelope. Jack looked at the photograph, then looked at Vlad with horrified eyes. "Jesus," he said.

Vlad said, "What the hell? Is this a loop? Am I a prisoner in a Moebius strip, or is it all a bad dream?"

Jack Stewart said, "No, it's not a bad dream. I'm sorry, I wish it were. I still don't know what it means, but it's not what we thought it meant – what we were *told* it meant. We're in another country from now on. A country with strange inhabitants and unknown boundaries."

IV.   Bagnell's Quest

Bagnell was walking, on his way to see Larraby again.

Who first developed the notion of The Phenomenon of the One-Legged Man in the Blue Baseball Cap? Bagnell did not know, but he knew the phenomenon well enough. You never saw such a person in your life, the story went, and the first day you see him, you see two more. Not merely *two*, mind you, but *two more*. Walking past the row of old stores which had, almost too late, been saved from destruction by a committee of concerned citizens – concerned, and prosperous – called Rowan Row, simply because it was on Rowan Street; walking along on the other side of the street, Bagnell looked up. He looked up with a jerk of his head; he had not intended to stop, for he had walked slowly past the old buildings earlier, had looked in the shop windows, seen nothing he wanted to examine closely; he looked up now with a jerk of his head. Had he seen, could he have seen a sign reading *Paper-Man*? He had not. Not quite.

The shop buildings were all of brick and one story high, and dated from the 1830s. Some attempt had been made to preserve or restore the period flavor: where the tobacco store had been was a tobacco store now, and outside it was a wooden Indian. *Apothecary's* had a row of very attractive apothecary's jars on display, plus antique equipment in a glass case, and as for the rest, offered exactly what was sold in any other drugstore.

PasTime Paper Antiques, the sign read; which Bagnell had seen out of the corner of his ever-ready-to-deceive-you eyes. It had not caught his attention at first because it was, actually, above eye-level on its own side of the street. He stared a moment. He crossed the street. In the window were such things as well-weathered marriage documents illuminated in color in the Pennsylvania Dutch *fraktur* style, with flowering trees never seen even in botanical gardens, on the boughs of which were *distelfinks*, birds unknown to ornithology. There were a pair of US Navy certificates identifying Chauncey Casey as *Caulker* and Clarence Casey as *Sailmaker*, dated in the 1890s. There were a few posters in extravagant tints, and a small sedate notice, *more inside*. Bagnell noticed a selection of lacy valentines.

Bagnell noticed the Paper-Man in the very front part of the window.

An old-fashioned bell bobbed and dipped and rang as Bagnell swung the door widely open. An informally-neatly-dressed gentleman in perhaps his early forties appeared from behind an oriental screen. "If there were a time-travel machine," the man said, quizzing his eyebrows, "I'd go back and murder whoever it was who cut something out of this copy of *Godey's Ladies' Book*, October 1842. Just imagine. Does this interest you? Yours for a dollar." He thrust it forward, but Bagnell did not thrust a dollar at him.

"I'd like to see one of the daguerreotypes in the window," Bagnell said. He realized that he was speaking very fast. He realized that he was breathing very fast. "The second one from the right."

314   *AVRAM DAVIDSON & GRANIA DAVIS*

"Certainly. – Please help yourself," the man gestured to two bowls on a little table, and went forward to the window. With great control, Bagnell did not go with him, did not even turn to watch him. He examined the bowls. One contained small candies; the other was full of business cards reading:

PasTime Paper Antiques
Number 7, Rowan Row
Mr Sydney, Proprietor

Mr Sydney, Proprietor, returned. He held in his hand what looked like a tiny book, and handed it to Bagnell, who at once unclasped the tiny hook and reopened it: it was the right one. It was the likeness of a young man in uniform, in no way remarkable, one might see him or his mates today drinking canned beer and watching television anywhere in town. Anywhere in the United States. "That is real leather and real brass, the casing, I mean, hardly to be found anymore anywhere; and the same goes for the satin facing the picture."

Bagnell asked the price, and Mr Sydney slipped behind the screen and returned with a loose-leaf notebook which he now consulted. "Ah, yes. The collection of six daguerreotypes, I must tell you that they are actually ambrotypes, a slightly later process, but I follow your own usage which is my own as well; the collection of six daguerreotypes are for sale at $1,000, plus, alas, State sales tax of 3.7 percent. Sell only the single one? Oh I am *afraid* not. They are after all a collection, and I couldn't sell just one. Not for less than $200, that is. And no, we don't take credit cards or out-of-state checks. Sorry. These are after all collectors' items, and a *very* good investment." He proceeded to tell Bagnell about one such which had appreciated even as it sat in the window; adding, "Though if these are still here when the weather gets hotter, of course I will bring them inside because I am afraid of them fading."

Curator Luke Larraby gave a grunt of surprise at seeing Bagnell again so soon, but he was not uncivil, and listened to him without interruption. He said, "Calm down, we're not used to excitement here, in fact haven't had any since the Yankee army passed through town, thank the Lord they didn't even stop to burn it.

Excitement, yes. I don't feel I can discount the possibility that you are still in a state of excitement – even shock. It is a shocking sight, that photograph of mine – and those things I showed you. So . . . Oh of course I'll go stroll by and take a look at the one you say is in . . . where? Rowan Row. Oh." He looked at the card Bagnell gave him. "It would be one of the most remarkable coincidences if, actually, they were – Ho. Mr Sydney, yes. Know him. Done business with him, *business*, you get the point? Sydney is not running a junkyard. Now settle down. Rome wasn't built in a day. *Quit that fidgeting*."

Bagnell extended his stay at his motel, drove slowly back to the old Carolina Coast Museum, went up the blue slate steps, scooped and hollowed by the passing feet of a century. Larraby was there, and beckoned him in from inside his private office. "Aw right. Saw – it. What? *Course* it's the same face! Out*rage*ous coincidence! Against all known laws of probability. However. We must have a copy of Sydney's ambro and work from there. No other choice. And it's up to you to get him to let you make that copy. They're not photographic negatives, you know that, of course. We'll have to photograph it and produce our own negative. Enlarge it. Well – enlarge them *both*. Go over them with magnifying lens and fine-tooth comb. Have *you* got $200 cash on you, by the way? Ha. *Thought* not."

Bagnell found himself breathing rapidly again. "Look here, Luke" – a silvery-tufted eyebrow shot up, but Larraby listened, – "this is absolutely the first time it's been even possible to *think* of its being even possible to provide any element of pre-history of a Paper-Man, and you *can't* let it go by and risk losing it forever."

Larraby, still calm in his naturally-cool old-fashioned office, with sepia-tinted framed photographs of his predecessors on its walls; Larraby, still calm, said it was Bagnell's fault for showing enthusiasm. "However. I understand your emotion. Still, why he wants $200, $200 for a daguerreotype of a nobody, for that price you ought to get one of Lola Montez naked – and I have not *got* that $200 in my budget."

Bagnell gnawed his neat mustache. "Well, how much *have* you got that you can spend to borrow the picture, just borrow it and have it copied? I mean, you absorb the copying costs, and I'm sure I can manage a pro rata share of it – how much?"

The old curator sighed and canted his head and looked at his wall calendar. "Oh . . . $50? *Tops*."

Mr Sydney was cautious. Mr Sydney smelled something. Bagnell offered to have it cleaned for him. "No charge."

"*Cleaned*? It's as clean as a whistle! Look at it. Beautiful condition. What –"

"Okay. I'll come clean with you."

"Now we're talking."

"The Carolina Coast Museum –"

"The Carolina Coast Mu – Oh, Lord, *they* don't have a *button*! Nothing doing. Oh, well, what's your offer?"

"An offer of $50 just to –"

Mr Sydney's shock was not assumed. "Fifty *doll*ars! *No* no. Out of the –"

"– just to borrow it for one week for purposes of comparison with another picture."

This was unexpected. Mr Sydney seemed genuinely uncertain. "And what do I do if someone comes in off the Row and asks, 'where's the old snapshot of the boy in uniform, used to be in between Baby Phoebe and Grampa Jukes?' "

"You say 'It's being cleaned. Would you like to put down a deposit? It will be cleaned for you. Free.' "

It was immediately clear that Mr Sydney liked this image. He nodded. His mouth moved, evidently silently repeating the words. "You have a suggestion there. Not bad. Very well. I feel able to do it for you and the museum, but for $75. Impossible for less: risk factor."

Slowly, Bagnell emptied his pockets. There was the fairly crisp $50. And, also, there was a limp $20, and two dim ones, and 50 cents. His sigh was quite immediate. So was Mr Sydney's reaction. "Oh, very well, the Firm will settle for $70, and will cover State tax. The Firm is not hard-hearted. Keep the two-fifty for lunch. The Museum will probably offer you possum *à la taxidermy*. Oh, and I shall require you to show some ID and to sign a little piece of paper, and then shall I gift-wrap it for you? No? But remember now: *Not more than one week*."

"Company in the parlor," Curator Larraby said, briskly.

Bagnell blinked. "An odd phrase to come from a self-admitted church member."

Company, in the small lecture-room (doors locked), consisted of Hughes of the Southeastern Interstate Criminology Institute (commonly called the Crim Lab), and Dr Preston Budworth of every hospital in town. "My colleagues insist that the best specialty is dermatology. They say, 'The patients never die and they never get cured; they just keep coming back.' And I say, 'True, but plastic surgeons make more. Oh boy, yes. Of course, we work *hard* for it, oh, it's hell on the feet.' "

He said no more for the moment, the lights having then been turned off; then he said, "Jesus *Christ*!" – the slide of the Paper-Man's head having briefly flashed on the screen. "Course, I've seen worse," said Dr Budworth. "Oh, lots worse. But seen nothing the same. What in salvation *is* it?" The copy of the ambrotype next appeared. "Soldier boy, hey?" It remained a while, then the severed head, with its cold, sly sneer, came back to grimace at them. Dr Budworth cleared his throat and said, "Looks as though he'd been shot dead at Gettysburg and had his picture taken at Appomattox."

In a voice slow and heavy, Larraby said, "Perhaps you're right."

There was a silence then, broken by Hughes asking, "Is this your question, Curator? 'Are these two pictures of the same man?' Is that it?" Larraby said, yes, that was it. Was asked to show both slides side by side. Did so. Hughes then said he thought they might well be. "For example, that drooping – Oh, excuse me, Dr Budworth." But Budworth told him to go on. "– that drooping eyelid. And then you observe the crease in the ear lobe. Can you see that really very slight scar on the cheekbone, on the opposite side from the drooping eyelid? And, ah, of course in the, I assume, post-mortem photo, some of the teeth are exposed, and you see that the left canine is crooked and protrudes. Of course in the one in uniform, he has his mouth closed, but there is still a slight protrusion just over where that canine would be.

"Now, these are technical observations, though not very technical, and of course my simple guess would have been anyway that it is the same person, some years apart, though I wouldn't offhand guess how many. Not more than ten, I'd say. Maybe even five, or a bit less, since . . . war being war, you know . . ."

The "post-mortem" photo, a perfectly correct description, certainly, had been cropped in the copying process, and it was not evident that the head was separate from the torso. If Hughes suspected anything, Hughes was not saying. To Bagnell, trying to put aside what he knew, merely the difference in the photographic techniques, more than a century apart, was obvious.

Preston Budworth's comments were more technical, but he came to the same conclusion. "Of course I would want to make measurements and enlarge the pictures even more, on as close to even-scale as possible, before I'd sign my name to anything, not that I'm going to, anyway. Historical detective work is lots of fun, of course, and nobody waiting to sue you for malpractice. Well. I wouldn't want to ask where you got that ghouly-looking one from."

Promptly, Hughes said, "*I* would. I *will*. *Where?*"

But they did not tell him. Not yet.

Military historians identified uniform coat and badges as those of the 23rd Patriot Rifles. Phone calls in all directions finally produced Charles O'Neill Sturtevant, Col., USA (Ret.), who had an enormous collection of Civil War photographs. And –

"Mind you, young man, it's a *loan*. Your balls are in bond for it."

"Yes, Colonel, of course, any time you like, sir," babbled Bagnell, scarcely knowing what he was saying.

On that red-letter day, against what awesome odds, Ed Bagnell found what he was hoping for: printed off a cracked wet-plate, though only slightly cracked, the likenesses of three young men, frozen stolid, hands on knees; and on the back the signatures – two florid and scrawly/scrolly, one awkward and cramped – Corporal W.M. Ewing. Private Elwen Michaels. Private Ephraim Mackilwhit.

Now for the first time, there was a *name*.

The 23rd Patriot Rifles had been enlisted in Gainsboro, as far to the South as it was perhaps possible for a Northern town to be, and there Bagnell went as fast as was consistent with speed laws, and energy consistent with small packets of crackers-and-cheese sold in gas stations. In the Gainsboro phone book he pushed a restless finger down the columns in search of people named Mackilwhit.

He found not one.

That is, the current one contained not one. At the public library, in the reference room: "Out-of-date telephone directories? Nooo. We don't keep them."

"Oh . . ." Sinking voice, sinking feeling.

"But I'll tell you who *does*. Mr Rodeheaver does. I'll write down the address for you."

Homer would have felt at home in the old room where Mr Rodeheaver worked. Bagnell felt that if he had wanted the directory for Fusby-le-Mud, 1901, it would have been there. Mr Rodeheaver perhaps collected them, perhaps compiled mailing lists, or traced missing heirs. Bagnell didn't care. Mr Rodeheaver was getting on in years and he listened patiently; then he asked, "What's it worth to you?"

"Worth –?"

"Is it worth five dollars?"

Mr Rodeheaver began to pull down old phone books and pile them on his dusty desk; beckoned Bagnell to come look. Waited while he did. Ceasing three years before, but as far back from then, farther back than Bagnell cared to go, a Mrs Lambert Mackilwhit had lived at 269 Longfellow Avenue. Bagnell copied the address, handed the man a crumpled five-dollar bill.

"Well, there's lunch," said Mr Rodeheaver.

Did she still live there? Had she died three years ago? Had she just given up her phone, there being too few left alive to call her? Or, perhaps, there had been some difficulty about a bill, and she had let her listing lapse, and had a phone installed in the name of a neighbor, friend, or . . . well, probably not. But. Hurt to try? Might find a lead. Leads *had* been found, one after another.

Two-sixty-nine was in rather better shape than the other houses, which had all once been neat and bright . . . long ago . . . and Mrs Mackilwhit lived in a little room on the top floor, whither he was directed by a series of ageless women in cotton house-dresses, of whom each seemed to have three children and one *in utero*. But Mrs Mackilwhit was not ageless. Mrs. Mackilwhit was very aged indeed, and her skin hung in heavy flaps.

Did she know of an Ephraim Mackilwhit, who had served in the Civil War? A silence. The room smelled, rather, but of nothing worse than old people's flesh and of cabbage, and perhaps it was only the neighbors' cabbage. The room contained what was left of her life as it had drawn in upon itself, decade after decade; there was hardly room enough to move, although no doubt the woman who lived there had moved enough. She sat in her chair and she did not move now, and she stared at nothing which other people could see.

Silence. Then – "He disappeared," she said at last. "Lambert's, my husband's aunts, used to speak of him. He was the black sheep of the family. He went away and he never came back. Yes. He disappeared."

Bagnell had brought another picture along, of another group of soldiers, as a sort of control, and now he put both in her hands. "Might you recognize a family resemblance?"

She pushed one away after a glance, but the other one she looked at long and long. "A family resemblance. Yes. The one at the end. On the right. He has Lambert's look. Yes. He has Lambert's look." And, very silently, her slow tears rained along the ruined landscape of her face.

A family resemblance. *Is not Ephraim a beloved child*? And what had he come to? A thing in three boxes: shrivelled, withered, broken, and foul. But now at last, thank God forever dead.

Bagnell to Larraby: "*Where* was Ephraim Mackilwhit . . . that is, where was the Paper-Man found? Come clean."

"Basement storeroom, in an old private girls' school in Gainsboro, couple years ago. Mustee was picking up a little extra money there as a weekend relief watchman," said Larraby.

Thither went Dr Claire Zimmerman, at Bagnell's request, to interview the headmistress, Mrs Sidwell:

"Yes, this *is* one of the oldest houses in town. It is well-preserved, and consequently required no major restorations. It has made an excellent private school building." Mrs Sidwell stopped and thought. "Do I recall anything *odd* happening a couple of years ago? Well, there was a . . . I suppose the word I have to use is *prank*. It's difficult to say when a prank gets out of hand and becomes . . . something more. Dr Rose Bennett asked me into her Advanced English class during a morning break. She said there was something on the blackboard she didn't like. Of course I expected what we used to call a naughty word. *Are* there anymore naughty words? I haven't quite grown used to hearing sweet girls talking like sailors. Well, no, it wasn't a naughty word. The words *Nothing but Death* were written on the blackboard, and the writing was odd . . . somehow *wrong*. The next day the same words were written on a blackboard in room A-6, and the following morning, there it was again. Security and maintenance promised to keep a close watch on room A-6, and the next day the words *Nothing but Death* appeared in room C-12! When that happened, *every*body began to get nervous. Well, we photographed the words, sponged all the blackboards, and read the riot act to security and maintenance, but still it appeared. Of course you'd like to see it . . ." Mrs Sidwell rummaged in a drawer and handed an enlarged photograph to Claire, who studied it intently.

"Then Rose Bennett remembered that those were Jane Austen's dying words. But the handwriting bore no resemblance to samples of Jane Austen's, and we weren't even teaching Jane Austen that year. So our school was being haunted by a spectre with a good knowledge of early 19th century English literature. But who?"

"Judging from the cramped and wavering writing, it must have been somebody very sick, or very tired," said Claire.

"Oh my, I don't like the sound of that, though you're probably right. I must say, the whole thing gave me the creeps. Do you think somebody very *old* wrote it? The writing looks so weak and old fashioned. But why would an old person come creeping in like that? I asked Rose Bennett what the class had been discussing, the day before the words appeared. She remembered that she had asked them; 'If you could be granted only one wish, what would you wish for?" The next morning, the words began to appear: *Nothing but death*. Then just as suddenly, it stopped."

Claire examined the photograph closely. "What's that down at the bottom of the blackboard? It looks like the letters 'E.M.' in the same writing."

"Oh yes, sometimes that appeared too. But nobody knew what it meant," said Mrs Sidwell. And then the bell rang and she had to go.

Vlad Smith and Jack Stewart were bedded down in an old-fashioned Tourist Guesthouse for the night. It was owned by Mrs Warrington, who looked like a gentlewoman in reduced circumstances. A bottle and glasses stood on the table next to a small pile of rather unprofessional-looking printed matter.

Jack tugged a comb through his tangled molasses curls and picked one up. "Nice old guy who gave us these," he said. "Mr Pabrocky. All these years he's been sending you these things and then all of a sudden you turn up on his doorstep. *The News Bulletin of the Atlantic Folk Lore,* two words and no hyphen, very dubious usage, *Club,*" he read. "Volume XV, number 11, to be precise. 'WHO'S BOSS IN YOUR WALL?' Cute, hey? *There is a story told particularly in the south eastern and south central states of a spook or specter or bogle or hant who inhabitants houses and other older, usually, buildings. He is musty and gant and lives in the walls and floors and empty rooms and is seldom seen. The description is that he is skeletal but unlike other such myths he is depicted as wearing old clothes and is afraid of cats and fires. Perhaps because he is all dried up? It is quite a task to look this subject up in indexes and bibliographies, for one thing because it has so many names and for another so little seems to have been published. So we urge our members to make inquiries wherever they happen to be. Perhaps our little amateur News Bulletin may provide some information which the learned quarterlies have not. This folk tale figure is called 'Paper-Man' because he lives behind the wall paper which used to be on every wall but now no longer owing to the high cost and labor and also, we assume, because of a prejudice that 'Bugs' breed there. This creature issues a noise which is variously described as clicking or clattering or even rustling. Hence the various names of 'Rustler' or 'Clicker' as well as 'the Boss in the Wall.' Another name is 'House Devil' and Mary Mae Subchak reports she has heard it referred to as 'the Devil in the Wall.' "*

Stewart next applied his lips to a glass, then said, "Well, I would give this a . . . a B-minus. You, Dr Smith? Trouble with amateurs, they are always reinventing the wheel."

"MORE ON PAPER-MAN NAMES (CONT.)" Jack read.

"We find that the so-called 'Minorcan' descended people of St Augustine, Fla., employ the name or term 'Clicky Dicky.' Alas for our hopes that we might find some such Spanish survival variants. Crossing the peninsula to Pensacola, we note that 'Clicky Dicky' has become 'Tricky Dicky,' a term extending as far south on that coast as Tampa. We were unable to find this legend at all in St Petersburg, Fla, an absence tentatively attributed to the Northern-Origin of so Many of The People in the 'Winter Capital'. Mr

Pabrocky has suggested, with the well-known twinkle in his eye, that it is remarkable nonetheless that neither 'Clicker' nor 'Clicky Dicky' is to be found where there are so many Senior Citizens (of whom he is one!), considering how many of them have the medically well-known condition, 'a clicking knee-cap'! Humor apart, this does raise the QUESTION, if the 'clicking' attributed to the specter comes from the sound of teeth as had generally been believed or to some other source. Hmmm." Jack put the *News Bulletin* down.

Vlad sighed wearily. "Is there any more brandy in the bottle?"

There was no more brandy in the bottle. They argued back and forth about opening another bottle. Each took both sides. Then they opened another bottle.

"Should we read more mind-improving books now?" asked Jack.

Vlad said he'd rather *write* a mind-improving book called, "*The Myth of the Paper-Man Examined and Refuted*. Even that title shows how far I've come in my thinking. A month ago I'd no more have needed to refute it than I would have refuted Dracula or Frankenstein. Household words; everybody knows about them, but nobody *believes* in them, or cowers in *fear* of them."

Jack slipped a cassette of Buxtehude's *Misa Brevis* into his lil ole cassette player. His movements made goofy shadows on the wall. "That nice?" he asked.

"More than nice, it's ravishing," said Vlad sleepily. "When it's over, play it again, Sam."

Perhaps Sam had played it again, but now it was not playing. A shadow was playing on the floor, which *goofy* would not describe. It looked like the shadow of an enormous four-legged spider gliding upside down across the floor. Whatever it was looked horrible. Dear god, would he forever be seeing horrid and impossible things?

Jack was sitting up in his bed with his face gone ghastly. Then he leaped out of his bed and out of their room, and went roaring and running down the hallway. "Where did it go? Did you *see* it, Vlad? It ran along the *ceiling*!" Jack dragged a table and chair into the hallway and started to climb on it.

Mrs Warrington appeared, with her hair in a gray-streaked braid, and a man's bathrobe over her nightgown. She stretched out her hands and called, "Mr Stewart! You must stop this *now*!"

"Miz Warrington! Where did it go? Where did it come from? What *lives* in this hallway?"

Many expressions passed rapidly over her worn face, but now they settled into one expression: a gentlewoman in reduced circumstances. "Mr Stewart," she said in a quick but firm and level voice, "I am very sorry that you had a bad dream, but I will not be shouted at in my own house, and I refuse to hold a conversation with a strange man in his underwear. Please take the table and chair *back*, sir!"

"No I *won't*, Miz Warrington, not yet. Please excuse me ma'am," said Jack, as he climbed onto the table and chair, and began to examine the imperfect surface of the ceiling.

Mrs Warrington was actually wringing her hands. "What is he *doing*? Can't you make him *stop*, Professor Smith? You have terrified me with those awful yells, and now *this*! What is it?"

Jack said in doleful tones, "It didn't rattle or click, but I know what it is, ma'am, and I reckon you know too."

The woman's face seemed to collapse in upon itself, and she tottered and leaned against the wall, for just a moment, then sprang away as though it were red-hot. Her voice was now trembling but fierce. "This guesthouse is all I have to live on. I don't know who you are, but I want you to get out right *now*. I don't want your money, please *go*!"

They went as soon as they could dress and pack. Without discussion they left money on the table. Then they got into the car and drove in silence, with Vlad behind the wheel. His sallow face was weary, and his blue-gray eyes were troubled and gray.

"What did you see?" Vlad finally asked.

"I woke up and saw this *thing* scuttling across the ceiling. Something like a man, but horribly bony and filthy, and utterly nasty in some way I can't describe. You?"

"I just saw the shadow," said Vlad. "I never heard of one on the ceiling."

"It was clinging by its long nails to the tiny gaps in the plaster, and the flaps of torn clothing swayed, and that vile body swayed too. I don't know where it came from, or where it went to. There's no window or hatchway, only a little ventilation slit that maybe a rat could get through, but not a *man*."

Eventually they stopped at the brightest and newest motel they could find, with walls too thin for even a roach to hide.

Mr Pabrocky's *News Bulletin* led Vlad and Jack to a privately-endowed art museum. They were repeating a list of names to the "museum lady", and the list had begun to seem very tiresome and, indeed, loathsome. ". . . or the Boss in the Wall . . .?" Vlad finished the list, and a look of great surprise came over her face.

She said, "Of *course*. Hobson's Ghost. You know that all institutions have their skeletons in the closet. That one is ours. Long ago we bought what is known as a 'primitive' portrait, meaning it was painted by a self-taught, itinerant artist. It showed a woman sitting in a room. Evidently something was painted into the picture which wasn't apparent. Something was painted over, and then the over-paint sloughed off. It rose to the surface like a ghost, and it was ghost-like, and quite famous for a while. But finally we had to take the picture off exhibition because parents complained that it scared their children – and it probably scared *them*. On the old acquisition slip is written *Hobson*. We aren't sure if that's the subject or the artist, and faintly penciled in is *Boss in the Wall*. Whatever *that* means. Would you like to see it?"

Primitive it certainly was. A late middle-aged woman sat stiffly in a chair in an old-fashioned room. Her skirt was long and black, her shawl was white, and her face was stiff. Above her was something gray and ghastly that seemed to ooze from a panel in the wall. It looked like the bleached carapace of a long-dead spider, with bared teeth, and skeletal hands with clawing nails. Its expression was both fearful and malignant. *Hobson's Ghost*.

"Oh god, yes," said Vlad in a sick, weak voice. "That's it . . . a Boss in the Wall. Do you know any more about it?"

"Well, there is an old story about a Henry and Hannah Hobson, who were settlers over in Blainesville. He was a wi-dower, she a widow. He wanted to move west to live with his children. She wanted to move east to live with *her* children. Folks didn't divorce or separate in those days, so they quarreled day and night. Then either he got sick and she let him die without calling a doctor, or she slowly poisoned his food. Anyway, his last words were that he'd never leave the house alive – and neither would she. And after he died, she never *did* leave. She packed more than once, but never left. Then old Hobson began to haunt her. One time or another, that wretched woman lived in every room of the house. No use. He'd find her, so in the end she hanged herself. There's even an old song about it." The museum lady began to sing in a wavering voice:

"*How the night winds howl, for death seems near to me.*
  Beware, Mr Hobson, do not drink that tea!
I fear my time is fleeting, and death comes in a rush.
  Beware, Mr Hobson, do not sup that mush!
I fear my bad wife Hannah, and I fear my time has come.
  Beware, Mr Hobson, do not drink that rum!
So stand back good Christian people, and do not heed
  her calls.
  For to haunt my bad wife Hannah, I slink slowly
    through the walls!

Now Vlad and Jack were talking to Henry Wabershaw. "I'm named for my grandfather's old Russian friend, Vladimir, for Smithville is full of Edgars, but how many *Vlad* Smiths are there?" said Vlad.

If, inside of Wabershaw's great fat man's body there was a thin man screaming to get out, the screaming was inaudible to either Vlad or Jack. "You fellows from The Committee?" asked Wabershaw, in a small voice almost stifled by his immense flesh.

"The committee?" asked Vlad. "That makes as much sense as 'Larraby's got one.' "

Perhaps Wabershaw understood the nuances of the remark and perhaps he did not. What he said was, "So you know about Larraby, hmm?" He nodded the small face set inside the very large one, and gave them an odd look. After a moment he sighed and said, "I'm sorry I can't ask you boys to have a bite to eat, but there's not a bite in the house." He gazed at them as if he had given a sign and were waiting for a countersign.

Vlad and Jack had been warned that the way to Wabershaw's heart and head was through his stomach, for he was surely eating himself to death. So they were prepared. Stewart now said, "As to that, Mr Wabershaw, as we hadn't yet had our dinner, we took the liberty of bringing a little something along, and wondered if you'd have some with us." He lifted the large paper sacks onto the table.

"Why, *fried* chicken! I always say that fried chicken is the friend of man. And how I love potato salad! *Three* kinds of bread, *real* butter, French mustard, and look at these tempting cold cuts! Oh, I am very fond of raspberry soda. And what might be in this other bag? *Chinese* food! Is there anything nicer than Chinese food?" Then he peeped into a cardboard box and exclaimed with almost erotic glee, "What a *lovely* cake!" Pieces of fried chicken were already on the way to his turtle-like mouth when he paused and said, "*You* boys aren't from The Committee. Catch any of them giving anything – they just *take*! Bagnell, Calloway, Zimmerman, Elbaum, Branch, and the rest of that bunch. They want it *all* for themselves."

"*Branch*!" cried Vlad.

By and by the galloping consumption of food slowed down to a mere nibbling. Wabershaw surveyed the wreckage on the table with elephantine calm and said, "Happiest day in my life."

"Which day was that?" asked Vlad.

"When I first realized that the Boss in the Wall was *real*! Why? Because on that day I knew for sure that I was not going crazy."

"I can appreciate that," said Vlad with heartfelt sincerity.

"When you've been hearing things you can't see, and seeing things you can't believe, why, a fear builds up inside you and your life sort of slumps sideways into a different universe. I tried staying away from home, sleeping in the office and sleeping in hotels. I tried getting drunk and staying drunk, and I lost my good job as State Historian. I was hospitalized twice for nervous breakdowns, and in the hospital I began to put on flesh. Then one day I realized I was *not* crazy, so I came home. And I found a man with trained ferrets, and we sent those ferrets into the walls. Then we heard a terrible thrashing sound in the storeroom, and by the time we got there it was dead – but it had bit some of the ferrets to pieces. The man was pretty mad, and made me pay plenty for the loss of his critters. But I rejoiced, for just the sight and smell of that House-Devil proved I wasn't crazy. I burned it in the fireplace, for it was very dry. And now I keep openings in the walls for my cats, who can git to any part of this house, and who serve to give warning if needed. You can feel *safe* here, professors. This house has been purged. This house is *pure*."

Vlad recalled Pappa John's words to Uncle Mose. "*Git you a cat.*"

Then Wabershaw placed his vasty paw over Vlad's very ordinary hand, in a reassuring way that persuaded Vlad that once upon a time, before he became an eccentric though harmless monster, Henry Wabershaw must have been a very nice fellow. He said, "So now I stay home, for I no longer fear for my sanity. And I don't drink any more – I just eat."

Vlad said, "You have come face to face with the same thing which persuaded us that this myth is no myth – namely, we have also *seen* the creatures. Now the question is how did they come to exist? For if we know what started them, maybe we'll know how to stop them."

Wabershaw shifted his great weight in his reinforced chair, reached in a drawer and handed Vlad a manila envelope. "Seen anything like this?" he asked, as Vlad removed a sheaf of papers labeled *First Draft of the Interim Committee Report.*

Vlad made a sound of surprise, for the papers were in the same format as those Bagnell had left behind in the nightstand of the Sumner College guesthouse. He began to read:

". . . *They are commonly known as Rattlers or Rustlers but, in places as far apart as San Francisco and St. Louis, the favorite term is Clickers. In certain border states, the obscure Hyett is found, which may be related to Rawheaded Bloody Bones. In Biloxi, the favored terms are Boss-Devil, or Devil in the Wall. Dr Allan Lee Murrow, the great Southern folklorist says this may be an extension of the zomby legends, or that the zomby may have its origins here. Dr Robert Allbright notes the Yazoo Delta fable that Hyetts died of yellow fever or plague, and eat human flesh.*

"*Hamling Calloway M.D. raises the question of whether there might be an unidentified retro-virus or microorganism, somehow associated with the great plagues (perhaps as a 'fellow traveler'), which might in some way cause the phenomena that lie at the bottom of these tales. Something which resembles life; some unrecognized viral wasting syndrome or plague which causes pseudo-life. And if so, is this plague still active – now?*"

Vlad let the papers drop on the still-littered table, sighed and rubbed his eyes. "What do *you* think?" he asked Wabershaw.

"Professors, as near as I am confident, there is a disease, never diagnosed, which simulates death – and which then simulates *life*.

And which still, from time to time, simulates it *now*. From the time when their normal body processes sink below a certain point, those old Paper-Men are neither alive as we know it, nor dead as we know it. They lie motionless behind countless walls, not crumbling to dust, until something *disturbs* them, and then they go clickin' and clattering, and rustlin' and rattling – until their clock runs down again. Then they go back inside the walls until something winds them up again. I have often wondered how many of those poor old derelicts we see nodding and mumbling in doorways of old buildings, are in fact suffering from Paper-Man's disease. They wrap themselves in rags and newspapers to stay warm, and crawl into a niche in some wall. They keep themselves 'alive' with an occasional rat, for rats are known to run along walls, and they sink into a hibernating state until something wakes them – then they attack. I knew all this before those fancy committee fellows did. I tried to tell them, but they wouldn't listen, *they* knew better. Well, hell with'm. Young Professor Stewart, there's a gallon of sweet melk in the ice-box, if you'd be so kind to bring it out."

V. The Committee

Gertrude (Mrs Harry Brown) Roberts had finally, after years of trying everything in the pharmacopeia, found something which would put her to sleep and keep her to sleep. Ten minutes after she had taken it – an interval long enough to read her nightly number of lines from the Bible and to say her prayers (she now left the Catholics and Episcopalians for last, as she drifted into slumber) – her toothless mouth would open in her bony face and she would begin to snore. This, as it usually woke him up, was her old husband's signal that he was once again a free man for the night.

"So, Gertrude Sayer," he hissed at the unresponsive body on the far side of the bed; "taking more than a thimbleful of brandy is *wrong*, is it? But doping your soul into subconsciousness with that chemical counterfeit of poppy and mandragore is all right, is it? Stuff! Poppycock! But just like a Sayer!"

Old Harry Roberts got out of bed; the night air being just a bit chill, he put on his second-best frock coat (the one he saved for commencements and inaugurations, saving the very best one for

Board meetings) over his nightshirt, and shuffled along the street in his carpet slippers. There were no passers-by and had there been, few would have given him a second glance and had any done so it would have been a glance of approval. New England still dearly cherished its eccentrics . . . had any identified him as one.

H. Brown Roberts was soon at a certain side-door to the General Museum of the Province of Rhode-Island and Providence Plantations, of which he was still Librarian Emeritus and a member of the Budget Committee. He let himself in with his keys. A moment later he was once again deep into the immense annals of the Underground Railroad, on which he had long planned a series of books, and thus he stayed. From time to frequent time he muttered to himself about the Fugitive Slave Act and the Free Soil Whigs, and his great grandmother Brown and his great grandfather Roberts, both of whom were conductors on the Underground Railroad; when glancing up he observed one of the passengers.

"Oh, my poor fellow!" H.B.R. exclaimed, rising to his feet. "Are you one of the stowaways aboard the cotton-boat from Charleston? Never do fear, we shall see you safe to Canada . . . but perhaps you are hungry, did they give you some hot victuals in the kitchen? What? Not? Well just you come with me." The hallway seemed a trifle strange to him, as he padded along it, followed by the silent figure. Presently they entered another room, which he did not precisely recognize as either a part of the old Roberts or of the old Brown house . . . though to be sure, some of the furnishings . . . It was not the kitchen, whatever it was, although . . . "Ha! There is the porcelain ginger-jar which Merchant Houqua of the Hong gave to Reuben Roberts. Hmm, I believe that in this cabinet one should find . . . Drat, it is locked! Pshaw! Have you, perchance with you, no, I suppose not, a lever with a thin end to it?"

The dark and silent stowaway produced an enormous screwdriver, and had the cabinet opened in a second. Inside, however, was no bread, no cold meat or mutton soup, no hasty pudding. What there was in it were two bottles of brandy. Seizing first one and then the other, the liberated three-fifths of a person smote the bottom of each bottle a great blow with the flat of his great hand, neatly popped each cork; and handed one bottle to Dr H. Brown Roberts.

"An excellent stratagem! Yes, yes. Hmm, no glasses, I suppose, in the cotton fields away." He raised his bottle and sniffed. "An excellent Fundador. Ha hm. Here is to your good health, my man and my brother, and to your prosperity in Nova Scotia. Ah, ha, *mmm*."

The dark stranger was an excellent guest, that is, he neither interrupted nor made any comment himself. When his voice was heard for the first time, it was deep and rough: "I wants that *head*."

"Oh you do, do you? Do you? If you expect to trade it to the Bluenoses for rum, let me tell you that a quarter-quintal of codfish would be a likelier item." Harry Roberts looked at his guest and had another tot from the brandy bottle, and why not? – he was already saved, wasn't he? Yes he was. "Well, it doesn't signify and I see no reason why you shouldn't have it, for the acquisition was never authorized. Want that head? With taste and scent, no argument. Old Reuben Roberts brought one back from the Moluccas packed in cloves once. Well, the cloves were from the Moluccas." They were walking down the hall by now. "Here we are; I have a key to the door, mm-hm, but my key no longer fits *this* lock, for Selby Silas, wretched fellow, had the lock changed, confound him, a *Methodist*!"

A few wrenches with the huge screwdriver, and another cabinet was open. A hideous odor filled the room; there was the head, and the supposed follower of the Drinking Gourd gave a grunt of recognition. "Don't touch it, my good fellow, they will scarcely let you on the cars if you reek of it, and certainly it would frighten the horses. Hmm. Ah! Scrape it off the shelf into these plastic bags and tie a knot. Drop them into this one. Tie another knot. And another. Ha, Selby Silas, his face will be a *sight*! Well, was it an authorized acquisition? No it was *not*! You are going now? Avoid Boston, the cotton-brokers are hand in glove with the – well, I needn't tell *you*. Travel only at night, and take the back roads to Amherst. Rattle on the rear-windows of Moses Stuart, the house with the high stone fence." The Librarian Emeritus affixed a small piece of paper (from the waste-basket, its back was unused) to the cabinet door with a very tiny piece of Scotch tape, wrote APRIL FOOL on it, and decided to go home.

Harry Roberts, who rumor had it owned half the mortgages in Newport, hid the bottle behind great grand-uncle Erastus Everett's second edition of *Johnson's Lives of the Poets*, where Gertrude eventually found it, as she eventually found everything. She never said a word, but decided it was time to bake fruit-cake. The raisins were getting dry anyway, and, with the windfall of the Spanish brandy, the cake should be just about ready to eat by Christmas.

The Mustee had not, as a matter of fact, planned on taking the horse-cars; or whatever remnants of the railroad which capital, management, labor, or government had left of the system. He made his way to a certain section of town, and there he walked slowly up and down the emptied streets, looking at license plates. The furthest southern origin he could find was New York, so, with a shrug, and a rather rapid use of the useful screwdriver, he let himself into the small truck's cab, dropped his burden between his knees, and applied his lips to the brandy bottle. Then he simply settled into his seat. And waited. After a while someone else, humming a frolicsome air, also entered the truck-cab, though from the other side, and, catching sight of his passenger, attempted to tumble out backwards. A very long, very strong arm caught and drew him back in. "We goin *sout*," said the Mustee.

"Yes*sir*, Big Blood," the driver said. "We goin' south. No doubt 'bout that."

Crossing into New York City in the gritty light of dawn, the driver realized that although his passenger was either dead or dead drunk, the truck was not his own. He therefore parked the vehicle in front of its owner's garage, gestured to the owner, and called, "You got it." Then he left the truck, turned a corner, and ran like hell.

The owner did not put down his coffee. He languidly eyed the truck, languidly kicked a tire, locked the garage, and ambled off to breakfast.

The truck was already under the scrutiny of the pioneer squad of a social group, called many amusing names by those who were not themselves members. Though not . . . as a rule . . . in the presence of the social group, all of whom hailed from a lovely tropical hamlet near Ponce. The group members called themselves *The Christian Heroes*. They cared little that the religious practices of their native hamlet were not up to the highest standards of Orthodoxy. And little cared their fathers and their mothers.

The pioneer squad of the Heroes advanced, peered into the truck and its cab. Reported that the truck itself was empty, but that the cab contained a comatose Black man holding onto an empty brandy bottle and a plastic bag (the Taino and Arawack presence in their native island had been absorbed too long ago for them to recognize the Mustee as half-Indian); in fact the slack of the bag was wound tightly around his hand. The Christian Heroes held a brief council, then deployed their forces. "*Andale! La bolsa!*" cried the smallest Hero, as he was hoisted into the open cab window, with a very sharp knife, and very deftly cut the plastic and snatched the bag away.

A jacket was tossed over the plastic bag. The Heroes wandered away and eventually returned to their headquarters, a semi-occupied storeroom behind a small *botanica*, whose proprietor was an honorary Hero. There the reeking bag or bags were opened. Alas! No grass! Some of the Heroes uttered exclamations, not of enthusiasm.

But the honorary member, with a look of the utmost gravity, had his own exclamation to utter, as he knelt and crossed himself, "*Esta la cabeza de Santo Mumbo!*"

Something of Africa was after all recognized in the eclectic pantheon of the Christian Heroes. One by one, the others knelt down and followed his example.

Sergeant Reilly said, "Urright, here's anudda one, from one o' dem buhyn-dout houses on Corona Street. Tullaphone call says dey, om, wuhyshippin da Devil's head wit dead chickens, and alla dat blasphemy stuff." He gave his own head an angry shake as though regretful that all of that blasphemy stuff had not constituted an indictable offense in New York State since 1797 (*People v. Jemima Wilkerson*); "So, om, Lopez? Levine? And take the visitin Royal Canadian witchuz and tull um t'muffle his hawss's hoofs. Hoar, hoar!" Reilly went back to his coffee.

"Worshipping the Devil's Head!" exclaimed Corporal Clanranald. "Eh?"

All the police repeated, "*Eh?*" in chorus, and laughed heartily.

All had been very interested that a corporal from the RCMP would be with them a little while as part of a crash course in Urban Crime. All had been disappointed that the corporal had not worn his scarlet mountie coat, but his accent was meat for much merriment.

Corporal Clanranald, of, originally, Trail, B.C., to whom Urban Crime had largely meant drunken peasoupers peeing in the streets and drunken Indians ineptly trying to take the tires off cars not theirs and mashing their fingers in the process, and drunken Manitoba-French Metis singing *Voyageur* songs under the street lamps at 2:00 a.m. – to Corporal Clanranald, New York City Urban Crime was Something Else. But even so, "worshiping the Devil's head" was something else *yet*. The benign Sunday Schools of the United Church of Canada had not prepared him for metropolitan diabolism.

The police car slowed down in that Borough where Thomas Wolfe had long ago heard the peaceful sound of a million Jews turning the pages of the Sunday *Times*. Times had changed. "Here we are, Corp, see? Some kid, I guess he was laying chicky, he just run in t'give the word . . ." Then, and only then, as the car was parked in front of a smoke-streaked apartment-building, whose doorless door-way was heaped with rubbish, did they briefly turn on the siren.

Absolute shells, wreckages of other fires, or mere heaps of rubble, cellars of demolished houses, houses which had been burned repeatedly long after any insurance could possibly have been issued: this is what else they saw on Corona Street in that block.

Visiting RCMP Corporal Clanranald, hissed and pointed, "Look, they're running out the back and getting away!"

"Fine, we don't want 'em," said Lopez.

"The Tombs is full enough as it is." Levine said.

The three men got out of the car and gingerly entered the building. Stale reek of smoke still clung to it. Doorways gaped. Now suddenly galvanized, Lopez and Levine loudly clumped their feet on the steps, called out, "*Police*!" A last clatter of their feet; then silence.

On the second floor an entire wall had been knocked out, and in the large room which had resulted they found the evidence of the ceremony they had interrupted. On the walls were holy pictures of Mother Mary and the Caribbean Indian Saint, Maria Lionza, riding nude upon her horse; all affixed with thumb-tacks or scotch tape. On one wall hung a crucifix. In front of the crucifix was a table and in front of the table lay three headless black chickens and three headless white chickens. Their heads were on the table, so was smoldering incense, so were piles of wilting fruit and flowers, and little bowls piled with unknown substances, also cigars and candles red and yellow and blue and black. So was –

Clanranald pointed. "My *God*! What is – *that*?"

In the center of the table it sat. Its mouth was smeared with fresh blood, and it seemed to leer at them out of the side of its single open eye. Slyly.

"Oh, that's *horr*ible! What *is* it?"

"Werentcha *lis*tening? That's the Devil's head. It looks like it, too," said Levine. "Gevalt, whadid they do, somebody rob a *grave*? Stay here, Royal, will ya? We gotta look around and radio da phatagraphers. Be right back . . ."

Malcolm Clanranald would easily have preferred to do other things than stay there, but he stayed as ordered, as he told himself, he would have done in the frozen northern Yukon. It was then, under the unremittent gaze of the horrid head on the . . . table . . . *altar*? . . . he bethought himself of his own small personal camera; and took it from his pocket, and snapped a few photographs to show the folks in B.C. before Lopez and Levine returned, eventually followed by the official police photographers.

What became of the head after its removal to the New York Police Lab, he never learned. For soon the course in Urban Crime was completed, and Clanranald was back in Canada. There he developed the photographs himself, and there one of the folks in BC had connections with a sensationalist newspaper. The corporal was not an especially talented photographer and most of the shots were ho-hum. But one single one was clear enough and ghastly enough to be picked up by a press syndicate.

So for the first time, in newspapers throughout North America, appeared the likeness of a Paper-Man's head. Though none of the caption-writers called it by that name.

Genevieve Silas, Selby's widowed sister-in-law and housekeeper, had made fish cakes and baked beans for breakfast again – often had he told her that he detested them at all times, and especially for breakfast: uselessly. So he was not in the best mood when the phone rang. "Silas here."

"Yeah, well this is Riordon here. What the hell have you been doing with the *head* I examined? What's it doing in New *York*?"

It took a few seconds for Silas to isolate this Riordon from the vast number of tribesmen of that name. "*Do*ing with it, my dear Doctor Riordon; the object is in a locked cabinet in a locked room, and has certainly not been in New York City."

The dental surgeon's voice cut in on his polite protest. "*Worshipping the Devil's Head*, the papers say."

"Well, they do sometimes turn up as cult objects, *yes*, but I never heard of one in New *York*!"

Riordon did not believe him, and Riordon did not believe that he had seen no such picture in the newspaper. Riordon said the New York City police had somehow had the teeth examined by someone who *knew* something. And this someone said that the teeth of this evidently ancient head had been not only recently drilled, but drilled by the new experimental Davenport drill, "and you know how many of *them* there are. Damned few. If this gets traced to me, well, God won't help you." With these cryptic words, Edward L. Riordon, doctor of dental medicine, hung up.

Silas was in every way amazed. His stomach ached and rumbled as he consulted the pile of unread newspapers on the reading desk. There it was: MYSTERY GROWS AROUND "DEVIL'S HEAD". Silas hardly remembered running down the hall, but he remembered *some*one running down the hall, and fumbling with the key in the lock of the outer door. One good look showed him the cabinet whose lock had been jimmied open, and the tiny note saying *APRIL FOOL*. Was there anything he could do which would be of the least help and comfort to him? Selby Silas knew well that there was nothing he could do.

As for the Mustee, Larraby grilled him until he was scorched on both sides. He told Larraby that he could handle the Red men and he could handle the Black men and Paper-Men, but he could not handle the New York Police men. This was perhaps the truth, though certainly not the whole truth; but then the Mustee wasn't under oath.

"You owe me a head," said Larraby.

What else could he have said?

Edward Bagnell unfolded his morning paper, and was jolted fully awake. There was the Paper-Man's head . . . the Devil's head . . . Ephraim Mackilwhit's head gazing at him slyly. Bagnell realized that the dreadful secret, so long concealed, had begun to escape from its dreadfully long concealment.

Professor Vlad Smith was not reading the newspapers.

Jack Stewart had said that they were close to his home, and he wanted to spend a few days with his family, who hadn't seen him since winter vacation. So Vlad dropped him off and continued alone.

Later he phoned his own family and, to his pleasure and surprise, Elsa answered the phone. "Bella is a little better, thank God. She's seeing a psychiatrist, who has her on a low dose of medication, but I wish she wasn't so *listless*!" Elsa said.

This last word, with its tone of emotion, however unhappy, gave Vlad hope that Elsa was starting to *feel* again – and that eventually her feelings might again include him.

Vlad recalled that one of the names Wabershaw had mentioned as part of the secretive committee was Zimmerman, and he guessed that this was Claire Zimmerman, a woman he had often enjoyed meeting at folklore conferences. She lived nearby and perhaps she could help him. "Hello, Claire."

"Why . . . Vlad *Smith*!" A big hug.

"Excuse the abrupt appearance at this hour. I tried three times to phone you, but the line . . ."

"I just made fresh coffee, and have a slice of cake." She handed him coffee and cake, and their hands brushed. Vlad had never before noticed how soft her hands were, or how her sleek dark hair framed her round and downy cheeks. Better to *stop* noticing. "I'm researching that old legend, the Paper-Man or Boss in the Wall . . ."

"Oh, I suppose you saw the picture in the paper. Ghastly thing." She handed him a folded newspaper, and this time he didn't even notice that their hands brushed. Vlad stared with startled blue-gray eyes at the newspaper photo of the "Devil's Head," while Claire rattled on with just a slight nervous edge in her voice.

"You *had* seen it, hadn't you? I mean, I assumed that's what you came to talk about, because of my research project with old news clippings and all. Well, that photo *is* startling, but nothing new, really, nothing new at all. Here, let me show you some examples." She pulled a file of photocopies off a shelf. "Look at this one, from the New Orleans *Daily Picayune*, dated March 12, 1871. Right next to an ad for Ayer's medicinal Sarsaparilla, and another ad for a hot spring cure for opium habits; the headline is '*Kneeling Down to Idols*.' It says, '*In a dark row of tenements on Dumaine Street, is a very old building with crumbling walls overgrown with wild creepers. Rain drops fall through the roof without restraint. A low, heavy doorway admits the visitor to a gloomy cell with a hard earthen floor. In one corner of the room is a bundle of rags, and on the wretched pallet reposes a half-naked Voudon doctor, beneath the idol of some heathenish divinity . . .*' It goes on like that for quite a while, but you see this sort of thing is *not* new, Vlad, not at all."

Vlad impulsively cupped her round and warm cheeks in his two long hands. "The legends aren't new, Claire. What's new is that the legends are *real*, and *you* know it and the committee knows it, and I *need* to know what's going on!"

Vlad told her all that had happened, and when he finished she sipped her coffee silently for a moment, then said in a soft voice, "I didn't *know* Vlad, I'm so sorry this happened to your family, and to you, because I've always liked you. You're great at puncturing stuffed shirts at conferences. Oh hell, take this memo. It has the date and location of the next committee meeting – and tell 'em Claire sent you."

Vlad thanked her. Then he thanked her again. Then he said it was getting late and started towards the door. Then he turned and thanked her again, and took her hand. Then their lips brushed, and her open mouth was soft and *warm*.

Later that night, Vlad read from the *Interim Committee Report*:

"It is said that the Gullahs of the Georgia coast sometimes refer to them as *Thunder People*, because of the belief that they are seen more often during thunderstorms. Dr Allbright suggests that they may seize upon these deafening noises to cover their own well-known and well-feared sounds. Or perhaps the Boss in the Wall is discomfited by the falling of the barometer, and is impelled to move and to stir about.

"In certain border states, the obscure term *Hyett* is found, which may be related to a little-known tale. There was a banker named Williams who had a wife named Dorcas and a daughter named Mary Martha. The family was prosperous, and Dorcas always liked to see a good plate of victuals on the table, and had a closet full of good black silk dresses. After Williams died of consumption, it was discovered that most of the bank's assets had been invested in beautifully engraved, but worthless bonds. In all the excitement and tumult which followed, nobody gave much thought to the Widow Williams and her daughter.

"During the next few months, six babies were reported missing from sharecroppers' shacks in the vicinity. Perhaps the number was more, for the poor sometimes counted their blessings in the way of children, and concluded that they had been overblessed. The word *Gypsies* was mentioned, and many a mother threw up her hands in horror.

"Constable Stebbins was sent to investigate, a rough but kindly man. It occurred to him that Mrs and Miss Williams had not been seen lately, and he went to inquire if they had been bothered by any frightening strangers. He went to the back of the house, and its neglected condition made him feel uneasy. But Miss Mary Williams assured him that she and her mother were quite all right, and that they had seen no suspicious characters or small children around. Her complexion was very pale, and there was a slight smile on her lips.

"Then the Constable noted something red beneath the edge of a large towel in the kitchen, and he recalled that one of the missing children had been wearing a red dress. He lifted the towel – and found a basket full of babies' clothes. Then Miss Mary Williams looked at him with her small little smile, and said, 'Mother was very hungry.'

"No such shocking event had ever occurred in the county, as the news that Mary Williams had drowned at least six small children, and carried them home in her shawl to be eaten. The people screamed for her blood. How much did old Mrs Williams know? All she said was, 'Nobody cared about me and my baby.' Mary Williams was sentenced to be hanged, and her mother was sent to a lunatic asylum for life. Miss Williams' last words were, 'Will they feed mother good there?'

"Mrs Dorcas Williams was allowed to bring her best black silk dresses to the asylum, and they say that she sat in a certain chair in the ward, without speaking a word, for thirty-seven years. They say that she ate hearty, and never spotted her black silk dress.

"Mrs Williams' family name was *Hyett*, and any small child in the region will run screaming if one says: 'Mother Hyett was very hungry.' "

Vlad picked up Jack from his family's home, and said that they were off to a meeting of the mysterious committee.

The man at the head of the table said that, like the interesting club in New York City whose only rule was that there were no rules, this committee had no name, no schedule of meetings – this was either its third, tenth, or twelfth session, depending on how you looked at it – and no formal chair. "And if anyone else would rather chair this, speak up, I'll gracefully yield." No one spoke up.

Then the people around the table looked up to see two other people who hadn't been present before. "What the hell," said Bagnell. "You're not supposed to be here, you know."

"I know," said Vlad Smith. "Do you still doubt what I saw?"

Said Bagnell, "I never doubted it."

"Why the secrecy, Branch, why?" asked Vlad.

"I was trying to protect you," said Dave Branch.

"Like hell," said Jack Stewart. "You were all trying to protect your frigging academic turf."

The men faced each other silently for a moment.

"Who told you?" asked Bagnell.

"*I* told them," said Claire Zimmerman. "They are here at *my* invitation, because they *belong* here. So let's stop squabbling over which kids are allowed in the clubhouse, and get on with it."

Having no other choice, they got on with it.

The man at the head of the table, whom Branch identified for Vlad and Jack as Augustus Elbaum, had a reddish grizzled beard. He sighed and said, "All right. On the principle that it doesn't matter where you begin to measure the circumference of a circle, as usual we'll begin anywhere. Notes and queries have been sent to me, and I've answered some and sent some around. We'll go over a few of them anyway." He paused and looked around the table, then continued.

"The trouble is, you know, we are getting in over our depths. *We* began as a group of folklorists, most of us trained to classify and catalog: 'Oh, this is obviously a version of Childe Ballad number such-and-such.' Now we've got historians, criminologists, physicians – and we just keep getting in deeper and deeper. *We may already be in over our heads.* Seen the newspapers? Seen a certain picture of a certain head?"

A stir in the chamber. Not a particularly stately chamber. One might expect to see it contain a meeting of insurance salesmen looking at graphs. A stir, and a woman said, "This is . . . definitely a . . . one of ours?"

Bagnell said almost wearily, "It is definitely one of ours. By and by we'll show you another photograph. You'll need no convincing. But how it got to be part of a Caribbean cult ceremony in New York, I have no idea. Perhaps just as well because if I *had* an idea, so would the press." He eased his long, lanky body back into his chair.

Elbaum began to pick up papers and read aloud. " '*Could the jerky gait ascribed to the String-Fellow be explained by the shortening of tendons? If so, which tendons and how do they shrink?*' Would you give that one some thought, Doctor Calloway?"

"Okay, Gus. Yes, get back to you on it."

In the silence right after, the incessant sound of the airconditioning made itself heard. Before Elbaum could read another slip of paper, there was a vocal query in the bland, blank room. "What became of the mental patient, Hillsmith, who –?"

Bagnell stirred and spoke. "Yes, I investigated that myself. Oh, Hillsmith is certainly insane, with a horrible and disturbing delusion. On one level it's a mad reiteration of parts of the Bible. Particularly the vision of Ezekial in the valley of the dry bones. No doubt about *that*. But, on another level, per*haps* it was triggered by the actual sighting of dormant Paper-Men, a whole group of them maybe, in a very old house, suddenly coming *alive*, so to speak, and beginning to move. Enough to knock anybody off the steady spin around his mental axis."

Claire said softly and thoughtfully, her black hair hugging her round face, "Dr Elbaum, I've been wondering why – so far – there only seem to be Paper-*Men*. Why hasn't there been a single report of a Paper-*Woman*? This is hardly an Equal Opportunity issue, but still I wonder, don't you?"

Elbaum poured a glass of water and after a moment said, "We just don't *know*. That's a measure of our ignorance, not our knowledge. Why do women get pregnant and men have prostate trouble? We all know why, but with this other we can't and *don't* see why. One of many things for which we have no answer, but that's not to say we don't have a question. Why do sightings of Paper-Men occur most frequently just before outbreaks of *war*? Does the hostility and tension in the air stir them? Do our current tensions explain the upsurge of recent sightings? We have far more questions than we have answers."

A pale woman in an odd sort of hat scratched some notes on a pad and spoke, "If the disease model is correct, all the life processes would be slowed down . . . metabolism . . . pulse . . . peristalsis . . . mental functioning . . . extreme desiccation. Could the Paper-Man possibly *speak*? When he's jolted from his dormant state, or when he's still in the transition from life to pseudo-life, could he *talk* to us?"

"Impossible," said someone. There were murmurs of discussion in the meeting room. ". . . mmm . . . nnn . . ."

Someone else said, "There would be no pulse as we know it, I should think. The hedgehog in hibernation may be said to cease breathing. Hibernating hedgehogs have been submerged in water for over half an hour and they didn't drown, they just got wet."

Silence. The air a dull cool which did not refresh.

"I'd say . . . from what I've heard and read and thought about . . . it seems to me that some of them died despairing and some died hating . . . and those ones that are most dangerous died hating."

Someone who had been drinking water suddenly put it down and asked, hastily, "Oh say, Gus. Rats? About those rats –"

About the rats . . .

Elbaum wondered aloud, "Where to begin, where to begin?" Then said that he would begin by considering not merely *no* supernatural explanation, but no explanation that could not be made in only moderately non-conventional terms.

"Okay . . . about them eating rats; let's say we have someone named Jack Jones in, say, Memphis in 1845, suffering from any one of a number of possible diseases causing intense cramps and vomiting. Say there's been an outbreak of cholera. Or plague. Everyone will at once assume he's got the pest . . . and everyone will clear out, *fast*. So now assume that he is a stranger in

Memphis, and he's all alone in some shack, some whore's crib. Okay. Time passes. No one comes *near* him. He might very well have died, but, somehow, he *does*n't die. After a week or two he's probably on the floor and he may be partially naked, hell, even entirely naked. Need I say that he's terribly emaciated, puking and nearly dead, glarey-eyed and gaunt and very likely more than a bit out of his mind. He's famished, famished. If there'd been a crust of bread, a cheese rind or a bacon rind, why, he'd already eaten *that* long ago, as soon as he *could* eat. Then along comes a rat. A rat *creeps* along the wall as rats do."

Elbaum sipped from a coffee cup, gazed around the meeting room and continued. "Now I have never tried to catch a rat with my bare hands, and I grant you that it's hard for even a healthy man to catch a rat. And Jack Jones is not in good health *at all*. But. I give you *this* thought. Perhaps the *rat is not in good health either*. Rats get sick and rats die, sometimes where people can see them. If a plague was on, more rats would be dying openly. Perhaps the rat is nearly dead from plague – or maybe it's got *something related to Paper-Man's disease*. Jack Jones eats the rat, or laps its blood – and, his immune system already weakened, of course picks up whatever sickness the rat has.

"Now let's say that by and by someone else is sneaking around, looking for something to steal in a presumably empty shack. Now, who is this potential thief? It could be some low-down, uneducated, ignorant, ignoble, dim-witted, down-and-out fellow named, mm, Anse Drobble. He comes sneaking up to this shack. He peeps inside. He sees a sort of living skeleton with glaring eyes biting into a rat. What do you think Anse Drobble does? Do you think that he *tar*ries? That Anse Drobble comes forward and says, 'Worthy and suffering Christian brother, allow me to give you succor and sustenance'? Hell no. Anse Drobble never gave *any*body *any*thing . . . except maybe the clap. He runs off and his poor maggoty mind is going to report, '*I seed a daid man eating a rat!*'

"Even though it's now believed that the Boss in the Wall never actually *eats* the rat, *merely he laps its blood*. Easier than chewing with wasted jaw muscles, and easier to digest, as well.

"Multiply this one instance by hundreds, and our rat-eating legend takes off."

Hamling Calloway M.D. looked down along the table provided with, at intervals, the pads of paper, the short sharp pencils, the glasses of water. The table might have been set for a meeting about changing zoning laws, or a discussion of splitting a stock. "Gus, the picture you have just drawn, why it's very vivid. No reason why it couldn't be perfectly correct. So let us not linger. I'd like to move along to, why certainly not to a supernatural explanation, but to one which is certainly impossible to explain in fairly, or even unfairly, conventional terms."

Elbaum absently stroked his short and grizzled beard with its still-visible streaks of red. "What do you –"

"What do I *mean*? Well, what *happened* to Jack Jones? What *became* of him? Back then in Memphis, in 1845? After he'd recovered enough to eat his rat, or, rather, lap its blood . . . what *happened* to him?"

Elbaum suggested that any number of things might have happened. He might have recovered after his nip of rat blood, and gotten dressed and on his feet and returned to the cotton farm or the river boat. "Maybe. But maybe Jack Jones never quite died, but never quite recovered from his rat-borne disease. Maybe he became an outcast and a skulker and a lurker. Imagine *that* if you can. Growing older and filthier and more emaciated, creeping from one abandoned house to another, living off scraps and rats. Never able to be anything *but* emaciated. Sometimes hiding in the walls . . . a boss in the wall, but a boss nowhere else. And maybe, in colder weather, wrapping his wasted body in layer after layer of old newspapers to keep out the cold, as all his physiological functions declined."

Elbaum again stroked his reddish-gray beard. "Imagine this in hundreds of cities and towns, not just in the 1800s, but *now*. We know that most derelicts we see in doorways are suffering from the diseases of alcoholism or schizophrenia, or from a diseased society – but some may be slowly *wasting away from Paper-Man's disease*. That could explain why there are always more 'Bosses' forming, even though so many get killed off. And that could explain why the Boss in the Wall legend appears everywhere, and never dies out."

A woman in the far corner now lifted her head and cleared her throat with an odd sort of sound. Vlad had not really registered her presence, and, judging by a sudden shuffling and half-turning on the part of others, there were a number of them who had now suddenly remembered that they had forgotten. Jack Stewart said later that she had instantly reminded him of "Aunt Pearline, the one you never see except at a funeral and you see her at *every* funeral, including the ones you try to keep quiet."

Vlad (in a whisper): "Ed. Who is she?"

Bagnell: (writing his reply on a pad): Dr Isabella Crokeshank. *Rats*.

She was by no means a young woman. She cleared her throat again with that odd sort of squeak, and touched her lips with a tissue. They were probably, by now, by nature, pale lips; but Dr Isabelle Crokeshank had been a young woman when young women were first able to combine make-up and respectability; and, however odd it seemed, her withered lips were still, in the manner of her youth, rouged red with lipstick. Bright, against that pallid face. Bright red.

At last she spoke. "What Dr Elbaum says is logical, very logical. Now, I was first drawn into this . . . somewhat clandestine project here, purely because I might learn something which might lead to some explanation of the irregularly regular appearances of exsanguinated rats. I was skeptical. Perhaps more than I need have been. There are some weird and wonderful things about rats. Don't let me go on for too long, it's more than a discipline, it's an obsession. *But* have you ever heard of a Rat King? I see few of you have. I refer you to my work called 'Tail-Tied kings'. Well, it's not a king of the rats, *not* an individual rat but a group of rats. This . . . *King*. Oh, from time to time there have been found, in Europe, in America, a number of rats of both sexes which are bound together by, literally, their tales being *tied* together. No string or cord, just the tails themselves. I long ago ruled out hoaxes; for one thing they have been found in places ordinarily inaccessible to humans, found when buildings are being demolished, for example. Now what has caused this phenomenon?"

Dr Isabelle Crokeshank paused and drank water. No one moved. "Well now, how, for example, did they live? Obtain food? Water? Evidently this was brought by mouth by other rats. The only theory ever really seriously considered was that other rats had selected them as a sort of gene pool, breeding pool, while they were very young, and by tooth and claw and paw had made those knots. The matter certainly remains not proven. During the course of this conference a notion came to me. It is only a notion. *Is* it possible, I have asked myself, that this . . . your . . . the Boss in the Wall? The Paper-Man? Is *that* what made them? Could those . . . oh . . . dare I borrow from another legend a term, *the un-dead*? Could *they* have tied the rats' tails together? Taken young rats and done that? Leaving up to the rat-groups the perhaps instinctively-performed job of bringing food, perhaps food dipped in water?

"So that when and if the Boss in the Wall wanted a rat . . . it had only to go and *get* one . . .?"

Perhaps the silence shuddered. No one offered an answer. No one said a word or made another sound. For a while.

Dr. Elbaum looked at his watch. Then he said, "It's two o'clock. I believe that Dr Dave Branch and Dr Ed Bagnell – Boys . . .?"

They nodded. Got up. Bagnell set up a screen while Branch got the projector ready. Branch's narrow face was usually grave. Now it was somber. "All right," he said, nodding. Bagnell turned out the lights. Branch said, "We are about to show a photograph of perhaps the only intact Boss in the Wall – oh, I don't know why I prefer that name – or Paper-Man. Not a head alone. It's even less of a pretty sight, so all those suspecting they may be faint of heart may leave."

Nobody left.

"All right, here we go, at the count of three: one . . . two . . . three . . ."

The image on the screen was very blurred and only gradually became clear. Very clear. The photograph was actually two photographs, side by side on one slide. *Fore*. The mouth seemed fallen open. One eye looked right at them, one eye was rolled up. One clawed hand was at chest-level. The other seemed to gesture from alongside the ear. Only shreds of clothing were left and in some places only shreds of paper, with here and there only a patch of it adhering to a skin which clung to the bones like crepe paper.

Aft. There was more paper on the backside, and, along the backbone this seemed deeply depressed on either side. The skin on the lower extremities seemed more tightly fitted, though the left leg and buttock appeared much torn; it was not evident, how.

"Well. Had enough? Too bad." The screen went blank, Branch moved to another projector. "All those who now know that they are faint of heart may now leave. What we are now about to show purports to be the only *moving picture* of a Boss in the Wall." Evidently somebody wanted to; there was a scuffle of a chair being pushed back, the dimness was relieved for an odd moment as a door opened, shut. "Here we go, at the count of three . . ."

The film was badly made. It was jerky and dim and it flickered. It was, also, totally and horribly convincing. In a voice which, low as it was, carried, Branch said, "I'm not allowed to tell you where, when, *how* it was shot." The lights came on again.

Elbaum spoke up after a moment. "My question now is: is there anybody here, anyone amongst us, who still doubts the actual and physical, factual, tangible existence of the creature known as the Paper-Man or The Boss in the Wall?"

A massive black man with an immense face opened his massive mouth and spoke in an immense bass organ note, "Let the record state that Bishop Burton Blankenship has no doubt and never had. I now yield."

". . . don't know how anybody *could* . . . any longer . . . after that movie . . ."

Hughes of the Criminology Lab, dapper, calm, seeming not in the least worried or upset, Hughes said, "Ah yes, that movie. Impressive. How do we know it's the real thing?"

". . . well . . ."

Hughes lightly stroked his mustache, slightly smiled; then said, "I trust that no one trained in a scientific discipline is going to say to anyone else trained in a scientific discipline, 'You'll just have to take my word for it.' You, Dr Dave Branch, have declared that there are things about the film which you can't or *won't* tell us. How can you really expect us to bring in any other verdict except the Scottish one, 'Not proven?' "

". . . well . . ."

"How can you be certain that you yourself have not been hoaxed? You can't, I think. After all, what are generally called 'special effects' have been around a pretty long time. Isn't that so? Not all hoaxes are done for money. Or notoriety. Or this. Or that. I believe, and it's an educated belief, that most hoaxes are done because the hoaxer *liked* that particular hoax. People whom I trust, as I trust you, have been known to be taken in by doctored evidence. So I say I have to withhold my judgment. I, don't, *know*."

The pause after he concluded was punctuated by a small sub-vocal sound from a middle-aged man in – despite the summer's heat – a dark suit and white shirt. He now looked up and with slightly raised eyebrows looked around, not as if he were waiting for others, but as though the others were waiting for him. The technique worked, and Dr Darnell Frost began to speak. There was something in his manner which reminded Vlad of certain members of the clergy; of those few denominations which do not have a paid ministry, and thus have to earn their income by worldly means. When they served in the marketplace there was nevertheless a touch of the pulpit in their manner; and, when they served in the pulpit, a touch of the marketplace.

He spoke in a manner both rapid and clear; his sparse hair was reddish-gold, and he wore gold-rimmed eyeglasses. "Perhaps we have been too much carried away by the unpleasant aspects of our subject. Is this possible? Our subject is not really a damned soul, after all, he's a very – a most unfortunate human being. But nonetheless a human being. He is the victim, it seems likely, of a dread, a very dread disease. Like old Tithonus, he has been cursed with eternal life without eternal youth. We don't know how many he may be, but he is not a demon cast out of a herd of swine; he is simply an unfortunate human being to whom something extra-ordinary has happened. He is our fellow countryman, and in at least one instance he has fought in our country's wars, wearing the indigo uniform. We all know there was an old farmhouse right in the middle of the battle of Bull Run, and an old woman died there during the battle. How can we know who else crawled into that house to die – or to not die? How can we not have compassion for him, as our brother?"

Vlad saw Bagnell and Branch match eyes. Whatever Darnell Frost was up to, it was something a vast deal different from what the others had been up to.

Frost went on in his rapid way, one word almost overtaking the other. "Is his disease – let's call it Paper-Man's Disease – is it worse than leprosy? At one time the unfortunate victims of leprosy were isolated from society forever. We winced when we saw their dreadful deformities and heard their warning bells.

If they did not submit, they were hunted down. But that is mercifully a thing of the past, and oh what a good thing that it is. They aren't even called lepers now, they are victims of Hansen's Bacillus. We don't cast them *out*," Frost declared, shaking his head. "We beckon them *in* and *treat* them. Yes we do. *Am I not also a man and a brother*? Is not the victim of Paper-Man's Disease a man and a brother like the victim of Hansen's Disease? Why, yes he is. I appeal to us all to rise to the incredible challenge which this study presents. I am speaking not only of compassion, but of *profit*. You ask – What? *Profit*? You wonder how I can be so bold, but I say that we must not feel afraid but hopeful. For this wretched and unfortunate creature has, I truly believe, a precious secret locked within his body, the most precious secret any creature may have. The secret that every living being desires; my friends and colleagues. What secret is that? Why it is so obvious, why haven't I heard it from anyone gathered here? The precious secret which, like the ugly and venomous toad, the Paper-Man bears in his body – why of course that secret is *life*!"

By now all eyes were on Dr Darnell Frost.

"That secret, my friends, my colleagues, is *life*! Oh I don't dare say eternal life, no I don't, but is a life span prolonged for let's say a century and a half, is such a life span *nothing*?"

Vlad rose to his feet, as the bile rose in his mouth. "My god, man, such a life is *worse* than nothing," he shouted.

Frost waved him gently down. "Be patient with me, dear sir, and then it will be your turn. I've been patient with all of you. The Paper-Man's life has been sad and terrible, true, but I say it need not be! I say why weepest thou? Arise, now, and gird up thy loins! We are men and women . . . people of *science*! We do not take the past for granted. We must not tarry. We have tasks of the topmost priority, friends and colleagues. We must track the Paper-Man in every hidden wall and closet and doorway, in every wretched building and slum that he inhabits. We must take hold of him gently and lead him to refuge, where he may be studied with every merciful consideration, like every other victim of a baffling disease. After full-scale research which will surely discover his secret, we will *share* this secret with our fellow men and women. My dearest friends, we have no choice, it's not a thing which permits of hesitation, and we must share it with all humankind –

and we will share the glory and the profit among ourselves. *There.*" He slapped his neat stack of notes on the table and looked around the room. Dr Darnell Frost had staked his claim.

The room was in commotion. Calloway was on his feet, shouting. Branch was pounding his fist on the table, shouting, "What are you going to do, milk them like *snakes*?"

Vlad's startled blue-gray eyes met Jack's – both men looked shocked, troubled. "I think we've found the kernel in the nut," said Vlad. "He *can't be serious*."

"Frost sees himself in the newspapers," said Jack Stewart. "On the cover of *Time*. Or even more in the *Readers Digest*, which is what *he* probably reads. He doesn't know what kinds of worms are in that can, and he doesn't want to know either."

Branch leaned over to Vlad; grimly he said, "Well, now you know why I didn't want to tell you before . . . why I wanted to protect you. Have you seen enough? Are you happy now?"

Vlad said, "I wasn't happy before, but I've seen enough for now."

"– details must be worked out as we go along, doctors, professors, admittedly there is an *immense* amount of work, but –"

Frost had staked his claim. Who knew where the assay office was? It could hardly be said yet that the rush was on, but certainly the brawling had already started in the mining camp.

VI. The Old, Old House Revealed

Why had Hillsmith not received his usual dose of Thorazine? No one really knew. Doors would slam and heads would roll, thorough investigations be made: the facts would never be discovered. Things sometimes happened which should not. Confusion followed. For in fact the hospital was always overcrowded and understaffed. Even the locked ward could not always be kept locked; could every linen locker?

Hillsmith, for once alert and cunning, had turned into a quick-change artist. Finding the ward briefly unlocked, he slipped into the staff physician's shower-room, and emerged with the clothing and ID badge of someone in the shower. Properly clad and badged, he calmly strolled along, looking here and there and, sure enough: "*There's* my bag," he said, aloud, but not loudly.

The car keys were in the bag, and the gate guard, due for retirement, had other things on his mind. Never mind the gate guard. Hillsmith didn't.

He got as far as Bewdley Hill when the car ran out of gas. Hillsmith continued on foot. He persuaded young Eddy Fritz at the gas station to keep the doctor bag as security for a can of gas.

It was always a question around Bewdley Hill; was that Nasser Fauntleroy boy *crazy*, or just plain *mean*? Nasser greeted Hillsmith at first sight with a loud cry of "*Hey*, Doctor Flim-Flam! Watchew wearing them funny clothes for, Doctor Floy-Floy? I says hey! *Hey*!"

This getting no response (and perhaps desiring none), he fell into step a safe distance behind, and began following his latest victim in an exaggerated version of the victim's gait, all the while jeering and hooting and mocking. In fact it was almost impossible to get rid of him. If ignored, he kept on. If confronted, he increased his attack. If smiled at, he became more brutal. He had been known to follow someone for miles.

Hillsmith kept on, carrying the can of gas. So did Nasser Fauntleroy, flinging out fists and feet, breaking out when he saw fit. Hillsmith turned up River Road, and up a lane containing a certain old house. He began to gather wooden rubble from the littered lane. At this point a curious change came over Nasser Fauntleroy. His stiff-legged steps faltered, and he looked all around. He slowed. He made many faces. He never entirely stopped, but he did, however, fall quite quiet.

Vlad had seen enough, and now he wanted only to see his family. His favorite niece, Elizabeth, answered the phone. "How's your Aunt Elsa?" asked Vlad.

"She's playing gawlf. They're all playing gawlf." said Elizabeth.

"Say, that's great!" Vlad exclaimed. "And Bella?"

"She's taking her nap on the screened porch."

"Cooler, eh?"

"Well, she won't sleep *in*side."

Vlad winced. "Is she having any of her attacks?"

"Nope," said Elizabeth.

"Does she smile and laugh?"

"Nope."

"Does she eat or *talk*?"

"Little bit."

"Listen, I'm coming to pick her up . . . to take her for a drive, okay?

There commenced a pause and a series of squalid sounds which Vlad analyzed as those of a teenager eating an apple. Then: "Yeah, I guess so, okay."

Vlad dropped off Jack Stewart to attend to some business of his own, and went to pick up Bella. After he drove for a while with the quiet and withdrawn child beside him in the car, he had the great and good idea of returning to the old house. Bella would see the place in the sunlight, as he had first seen it – when the creature would be quiescent – and she would realize there was nothing to fear. It seemed worth a try; all the psychologists and medications clearly weren't helping. Bella did not recognize the old house, so Vlad took her inside, to the room where the tragedy had occurred.

Hillsmith paused in the lane in front of the old house, and eyed a car parked near the overgrown drive. Then he continued his stride. There was a lot of debris in the yard: fragments of furniture, frayed boards, sloughed shingles and the like. Hillsmith gathered and put some of this under his arm, and, walking tiptoed, went up to the house. Fauntleroy did the same. Still he kept silent.

Hillsmith carried the rubble to the verandah surrounding the old house, and made a neat trail of wooden debris all the way around. Then he paused to listen at the walls. Was there, in the sultry silence of the ebbing day, was there any sound at all? If so, was it made by the wind in the huge old trees? Was there any other sound? A rustle? A click?

Nasser Fauntleroy mocked his movements in silence. Why did he not leave? He was certainly in no way at ease.

What is there which makes them both stop now? Perhaps Nasser Fauntleroy stops because Hillsmith stops, but why does Hillsmith stop? Why does he scan the moldering wall so carefully? Hillsmith picks up his can and runs. Hillsmith runs and runs, a-teeter and a-totter, around the verandah, and it is a marvel how thin a stream of fluid he has managed to spill, almost to spray, along the base of the walls as he runs and runs, tossing lit matches like fireflies.

Then with no warning, with no word, with no sound, Hillsmith seems to leave the floor to hurtle through the air, to burst through the rotting wall, to seize – suddenly – something in both his hands – something which rustles . . . and rattles . . . and clicks . . . and kicks . . . and struggles . . . and slips out of Hillsmith's grip as Hillsmith staggers and half-falls to the ground. Does Nasser Fauntleroy scream? If not, who then did?

Once again, Vlad Smith heard his small daughter's shrill scream, and felt her body arch in his arms. Did he smell smoke or was that the stench of . . .? Did he hear the crackle of flames or was that the clicking sound of . . .? "My god," he whispered, and he felt his body grow cold. They poured out of cracks in the walls as if a roaches' nest had been disturbed. They surrounded him with their horrible stenches and their horrible sounds; then they clambered, roachlike, up the walls towards the ceiling.

Now Vlad saw the smoke and the flames through the window, and he knew what had wakened them, and he knew they had to get out. But a Paper-Man lay on the floor in the doorway, blocking their escape. It began to crawl towards them with its terrible claws extended, shedding scraps of rotting paper as it moved. Its stinking odor hit Vlad in waves. He watched for a moment, and willed his stomach to be still. He recalled that the best way to kill a Paper-Man is to break its neck. Vlad dashed forward and aimed a long-unused soccer kick at the creature's head. Something snapped lightly and rolled. It was the head, which stared with open eyes at him and writhed its lips at him and clicked its foul teeth at him.

Then the headless body in the doorway, in its reeking and tattered clothes, the shattered body began to writhe and crawl. Its hands went scrabbling and pawing and feeling . . . feeling for the missing head. Vlad knew it must not find the head. He broke the window with a single kick, seized the head by its scant and filthy hair, and threw it out into the flames. Still the headless thing in the doorway twitched and flung its scrannel arms around, and lunged. Then there was a sound like a breaking stick, and the thing in the doorway was still. Choking smoke filled the room, as Vlad, shielding whimpering Bella in his arms, leaped over the

Paper-Man's body, and raced out of the old house . . . into the front yard.

A large yard it is, and one in which many splendid carriages had come, one after the other, one after the other . . . and then had ceased to come. At all. Long years ago.

Outside it is by now the long summer twilight.

Hillsmith walks along the old carriage-drive, now a neglected lane, to the large Oak tree draped with Spanish Moss, very near where the street begins; and there he leans, against the tree, facing the house. He waits. Waits.

Hillsmith was still there long after the night air was filled with smoke and noise. Now there were many people with him, and police cars and fire-engines and ambulances. Many people by then were there, shouting and screaming and pointing as the flames poured forth from every window of the old, old house. "*Purified by fire!*" Hillsmith cried. Again. Again. He felt weak, he tottered.

A man's large arm went around his waist, and Hillsmith found it immensely comforting. "*Purified by fire!*" he cried . . . again, again, in a voice gone weak.

"Easy now, Mr Hillsmith. Easy. Lean against me, now . . . That's right. You know me, Mr Hillsmith?"

"Dr Eberhardt?"

"That's right. That's right. You set this fire, right? Why did you –?" His voice stopped abruptly. Every voice of the growling, howling multitude stopped. Abruptly. Atop the roof of the house, like a spectacle prepared to amuse some King of Ghouls, appeared a row of figures . . . dancing . . . stamping . . . pirouetting . . . flinging out gant arms and lifting gant legs . . .

"Good *Lord*!" cried Eberhardt. The crowd began its growl again.

Lifting gant legs and flinging gant arms in mad disco-ordinate movement; stamping and dancing, and all silent. Silently dancing.

And all ablaze – dancing on the rooftop all ablaze – all ablaze.

After a while the roof fell in, and the crowd groaned. Steam and vapor from the fire-hoses began to hide it all from sight.

Hillsmith said, really gently, to Dr Eberhardt, "You see

why? Purified by fire. No longer human. Abominations, they were."

From a corner of the yard, the ambulance crew dragged someone. Someone kicking . . . dancing . . . flinging arms and legs about. Someone crying and screaming. Screams and cries. "Dry bones live! Dry bones *live*!" screamed Nasser Fauntleroy, as they lifted him and carried him away. "*Dry bones live!*"

Hillsmith said, so softly that Dr Eberhardt had to put his ear up close, ". . . purified by fire . . ."

Vlad wrapped Bella in his jacket, and from the bottom of the jacket a pair of very small feet projected. "Bella, my god. Bella!"

She opened her eyes and rolled them up until only the whites showed. Then she rolled them down. Then she looked at him directly with wide blue-grey eyes, and shook her head and said, "No." Then she reached her arms to him, and he couldn't say anything at all.

"Was that a bad dream, daddy?" she asked, into his ear.

"Something like that."

"It was *very* bad. I don't like it here. Let's go home."

To say that the office looked dirty and shabby was to say that water looked liquid and wet. Newspapers, documents, magazines, clippings, files and folders lay stacked and slipped and scattered. Someone was thrusting his hand into a large manila envelope. Someone was turning the pages of an old illustrated publication. Someone was going through a scrapbook, moistening loose corners with a small glue-brush. On one webby wall was a sign, THE CONTRACT NEVER EXPIRES. *None of the men was working hard or working fast, none of them seemed interested in what he was doing, and whatever they were all doing they gave the impression of having been doing it for a long, long time. One man ruffled through the clippings taken from the manila envelope. Stopped. Went back a few clippings. Opened a drawer and removed an album, opened it. Turned pages. Put the album down and read the clipping. Cleared his throat. Another man looked up, said, after a moment,* "What."

The first man said, "Mackilwhit's head."

The second stared. "Mackilwhit's head?"

"Yeah."

The second man said, "Where's the rest of him."

The first man slightly shrugged. "Doesn't say."

"Mackilwhit. He went into the wall. Yeah. In the wall."

The first man fumbled till he found what seemed an old handpenned list. From his rat's nest of a desk he selected a worn-down pencil, the point of which he moistened in his mouth. Then he let his finger find a line. Slowly, as though he had all the time in the world, he made a pencil-mark through it.

"Well," the man said, "he's out now."

And he dwelleth in desolate cities, and in houses which no man inhabiteth . . .

– Job xv, 28

HARLAN ELLISON

Objects of Desire in the Mirror Are Closer Than They Appear

THE GREAT FANTASIST Theodore Sturgeon once remarked, "Anywhere you go in the world, if there are at least two writers in the group, they'll wind up having a conversation about Harlan Ellison."

Although that well-known epigram may be more than slightly apocryphal, there is still no denying the fact that Ellison is certifiably a legend in his own lifetime.

He has won more awards in the genres of imaginative fiction than any other living author – including the Hugo, Nebula, Edgar, Writer's Guild of America, World Fantasy and Bram Stoker; so many in fact, that they now merely give him prestigious Lifetime Achievement Awards.

Since making his professional début in a 1956 edition of *Infinity Science Fiction*, he has published countless acclaimed novels and short stories, appeared in *The Best American Short Stories* collection, won Audie awards for spoken-word recordings and Writers Guild Awards for Most Outstanding Teleplay, written fiction in bookstore windows in plain view of amazed onlookers (including the memorable piece that follows), edited such landmark science fiction anthologies as *Dangerous Visions* (1967) and *Again, Dangerous Visions* (1972), discovered and promoted new writers such as Dan Simmons and Poppy Z. Brite, and produced numerous movie and TV scripts and essays and columns and articles and reviews . . .

At the same time Ellison sued the producers of *The Terminator* for plagiarism – and won; travelled 3000 miles to punch in the mouth a writer who had spoken ill of one of his friends, and is renowned for speaking his mind at public gatherings.

Such is the stuff of which legends are truly made.

W E FOUND THE POOR OLD GUY lying in garbage and quite a lot of his own blood in the alley next to the Midnight Mission. His shoes had been stolen – no way of knowing if he'd been wearing socks – and whatever had been in the empty, dirty paper bag he was clutching. But his fingernails were immaculate, and he had no beard stubble. Maybe sixty, maybe older. No way of telling at a cold appraisal.

There were three young women down on their knees, weeping and flailing toward the darkening sky. It was going to rain, a brick-mean rain. Bag ladies in an alley like that, yeah, no big surprise . . . but these weren't gap-toothed old scraggy harridans. I recognized two of them from commercials; I think the precise term is *supermodel*. Their voices outshone the traffic hissing past the alley mouth. They were obviously very broken up at the demise of this old bum.

We strung the yellow tape; and we started assembling whatever was going to pass for witnesses; and then, without any further notice, the sky ruptured and in an instant we were all drenched. The old man's blood sluiced away in seconds, and the alley was that slick, pretty, shiny black again. So much for ambient clues.

We moved inside.

The smell of Lysol and sour mash was charming. I remember once, when I was a little kid, I shinnied up an old maple tree and found a bird nest that had recently been occupied by, I don't know, maybe robins, maybe crows, or something, and it had a smell that was both nasty and disturbing. The inside of the room they let us use for our interrogation smelled not much the same, but it had the same two qualities: nasty, and unsettling.

"Lieutenant," one of the uniforms said, behind me; and I turned and answered, "Yeah?" Not the way I usually speak, but this was about as weird a venue, as troubling a set of circumstances as any I'd handled since I'd been promoted to Homicide. "Uh, excuse me, Lieutenant, but what do you want us to do with these three ladies?"

I looked over at them, huddling near the door, and for a moment I hated them. They were taller than I, they were prettier than I, they were certainly wealthier than I, they had no hips and their asses were smaller than mine, and they dressed a lot better. I won't compare cup size: at least I had them beat in that capacity.

"Keep them from talking to each other, but be easy with 'em. I think they're famous, and we've got enough problems in the Department this week." I was talking, of course, about the serial hooker-slayer who had been leaving bits of unrecognizable meat all over town for the preceding six months. Then I went to work. Bird nest smell. Not nice.

The first half dozen were either too wetbrain or demented even to grasp what I was asking them. Clearly, none of them had been out in that alley. But someone *had* been; the old man probably didn't cut his own throat. I'd say definitely, not even possibly.

The first bit of remark that bore any relation to a lead, was the ramble of a guy in his thirties, broke-down like the rest of them, but apparently not as long in the life as his peers. He had been an aerospace worker, laid off at Boeing a few years earlier in one of the periodic "downsizing" ploys.

His name was Richard. He mumbled his last name and I wrote it on my pad, but I paid less attention than I might've, had he been a real suspect, when he said, "Wull, I seen the green light."

"Green light?"

"Richard. Muh name's Richard."

"Yeah, I got that part. You said 'a green light.' "

"Uh-huh. It was a light, out there, with him, y'know the dead guy?"

I said, yeah, I know the dead guy. "And there was this light. And it was green."

"Uh-huh."

I contemplated a career in orthodonture, as I was already pulling teeth. "Well, look, Richard, you can be of great help to us in solving this murder, if you could just tell me *exactly* what you saw. Out there. In the alley. The green light. Okay?"

He nodded, the poor sonofabitch; and I confess I felt my heart go out to him. He actually was doing the best he could, and I didn't want to push him any more fiercely than common decency would permit. It is probably toasty warm inclinations of a similar sort that will forever block me from becoming one of the Bosses. Oh, well, Lieutenant is a perfectly decent rank to die with.

"I wuz, er, uh . . ." I read embarrassment.

"Go ahead, Richard, just tell me. Don't be embarrassed."

"Wull, I wuz takin' a leak out back. Around the corner in the alley, but back around the corner, y'know? Back behind where the dumpsters are. An' I wasn't watchin' nothin' else but my own business, an' I heard these girls singing and laughin', and I wuz 'fraid they might come over 'round the corner an' see me wit' my di . . . with my pants unzipped . . ."

"The green light, Richard? Remember: the green light?"

"Uh-huh, I wuz gettin' to that. I zipped up so fast I kinda wet myself, an' I turned around to the back over there, an' all of a sudden there was this green light, big green light, an' I heard the girls screamin' and there was some kinda music, I guess it wuz, an' then allmigawd it was really loud, the girls' screamin', an' I ducked outta there, and went around the dumpsters onna other side, and went over to the fence an' crawled over and come back to the Mission, b'cuz I din't want to get involved, cuz . . ."

He stopped talking. I had dropped my pencil. I bent to pick it up where it had rolled, next to his right foot. I saw his shoes. When I straightened, I looked him in the eye and said, "But you went out there afterward, didn't you, Richard?"

"Nuh-*uh*!" He shook his head violently, but I was looking him right in the eye.

"Before the police came, you went out again, didn't you, Richard?"

His lower lip started to tremble. I felt sorry as hell for the poor slob. He was somebody's son, somebody's brother, maybe even somebody's husband, once upon a layoff; and he was soaked to the skin with cheap wine; and he was scared.

"C'mon, Richard . . . I *know* you went back, so you might as well tell me what else you remember."

He murmured something so softly, and with such embarrassment, that I had to ask him gently to repeat: "I found the big knife."

"And you took it?"

"Yes'm."

"When you took his shoes."

"Yes'm."

"And anything else?"

"No'mum. I'm sorry."

"That's all right, Richard. Now I want you to go and get me the big knife, and bring it right straight back to this room, and give it to me. I'll have one of the officers go with you."

"Yes'm."

I called for Napoli, and told him to take Richard out to the common room, to retrieve "the big knife". As they started for the door of the smelly little room, Richard turned back to me and started to say, "You gonna take . . ."

And I stopped him. "No, Richard, no I'm not going to take back those nice shiny new shoes. They look very comfortable, and they're yours. In exchange for the big knife."

He smiled weakly, like a child who knows he's done wrong, is truly abject about it, but is grateful for being let off with just a reprimand.

When he came back, Napoli was carrying "the big knife." I'd expected a grav-knife or a butterfly, something street standard. This was a rusty machete. A big, wide-bladed, cut-down-the-sugar-cane machete. The blood that was dried on the blade, all the way up to the handle, was – for certain – some of the same that had been, until recently, billeted in the carotid artery of that old man.

I took the machete gingerly. Napoli had tied a string around the base of the haft, to preserve Richard's – and any others' – prints. I lowered the killing weapon to the table using only the string noose. Then I went back to questioning Richard.

He'd thought he could sell it for some sneaky pete. That's all there was to it. The shoes, because he needed them; and the knife, because it had been left lying there next to the body.

He tried to tell me the story a dozen different ways, but it was always the same. Taking a leak, seeing the green light, running away, coming back and taking the old man's shoes (and socks, as it turned out), swiping the machete while the three women bawled and screamed.

And he went on. For some long while. I gave him a five dollar bill, and told him to get a good dinner over at The Pantry. I'm not ready for this line of work. It's only eleven years; I'm not ready.

Days or weeks or millennia later, or maybe it only seemed as quick as that, I was back at the Precinct. I turned the big knife over to Forensics. My feet hurt, and there was a patina of Post-Its all over my desk . . . and faxes . . . and memos enough to choke a Coke machine. But the only urgent one was from the M.E. So I handed all the others off to Napoli, and told him to get them squared away, while I went downtown and had a chat with Dear Old Doc Death, our coroner. The Boss saw me heading out, and he put those two fingers in his mouth and whistled me to a halt, and yelled across the squadroom, "Have you eaten?"

"Since what time?" I answered.

"Since ever. Go get some dinner."

"I got to go downtown to see Dear Old Doc Death."

"Jacobs," he said, without room for argument, "do as I tell you." I said, yessir, and I went to The Pantry and had a T-bone. Richard of the green light was there, having a meal. He looked happy in his new shoes. I felt a lot better about the universe after that. In your heart of hearts, you think a Richard kind of rummy is going to stoke up on some sweet lucy or a tankard of muscatel, and so you just don't dip into the wallet for somebody like that. But every once in a sometime they fool you. This Richard was eating well, so I told the guy behind the cash register not to take his money, that I was paying for it, and Richard could maybe have a second meal, or buy a hat, or get a life. It was easier, after that, to go downtown.

"Not only has his throat been cut literally from ear to ear practically excising his head from his neck, not only was the rip strong and deep enough to sever the carotid, the jugular *and* the trachea – we're talking someone with heavy-duty *power*! – but I put his age at something over a hundred, maybe a hundred and two, a hundred and ten, maybe a hundred fifty, there's no way of judging something like this, I've never seen anything like it in all my years; but I have to *tell* you that this one-hundred-and-two-year-old corpse, this old man lying here all blue and empty, this old man . . . is pregnant."

Dear Old Doc Death had hair growing out of his ears. He had

a gimp on his starboard side. He did tend to drool and spit a mite when he was deep in conversation or silent communication with (I supposed) the spirits of the departed. But he was an award-winning sawbones. He could smell decay before the milk went sour, before the rot started to manifest itself. If he said this headless horseman was over a hundred years old, I might wrinkle my brow – and have to lave myself with vitamin E moisturizer later that night – but I'd make book he was dead on. Not a good choice of phrase, dead on. Right. I'd bet he was right. Correct.

"What're we talking here, Doc, some kind of artificial insemination?"

He shook his head. "No, not that easy." He breathed heavily, as if he didn't want to move forward with the story. But I caught a whiff of dinner-breath, anyway. Then he spoke very softly, sort of motioning me in closer. Fettucine Alfredo. "Look, Francine, I've been at this forever. But with all I've seen, all I've known of the variety of the human condition . . . never anything like this. The man has two complete sets of internal organs. Two hearts. Two livers, kidneys, alimentary canals, sixteen sinuses, two complete nervous systems – interlocked and twisting around each other like some insane roller coasters – and one of those sets is female, and the other is male. What we have here is –"

"Hermaphrodite?"

"No, goddamit!" He actually snapped at me. "Not some freak of nature, not some flunked transvestism exercise. What I'm describing to you, Francine, is two complete bodies jammed neatly and working well into one carcass. And the woman in there is about three months' gone with child. I'd say it would have been a perfectly normal – but how am I to know, really – a perfectly normal little girl. Now, all three of them are dead."

We talked for a lot longer. It never got any clearer. It never got any easier to believe. If it had come from anyone but Dear Old Doc Death, I'd've had the teller of the tale wrapped in the big Band-Aid. But who could doubt a man with that much moss coming out of his earholes?

One of the supermodels was Hypatia. Like Iman or Paulina or Vandela. One name. Maybe before the advent of blusher she was something additional, something Polish or Trinidadian, but to eyes that rested on glossy pages of fashion magazines, she was one name. Hypatia.

Candor: I wanted to kill her. No one of the same sex is supposed to look that good after wallowing in an alley, on her knees, in the rain and garbage, amid blood and failure.

"Care to tell me about it?"

She stared back at me across a vast, windy emptiness. I sighed softly. Just once, lord, I thought, just once give me Edna St. Vincent Millay to interrogate, and not Betty Boop.

"I don't know what you mean," she said. Gently. I almost believed she didn't have a clue.

"Well, how about this for a place to begin: you are a pretty famous celebrity, make many hundreds of thousands of dollars just to smile at a camera for a few hours, and you're wearing a Halston suit I'd price at maybe six-five or seven thousand dollars. And you were on Skid Row, outside the Midnight Mission – where the name Donna Karan has never been spoken – kneeling in a pool of blood spilled by an old, old man, and you're crying as if you'd lost your one great love."

"I did."

The other two were equally as helpful. Camilla DelFerro was brave, but barely coherent. She was so whacked, she kept mixing her genders, sometimes calling him "her." Angie Rose just kept bawling. They were no help. They just kept claiming they'd loved the old guy, that they couldn't go on without him, and that if they could be permitted, if it wasn't an inconvenience, they would all three like to be buried with him. Dead or alive, our option. Whacked; we're talking whacked here.

And they mentioned, in passing, the green light.

Don't ask.

When I turned in my prelim, the Boss gave me one of his looks. Not the one that suggests you're about to be recycled, or the one that says it's all over for you . . . the one that says if I had a single wish, it would be that you hadn't put these pages in front of me. He sighed, shoved back his chair, and took off his glasses, rubbing those two red spots on the wings of his nose where the frames pinched. "No one saw anything else? No one with a grudge, a score to settle, a fight over a bottle of wine, a pedestrian pissed off the old guy tried to brace him for loose change?"

I spread my hands. "You've got it there, all of it. The women are of no earthly help. They just keep saying they loved him, and that they can't live without him. In fact, we've got two of them on suicide watch. They might just *not* want to live without him. Boss, I'm at a total loss on this one."

He shoved back from the desk, slid down the chair till his upper weight was resting on his coccyx, and stared at me.

"What?"

He waggled his head, as if to say *nothing, nothing at all.* He reached out an enormous catcher's mitt of a hand and tore a little square off his notepad, wadded it, and began to chew it. Never understood that: kids in home-room with spit-wads, office workers with their minds elsewhere, people chewing paper. Never could figure that out.

"So, if it's nothing, Boss, why d'you keep staring at me like I just fell off the moon or something?"

"When was the last time you got laid, Jacobs?"

I was truly and genuinely shocked. The man was twice, maybe three or four times my age; he walked with a bad limp from having taken an off-duty slug delivered by a kid messing with a 7-Eleven; he was married, with great-grandchildren stacked in egg-crates; and he was Eastern Orthodox Catholic; and he bit his nails. And he chewed paper. I was truly, even genuinely, shocked.

"Hey, don't we have enough crap flying loose in this house without me having to haul your tired old ass up on sexual *hare*-assment?"

"You wish." He spat soggy paper into the waste basket. "So? Gimme a date, I'll settle for a ballpark figure. Round it off to the nearest decade."

I didn't think this was amusing. "I live the way I like."

"You live like shit."

I could feel the heat in my cheeks. "I don't have to –"

"No; you don't. But I've watched you for a long time, Francine. I knew your step-father, and I knew Andy . . ."

"Leave Andy out of it. What's done is done."

"Whatever. Andy's gone, a long time now he's been gone, and I don't see you moving along. You live like an old lady, not even with the cat thing; and one of these days they'll find your desiccated corpse stinking up the building you live in, and they'll bust open the door, and there you'll be, all leathery and oozing parts, in rooms filled with old Sunday newspaper sections, like those two creepy brothers . . .”

"The Collyer Brothers."

"Yeah. The Collyer Brothers."

"I don't think that'll happen."

"Right. And I never thought we'd elect some half-assed actor for President."

"Clinton wasn't an actor."

"Tell that to Bob Dole."

It was wearing thin. I wanted out of there. For some reason all this sidebar crap had wearied me more than I could say. I felt like shit again, the way I'd felt before dinner. "Are you done beating up on me?" He shook his head slowly, wearily.

"Go home. Get some sleep. Tomorrow we'll start all over." I thanked him, and I went home. Tomorrow, we'll start all over. Right at the level of glistening black alleys. I felt like shit.

I was dead asleep, dreaming about black birds circling a garbage-filled alley. The phone made that phlegm-ugly electronic sound its designers thought was reassuring to the human spirit, and I grabbed it on the third. "Yeah?" I wasn't as charming as I might otherwise have been. The voice on the other end was Razzia down at the house. "The three women . . . them models . . .?"

"Yeah, what about them?"

"They're gone."

"So big deal. They were material witnesses, that's all. We know where to find 'em."

"No, you don't understand. They're *really* gone. As in 'vanished.' Poof! Green light . . . and gone."

I sat up, turned on the bed lamp. "Green light?"

"Urey had 'em in tow, he was takin' 'em down the front steps, and there was this green light, and Urey's standin' there with his dick in his mitt." He coughed nervously. "In a manner 'a speakin'."

I was silent.

"So, uh, Lootenant, they're, uh, like no longer wit' us."

"I got it. They're gone. Poof."

I hung up on him, and I went back to sleep. Not immediately, but I managed. Why not. There was a big knife with a tag on it, in a brown bag, waiting for me; and some blood simples I already knew; there were three supermodels drunk with love who now had vanished in front of everyone's eyes; and we still had an old dead man with his head hanging by a thread.

The Boss had no right to talk to me like that.

I didn't collect old newspapers. I had a subscription to *Time*. And the J. Crew catalogue.

And it was that night, in dreams, that the one real love of my life came to me.

As I lay there, turning and whispering to myself, a woman in her very early forties, tired as hell but quite proud of herself, only eleven years on the force and already a Lieutenant of Homicide, virtually unheard-of, I dreamed the dream of true love.

She appeared in a green light. I understood that . . . it was part of the dream, from the things the bum Richard had said, that the women had said. In a green light, she appeared, and she spoke to me, and she made me understand how beautiful I really was. She assured me that Angie Rose and Hypatia and Camilla had told her how lovely I was, and how lonely I was, and how scared I was . . . and we made love.

If there is an end to it all, I have seen it; I have been there, and I can go softly, sweetly. The one true love of my life appeared to me, like a goddess, and I was fulfilled. The water was cool and clear and I drank deeply.

I realized, as I had not even suspected, that I was tired. I was exhausted from serving time in my own life. And she asked me if I wanted to go away with her, to a place where the winds were cinnamon-scented, where we would revel in each other's adoration till the last ticking moment of eternity.

I said: take me away.

And she did. We went away from there, from that sweaty bedroom in the three-room apartment, before dawn of the next day when I had to go back to death and gristle and puzzles that could only be solved by apprehending monsters. And we went away, yes, we did.

I am very old now. Soon I will no doubt close my eyes in a sleep even more profound than the one in which I lay when she came to release me from a life that was barely worth living. I have been in this cinnamon-scented place for a very long time. I suppose time is herniated in this venue, otherwise she would not have been able to live as long as she did, nor would she have been able to move forward and backward with such alacrity and ease. Nor would the twisted eugenics that formed her have borne such elegant fruit.

I could have sustained any indignity. The other women, the deterioration of our love, the going-away and the coming back, knowing that she . . . or he, sometimes . . . had lived whole lives in other times and other lands. With other women. With other men.

But what I could not bear was knowing the child was not mine. I gave her the best eternity of my life, yet she carried that damned thing inside her with more love than *ever* she had shown me. As it grew, as *it* became the inevitable love-object, I withered.

Let her travel with them, whatever love-objects she could satisfy, with whatever was in that dirty paper bag, and let them wail if they choose . . . but from this dream neither he nor she will ever rise. I am in the green light now, with the machete. It may rain, but I won't be there to see it.

Not this time.

PETER STRAUB

Mr Clubb and Mr Cuff

PETER STRAUB IS THE AUTHOR OF a number of best-selling novels, including *Ghost Story*, *Shadowland*, *Koko*, *The Throat* and *The Hellfire Club*. He has won the Bram Stoker Award, the British Fantasy Award, two World Fantasy Awards and the International Horror Guild Award (for "Mr Clubb and Mr Cuff"). He also received the Life Achievement Award at the 1997 World Horror Convention.

More recently he published a new novel, *Mr X*, and the novella *Pork Pie Hat* appeared as part of Orion's Criminal Records series. A new collection of shorter fiction, *Magic Terror*, is forthcoming.

About the following powerful novella, the author explains, "I had been thinking about what I might do with Herman Melville's great story 'Bartleby the Scrivener' when Otto Penzler asked me to contribute to an anthology based on the theme of revenge. 'All right,' I thought, 'let's do a "Bartleby" about revenge.'

"I had to do *something* with 'Bartleby', anyhow, as I hadn't been able to think about anything else since I reread it. Plus the idea of revenge exacted by revenge itself, which is the only kind of revenge interesting enough to write about, seemed to fit pretty well into a story about a man who cannot rid himself of a mysterious employee. Once I started, the entire story seemed to fall happily into place. I should add that the lyrical descriptions of cigar-smoke are jokes about connoisseurship."

I.

I never intended to go astray, nor did I know what that meant. My journey began in an isolated hamlet notable for the piety of its inhabitants, and when I vowed to escape New Covenant I assumed that the values instilled within me there would forever be my guide. And so, with a depth of paradox I still only begin to comprehend, they have been. My journey, so triumphant, also *so* excruciating, is both *from* my native village and *of* it. For all its splendor, my life has been that of a child of New Covenant.

When in my limousine I scanned the *Wall Street Journal*, when in the private elevator I ascended to the rosewood-paneled office with harbor views, when in the partners' dining room I ordered squab on a mesclun bed from a prison-rescued waiter known to me alone as Charlie-Charlie, also when I navigated for my clients the complex waters of financial planning, above all when before her seduction by my enemy Graham Leeson I returned homeward to luxuriate in the attentions of my stunning Marguerite, when transported within the embraces of my wife, even then I carried within the frame houses dropped like afterthoughts down the streets of New Covenant, the stiff faces and suspicious eyes, the stony cordialities before and after services in the grim great Temple – the blank storefronts along Harmony Street – tattooed within me was the ugly, enigmatic beauty of my birthplace. Therefore I believe that when I strayed, and stray I did, make no mistake, it was but to come home, for I claim that the two strange gentlemen who beckoned me into error were the night of its night, the dust of its dust. In the period of my life's greatest turmoil – the month of my exposure to Mr Clubb and Mr Cuff, "Private Detectives Extraordinaire," as their business card described them – in the midst of the uproar I felt that I saw *the contradictory dimensions of . . .*

of . . .

I felt I saw . . . had seen, had at least glimpsed . . . what a wiser man might call . . . try to imagine the sheer difficulty of actually writing these words . . . the Meaning of Tragedy. You smirk, I don't blame you, in your place I'd do the same, but I assure you I saw *something*.

I must sketch in the few details necessary to understand my story. A day's walk from New York state's Canadian border,

New Covenant was (and still is, still is) a town of just under a thousand inhabitants united by the puritanical Protestantism of the Church of the New Covenant, whose founders had broken away from the even more puritanical Saints of the Covenant. (The Saints had proscribed sexual congress in the hope of hastening The Second Coming.) The village flourished during the end of the nineteenth century, and settled into its permanent form around 1920.

To wit: Temple Square, where the Temple of the New Covenant and its bell tower, flanked left and right by the Youth Bible Study Center and the Combined Boys and Girls Elementary and Middle School, dominate a modest greensward. Southerly stand the shop fronts of Harmony Street, the bank, also the modest placards indicating the locations of New Covenant's doctor, lawyer, and dentist; south of Harmony Street lie the two streets of frame houses sheltering the town's clerks and artisans, beyond these the farms of the rural faithful, beyond the farmland deep forest. North of Temple Square is Scripture Street, two blocks lined with the residences of the Reverend and his Board of Brethren, the aforementioned doctor, dentist, and lawyer, the President and Vice-President of the bank, also the families of some few wealthy converts devoted to Temple affairs. North of Scripture Street are more farms, then the resumption of the great forest in which our village described a sort of clearing.

My father was New Covenant's lawyer, and to Scripture Street was I born. Sundays I spent in the Youth Bible Study Center, weekdays in the Combined Boys and Girls Elementary and Middle School. New Covenant was my world, its people all I knew of the world. Three-fourths of all mankind consisted of gaunt, bony, blond-haired individuals with chiseled features and blazing blue eyes, the men six feet or taller in height, the women some inches shorter – the remaining fourth being the Racketts, Mudges, and Blunts, our farm families, who after generations of intermarriage had coalesced into a tribe of squat, black-haired, gap-toothed, moon-faced males and females seldom taller than five feet, four or five inches. Until I went to college I thought that all people were divided into the races of town and barn, fair and dark, the spotless and the mud-spattered, the reverential and the sly.

Though Racketts, Mudges and Blunts attended our school and

worshipped in our Temple, though they were at least as prosperous as we in town save the converts in their mansions, we knew them tainted with an essential inferiority. Rather than intelligent they seemed *crafty*, rather than spiritual, *animal*. Both in classrooms and Temple, they sat together, watchful as dogs compelled for the nonce to be "good," now and again tilting their heads to pass a whispered comment. Despite Sunday baths and Sunday clothes, they bore an uneraseable odor redolent of the barnyard. Their public self-effacement seemed to mask a peasant amusement, and when they separated into their wagons and other vehicles, they could be heard to share a peasant laughter.

I found this mysterious race unsettling, in fact profoundly annoying. At some level they frightened me – I found them compelling. Oppressed from my earliest days by life in New Covenant, I felt an inadmissible fascination for this secretive brood. Despite their inferiority, I wished to know what they knew. Locked deep within their shabbiness and shame I sensed the presence of a freedom I did not understand but found *thrilling*.

Because town never socialized with barn, our contacts were restricted to places of education, worship, and commerce. It would have been as unthinkable for me to take a seat beside Delbert Mudge or Charlie-Charlie Rackett in our fourth-grade classroom as for Delbert or Charlie-Charlie to invite me for an overnight in their farmhouse bedrooms. Did Delbert and Charlie-Charlie actually have bedrooms, where they slept alone in their own beds? I recall mornings when the atmosphere about Delbert and Charlie-Charlie suggested nights spent in close proximity to the pig pen, others when their worn dungarees exuded a freshness redolent of sunshine, wildflowers and raspberries.

During recess an inviolable border separated the townies at the northern end of our play area from the barnies at the southern. Our play, superficially similar, demonstrated our essential differences, for we could not cast off the unconscious stiffness resulting from constant adult measurement of our spiritual worthiness. In contrast, the barnies did not play at playing but actually *played*, plunging back and forth across the grass, chortling over victories, grinning as they muttered what must have been jokes. (We were not adept at jokes.) When school closed at end of day, I tracked the homebound progress of Delbert, Charlie-Charlie and clan with envious eyes and a divided heart.

Why should they have seemed in possession of a liberty I desired? After graduation from Middle School, we townies progressed to Shady Glen's Consolidated High, there to monitor ourselves and our fellows while encountering the temptations of the wider world, in some cases then advancing into colleges and universities. Having concluded their educations with the seventh grade's long division and "Hiawatha" recitations, the barnies one and all returned to their barns. Some few, some very few, of *us*, among whom I had determined early on to be numbered, left for good, thereafter to be celebrated, denounced, or mourned. One of *us*, Caleb Thurlow, violated every standard of caste and morality by marrying Munna Blunt and vanishing into barnie-world. A disgraced, disinherited pariah during my childhood, Thurlow's increasingly pronounced stoop and decreasing teeth terrifyingly mutated him into a blond, wasted barnie-parody on his furtive annual Christmas appearances at Temple. One of *them*, one only, my old classmate Charlie-Charlie Rackett, escaped his ordained destiny in our twentieth year by liberating a plow horse and Webley-Vickers pistol from the family farm to commit serial armed robbery upon Shady Glen's George Washington Inn, Town Square Feed & Grain, and Allsorts Emporium. Every witness to his crimes recognized what, if not who, he was, and Charlie-Charlie was apprehended while boarding the Albany train in the next village west. During the course of my own journey from and of New Covenant, I tracked Charlie-Charlie's gloomy progress through the way stations of the penal system until at last I could secure his release at a parole hearing with the offer of a respectable job in the financial planning industry.

I had by then established myself as absolute monarch of three floors in a Wall Street monolith. With my two junior partners, I enjoyed the services of a fleet of paralegals, interns, analysts, investigators, and secretaries. I had chosen these partners carefully, for as well as the usual expertise, skill and dedication, I required other, less conventional qualities.

I had sniffed out intelligent but unimaginative men of some slight moral laziness; capable of cutting corners when they thought no one would notice; controlled drinkers and secret drug-takers: juniors with reason to be grateful for their positions.

I wanted no *zealousness*. My employees were to be steadfastly incurious and able enough to handle their clients satisfactorily, at least with my paternal assistance.

My growing prominence had attracted the famous, the established, the notorious. Film stars and athletes, civic leaders, corporate pashas, and heirs to longstanding family fortunes regularly visited our offices, as did a number of conspicuously well-tailored gentlemen who had accumulated their wealth in a more colorful fashion. To these clients I suggested financial stratagems responsive to their labyrinthine needs. I had not schemed for their business. It simply *came to me*, willy-nilly, as our Temple held that salvation came to the elect. One May morning, a cryptic fellow in a pin-striped suit appeared in my office to pose a series of delicate questions. As soon as he opened his mouth, the cryptic fellow summoned irresistably from memory a dour, squinting member of the Board of Brethren of New Covenant's Temple. I *knew* this man, and instantly I found the tone most acceptable to him. Tone is all to such people. After our interview he directed others of his kind to my office, and by December my business had tripled. Individually and universally these gentlemen pungently reminded me of the village I had long ago escaped, and I cherished my suspicious buccaneers even as I celebrated the distance between my moral life and theirs. While sheltering these self-justifying figures within elaborate trusts, while legitimizing subterranean floods of cash, I immersed myself within a familiar atmosphere of pious denial. Rebuking home, I *was* home.

Life had not yet taught me that revenge inexorably exacts its own revenge.

My researches eventually resulted in the hiring of the two junior partners known privately to me as Gilligan and Captain. The first, a short, trim fellow with a comedian's rubber face and dishevelled hair, brilliant with mutual funds but an ignoramus at estate planning, each morning worked so quietly as to become invisible. To Gilligan I had referred many of our actors and musicians, and those whose schedules permitted them to attend meetings before the lunch hour met their soft-spoken advisor in a dimly lighted office with curtained windows. After lunch, Gilligan tended toward the vibrant, the effusive, the extrovert. Red-faced and sweating, he loosened his tie, turned on a powerful sound system and ushered emaciated musicians with haystack hair into the atmosphere of a backstage party. Morning Gilligan spoke in whispers; Afternoon Gilligan batted our secretaries' shoulders as he bounced office-ward down the corridors. I snapped him up as soon as one of my competitors let him go, and he proved a perfect complement to the Captain. Tall, plump, silver-haired, this gentleman had come to me from a specialist in estates and trusts discomfited by his tendency to become pugnacious when outraged by a client's foul language, improper dress, or other offenses against good taste. Our tycoons and inheritors of family fortunes were in no danger of arousing the Captain's ire, and I myself handled the unshaven film stars' and heavy metallists' estate planning. Neither Gilligan nor the Captain had any contact with the cryptic gentlemen. Our office was an organism balanced in all its parts. Should any mutinous notions occur to my partners, my spy the devoted Charlie-Charlie Rackett, to them as Charles the Perfect Waiter, every noon silently monitored their every utterance while replenishing Gilligan's wine glass. My marriage of two years seemed blissfully happy, my reputation and bank account flourished alike, and I anticipated perhaps another decade of labor followed by luxurious retirement. I could not have been less prepared for the disaster to come.

Mine, as disasters do, began at home. I admit my contribution to the difficulties. While immersed in the demands of my profession, I had married a beautiful woman twenty years my junior. It was my understanding that Marguerite had knowingly entered into a contract under which she enjoyed the fruits of income and social position while postponing a deeper marital communication until I cashed in and quit the game, at which point she and I could travel at will, occupying grand hotel suites and staterooms while acquiring every adornment which struck her eye. How could an arrangement so harmonious have failed to satisfy her? Even now I feel the old rancor. Marguerite had come into our office as a faded singer who wished to invest the remaining proceeds from a five- or six-year-old "hit," and after an initial consultation Morning Gilligan whispered her down the corridor for my customary lecture on estate tax, trusts, so forth and so on, in her case due to the modesty of the funds in question mere show. (Since during their preliminary discussion she had casually employed the Anglo-Saxon monosyllable for excrement, Gilligan dared not subject her to the Captain.) He escorted her into my chambers, and I glanced up with the customary show of interest. You may imagine a thick bolt of lightning slicing through a double-glazed office window, sizzling across the width of a polished teak desk, and striking me in the heart.

Already I was lost. Thirty minutes later I violated my most sacred edict by inviting a female client to a dinner date. She accepted, damn her. Six months later, Marguerite and I were married, damn us both. I had attained everything for which I had abandoned New Covenant, and for twenty-three months I inhabited the paradise of fools.

I need say only that the usual dreary signals, matters like unexplained absences, mysterious telephone calls abruptly terminated upon my appearance, and visitations of a melancholic, distracted *daemon*, forced me to set one of our investigators on Marguerite's trail, resulting in the discovery that my wife had been two-backed-beasting it with my sole professional equal, the slick, the smooth Graham Leeson, to whom I, swollen with uxorious pride a year after our wedding day, had introduced her during a function at the Waldorf-Astoria Hotel. I know what happened. I don't need a map. Exactly as I had decided to win her at our first meeting, Graham Leeson vowed to steal Marguerite from me the instant he set his handsome blue eyes on her between the fifty-thousand-dollar tables on the Starlight Roof.

My enemy enjoyed a number of natural advantages. Older than she by but ten years to my twenty, at six-four three inches taller than I, this reptile had been blessed with a misleadingly winning Irish countenance and a full head of crinkly red-blond hair. (In contrast, my white tonsure accentuated the severity of the all-too Cromwellian townie face.) I assumed her immune to such obvious charms, and I was wrong. I thought Marguerite could not fail to see the meagerness of Leeson's inner life, and I was wrong again. I suppose he exploited the inevitable temporary isolation of any spouse to a man in my position. He must have played upon her grudges, spoken to her secret vanities. Cynically, I am sure, he encouraged the illusion that she was an "artist." He flattered, he very likely wheedled. By every shabby means at his disposal he had overwhelmed her, most crucially by screwing her brains out three times a week in a corporate suite at a Park Avenue hotel.

After I had examined the photographs and other records arrayed before me by the investigator, an attack of nausea brought my dizzied head to the edge of my desk; then rage stiffened my backbone and induced a moment of hysterical blindness. My marriage was dead, my wife a repulsive stranger. Vision returned a second or two later. The checkbook floated from the desk drawer, the Waterman pen glided into position between thumb and forefinger, and while a shadow's efficient hand inscribed a check for ten thousand dollars, a disembodied voice informed the hapless investigator that the only service required of him henceforth would be eternal silence.

For perhaps an hour I sat alone in my office, postponing appointments and refusing telephone calls. In the moments when I had tried to envision my rival, what came to mind was some surly drummer or guitarist from her past, easily intimidated and readily bought off. In such a case, I should have inclined toward mercy. Had Marguerite offered a sufficiently self-abasing apology, I would have slashed her clothing allowance in half, restricted her public appearances to the two or three most crucial charity events of the year and perhaps as many dinners at my side in the restaurants where one is "seen", and insured that the resultant mood of sackcloth and ashes prohibited any reversion to bad behavior by intermittent use of another investigator.

No question of mercy, now. Staring at the photographs of my life's former partner entangled with the man I detested most in the world, I shuddered with a combination of horror, despair, loathing, and – appallingly – an urgent spasm of sexual arousal. I unbuttoned my trousers, groaned in ecstatic torment, and helplessly ejaculated over the images on my desk. When I had recovered, weak-kneed and trembling I wiped away the evidence, fell into my chair, and picked up the telephone to request Charlie-Charlie Rackett's immediate presence in my office.

The cryptic gentlemen, experts in the nuances of retribution, might seem more obvious sources of assistance, but I could not afford obligations in that direction. Nor did I wish to expose my humiliation to clients for whom the issue of respect was all-important. Devoted Charlie-Charlie's years in the jug had given him an extensive acquaintanceship among the dubious and irregular, and I had from time to time commandeered the services of one or another of his fellow yardbirds. My old companion sidled around my door and posted himself before me, all dignity on the outside, all curiosity within.

"I have been dealt a horrendous blow, Charlie-Charlie," I said, "and as soon as possible I wish to see one or two of the best."

Charlie-Charlie glanced at the folders. "You want serious people," he said, speaking in code. "Right?"

"I must have men who can be serious when seriousness is necessary," I said, replying in the same code.

While my lone surviving link to New Covenant struggled to understand this directive, it came to me that Charlie-Charlie had now become my only true confidant, and I bit down on an upwelling of fury. I realized that I had clamped shut my eyes, and opened them upon an uneasy Charlie-Charlie.

"You're sure," he said.

"Find them," I said, and to restore some semblance of our conventional atmosphere asked, "The boys still okay?"

Telling me that the juniors remained content, he said, "Fat and happy. I'll find what you want, but it'll take a couple of days."

I nodded, and he was gone.

For the remainder of the day I turned in an inadequate impersonation of the executive who usually sat behind my desk and, after putting off the moment as long as reasonably possible, buried the awful files in a bottom drawer and returned to the townhouse I had purchased for my bride-to-be and which, I remembered with an unhappy pang, she had once in an uncharacteristic moment of cuteness called "our townhome."

Since I had been too preoccupied to telephone wife, cook, or butler with the information that I would be late at the office, when I walked into our dining room the table had been laid with our china and silver, flowers arranged in the centerpiece, and in what I took to be a new dress, Marguerite glanced mildly up from her end of the table and murmured a greeting. Scarcely able to meet her eyes, I bent to bestow the usual homecoming kiss with a mixture of feelings more painful than I previously would have imagined myself capable. Some despicable portion of my being responded to her beauty with the old husbandly appreciation even as I went cold with the loathing I could not permit myself to show. I hated Marguerite for her treachery, her beauty for its falsity, myself for my susceptibility to what I knew was treacherous and false. Clumsily, my lips brushed the edge of an azure eye, and it came to me that she may well have been with Leeson while the investigator was displaying the images of her degradation.

Through me coursed an involuntary tremor of revulsion with, strange to say, at its center a molten erotic core. Part of my extraordinary pain was the sense that I too had been contaminated: a layer of illusion had been peeled away, revealing monstrous blind groping slugs and maggots.

Having heard voices, Mr Moncrieff, the butler I had employed upon the abrupt decision of the Duke of Denbigh to cast off worldly ways and enter an order of Anglican monks, came through from the kitchen and awaited orders. His bland, courteous manner suggested as usual that he was making the best of having been shipwrecked on an island populated by illiterate savages. Marguerite said that she had been worried when I had not returned home at the customary time.

"I'm fine," I said. "No, I'm not fine. I feel unwell. Distinctly unwell. Grave difficulties at the office." With that I managed to make my way up the table to my chair, along the way signalling to Mr Moncrieff that the Lord of the Savages wished him to bring in the pre-dinner martini and then immediately begin serving whatever the cook had prepared. I took my seat at the head of the table, and Mr Moncrieff removed the floral centerpiece to the sideboard. Marguerite regarded me with the appearance of probing concern. This was false, false, false. Unable to meet her eyes, I raised mine to the row of Canalettos along the wall, then the intricacies of the plaster molding above the paintings, at last to the chandelier depending from the central rosette on the ceiling. More had changed than my relationship with my wife. The molding, the blossoming chandelier, even Canaletto's Venice resounded with a cold, selfish lovelessness.

Marguerite remarked that I seemed agitated.

"No, I am not," I said. The butler placed the ice-cold drink before me, and I snatched up the glass and drained half its contents. "Yes, I am agitated, terribly," I said. "The difficulties at the office are more far-reaching than I intimated." I polished off the martini and tasted only glycerine. "It is a matter of betrayal and treachery made all the more wounding by the closeness of my relationship with the traitor."

I lowered my eyes to measure the effect of this thrust to the vitals on the traitor in question. She was looking back at me with a flawless imitation of wifely concern. For a moment I doubted her unfaithfulness. Then the memory of the photographs in my

bottom drawer once again brought crawling into view the slugs
and maggots. "I am sickened unto rage," I said, "and my rage
demands vengeance. Can you understand this?"

Mr Moncrieff carried into the dining room the tureens or
serving dishes containing whatever it was we were to eat that
night, and my wife and I honored the silence which had become
conventional during the presentation of our evening meal. When
we were alone again, she nodded in affirmation.

I said, "I am grateful, for I value your opinions. I should like
you to help me reach a difficult decision."

She thanked me in the simplest of terms.

"Consider this puzzle," I said. "Famously, vengeance is the
Lord's, and therefore it is often imagined that vengeance exacted
by anyone other is immoral. Yet if vengeance is the Lord's, then a
mortal being who seeks it on his own behalf has engaged in a
form of worship, even an alternate version of prayer. Many good
Christians regularly pray for the establishment of justice, and
what lies behind an act of vengeance but a desire for justice? God
tells us that eternal torment awaits the wicked. He also demon-
strates a pronounced affection for those who prove unwilling to
let Him do all the work."

Marguerite expressed the opinion that justice was a fine thing
indeed, and that a man such as myself would always labor in its
behalf. She fell silent and regarded me with what on any night
previous I would have seen as tender concern. Though I had not
yet so informed her, she declared, the Benedict Arnold must have
been one of my juniors, for no other employee could injure me so
greatly. Which was the traitor?

"As yet I do not know," I said. "But once again I must be
grateful for your grasp of my concerns. Soon I will put into
position the bear-traps which will result in the fiend's exposure.
Unfortunately, my dear, this task will demand all of my energy
over at least the next several days. Until the task is accomplished,
it will be necessary for me to camp out in the — Hotel." I named
the site of her assignations with Graham Leeson.

A subtle, momentary darkening of the eyes, her first genuine
response of the evening, froze my heart as I set the bear-trap into
place. "I know, the —'s vulgarity deepens with every passing
week, but Gilligan's apartment is but a few doors north, the
Captain's one block south. Once my investigators have installed

their electronic devices, I shall be privy to every secret they possess. Might you not enjoy spending several days at Green Chimneys? The servants have the month off, but you might enjoy the solitude there more than you would being alone in town."

Green Chimneys, our country estate on a bluff above the Hudson River, lay two hours away. Marguerite's delight in the house had inspired me to construct on the grounds a fully-equipped recording studio, where she typically spent days on end, trying out new "songs".

Charmingly, she thanked me for my consideration and said that she would enjoy a few days in seclusion at Green Chimneys. After I had exposed the traitor, I was to telephone her with the summons home. Accommodating on the surface, vile beneath, these words brought an anticipatory tinge of pleasure to her face, a delicate heightening of her beauty I would have, very likely *had*, misconstrued on earlier occasions. Any appetite I might have had disappeared before a visitation of nausea, and I announced myself exhausted. Marguerite intensified my discomfort by calling me her poor darling. I staggered to my bedroom, locked the door, threw off my clothes, and dropped into bed to endure a sleepless night. I would never see my wife again.

II.

Sometime after first light I had attained an uneasy slumber; finding it impossible to will myself out of bed on awakening, I relapsed into the same restless sleep. By the time I appeared within the dining room, Mr Moncrieff, as well-chilled as a good Chardonnay, informed me that Madame had departed for the country some twenty minutes before. Despite the hour, did Sir wish to breakfast? I consulted, trepidatiously, my wristwatch. It was ten-thirty: my unvarying practice was to arise at six, breakfast soon after, and arrive in my office well before seven. I rushed downstairs, and as soon as I slid into the back seat of the limousine forbade awkward queries by pressing the button to raise the window between the driver and myself.

No such mechanism could shield me from Mrs Rampage, my secretary, who thrust her head around the door a moment after I had expressed my desire for a hearty breakfast of poached eggs, bacon, and whole-wheat toast from the executive dining room.

All calls and appointments were to be postponed or otherwise put off until the completion of my repast. Mrs Rampage had informed me that two men without appointments had been awaiting my arrival since eight a.m. and asked if I would consent to see them immediately. I told her not to be absurd. The door to the outer world swung to admit her beseeching head. "Please," she said. "I don't know who they are, but they're *frightening* everybody."

This remark clarified all. Earlier than anticipated, Charlie-Charlie Rackett had deputized two men capable of seriousness when seriousness was called for. "I beg your pardon," I said. "Send them in."

Mrs Rampage withdrew to lead into my sanctum two stout, stocky, short, dark-haired men. My spirits had taken wing the moment I beheld these fellows shouldering through the door, and I rose smiling to my feet. My secretary muttered an introduction baffled as much by my cordiality as by her ignorance of my visitors' names.

"It is quite all right," I said. "All is in order, all is in train." New Covenant had just walked in.

Barnie-slyness, barnie-freedom, shone from their great round gap-toothed faces: in precisely the manner I remembered, these two suggested mocking peasant violence scantily disguised by an equally mocking impersonation of convention. Small wonder that they had intimidated Mrs Rampage and her underlings, for their nearest exposure to a like phenomenon had been with our musicians, and when offstage they were pale, emaciated fellows of little physical vitality. Clothed in black suits, white shirts and black neckties, holding their black derbies by their brims and turning their gappy smiles back and forth between Mrs Rampage and myself, these barnies had evidently been loose in the world for some time. They were perfect for my task. *You will be irritated by their country manners, you will be annoyed by their native insubordination*, I told myself, *but you will never find men more suitable, so grant them what latitude they need*. I directed Mrs Rampage to cancel all telephone calls and appointments for the next hour.

The door closed, and we were alone. Each of the black-suited darlings snapped a business card from his right jacket pocket and extended it to me with a twirl of the fingers. One card read:

MR CLUBB AND MR CUFF
Private Detectives Extraordinaire
Mr Clubb

and the other:

MR CLUBB AND MR CUFF
Private Detectives Extraordinaire
Mr Cuff

I inserted the cards into a pocket and expressed my delight at making their acquaintance.

"Becoming aware of your situation," said Mr Clubb, "we preferred to report as quickly as we could."

"Entirely commendable," I said. "Will you gentlemen please sit down?"

"We prefer to stand," said Mr Clubb.

"I trust you will not object if I again take my chair," I said, and did so. "To be honest, I am reluctant to describe the whole of my problem. It is a personal matter, therefore painful."

"It is a domestic matter," said Mr Cuff.

I stared at him. He stared back with the sly imperturbability of his kind.

"Mr Cuff," I said, "you have made a reasonable, and as it happens, an accurate supposition, but in the future you will please refrain from speculation."

"Pardon my plain way of speaking, sir, but I was not speculating," he said. "Marital disturbances are domestic by nature."

"All too domestic, one might say," put in Mr Clubb. "In the sense of pertaining to the home. As we have so often observed, you find your greatest pain right smack-dab in the living room, as it were."

"Which is a somewhat politer fashion of naming another room altogether." Mr Cuff appeared to suppress a surge of barnie-glee.

Alarmingly, Charlie-Charlie had passed along altogether too much information, especially since the information in question should not have been in his possession. For an awful moment I imagined that the dismissed investigator had spoken to Charlie-Charlie. The man may have broadcast my disgrace to every person encountered on his final journey out of my office, inside the public elevator, thereafter even to the shoeshine "boys" and cup-rattling vermin lining the streets. It occurred to me that I might be forced to have the man silenced. Symmetry would then demand the silencing of valuable Charlie-Charlie. The inevitable next step would resemble a full-scale massacre.

My faith in Charlie-Charlie banished these fantasies by suggesting an alternate scenario and enabled me to endure the next utterance.

Mr Clubb said, "Which in plainer terms would be to say the bedroom."

After speaking to my faithful spy, the Private Detectives Extraordinaire had taken the initiative by acting as if *already employed* and following Marguerite to her afternoon assignation at the — Hotel. Here, already, was the insubordination I had forseen, but instead of the expected annoyance I felt a thoroughgoing gratitude for the two men leaning slightly toward me, their animal senses alert to every nuance of my response. That they had come to my office armed with the essential secret absolved me from embarrassing explanations; blessedly, the hideous photographs would remain concealed in the bottom drawer.

"Gentlemen," I said, "I applaud your initiative."

They stood at ease. "Then we have an understanding," said Mr Clubb. "At various times, various matters come to our attention. At these times we prefer to conduct ourselves according to the wishes of our employer, regardless of difficulty."

"Agreed," I said. "However, from this point forward I must insist –"

A rap at the door cut short my admonition. Mrs Rampage brought in a coffee pot and cup, a plate beneath a silver cover, a rack with four slices of toast, two jam-pots, silverware, a linen napkin, and a glass of water, and came to a halt some five or six feet short of the barnies. A sinfully arousing smell of butter and bacon emanated from the tray. Mrs Rampage deliberated between placing my breakfast on the table to her left or venturing into proximity to my guests by bringing the tray to my desk. I gestured her forward, and she tacked wide to port and homed in on the desk. "All is in order, all is in train," I said. She nodded and backed out – literally walked backwards until she reached the door, groped for the knob, and vanished.

I removed the cover from the plate containing two poached

eggs in a cup-sized bowl, four crisp rashers of bacon, and a mound of home fried potatoes all the more welcome for being a surprise gift from our chef.

"And now, fellows, with your leave I shall –"

For the second time my sentence was cut off in mid-flow. A thick barnie-hand closed upon the handle of the coffee pot and proceeded to fill the cup. Mr Clubb transported my coffee to his lips, smacked appreciatively at the taste, then took up a toast slice and plunged it like a dagger into my egg-cup, releasing a thick yellow suppuration. He crunched the dripping toast between his teeth.

At that moment, when mere annoyance passed into dumbfounded ire, I might have sent them packing despite my earlier resolution, for Mr Clubb's violation of my breakfast was as good as an announcement that he and his partner respected none of the conventional boundaries and would indulge in boorish, even disgusting behavior. I very nearly did send them packing, and both of them knew it. They awaited my reaction, whatever it should be. Then I understood that I was being tested, and half of my insight was that ordering them off would be a failure of imagination. I had asked Charlie-Charlie to send me serious men, not Boy Scouts, and in the rape of my breakfast were depths and dimensions of seriousness I had never suspected. In that instant of comprehension, I believe, I virtually knew all that was to come, down to the last detail, and gave a silent assent. My next insight was that the moment when I might have dismissed these fellows with a conviction of perfect rectitude had just passed, and with the sense of opening myself to unpredictable adventures I turned to Mr Cuff. He lifted a rasher from my plate, folded it within a slice of toast, and displayed the result.

"Here are our methods in action," he said. "We prefer not to go hungry while you gorge yourself, speaking freely, for the one reason that all of this stuff represents what you ate every morning when you were a kid." Leaving me to digest this shapeless utterance, he bit into his impromptu sandwich and sent golden-brown crumbs showering to the carpet.

"For as the important, abstemious man you are now," said Mr Clubb, "what do you eat in the mornings?"

"Toast and coffee," I said. "That's about it."

"But in childhood?"

"Eggs," I said. "Scrambled or fried, mainly. And bacon. Home-fries, too." Every fatty, cholesterol-crammed ounce of which, I forbore to add, had been delivered by barnie-hands directly from barnie-farms. I looked at the rigid bacon, the glistening potatoes, the mess in the egg-cup. My stomach lurched.

"We prefer," Mr Clubb said, "that you follow your true preferences instead of muddying mind and stomach by gobbling this crap in search of a inner peace which never existed in the first place, if you can be honest with yourself." He leaned over the desk and picked up the plate. His partner snatched a second piece of bacon and wrapped it within a second slice of toast. Mr Clubb began working on the eggs, and Mr Cuff grabbed a handful of home-fried potatoes. Mr Clubb dropped the empty egg cup, finished his coffee, refilled the cup, and handed it to Mr Cuff, who had just finished licking the residue of fried potato from his free hand.

I removed the third slice of toast from the rack. Forking home fries into his mouth, Mr Clubb winked at me. I bit into the toast and considered the two little pots of jam, greengage, I think, and rosehip. Mr Clubb waggled a finger. I contented myself with the last of the toast. After a while I drank from the glass of water. All in all I felt reasonably satisfied, and, but for the deprivation of my customary cup of coffee, content with my decision. I glanced in some irritation at Mr Cuff. He drained his cup, then tilted into it the third and final measure from the pot and offered it to me. "Thank you," I said. Mr Cuff picked up the pot of greengage jam and sucked out its contents, loudly. Mr Clubb did the same with the rosehip. They sent their tongues into the corners of the jam-pots and cleaned out whatever adhered to the sides. Mr Cuff burped. Overlappingly, Mr Clubb burped.

"Now, that is what I call by the name of breakfast, Mr Clubb," said Mr Cuff. "Are we in agreement?"

"Deeply," said Mr Clubb. "That is what I call by the name of breakfast now, what I have called by the name of breakfast in the past, and what I shall continue to call by that sweet name on every morning in the future." He turned to me and took his time, sucking first one tooth, then another. "Our morning meal, sir, consists of that simple fare with which we begin the day, except when in all good faith we wind up sitting in a waiting room with our stomachs growling because our future client has chosen to skulk in late for work." He inhaled. "Which was for the same exact reason which brought him to our attention in the first place and for which we went without in order to offer him our assistance. Which is, begging your pardon, sir, the other reason for which you ordered a breakfast you would ordinarily rather starve than eat, and all I ask before we get down to the business at hand is that you might begin to entertain the possibility that simple men like ourselves might possibly understand a thing or two."

"I see that you are faithful fellows," I began.

"Faithful as dogs," broke in Mr Clubb.

"And that you understand my position," I continued.

"Down to its smallest particulars," he interrupted again. "We are on a long journey."

"And so it follows," I pressed on, "that you must also understand that no further initiatives may be taken without my express consent."

These last words seemed to raise a disturbing echo, of what I could not say but an echo nonetheless, and my ultimatum failed to achieve the desired effect. Mr Clubb smiled and said, "We intend to follow your inmost desires with the faithfulness, as I have said, of trusted dogs, for one of our sacred duties is that of bringing these to fulfillment, as evidenced, begging your pardon, sir, in the matter of the breakfast our actions spared you from gobbling up and sickening yourself with. Before you protest, sir, please let me put to you the question of you how you think you would be feeling right now if you had eaten that greasy stuff all by yourself?"

The straightforward truth announced itself and demanded utterance. "Poisoned," I said. After a second's pause, I added, "Disgusted."

"Yes, for you are a better man than you know. Imagine the situation. Allow yourself to picture what would have transpired had Mr Cuff and myself not acted on your behalf. As your heart throbbed and your veins groaned, you would have taken in that while you were stuffing yourself the two of us stood hungry before you. You would have remembered that good woman informing you that we had patiently awaited your arrival since eight this morning, and at that point, sir, you would have experienced a self-disgust which would forever have tainted our relationship. From that point forth, sir, you would have been incapable of receiving the full benefits of our services."

I stared at the twinkling barnie. "Are you saying that if I had eaten my breakfast you would have refused to work for me?"

"You did eat your breakfast. The rest was ours."

This statement was so literally true that I burst into laughter and said, "Then I must thank you for saving me from myself. Now that you may accept employment, please inform me of the rates for your services."

"We have no rates," said Mr Clubb.

"We prefer to leave compensation to the client," said Mr Cuff.

This was crafty even by barnie-standards, but I knew a counter-move. "What is the greatest sum you have ever been awarded for a single job?"

"Six hundred thousand dollars," said Mr Clubb.

"And the smallest?"

"Nothing, zero, *nada*, zilch," said the same gentleman.

"And your feelings as to the disparity?"

"None," said Mr Clubb. "What we are given is the correct amount. When the time comes, you shall know the sum to the penny."

To myself I said, *So I shall, and it shall be nothing*; to them, "We must devise a method by which I may pass along suggestions as I monitor your ongoing progress. Our future consultations should take place in anonymous public places on the order of street corners, public parks, diners, and the like. I must never be seen in your office."

"You must not, you could not," said Mr Clubb. "We would prefer to install ourselves here within the privacy and seclusion of your own beautiful office."

"Here?" He had once again succeeded in dumbfounding me.

"Our installation within the client's work space proves so advantageous as to overcome all initial objections," said Mr Cuff. "And in this case, sir, we would occupy but the single corner behind me where the table stands against the window. We would come and go by means of your private elevator, exercise our natural functions in your private bathroom, and have our simple meals sent in from your kitchen. You would suffer no interference or awkwardness in the course of your business. So we prefer to do our job here, where we can do it best."

"You prefer to move in with me," I said, giving equal weight to every word.

"Prefer it to declining the offer of our help, thereby forcing you, sir, to seek the aid of less reliable individuals."

Several factors, first among them being the combination of delay, difficulty, and risk involved in finding replacements for the pair before me, led me to give further thought to this absurdity. Charlie-Charlie, a fellow of wide acquaintance among society's shadow-side, had sent me his best. Any others would be inferior. It was true that Mr Clubb and Mr Cuff could enter and leave my office unseen, granting us a greater degree of security possible in diners and public parks. There remained an insuperable problem.

"All you say may be true, but my partners and clients alike enter this office daily. How do I explain the presence of two strangers?"

"That is easily done, Mr Cuff, is it not?" said Mr Clubb.

"Indeed it is," said his partner. "Our experience has given us two infallible and complementary methods. The first of these is the installation of a screen to shield us from the view of those who visit this office."

I said, "You intend to hide behind a screen."

"During those periods when it is necessary for us to be on site."

"Are you and Mr Clubb capable of perfect silence? Do you never shuffle your feet, do you never cough?"

"You could justify our presence within these sacrosanct confines by the single manner most calculated to draw over Mr Clubb and myself a blanket of respectable, anonymous impersonality."

"You wish to be introduced as my lawyers?" I asked.

"I invite you to consider a word," said Mr Cuff. "Hold it steadily in your mind. Remark the inviolability which distinguishes those it identifies, measure its effect upon those who hear it. The word of which I speak, sir, is this: consultant."

I opened my mouth to object and found I could not.

Every profession occasionally must draw upon the resources of impartial experts – consultants. Every institution of every kind has known the visitations of persons answerable only to the top and given access to all departments – consultants. Consultants are *supposed* to be invisible. Again I opened my mouth, this time to say, "Gentlemen, we are in business." I picked up my telephone

and asked Mrs Rampage to order immediate delivery from
Bloomingdale's of an ornamental screen and then to remove
the breakfast tray.

Eyes a-gleam with approval, Mr Clubb and Mr Cuff stepped
forward to shake my hand.

"We are in business," said Mr Clubb.

"Which is by way of saying," said Mr Cuff, "jointly dedicated
to a sacred purpose."

Mrs Rampage entered, circled to the side of my desk, and gave
my visitors a glance of deep-dyed wariness. Mr Clubb and Mr
Cuff clasped their hands before them and looked heavenward.
"About the screen," she said. "Bloomingdale's wants to know if
you would prefer one six feet high in a black and red Chinese
pattern or one ten feet high, Art Deco, in ochres, teals, and
taupes."

My barnies nodded together at the heavens. "The latter, please,
Mrs Rampage," I said. "Have it delivered this afternoon, regardless of cost, and place it beside the table for the use of these
gentlemen, Mr Clubb and Mr Cuff, highly regarded consultants
to the financial industry. That table shall be their command
post."

"Consultants," she said. "Oh."

The barnies dipped their heads. Much relaxed, Mrs Rampage
asked if I expected great changes in the future.

"We shall see," I said. "I wish you to extend every cooperation
to these gentlemen. I need not remind you, I know, that change is
the first law of life."

She disappeared, no doubt on a beeline for her telephone.

Mr Clubb stretched his arms above his head. "The preliminaries are out of the way, and we can move to the job at hand. You,
sir, have been most *exceedingly*, most *grievously* wronged. Do I
overstate?"

"You do not," I said.

"Would I overstate to assert that you have been injured, that
you have suffered a devastating wound?"

"No, you would not," I responded, with some heat.

Mr Clubb settled a broad haunch upon the surface of my desk.
His face had taken on a grave, sweet serenity. "You seek redress.
Redress, sir, is a *correction*, but it is nothing more. You imagine
that it restores a lost balance, but it does nothing of the kind. A

crack has appeared on the earth's surface, causing widespread loss of life. From all sides are heard the cries of the wounded and dying. It is as though the earth itself has suffered an injury akin to yours, is it not?"

He had expressed a feeling I had not known to be mine until that moment, and my voice trembled as I said, "It is exactly."

"Exactly," he said. "For that reason I said *correction* rather than *restoration*. Restoration is never possible. Change is the first law of life."

"Yes, of course," I said, trying to get down to brass tacks.

Mr Clubb hitched his buttock more comprehensively onto the desk. "What will happen will indeed happen, but we prefer our clients to acknowledge from the first that, apart from human desires being a deep and messy business, outcomes are full of surprises. If you choose to repay one disaster with an equal and opposite disaster, we would reply, in our country fashion, there's a calf that won't suck milk."

I said, "I know I can't pay my wife back in kind, how could I?"

"Once we begin," he said, "we cannot undo our actions."

"Why should I want them undone?" I asked.

Mr Clubb drew up his legs and sat cross-legged before me. Mr Cuff placed a meaty hand on my shoulder. "I suppose there is no dispute," said Mr Clubb, "that the injury you seek to redress is the adulterous behavior of your spouse."

Mr Cuff's hand tightened on my shoulder.

"You wish that my partner and myself punish your spouse."

"I didn't hire you to read her bedtime stories," I said.

Mr Cuff twice smacked my shoulder, painfully, in what I took to be approval.

"Are we assuming that her punishment is to be of a physical nature?" asked Mr Clubb. His partner gave my shoulder another all-too hearty squeeze.

"What other kind is there?" I asked, pulling away from Mr Cuff's hand.

The hand closed on me again, and Mr Clubb said, "Punishment of a mental or psychological nature. We could, for example, torment her with mysterious telephone calls and anonymous letters. We could use any of a hundred devices to make it impossible for her to sleep. Threatening incidents could be staged so often as to put her in a permanent state of terror."

"I want physical punishment," I said.

"That is our constant preference," he said. "Results are swifter and more conclusive when physical punishment is used. But again, we have a wide spectrum from which to choose. Are we looking for mild physical pain, real suffering, or something in between, on the order of, say, broken arms or legs?"

I thought of the change in Marguerite's eyes when I named the — Hotel. "Real suffering."

Another bone-crunching blow to my shoulder from Mr Cuff and a wide, gappy smile from Mr Clubb greeted this remark. "You, sir, are our favorite type of client," said Mr Clubb. "A fellow who knows what he wants and is unafraid to put it into words. This suffering, now, did you wish it in brief or extended form?"

"Extended," I said. "I must say that I appreciate your thoughtfulness in consulting with me like this. I was not quite sure what I wanted of you when first I requested your services, but you have helped me become perfectly clear about it."

"That is our function," he said. "Now, sir. The extended form of real suffering permits two different conclusions, gradual cessation or termination. Which is your preference?"

I opened my mouth and closed it. I opened it again and stared at the ceiling. Did I want these men to murder my wife? No. Yes. No. Yes, but only after making sure that the unfaithful trollop understood exactly why she had to die. No, surely an extended term of excruciating torture would restore the world to proper balance. Yet I wanted the witch dead. But then I would be ordering these barnies to kill her. "At the moment I cannot make that decision," I said. Irresistibly, my eyes found the bottom drawer containing the file of obscene photographs. "I'll let you know my decision after we have begun."

Mr Cuff dropped his hand, and Mr Clubb nodded with exaggerated, perhaps ironic slowness. "And what of your rival, the seducer, sir? Do we have any wishes in regard to that gentleman, sir?"

The way these fellows could sharpen one's thinking was truly remarkable. "I most certainly do," I said. "What she gets, he gets. Fair is fair."

"Indeed, sir," said Mr Clubb, "and, if you will permit me, sir, only fair is fair. And fairness demands that before we go any deeper into the particulars of the case we must examine the evidence as presented to yourself, and when I speak of fairness, sir, I refer to fairness particularly to yourself, for only the evidence seen by your own eyes can permit us to view this matter through them."

Again, I looked helplessly down at the bottom drawer. "That will not be necessary. You will find my wife at our country estate, Green . . ."

My voice trailed off as Mr Cuff's hand ground into my shoulder while he bent down and opened the drawer.

"Begging to differ," said Mr Clubb, "but we are now and again in a better position than the client to determine what is necessary. Remember, sir, that while shame unshared is toxic to the soul, shame shared is the beginning of health. Besides, it only hurts for a little while."

Mr Cuff drew the file from the drawer.

"My partner will concur that your inmost wish is that we examine the evidence," said Mr Clubb. "Else you would not have signalled its location. We would prefer to have your explicit command to do so, but in the absence of explicit, implicit serves just about as well."

I gave an impatient, ambiguous wave of the hand, a gesture they cheerfully misunderstood.

"Then all is . . . how do you put it, sir? 'All is . . .' "

"All is in order, all is in train," I muttered.

"Just so. We have ever found it beneficial to establish a common language with our clients, in order to conduct ourselves within terms enhanced by their constant usage in the dialogue between us." He took the file from Mr Cuff's hands. "We shall examine the contents of this folder at the table across the room. After the examination has been completed, my partner and I shall deliberate. And then, sir, we shall return for further instructions."

They strolled across the office and took adjoining chairs on the near side of the table, presenting me with two identical, wide, black-clothed backs. Their hats went to either side, the file between them. Attempting unsuccessfully to look away, I lifted my receiver and asked my secretary who if anyone had called in the interim and what appointments had been made for the morning.

Mr Clubb opened the folder and leaned forward to inspect the topmost photograph.

My secretary informed me that Marguerite had telephoned from the road with an inquiry concerning my health. Mr Clubb's back and shoulders trembled with what I assumed was the shock of disgust. One of the scions was due at two p.m., and at four a cryptic gentleman would arrive. By their works shall ye know them, and Mrs Rampage proved herself a diligent soul by asking if I wished her to place a call to Green Chimneys at three o'clock. Mr Clubb thrust a photograph in front of Mr Cuff. "I think not," I said. "Anything else?" She told me that Gilligan had expressed a desire to see me privately – meaning, without the Captain – sometime during the morning. A murmur came from the table. "Gilligan can wait," I said, and the murmur, expressive I had thought of dismay and sympathy, rose in volume and revealed itself as amusement.

They were chuckling – even chortling!

I replaced the telephone and said, "Gentlemen, please, your laughter is insupportable." The potential effect of this remark was undone by its being lost within a surge of coarse laughter. I believe that something else was at that moment lost . . . some dimension of my soul . . . an element akin to pride . . . akin to dignity . . . but whether the loss was for good or ill, then I could not say. For some time, in fact an impossibly lengthy time, they found cause for laughter in the wretched photographs. My occasional attempts to silence them went unheard as they passed the dread photographs back and forth, discarding some instantly and to others returning for a second, even a third, even a fourth and fifth, perusal.

And then at last the barnies reared back, uttered a few nostalgic chirrups of laughter, and returned the photographs to the folder. They were still twitching with remembered laughter, still flicking happy tears from their eyes, as they sauntered grinning back across the office and tossed the file onto my desk. "Ah me, sir, a delightful experience," said Mr Clubb. "Nature in all her lusty romantic splendor, one might say. Remarkably stimulating, I could add. Correct, sir?"

"I hadn't expected you fellows to be stimulated to mirth," I grumbled, ramming the foul thing into the drawer and out of view.

"Laughter is merely a portion of the stimulation to which I refer," he said. "Unless my sense of smell has led me astray, a thing I fancy it has yet to do, you could not but feel another sort of arousal altogether before these pictures, am I right?"

I refused to respond to this sally but feared that I felt the blood rising to my cheeks. Here they were again, the slugs and maggots.

"We are all brothers under the skin," said Mr Clubb. "Remember my words. Shame unshared poisons the soul. And besides, it only hurts for a little while."

Now I could not respond. What was the "it" which hurts only for a little while – the pain of cuckoldry, the mystery of my shameful response to the photographs, or the horror of the barnies knowing what I had done?

"You will find it helpful, sir, to repeat after me: *It only hurts for a little while.*"

"It only hurts for a little while," I said, and the naive phrase reminded me that they were only barnies after all.

"Spoken like a child," Mr Clubb most annoyingly said, "in as it were the tones and accents of purest innocence," and then righted matters by asking where Marguerite might be found. Had I not mentioned a country place named Green . . .?

"Green Chimneys," I said, shaking off the unpleasant impression which the preceding few seconds had made upon me. "You will find it at the end of — Lane, turning right off — Street just north of the town of —. The four green chimneys easily visible above the hedge along— Lane are your landmark, though as it is the only building in sight you can hardly mistake it for another. My wife left our place in the city just after ten this morning, so she should be getting there . . ." I looked at my watch. ". . . in thirty to forty-five minutes. She will unlock the front gate, but she will not relock it once she has passed through, for she never does. The woman does not have the self-preservation of a sparrow. Once she has entered the estate, she will travel up the drive and open the door of the garage with an electronic device. This door, I assure you, will remain open, and the door she will take into the house will not be locked."

"But there are maids and cooks and laundresses and bootboys and suchlike to consider," said Mr Cuff. "Plus a major-domo to conduct the entire orchestra and go around rattling the doors to make sure they're locked. Unless all of these parties are to be absent on account of the annual holiday."

"The servants have the month off," I said.

"A most suggestive consideration," said Mr Clubb. "You possess a devilish clever mind, sir."

"Perhaps," I said, grateful for the restoration of the proper balance. "Marguerite will have stopped along the way for groceries and other essentials, so she will first carry the bags into the kitchen, which is the first room to the right off the corridor from the garage. Then I suppose she will take the staircase up to her bedroom and air it out." I took pen and paper from my topmost drawer and sketched the layout of the house as I spoke. "She may go around to the library, the morning room, and the drawing room, opening the shutters and a few windows. Somewhere during this process, she is likely to use the telephone. After that, she will leave the house by the rear entrance and take the path along the top of the bluff to a long, low building which looks like this."

I drew in the well-known outlines of the studio in its nest of trees on the bluff above the Hudson. "It is a recording studio I had built for her convenience. She may well plan to spend the entire afternoon inside it, and you will know if she is there by the lights." Then I could see Marguerite smiling to herself as she fit her key into the lock on the studio door, see her let herself in and reach automatically for the light switch, and a wave of emotion rendered me speechless.

Mr Clubb rescued me by asking, "It is your feeling, sir, that when the lady stops to use the telephone she will be placing a call to that energetic gentleman?"

"Yes, of course," I said, only barely refraining from adding *you dolt*. "She will seize the earliest opportunity to inform him of their good fortune."

He nodded with the extravagant caution I was startled to recognize from my own dealings with backward clients. "Let us pause to see all 'round the matter, sir. Will the lady wish to leave a suspicious entry in your telephone records? Isn't it more likely that the person she telephones will be you, sir? The call to the athletic gentleman will already have been placed, according to my way of seeing things, either from the roadside or the telephone in the grocery where you have her stop to pick up her essentials."

Though disliking these references to Leeson's physical condition, I admitted that he might have a point.

"So, in that case, sir, and I know that a mind as quick as yours has already overtaken mine, you would want to express yourself with the utmost cordiality when the missus calls again, so as not to tip your hand in even the slightest way. But that I'm sure goes without saying, after all you have been through, sir."

Without bothering to acknowledge this, I said, "Shouldn't you fellows really be leaving? No sense in wasting time, after all."

"Precisely why we shall wait here until the end of the day," said Mr Clubb. "In cases of this unhappy sort, we find it more effective to deal with both parties at once, acting in concert when they are in prime condition to be taken by surprise. The gentleman is liable to leave his place of work at the end of the day, which implies to me that he is unlikely to appear at your lovely country place at any time before seven this evening, or, which is more likely, eight. At this time of the year, there is still enough light at nine o'clock to enable us to conceal our vehicle on the grounds, enter the house, and begin our business. At eleven o'clock, sir, we shall call with our initial report and request additional instructions."

I asked the fellow if he meant to idle away the entire afternoon in my office while I conducted my business.

"Mr Cuff and I are never idle, sir. While you conduct your business, we will be doing the same, laying out our plans, refining our strategies, choosing our methods and the order of their use."

"Oh, all right," I said, "but I trust you'll be quiet about it."

At that moment, Mrs Rampage buzzed to say that Gilligan was before her, requesting to see me immediately, proof that bush telegraph is a more efficient means of spreading information than any newspaper. I told her to send him in, and a second later the morning Gilligan, pale of face, dark hair tousled but not as yet completely wild, came treading softly toward my desk. He pretended to be surprised that I had visitors and pantomimed an apology which incorporated the suggestion that he depart and return later. "No, no," I said, "I am delighted to see you, for this gives me the opportunity to introduce you to our new consultants, who will be working closely with me for a time."

Gilligan swallowed, glanced at me with the deepest suspicion, and extended his hand as I made the introductions. "I regret that I am unfamiliar with your work, gentlemen," he said. "Might I ask the name of your firm? Is it Locust, Bleaney, Burns or Charter, Carter, Maxton, and Coltrane?"

By naming the two most prominent consultancies in our industry, Gilligan was assessing the thinness of the ice beneath his feet: LBB specialized in investments, CCM&C in estates and trusts. If my visitors worked for the former, he would suspect that a guillotine hung above his neck; if the latter, the Captain was liable for the chop. "Neither," I said. "Mr Clubb and Mr Cuff are the directors of their own concern, which covers every aspect of the trade with such tactful professionalism that it is known to but the few for whom they will consent to work."

"Excellent," Gilligan whispered, gazing in some puzzlement at the map and floor plan atop my desk. "Tip-top."

"When their findings are given to me, they shall be given to all. In the meantime. I would prefer that you say as little as possible about the matter. Though change is a law of life, we wish to avoid unnecessary alarm."

"You know that you can depend on my silence," said Morning Gilligan, and it was true, I did know that. I also knew that his alter ego, Afternoon Gilligan, would babble the news to everyone who had not already heard it from Mrs Rampage. By six p.m., our entire industry would be pondering the information that I had called in a consultancy team of such rarified accomplishments *that they chose to remain unknown but to the very few*. None of my colleagues could dare admit to an ignorance of Clubb & Cuff, and my reputation, already great, would increase exponentially.

To distract him from the floor plan of Green Chimneys and the rough map of my estate, I said, "I assume some business brought you here, Gilligan."

"Oh! Yes – yes – of course," he said, and with a trace of embarrassment brought to my attention the pretext for his being there, the ominous plunge in value of an overseas fund in which we had advised one of his musicians to invest. Should we recommend selling the fund before more money was lost, or was it wisest to hold on? Only a minute was required to decide that the musician should retain his share of the fund until next quarter, when we anticipated a general improvement, but both Gilligan and I were aware that this recommendation call could easily have been handled by telephone, and soon he was moving toward the door, smiling at the barnies in a pathetic display of false confidence.

The telephone rang a moment after the detectives had returned to the table. Mr Clubb said, "Your wife, sir. Remember: the utmost cordiality." Here was false confidence, I thought, of an entirely different sort. I picked up the receiver to hear Mrs Rampage tell me that my wife was on the line.

What followed was a banal conversation of the utmost *duplicity*. Marguerite pretended that my sudden departure from the dinner table and my late arrival at the office had caused her to fear for my health. I pretended that all was well, apart from a slight indigestion. Had the drive up been peaceful? Yes, the highways had been surprisingly empty. How was the house? A little musty, but otherwise fine. She had never quite realized, she said, how very large Green Chimneys was until she walked around in it, knowing she was going to be there alone. Had she been out to the studio? No, but she was looking forward to getting a lot of work done over the next three or four days and thought she would be working every night, as well. (Implicit in this remark was the information that I should be unable to reach her, the studio being without a telephone.) After a moment of awkward silence, she said, "I suppose it is too early for you to have identified your traitor." It was, I said, but the process would begin that evening. "I'm so sorry you have to go through this," she said. "I know how painful the discovery was for you, and I can only begin to imagine how angry you must be, but I hope you will be merciful. No amount of punishment can undo the damage, and if you try to exact retribution you will only injure yourself. The man is going to lose his job and his reputation. Isn't that punishment enough?" After a few meaningless pleasantries the conversation had clearly come to an end, although we still had yet to say good-bye. Then an odd thing happened to me. I nearly said, *Lock all the doors and windows tonight and let no one in*. I nearly said, *You are in grave danger and must come home*. With these words rising in my throat, I looked across the room at Mr Clubb and Mr Cuff, and Mr Clubb winked at me. I heard myself bidding Marguerite farewell, and then heard her hang up her telephone.

"Well done, sir," said Mr Clubb. "To aid Mr Cuff and myself in the preparation of our inventory, can you tell us if you keep certain staples at Green Chimneys?"

"Staples?" I said, thinking he was referring to foodstuffs.

"Rope?" he asked. "Tools, especially pliers, hammers, and

screwdrivers? A good saw? A variety of knives? Are there by any chance firearms?"

"No firearms," I said. "I believe all the other items you mention can be found in the house."

"Rope and tool chest in the basement, knives in the kitchen?"

"Yes," I said, "precisely." I had not ordered these barnies to murder my wife, I reminded myself; I had drawn back from that precipice. By the time I went into the executive dining room for my luncheon, I felt sufficiently restored to give Charlie-Charlie that ancient symbol of approval, the thumbs-up sign.

III.

When I returned to my office the screen had been set in place, shielding from view the detectives in their preparations but in no way muffling the rumble of comments and laughter they brought to the task. "Gentlemen," I said in a voice loud enough to be heard behind the screen – a most unsuitable affair decorated with a pattern of alternating ocean liners, martini glasses, champagne bottles and cigarettes – "you must modulate your voices, as I have business to conduct here as well as you." There came a somewhat softer rumble of acquiescence. I took my seat to discover my bottom desk drawer pulled out, the folder absent. Another roar of laughter jerked me once again to my feet.

I came around the side of the screen and stopped short. The table lay concealed beneath drifts and mounds of yellow legal paper covered with lists of words and drawings of stick figures in varying stages of dismemberment. Strewn through the yellow pages were the photographs, loosely divided into those in which either Marguerite or Graham Leeson provided the principal focus. Crude genitalia had been drawn, without reference to either party's actual gender, over and atop both of them. Aghast, I leaned over and began gathering up the defaced photographs. "I must insist . . ." I said. "I really must insist, you know . . ."

Mr Clubb immobilized my wrist with one hand and extracted the photographs with the other. "We prefer to work in our time-honored fashion," he said. "Our methods may be unusual, but they are ours. But before you take up the afternoon's occupations, sir, can you tell us if items on the handcuff order might be found in the house?"

"No," I said. Mr Cuff pulled a yellow page before him and wrote *handcuffs*.

"Chains?" asked Mr Clubb.

"No chains," I said, and Mr Cuff added *chains* to his list.

"That is all for the moment," said Mr Clubb, and released me.

I took a step backwards and massaged my wrist, which stung as if from rope-burn. "You speak of your methods," I said, "and I understand that you have them. But what can be the purpose of defacing my photographs in this grotesque fashion?"

"Sir," said Mr Clubb in a stern, teacherly voice, "where you speak of defacing, we use the term enhancement. Enhancement is a tool we find vital to the method known by the name of Visualization."

I retired defeated to my desk. At five minutes before two, Mrs Rampage informed that the Captain and his scion, a thirty-year-old inheritor of a great family fortune named Mr Chester Montfort d'M—, awaited my pleasure. Putting Mrs Rampage on hold, I called out, "Please do give me absolute quiet, now. A client is on his way in."

First to appear was the Captain, his tall, rotund form as alert as a pointer's in a grouse field as he led in the taller, inexpressibly languid figure of Mr Chester Montfort d'M—, a person marked in every inch of his being by great ease, humor, and stupidity. The Captain froze to gape horrified at the screen, but Montfort d'M— continued round him to shake my hand and say, "Have to tell you, I like that thingamabob over there immensely. Reminds me of a similar thingamabob at the Beeswax Club a few years ago, whole flocks of girls used to come tumbling out. Don't suppose we're in for any unicycles and trumpets today, eh?"

The combination of the raffish screen and our client's unbridled memories brought a dangerous flush to the Captain's face, and I hastened to explain the presence of top-level consultants who preferred to pitch tent on-site, as it were, hence the installation of a screen, all the above in the service of, well, *service*, an all-important quality we . . .

"By Kitchener's mustache," said the Captain. "I remember the Beeswax Club. Don't suppose I'll ever forget the night Little Billy Pegleg jumped up and . . ." The color darkened on his cheeks, and he closed his mouth.

From behind the screen, I heard Mr Clubb say, "Visualize *this*." Mr Cuff chuckled.

The Captain recovered himself and turned his sternest glare upon me. "Superb idea, consultants. A white-glove inspection tightens up any ship." His veiled glance toward the screen indicated that he had known of the presence of our "consultants" but, unlike Gilligan, had restrained himself from thrusting into my office until given legitimate reason. "That being the case, is it still quite proper that these people remain while we discuss Mr Montfort d'M—'s confidential affairs?"

"Quite proper, I assure you," I said. "The consultants and I prefer to work in an atmosphere of complete cooperation. Indeed, this arrangement is a condition of their accepting our firm as their client."

"Indeed," said the Captain.

"Top of the tree, are they?" said Mr Montfort d'M—. "Expect no less of you fellows. Fearful competence. *Terrifying* competence."

Mr Cuff's voice could be heard saying, "Okay, visualize *this*." Mr Clubb uttered a high-pitched giggle.

"Enjoy their work," said Mr Montfort d'M—.

"Shall we?" I gestured to their chairs. As a young man whose assets equalled fifteen to twenty billion dollars (depending on the condition of the stock market, the value of real estate in half a dozen cities around the world, global warming, forest fires and the like) our client was as catnip to the ladies, three of whom he had previously married and divorced after siring a child upon each, resulting in a great interlocking complexity of trusts, agreements, and contracts, all of which had to be re-examined on the occasion of his forthcoming wedding to a fourth young woman, named like her predecessors after a semi-precious stone. Due to the perspicacity of the Captain and myself, each new nuptial altered the terms of those previous so as to maintain our client's liability at an unvarying level. Our computers had enabled us to generate the documents well before his arrival, and all Mr Montfort d'M— had to do was listen to the revised terms and sign the papers, a task which generally induced a slumberous state except for those moments when a prized asset was in transition.

"Hold on, boys," he said ten minutes into our explanations, "you mean Opal has to give the race horses to Garnet, and in return she gets the teak plantation from Turquoise, who turns around and gives Opal the ski resort in Aspen? Opal is crazy about those horses, and Turquoise just built a house."

I explained that his second wife could easily afford the purchase of a new stable with the income from the plantation and his third would keep her new house. He bent to the task of scratching his signature on the form. A roar of laughter erupted behind the screen. The Captain glanced sideways in displeasure, and our client looked at me blinking. "Now to the secondary trusts," I said. "As you will recall, three years ago . . ."

My words were cut short by the appearance of a chuckling Mr Clubb clamping an unlighted cigar in his mouth, a legal pad in his hand, as he came toward us. The Captain and Mr Montfort d'M— goggled at him, and Mr Clubb nodded. "Begging your pardon, sir, but some queries cannot wait. Pickaxe, sir? Dental floss? Awl?"

"No, yes, no," I said, and then introduced him to the other two men. The Captain appeared stunned, Mr Montfort d'M— cheerfully puzzled.

"We would prefer the existence of an attic," said Mr Clubb.

"An attic exists," I said.

"I must admit my confusion," said the Captain. "Why is a consultant asking about awls and attics? What is dental floss to a consultant?"

"For the nonce, Captain," I said, "these gentlemen and I must communicate in a form of cipher or code, of which these are examples, but soon . . ."

"Plug your blow-hole, Captain," broke in Mr Clubb. "At the moment you are as useful as wind in an outhouse, always hoping you will excuse my simple way of expressing myself."

Sputtering, the Captain rose to his feet, his face rosier by far than during his involuntary reminiscence of what Little Billy Pegleg had done one night at the Beeswax Club.

"Steady on," I said, fearful of the heights of choler to which indignation could bring my portly, white-haired, but still powerful junior.

"Not on your life," bellowed the Captain. "I cannot brook . . . cannot tolerate . . . If this ill-mannered dwarf imagines excuse is possible after . . ." He raised a fist. Mr Clubb said, "Pish tosh," and placed a hand on the nape of the Captain's neck. Instantly, the Captain's eyes rolled up, the color drained from his face, and he dropped like a sack into his chair.

"Hole in one," marvelled Mr Montfort d'M—. "World class. Old boy isn't dead, is he?"

The Captain exhaled uncertainly and licked his lips.

"With my apologies for the unpleasantness," said Mr Clubb, "I have only two more queries at this juncture. Might we locate bedding in the aforesaid attic, and have you an implement such a match or a lighter?"

"There are several old mattresses and bedframes in the attic," I said, "but as to matches, surely you do not . . ."

Understanding the request better than I, Mr Montfort d'M— extended a golden lighter and applied an inch of flame to the tip of Mr Clubb's cigar. "Didn't think that part was code," he said. "Rules have changed? Smoking allowed?"

"From time to time during the workday my colleague and I prefer to smoke," said Mr Clubb, expelling a reeking miasma across the desk. I had always found tobacco nauseating in its every form, and in all parts of our building smoking had of course long been prohibited.

"Three cheers, my man, plus three more after that," said Mr Montfort d'M—, extracting a ridged case from an inside pocket, an absurdly phallic cigar from the case. "I prefer to smoke, too, you know, especially during these deadly conferences about who gets the pincushions and who gets the snuffboxes. Believe I'll join you in a corona." He submitted the object to a circumcision, _snick-snick_, and to my horror set it alight. "Ashtray?" I dumped paper clips from a crystal oyster shell and slid it toward him. "Mr Clubb, is it? Mr Clubb, you are a fellow of wonderful accomplishments, still can't get over that marvelous whopbopaloobop on the Captain, and I'd like to ask if we could get together some evening, cigars and cognac kind of thing."

"We prefer to undertake one matter at a time," said Mr Clubb. Mr Cuff appeared beside the screen. He, too, was lighting up eight or nine inches of brown rope. "However, we welcome your appreciation and would be delighted to swap tales of derring-do at a later date."

"Very, very cool," said Mr Montfort d'M—, "especially if you could teach me how to do the whopbopaloobop."

"This is a world full of hidden knowledge," Mr Clubb said. "My partner and I have chosen as our sacred task the transmission of that knowledge."

"Amen," said Mr Cuff.

Mr Clubb bowed to my awed client and sauntered off. The Captain shook himself, rubbed his eyes, and took in the client's cigar. "My goodness," he said. "I believe . . . I can't imagine . . . heavens, is smoking permitted again? What a blessing." With that, he fumbled a cigarette from his shirt pocket, accepted a light from Mr Montfort d'M—, and sucked in the fumes. Until that moment I had not known that the Captain was an addict of nicotine.

For the remainder of the hour a coiling layer of smoke like a low-lying cloud established itself beneath the ceiling and increased in density as it grew toward the floor while we extracted Mr Montfort d'M—'s careless signature on the transfers and assignments. Now and again the Captain displaced one of a perpetual chain of cigarettes from his mouth to remark upon the peculiar pain in his neck. Finally I was able to send client and junior partner on their way with those words of final benediction, "All is in order, all is in train," freeing me at last to stride about my office flapping a copy of *Institutional Investor* at the cloud, a remedy our fixed windows made more symbolic than actual. The barnies further defeated the effort by wafting ceaseless billows of cigar effluvia over the screen, but as they seemed to be conducting their business in a conventionally businesslike manner I made no objection and retired in defeat to my desk for the preparations necessitated by the arrival in an hour of my next client, Mr Arthur "This Building Is Condemned" C—, the most cryptic of all the cryptic gentlemen.

So deeply was I immersed in these preparations that only a polite cough and the supplication of "Begging your pardon, sir" brought to my awareness the presence of Mr Clubb and Mr Cuff before my desk. "What is it now?" I asked.

"We are, sir, in need of creature comforts," said Mr Clubb. "Long hours of work have left us exceeding dry in the region of the mouth and throat, and the pressing sensation of thirst has made it impossible for us to maintain the concentration required to do our best."

"Meaning a drink would be greatly appreciated, sir," said Mr Cuff.

"Of course, of course," I said. "You should have spoken earlier. I'll have Mrs Rampage bring in a couple of bottles of water. We have San Pellegrino and Evian. Which would you prefer?"

With a smile almost menacing in its intensity, Mr Cuff said, "We prefer drinks when we drink. *Drink* drinks, if you take my meaning."

"For the sake of the refreshment found in them," said Mr Clubb, ignoring my obvious dismay. "I speak of refreshment in its every aspect, from relief to the parched tongue, taste to the ready palate, warmth to the inner man, and to the highest of refreshments, that of the mind and soul. We prefer bottles of gin and bourbon, and while any decent gargle would be gratefully received, we have like all men who partake of grape and grain our favorite tipples. Mr Cuff is partial to JW Dant bourbon, and I enjoy a glass of Bombay gin. A bucket of ice would not go amiss, and I could say the same for a case of ice-cold Old Bohemia beer. As a chaser."

"You consider it a good idea to consume alcohol before embarking on . . ." I sought for the correct phrase. "A mission so delicate?"

"We consider it an essential prelude. Alcohol inspires the mind and awakens the imagination. A fool dulls both by over-indulgence, but up to that point, which is a highly individual matter, there is only enhancement. Through history, alcohol has been known for its sacred properties, and the both of us know during the sacrament of Holy Communion, priests and reverends happily serve as bartenders, passing out free drinks to all comers, children included."

"Besides that," I said after a pause, "I suppose you would prefer not to be compelled to quit my employment after we have made such strides together."

"We are on a great journey," he said.

I placed the order with Mrs Rampage, and fifteen minutes later into my domain entered two ill-dressed youths laden with the requested liquors and a metal bucket in which the necks of beer bottles protruded from a bed of ice. I tipped the louts a dollar apiece, which they accepted with boorish lack of grace. Mrs Rampage took in this activity with none of the revulsion for the polluted air and spirituous liquids I had anticipated.

The louts slouched away through the door she held open for them; the chuckling barnies disappeared from view with their refreshments; and, after fixing me for a moment of silence, her eyes alight with an expression I had never before observed in them, Mrs Rampage ventured the amazing opinion that the recent relaxation of formalities should prove beneficial to the firm as a whole and added that, were Mr Clubb and Mr Cuff responsible for the reformation, they had already justified their reputation and would assuredly enhance my own.

"You believe so," I said, noting with momentarily delayed satisfaction that the effects of Afternoon Gilligan's indiscretions had already begun to declare themselves.

Employing the tactful verbal formula for *I wish to speak exactly half my mind and no more*, Mrs Rampage said, "May I be frank, sir?"

"I depend on you to do no less," I said.

Her carriage and face at that moment became what I can only describe as girlish – years seemed to drop away from her. "I don't want to say too much, sir, and I hope you know how much everyone understands what a privilege it is to be a part of this firm." Like the Captain but more attractively, she blushed. "Honest, I really mean that. Everybody knows that we're one of the two or three companies best at what we do."

"Thank you," I said.

"That's why I feel I can talk like this," said my ever-less-recognizable Mrs Rampage. "Until today, everybody thought if they acted like themselves, the way they really were, you'd fire them right away. Because, and maybe I shouldn't say this, maybe I'm way out of line, sir, but it's because you always seem, well, so proper you could never forgive a person for not being as dignified as you are. Like the Captain is a heavy smoker and everybody knows it's not supposed to be permitted in this building, but a lot of companies here let their top people smoke in their offices as long as they're discreet because it shows they appreciate those people, and that's nice because it shows if you get to the top you can be appreciated, too, but here the Captain has to go all the way to the elevator and stand outside with the file clerks if he wants a cigarette. And in every other company I know the partners and important clients sometimes have a drink together and nobody thinks they're committing a terrible sin. You're a religious man, sir, we look up to you so much, but I think you're going to find that people will respect you even more once it gets out that you loosened the rules a little bit." She gave me a look in which I read that she feared having spoken too freely. "I just wanted to say that I think you're doing the right thing, sir."

What she was saying, of course, was that I was widely regarded as pompous, remote, and out of touch. "I had not known that my employees regarded me as a religious man," I said.

"Oh, we all do," she said with almost touching earnestness. "Because of the hymns."

"The hymns?"

"The ones you hum to yourself when you're working."

"Do I, indeed? Which ones?"

"*Jesus Loves Me, The Old Rugged Cross, Abide With Me*, and *Amazing Grace*, mostly. Sometimes *Onward Christian Soldiers*."

Here, with a vengeance, were Temple Square and Scripture Street! Here was the the Youth Bible Study Center, where the child-me had hours on end sung these same hymns during our Sunday School sessions! I did not to know what to make of the new knowledge that I hummed them to myself at my desk, but it was some consolation that this unconscious habit had at least partially humanized me to my staff.

"You didn't know you did that? Oh, sir, that's so *cute*!"

Sounds of merriment from the far side of the office rescued Mrs Rampage from the fear that this time she had truly overstepped the bounds, and she made a rapid exit. I stared after her for a moment, at first unsure how deeply I ought regret a situation in which my secretary found it possible to describe myself and my habits as *cute*, then resolving that it probably was, or eventually would be, all for the best. "All is in order, all is in train," I said to myself. "It only hurts for a little while." With that, I took my seat once more to continue delving into the elaborations of Mr "This Building Is Condemned" C—'s financial life.

Another clink of bottle against glass and ripple of laughter brought with them the long-delayed recognition that this particular client would never consent to the presence of unknown "consultants". Unless the barnies could be removed for at least an hour, I should face the immediate loss of a substantial portion of my business.

"Fellows," I cried, "come up here now. We must address a most serious problem."

Glasses in hand, cigars nestled into the corners of their mouths,

Mr Clubb and Mr Cuff sauntered into view. Once I had explained the issue in the most general terms, the detectives readily agreed to absent themselves for the required period. Where might they install themselves? "My bathroom," I said. "It has a small library attached, with a desk, a work table, leather chairs and sofa, a billiard table, a large-screen cable television set and a bar. Since you have not yet had your luncheon, you may wish to order whatever you like from the kitchen."

Five minutes later, bottles, glasses, hats, and mounds of paper arranged on the bathroom table, the bucket of beer beside it, I exited through the concealed door to the right of my desk as Mr Clubb ordered up from my doubtless astounded chef a meal of chicken wings, french fries, onion rings and T-bone steaks, medium well. With plenty of time to spare, I immersed myself again in details only to be brought up short by the recognition that I was humming, none too quietly, that most innocent of hymns, *Jesus Loves Me*. And then, precisely at the appointed hour, Mrs Rampage informed me of the arrival of my client and his associates, and I bade her bring them through.

A sly, slow-moving whale encased in an exquisite double-breasted black pinstripe, Mr "This Building Is Condemned" C— advanced into my office with his customary *hauteur* and offered me the customary nod of the head while his three "associates" formed a human breakwater in the center of the room. Regal to the core, he affected not to notice Mrs Rampage sliding a black leather chair out of the middle distance and around the side of the desk until it was in position, at which point he sat himself in it without looking down. Then he inclined his slablike head and raised a small, pallid hand. One of the "associates" promptly moved to open the door for Mrs Rampage's departure. At this signal, I sat down, and the two remaining henchmen separated themselves by a distance of perhaps eight feet. The third closed the door and stationed himself by his general's right shoulder. These formalities completed, my client shifted his close-set obsidian eyes to mine and said, "You well?"

"Very well, thank you," I replied according to ancient formula. "And you?"

"Good," he said. "But things could still be better." This, too, followed long-established formula, but his next words were a startling deviation. He took in the stationary cloud and the corpse

of Montfort d'M—'s cigar rising like a monolith from the reef of
cigarette butts in the crystal shell, and, with the first genuine smile
I had ever seen on his pockmarked, small-featured face, said, "I
can't believe it, but one thing just got better already. You eased up
on the stupid no-smoking rule which is poisoning this city, good
for you."

"It seemed," I said, "a concrete way in which to demonstrate
our appreciation for the smokers among those clients we most
respect." When dealing with the cryptic gentlemen, one must not
fail to offer intervallic allusions to the spontaneous respect in
which they are held.

"Deacon," he said, employing the sobriquet he had given me
on our first meeting, "you being one of a kind at your job, the
respect you speak of is mutual, and besides that, all surprises
should be as pleasant as this." With that, he snapped his fingers at
the laden shell, and as he produced a ridged case similar to but
more capacious than Mr Montfort d'M—'s, the man at his
shoulder whisked the impromptu ashtray from the desk, deposited its contents in the *poubelle*, and repositioned it at a point on
the desk precisely equidistant from us. My client opened the case
to expose the six cylinders contained within, removed one, and
proffered the remaining five to me. "Be my guest, Deacon," he
said. "Money can't buy better Havanas."

"Your gesture is much appreciated," I said. "However, with all
due respect, at the moment I shall choose not to partake."

Distinct as a scar, a vertical crease of displeasure appeared on
my client's forehead, and the ridged case and its five inhabitants
advanced an inch toward my nose. "Deacon, you want me to
smoke alone?" asked Mr "This Building Is Condemned" C—.
"This here, if you were ever lucky enough to find it at your local
cigar store, which that lucky believe me you wouldn't be, is
absolutely the best of the best, straight from me to you as what
you could term a symbol of the cooperation and respect between
us, and at the commencement of our business today it would
please me greatly if you would do me the honor of joining me in a
smoke."

As they say, or, more accurately, as they used to say, needs
must when the devil drives, or words to that effect. "Forgive me,"
I said, and drew one of the fecal things from the case. "I assure
you, the honor is all mine."

Mr "This Building Is Condemned" C— snipped the rounded end from his cigar, plugged the remainder in the center of his mouth, then subjected mine to the same operation. His henchman proffered a lighter, Mr "This Building Is Condemned" C— bent forward and surrounded himself with clouds of smoke, in the manner of Bela Lugosi materializing before the brides of Dracula. The henchmen moved the flame toward me, and for the first time in my life I inserted into my mouth an object which seemed as large around as the handle of a baseball bat, brought it to the dancing flame, and drew in that burning smoke from which so many other men before me had derived pleasure.

Legend and common sense alike dictated that I should sputter and cough in an attempt to rid myself of the noxious substance. Nausea was in the cards, also dizziness. It is true that I suffered a degree of initial discomfort, as if my tongue had been lightly singed or seared, and the sheer unfamiliarity of the experience – the thickness of the tobacco-tube, the texture of the smoke, as dense as chocolate – led me to fear for my well-being. Yet, despite the not altogether unpleasant tingling on the upper surface of my tongue, I expelled my first mouthful of cigar smoke with the sense of having sampled a taste every bit as delightful as the first sip of a properly made martini. The thug whisked away the flame, and I drew in another mouthful, leaned back, and released a wondrous quantity of smoke. Of a surprising smoothness, in some sense almost cool rather than hot, the delightful taste defined itself as heather, loam, morel mushrooms, venison, and some distinctive spice akin to coriander. I repeated the process, with results even more pleasurable – this time I tasted a hint of black butter sauce. "I can truthfully say," I told my client, "that never have I met a cigar as fine as this one."

"You bet you haven't," said Mr "This Building Is Condemned" C—, and on the spot presented me with three more of the precious objects. With that, we turned to the tidal waves of cash and the interlocking corporate shells, each protecting another series of interconnected shells which concealed yet another, like Chinese boxes.

The cryptic gentlemen one and all appreciated certain ceremonies, such as the appearance of espresso coffee in thimble-sized porcelain cups and an accompanying assortment of *biscotti* at the halfway point of our meditations. Matters of business being

forbidden while coffee and cookies were dispatched, the conversation generally turned to the conundrums posed by family
life. Since I had no family to speak of, and, like most of his kind,
Mr "This Building Is Condemned" C— was richly endowed with
grandparents, parents, uncles, aunts, sons, daughters, nephews,
nieces, and grandchildren, these remarks on the genealogical
tapestry tended to be monologic in nature, my role in them
limited to nods and grunts. Required as they were more often
by the business of the cryptic gentlemen than was the case in other
trades or professions, funerals were another ongoing topic. Taking tiny sips of his espresso and equally maidenish nibbles from
his favorite sweet-meats (Hydrox and Milano), my client favored
me with the expected praises of his son, Arthur Jr (Harvard
graduate school, English Lit.), lamentations over his daughter,
Fidelia (thrice-married, never wisely), hymns to his grandchildren
(Cyrus, Thor, and Hermione, respectively, the genius, the dreamer, and the despot), and then proceeded to link his two unfailing
themes by recalling the unhappy behavior of Arthur Jr at the
funeral of my client's uncle and a principal figure in his family's
rise to an imperial eminence, Mr Vincente "Waffles" C—.

The anecdote called for the beheading and ignition of another
magnificent stogie, and I greedily followed suit.

"Arthur Jr.'s got his head screwed on right, and he's got the
right kinda family values," said my client. "Straight As all
through school, married a standup dame with money of her
own, three great kids, makes a man proud. Hard worker. Got
his head in a book morning to night, human encyclopedia type
guy, up there at Harvard, those professors, they love him. Kid
knows how you're supposed to act, right?"

I nodded and filled my mouth with another fragrant draught.

"So he comes to my uncle Vincente's funeral all by himself,
which troubles me. On top of it doesn't show the proper respect
to old Waffles, who was one hell of a man, there's guys still
pissing blood on account of they looked at him wrong forty years
ago, on top a that, I don't have the good feeling I get from taking
his family around to my friends and associates and saying, so look
here, this here is Arthur Jr, my Harvard guy, plus his wife Hunter
whose ancestors I think got here even before that rabble on the
Mayflower, plus his three kids – Cyrus, little bastard's even
smarter than his dad, Thor, the one's got his head in the clouds,

which is okay because we need people like that, too, and Hermione, who you can tell just by looking at her she's mean as a snake and is gonna wind up running the world some day. So I say, Arthur Jr, what the hell happened, everybody else get killed in a train wreck or something? He says, No, Dad, they just didn't wanna come, these big family funerals, they make 'em feel funny, they don't like having their pictures taken so they show up on the six o'clock news. Didn't wanna come, I say back, what kinda shit is that, you shoulda made 'em come, and if anyone took their pictures when they didn't want, we can take care of that, no trouble at all. I go on like this, I even say, what good is Harvard and all those books if they don't make you any smarter than this, and finally Arthur Jr's mother tells me, put a cork in it, you're not exactly helping the situation here.

"So what happens then? Insteada being smart like I should, I go nuts on account of I'm the guy who pays the bills, that Harvard up there pulls in the money better than any casino I ever saw, and you want to find a real good criminal, get some Boston WASP in a bow tie, and all of a sudden nobody listens to me! I'm seeing red in a big way here, Deacon, this is my uncle Vincente's funeral, and insteada backing me up his mother is telling me I'm not *helping*. I yell, You want to help? Then go up there and bring back his wife and kids, or I'll send Carlo and Tommy to do it. All of a sudden I'm so mad I'm thinking these people are insulting me, how can they think they can get away with that, people who insult me don't do it twice – and then I hear what I'm thinking, and I do what she said and put a cork in it, but it's too late, I went way over the top and we all know it.

"Arthur Jr takes off, and his mother won't talk to me for the whole rest of the day. Only thing I'm happy about is I didn't blow up where anyone else could see it. Deacon, I know you're the type guy wouldn't dream of threatening his family, but if the time ever comes, do yourself a favor and light up a Havana instead."

"I'm sure that is excellent advice," I said.

"Don't let the thought cross your mind. Anyhow, you know what they say, it only hurts for a little while, which is true as far as it goes, and I calmed down. Uncle Vincente's funeral was beautiful. You woulda thought the Pope died. When the people are going out to the limousines, Arthur Jr is sitting in a chair at the back of the church reading a book. Put that in your pocket, I say,

wanta do homework, do it in the car. He tells me it isn't homework, but he puts it in his pocket and we go out to the cemetery.
His mother looks out the window the whole time we're driving to
the cemetery, and the kid starts reading again. So I ask what the
hell is it, this book he can't put down? He tells me but it's like he's
speaking some foreign language, only word I understand is 'the,'
which happens a lot when your kid reads a lot of fancy books,
half the titles make no sense to an ordinary person. Okay, we're
out there in Queens, goddam graveyard the size of Newark, FBI
and reporters all over the place, and I'm thinking maybe Arthur Jr
wasn't wrong after all, Hunter probably hates having the FBI take
her picture, and besides that little Hermione probably would a
mugged one of 'em and stole his wallet. So I tell Arthur Jr I'm
sorry about what happened. I didn't really think you were going
to put me in the same grave as Uncle Waffles, he says, the
Harvard smart-ass. When it's all over, we get back in the car,
and out comes the book again. We get home, and he disappears.
We have a lot of people over, food, wine, politicians, old-timers
from Brownsville, Chicago people, Detroit people, LA people,
movie directors, cops, actors I never heard of, priests, bishops, the
guy from the Cardinal. Everybody's asking me, Where's Arthur,
Jr? I go upstairs to find out. He's in his old room, and he's still
reading that book. I say, Arthur Jr, people are asking about you, I
think it would be nice if you mingled with our guests. I'll be right
down, he says, I just finished what I was reading. Here, take a
look, you might enjoy it. He gives me the book and goes out of the
room. So I'm wondering – what the hell *is* this, anyhow? I take it
into the bedroom, toss it on the table. About ten-thirty, eleven
that night, everybody's gone, kid's on the shuttle back to Boston,
house is cleaned up, enough food in the refrigerator to feed the
whole bunch all over again, I go up to bed. Arthur Jr's mother still
isn't talking to me, so I get in and pick up the book. Herman
Melville is the name of the guy, and I see that the story the kid was
reading is called 'Bartleby the Scrivener.' So I decide I'll try it.
What the hell, right? You're an educated guy, you ever read that
story?"

    "A long time ago," I said. "A bit . . . *odd*, isn't it?"

    "Odd? That's the most terrible story I ever read in my whole
life! This dud gets a job in a law office and decides he doesn't
want to work. Does he get fired? He does not. This is a story? You

hire a guy who won't do the job, what do you do, pamper the asshole? At the end, the dud ups and disappears and you find out he used to work in the dead letter office. Is there a point here? The next day I call up Arthur Jr, say, could he explain to me please what the hell that story is supposed to mean? Dad, he says, it means what it says. Deacon, I just about pulled the plug on Harvard right then and there. I never went to any college, but I do know that nothing means what it says, not on this planet."

This reflection was accurate when applied to the documents on my desk, for each had been encoded in a systematic fashion which rendered their literal contents deliberately misleading. Another code had informed both of my recent conversations with Marguerite. "Fiction is best left to real life," I said.

"Someone shoulda told that to Herman Melville," said Mr Arthur "This Building Is Condemned" C—.

Mrs Rampage buzzed me to advise that I was running behind schedule and enquire about removing the coffee things. I invited her to gather up the debris. A door behind me opened, and I assumed that my secretary had responded to my request with an alacrity remarkable even in her. The first sign of my error was the behavior of the three other men in the room, until this moment no more animated than marble statues. The thug at my client's side stepped forward to stand behind me, and his fellows moved to the front of my desk. "What the hell is this shit?" said the client, because of the man in front of him unable to see Mr Clubb and Mr Cuff. Holding a pad bearing one of his many lists, Mr Clubb gazed in mild surprise at the giants flanking my desk and said, "I apologize for the intrusion, sir, but our understanding was that your appointment would be over in an hour, and by my simple way of reckoning you should be free to answer a query as to steam irons."

"What the hell *is* this shit?" said my client, repeating his original question with a slight tonal variation expressive of gathering dismay.

I attempted to salvage matters by saying, "Please allow me to explain the interruption. I have employed these men as consultants, and as they prefer to work in my office, a condition I of course could not permit during our business meeting, I temporarily relocated them in my washroom, outfitted with a library adequate to their needs."

"Fit for a king, in my opinion," said Mr Clubb.

At that moment the other door into my office, to the left of my desk, opened to admit Mrs Rampage, and my client's guardians inserted their hands into their suit jackets and separated with the speed and precision of a dance team.

"Oh, my," said Mrs Rampage. "*Excuse* me. Should I come back later?"

"Not on your life, my darling," said Mr Clubb. "Temporary misunderstanding of the false alarm sort. Please allow us to enjoy the delightful spectacle of your feminine charms."

Before my wondering eyes, Mrs Rampage curtseyed and hastened to my desk to gather up the wreckage.

I looked toward my client and observed a detail of striking peculiarity, that although his half-consumed cigar remained between his lips, four inches of cylindrical ash had deposited a grey smear on his necktie before coming to rest on the shelf of his belly. He was staring straight ahead with eyes grown to the size of quarters. His face had become the color of raw pie crust.

Mr Clubb said, "Respectful greetings, sir."

The client gargled and turned upon me a look of unvarnished horror.

Mr Clubb said, "Apologies to all." Mrs Rampage had already bolted. From unseen regions came the sound of a closing door.

Mr "This Building Is Condemned" C— blinked twice, bringing his eyes to something like their normal dimensions. With an uncertain hand but gently, as if it were a tiny but much-loved baby, he placed his cigar in the crystal shell. He cleared his throat; he looked at the ceiling. "Deacon," he said, gazing upward. "Gotta run. My next appointment musta slipped my mind. What happens when you start to gab. I'll be in touch about this stuff." He stood, dislodging the ashen cylinder to the carpet, and motioned his gangsters to the outer office.

IV.

Of course at the earliest opportunity I interrogated both of my detectives about this turn of events, and while they moved their mountains of paper, bottles, buckets, glasses, hand-drawn maps, and other impedimenta back behind the screen, I continued the questioning. No, they averred, the gentlemen at my desk was not a gentleman whom previously they had been privileged to look upon, acquaint themselves with, or encounter in any way whatsoever. They had never been employed in any capacity by the gentleman. Mr Clubb observed that the unknown gentleman had been wearing a conspicuously handsome and well-tailored suit.

"That is his custom," I said.

"And I believe he smokes, sir, a noble high order of cigar," said Mr Clubb with a glance at my breast pocket. "Which would be the sort of item unfairly beyond the dreams of honest laborers such as ourselves."

"I trust that you will permit me," I said with a sigh, "to offer you the pleasure of two of the same." No sooner had the offer been accepted, the barnies back behind their screen, than I buzzed Mrs Rampage with the request to summon by instant delivery from the most distinguished cigar merchant in the city a box of his finest. "Good for you, boss!" whooped the new Mrs Rampage.

I spent the remainder of the afternoon brooding upon the reaction of Mr Arthur "This Building Is Condemned" C— to my "consultants." I could not but imagine that his hasty departure boded ill for our relationship. I had seen terror on his face, and he knew that *I* knew what I had seen. An understanding of this sort is fatal to that nuance-play critical alike to high-level churchmen and their outlaw counterparts, and I had to confront the possibility that my client's departure had been of a permanent nature. Where Mr "This Building Is Condemned" C— went, his colleagues of lesser rank, Mr Tommy "I Believe in Rainbows" B—, Mr Anthony "Moonlight Becomes You" M—, Mr Bobby "Total Eclipse" G—, and their fellow Archbishops, Cardinals, and Papal Nuncios would assuredly follow. Before the close of the day, I would send a comforting fax informing Mr "This Building Is Condemned" C— that the consultants had been summarily released from employment. I would be telling only a "white" or provisional untruth, for Mr Clubb and Mr Cuff's task would surely be completed long before my client's return. All was in order, all was in train, and as if to put the seal upon the matter, Mrs Rampage buzzed to enquire if she might come through with the box of cigars. Speaking in a breathy timbre I had never before heard from anyone save Marguerite in the earliest, most blissful days of our marriage, Mrs Rampage added that she had some surprises for me, too. "By this point," I said, "I expect no less." Mrs Rampage *giggled*.

The surprises, in the event, were of a satisfying practicality. The good woman had wisely sought the advice of Mr Montfort d'M—, who, after recommending a suitably aristocratic cigar emporium and a favorite cigar, had purchased for me a rosewood humidor, a double-bladed cigar cutter, and a lighter of antique design. As soon Mrs Rampage had been instructed to compose a note of gratitude embellished in whatever fashion she saw fit, I arrayed all but one of the cigars in the humidor, decapitated that one, and set it alight. Beneath a faint touch of fruitiness like the aroma of a blossoming pear tree, I met in successive layers the tastes of black olives, aged Gouda cheese, pine needles, new leather, miso soup, either sorghum or brown sugar, burning peat, library paste and myrtle leaves. The long finish intriguingly combined Bible paper and sunflower seeds. Mr Montfort d'M— had chosen well, though I regretted the absence of black butter sauce.

Feeling comradely, I strolled across my office towards the merriment emanating from the far side of the screen. A superior cigar, even if devoid of black butter sauce, should be complemented by a worthy liquor, and in the light what was to transpire during the evening I considered a snifter of Mr Clubb's Bombay gin not inappropriate. "Fellows," I said, tactfully announcing my presence, "are preparations nearly completed?"

"That, sir, they are," said one or another of the pair.

"Welcome news," I said, and stepped around the screen. "But I must be assured –"

I had expected disorder, but nothing approaching the chaos before me. It was as if the detritus of New York City's half-dozen filthiest living quarters had been scooped up, shaken and dumped into my office. Heaps of ash, bottles, shoals of papers, books with stained covers and broken spines, battered furniture, broken glass, refuse I could not identify, refuse I could not even *see*, undulated from the base of the screen, around and over the table, heaping itself into landfill-like piles here and there, and washed against the plate-glass windows. A jagged, five-foot opening gaped in a smashed pane. Their derbies perched on their heads, islanded in their chairs, Mr Clubb and Mr Cuff leaned back, feet up on what must have been the table.

"You'll join us in a drink, sir," said Mr Clubb, "by way of

wishing us success and adding to the pleasure of that handsome smoke." He extended a stout leg and kicked rubble from a chair. I sat down. Mr Clubb plucked an unclean glass from the morass and filled it with Dutch gin or genever from one of the minaret-shaped stone flagons I had observed upon my infrequent layovers in Amsterdam, the Netherlands. Mrs Rampage had been variously employed during the barnies' sequestration. Then I wondered if Mrs Rampage might not have shown signs of intoxication during our last encounter.

"I thought you drank Bombay," I said.

"Variety is, as they say, life's condiment," said Mr Clubb, and handed me the glass.

I said, "You have made yourselves quite at home."

"I thank you for your restraint," said Mr Clubb. "In which sentiment my partner agrees, am I correct, Mr Cuff?"

"Entirely," said Mr Cuff. "But I wager you a C-note to a see-gar that a word or two of reassurance is in order."

"How right that man is," said Mr Clubb. "He has a genius for the truth I have never known to fail him. Sir, you enter our workspace to come upon the slovenly, the careless, the unseemly, and your response, which we comprehend in every particular, is to recoil. My wish is that you take a moment to remember these two essentials: one, we have, as aforesaid, our methods which are ours alone, and two, having appeared fresh on the scene, you see it worse than it is. By morning tomorrow, the cleaning staff shall have done its work."

"I suppose you have been Visualizing," I said, and quaffed genever.

"Mr Cuff and I," he said, "prefer to minimize the risk of accidents, surprises, and such by the method of rehearsing our as you might say performances. These poor sticks, sir, are easily replaced, but our work once under way demands completion and cannot be duplicated, redone, or undone."

I recalled the all-important guarantee. "I remember your words," I said, "and I must be assured that you remember mine. I did not request termination. During the course of the day my feelings on the matter have intensified. Termination, if by that term you meant . . ."

"Termination is termination," said Mr Clubb.

"*Ex*termination," I said. "Cessation of life due to external forces. It is not my wish, it is unacceptable, and I have even been thinking that I overstated the degree of physical punishment appropriate in this matter."

"Appropriate?" said Mr Clubb. "When it comes to desire, 'appropriate' is a concept without meaning. In the sacred realm of desire, 'appropriate,' being meaningless, does not exist. We speak of your inmost wishes, sir, and desire is an extremely *thingy* sort of thing."

I looked at the hole in the window, the broken bits of furniture and ruined books. "I think," I said, "that permanent injury is all I wish. Something on the order of blindness or the loss of a hand."

Mr Clubb favored me with a glance of humorous irony. "It goes, sir, as it goes, which brings to mind that we have but an hour more, a period of time to be splendidly improved by a superior Double Corona such as the fine example in your hand."

"Forgive me," I said. "And might I then request . . . ?" I extended the nearly empty glass, and Mr Clubb refilled it. Each received a cigar, and I lingered at my desk for the required term, sipping genever and pretending to work until I heard sounds of movement. Mr Clubb and Mr Cuff approached. "So you are off," I said.

"It is, sir, to be a long and busy night," said Mr Clubb. "If you take my meaning."

With a sigh I opened the humidor. They reached in, snatched a handful of cigars apiece, and deployed them into various pockets. "Details at eleven," said Mr Clubb.

A few seconds after their departure, Mrs Rampage informed that she would be bringing through a fax communication just received.

The fax had been sent me by Chartwell, Munster and Stout, a legal firm with but a single client, Mr Arthur "This Building Is Condemned" C—. Chartwell, Munster and Stout regretted the necessity to inform me that their client wished to seek advice other than my own in his financial affairs. A sheaf of documents binding me to silence as to all matters concerning the client would arrive for my signature the following day. All records, papers, computer discs, and other data were to be referred post haste to their offices. I had forgotten to send my intended note of client-saving reassurance.

V.

What an abyss of shame I must now describe, at every turn what humiliation. It was at most five minutes past six p.m. when I learned of the desertion of my most valuable client, a turn of events certain to lead to the loss of his cryptic fellows and some forty per cent of our annual business. Gloomily I consumed my glass of Dutch gin without noticing that I had already far exceeded my tolerance. I ventured behind the screen and succeeded in unearthing another stone flagon, poured another measure and gulped it down while attempting to demonstrate numerically that (a) the anticipated drop in annual profit could not be as severe as feared, and (b) if it were, the business could continue as before, without reductions in salary, staff and benefits. Despite ingenious feats of juggling, the numbers denied (a) and mocked (b), suggesting that I should be fortunate to retain, not lose, forty per cent of present business. I lowered my head to the desk and tried to regulate my breathing. When I heard myself rendering an off-key version of "Abide With Me," I acknowledged that it was time to go home, got to my feet and made the unfortunate decision to exit through the general offices on the theory that a survey of my presumably empty realm might suggest the sites of pending amputations.

I tucked the flagon under my elbow, pocketed the five or six cigars remaining in the humidor, and passed through Mrs Rampage's chamber. Hearing the abrasive music of the cleaners' radios, I moved with exaggerated care down the corridor, darkened but for the light spilling from an open door thirty feet before me. Now and again, finding myself unable to avoid striking my shoulder against the wall, I took a medicinal swallow of genever. I drew up to the open door and realized that I had come to Gilligan's quarters. The abrasive music emanated from his sound system. *We'll get rid of that, for starters*, I said to myself, and straightened up for a dignified navigation past his doorway. At the crucial moment I glanced within to observe my jacketless junior partner sprawled, tie undone, on his sofa beside a scrawny ruffian with a quiff of lime-green hair and attired for some reason in a skin-tight costume involving zebra stripes and many chains and zippers. Disreputable creatures male and female occupied themselves in the background. Gilligan shifted his head, began to smile, and at the sight of me turned to stone.

"Calm down, Gilligan," I said, striving for an impression of sober paternal authority. I had recalled that my junior had scheduled a late appointment with his most successful musician, a singer whose band sold millions of records year in and year out despite the absurdity of their name, the Dog Turds or the Rectal Valves, something of that sort. My calculations had indicated that Gilligan's client, whose name I recalled as Cyril Futch, would soon become crucial to the maintenance of my firm, and as the beaky little rooster coldly took me in I thought to impress upon him the regard in which he was held by his chosen financial planning institution. "There is, I assure you, no need for alarm, no, certainly not, and in fact, Gilligan, you know, I should be honored to seize this opportunity of making the acquaintance of your guest, whom it is our pleasure to assist and advise and whatever."

Gilligan reverted to flesh and blood during the course of this utterance, which I delivered gravely, taking care to enunciate each syllable clearly in spite of the difficulty I was having with my tongue. He noted the bottle nestled into my elbow and the lighted cigar in the fingers of my right hand, a matter of which until that moment I had been imperfectly aware. "Hey, I guess the smoking lamp is lit," I said. "Stupid rule anyhow. How about a little drink on the boss?"

Gilligan lurched to his feet and came reeling toward me.

All that followed is a montage of discontinuous imagery. I recall Cyril Futch propping me up as I communicated our devotion to the safeguarding of his wealth, also his dogged insistence that his name was actually Simon Gulch or Sidney Much or something similar before he sent me toppling onto the sofa; I see an odd little fellow with a tattooed head and a name like Pus (there was a person named Pus in attendance, though he may not have been the one) accepting one of my cigars and eating it; I remember inhaling from smirking Gilligan's cigarette and drinking from a bottle with a small white worm lying dead at its bottom and snuffling up a white powder recommended by a female Turd or Valve; I remember singing "The Old Rugged Cross" in a state of partial undress. I told a face brilliantly lacquered with make-up that I was "getting a feel" for "this music." A female Turd or Valve, not the one who had recommended the powder but one in a permanent state of hilarity I found endearing, assisted me into my limousine and on the homeward journey experimented with its many buttons and controls. Atop the townhouse steps, she removed the key from my fumbling hand gleefully to insert it into the lock. The rest is welcome darkness.

VI.

A form of consciousness returned with a slap to my face, the muffled screams of the woman beside me, a bowler-hatted head thrusting into view and growling, "The shower for you, you damned idiot." As a second assailant whisked her away, the woman, whom I thought to be Marguerite, wailed. I struggled against the man gripping my shoulders, and he squeezed the nape of my neck.

When next I opened my eyes, I was naked and quivering beneath an onslaught of cold water within the marble confines of my shower cabinet. Charlie-Charlie Rackett leaned against the open door of the cabinet and regarded me with ill-disguised impatience. "I'm freezing, Charlie-Charlie," I said. "Turn off the water."

Charlie-Charlie thrust an arm into the cabinet and became Mr Clubb. "I'll warm it up, but I want you sober," he said. I drew myself up into a ball.

Then I was on my feet and moaning while I massaged my forehead. "Bath time all done now," called Mr Clubb. "Turn off the wa-wa." I did as instructed. The door opened, and a bath towel unfurled over my left shoulder.

Side by side on the bedroom sofa and dimly illuminated by the lamp, Mr Clubb and Mr Cuff observed my progress toward the bed. A black leather satchel stood on the floor between them. "Gentlemen," I said, "although I cannot presently find words to account for the condition in which you found me, I trust that your good nature will enable you to overlook . . . or ignore . . . whatever it was that I must have done . . . I cannot quite recall the circumstances."

"The young woman has been sent away," said Mr Clubb, "and you need never fear any trouble from that direction, sir."

"The young woman?" I asked, and remembered a hyperactive figure playing with the controls in the back of the limousine. This opened up a fragmentary memory of the scene in Gilligan's office, and I moaned aloud.

"None too clean, but pretty enough in a ragamuffin way," said Mr Clubb. "The type denied a proper education in social graces. Rough about the edges. Intemperate in language. A stranger to discipline."

I groaned – to have introduced such a creature to my house!

"A stranger to honesty, too, sir, if you'll permit me," said Mr Cuff. "It's addiction turns them into thieves. Give them half a chance, they'll steal the brass handles off their mothers' coffins."

"Addiction?" I said. "Addiction to what?"

"Everything, from the look of the bint," said Mr Cuff. "Before Mr Clubb and I sent her on her way, we retrieved these items doubtless belonging to you, sir." While walking toward me he removed from his pockets the following articles: my wristwatch, gold cufflinks, wallet, the lighter of antique design given my by Mr Montfort d'M—, likewise the cigar cutter, and the last of the cigars I had purchased that day. "I thank you most gratefully," I said, slipping the watch on my wrist and all else save the cigar into the pockets of my robe. It was, I noted, just past four o'clock in the morning. The cigar I handed back to him with the words, "Please accept this as a token of my gratitude."

"Gratefully accepted," he said. Mr Cuff bit off the end, spat it onto the carpet, and set the cigar alight, producing a nauseating quantity of fumes.

"Perhaps," I said, "we might postpone our discussion until I have had time to recover from my ill-advised behavior. Let us reconvene at . . ." A short period was spent pressing my hands to my eyes while rocking back and forth. "Four this afternoon?"

"Everything in its own time is a principle we hold dear," said Mr Clubb. "And this is the time for you to down aspirin and alka-seltzer, and for your loyal assistants to relish the hearty breakfasts the thought of which sets our stomachs to growling. A man of stature and accomplishment like yourself ought to be able to overcome the effects of too much booze and attend to business, on top of the simple matter of getting his flunkies out of bed so they can whip up the bacon and eggs."

"Because a man such as that, sir, keeps ever in mind that business faces the task at hand, no matter how lousy it may be," said Mr Cuff.

"The old world is in flames," said Mr Clubb, "and the new one is just being born. Pick up the phone."

"All right," I said, "but Mr Moncrieff is going to *hate* this. He worked for the Duke of Denbigh, and he's a terrible snob."

"All butlers are snobs," said Mr Clubb. "Three fried eggs apiece, likewise six rashers of bacon, home-fries, toast, hot coffee, and for the sake of digestion a bottle of your best cognac."

Mr Moncrieff picked up his telephone, listened to my orders and informed me in a small, cold voice that he would speak to the cook. "Would this repast be for the young lady and yourself, sir?" he asked.

With a wave of guilty shame which intensified my nausea, I realized that Mr Moncrieff had observed my unsuitable young companion accompanying me upstairs to the bedroom. "No, it would not," I said. "The young lady, a client of mine, was kind enough to assist me when I was taken ill. The meal is for two male guests." Unwelcome memory returned the spectacle of a scrawny girl pulling my ears and screeching that a useless old fart like me didn't deserve her band's business.

"The phone," said Mr Clubb. Dazedly I extended the receiver.

"Moncrieff, old man," he said, "amazing good luck, running into you again. Do you remember that trouble the Duke had with Colonel Fletcher and the diary? . . . Yes, this is Mr Clubb, and it's delightful to hear your voice again . . . He's here, too, couldn't do anything without him . . . I'll tell him . . . Much the way things went with the Duke, yes, and we'll need the usual supplies . . . Glad to hear it . . . The dining room in half an hour." He handed the telephone back to me and said to Mr Cuff, "He's looking forward to the pinochle, and there's a first-rate Petrus in the cellar he knows you're going to enjoy."

I had purchased six cases of 1928 Chateau Petrus at an auction some years before and was holding it while its already immense value doubled, then tripled, until perhaps a decade hence, when I would sell it for ten times its original cost.

"A good drop of wine sets a man right up," said Mr Cuff. "Stuff was meant to be drunk, wasn't it?"

"You know Mr Moncrieff?" I asked. "You worked for the Duke?"

"We ply our humble trade irrespective of nationality and borders," said Mr Clubb. "Go where we are needed, is our motto. We have fond memories of the good old Duke, who showed himself to be quite a fun-loving, spirited fellow, sir, once you got past the crust, as it were. Generous, too."

"He gave until it hurt," said Mr Cuff. "The old gentleman cried like a baby when we left."

"Cried a good deal before that, too," said Mr Clubb. "In our experience, high-spirited fellows spend a deal more tears than your gloomy customers."

"I do not suppose you shall see any tears from me," I said. The brief look which passed between them reminded me of the complicitous glance I had once seen fly like a live spark between two of their New Covenant forbears, one gripping the hind legs of a pig, the other its front legs and a knife, in the moment before the knife opened the pig's throat and an arc of blood threw itself high into the air. "I shall heed your advice," I said, "and locate my analgesics." I got on my feet and moved slowly to the bathroom. "As a matter of curiosity," I said, "might I ask if you have classified me into the high-spirited category, or into the other?"

"You are a man of middling spirit," said Mr Clubb. I opened my mouth to protest, and he went on, "But something may be made of you yet."

I disappeared into the bathroom. *I have endured these moon-faced yokels long enough*, I told myself, *hear their story, feed the bastards, then kick them out.*

In a condition more nearly approaching my usual self, I brushed my teeth and splashed water on my face before returning to the bedroom. I placed myself with a reasonable degree of executive command in a wing chair, folded my pinstriped robe about me, inserted my feet into velvet slippers, and said, "Things got a bit out of hand, and I thank you for dealing with my young client, a person with whom in spite of appearances I have a professional relationship only. Now we may turn to our real business. I trust you found my wife and Leeson at Green Chimneys. Please give me an account of what followed. I await my report."

"Things got a bit out of hand," said Mr Clubb. "Which is a way of describing something that can happen to us all, and for which no one can be blamed. Especially Mr Cuff and myself, who are always careful to say right smack at the beginning, as we did with you, sir, what ought to be so obvious as not need saying at all, that our work brings about permanent changes which can never be undone. Especially in the cases when we specify a time to make our initial report and the client disappoints us at the said time. When we are let down by our client, we must go forward and complete the job to our highest standards with no rancor or ill-will, knowing that there are many reasonable explanations of a man's inability to get to a telephone."

"I don't know what you mean by this self-serving doubletalk," I said. "We had no arrangement of that sort, and your effrontery forces me to conclude that you failed in your task."

Mr Clubb gave me the grimmest possible suggestion of a smile. "One of the reasons for a man's failure to get to a telephone is a lapse of memory. You have forgotten my informing you that I would give you my initial report at eleven. At precisely eleven o'clock I called, to no avail. I waited through twenty rings, sir, before I abandoned the effort. If I had waited through a hundred, sir, the result would have been the same, on account of your decision to put yourself into a state where you would have had trouble remembering your own name."

"That is a blatant lie," I said, then remembered. The fellow had in fact mentioned in passing something about reporting to me at that hour, which must have been approximately the time when I was regaling the Turds or Valves with "The Old Rugged Cross." My face grew pink. "Forgive me," I said. "I am in error, it is just as you say."

"A manly admission, sir, but as for forgiveness, we extended that quantity from the git-go," said Mr Clubb. "We are your servants, and your wishes are our sacred charge."

"That's the whole ball of wax in a nutshell," said Mr Cuff, giving a fond glance to the final inch of his cigar. He dropped the stub onto my carpet and ground it beneath his shoe. "Food and drink to the fibers, sir," he said.

"Speaking of which," said Mr Clubb. "We will continue our report in the dining room, so as to dig into the feast ordered up by that wondrous villain, Reggie Moncrieff."

Until that moment I believe that it had never quite occurred to me that my butler possessed, like other men, a Christian name.

VII.

"A great design directs us," said Mr Clubb, expelling morsels of his cud. "We poor wanderers, you and me and Mr Cuff and the milkman too, only see the little portion right in front of us. Half the time we don't even see that in the right way. For sure we don't have a Chinaman's chance of understanding it. But the design is ever-present, sir, a truth I bring to your attention for the sake of the comfort in it. Toast, Mr Cuff."

"Comfort is a matter cherished by all parts of a man," said Mr Cuff, handing his partner the rack of toasted bread. "Most particularly that part known as his soul, which feeds upon the nutrient adversity."

I was seated at the head of the table and flanked by Mr Clubb and Mr Cuff. The salvers and tureens before us overflowed, for Mr Moncrieff, who after embracing each barnie in turn and then entering into a kind of conference or huddle, had summoned from the kitchen a meal far surpassing their requests. Besides several dozen eggs and perhaps two packages of bacon, he had arranged a mixed grill of kidneys, lamb's livers and lamb chops, and strip steaks, as well as vats of oatmeal and a pasty concoction he described as "kedgeree – as the old Duke fancied it."

Sickened by the odors of the food, also by the mush visible in my companions' mouths, I tried once more to extract their report. "I don't believe in the grand design," I said, "and I already face more adversity than my soul could find useful. Tell me what happened at the house."

"No mere house, sir," said Mr Clubb. "Even as we approached along — Lane, Mr Cuff and I could not fail to respond to its magnificence."

"Were my drawings of use?" I asked.

"They were invaluable." Mr Cuff speared a lamb chop and raised it to his mouth. "We proceeded through the rear door into your spacious kitchen or scullery. Wherein we observed evidence of two persons having enjoyed a dinner enhanced by a fine wine and finished with a noble champagne."

"Aha," I said.

"By means of your guidance, Mr Cuff and I located the lovely staircase and made our way to the lady's chamber. We effected an entry of the most praiseworthy silence, if I may say so."

"That entry was worth a medal," said Mr Cuff.

"Two figures lay slumbering upon the bed. In a blamelessly professional manner we approached, Mr Cuff on one side, I on the other. In the fashion your client of this morning called the whopbopaloobop, we rendered the parties in question even more unconscious than previous, thereby giving ourselves a good fifteen minutes for the disposition of instruments. We take pride in being careful workers, sir, and like all honest craftsmen we respect our tools. We bound and gagged both parties in timely fashion. Is the male party distinguished by an athletic past?" Suddenly alight with barnieish glee, Mr Clubb raised his eyebrows and washed down the last of his chop with a mouthful of cognac.

"Not to my knowledge," I said. "I believe he plays a little racquetball and squash, that kind of thing."

He and Mr Cuff experienced a moment of mirth. "More like weightlifting or football, is my guess," he said. "Strength and stamina. To a remarkable degree."

"Not to mention considerable speed," said Mr Cuff with the air of one indulging a tender reminiscence.

"Are you telling me that he got away?" I asked.

"No one gets away," said Mr Clubb. "That, sir, is Gospel. But you may imagine our surprise when for the first time in the history of our *consultancy*," and here he chuckled, "a gentleman of the civilian persuasion managed to break his bonds and free himself of his ropes whilst Mr Cuff and I were engaged in the preliminaries."

"Naked as jaybirds," said Mr Cuff, wiping with a greasy hand a tear of amusement from one eye. "Bare as newborn lambie-pies. There I was, heating up the steam-iron I'd just fetched from the kitchen, sir, along with a selection of knives I came across in exactly the spot you described, most grateful I was, too, squatting on my haunches without a care in the world and feeling the first merry tingle of excitement in my little soldier –"

"What?" I said. "You were naked? And what's this about your little soldier?"

"Hush," said Mr Clubb, his eyes glittering. "You refuse, I

refuse, it's all the same. Nakedness is a precaution against fouling our clothing with blood and other bodily products, and men like Mr Cuff and myself take pleasure in the exercise of our skills. In us, the inner and the outer man are one and the same."

"Are they, now?" I said, marvelling at the irrelevance of this last remark. It then occurred to me that the remark might have been relevant after all – most unhappily so.

"At all times," said Mr Cuff, amused by my having missed the point. "If you wish to hear our report, sir, reticence will be helpful."

I gestured for him to go on with the story.

"As said before, I was squatting in my birthday suit by the knives and the steam iron, not a care in the world, when I heard from behind me the patter of little feet. *Hello*, I say to myself, *what's this?*, and when I look over my shoulder here is your man, bearing down on me like a steam engine. Being as he is one of your big, strapping fellows, sir, it was a sight to behold, not to mention the unexpected circumstances. I took a moment to glance in the direction of Mr Clubb, who was busily occupied in another quarter, which was, to put it plain and simple, the bed."

Mr Clubb chortled and said, "By way of being in the line of duty."

"So in a way of speaking I was in the position of having to settle this fellow before he became a trial to us in the performance of our duties. He was getting ready to tackle me, sir, which was what put us in mind of football being in his previous life, tackle the life out of me before he rescued the lady, and I got hold of one of the knives. Then, you see, when he came flying at me that way all I had to do was give him a good jab in at the bottom of the throat, a matter which puts the fear of God into the bravest fellow. It concentrates all their attention, and after that they might as well be little puppies for all the harm they're likely to do. Well, this boy was one for the books, because for the first time in I don't know how many similar efforts, a hundred –"

"I'd say double at least, to be accurate," said Mr Clubb.

"– in at least a hundred, anyhow, avoiding immodesty, I underestimated the speed and agility of the lad, and instead of planting my weapon at the base of his neck stuck him in the side, a manner of wound which in the case of your really *aggressive* attacker, who you come across in about one out of twenty, is about as effective as a slap with a powder puff. Still, I put him off his stride, a welcome sign to me that he had gone a bit loosey-goosey over the years. Then, sir, the advantage was mine, and I seized it with a grateful heart. I spun him over, dumped him on the floor, and straddled his chest. At which point I thought to settle him down for the evening by taking hold of a cleaver and cutting off his right hand with one good blow.

"Ninety-nine times out of a hundred, sir, chopping off a hand will take the starch right out of a man. He settled down pretty well. It's the shock, you see, shock takes the mind that way, and because the stump was bleeding like a bastard, excuse the language, I did him the favor of cauterizing the wound with the steam iron because it was good and hot, and if you sear a wound there's no way that bugger can bleed any more. I mean, the *problem* is *solved*, and that's a fact."

"It has been proved a thousand times over," said Mr Clubb.

"Shock being a healer," said Mr Cuff. "Shock being a balm like salt water to the human body, yet if you have too much of either, the body gives up the ghost. After I seared the wound, it looked to me like he and his body got together and voted to take the next bus to what is generally considered a better world." He held up an index finger and stared into my eyes while forking kidneys into his mouth. "This, sir, is a *process*. A *process* can't happen all at once, and every reasonable precaution was taken. Mr Clubb and I do not have, nor ever have had, the reputation for carelessness in our undertakings."

"And never shall," said Mr Clubb. He washed down whatever was in his mouth with half a glass of cognac.

"Despite the *process* underway," said Mr Cuff, "the gentleman's left wrist was bound tightly to the stump. Rope was again attached to the areas of the chest and legs, a gag went back into his mouth, and besides all that I had the pleasure of whapping my hammer once and once only on the region of his temple, for the purpose of keeping him out of action until we were ready for him in case he was not boarding the bus. I took a moment to turn him over and gratify my little soldier, which I trust was in no way

exceeding our agreement, sir." He granted me a look of the purest
innocence.

"Continue," I said, "although you must grant that your tale is
utterly without verification."

"Sir," said Mr Clubb, "we know one another better than that."
He bent over so far that his head disappeared beneath the table,
and I heard the undoing of a clasp. Resurfacing, he placed
between us on the table an object wrapped in one of the towels
Marguerite had purchased for Green Chimneys. "If verification is
your desire, and I intend no reflection, sir, for a man in your line
of business has grown out of the habit of taking a fellow at his
word, here you have wrapped up like a birthday present the finest
verification of this portion of our tale to be found in all the
world."

"And yours to keep, if you're taken that way," said Mr Cuff.

I had no doubts whatsoever concerning the nature of the
trophy set before me, and therefore I deliberately composed
myself before pulling away the folds of toweling. Yet for all
my preparations the spectacle of the actual trophy itself affected
me more greatly than I would have thought possible, and at the
very center of the nausea rising within me I experienced the first
faint stirrings of my enlightenment. *Poor man*, I thought, *poor
mankind*.

I refolded the material over the crab-like thing and said,
"Thank you. I meant to imply no reservations concerning your
veracity."

"Beautifully said, sir, and much appreciated. Men like ourselves, honest at every point, have found that persons in the habit
of duplicity often cannot understand the truth. Liars are the bane
of our existence. And yet, such is the nature of this funny old
world, we'd be out of business without them."

Mr Cuff smiled up at the chandelier in rueful appreciation of
the world's contradictions. "When I replaced him on the bed, Mr
Clubb went hither and yon, collecting the remainder of the tools
for the job at hand."

"When you say you replaced him on the bed," I broke in, "is it
your meaning –"

"Your meaning might differ from mine, sir, and mine, being
that of a fellow raised without the benefits of a literary education,
may be simpler than yours. But bear in mind that every guild has

its legacy of customs and traditions which no serious practitioner can ignore without thumbing his nose at all he holds dear. For those brought up into our trade, physical punishment of a female subject invariably begins with the act most associated in the feminine mind with humiliation of the most rigorous sort. With males the same is generally true. Neglect this step, and you lose an advantage which can never be regained. It is the foundation without which the structure cannot stand, and the foundation must be set in place even when conditions make the job distasteful, which is no picnic, take my word for it." He shook his head and fell silent.

"We could tell you stories to curl your hair," said Mr Clubb. "Matter for another day. It was on the order of nine-thirty when our materials had been assembled, the preliminaries taken care of, and business could begin in earnest. This is a moment, sir, ever cherished by professionals such as ourselves. It is of an eternal freshness. You are on the brink of testing yourself against your past achievements and those of masters gone before. Your skill, your imagination, your timing and resolve will be called upon to work together with your hard-earned knowledge of the human body, because it is a question of being able to sense when to press on and when to hold back, of I can say having that instinct for the right technique at the right time you can build up only through experience. During this moment you hope that the subject, your partner in the most intimate relationship which can exist between two people, owns the spiritual resolve and physical capacity to inspire your best work. The subject is our instrument, and the nature of the instrument is vital. Faced with an out-of-tune, broken-down piano, even the greatest virtuoso is up shit creek without a paddle. Sometimes, sir, our work has left us tasting ashes for weeks on end, and when you're tasting ashes in your mouth you have trouble remembering the grand design and your wee part in that majestical pattern."

As if to supplant the taste in question and without benefit of knife and fork, Mr Clubb bit off a generous portion of steak and moistened it with a gulp of cognac. Chewing with loud smacks of the lips and tongue, he thrust a spoon into the kedgeree and began moodily slapping it onto his plate while seeming for the first time to notice the Canalettos on the walls.

"We started off, sir, as well as we ever have," said Mr Cuff, "and better than most times. The fingernails was a thing of rare beauty, sir, the fingernails was prime. And the hair was on the same transcendant level."

"The fingernails?" I asked. "The hair?"

"Prime," said Mr Clubb with a melancholy spray of food. "If they could be done better, which they could not, I should like to be there as to applaud with my own hands."

I looked at Mr Cuff, and he said, "The fingernails and the hair might appear to be your traditional steps two and three, but they are in actual fact steps one and two, the first procedure being more like basic groundwork than part of the performance-work itself. Doing the fingernails and the hair tells you an immense quantity about the subject's pain level, style of resistance, and aggression/passivity balance, and that information, sir, is your virtual Bible once you go past step four or five."

"How many steps are there?" I asked.

"A novice would tell you fifteen," said Mr Cuff. "A competent journeyman would say twenty. Men such as us know there to be at least a hundred, but in their various combinations and refinements they come out into the thousands. At the basic or kinder-garten level, they are, after the first two: foot-soles; teeth; fingers and toes; tongue; nipples; rectum; genital area; electrification; general piercing; specific piercing; small amputation; damage to inner organs; eyes, minor; eyes, major; large amputation; local flaying; and so forth."

At mention of "tongue", Mr Clubb had shoved a spoonful of kedgeree into his mouth and scowled at the two paintings directly across from him. At "electrification", he had thrust himself out of his chair and crossed behind me to scrutinize them more closely. While Mr Cuff continued my education, he twisted in his chair to observe his partner's actions, and I did the same.

After "and so forth", Mr Cuff fell silent. The two of us watched Mr Clubb moving back and forth in evident agitation between the two large paintings. He settled at last before a depiction of a regatta on the Grand Canal and took two deep breaths. Then he raised his spoon like a dagger and drove it into the painting to slice beneath a handsome ship, come up at its bow, and continue cutting until he had deleted the ship from the painting. "Now that, sir, is local flaying," he said. He moved to the next picture, which gave a view of the Piazetta. In seconds he had sliced all the canvas from the frame. "And that, sir, is what is meant by general flaying." He crumpled the canvas in his hands, threw it to the ground, and stamped on it.

"He is not quite himself," said Mr Cuff.

"Oh, but I am, I am myself to an alarming degree, I am," said Mr Clubb. He tromped back to the table and bent beneath it. Instead of the second folded towel I had anticipated, he produced his satchel and used it to sweep away the plates and serving dishes in front of him. He reached within and slapped down beside me the towel I had expected. "Open it," he said. I unfolded the towel. "Are these not, to the last particular, what you requested, sir?"

It was, to the last particular, what I had requested. Marguerite had not thought to remove her wedding band before her assignation, and her . . . I cannot describe the other but to say that it lay like the egg perhaps of some small sandbird in the familiar palm. Another portion of my eventual enlightenment moved into place within me, and I thought: *here we are, this is all of us, this crab and this egg.* I bent over and vomited beside my chair. When I had finished, I grabbed the cognac bottle and swallowed greedily, twice. The liquor burned down my throat, struck my stomach like a branding iron, and rebounded. I leaned sideways and, with a dizzied spasm of throat and guts, expelled another reeking contribution to the mess on the carpet.

"It is a Roman conclusion to a meal, sir," said Mr Cuff.

Mr Moncrieff opened the kitchen door and peeked in. He observed the mutilated paintings and the two objects nested in the striped towel and watched me wipe a string of vomit from my mouth. He withdrew for a moment and reappeared holding a tall can of ground coffee, wordlessly sprinkled its contents over the evidence of my distress, and vanished back into the kitchen. From even the depths of my wretchedness I marvelled at the perfection of this display of butler decorum.

I draped the toweling over the crab and the egg. "You are conscientious fellows," I said.

"Conscientious to a fault, sir," said Mr Cuff, not without a touch of kindness. "For a person in the normal way of living cannot begin to comprehend the actual meaning of that term,

nor is he liable to understand the fierce requirements it puts on
a man's head. And so it comes about that persons in the
normal way of living try to back out long after backing out is
possible, even though we explain exactly what is going to
happen at the very beginning. They listen, but they do not
hear, and it's the rare civilian who has the common sense to
know that if you stand in a fire you must be burned. And if
you turn the world upside-down, you're standing on your head
with everybody else."

"Or," said Mr Clubb, calming his own fires with another deep
draught of cognac, "as the Golden Rule has it, what you do is
sooner or later done back to you."

Although I was still one who listened but could not hear, a
tingle of premonition went up my spine. "Please go on with your
report," I said.

"The responses of the subject were all one could wish," said
Mr Clubb. "I could go so far as to say that her responses were
a thing of beauty. A subject who can render you one magnificent scream after another while maintaining a basic self-
possession and not breaking down is a subject highly attuned
to her own pain, sir, and one to be cherished. You see, there
comes a moment when they understand that they are changed
for good, they have passed over the border into another realm
from which there is no return, and some of them can't handle
it and turn, you might say, sir, to mush. With some it happens
right at the foundation stage, a sad disappointment because
thereafter all the rest of the work could be done by the crudest
apprentice. It takes some at the nipples stage, and at the
genital stage quite a few more. Most of them comprehend
irreversibility during the piercings, and by the stage of small
amputation ninety per cent have shown you what they are
made of. The lady did not come to the point until we had
begun the eye-work, and she passed with flying colors, sir. But
it was then the male upped and put his foot in it."

"And eye-work is delicate going," said Mr Cuff. "Requiring
two men, if you want it done even close to right. But I couldn't
have turned my back on the fellow for more than a minute and a
half."

"Less," said Mr Clubb, "And him lying there in the corner
meek as a baby. No fight left in him at all, you would have said.

You would have said, that fellow there is not going to risk so much as opening his eyes until he's made to do it."

"But up he gets, without a rope on him, sir," said Mr Cuff, "which you would have said was far beyond the powers of a fellow who had recently lost a hand."

"Up he gets and on he comes," said Mr Clubb. "In defiance of all of Nature's mighty laws. Before I know what's what, he has his good arm around Mr Cuff's neck and is earnestly trying to snap that neck while beating Mr Cuff about the head with his stump, a situation which compels me to set aside the task at hand and take up a knife and ram it into his back and sides a fair old number of times. The next thing I know, he's on *me*, and it's up to Mr Cuff to peel him off and set him on the floor."

"And then, you see, your concentration is gone," said Mr Cuff. "After something like that, you might as well be starting all over again at the beginning. Imagine if you are playing a piano about as well as ever you did in your life, and along comes another piano with blood in its eye and jumps on your back. It was pitiful, that's all I can say about it. But I got the fellow down and jabbed him here and there until he was still, and then I got the one item we count on as a sure-fire last resort for incapacitation."

"What is that item?" I asked.

"Dental floss," said Mr Clubb. "Dental floss cannot be overestimated as a particular in our line of work. It is the razor-wire of everyday life, and fishing-line cannot hold a candle to it, for fishing-line is dull, but dental floss is both *dull* and *sharp*. It has a hundred uses, and a book should be written on the subject."

"What do you do with it?" I asked.

"It is applied to a male subject," he said. "Applied artfully and in a manner perfected only over years of experience. The application is of a lovely *subtlety*. During the process, the subject must be in a helpless, preferably an unconscious, position. When the subject regains the first fuzzy inklings of consciousness, he is aware of no more than a vague discomfort like unto a form of numb tingling, similar to when a foot has gone asleep. In a wonderfully short period of time, that discomfort builds up itself, ascending to mild pain, real pain, *severe* pain, and then outright agony. And then it goes past agony. The final stage is a mystical condition I don't think there is a word for which, but it close resembles ecstasy. Hallucinations are common. Out-of-body experiences are common. We have seen men speak in tongues, even when tongues were strictly speaking organs they no longer possessed. We have seen wonders, Mr Cuff and I."

"That we have," said Mr Cuff. "The ordinary civilian sort of fellow can be a miracle, sir."

"Of which the person in question was one, to be sure," said Mr Clubb. "But he has to be said to be in a category all by himself, a man in a million you could put it, which is the cause of my mentioning the grand design ever a mystery to us who glimpse but a part of the whole. You see, the fellow refused to play by the time-honored rules. He was in an awesome degree of suffering and torment, sir, but he would not do us the favor to lie down and quit."

"The mind was not right," said Mr Cuff. "Where the proper mind goes to the spiritual, sir, as just described, this was that one mind in *ten* million, I'd estimate, which moves to the animal at the reptile level. If you cut off the head of a venomous reptile and detach it from the body, that head will still attempt to strike. So it was with our boy. Bleeding from a dozen wounds. Minus one hand. Seriously concussed. The dental floss murdering all possibility of thought. Every nerve in his body howling like a banshee. Yet up he comes with his eyes red and the foam dripping from his mouth. We put him down again, and I did what I hate, because it takes all feeling away from the body along with the motor capacity, and cracked his spine right at the base of the head. Or would have, if his spine had been a normal thing instead of solid steel in a thick india-rubber case. Which is what put us in mind of weight-lifting, sir, an activity resulting in such development about the top of the spine you need a hacksaw to get even close to it."

"We were already behind schedule," said Mr Clubb, "and with the time required to get back into the proper frame of mind, we had at least seven or eight hours of work ahead of us. And you had to double that, because while we could knock the fellow out, he wouldn't have the decency to *stay* out more than a few minutes at a time. The natural thing, him being only the secondary subject, would have been to kill him outright so we could get on with the real job, but improving our working conditions by that fashion would require an amendment to our contract. Which comes under the heading of Instructions from the Client."

"And it was eleven o'clock," said Mr Cuff.

"The exact time scheduled for our conference," said Mr Clubb. "My partner was forced to clobber the fellow into senselessness, how many times was it, Mr Cuff, while I prayed for our client to do us the grace of answering his phone during twenty rings?"

"Three times, Mr Clubb, three times exactly," said Mr Cuff. "The blow each time more powerful than the last, which combining with his having a skull made of granite led to a painful swelling of my hand."

"The dilemma stared us in the face," said Mr Clubb. "Client unreachable. Impeded in the performance of our duties. State of mind, very foul. In such a pickle, we could do naught but obey the instructions given us by our hearts. *Remove the gentleman's head*, I told my partner, *and take care not be bitten once it's off*. Mr Cuff took up an axe. Some haste was called for, the fellow just beginning to stir again. Mr Cuff moved into position. Then from the bed, where all had been lovely silence but for soft moans and whimpers, we hear a god-awful yowling ruckus of the most desperate and importunate protest. It was of a sort to melt the heart, sir. Were we not experienced professionals who enjoy pride in our work, I believe we might have been persuaded almost to grant the fellow mercy, despite his being a pest of the first water. But now those heart-melting screeches reach the ears of the pest and rouse him into movement just at the moment Mr Cuff lowers the boom, so to speak."

"Which was an unfortunate bit of business," said Mr Cuff. "Causing me to catch him in the shoulder, causing him to rear up, causing me to lose my footing what with all the blood on the floor, then causing a tussle for possession of the axe and myself suffering several kicks to the breadbasket. I'll tell you, sir, we did a good piece of work when we took off his hand, for without the nuisance of a stump really being useful only for leverage, there's no telling what that fellow might have done. As it was, I had the devil's own time getting the axe free and clear, and once I had done, any chance of making a neat, clean job of it was long gone. It was a slaughter and an act of butchery with not a bit of finesse or sophistication to it, and I have to tell you, such a thing is both an embarrassment and an outrage to men like ourselves. Turning a subject into hamburger by means of an axe is a violation of all our training, and it is not why we went into this business."

"No, of course not, you are more like artists than I had imagined," I said. "But in spite of your embarrassment, I suppose you went back to work on . . . on the female subject."

"We are not *like* artists," said Mr Clubb, "we *are* artists, and we know how to set our feelings aside and address our chosen medium of expression with a pure and patient attention. In spite of which we discovered the final and insurmountable frustration of the evening, and that discovery put paid to all our hopes."

"If you discovered that Marguerite had escaped," I said, "I believe I might almost, after all you have said, be –"

Glowering, Mr Clubb held up his hand. "I beg you not to insult us, sir, as we have endured enough misery for one day. The subject had escaped, all right, but not in the simple sense of your meaning. She had escaped for all eternity, in the sense that her soul had taken leave of her body and flown to those realms at whose nature we can only make our poor, ignorant guesses."

"She died?" I asked. "In other words, in direct contradiction of my instructions, you two fools killed her. You love to talk about your expertise, but you went too far, and she died at your hands. I want you incompetents to leave my house immediately. Begone. Depart. This minute."

Mr Clubb and Mr Cuff looked into each other's eyes, and in that moment of private communication I saw an encompassing and universal sorrow which utterly turned the tables on me: before I was made to understand how it was possible, I saw that the only fool present was myself. And yet the sorrow included all three of us, and more besides.

"The subject died, but we did not kill her," said Mr Clubb. "We did not go, nor have we ever gone, too far. The subject chose to die. The subject's death was an act of suicidal will. Can you hear me? While you are listening, sir, is it possible, sir, for you to open your ears and hear what I am saying? She who might have been in all of our long experience the noblest, most courageous subject we ever will have the good fortune to be given witnessed the clumsy murder of her lover and decided to surrender her life."

"Quick as a shot," said Mr Cuff. "The simple truth, sir, is that otherwise we could have kept her alive for about a year."

"And it would have been a rare privilege to do so," said Mr Clubb. "It is time for you to face facts, sir."

"I am facing them about as well as one could," I said. "Please tell me where you disposed of the bodies."

"Within the house," said Mr Clubb. Before I could protest, he said, "Under the wretched circumstances, sir, including the continuing unavailability of the client and the enormity of the personal and professional let-down felt by my partner and myself, we saw no choice but to dispose of the house along with the telltale remains."

"Dispose of Green Chimneys?" I said, aghast. "How could you dispose of Green Chimneys?"

"Reluctantly, sir," said Mr Clubb "With heavy hearts and an equal anger. With also the same degree of professional unhappiness experienced previous. In workaday terms, by means of combustion. Fire, sir, is a substance like shock and salt water, a healer and a cleanser, though more drastic."

"But Green Chimneys has not been healed," I said. "Nor has my wife."

"You are a man of wit, sir, and have provided Mr Cuff and myself many moments of precious amusement. True, Green Chimneys has not been healed, but cleansed it has been, root and branch. And you hired us to punish your wife, not heal her, and punish her we did, as well as possible under very trying circumstances indeed."

"Which circumstances include our feeling that the job ended before its time," said Mr Cuff. "Which circumstance is one we cannot bear."

"I regret your disappointment," I said, "but I cannot accept that it was necessary to burn down my magnificent house."

"Twenty, even fifteen years ago, it would not have been," said Mr Clubb. "Nowadays, however, that contemptible alchemy known as Police Science has fattened itself up into such a gross and distorted breed of sorcery that a single drop of blood can be detected even after you scrub and scour until your arms hurt. It has reached the hideous point that if a constable without a thing in his head but the desire to imprison honest fellows employed in an ancient trade finds two hairs at what is supposed to be a crime scene, he waddles along to the laboratory and instantly a loathsome sort of wizard is popping out to tell him that those same two hairs are from the heads of Mr Clubb and Mr Cuff, and I exaggerate, I know, sir, but not by much."

"And if they do not have our names, sir," said Mr Cuff, "which they do not and I pray never will, they ever after have our particulars, to be placed in a great universal file against the day when they *might* have our names, so as to look back into that cruel file and commit the monstrosity of unfairly increasing the charges against us. It is a malignant business, and all sensible precautions must be taken."

"A thousand times I have expressed the conviction," said Mr Clubb, "that an ancient art ought not be against the law, nor its practitioners described as criminals. Is there even a name for our so-called crime? There is not. GBH they call it, sir, for Grievous Bodily Harm, or, even worse, Assault. We do not Assault. We induce, we instruct, we instill. Properly speaking, these cannot be crimes, and those who do them cannot be criminals. Now I have said it a thousand times and one."

"All right," I said, attempting to speed this appalling conference to its end, "you have described the evening's unhappy events. I appreciate your reasons for burning down my splendid property. You have enjoyed a lavish meal. All remaining is the matter of your remuneration, which demands considerable thought. This night has left me exhausted, and after all your efforts, you, too, must be in need of rest. Communicate with me, please, in a day or two, gentlemen, by whatever means you choose. I wish to be alone with my thoughts. Mr Moncrieff will show you out."

The maddening barnies met this plea with impassive stares and stoic silence, and I renewed my silent vow to give them nothing – not a penny. For all their pretensions, they had accomplished naught but the death of my wife and the destruction of my country house. Rising to my feet with more difficulty than anticipated, I said, "Thank you for your efforts on my behalf."

Once again, the glance which passed between them implied that I had failed to grasp the essentials of our situation.

"Your thanks are gratefully accepted," said Mr Cuff, "though, dispute it as you may, they are premature, as you know in your soul. This morning we embarked upon a journey of which we have yet more miles to go. In consequence, we prefer not to leave. Also, setting aside the question of your continuing education, which if we do not address will haunt us all forever, residing here with you for a sensible period out of sight is the best protection from law enforcement we three could ask for."

"No," I said, "I have had enough of your education, and I need no protection from officers of the law. Please, gentlemen, allow me to return to my bed. You may take the rest of the cognac with you as a token of my regard."

"Give it a moment's reflection, sir," said Mr Clubb. "You have announced the presence of high-grade consultants and introduced these same to staff and clients both. Hours later, your spouse meets her tragic end in a conflagration destroying your upstate manor. On the very same night also occurs the disappearance of your greatest competitor, a person certain to be identified before long by a hotel employee as a fellow not unknown to the late spouse. Can you think it wise to have the high-grade consultants vanish right away?"

I did reflect, then said, "You have a point. It will be best if you continue to make an appearance in the office for a time. However, the proposal that you stay here is ridiculous." A wild hope, utterly irrational in the face of the grisly evidence, came to me in the guise of doubt. "If Green Chimneys has been destroyed by fire, I should have been informed long ago. I am a respected figure in the town of —, personally acquainted with its Chief of Police, Wendall Nash. Why has he not called me?"

"Oh, sir, my goodness," said Mr Clubb, shaking his head and smiling inwardly at my folly, "for many reasons. A small town is a beast slow to move. The available men have been struggling throughout the night to rescue even a jot or tittle portion of your house. They will fail, they have failed already, but the effort will keep them busy past dawn. Wendall Nash will not wish to ruin your night's sleep until he can make a full report." He glanced at his wristwatch. "In fact, if I am not mistaken . . ." He tilted his head, closed his eyes, and raised an index finger. The telephone in the kitchen began to trill.

"He has done it a thousand times, sir," said Mr Cuff, "and I have yet to see him strike out."

Mr Moncrieff brought the instrument through from the kitchen, said, "For you, sir," and placed the receiver in my waiting hand. I uttered the conventional greeting, longing to hear the voice of anyone but . . .

"Wendall Nash, sir," came the Chief's raspy, high-pitched drawl. "Calling from up here in —. I hate to tell you this, but I have some awful bad news. Your place Green Chimneys started burning sometime around midnight last night, and every man-jack we had got put on the job and the boys worked like dogs to save what they could, but sometimes you can't win no matter what you do. Me personally, I feel terrible about this, but, tell you the truth, I never saw a fire like it. We nearly lost two men, but it looks like they're going to come out of it okay. The rest of our boys are still out there trying to save the few trees you got left."

"Dreadful," I said. "Please permit me to speak to my wife."

A speaking silence followed. "The missus is not with you, sir? You're saying she was inside there?"

"My wife left for Green Chimneys this morning. I spoke to her there in the afternoon. She intended to work in her studio, a separate building at some distance from the house, and it is her custom to sleep in the studio when working late." Saying these things to Wendall Nash, I felt almost as though I were creating an alternative world, another town of — and another Green Chimneys, where another Marguerite had busied herself in the studio, and there gone to bed to sleep through the commotion. "Have you checked the studio? You are certain to find her there."

"Well, I have to say we didn't, sir," he said. "The fire took that little building pretty good, too, but the walls are still standing and you can tell what used to be what, furnishing-wise and equipment-wise. If she was inside it, we'd of found her."

"Then she got out in time," I said, and instantly it was the truth: the other Marguerite had escaped the blaze and now stood, numb with shock and wrapped in a blanket, unrecognized amidst the voyeuristic crowd always drawn to disasters.

"It's possible, but she hasn't turned up yet, and we've been talking to everybody at the site. Could she have left with one of the staff?"

"All the help is on vacation," I said. "She was alone."

"Uh huh," he said. "Can you think of anyone with a serious grudge against you? Any enemies? Because this was not a natural-type fire, sir. Someone set it, and he knew what he was doing. Anyone come to mind?"

"No," I said. "I have rivals, but no enemies. Check the hospitals and anything else you can think of, Wendall, and I'll be there as soon as I can."

"You can take your time, sir," he said. "I sure hope we find her, and by late this afternoon we'll be able to go through the ashes." He said he would give me a call if anything turned up in the meantime.

"Please, Wendall," I said, and began to cry. Muttering a consolation I did not quite catch, Mr Moncrieff vanished with the telephone in another matchless display of butler *politesse*.

"The practise of hoping for what you know you cannot have is a worthy spiritual exercise," said Mr Clubb. "It brings home the vanity of vanity."

"I beg you, leave me," I said, still crying. "In all decency."

"Decency lays heavy obligations on us all," said Mr Clubb. "And no job is decently done until it is done completely. Would you care for help in getting back to the bedroom? We are ready to proceed."

I extended a shaky arm, and he assisted me through the corridors. Two cots had been set up in my room, and a neat array of instruments – "staples" – formed two rows across the bottom of the bed. Mr Clubb and Mr Cuff positioned my head on the pillows and began to disrobe.

VIII.

Ten hours later, the silent chauffeur aided me in my exit from the limousine and clasped my left arm as I limped toward the uniformed men and official vehicles on the far side of the open gate. Blackened sticks which had been trees protruded from the blasted earth, and the stench of wet ash saturated the air. Wendall Nash separated from the other men, approached, and noted without comment my garb of grey Homburg hat, pearl-grey cashmere topcoat, heavy gloves, woolen charcoal-grey pinstriped suit, sunglasses, and Malacca walking stick. It was the afternoon of a midsummer day in the upper eighties. Then he looked more closely at my face. "Are you, uh, are you sure you're all right, sir?"

"In a manner of speaking," I said, and saw him blink at the oozing gap left in the wake of an incisor. "I slipped at the top of a marble staircase and tumbled down all forty-six steps, resulting in massive bangs and bruises, considerable physical weakness, and the persistent sensation of being uncomfortably cold. No broken bones, at least nothing major." Over his shoulder I stared at four isolated brick towers rising from an immense black hole in the ground, all that remained of Green Chimneys. "Is there news of my wife?"

"I'm afraid, sir, that –" Nash placed a hand on my shoulder, causing me to stifle a sharp outcry. "I'm sorry, sir. Shouldn't you be in the hospital? Did your doctors say you could come all this way?"

"Knowing my feelings in this matter, the doctors insisted I make the journey." Deep within the black cavity, men in bulky orange space-suits and space-helmets were sifting through the sodden ashes, now and then dropping unrecognizable nuggets into heavy bags of the same color. "I gather that you have news for me, Wendall," I said.

"Unhappy news, sir," he said. "The garage went up with the rest of the house, but we found some bits and pieces of your wife's little car. This here was one incredible hot fire, sir, and by hot I mean *hot*, and whoever set it was no garden-variety firebug."

"You found evidence of the automobile," I said. "I assume you also found evidence of the woman who owned it."

"They came across some bone fragments, plus a small portion of a skeleton," he said. "This whole big house came down on her, sir. These boys are experts at their job, and they don't hold out hope for coming across a whole lot more. So if your wife was the only person inside . . ."

"I see, yes, I understand," I said, staying on my feet only with the support of the Malacca cane. "How horrid, how hideous that it should all be true, that our lives should prove such a *littleness* . . ."

"I'm sure that's true, sir, and that wife of yours was a, was what I have to call a special kind of person who gave pleasure to us all, and I hope you know that we all wish things could of turned out different, the same as you."

For a moment I imagined that he was talking about her recordings. And then, immediately, I understood that he was laboring to express the pleasure he and the others had taken in what they, no less than Mr Clubb and Mr Cuff but much, much more than I, had perceived as her essential character.

"Oh, Wendall," I said into the teeth of my sorrow, "it is not possible, not ever, for things to turn out different."

He refrained from patting my shoulder and sent me back to the rigors of my education.

IX.

A month – four weeks – thirty days – seven hundred and twenty hours – forty-three thousand, two hundred minutes – two million, five hundred and ninety-two thousand seconds – did I spend under the care of Mr Clubb and Mr Cuff, and I believe I proved in the end to be a modestly, moderately, middlingly satisfying subject, a matter in which I take an immodest and immoderate pride. "You are little in comparison to the lady, sir," Mr Clubb once told me while deep in his ministrations, "but no one could say that you are nothing." I, who had countless times put the lie to the declaration that they should never see me cry, wept tears of gratitude. We ascended through the fifteen stages known to the novice, the journeyman's further five, and passed, with the frequent repetitions and backward glances appropriate for the slower pupil, into the artist's upper eighty, infinitely expandable by grace of the refinements of his art. We had the little soldiers. We had *dental floss*. During each of those forty-three thousand, two hundred minutes, throughout all two million and nearly six hundred thousand seconds, it was always deepest night. We made our way through perpetual darkness, and the utmost darkness of the utmost night yielded an infinity of textural variation, cold, slick dampness to velvety softness to leaping flame, for it was true that no one could say I was nothing.

Because I was not nothing, I glimpsed the Meaning of Tragedy. Each Tuesday and Friday of these four sunless weeks, my consultants and guides lovingly bathed and dressed my wounds, arrayed me in my warmest clothes (for I never after ceased to feel the blast of arctic wind against my flesh), and escorted me to my office, where I was presumed much reduced by grief as well as certain household accidents attributed to grief.

On the first of these Tuesdays, a flushed-looking Mrs Rampage offered her consolations and presented me with the morning newspapers, an inch-thick pile of faxes, two inches of legal documents, and a tray filled with official-looking letters. The newspapers described the fire and eulogized Marguerite; the increasingly threatening faxes declared Chartwell, Munster and Stout's intention to ruin me professionally and personally in the face of my continuing refusal to return the accompanying documents along with all records having reference to their client; the documents were those in question; the letters, produced by the various legal firms representing all my other cryptic gentlemen, deplored the (unspecified) circumstances necessitating their clients' universal desire for change in re financial management. These lawyers also desired all relevant records, discs, etc., etc., urgently. Mr Clubb and Mr Cuff roistered behind their screen. I signed the documents in a shaky hand and requested Mrs Rampage to have these delivered with the desired records to Chartwell, Munster and Stout. "And dispatch all these other records, too," I said, handing her the letters. "I am now going in for my lunch."

Tottering toward the executive dining room, now and then I glanced into smoke-filled offices to observe my much-altered underlings. Some of them appeared, after a fashion, to be working. Several were reading paperback novels, which might be construed as work of a kind. One of the Captain's assistants was unsuccessfully lofting paper airplanes toward his wastepaper basket. Gilligan's secretary lay asleep on her office couch, and a Records clerk lay sleeping on the file-room floor. In the dining room, Charlie-Charlie Rackett hurried forward to assist me to my accustomed chair. Gilligan and the Captain gave me sullen looks from their usual lunchtime station, an unaccustomed bottle of Scotch whiskey between them. Charlie-Charlie lowered me into my seat and said, "Terrible news about your wife, sir."

"More terrible than you know," I said.

Gilligan took a gulp of whiskey and displayed his middle finger, I gathered to me rather than Charlie-Charlie.

"Afternoonish," I said.

"Very much so, sir," said Charlie-Charlie, and bent closer to the brim of the Homburg and my ear. "About that little request you made the other day. The right men aren't nearly so easy to find as they used to be, sir, but I'm still on the job."

MR CLUBB AND MR CUFF

My laughter startled him. "No squab today, Charlie-Charlie. Just bring me a bowl of tomato soup."

I had partaken of no more than two or three delicious mouthfuls when Gilligan lurched up beside me. "Look here," he said, "it's too bad about your wife and everything, I really mean it, honest, but that drunken act you put on in my office cost me my biggest client, not to forget that you took his girl friend home with you."

"In that case," I said, "I have no further need of your services. Pack your things and be out of here by three o'clock."

He listed to one side and straightened himself up. "You can't mean that."

"I can and do," I said. "Your part in the grand design at work in the universe no longer has any connection with my own."

"You must be as crazy as you look," he said, and unsteadily departed.

I returned to my office and gently lowered myself into my seat. After I had removed my gloves and accomplished some minor repair work to the tips of my fingers with the tape and gauze pads thoughtfully inserted by the detectives into the pockets of my coat, I slowly drew the left glove over my fingers and became aware of feminine giggles amidst the coarser sounds of male amusement behind the screen. I coughed into the glove and heard a tiny shriek. Soon, though not immediately, a blushing Mrs Rampage emerged from cover, patting her hair and adjusting her skirt. "Sir, I'm so sorry, I didn't expect . . ." She was staring at my right hand, which had not as yet been inserted into its glove.

"Lawnmower accident," I said. "Mr Gilligan has been released, and I should like you to prepare the necessary papers. Also, I want to see all of our operating figures for the past year, as significant changes have been dictated by the grand design at work in the universe."

Mrs Rampage flew from the room, and for the next several hours, as for nearly every remaining hour I spent at my desk on the Tuesdays and Thursdays thereafter, I addressed with a carefree spirit the details involved in shrinking the staff to the smallest number possible and turning the entire business over to the Captain. Graham Leeson's abrupt disappearance greatly occupied the newspapers, and when not occupied as described I read that my arch-rival and competitor had been a notorious Don

Juan, i.e. a compulsive womanizer, a flaw in his otherwise immaculate character held by some to have played a substantive role in his sudden absence. As Mr Clubb had predicted, a clerk at the – Hotel revealed Leeson's sessions with my late wife, and for a time professional and amateur gossip-mongers alike speculated that he had caused the disastrous fire. This came to nothing. Before the month had ended, Leeson-sightings were reported in Monaco, the Swiss Alps and Argentina, locations accommodating to sportsmen – after four years of varsity football at the University of Southern California, Leeson had won a Olympic silver medal in weightlifting while earning his MBA at Wharton.

In the limousine at the end of each day, Mr Clubb and Mr Cuff braced me in happy anticipation of the lessons to come as we sped back through illusory sunlight toward the real darkness.

X.   The Meaning of Tragedy

Everything, from the designs of the laughing gods down to the lowliest cells in the human digestive tract, is changing all the time, every particle of being large and small is eternally in motion, but this simple truism, so transparent on its surface, evokes immediate headache and stupefaction when applied to itself, not unlike the sentence, "Every word that comes out of my mouth is a bald-faced lie." The gods are ever laughing while we are always clutching our heads and looking for a soft place to lie down, and what I glimpsed in my momentary glimpses of the meaning of tragedy preceding, during, and after the experience of *dental floss* was so composed of paradox that I can state it only in cloud- or vapor form, as:

> The meaning of tragedy is: *all is in order, all is in train*.
> The meaning of tragedy is: *it only hurts for a little while*.
> The meaning of tragedy is: *change is the first law of life*.

XI.

So it took place that one day their task was done, their lives and mine were to move forward into separate areas of the grand design, and all that was left before preparing my own departure was to stand, bundled-up against the nonexistent arctic wind, on the bottom step and wave farewell with my remaining hand while shedding buckets and bathtubs of tears with my remaining eye. Chaplinesque in their black suits and bowlers, Mr Clubb and Mr Cuff ambled cheerily toward the glittering avenue and my bank, where arrangements had been made for the transfer into their hands of all but a small portion of my private fortune by my private banker, virtually his final act in that capacity. At the distant corner, Mr Clubb and Mr Cuff, by then only tiny figures blurred by my tears, turned, ostensibly to bid farewell, actually, as I knew, to watch as I mounted my steps and went back within the house, and with a salute I honored this last painful agreement between us.

A more pronounced version of the office's metamorphosis had taken place inside my townhouse, but with the relative ease practice gives even to one whose step is halting, whose progress is interrupted by frequent pauses for breath and the passing of certain shooting pains, I skirted the mounds of rubble, the dangerous loose tiles and more dangerous open holes in the floor, the regions submerged underwater, and toiled up the resilient staircase, moved with infinite care across the boards bridging the former landing, and made my way into the former kitchen, where broken pipes and limp wires protruding from the lathe marked the sites of those appliances rendered pointless by the gradual disappearance of the household staff. (In a voice choked with feeling, Mr Moncrieff, Reggie Moncrieff, Reggie, the last to go, had informed me that his last month in my service had been "As fine as my days with the Duke, sir, every bit as noble as ever it was with that excellent old gentleman.") The remaining cupboard yielded a flagon of genever, a tumbler, and a Montecristo torpedo, and with the tumbler filled and the cigar alight I hobbled through the devastated corridors toward my bed, there to gather my strength for the ardors of the coming day.

In good time, I arose to observe the final appointments of the life soon to be abandoned. It is possible to do up one's shoelaces and knot one's necktie as neatly with a single hand as with two, and shirt buttons eventually become a breeze. Into my travelling bag I folded a few modest essentials atop the flagon and the cigar box, and into a pad of shirts nestled the black lucite cube prepared at my request by my instructor-guides and containing, mingled with the ashes of the satchel and its contents, the few bony nuggets rescued from Green Chimneys. The travelling bag accompanied me first to my lawyer's office, where I signed papers making over the wreckage of the townhouse to the European gentleman who had purchased it sight unseen as a "fixer-upper" for a fraction of its (considerably reduced) value. Next I visited the melancholy banker and withdrew the pittance remaining in my accounts. And then, glad of heart and free of all unnecessary encumbrance, I took my place in the sidewalk queue to await transportation by means of a kindly kneeling bus to the great terminus where I should employ the ticket reassuringly lodged within my breast pocket.

Long before the arrival of the bus, a handsome limousine crawled past in the traffic, and glancing idly within, I observed Mr Chester Montfort d'M— smoothing the air with a languid gesture while in conversation with the two stout, bowler-hatted men on his either side. Soon, doubtless, he would begin his instructions in the whopbopaloobop.

XII.

What is a pittance in a great city may be a modest fortune in a hamlet, and a returned prodigal might be welcomed far in excess of his true deserts. I entered New Covenant quietly, unobtrusively, with the humility of a new convert uncertain of his station, inwardly rejoicing to see all unchanged from the days of my youth. When I purchased a dignified but unshowy house on Scripture Street, I announced only that I had known the village in my childhood, had travelled far, and now in my retirement wished no more than to immerse myself in the life of the community, exercising my skills only inasmuch as they might be requested of an elderly invalid. How well the aged invalid had known the village, how far and to what end had he travelled, and the nature of his skills remained unspecified. Had I not attended daily services at the Temple, the rest of my days might have passed in pleasant anonymity and frequent perusals of a little book I had obtained at the terminus, for while my surname was so deeply of New Covenant that it could be read on a dozen headstones in the Temple graveyard, I had fled so early in life and so long ago that my individual identity had been entirely forgotten. New Covenant is curious – intensely curious – but it does not wish to pry. One fact and one only led to the metaphoric slaughter of the fatted calf and the prodigal's elevation. On the day when, some five or six months after his installation on Scripture Street, the afflicted newcomer's faithful Temple attendance was rewarded with an invitation to read the Lesson for the Day, Matthew 5: 43–48, seated amidst numerous offspring and offspring's offspring in the barnie-pews for the first time since an unhappy tumble from a hayloft was Delbert Mudge.

My old classmate had weathered into a white-haired, sturdy replica of his own grandfather, and although his hips still gave him considerable difficulty his mind had suffered no comparable stiffening. Delbert knew my name as well as his own, and though he could not connect it to the wizened old party counseling him from the lectern to embrace his enemies, the old party's face and voice so clearly evoked the deceased lawyer who had been my father that he recognized me before I had spoken the whole of the initial verse. The grand design at work in the universe once again could be seen at its mysterious work: unknown to me, my entirely selfish efforts on behalf of Charlie-Charlie Rackett, my representation to his parole board and his subsequent hiring as my spy, had been noted by all of barnie-world. I, a child of Scripture Street, had become a hero to generations of barnies! After hugging me at the conclusion of the fateful service, Delbert Mudge implored my assistance in the resolution of a fiscal imbroglio which threatened his family's cohesion. I of course assented, with the condition that my services should be free of charge. The Mudge imbroglio proved elementary, and soon I was performing similar services for other barnie clans. After listening to a half-dozen accounts of my miracles while setting broken barnie-bones, New Covenant's physician visited my Scripture Street habitation under cover of night, was prescribed the solution to his uncomplicated problem, and sang my praises to his fellow townies. Within a year, by which time all New Covenant had become aware of my "tragedy" and consequent "reawakening", I was managing the Temple's funds as well as those of barn and town. Three years later, our Reverend having in his ninety-first year, as the Racketts and Mudges put it, "woke up dead", I submitted by popular acclaim to appointment in his place.

Daily, I assume the honored place assigned me. Ceremonious vestments assure that my patchwork scars remain unseen. The lucite box and its relics are interred deep within the sacred ground beneath the Temple where I must one day join my predecessors – some bony fragments of Graham Leeson reside there, too, mingled with Marguerite's more numerous specks and nuggets. Eyepatch elegantly in place, I lean forward upon the Malacca cane and, while flourishing the stump of my right hand as if in demonstration, with my ruined tongue whisper what I know none shall understand, the homily beginning, *It only* . . . To this I append in silent exhalation the two words concluding that little book brought to my attention by an agreeable murderer and purchased at the great grand station long ago, these: *Ah, humanity!*

STEPHEN JONES & KIM NEWMAN

Necrology: 1998

THE FOLLOWING WRITERS, ARTISTS, PERFORMERS AND TECHNI-CIANS who made significant contributions to the horror, science fiction and fantasy genres during their lifetimes (or left their mark on popular culture in other ways) died in 1998 . . .

AUTHORS/ARTISTS

Prolific author **Walter D. Edmonds**, best remembered for his 1930s bestseller *Drums Along the Mohawk* (filmed by John Ford in 1939) died on January 24th, aged 94.

Cartoonist and dust jacket illustrator "**Ionicus**" (Joshua Charles Armitage) died on January 29th, aged 84. He trained at the Liverpool School of Art and, following service in the Royal Navy during World War II, began contributing cartoons to *Punch* magazine. He produced fifty-eight covers for the Penguin P.G. Wodehouse series, but it is his sixty-five dust jacket paintings for William Kimber's ghost story collections and anthologies between 1974–88 – by R. Chetwynd-Hayes, James Turner, Denys Val Baker, Amy Myers and others – for which he will be remembered.

Thriller writer **Lawrence Sanders** died on February 7th, aged 78. Best known for his novels *The Anderson Tapes* and *The First Deadly Sin* (filmed in 1972 and 1980, respectively), he also wrote such borderline-SF titles as *The Tomorrow File* and *The Passion* *of Molly T*, plus the fantasy *Dark Summer* under the pseudonym "Mark Upton".

Fantasy and science fiction writer (Patricia) **Jo Clayton** died of multiple myeloma on February 13th, two days before her 59th birthday. Despite being hospitalized for more than a year and a half and suffering from advanced bone cancer, she completed the second volume (*Drum Calls*) and part of the third book in her "Drums" trilogy, along with a number of short stories. Among her thirty-five published novels are *Diadem from the Stars* (1977), *Moongather*, *Drinker of Souls*, *Skeen's Leap*, *Shadowplay*, *Wild Magic*, *Dancer's Rise*, *Fire in the Sky* and *Drum Warning*.

Games designer and fantasy novelist **Sean A. Moore** was killed in a single-car accident in the early evening hours of February 23rd. The creator of the bestselling computer game, *Ultimate Wizard*, he was 33 and had recently quit his job to become a full-time writer. His books included *Conan the Hunter*, *Conan and the Shaman's Curse*, *Conan and the Grim Gray God* and the novelisation of the 1997 movie *Kull the Conqueror* (he also worked uncredited on the script).

Cuban-born cartoonist **Antonio Prohias**, who drew the "Spy vs. Spy" strip for *Mad* magazine from 1961 until he retired in 1991, died from cancer on February 24th in Florida. He was 77.

Rockin' Sidney Simien, who won a Grammy Award in 1985 for his zydeco hit "(Don't Mess With) My Toot Toot", died of lung cancer on February 25th, aged 59.

Beat poet **Jack Micheline**, a close friend of Jack Kerouac, Gregory Corso and Bob Kaufman, who published more than twenty books of poetry, died in San Francisco on February 27th, aged 68.

Comics writer and editor **Archie Goodwin** (Archibald Goodwin) died on March 1st after a long battle with cancer. He was 60. In 1965 he entered the comics field as a writer and Editor-in-Chief of Warren Publication's *Creepy* and *Eerie* titles. He later worked at both Marvel and DC Comics, and scripted such newspaper strips as *Star Wars* and *Secret Agent X-9*.

43-year-old MS sufferer **Robert James Leake**, the seven-foot tall "professional monster" who appeared in numerous commercials and television shows as Dracula, the Frankenstein Monster and Darth Vader, died the same day, after entering hospital with a chest infection. He joined The Dracula Society in 1974 and held a variety of positions, including Honorary Secretary, archivist, media consultant and editor of the society's newsletter, *Voices from the Vaults*.

Following treatment for a series of aneurysms, playwright and screenwriter **Beverley Cross**, who was married to actress Dame Maggie Smith, died on March 20th, aged 66. His credits include the Ray Harryhausen fantasy adventures *Jason and the Argonauts*, *Sinbad and the Eye of the Tiger* and *Clash of the Titans*.

Rozz Williams, the songwriter and musician who founded Gothic rock group Christian Death, hanged himself on April 1st at his home in West Hollywood. He was 34.

Puerto Rico-born science fiction illustrator **Alex Schomburg** died on April 7th, aged 92. His career spanned seven decades and included the covers of Hugo Gernsback's science magazines in the 1920s, superhero titles from the Golden Age of comics, and pulp and digest SF magazine covers during the 1950s and 60s. *Croma: The Art of Alex Schomburg* was published in 1986, and he received a special Lifetime Achievement Award in SF Art at the 1989 World Science Fiction Convention.

Comic strip artist **Lee Elias** died at a nursing home on April 8th, aged 77. From 1952–55 he collaborated with Jack Williamson on the daily newspaper strip *Beyond Mars*. He also worked on *Terry and the Pirates* for many years.

Singer, photographer and vegetarian **Linda McCartney** died from breast cancer on April 17th, aged 56. Along with her husband Paul (whom she married in 1969) she was in the group Wings, and her photo of Clive Barker appeared on the dust jacket of *Weaveworld*.

American Gothic novelist and essayist **Wright Morris** died on April 25th, aged 88.

Carlos Castaneda, the author of a series of mystical novels about Yaqui Indian shaman Don Juan, died of liver cancer on April 27th. His age was uncertain, but he was somewhere between 68 and 74.

Veteran short story author and screenwriter (Drexel) **Jerome** (Lewis) **Bixby** died on April 28th from a heart attack after complications following quadruple bypass surgery. He was 75. The author of more than a thousand short stories, Bixby's first sale was to the pulp magazine *Planet Stories* in 1949, which he also edited from 1950–1 along with the first three issues of its companion title, *Two Complete Science-Adventure Books*. After working as an associate editor for *Galaxy, Thrilling Wonder Stories* and *Startling Stories*, he sold a number of screenplays to Hollywood, including *It! The Terror from Beyond Space, The Lost Missile* and *Curse of the Faceless Man*. His story "It's a Good Life" was adapted for TV's *Twilight Zone* and again for the 1983 movie, he wrote the original story for what later became *Fantastic Voyage*, and his *Star Trek* scripts include "Mirror Mirror" and "Day of the Dove". Some of his best fiction is collected in *Space by the Table* and *The Devil's Scrapbook*.

Prolific children's author **Mabel Esther Allan** died on May 14th, aged 83. Among her 180 books were the short ghost novel, *A Chill in the Lane, The Haunted Valley and Other Poems* and *A Strange Enchantment*.

British author and actor **Ivan Butler**, the last surviving cast member of the first commercial London stage production of *Dracula*, died on May 17th, aged 89. In 1929, Butler played Lord Godalming and then understudied the part of Dracula in Hamilton Deane's dramatization of Bram Stoker's novel. He went on to play every male part in the play, including the Count, and produced *Dracula* on the stage many times. In the early 1950s he had several plays presented on television by the BBC and in later years he was the author of such books as *The Horror Film, The Cinema of Roman Polanski* and *Cinema in Britain*.

Alan D. Williams, who edited half a dozen novels and the collection *Different Seasons* by Stephen King while at Viking Penguin, died of cancer the same day. He was 72.

Novelist, playwright and screenwriter **Wolf Mankowitz** died in County Cork, Ireland, on May 20th from cancer, aged 73. His screenplays include Hammer's *The Two Faces of Dr Jekyll* (aka *House of Fright*), *The Day the Earth Caught Fire* and *Casino Royale*. Among his books are the fantasies *A Kid for Two Farthings* and *A Night With Casanova*, the vampire novel *The Devil in Texas* (illustrated by Ralph Steadman), plus the biography *The Extraordinary Mr Poe*.

British novelist and playwright **Robert Muller** died on May 27th, aged 72. In 1977 he created and scripted seven of the eight episodes of the BBC TV series *Supernatural*, two of which starred his wife Billie Whitelaw. A tie-in paperback was published by Fontana.

Mary Elizabeth Grenander, a leading authority on Ambrose Bierce, died in her sleep on May 28th, aged 79. She edited and wrote the introduction for the 1995 book *Poems of Ambrose Bierce*.

Book editor **William Abrahams**, who worked for Atlantic Monthly Press and later for Holt, Reinhart and Winston and Dutton, died on June 2nd, aged 79. His authors included Pauline Kael and Joyce Carol Oates, and he presided over the annual O. Henry short story awards for more than three decades.

New York bookseller and publisher **Jack Biblo** died on June 5th, aged 92. With his business partner Jack Tannen he started Canaveral Press in the 1960s. Under the editorship of Richard A. Lupoff, Canaveral reprinted a number of Edgar Rice Burroughs books which had gone into public domain, eventually becoming the sole authorized hardcover publisher of Burroughs, along with titles by Lupoff, L. Sprague de Camp and E.E. Smith.

French novelist **Thomas Narcejac** died in Paris on June 9th, aged 89. He collaborated with Pierre Boileau on more than forty thrillers, including *Les Louves*, *Les Yeux Sans Visage* and *Body Parts*, which were all filmed.

Bestselling thriller writer (Ralph) **Hammond Innes** died June 10th, aged 84. He first novel, *The Doppelgänger* (1936), was an occult thriller, and his ghost story "South Sea Bubble" (from the Christmas 1973 *Punch*) has been anthologized often. He left behind an unexpected collection of rare stamps worth up to £11,000 as part of his £6.8 million estate.

Romantic bestseller **Dame Catherine Cookson** (Catherine Ann McMullen) died on June 11th, aged 91. She made her writing début at the age of 44, producing an average of two books a year. Her children's fantasy *Mrs. Flannagan's Trumpet* was published in 1976. She was awarded an OBE in 1985, and made a Dame in 1993.

Ann Elizabeth Dobbs, the only grandchild of *Dracula* author Bram Stoker and the last surviving link with his wife Florence, died at her home on June 15th, aged 81. She reportedly found her grandfather's novel too scary to read!

Playwright, screenwriter and lyricist **Edward Eliscu** died on June 18th, aged 96. He wrote the words to "Flying Down to Rio" and was blacklisted in the 1950s for his outspoken political views.

Michael D. Weaver, whose novels include *Mercedes Night* and the Norse werewolf trilogy, *Wolf-Dreams* (1987), *Nightreaver* and *Bloodfang*, died on July 5th when he drowned in three feet of water. He was 36.

Writer, editor and fan **Robert A.W.** ("Doc") **Lowndes** died on July 14th of renal cancer. He was 81. A founder member of New York's Futurians SF club in 1938, he began writing his own stories in the 1940s, often in collaboration with other authors. His novels include *The Mystery of the Third Mine* (1953), *Believer's World* and *The Puzzle Planet*, and a collection of his columns appeared under the title *Three Faces of Science Fiction* in 1973. Although Lowndes was editor of the Avalon Books hardcover science fiction line from 1955–70 and compiled *The Best of James Blish* in 1979, he is best remembered as a magazine editor, beginning with *Future Fiction* and *Science Fiction Quarterly* (both 1941–43), followed by *Dynamic Science Fiction* (1952–54) and *Science Fiction Stories/The Original Science Fiction Stories* (1954–60). During the 1960s he worked for Health Knowledge Inc., editing a series of digest magazines that included *The Magazine of Horror* (1963–71), *Startling Mystery Stories* (1966–71), *Famous Science Fiction* (1966–69) and *Bizarre Fantasy Tales* (1970–71). It was during this period that he published the young Stephen King's first two professional tales in 1967 and 1969 issues of *Startling Mystery Stories*.

Children's illustrator **Lillian Hoban**, who began her career in the 1960s illustrating the *Frances* books written by her husband Russell Hoban, died of a heart attack on July 17th, aged 73.

Screenwriter **John Hopkins**, who co-wrote the Bond film *Thunderball* and scripted *Murder by Decree*, died on July 23rd, aged 67.

French author, translator and editor **Alain Doremieux** died in his sleep on July 26th, aged 64. A former editor of the French editions of *The Magazine of Fantasy & Science Fiction* (aka *Ficcion*) and *Galaxy*, between 1991–96 he edited nine volumes of the horror anthology series *Territoires de I'Inquietude*, and in 1993 he was responsible for Steve Rasnic Tem's only collection to date, *Ombres sur la Route*.

Science fiction cover artist **Paul Lehr** died on July 27th, aged 67, six weeks after being diagnosed with pancreatic cancer. He received the Merit Award from the Society of Illustrators in 1980 and served as a judge for the L. Ron Hubbard Illustrators of Future contest since its inception.

Author and bookseller **Noel Lloyd** died on August 3rd, aged 73. With his partner Geoffrey Palmer he collaborated on thirty books, including the juvenile ghost story collections *Ghosts Go Haunting*, *Ghost Stories Round the World* and *The Obstinate Ghost and Other Ghostly Tales*. They also wrote the biography *E.F. Benson as He Was* (1988) and published a number of limited edition booklets by the author.

American author and playwright **Sigmund Miller**, who scripted the radio show *Inner Sanctum* in the 1940s, died of complications from pneumonia on August 5th, aged 87. He was blacklisted during the McCarthy era and moved to London, where he wrote movie scripts under a pseudonym.

Scriptwriter and producer **Arthur Rowe** died after a lengthy illness on August 6th, aged 74. He wrote the 1976 horror film *The Devil's Men* (aka *Land of the Minotaur*) starring Donald Pleasence and Peter Cushing, and episodes of *The Man from U.N.C.L.E.*, *Fantasy Island*, *The Bionic Woman*, *The Six Million Dollar Man*, *Mission Impossible* and *Kolchak: The Night Stalker*.

Lyricist **Marshall Barer** died of cancer on August 25th, aged 75. Better known for his Broadway musicals, he also wrote the *Mighty Mouse* theme song, "Here I Come to Save the Day", in the back of a taxicab.

Scriptwriter and novelist **Catherine Turney** died on September 9th, aged 91. A contract writer for MGM and Warner Bros. she wrote several episodes of TV's *One Step Beyond* and adapted her 1952 novel *The Other One* for the screen as *Back from the Dead* (1957).

Scriptwriter **Sam Locke**, whose career included the radio show *Inner Sanctum*, died on September 18th, aged 81. He also wrote scripts for TV shows and beach movies, as well as sketches for comedians Red Buttons and Ed Wynn.

TV scriptwriter and composer **Jeffrey Moss**, who created the Cookie Monster, Oscar the Grouch and other characters for Jim Henson's *Sesame Street*, died of cancer on September 24th, aged 56.

Illustrator **Julian Allen**, who collaborated with Bruce Wagner on the comic-strip *Wild Palms*, which became a TV mini-series produced by Oliver Stone, died of non-Hodgkin's lymphoma on

September 28th, aged 55. In 1994 he was commissioned by the American Postal Service to create a series of stamps featuring blues singers.

A former newspaper reporter turned Edgar Award-winning TV scriptwriter, **Adrian Spies** died during open heart surgery on October 2nd, aged 78. He scripted the 1966 *Star Trek* episode "Miri", which was banned for many years in Britain.

Chinese painter and sculptor **Chang Chong-Jen**, who inspired Belgium artist Hergé (Georges Remi) to create the character of Chang in the *Tintin* books, died on October 8th at a retirement home outside Paris. He was 93.

British thriller writer **Eric Ambler** died on October 22nd, aged 89. His books include *The Mask of Dimitrios* and *Journey Into Fear* (both filmed). In 1953 he was nominated for an Academy Award for the screenplay adaptation of Nicholas Monserrat's novel *The Cruel Sea*, he was named a Grand Master by the Mystery Writers of America in 1975, and received the O.B.E. in 1981.

Walter Kendrick, professor of English at Fordham University and an authority on Victorian literature, died of pancreatic cancer on October 25th, aged 51. His books include the 1991 study *The Thrill of Fear: 250 Years of Scary Entertainment*.

Two weeks after receiving the Order of Merit from the Queen, Britain's Poet Laureate **Ted Hughes** (Edward James Hughes) died from cancer on October 28th, aged 68. His books include *Tales of the Early World* and *Ffangs the Vampire Bat and the Kiss of Truth*. He had been married to two poets – Sylvia Plath and Assia Wevill – both of whom committed suicide.

American screenwriter, novelist and playwright **James Goldman** died of a heart attack the same day, aged 71. His credits include *The Lion in Winter*, *They Might Be Giants*, Stephen Sondheim's *Follies* and *Robin and Marian*.

Comics artist **Bob Kane**, who created caped crimefighter Batman with Bill Finger when he was just 24 years old, died on November 3rd, aged 83. Inspired by Zorro, The Shadow and the 1930 movie *The Bat Whispers*, the character made his début in the May 1939 issue of *Detective Comics* No.27, and later became a billion-dollar industry that encompassed numerous films and television series. Although his name appeared on the strip until 1964, much of the work was done by other artists whom Kane called his "ghosts".

British author **Rumer Godden**, whose books include *Black Narcissus* and *The River* (both filmed), died in Scotland on November 8th, aged 91. She also published a number of children's books and collections of poetry.

Canadian novelist and teacher **Wayland Drew** died on December 3rd after a lengthy illness suffering from Lou Gehrig's Disease. He was 66. Drew's first novel was published in 1973, and although best known for the post-apocalyptic "Erthring Cycle", he was also the author of such movie novelizations as *Dragonslayer*, *Willow* and **Batteries Not Included*.

Novelist and playwright **Robert Marasco**, whose first book was the haunted house novel *Burnt Offerings* (filmed in 1976), died of lung cancer on December 5th, aged 62. His surprise Broadway hit *Child's Play* (it ran for 343 performances) was filmed in 1972 by Sidney Lumet.

American comics illustrator **George Wilson**, whose work appeared in *Turok Son of Stone*, *Space Family Robinson* and *The Phantom*, died on December 7th, aged 77.

British book cover and comic-strip illustrator **Ron Turner** died on December 19th, aged 76. During the 1950s and 60s he worked on such strips as *Rick Random – Space Detective*, *The Daleks* and *Star Trek*, and more recently produced a series of covers for Gryphon Books.

American comics artist **Joe Orlando**, whose credits include *Tales from the Crypt*, *House of Mystery*, *Swamp Thing*, *Little Orphan Annie* and *Mad* magazine, died on December 23rd, aged 71.

68-year-old French writer and comic-strip artist **Jean-Claude Forest**, who created sexy 41st-century spacewoman Barbarella in 1962, died on December 30th from a respiratory illness. He acted as design consultant on the 1967 movie in which Jane Fonda portrayed his seductive character. In 1984 he was awarded the Grand Prize at the annual Angoulême comic strip festival.

ACTORS/ACTRESSES

The voice of cartoon characters Betty Boop, Olive Oyl and Sweet Pea, **Mae Questel** died on January 4th, aged 89. She played opposite Bela Lugosi (dressed as Dracula) in the 1933 novelty short *Hollywood on Parade No.8*, appeared in Woody Allen's

New York Stories and *Zelig*, and revived her Betty Boop characterisation for *Who Framed Roger Rabbit*.

Cher's ex-husband and business partner, a former mayor of Palm Springs and Republican Congressman, **Sonny Bono** (Salvatore Bono) was killed in a freak skiing accident on January 5th. He was 62. After rising to fame as half of the singing duo Sonny and Cher in 1965 with the hit "I Got You Babe", he appeared as a cartoon character in a 1972 *Scooby-Doo* TV movie and turned into a tree in the 1985 horror film *Troll*.

Veteran stuntman and actor **Joe Yrigoyen** died on January 11th, aged 87. He appeared in numerous serials, including *Fighting Devil Dogs*, *Daredevils of the Red Circle*, *Drums of Fu Manchu*, *The Masked Marvel*, *Secret Service in Darkest Africa*, *Captain America*, *The Crimson Ghost* and *Canadian Mounties vs. Atomic Invaders*.

83-year-old character actor **Emil Sitka**, who was a favourite foil of The Three Stooges, died on January 16th following a stroke. He appeared in thirty-five Stooges shorts between 1938–58, often playing dignified butlers, plus *The Three Stooges in Orbit*, *The Three Stooges Meet Hercules*, *Watermelon Man*, *Intruder* and TV's *My Favorite Martian*.

British actor **James Villiers** died on January 18th, aged 64. For Hammer he appeared in *The Damned* (aka *These Are the Damned*), *The Nanny* and *Blood from the Mummy's Tomb* (as the scheming Corbeck). His other film credits include *Repulsion*, *The Ruling Class*, *The Amazing Mr Blunden*, *Asylum*, *Spectre* and the Bond movie *For Your Eyes Only*.

American actor **Jack Lord** (John Joseph Ryan), who played Detective Steve McGarrett on TV's longest-running cop show, *Hawaii Five-O* (1968–79), died of congestive heart failure on January 21st, aged 77. His film roles include *Dr. No* and *The Name of the Game is Kill*, and he guested on such series as *One Step Beyond*, *The Invaders* and *The Man from U.N.C.L.E.*

German-born character actor **Ferdinand** (Ferdy) **Mayne** (Ferdinand Mayer-Boerckel) died in London of complications from Parkinson's Disease on January 30th, aged 81. He was a spoof vampire in *Dance of the Vampires* (aka *The Fearless Vampire Killers*) and Dracula in *The Vampire Happening*. His other films include *All Hallowe'en*, Hammer's *The Vampire Lovers*, *The Horror Star*, *Hawk the Slayer*, *Conan the Destroyer*, *Howling II*

Stirba – Werewolf Bitch, *My Lovely Monster* and *Warlock The Armageddon*. On TV he guest-starred in *The Avengers*, *The New Avengers*, *Monsters* and the 1986 Czechoslovakian/West German series *Frankenstein's Auntie*.

Character actor **Philip Abbott**, whose film credits include *The Invisible Boy*, *Hangar 18* and *The First Power*, died of cancer on February 22nd, aged 73. He played assistant director Arthur Ward on the ABC-TV series *The F.B.I.* (1965–74).

"The King of the One-Liners", comedian **Henny Youngman** died of pneumonia on February 24th, aged 92. The man who coined the phrase "Take my wife . . . please!" appeared in Herschell Gordon Lewis' *The Gore Gore Girls*, *History of the World Part 1* and *Amazon Women on the Moon*.

Hard-working supporting actor **J.T. Walsh** died of a heart attack while on vacation on February 27th, aged 54. He appeared in adaptations of Stephen King's *Misery* and *Needful Things*, *The Last Seduction*, *Miracle on 34th Street* (1994), *Outbreak*, *Breakdown* and *Pleasantville*, and starred as Colonel Frank Back in the 1996–97 TV series *Dark Skies*.

American actor **Donald Woods** died on March 5th, aged 88. He starred in William Castle's *13 Ghosts* and also appeared in *The Lost Volcano*, *The Beast from 20,000 Fathoms* and *Dimension 5*. On TV his credits include *Lights Out*, *Inner Sanctum*, *Men Into Space*, *Thriller* and *The Wild Wild West*.

Hollywood leading man **Lloyd** (Vernet) **Bridges**, the father of actors Jeff and Beau, died of complications from a heart condition at his home in Los Angeles on May 10th, aged 85. His many credits include *The Crime Doctor's Strangest Case*, *Here Comes Mr Jordan*, *Strange Confession* and *High Noon* (both with Lon Chaney, Jr.), *Rocketship X-M*, *The Deadly Dream*, *Haunts of the Very Rich*, *Airplane* and *Airplane II*, *Honey, I Blew up the Kid* and numerous TV shows, including the series *Sea Hunt* (1958–61). In the early 1950s he admitted to being a former member of the Communist Party and was a key witness before the House of Representatives Un-American Activities Committee.

American leading lady **Helen Westcott** died of cancer on March 17th, aged 70. She starred in *Abbott and Costello Meet Dr. Jekyll and Mr Hyde* (with Boris Karloff), *Whirlpool*, *Invisible Avenger* and *Monster on the Campus*.

American actress **Ramsay Ames**, who portrayed the reincarnated love of Lon Chaney, Jr's Kharis in *The Mummy's Ghost* (1944), died of lung cancer on March 21st, aged 78. She also co-starred with Chaney in *Calling Dr. Death* the previous year.

British actor **Daniel Massey**, the son of Raymond Massey and brother of Anna, died on March 25th of Hodgkin's Disease after a long illness. He was 64, and his credits include *Sabu and the Magic Ring*, *Fragment of Fear*, *Vault of Horror*, *Warlords of Atlantis*, *The Cat and the Canary* (1977) and the TV series *Sherlock Holmes* and *The Casebook of Sherlock Holmes*.

American character actor **Gene Evans** died of complications from heart disease on April 1st, aged 75. He starred in *Donovan's Brain*, *Behemoth the Sea Monster* (aka *The Giant Behemoth*), *Shock Corridor*, *A Knife for the Ladies*, *Devil Times Five* (aka *Peopletoys*) and was a regular on TV's *Matt Helm* (1975–76).

Country singer **Tammy Wynette** (Virginia Wynette Pugh) died from a blood clot in the lung on April 6th, aged 55. She had ten consecutive No. 1 hits in America (out of a total of twenty), the best-known being "Stand by Your Man". A year after her death, her body was exhumed and an autopsy performed at the request of her fifth husband, George Richey, after three of the singer's daughters filed a $50 million lawsuit for wrongful death, claiming she died because he did not seek medical attention for her.

Punk singer with The Plasmatics, **Wendy O. Williams** committed suicide the same day. She was 48, and appeared in the cult 1986 movie *Reform School Girls*.

Actor **Liam Sullivan**, who portrayed the villainous Sir Branton in the 1961 fantasy *The Magic Sword*, died of a heart attack on April 19th, aged 74. He also played a telepathic alien in the 1968 *Star Trek* episode "Plato's Stepchildren".

Variety performer **Peter Lind Hayes** died in a Las Vegas hospice on April 21st, aged 82. With his wife Mary Healy he starred in *The 5,000 Fingers of Dr. T* in 1953.

American actor **Frederic Downs**, whose credits include *Terror from the Year 5000*, died on April 24th, aged 81. For ten years he appeared on the sit-com *Days of Our Lives*.

Character actress **Maidie Norman**, who portrayed the maid in *What Ever Happened to Baby Jane?*, died of lung cancer on May 2nd, aged 85. Her other credits include *Airport '77* and TV's *Kung Fu*.

Child stage star and leading man of the 1930s **Gene Raymond**

(Raymond Guion) died from pneumonia in a Hollywood hospital on May 3rd, aged 89. His films include *Zoo in Budapest*, *7 Keys to Baldpate* and *Five Bloody Graves*. He was married to Jeanette MacDonald.

American leading lady and a former singer with Rudy Vallee's band, **Alice Faye** (Ann Leppert) died on May 9th, aged 83. She appeared in such films as *Sing Baby Sing*, *In Old Chicago*, *Hello Frisco Hello*, *Hollywood Cavalcade* and *Alexander's Ragtime Band*, before retiring from the screen in the mid-1940s. She remained active in radio with her husband, band leader Phil Harris, and returned to movies in 1976 with *Won Ton Ton, the Dog Who Saved Hollywood*.

"Ol' Blue Eyes", "The Chairman of the Board" and the leader of the "Rat Pack", singer and actor **Frank Sinatra** died of a heart attack on May 14th, aged 82. A former band singer and teenage heart-throb, he received twenty-five gold albums and appeared in such films as *The Manchurian Candidate*, *Suddenly*, *Around the World in Eighty Days*, *Road to Hong Kong* and *The First Deadly Sin*, winning the Academy Award for Best Supporting Actor for his role as Maggio in *From Here to Eternity*. His long-time friend Joey Bishop subsequently revealed that Sinatra paid for the funeral of Bela Lugosi, who died broke.

Veteran American character actor **Douglas V. Fowley** died on May 21st, aged 86. His numerous film appearances include *The Thin Man*, *Charlie Chan on Broadway*, *Docks of New Orleans*, *Night Life of the Gods*, *Charlie Chan at Treasure Island*, *Scared to Death* (with Bela Lugosi), *Mighty Joe Young*, *Tarzan's Peril*, *Singin' in the Rain*, *The Naked Jungle*, *Cat Women of the Moon*, *7 Faces of Dr. Lao*, *Homebodies* and *The White Buffalo*. In 1960 he produced and directed *Macumba Love* and regularly guested on such TV shows as *Topper*, *Kolchak: The Night Stalker*, *Kung Fu*, *Quark* and *Fantasy Island*.

49-year-old American comedy actor **Phil Hartman** was shot dead at his home on May 28th, apparently by his wife in a murder-suicide. Best known for his roles (1986–94) on TV's *Saturday Night Live*, *The Simpsons* (as the voice of Troy McClure and others) and the season-ender of *3rd Rock from the Sun*, he co-scripted *Pee-Wee's Big Adventure* and appeared in *Amazon Women on the Moon*, *Coneheads*, *So I Married an Ax Murderer*, *The Pagemaster* and *Small Soldiers*.

WWF wrestler **Sylvester Ritter** aka "Junkyard Dog" died on June 2nd, aged 44.

American leading lady **Josephine Hutchinson** died in a New York nursing home on June 4th, aged 94. She starred as Alice in a 1932 Broadway production of *Alice in Wonderland*, played Elsa von Frankenstein in the 1939 movie *Son of Frankenstein*, and appeared in an adaptation of Ray Bradbury's "I Sing the Body Electric" on TV's *The Twilight Zone*.

Character actress **Jeanette Nolan** died from a stroke on June 5th, aged 86. Over a seventy-year acting career she starred in such films as Orson Welles' *Macbeth* (1948), *My Blood Runs Cold*, *Chamber of Horrors*, *The Reluctant Astronaut*, *The Manitou* and *Cloak & Dagger* (with her husband John MacIntire), and appeared on TV in *Alfred Hitchcock Presents*, *Thriller*, *The Twilight Zone*, *The Man from U.N.C.L.E.*, *The Invaders*, *Night Gallery*, *The Sixth Sense*, *Fantasy Island*, *The Incredible Hulk* and *Goliath Awaits*.

Character actress **Theresa Merritt**, who played Aunt Em in the 1978 musical *The Wiz*, died after a long battle with skin cancer on June 12th, aged 75. Her other films include *Voodoo Dawn* and *The Serpent and the Rainbow*.

Mexican actor **Roberto Cañedo** died on June 16th. He appeared in numerous movies, including *Doctor of Doom*, *Santo contra el Estrangulador*, *Santo contra el Espectro de el Estrangulador*, *La Mujer Murcielago* and *Santo contra la Hija de Frankestein*.

Actor and singer **Felix Knight**, who appeared as Tom-Tom the Piper's Son in the 1934 Laurel and Hardy fantasy *Babes in Toyland*, died on June 18th, aged 89.

Irish-born American leading lady **Maureen O'Sullivan**, the mother of actress Mia Farrow, died from a heart attack on June 23rd, aged 87. Best remembered for her role as Jane opposite Johnny Weismuller's Tarzan in six films, she also appeared in *Just Imagine*, *A Connecticut Yankee* (1931), Tod Browning's *The Devil-Doll*, *Too Scared to Scream*, *Peggy Sue Got Married* and *Stranded*. She was married to director John Farrow.

Cowboy star **Roy Rogers** (Leonard Slye) died of congestive heart failure on July 6th, aged 86. A member of the singing Sons of the Pioneers in the 1930s, he appeared in more than one hundred movies and TV's *The Roy Rogers Show* (1951–56) with his horse Trigger (who died in 1966). A chain of fast-food restaurants was named after him in America.

Hugh Reilly, who played Timmy Martin's father Paul in the TV series *Lassie* (1958–64), died after a long battle with emphysema on July 17th. He was 82.

The same day saw the death from brain cancer of 64-year-old American character actor **Joseph Maher**, who played Warren Beatty's butler in *Heaven Can Wait*.

Hollywood leading man **Robert** (George) **Young** died on July 21st, aged 91. Although best known for his Emmy Award-winning TV shows *Life With Father* (1954–60) and *Marcus Welby, M.D.* (1969–76), he also appeared in *The Black Camel* (with Bela Lugosi), *The House of Rothschild* (with Boris Karloff), Tod Browning's *Miracles for Sale*, *The Canterville Ghost* (1943) and *The Enchanted Cottage*. Young battled alcoholism and depression throughout his life, and attempted suicide in 1991. In later years he advertised Sanka decaffeinated coffee on American TV.

British-born character actress **Binnie Barnes** (Gitelle Barnes), who went to Hollywood in the mid-1930s, died on July 27th, aged 95. Her films include *Murder at Covent Garden*, *The Three Musketeers* (1939) and *The Time of Their Lives*.

Buffalo Bob Smith (Robert E. Smith), the host and voice of the eponymous puppet star of the first TV programme specifically for children, *The Howdy Doody Show* (1947–60), died of lung cancer on July 30th, aged 80.

American TV actress **Sylvia Field Truex**, who portrayed Mrs. Wilson in the CBS series *Dennis the Menace* (1959–63), died on July 31st, aged 97.

Hungarian-born actress **Eva Bartok** (Eva Sjöke) died in a London hospital from heart failure after a long illness on August 1st, aged 72. Formerly married to actor Curt Jurgens, she starred in *The Crimson Pirate*, Hammer's *Spaceways*, *The Gamma People* and Mario Bava's *Blood and Black Lace*.

Twelve-time Emmy Award-winning children's TV presenter and ventriloquist **Shari Lewis**, who created the squeaky-voiced sock puppet Lamb Chop for the *Captain Kangaroo* show in 1957, died of uterine cancer and pneumonia on August 2nd, aged 65. A winner of a Peabody and the John F. Kennedy Center Award for Excellence and Creativity, at the time of her death she was producer and star of the PBS series *The Charlie Horse Music Pizza*.

The same day saw the death in a nursing home of 50-year-old **David-Allen "Chico" Ryan**, who sang and played bass with 1950s revival group Sha Na Na. He also appeared in the hit movie *Grease*.

44-year-old Canadian stuntman **Marc Akerstream** was killed on August 14th when a special effects explosion went wrong on the TV series *The Crow: Stairway to Heaven*. A piece of debris thrown into the air by the blast struck Akerstream on the head and he later died in hospital. The show is based on the 1994 movie *The Crow*, during the filming of which star Brandon Lee was killed in a freak firearms accident.

Stand-up comic and character actor **Phil Leeds** died on August 16th of pneumonia, aged 82. His film credits include *Rosemary's Baby* and *Ghost*, and he appeared in numerous TV sit-coms such as *Dream On*, *Ellen* and *Ally McBeal*.

49-year-old Indian actress **Persis Khambatta**, who starred as bald-headed navigator Lieutenant Ilia in *Star Trek the Motion Picture*, died of an apparent heart attack in a Bombay hospital on August 18th. However, some reports claimed that the 1965 Miss India had no history of heart trouble (despite having undergone a bypass operation in 1983) and that she had been murdered. Her other films include *The Man With the Power*, *Megaforce*, *Nighthawks*, *Warriors of the Lost World* and *First Strike*.

American actor **E. (Edda) G. (Gunnar) Marshall** died on August 24th after a short illness. He was 88, and his many film and TV appearances include *Vampire*, *Superman II*, *The Phoenix*, *Creepshow*, *Two Evil Eyes*, *The Tommyknockers*, *Under Siege*, *Lights Out* (with John Carradine), *Inner Sanctum*, *Studio One*: "Donovan's Brain", *Alfred Hitchcock Presents*, *Moment of Fear*, *Night Gallery* and *Tales from the Darkside*. He won two Emmys for his role as attorney Lawrence Preston in *The Defenders* (1961–65), and in 1988 the liberal actor formed the environmentalist Preservation Party to support anti-development candidates in New York.

Stage actor **Jerome Dempsey**, who won a Drama Desk Award for his performance as Van Helsing opposite Frank Langella in the 1977 Broadway production of *Dracula*, died of heart failure on August 26th, aged 69.

Russian-born character actor **Leonid Kinskey**, who played Sascha, the bartender of Rick's Café in *Casablanca*, died of a stroke on September 8th, aged 95. He also appeared in such TV shows as *The Man from U.N.C.L.E.* and the pilot of *Hogan's Heroes*.

American tough-guy actor of the 1940s and '50s **Dane Clark** (Bernard Zanville) died on September 11th, aged 85.

CNN correspondent **John Holliman**, who appeared as himself in the 1997 movie *Contact*, was killed in a car crash in Atlanta, Georgia, on September 12th. He was 49.

British character actress **Patricia Hayes** died on September 19th, aged 88. Her films include *The Neverending Story*, *The Terrornauts*, *Fragment of Fear* and *Willow*, and she appeared on TV in *Hammer House of Mystery and Suspense* and *The Tomorrow People*.

American TV actress **Mary Frann**, who portrayed Bob Newhart's wife in the CBS series *Newhart* (1982–90), died of a heart attack on September 23rd, aged 55.

British leading man **Marius Goring**, C.B.E. died of cancer on September 30th, aged 86. Best remembered for his roles in the Powell and Pressburger classics *A Matter of Life and Death* (aka *Stairway to Heaven*) and *The Red Shoes*, he also appeared in *The Case of the Frightened Lady* and starred in the BBC-TV series *The Expert* (1970–75). In 1929 he was a founding member of the actor's union Equity.

Singing cowboy **Gene Autry** died of lymphoma on October 2nd, three days after his 91st birthday. He made his movie début in 1934, and appeared in ninety-five movies, usually with his horse Champion, including the SF serial *The Phantom Empire*, *Mystery Mountain* and *Gold Town Ghost Riders*. He also recorded 635 songs, most notably "Back in the Saddle Again" and "Rudolph the Red-Nosed Reindeer' and co-wrote 'Here Comes Santa Claus". A clever businessman, he produced his own TV show (1950–56) and others, eventually creating a half-billion-dollar investment portfolio which included oil wells, hotels, television stations and the Anaheim Angels baseball team. He opened the Gene Autry Western Heritage Museum in Los Angeles' Griffith Park in 1988.

Lon Clark, who portrayed *Nick Carter, Master Detective* on radio from 1943–55, died the same day, aged 86.

70-year-old British-born actor and photographer **Roddy McDowall** died of cancer in his Los Angeles home on October 3rd, only two weeks after word of his terminal illness became public. A former child star, he moved to Hollywood in 1940 where his later roles tended towards the bizarre or psychotic. Best remembered as the star of the *Planet of the Apes* film and TV series (playing various intelligent simians), he also portrayed ham horror host Peter Vincent in *Fright Night* and *Fright Night Part 2*. His many other credits include *Macbeth* (1948), *Midnight Lace* (1960), *Shock Treatment* (1964), *The Loved One, It!*, the *Night Gallery* pilot, *Tam Lin* (which he also directed), *Laserblast, A Taste of Evil, The Legend of Hell House, Arnold, The Cat from Outer Space, Embryo, The Silent Flute* (aka *Circle of Iron*), *Charlie Chan and the Curse of the Dragon Queen, The Thief of Baghdad* (1978), *The Black Hole, The Martian Chronicles, Class of 1984, Dead of Winter, Doin' Time on Planet Earth, Mirror Mirror 2: Raven Dance, Cutting Class, Heads, The Alien Within* and *A Bug's Life*. He co-starred with Boris Karloff in TV's *Playhouse 90*: "Heart of Darkness" (1958), portrayed the untrustworthy Jonathan Willoway on *Fantastic Journey*, played the villainous Bookworm on *Batman*, was the voice of The Mad Hatter on *Batman: The Animated Series*, and guested on such shows as *The Twilight Zone, Alfred Hitchcock Hour, The Invaders, Journey to the Unknown, The Snoop Sisters, Nightmare Classics*: "Carmilla" and *Fantasy Island* (as the Devil).

Another original singing cowboy star, **Robert "Tex" Allen**, died on October 9th, aged 92. In Hollywood since the 1930s, his films include *Crime and Punishment* (with Peter Lorre) and *The Phantom Stallion*, and he had his own TV series, *Frontier Doctor*, in 1952.

Radio and TV announcer **Tony Marvin**, who was the official "voice" of the 1939 New York World's Fair, died in Florida on October 10th, aged 86. He was also the original voice of Tony the Tiger in the Kellogg's cereal commercials.

American leading man **Richard Denning** (Louis A. Denninger) died of cardiac arrest after a long battle with emphysema on October 11th, aged 85. His films include *The Creature from the Black Lagoon, Her Jungle Love, Unknown Island, Target Earth!, The Creature With the Atom Brain*, Roger Corman's *The Day the World Ended* and *The Black Scorpion*. He co-starred with

Vincent Price in *Twice Told Tales* and played Governor Philip Grey on TV's *Hawaii Five-O* (1968–79). He was married to actress Evelyn Ankers, who died in 1985.

Silent screen star **Molly O'Day**, who began her career in *Our Gang* films and worked with Laurel and Hardy, died on October 15th, aged 88.

British character actress **Joan Hickson**, best remembered for her portrayal of Agatha Christie's *Miss Marple* on TV (1984–91), died on October 17th, aged 92. She appeared with Basil Rathbone in *Love from a Stranger* and Vincent Price in *Theatre of Blood*. Her other credits include *Don't Take It to Heart*, *Seven Days to Noon*, *Mad About Men*, *No Haunt for a Gentleman*, *One of Our Dinosaurs is Missing* and the 1969 TV production of *Mystery and Imagination*: "Dracula".

Former ballet dancer and actor **Christopher Gable** died of cancer on October 23rd, aged 58. He appeared in *The Boy Friend*, *The Slipper and the Rose*, *The Lair of the White Worm* and *The Rainbow*. He was also artistic director of the Northern Ballet Theatre, whose 1999 London production of *Dracula* was dedicated to his memory.

British leading lady **Rosamund John**, whose films include *The Secret of the Loch* and *Green for Danger*, died on October 27th, aged 85.

Bob Trow, who for thirty years appeared as the gibberish-talking Robert Troll, Bob Dog and occasionally as himself on the children's TV show *Mister Rogers' Neighborhood*, died of a heart attack on November 2nd, aged 72.

American actress **Martha O'Driscoll**, who starred in *House of Dracula*, *Crazy House* and *The Ghost Catchers* for Universal, died on November 3rd, aged 76. For the last fifty years of her life, she was married to wealthy Chicago businessman Arthur Appleton after promising to give up show business for ever.

Japanese actress **Momoko Kochi**, who starred in the 1954 *Godzilla King of the Monsters*, died of intestinal cancer on November 5th, aged 66. Her other films include *Half Human*, *The Mysterians* and the 1995 *Godzilla vs. Destroyer*.

After a long illness, French leading man **Jean Marais** (Jean Marais-Villain) died in Cannes of pulmonary disease on November 8th, aged 84. A protégé of surrealist artist Jean Cocteau, he is best remembered for his role in Cocteau's *La Belle et la Bête* and

as the super-criminal *Fantomas* in three 1960s movies. He also
appeared in *L'Eternel Retour*, *Orphée*, *Le Testament d'Orphée*,
Donkey Skin and *Amour de Poche*.

British actress **Mary Millar** died of cancer on November 10th,
aged 62. She appeared in the London stage musical of *The
Phantom of the Opera* as the original Madame Giry, but is
probably best known as Rose in the BBC-TV sit-com *Keeping
Up Appearances*.

British actress **Valerie Hobson** died of a heart attack in London
on November 13th, aged 81. She appeared in *Bride of Frankenstein*, *WereWolf of London*, *The Great Impersonation*, *The
Mystery of Edwin Drood*, *Q Planes*, *Great Expectations*
(1946), *Kind Hearts and Coronets* and *The Rocking Horse
Winner* before retiring as an actress. She married her second
husband, Conservative MP John Profumo, in 1954. In 1963 he
was forced to resign in disgrace as Secretary of State for War over
an affair with call girl Christine Keeler, who was also involved
with a Soviet military attaché.

American character actor **Dick O'Neill** died of heart failure on
November 17th, aged 70. He appeared in added American
footage for the Japanese film *Gammera* and was decapitated
in *Wolfen*. Other credits include *Pretty Poison*, *The UFO Incident*, *It Happened One Christmas* and *Chiller*.

TV comedian **Flip Wilson** (Clerow Wilson) died of liver cancer
on November 25th, aged 64. He had his own Emmy Award-
winning variety show on NBC-TV in the early 1970s and often
guest-hosted *The Tonight Show*. In 1976 he appeared in a TV
movie of *Pinocchio*.

Silent film actress **Ruth Clifford** died on November 30th, aged
98. She starred in the SF film *The Invisible Ray* (1920) and later
became a character actress in such films as *Dante's Inferno*, *The
Searchers* and *Sunset Blvd*.

British actor **Michael Craze** died on December 7th, aged 56. He
played Ben Jackson on TV's *Doctor Who* (1966–67), and also
appeared in such films as *Neither the Sea Nor the Sand*, *Satan's
Slave* and *Terror*.

American character actor **Norman Fell**, best known for his role
as irritable landlord Stanley Roper in the 1970s TV sit-coms
Three's Company and *The Ropers*, died of multiple myeloma on
December 14th, aged 74. His other credits include the movies

C.H.U.D. II Bud the Chud, *The Boneyard*, *Hexed*, *Transylvania 6–5000*, *Stripped to Kill* and such TV shows as *Alfred Hitchcock Hour*, *The Wild Wild West*, *The Man from U.N.C.L.E.*, *The Invaders*, *The Bionic Woman* and *Bewitched*.

Hollywood leading lady **Irene Hervey** (Irene Herwick) died of heart failure on December 20th, aged 89. She appeared in *House of Fear* (1939), *Night Monster* (with Bela Lugosi and Lionel Atwill), *Gang Busters*, *Mr Peabody and the Mermaid*, *Play Misty for Me*, *Goliath Awaits* and the 1965 TV series *Honey West*.

Canadian-born leading man **David Manners** (Rauff de Ryther Duan Acklom), who was a cousin to Arthur Conan Doyle and claimed to be descended from William the Conqueror, died in a Santa Barbara nursing home on December 23rd. He was 98. In the 1930s he portrayed the hero in *Dracula*, *The Mummy*, *The Death Kiss*, *The Black Cat*, *The Moonstone* and *Mystery of Edwin Drood* before retiring from the screen. He successfully invested in property and also wrote several novels and two works of philosophy.

American actor (William Rukard) **Hurd Hatfield** died in Monktown, Ireland, on December 25th, aged 80. Best known for his starring role in the 1945 movie *The Picture of Dorian Gray*, he also portrayed Dracula on stage in America and appeared in *Tarzan and the Slave Girl*, *Mickey One*, *The Boston Strangler*, *The Norliss Tapes*, *The House and the Brain* and such TV series as *Lights Out*, *Suspense*, *Alfred Hitchcock Presents*, *Voyage to the Bottom of the Sea*, *The Wild Wild West*, *Search*, *Blacke's Magic* and *Knight Rider*.

FILM/TV TECHNICIANS

Italian director **Carlo Ludovico Bragaglia,** whose films include *The Loves of Hercules* (with Jayne Mansfield and Mickey Hargitay), died on January 4th following an operation for a broken hip. He was 103.

Production executive **Gary Nardino** died of a stroke on January 22nd, aged 62. His credits include *Star Trek II The Wrath of Khan* and *Star Trek III The Search for Spock*, plus such TV shows as *Mork & Mindy* and *Bill & Ted's Excellent Adventures*.

British producer, scriptwriter and former editor **Sidney Cole** died on January 25th, aged 89. He edited the 1940 *Gaslight*, was supervising editor for Ealing Studios' ghost story *Halfway House*, associate produced their horror classic *Dead of Night* and *The Man in the White Suit*, and scripted the fantasy *The Angel Who Pawned Her Harp*.

Production designer **Jack T. Collis**, who worked on *Voodoo Island*, *Frankenstein 1970* and *Macabre* during the late 1950s, died on February 1st, aged 75. His other credits include *Splash*, *Cocoon*, *The Running Man* and *Star Trek IV The Voyage Home*.

Script supervisor **Peggy Robertson** died on February 6th, aged 81. For many years she was Alfred Hitchcock's personal assistant and worked with the director on *Vertigo*, *Psycho* and *The Birds*, amongst other films, as well as the TV series *Alfred Hitchcock Presents*.

Cinematographer **Richard C. Glouner**, whose credits include the H.P. Lovecraft movie *The Dunwich Horror* and TV series *Logan's Run* and *V*, died on February 9th, aged 66.

Leonard Ho, co-founder of Hong Kong studios Golden Harvest, died of a heart attack on February 16th.

TV director **John Nicolella**, who made his movie début with *Kull the Conqueror* in 1997, died on February 21st, aged 52.

British film distributor **Michael Myers** died on February 22nd, aged 69. Because of his successful distribution of John Carpenter's previous film, *Assault on Precinct 13*, the director named the killer in *Halloween* after Myers as a mark of gratitude.

James Nelson Algar, who began his career as an animator on Disney's *Snow White and the Seven Dwarfs* (1937), died on February 26th, aged 85. He also directed the classic "The Sorcerer's Apprentice" sequence for *Fantasia*, and numerous episodes of *Disney True Life Adventures*.

Hollywood casting director **Leonard Murphy**, who cast the Munchkins in *The Wizard of Oz* (1939), died on March 4th, aged 87.

Hollywood make-up artist and hairstylist **George Masters** died of heart failure in Las Vegas on March 6th, aged 62. Over the years he worked with Marilyn Monroe (as her personal make-up artist), Ann-Margret, Lauren Bacall, Bo Derek, Marlene Dietrich and Sophia Loren, and turned Dustin Hoffman into *Tootsie*.

Marvin A. Davis, who died on March 8th, aged 87, joined Walt Disney Imagineering in 1953 and helped create almost every aspect of Disneyland. He won an Emmy for his art direction on TV's *Walt Disney's Wonderful World of Color*.

Academy Award-winning cinematographer **Charles** (Bryant) **Lang** died of pneumonia on April 3rd, aged 96. A self-described "women's photographer", his many credits include the 1934 *Death Takes a Holiday*, *Peter Ibbetson*, *Midnight*, *The Cat and the Canary* (1939), *The Ghost Breakers*, *The Uninvited*, *The Ghost and Mrs. Muir*, *Some Like it Hot* and *Wait Until Dark*. He received the American Society of Cinematographers' Lifetime Achievement Award in 1991.

French producer **Anatole Dauman** died of an apparent heart attack on April 8th in Paris, aged 73. Credited with discovering and developing several of the French "New Wave" directors of the 1950s and '60s, his films include *Last Year at Marienbad*, *La Jetée*, *In the Realm of the Senses*, *The Tin Drum*, *Wings of Desire*, *Immoral Tales* and *The Beast*.

Film editor **Louis "Duke" Goldstone**, who edited George Pal's *Destination Moon*, died of heart failure on April 16th, aged 84. He later became a TV director.

Producer and scriptwriter **Marvin Worth** died from complications from a bronchiovalvular carcinoma on April 22nd, aged 72. He scripted episodes of *Get Smart* and produced *Lenny*, Spike Lee's *Malcolm X* and the remake of *Diabolique*.

Producer **Jack Cummings** died the same day of cancer, aged 49. After starting out as an assistant director on *The Howling* and *Time Walker*, he produced *Highlander II The Quickening*, *The Addams Family* and Stephen King's *Needful Things*.

Producer, director and writer **Leslie Stevens** died of a heart attack following complications during emergency angioplasty on April 24th, aged 74. Best remembered as the producer of the classic 1960s SF series *The Outer Limits*, he also produced such popular TV shows as *Search*, *The Invisible Man*, *Gemini Man*, *Battlestar Galactica* and *Buck Rogers in the 25th Century*. In 1965 he scripted and directed the Esperanto movie *Incubus* starring William Shatner. He married actress Kate Manx in 1958, but she committed suicide when the marriage ended.

Film editor and director **Gene Fowler, Jr.** died on May 11th, aged 80. The director of such cult classics as *I Was a Teenage Werewolf* and *I Married a Monster from Outer Space*, he won an

Academy Award for the documentary *Seeds of Destiny*, which he made while he was an Army lieutenant in World War II, and was nominated for another Oscar for editing *It's a Mad, Mad, Mad World*.

71-year-old former actor, photographer, producer and director **John Derek** (Derek Harris) suffered a heart attack on May 20th and died two days later in hospital after lengthy surgery to unblock his clogged arteries. As an actor he appeared in *Rogues of Sherwood Forest*, *Mask of the Avenger*, *The Ten Commandments* (1956) and other films, before turning to directing with such movies as *Tarzan the Ape Man*, *Bolero* and *Ghosts Can't Do It*. Best remembered for marrying such beautiful actresses as French star Pati Behrs, Ursula Andress and Linda Evans, his death ended a twenty-two year-long Svengali-like relationship with his fourth wife, Bo.

British film and TV composer **Edwin Astley** died on May 19th, aged 76. His movie scores include *Devil Girl from Mars*, *The Woman Eater*, *Behemoth the Sea Monster* (aka *The Giant Behemoth*) and Hammer's *The Phantom of the Opera*, along with composing music for such TV series as *The Saint*, *Danger Man* (aka *Secret Agent*) and *Randall and Hopkirk (Deceased)* (aka *My Partner the Ghost*).

Veteran special effects cinematographer **Linwood G. Dunn** died of cancer on May 20th, aged 94. At RKO Radio since the late 1920s, he worked on *Bringing Up Baby*, *King Kong*, *Citizen Kane*, *She*, *Cat People*, *Mighty Joe Young*, *The Thing from Another World* and *The Devil's Rain*. In 1967 he was nominated for an Emmy Award for his work on the original *Star Trek* TV series, and in 1985 the Academy of Motion Picture Arts and Sciences presented him with its Gordon E. Sawyer Award for career contributions.

Spanish film director **Ricardo Franco**, the nephew of Jesús Franco, died of heart failure the same day. He was 48.

TV director **Robert Gist** died on May 21st, aged 74. He began his career as a child actor in *Miracle on 34th Street* (1947) and turned to directing in the early 1960s. Amongst his credits are the "Lizard's Leg and Owlet's Wing" episode of *Route 66* starring Boris Karloff, Peter Lorre and Lon Chaney, Jr., and the "Galileo Seven" episode of *Star Trek*.

Walt Disney layout artist and art director **Kendall O'Connor** died on May 27th, aged 90. He worked on *Snow White and the Seven Dwarfs*, *Fantasia*, *Cinderella*, *Alice in Wonderland*, *Peter Pan* and such TV specials as *Man in Space*, *Man and the Moon* and *Mars and Beyond*.

Make-up effects designer and actor **Mark Williams** died of respiratory failure the same day, aged 38. He worked on *The Brain*, *Blue Monkey*, *Aliens*, *The Fly*, *The Abyss*, *Return to Salem's Lot*, *Terminator 2 Judgment Day*, *Skeletons*, *Curse of the Puppet Master*, *Frankenstein Reborn*, *The Borrowers* (1997) and *Talisman* (which he also scripted). Named head of Full Moon Pictures' special effects department shortly before his death, he was also the effects design co-ordinator for rock acts such as Alice Cooper and Poison, and he published the comic books *Sisters of Mercy* and *Nightshade*.

Storyboard artist **Sherman Labby**, whose credits include *Blade Runner*, died on May 30th. He was 68.

Former chief executive of cartoon studio UPA, **Henry G. Saperstein** died of cancer on June 24th, aged 80. He was executive producer and US distributor of a number of Japanese SF films, including *Frankenstein Conquers the World*, *Monster Zero*, *War of the Gargantuas* and *Terror of Mechagodzilla*. His other credits include *Gay Purr-ee*, *What's Up, Tiger Lily?* and *Mr Magoo* (1997), and he was a consultant on the 1998 *Godzilla*.

Film editor **Thomas F. Boutross**, who co-directed *The Hideous Sun Demon* (aka *Blood on His Lips*) under the name "Thomas Cassarino", died of heart failure on June 26th, aged 69. He also edited *The Legend of Boggy Creek* and *The Town That Dreaded Sundown*.

Sheldon Tromberg, who founded the distribution company Boxoffice Attractions and produced the horror thriller *The Redeemer* in the 1970s, died of a heart attack on July 5th, aged 67.

Argentine producer and director **Alejandro Sessa**, who made a number of films with Roger Corman in the 1980s, died of heart failure on July 11th, aged 60.

Choreographer **Jerome Robbins** (Jerome Rabinowitz), who received an Emmy for making Mary Martin fly in the 1955 TV adaptation of *Peter Pan*, died of a stroke on July 29th, aged 79. He won five Tony Awards as a Broadway choreographer and director for such shows as *On the Town*, *The King and I* and

Fiddler on the Roof, and two Academy Awards for the movie *West Side Story* (which he co-directed).

Shanghai-born **Edmund Goldman**, who moved to Los Angeles and created independent film distribution company Manson International, died on August 5th, aged 92.

Also a reporter and critic for *Variety*, film publicist **Mike Kaplan** died of a heart attack on August 23rd, aged 80. Among the movies he worked on were *The Andromeda Strain*, *Jaws* and *The Sting*.

TV animation producer **Lee Gunther**, whose credits include *Transformers*, *G.I. Joe* and *The Pink Panther Show*, died of a stroke on August 25th, aged 63.

Michael Samuelson, the father of actress Emma Samms, died from a blood clot in the lung on August 27th, aged 67. Along with his brothers David and Tony, he built the family business into one of the world's biggest film equipment service companies.

Former actor turned Emmy Award-winning TV director **Leo Penn** died of lung cancer on September 5th, aged 77. The father of actors Sean and Chris, he was blacklisted in the late 1940s and '50s for his association with actors' trade unions and reinvented himself as a director for the 1959 series *Ben Casey*. He directed more than 400 hours of prime-time TV, including episodes of *The Bionic Woman*, *Columbo*, *Alfred Hitchcock Hour*, *Star Trek*, *Lost in Space*, *Voyage to the Bottom of the Sea*, *I Spy*, *The Girl from U.N.C.L.E.*, *Ghost Story*, *Switch* and the TV movie *The Dark Secret of Harvest Home*.

Japanese director **Akira Kurosawa** died of a stroke at his home in Tokyo on September 6th, aged 88. The winner of two Academy Awards for Best Foreign Language Film, his many distinguished movies include *Rashomon*, *Seven Samurai*, *Throne of Blood*, *The Hidden Fortress* (which significantly influenced George Lucas's *Star Wars*), *Yojimbo*, *Sanjuro*, *The Shadow Warrior*, *Ran* and *Dreams*. He worked closely with original *Godzilla* director Ishiro Honda on his later films.

Emmy Award-winning special visual effects director **Mark Zarate** died of complications following appendicitis surgery on September 18th, aged 39. His credits include ABC-TV's *Lois & Clark: The New Adventures of Superman*.

French film composer **Paul Misraki** died in Paris on October 29th, aged 90. He composed more than 100 scores for movies, including Jess Franco's *Attack of the Robots* and Jean-Luc Godard's *Alphaville*.

Actor, director and biographer **Peter Cotes**, who directed the first stage production of Agatha Christie's *The Mousetrap*, died November 10th.

70-year-old American producer and director **Alan J. Pakula** was killed in a freak car accident on November 19th when another vehicle sent a seven-foot steel pipe crashing through his windscreen while he was driving back to his home in Long Island, New York. It struck him on the head and he lost control of his car, crashing into a barrier and suffering a fatal heart attack. His films include *Rollover*, *The Parallax View*, *Dream Lover*, *All the President's Men* and *Klute*.

Italian costume designer **Enrico Sabbatini** was killed in a car accident in Morocco on November 25th. He was 66, and the films he worked on included *The Tenth Victim*, *Ghosts Italian Style* and *Illustrious Corpses*.

Academy Award-winning British cinematographer **Freddie Young** died on December 1st, aged 96. Best known for his work with David Lean on such films as *Lawrence of Arabia* and *Doctor Zhivago*, he also photographed *Gorgo*, *You Only Live Twice*, *The Asphyx*, *The Blue Bird* (1976) and *Sword of the Valiant*.

Associate producer **David Leigh Macleod**, whose credits include Warren Beatty's *Reds* and *Ishtar*, was found dead of undisclosed causes in Montreal on December 6th, aged 54. He'd spent nearly a decade in Canada as a fugitive after being indicted by a New York court on a string of paedophilia charges.

Academy Award-winning British film composer **John Addison** died of a stroke on December 7th, aged 78. He scored such films as *Seven Days to Noon*, *The Seven-Per-Cent Solution*, *Strange Invaders* and the 1990 TV movie of *The Phantom of the Opera*, and composed the theme for TV's *Murder, She Wrote*.

Ukrainian-born **Lord Lew Grade** (Lewis Winogradsky) died in London from heart failure on December 13th, aged 91. Raised in the slums of the East End, he became Britain's biggest entertainment impresario. As the founder of the UK's first commercially financed TV company, Associated Television (ATV), he was responsible for such popular series as *Robin Hood*, *Thunderbirds*, *The Saint*, *The Muppets* and *Space: 1999*. Among the movies he produced are *The Exorcist*, *Capricorn One*, *The Boys* *from Brazil*, *Raise the Titanic*, *The Legend of the Lone Ranger* and *The Dark Crystal*. He was knighted in 1963, won the Queen's award for industry in 1967, and given a life peerage in 1976.

Italian director **Vittorio Cottafavi**, whose films include *Hercules and the Captive Women* and *Goliath and the Dragon*, died the same day, aged 84.

Former actor turned director **Don Taylor** died of heart failure on December 29th, aged 78. His directing credits include *Escape from the Planet of the Apes*, *The Island of Dr. Moreau* (1977), *The Final Countdown*, *Damien Omen II* and episodes of *Alfred Hitchcock Presents*, *Night Gallery* and *Beasts*. He was married to actress Hazel Court.

Japanese director **Keisuke Kinoshita**, who directed the 1949 supernatural film *Yotsuya Kaidan* and *The Ballad of Narayama*, died of a stroke on December 29th, aged 86.

USEFUL ADDRESSES

T HE FOLLOWING LISTING OF ORGANIZATIONS, publications, dealers and individuals is designed to present readers with further avenues to explore. Although I can personally recommend all those listed on the following pages, neither myself nor the publisher can take any responsibility for the services they offer. Please also note that all the information below is subject to change without notice.

ORGANIZATIONS

The British Fantasy Society (http://www.herebedragons.co.uk/bfs) began in 1971 and publishes the bi-monthly *Prism UK: The British Fantasy Newsletter*, produces other special booklets, and organizes the annual British FantasyCon and semi-regular meetings in London. Yearly membership is £20.00 (UK), £25.00 (Europe) and £30.00 (America and the rest of the world) made payable in sterling to "The British Fantasy Society" and sent to The BFS Secretary, c/o 2 Harwood Street, Stockport, SK4 1JJ, UK. E-mail: syrinx.2112@btinternet.com

The Ghost Story Society (http://www.ash-tree.bc.ca/gss.html) publishes the excellent *All Hallows* magazine three times a year. The annual subscription is $25.00 (USA), Cdn$32.00 (Canada) or £16.00/$27.50 (rest of the world airmail). Write to joint organizers Barbara and Christopher Roden at "The Ghost Story Society", PO Box 1360, Ashcroft, British Columbia, Canada VOK 1AO. E-mail: ashtree@ash-tree.bc.ca

Horror Writers Association (http://www.horror.org/) was formed in the 1980s and is open to anyone seeking Active, Affiliate or Associate membership. The HWA publishes a regular

Newsletter and organizes the annual Bram Stoker Awards ceremony. Standard membership is $55.00 (USA), £38.00/$65.00 (overseas); Corporate membership is $100.00 (USA), £74.00/$120.00 (overseas), and Family Membership is $75.00 (USA), £52.00/$85.00 (overseas). Send to "HWA", 8490 Zephyr Street, Arvada, CO 80005, USA.

World Fantasy Convention (http://www.farrsite.com/wfc/) is an annual convention held in a different (usually American) city each year.

MAGAZINES

Cinefantastique is a monthly SF/fantasy/horror movie magazine with a "Sense of Wonder". Cover price is $5.95/Cdn$9.50/£4.20 and a 12-issue subscription is $48.00 (USA) or $55.00 (Canada and overseas) to PO Box 270, Oak Park, IL 60303, USA.

Interzone is Britain's leading magazine of science fiction and fantasy. Single copies are available for £3.00 (UK) or £3.50/$6.00 (overseas) or a 12-issue subscription is £32.00 (UK), £38.00/$60.00 (USA) or £38.00 (overseas) to "Interzone", 217 Preston Drove, Brighton, BN1 6FL, UK.

Locus (http://www.Locusmag.com) is the monthly newspaper of the SF/fantasy/horror field. $4.95 a copy, a 12-issue subscription is $43.00 (USA), $48.00 (Canada), $70.00 (Europe), $80.00 (Australia, Asia and Africa) to "Locus Publications", PO Box 13305, Oakland, CA 94661, USA or "Locus Subscription", Fantast (Medway) Ltd, PO Box 23, Upwell Wisbech, Cambs PE14 9BU, UK.

Necrofile (http://www.necropress.com) is a quarterly review of horror fiction. $3.00 a copy, a 4-issue subscription is $12.00 (USA), $15.00 (Canada) or $17.50 (overseas) in US funds only to "Necronomicon Press", P.O. Box 1304, West Warwick, RI 02893, USA.

Science Fiction Chronicle (http://www.sfsite.com/sfc) is a bimonthly news and reviews magazine that covers the SF/fantasy/horror field. $3.50/Cdn$4.95 a copy, a one-year subscription is $25.00 (first class USA), $26.75/Cdn$50.30 (Canada), £19.00 (UK) and $A47.00 (Australia). Make cheques payable to "Science Fiction Chronicle" and send to Science Fiction Chronicle, PO Box

022730, Brooklyn, NY 11202–0056, USA or payable to "Algol Press" and send to Rob Hansen, 144 Plashet Grove, East Ham, London E6 1AB, UK.

SFX (http://www.sfx.co.uk) is a monthly multi-media magazine of science fiction, fantasy and horror. Single copies are £3.25 or a 12-issue subscription is £28.00 (UK), £44.00 (Europe), £62.00 (USA) or £64.00 (rest of the world) to "Future Publishing", SFX Subscriptions, FREEPOST (BS900), Somerton, Somerset TA11 6BR, UK, or overseas subscribers to "Future Publishing", SFX Subscriptions, Cary Court, Somerton, Somerset TA11 6TB, UK.

Shivers (http://www.visimag.com) is the monthly magazine of horror entertainment. Single copies are £3.25 (UK)/$5.99 (USA)/Cdn$7.95 (Canada), and a yearly subscription is £36.00 (UK), $68.00 (USA), £46.00 (Europe airmail and rest of the world surface) or £50.00 (rest of the world airmail) to "Visual Imagination Limited", Shivers Subscription, PO Box 371, London SW14 8JL, UK, or PO Box 156, Manorville, NY 11949, USA.

Starburst (http://www.visimag.com) is a monthly magazine of sci-fi entertainment. Cover price is £2.99 (UK)/$4.99 (USA)/ Cdn$6.95 (Canada). Yearly subscriptions comprise 12 regular issues ("budget") or 12 regular issues and four quarterly Specials ("full") at £46.00 full/£32.00 budget (UK), $82.00 full/$53.00 budget (USA), £56.00 full/£39.00 budget (Europe airmail and rest of the world surface) or £71.00 full/£49.00 budget (rest of the world airmail) to "Visual Imagination Limited", Starburst Subscrition, PO Box 371, London SW14 8JL, UK, or PO Box 156, Manorville, NY 11949, USA.

The Third Alternative (http://www.purl.oclc.org/net/ ttaonline/index.html) is a quarterly magazine of "extraordinary" new fiction, interviews and articles. Cover price is £3.00, and a four-issue subscription is £11.00 (UK), £13.00 (Europe) or $22.00/£15.00 (America and rest of the world) to "TTA Press", 5 Martins Lane, Witcham, Ely, Cambs CB6 2LB, UK.

Video Watchdog (http://www.cinemaweb.com/videowd) is a bi-monthly magazine described as "the Perfectionist's Guide to Fantastic Video". $6.50 a copy, an annual 6-issue subscription is $24.00 bulk/$35.00 first class (USA), $33.00 surface/$45.00

airmail (overseas). US funds only to "Video Watchdog", PO Box 5283, Cincinnati, OH 45205–0283, USA.

BOOK DEALERS

Cold Tonnage Books offers excellent mail order new and used SF/ fantasy/horror, art, reference, limited editions etc. with regular catalogues. Write to Andy Richards, 22 Kings Lane, Windlesham, Surrey GU20 6JQ, UK. Credit cards accepted. Tel: +44 (0) 1276– 475388. E-mail: andy@coldtonnage.demon.co.uk

Ken Cowley offers mostly used SF/fantasy/horror/crime/ supernatural, collectibles, pulps etc. by mail order with occasional catalogues. Write to Trinity Cottage, 153 Old Church Road, Clevedon, North Somerset, BS21 7TU, UK. Tel: +44 (0) 1275– 872247.

Richard Dalby issues semi-regular mail order lists of used ghost and supernatural volumes at very reasonable prices. Write to 4 Westbourne Park, Scarborough, North Yorkshire YO 12 4AT, UK. Tel: +44 (0) 1723 377049.

Dark Delicacies is a friendly Burbank, California, store specialising in horror books, vampire merchandise and signings. It moved to a new location at the end of 1999. Credit cards accepted. E-mail: darkdel@darkdel.com

DreamHaven Books & Comics (http://www.visi.com/ dreamhvn/) store and mail order offers new and used SF/fantasy/horror/art and illustrated etc. with regular catalogues. Write to 912 West Lake Street, Minneapolis, MN 55408, USA. Credit cards accepted. Tel: (612) 823–6070. E-mail: dreamhvn @visi.com

Fantastic Literature (http://www.netcomuk.co.uk/~sgosden) mail order offers new and used SF/fantasy/horror etc. with regular catalogues. Write to Simon G. Gosden, 35 The Ramparts, Rayleigh, Essex SS6 8PY, UK. Credit cards accepted. Tel: +44 (0)1268–747564. E-mail: sgosden@netcomuk.co.uk

Fantasy Centre shop and mail order has mostly used SF/ fantasy/horror, art, reference, pulps etc. at reasonable prices with regular catalogues. Write to 157 Holloway Road, London N7 8LX, UK. Credit cards accepted. Tel/Fax: +44 (0)171–607 9433.

House of Monsters (http://www.visionvortex/houseofmonsters) is a small treasure-trove of a store only open at weekends from noon that specializes in horror movie memorabilia, toys, posters, videos, books and magazines. 1579 N. Milwaukee Avenue, Gallery 218, Chicago, IL 60614, USA. Credit cards accepted. Tel: (773) 292–0980. E-mail: Homonsters @aol.com

Mythos Books (http://www.abebooks.com/home/mythosbooks/) mail order presents books and curiosities for the Lovecraftian scholar and collectors of horror, weird and supernatural fiction with regular catalogues and e-mail updates. Write to 218 Hickory Meadow Lane, Poplar Bluff, MO 63901–2160, USA. Credit cards accepted. Tel: (573) 785–7710. E-mail: dwynn@ldd.net

PDW Books mail order offers many speciality press items plus new and used SF/fantasy/horror etc. with regular catalogues. Write to 3721 Minnehaha Avenue South, Minneapolis, MN 55406, USA. Tel: (612) 721–5996. E-mail: PDW@visi.com

Kirk Ruebotham offers out of print and used horror/SF/ fantasy/crime and related non-fiction, with regular catalogues. Write to 16 Beaconsfield Road, Runcorn, Cheshire WA7 4BX, UK. Tel: +44 (0)1928 560540. E-mail: kirk@ruebotham.freeserve.co.uk

Sugen & Co. are mail order dealers who specialize in used film and TV tie-ins, with regular catalogues. Write to Southwood House, Well, Bedale, North Yorkshire DL8 2RL, UK. Tel: +44 (0)1677 470079.

Zardoz Books (http://www.zardozbooks.co.uk) are mail order dealers in used vintage and collectable paperbacks, especially movie tie-ins, with regular catalogues. Write to 20 Whitecroft, Dilton Marsh, Westbury, Wilts BA13 4DJ, UK. Credit cards accepted. Tel: +44 (0)1373 865371. E-mail: 100124.262@ compuserve.com

MARKET INFORMATION AND NEWS

DarkEcho is an excellent free service offering news, views and information of the horror field every week through e-mail. To subscribe, e-mail editor Paula Guran at darkecho@aol.com with "Subscribe" as your subject or see http://www.darkecho.com for more information.

The Gila Queen's Guide to Markets (http://www.gilaqueen.com/) is a regular publication detailing markets for SF/fantasy/horror plus other genres, along with publishing news, contests, anthologies, updates, etc. A sample copy is $6.00 and subscriptions are $34.00 (USA), $38.00 (Canada) and $50.00 (overseas). Back issues are also available. Cheques or money orders should be in US dollars and sent to "The Gila Queen's Guide to Markets", PO Box 97, Newton, NJ 07860–0097, USA. E-mail: GilaQueen@aol.com or Kathryn@gilaqueen.com In the UK *The Gila Queen* is distributed by: BBR Distribution (http://www.bbr-online.com). Contact Chris Reed, PO Box 625, Sheffield, S1 3GY UK. E-mail: c.s.reed@bbr-online.com

Hellnotes (http://www.hellnotes.com) is described as "Your Insider's Guide to the Horror Field". This weekly Newsletter is available on e-mail for $15.00 per year or hardcopy subscriptions are available for $40 per year. To subscribe by credit card, go to: http://www.hellnotes.com/subscrib.htm To subscribe by mail, send US check or money order (made out to "David B. Silva") to: Hellnotes, 27780 Donkey Mine Road, Oak Run, CA 96069, USA. Tel/Fax: (916) 472–1050. E-mail: dbsilva@hellnotes.com or pfolson@up.net The Hellnotes Bookstore can be found at http://www.hellnotes.com/book_store

Horroronline.com (http://www.universalstudios.com/horror) describes itself as "the horror fan's number one resource for news and information about dark entertainment" on the Internet. It includes reviews, articles, interviews and features on current film, video, comics, games and literature, including more than 1,200 horror movie reviews.

Scavenger's Newsletter (http://www.cza.com/scav/index.html) is a monthly newsletter for SF/fantasy/horror writers with an interest in the small press. News of markets, along with articles, letters and reviews. A sample copy is $2.50 (USA/Canada) and £2.40/$3.00 (overseas). An annual subscription is $18.00 (USA), $21.00 (Canada) and £22.80/$27.00 (overseas). *Scavenger's Scrapbook* is a twice yearly round-up, available for $4.00 (USA/Canada) and $5.00 (overseas). A year's subscription to the *Scrapbook* is $7.00 (USA/Canada) and $8.00 (overseas). Make cheques or money orders in US funds payable to "Janet

Fox" and send to 519 Ellinwood, Osage City, KS 66523–1329, USA. E-mail: foxscav1@jc.net. In the UK contact Chris Reed, BBR Distribution, PO Box 625, Sheffield S1 3GY, UK. (http://www.bbr-online.com). E-mail: c.s.reed@bbr-online.com